W9-BGM-778

THE
HIGHLANDER'S
LAST SONG

THE
GENTLEWOMAN'S
CHOICE

Two books in one special volume
George MacDonald's

THE
HIGHLANDER'S
LAST SONG

THE
GENTLEWOMAN'S
CHOICE

Edited by Michael R. Phillips

Bethany House Publishers
Minneapolis, Minnesota 55438
A division of Bethany Fellowship, Inc.

Originally published as *What's Mine's Mine* in 1886 by Kegan Paul, Trench &
Co. Publishers, London.

Copyright © 1986
Michael R. Phillips
All Rights Reserved

Published by Bethany House Publishers
A Division of Bethany Fellowship, Inc.
6820 Auto Club Road, Minneapolis, Minnesota 55438

Printed in the United States of America
First combined edition for Christian Herald Family Bookshelf: 1987

Library of Congress Cataloging-in-Publication Data

MacDonald, George, 1824–1905.
  The highlander's last song.

  Rev. ed. of: What's mine's mine.
  I. Phillips, Michael R., 1946–   II. MacDonald George, 1824–1905.
What's mine's mine.   III. Title.
PR 4967.H53   1986   823'.8   86-11739
ISBN 0-87123-658-3

THE
HIGHLANDER'S
LAST SONG

GEORGE MACDONALD
THE
HIGHLANDER'S LAST SONG

Michael R. Phillips, Editor

BETHANY HOUSE PUBLISHERS
MINNEAPOLIS, MINNESOTA 55438
A Division of Bethany Fellowship, Inc.

Originally published as *What's Mine's Mine* in 1886 by Kegan Paul, Trench & Co. Publishers, London.

Published by Bethany House Publishers
A Division of Bethany Fellowship, Inc.
6820 Auto Club Road, Minneapolis, Minnesota 55438

Printed in the United States of America

Library of Congress Cataloging-in-Publication Data

MacDonald, George, 1824-1905.
  The highlander's last song.

    Rev. ed. of: What's mine's mine.
    I. Phillips, Michael R., 1946-   . II. MacDonald George, 1824-1905.
What's mine's mine. III. Title.
PR4967.H53   1986   823'.8   86-11739
ISBN 0-87123-658-3

Contents

Scottish Romances by George MacDonald retold for today's reader by Michael Phillips:

The Fisherman's Lady
The Marquis' Secret
The Baronet's Song
The Shepherd's Castle
The Tutor's First Love
The Musician's Quest
The Maiden's Bequest
The Curate's Awakening
The Lady's Confession
The Baron's Apprenticeship
The Highlander's Last Song

Introduction _____

I occasionally wonder what more can be said to introduce George MacDonald and his remarkable works. And yet I continue to discover every book to be so unique in itself that words to commend them almost write themselves. If you have not read any of MacDonald's books in this series and are unfamiliar with his life and background, I urge you to read the Introduction to *The Fisherman's Lady*, the first book.

The Highlander's Last Song, originally published in 1886 as *What's Mine's Mine* and now reissued in the Bethany House Classic Reprint Series, has long been one of my favorites. But its attraction to me has also been one of the reasons I delayed so long in choosing it as a selection for this series; I questioned whether its unique *flavor* would be sufficient to "grab" twentieth-century readers—sad to say, always a necessity in this modern age. But it was precisely the book's *flavor* and *tone* which always intrigued me, which got under my skin and caused MacDonald's perspectives to influence me long after I had forgotten the specifics of the plot itself.

Several features set *The Highlander's Last Song* apart from the body of MacDonald's other work. Certainly the parallel between his beloved brother John and the character of Ian is noteworthy, for John MacDonald spent time in Russia and was forced to leave under almost identical circumstances. In addition he and his brother enjoyed a relationship similar to that of Alister and Ian. But more particularly it is a story of the *land* of Scotland—specifically the highlands along the northwest coast.

MacDonald's fascination with the land is clearly demonstrated in *The Highlander's Last Song*. Anyone who has read MacDonald, thoroughly, recognizes that nature always spoke to him about the character of the God he served. All his books resound with his love for the earth, the sky, the seas, the mountains, the heavens, the animal creation. And working in combination with his imaginative genius, MacDonald's descriptive passages are among the most moving to be found anywhere because to him nature was *alive* with the pulsating life of its Creator.

The Highlander's Last Song takes that love of nature a step further, because it is a story in which a Scottish clan's love for their homeland *is* the central theme. Thus the descriptions of Strathruadh and the interplay of the hills and the valley with the lives of the once mighty clan

Ruadh are integral to the very plot. Though Strathruadh itself is a fictional location, MacDonald, as was his habit, drew on actual place names in a given locality to fabricate the names and places for his stories. Thus we are able to fix the locale for the book—working from detailed maps of the area where to this day the Gaelic name "Ruadh" survives in many valley, hill, glen, and stream names of various forms—on the western coast of mainland Scotland, directly west of Inverness. It is a rugged land, sparsely populated, with fierce winters and stubborn soil which, when suitable ground for growing crops can be found, does not easily yield its bounty to those who choose to make these highlands their home.

But for centuries (roughly between the years 900 and 1800) many determined Scots of Celtic background *did* make the Scottish highlands their home. From past ages these strong and independent Scots—in whose veins flowed the blood of the Scandanavian Vikings, the mysterious Picts, and the Celts who had migrated from Europe before recorded history could even chronicle their movements—had banned together in large, familial tribes, or "clans." And the persistent unity within these clans—often expressed as bitter and warring hatred against rival clans—bound the people of the Scottish highlands together. Though as a nation Scotland first had to solidify its independence, then fight long and hard against England to keep it, and finally was united with her neighbor to the south in the seventeenth century, throughout it all the highland clans marched to their own independent tune, led by their chiefs and accompanied by the wail of bagpipes. They were part of the Scottish nation on one level, but on another, deeper level, were their own independent entity within the whole. Attempts to subdue the clan leaders throughout the years resulted only in bloodshed, for they were not a people to be overpowered by force.

Change, however, could not be held back; if force could not subdue the highlanders, economics ultimately did. Landowners from the south, attracted by cheap land prices, good hunting, and wide spaces where sheep could be raised inexpensively, began buying large plots of land in the north. Furthermore, those landowners who had long rented out small parcels to struggling crofters began to see that they could fatten their profits considerably by converting their property to grazing land for sheep, hardy creatures requiring little maintenance, whose wool fetched premium prices. For these and other complex reasons, in the late eighteenth century "the highland clearances" began; massive numbers of poor farmers were expelled from their homes and farms in favor of sheep, which needed a great deal of acreage to feed upon. Between 1800 and 1820 whole villages and clans were relocated, sometimes under cruel conditions and treatment, leaving the highlands desolate of the clans which had once so colorfully and energetically peopled them. The clan system was not able to withstand the onset of industrialization and many highlanders emigrated to Canada, some to fishing villages on Scotland's eastern coast, others to the south of Scotland; still others were scattered and the clan bonds broken forever. This is Scotland as it really was for many of its people.

But no MacDonald book is without deep undercurrents of abiding spiritual truth which emerge from the context of the historical setting of the story itself. In the growth of young Alister Macruadh, clan chief and central character of *The Highlander's Last Song*, a number of penetrating eternal principles convict the modern reader, driving us back to the solid bedrock upon which our faith is based. Determined and passionate, Alister must wage a fierce battle with his pride, asking himself what subtle disguises Mammon has put on to tempt him away from the highest calling of all—total submission to Christ. The choice faced by Alister is as complex an issue as MacDonald ever raised, fully justifying any attempt to rationalize away the spiritual element and settle for what might be acceptable "in the world's eyes." Yet Alister's resolve in the end to lay everything on the altar of dependence upon God's provision rather than man's initiative serves as an unforgettable and powerful model of true self-denying practical commitment to our Lord.

The Highlander's Last Song, then, is the story of a chief's love and devotion to his people, a story of the sacrificial commitment which undergirds the responsibility he feels for those that look to him for leadership, and the story of a young man's journey into the upper regions of freedom from self. For MacDonald was always anxious to show that even the righteous have a continuing need to purge themselves of anything standing in the way of God's perfect will for them. God's work in an individual heart is never complete, no matter how selfless that heart may seem to be.

But in the midst of these everlasting lessons we take from our reading, at the same time this is a historical novel, accurate in its portrayal of that portion of Scottish history during which the leaders of dying remnants of once-proud clans had to face the future and decide what was best for their people. This book offers us, along with a variety of characters, a portrayal, not only of Christ, but of the homeland which played such a vital part in MacDonald's own life and development, his personal, spiritual, literary, and ancestral roots.

Though the Gaelic place names still abound, and though in isolated pockets of Scotland (mostly in remote glens of the Western Isles) the Gaelic can still be heard, the sound of the ancient Celtic language has gone. And with it has gone the clan culture. Only faint echoes remain, echoes which exist only in the memory of those who love the heritage represented by this people and their strange but flowery tongue. The clan Ruadh, and all those who bore the name Macruadh ("son of Ruadh"), live on for us through George MacDonald's imagination, typifying a folk culture of a remote and distant land that is no more.

Michael Phillips
1707 E St.
Eureka, CA 95501

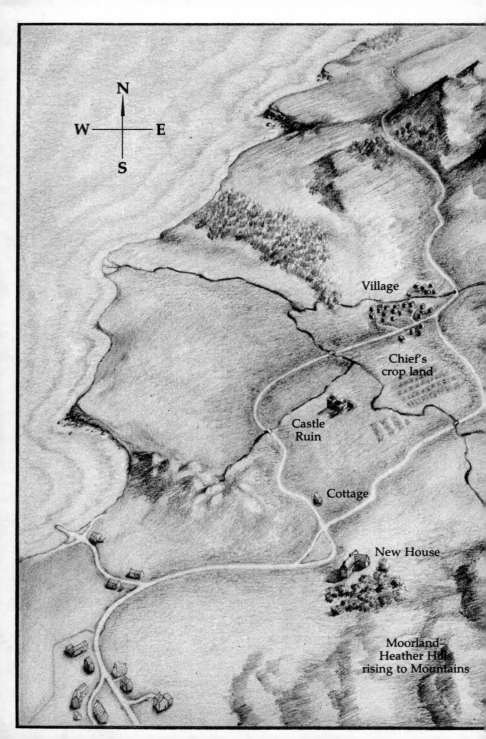

The Tomb

STRATHRUADH

1 / The Peregrine Palmer Family _____

A large fire blazed in the low round-backed grate. A snowy cloth of fine linen covered the large, well-appointed table—its silver bright, its china ornate though not elegant, its ham neither too fat nor too lean. A family of six sat eating breakfast.

Their finery presented a stark contrast to the rugged beauty surrounding them. What could they be doing in such a handsomely furnished dining room in this vast northern wasteland? Could they belong—notwithstanding the expensive oak sideboard, the heavy chairs backed in morocco leather, and the other accouterments of what appeared to be a London house inhabited by rich middle-class people—to the clan Ruadh whose very poverty bound its people together? It seemed unlikely.

Beyond the window the western seas lay clear and cold, broken with islands scattered thinly to the horizon. The ocean looked like a wild yet peaceful mingling of lake and land. Some of the islands were green from shore to shore; others were mere rocks with a bold front to the sea. Over the pale blue sea hung the pale blue sky, flecked with a few cold white clouds high above, looking as if they disowned the earth below. A keen wind was blowing, crisping the surface of the sea in patches—a pretty large crisping to be seen from the house, for the window looked out over several hills to the sea. Life—quiet yet eager—was all about; the solitude itself was alive. Its life needed nothing from beyond, independent even of the few fishing boats whose red and brown sails here and there broke the blue of the water.

Out the window on the other side were visible hills of heather rolling away eastward, some distance away beginning to rise into mountains, and farther yet, on the horizon, showing snow on their crests. It was a solemn and very still region—not a pretty country, but great: beautiful with the display of color and variety. Far in the distance, where the mountains and clouds have business together, its aspect rose to grandeur. At first glance one would hardly discover a single tree. Another look, however, would reveal a solitary clump of firs on a hill not far from the house, a hill steeper than most of them and green to the top.

At the breakfast table sat four girls—the first, one of the prettiest imaginable. Her skin was fair, yet with a glowing tinge. Her hair was brown with just a suspicion of red, waving to a curl at the ends. Her mouth was straight and thin-lipped, and seemed to dissolve into a bewitching smile, revealing perfect teeth. She was of medium height and quite graceful.

Near her at the table sat one who looked so different you could hardly believe they belonged to the same family. She was younger and taller—not ungraceful, though by no means beautiful. Her eyes, though dark, were full of the light that tries to see—questioning eyes. Her hair was long and black, her complexion dark, with something of a freckly unevenness. Hardly more than a girl, she was not so pretty or graceful as her sister.

One truth about a plain face rarely occurs to most: the plainness itself carries with it the potential for further maturation. Since this kind of face takes more developing for the completion of the idea lying beneath its surface, it may in the end result in a greater beauty. Any young man of aspiration in the matter of beauty, therefore, would be well advised to choose a plain woman for his wife—if she be lovely in his eyes. For the loveliness, which is within her, will be victorious over the plainness; and her face, still far from complete, has room for completion on a much grander scale than most handsome faces. But few are prophets enough for a plain face. A keen surprise of beauty waits many a man if he be pure enough to observe the transfiguration of the plain face he has loved.

This plain face was a solemn one, and the solemnity suited the plainness. It was not especially expressive—there was more of the latent power in it, while her sister's had more expression than power of any kind. Both were ladylike; whether they were ladies or not, the reader may determine.

There were two younger girls at the table, of whom I will say nothing more than that one of them looked awkward, promised to be handsome, and was apparently a good soul. The other was pretty and pert.

The mother, a woman with many autumnal reminders of spring about her, sat at the head of the table, regarding her queendom with a smile. She had the look of a woman on good terms with her motherhood, her society, and the universe.

The governor sitting opposite her—for so was the head of the family styled—was the only one at the table whose countenance displayed a shadow. He had tried to get into Parliament and had not succeeded, but he did not look discontented. Indeed, there was a certain radiance of success about him. Yet about the horizon of his thick, dark eyebrows seemed to hang a thundery atmosphere. In his youth he had probably been very nice-looking, but he had grown a trifle fat. In good health and when things went well, as they had mostly done with him, he was sweet-tempered. What he might be under other conditions was seldom asked.

He had a good opinion of himself—on what grounds I do not know. He was rich, and no more fertile soil exists for growing a good opinion of one's self than that.

Mr. Peregrine Palmer had finished his breakfast and sat for a while looking at nothing in particular, plunged deep in thought about nothing at all. He was a little above average height and looked not much older than his wife. His black hair had but begun to be touched with silver; he seemed a man without an atom of care more than reasonable. His speech was like that of an Englishman, for although born in Glasgow he had been to Oxford. He spoke respectfully to his wife and with a pleasant playfulness to his daughters.

Peregrine's grandfather had begun to make the family fortune by developing a little secret still in a remote Scottish highland glen—which had acquired a reputation for its whiskey—into a large, successful distillery. Both he and his son made money by it, as had Peregrine also. For all three of them, making money was the great calling of life. They were diligent in business, fervent in spirit, served mammon with all their hearts, and founded their claims to consideration on that fact. Neither Jacob nor John Palmer's worst enemy had ever called either a hypocrite. Both had gone regularly to church. Peregrine had even built a church and a school. He did not now take any active part in the distillery but invested his money in other ways—in making more money, for he had a genuine skill for business.

At college, Mr. Palmer had fallen in with a friend who saw no small amount of wit in his name. "Your father must have been a bit of a humorist," he said, "to name you Peregrine. It looks rather like a paternal joke."

"I don't know quite what you mean," said Peregrine. The fact was he had no glimmering idea of what he meant.

"Don't you see? *Peregrine* means pilgrim, from the Latin, *peregrinus*. But *Palmer* also means pilgrim. The palmer was a pilgrim who went to the holy land and when he came home he carried a palm branch to show where he had been. Thus, the interpretation of your name is *Pilgrim Pilgrim!*"

Henceforth, he was all the better pleased with his name, for he fancied in it something of the dignity of a double surname.

When their first child was born, the father thought long and hard for a suitable name for him, searching through old botany books for the scientific names of different palms. His wife, however, helped him out of his difficulty. As a child she had been encouraged to read an old-fashioned book called *The Pilgrim's Progress*, which her husband had never seen. Neither did he read it now, but accepted her suggestion and named the boy Christian. When a daughter came she was Christina. They named their second son Valentine, after Mr. Valiant-for-truth. Their second daughter was Mercy; and for the third and fourth, Hope and Grace seemed near enough.

So the family—whose mother's name was Miriam—had a cool glow of Puritanism about it, though nothing was further from the thoughts of any of them than what their names signified.

Mr. Palmer rose from the table with a merry remark on the prolongation of the meal by his girls, and went toward the door.

"Are you going to shoot?" asked his wife.

"Not today. But I am going to look after my guns."

She was referring to grouse shooting, the ostensible reason for her husband's presence there. But he did not really care much for the sport. Had he cared nothing for it at all, he would have been there all the same. Other people in his social position shot grouse, and he liked to do what other people did. If ever he tried the gate of heaven, it would be because other people did. But the primary reason for his being so far in the north was an opportunity to buy a nice piece of property very cheap—a fine property of mist and cloud, heather and rock, mountain and moor, and with no reputation for grouse to raise its price.

The words "my estate" sounded good to his ear, and after a good time of renovation he would be able to lease it out at a healthy profit. No sooner had the property been purchased than his wife and daughters were eager to visit it, and the man of business perceived that it would cost him much less if they spent their summers there instead of on the Continent. He therefore proceeded at once to enlarge the house and make it comfortable.

They had arrived the day before.

2 / The Girls' First Walk

The governor did not care much about walking and the mother had things to see to inside. Therefore the young people would have to explore by themselves. They put on their hats and went out.

The temperature was keen even though it was the middle of August. There was a certain sense of sadness in the pale sky and its cold brightness; but these young people felt no cold and perceived no sadness. The air was exhilarating and they breathed deep breaths of pleasure. They did not know nature, but she had an effect on them nevertheless, unmindful whether they knew what she was about or not.

But not one of them was capable of enjoying anything by herself. Together they were unable to enjoy much. So—like the miser who, when he cannot enjoy his money, desires more—they began to desire more company to share in the already withering satisfaction of their new possession. Enjoyment, not the lack of it, should make us desirous to share. To enjoy alone is to be capable of sharing.

The girls grew weary of the show around them because it was so quiet, so unaware of their presence, so motionless, so monotonous. Endless change was going on, but it was too slow for them to see. Before half an hour had passed they had begun to think with regret of Piccadilly and Regent Street. Doubtless humanity is better company than a bare hillside. But it all depends on how near we come to the humanity, and how near we come to the hill. But *seeing* neither humanity nor hillside, the girls went on and on, however, led mainly by the animal delight of motion, the two younger girls making many diversions up and down the little hills and valleys, shrieking aloud at everything that pleased them.

The house they had just left stood on the projecting shoulder of a hill, here and there planted with firs. There was a thicket of hardy trees at the back of the house, while toward the south less hardy ones grew in the shrubbery. The carriage drive to the house joined two not very distant points on the same road—a rough, country road, a good deal rutted and seldom repaired. Opposite the gates rose the steep slope of a heathery hill, along the flank of which the girls were now walking. On their right lay a piece of rough moorland, covered with heather, patches of bracken, and coarse grass. A few yards to the right, it sank in a steep descent. Such was the ground for some distance along the road—on one side the hill, on the other a narrow level, then an abrupt descent, as the road itself descended gradually toward a valley.

As they advanced they caught sight of a ruin rising above the brow of the descent. The two younger girls darted across the heather toward it; the two elder continued their walk along the road.

"I wonder what we shall see round the corner there," said Mercy, the younger of the two.

"The same over again, I suppose," answered Christina. "What a rough road it is! I've nearly twice sprained my ankle!"

As they descended the hill following the course of the road, the hillside to their left grew higher and higher while the valley, in front and on the right, opened gradually, showing a glimpse of a small stream cantering steadily toward the sea—now tumbling over a rock, now sullen in a brown pool. Arriving at length at a shoulder of the hill round which the road turned, a whole mile of the brook lay before them. It came down a narrow valley, with patches of meadow in the bottom. Immediately below them the valley was of some width with good land from side to side, where green oats waved their feathery grace and the yellow barley was nearly ready for the sickle. But the fertile valley held no more charm for them than the barren hill. Their talk was of the last ball they had attended.

The sisters were about as good friends as such shallow creatures could be; and they would be such friends all their lives if neither grew to anything better, or if no jealousy or difference of social position through marriage intervened. They loved each other, if not tenderly, yet with the genuineness of healthy family habit—a good thing, for it keeps the door open for something better. Habit is but the merest shadow of reality. Still it is not a small thing, as families go, if sisters and brothers do not dislike each other.

They had been criticizing certain of the young men they had met at the ball. Being so superficial in their development, what else did they have to talk about but clothes and balls and young men? But now they had come to a point of the road not far from the ruin to which the children had run across the heather.

"Look, Chrissy! It is an old castle!" said Mercy. "I wonder whether it's on our land."

"Not much to be proud of," replied the other. "It is nothing but the walls of a square house."

"Not just a common square house. Just look at it! I wonder how it is that all the old castles get deserted."

"Because they are old. It's well to desert them because they get so old and tumbled down."

"I love old things," said Mercy.

"I am different from you," rejoined Christina. "I like things as new as I can have them."

"I like new things well enough, Chrissy—you know I do. It is natural. The earth herself has new clothes once a year. Although it is but once a year, I grant."

"Often enough for an old granny like her!"

"Look, what a pretty cottage—down there, halfway to the burn! It's like an English cottage. Those we saw as we came were either like a piece of the earth or so white as to look ghastly. This one looks neat and comfortable and has trees about it."

The ruin, once a fortified house and called a castle, stood on a sloping root or spur that ran from the hill down to the bank of the stream. On the same spur, halfway to the burn, stood a low, stone, thatched cottage with a little grove of strong fir trees about it. The cottage stood toward the east side of the sinking ridge, which had a steep descent both east and west to the fields below. The slopes were green with sweet grass and apparently smooth as a lawn. Not far from where the cottage seemed to nest, the burn turned abruptly and flowed along the side of the ridge to the end of it and then on to the sea. The girls stood for a moment looking.

"It's really quite pretty," said Christina with condescension. "It actually has something of what one misses here so much—a certain cozy look. If there were just more trees around here. Oh, these wretched bare hills!"

"Wait till the heather is out. Then you will have color to make up for the barrenness."

They were now at the part of the road which crossed the descending spur as it left the hillside. Here they stopped again and looked down the rocky slope. There was hardly anything green between them and the old ruin, but beyond the ruin the green began again. Catching sight of Hope and Grace as they ran about the ruin, they went to join them. Through a gap that might once have been a door they entered. Finding in one corner a broken stair, they clambered up to a gap in the east wall. As they reached it they heard the sound of a horse's hoofs. Looking down the road they saw a gig approaching with two men. It had reached a part not so steep and was coming at a trot.

"Why!" exclaimed Christina, "there's Valentine—and someone with him!"

"I heard the governor say to Mama," returned Mercy, "that Val was going to bring a college friend of his and Christian's with him—'for a shoot at the grouse,' he said. I wonder what he will be like."

"He's a big, good-looking fellow," said Christina. "And mind you,

I was the first to discover it," she added.

They scrambled down from their lookout among the broken stones of the ruin and hastened back to the road.

The gig came up and stopped. Valentine threw the reins to his companion, jumped out, embraced his sisters, and seemed glad to see them. Had he met them after a similar span of time at home, he would have given them a cooler greeting, but he had traveled so many miles that they seemed not to have met for quite a long time.

"My friend, Mr. Sercombe," he said, jerking his head toward the gig with informal introduction.

Mr. Sercombe raised his hat and acquaintance was made.

"We'll drive on, Sercombe," said Valentine, jumping back up. "We're half dead with hunger, Chris. Do you think we'll find anything to eat?"

"Judging by what we left at breakfast," replied Christina, "I should say there would be enough for at least one of you. But you had better go and see."

3 / The Shop in the Village_____

The sun had been set for an hour and the night was already growing rather dark, notwithstanding the long twilight of these northern regions. A blanket of clouds had gathered and a few stray drops had begun to fall from it. A thin wind now and then woke to give a feeble puff. But just as soon, it seemed to change its mind and resolve not to blow, but let the rain come down. A muddy road wound through huts of turf—one or two of clay, and one or two of stone, which were more like cottages. Hardly one had a window two feet square and many of their windows had no glass. In almost all of them the only chimney was little more than a hole in the middle of the thatch. Left without an ordered path to its outlet—by virtue of the absence of glass in the windows—the smoke from the peat fires preferred a circuitous route and lingered on its way, filling the air with the wholesome and pleasant smell of peat. Outside were no lamps; the road was unlighted except by the few rays that here and there crept from a window. A drearier-looking spot for human abode it would be difficult to imagine.

One of the better cottages sent out a little more light, though it was only from a tallow candle, through the upper half of a door divided horizontally. The one window of that same cottage was filled with all sorts of little things for sale. Small and inconvenient for the humblest commerce, this was not merely the best; it was the only shop in the hamlet.

There were two persons inside, one in front and one behind the counter. The latter was a young woman, the former a man.

He was leaning over the counter and seemed quite at home, yet the young woman treated him with a marked, though unembarrassed respect. The man was dark. His coat was of some rough brown material, probably dyed and woven in the village, and he wore a kilt of tartan. They were more than well-worn—looking even in that poor light a little shabby. On his head was the highland bonnet called a glengarry. His eyes appeared very dark, but in the daylight were greenish-hazel. Usually he talked with the girl in Gaelic, but was on this night speaking English.

"And when was it you heard from Lachlan, Annie?" he asked.

After a moment's pause, during which she had been putting away things in a drawer behind the counter, she responded.

"Last Thursday it was, sir. You know we hear every month. Sometimes oftener."

"Yes; I know that. I hope the dear fellow is well?"

"He is quite well and of good hope. He says he will soon come and see us."

"And take you away, Annie?"

"Well, sir," returned Annie after a moment's hesitation, "he does not *say* so."

"If he did not mean it, he would be a rascal, and I should have to kill him. But I would bet my life on Lachlan's honesty!"

"Thank you, sir. He would lay down his for you."

"Not if you said to him, *Don't!*—eh, Annie?"

"But he would, Macruadh!" returned the young woman. "Are you not his chief?"

"Ah, that is all over now, my girl. There are no chiefs and no clans anymore! The chiefs sell their land, like Esau, for a mess of pottage. And the Sasunnach who buys it claims rights over them that never grew on the land or were hid in its caves! Thank God, the poor man is not their slave, but he is worse off, for they will not let him eat, and he has nowhere to go. My heart is ready to break for my people. Sometimes I feel as if I would gladly die."

"Oh, sir, don't say that!" expostulated the young woman with trembling voice. "Every heart in Glenruadh is glad when it goes well with the Macruadh."

"Yes, yes; I know you all love my father's son and my uncle's nephew. But how can it go well with the Macruadh when it goes badly with his clan? There is no way now for a chief to be father of his family; we are all poor together. Well, a man must be an honest man, even if there be no way but ruin. God knows, as we've all heard my father say a hundred times from the pulpit, there's no ruin but dishonesty!"

A pause followed.

"There are strangers at the New House, we hear," said Annie.

"From a distance I saw some young ladies, and one or two men. I don't desire to see more of them. God forbid I should wish any of them harm. But I don't like to see them here. I am afraid it is pride. They are rich, I hear, so we shall not be troubled with attention from them. They will look down on us—"

"Look down on the Macruadh!" exclaimed Annie, as if she could not believe her ears.

"—not that I should heed that," he went on. "A cock on the barn roof looks down on you and you don't feel offended. What I do dread is looking down on them. There is something in me that can hate, Annie, and I am afraid of it. There's something about the land—I don't care about the money. But I feel like a miser about the land. I don't mean *any* land. I would care nothing about buying land unless it had once been ours. But what came down to me from my own people—with my own people upon it—I would rather turn the spigot of the molten gold and let it run down into a bottomless pit than to let a foot of such land slip away from me. I feel it a disgrace to have lost it, though I never had it."

"Indeed, Macruadh," said Annie, "it is a hard time! There is no money in the country. And so many of the people are following Lachlan."

"I shall miss you, Annie."

"You are very kind to us all, sir."

"Are you not all my own? And you, I have to take care of for Lachlan's sake besides. He left you to my charge—as if that had been necessary, the foolish fellow, when we are foster brothers!"

Again came a pause.

"Not a gentleman farmer left from one end of the strath to the other!" said the chief at length. "When Ian is at home we feel just like two old turkeys left alone in the yard."

"Say two golden eagles, sir, on the cliff of the rock."

"Don't compare us to the eagle, Annie. I do not love the bird. He is very proud and greedy and cruel and never will know the hand that tames him. He is the bird of the monarch or the earl, not the bird of the father of his people. But he is beautiful, and I have no wish to kill him."

"They shot another, the female bird, last week. All the birds are going! Soon there will be nothing but the great sheep and the little grouse. The capercailzie's gone and the ptarmigan's gone!"

"The ptarmigan's not gone yet, Annie, though there are not many. And for the capercailzie, only one who loves them will be left to see before long."

"How is my lady, your mother?"

"Pretty well, thank you—wonderfully cheerful. It is time I went home to her. Lachlan would think I was treating him false and playing at love with you on my own account.

"No fear! He would know better than that. He would know, too, that if I did not belong to Lachlan, I would not let my chief humble himself."

"You're one of the old sort, Annie! Good night! Mind you, tell Lachlan I never miss a chance of looking in to see how you are getting on."

"I will. Good night, Macruadh."

They shook hands over the counter, and the young chief took his departure.

As he stood up he displayed a fine, powerful frame, over six feet in height, and perfectly poised. With a great easy stride he swept silently out of the shop. Neither from his gait nor his look would one have guessed that he had been all day at work on the remnant of property he could still call his own.

To an English gentleman it would have seemed strange that one who had come from such a line of patriarchal ancestors, and who held the land of the country, should talk with such familiarity with a girl in a humble little shop in a most miserable hamlet. It would have seemed stranger yet that such a man should toil at the labor the soul of a gentleman despises. But there are great and small in every class—here and there a ploughman who understands the poets, here and there a large-minded shopkeeper, and here and there an unselfish duke. Less worldly *cleverness* is required for country affairs, and so they leave more room for thinking. Doubtless many of the youth's ancestors would likewise have held such labor unworthy of a gentleman. But this, the last Macruadh, was not like most of his pedigree, and had now and then a peep into the kingdom of heaven.

4 / The Chief

The Macruadh strode into the dark and down the village, wasting no time in picking his way, and from there into the yet deeper dark of the moorland hills. The rain was beginning to come down in earnest, but he did not heed it; he was a thoroughbred and feared no element. An umbrella was to him a ludicrous thing: how could a little rain—as he would have called it had it come down in torrents—hurt anyone?

The Macruadh, as the few who yet held by the fast-vanishing skirt of clanship called him, was the son of the last minister of the parish— a godly man who lived that which he was unable to explain. He was a genial, friendly, and by nature even merry man, always ready to share what he had, and making no show of having what he had not, either in wisdom, knowledge, or earthly goods. His father and uncle had been owners of the property and chiefs of the clan, much beloved by the poor and misunderstood by most of the more well-to-do.

Some years earlier an ambitious hunger after greater things had arisen in the land, and with it a mass emigration toward the south. The uncle of the present Macruadh did all he could to keep his people at home, living on but a couple hundred pounds a year himself and leasing out many of his farms at lower rents. But to no avail. One after another departed until his land lay nearly waste. He grew very poor, mourning far more over his clan and his country than his poverty.

At length he believed himself compelled, for the good of his people, to part with all but a mere remnant of the property. From the man to whom he sold it, Mr. Peregrine Palmer bought it at twice the original price, still a good bargain. But the laird was disappointed as he saw more and more of the peasantry emigrate or driven to other parts of the country. The laird, a bachelor, eventually retired to the humble cottage of his brother, the pastor, just married rather late in life. Here he found every comfort love could give. But the thought that he could have done better for his people by retaining the land soon wore him out and, the purchase money dwindling, at last he died.

What remained of the property came to the minister. As for the chieftainship, that had almost died before the chief. But now because of the reverence felt for the minister, it revived and later took a higher form. When the minister died, his son regarded the chieftainship as sacred. In the eyes of the people, the authority of the chief and the

29

influence of the minister seemed reborn in Alister, despite his youth. The love the people bore his father, both pastor and chief, crowned Alister's head and heart. Scarcely a man or woman of the poor remnant of the clan did not love young Macruadh.

And he responded in truth to that love. With a renewed sense that all things had to be made new, he began with his own person and family and the remnant of the clan, to restore a vitality—however small—to that most ancient of governments, the patriarch. There may have been youthful presumption and some folly in the notion, but the idea sprang from the simple sense of responsibility he felt bound to undertake as the person upon whom had come the headship, however shadowy, of a house, ruinous indeed, but not yet razed.

The ruin on the ridge stood as the symbol of the family condition. It had, however, been a ruin longer than anyone alive could remember. Alister's uncle had lived in a house on the spot where Mr. Peregrine Palmer's now stood. The man who bought the house had pulled it down to build that which Mr. Palmer had since enlarged. It had been a humble affair—a great cottage in stone, much in the style of that in which the young chief now lived—only six times the size, with a large hall, indispensable to the notion of a chief's residence. Some would have said it was a kitchen; but it was the sacred heart of the house where loving hospitality was always given. Food and drinks were ample for any visitor, however poor. When the old house had to make room for the new, the seasoned wood from the last barrels of claret, which always stood on tap amid the peat smoke, was used as fuel to cook a few meals for mason and carpenter.

The property of Clanruadh, for it was regarded as clan property because it belonged to the chief, had at one time stretched out of sight in all directions. Nobody could have told exactly how far it went, for the undrawn boundary lines lay in regions of mist and cloud, in regions of stone and rock and desert to which a red deer, not to mention a stray sheep, rarely ascended. At one time it took in a portion of every hill to be seen from the spot where the ruin stood. Now the chief had only a small farm, consisting of some fair soil on the slope of a hill, some very good in the valley on both sides of the burn, and a hill pasture. The pasture, however, was hardly worth measuring in acres, for it abounded in rocks and heather, with patches of coarse grass here and there and some good high-valley grass for the small black cattle and black-faced sheep in summer. Beyond periodic burnings of the heather, this high pastureland received no attention except from the fog, the snow, the rain, the sun, and the sweet air. A few grouse and black game bred on it, along with mountain rabbits and wildcats and various vermin.

So tender of life was the Macruadh that he did not like killing even a fox or a hooded crow unless compelled. He never shot a bird for sport, or would let another shoot one, although the poorest would sometimes beg a bird or two from him for food, a request always granted. To him, the creatures seemed a part of his clan; he had to protect them, too, from a greedy world. But as the deer and birds ranged where they would, he could not do much for them.

Regret, not bitterness, stirred the mind of Alister Macruadh when he thought of the change that had passed on everything around him. He had been too well taught for grumbling—least of all at what was plainly the will of the Supreme. However man might be to blame, the thing was there.

Alister had no personal regrets. He was able to understand something of the signs of the times. He saw that nothing could bring back the old way—and nothing comes back—at least in the same form. He saw also that if patriarchal ways were ever to return, they must rise out of loftier principles—must begin afresh. At his age, Alister could not have generated such thoughts except for the wisdom that had preceded him—first the large-mindedness of his father, who was capable even of discarding his prejudices where he saw they might mislead him; and next, the response of his mother to her husband. Isobel Macruadh was a woman of real thinking power. Her sons being but boys when their father died, she at once took the part of mediator between the mind of the father and that of his sons. Besides guiding them on the same principles, she often told them things their father had said.

One of the chief lessons he had left them was his verbal opposition to the growing disregard for integrity in human relations. He maintained that the conditions of fulfilling an agreement between men was of the highest consequence, as was one's inner attitude toward every other with whom he entered into such a pact. "In the possibility of any bargain," he had said, "are involved eternal conditions: relationship, brotherhood. Even to give with an improper attitude, to be kind while harboring a protest in your heart, is an injury, charity without love, salt without the saltiness. If we spend our lives on mere charity, we will never overtake the neglected claims that fall to us—claims between brothers, such as those from the very beginning of the relations of men. If a man justifies his self-centeredness by saying, 'I have not been unjust; I owed the man nothing,' he sides with death—says with the murderer, 'Am I my brother's keeper?' and builds the tombs of those his father slew."

In young Alister Macruadh's heart, the fatherly relation of the strong to the weak survived the disappearance of most of the outward signs of clan-kindred. In him, the chieftainship was elevated to a higher level. The more the outward, visible fact of chief-ness died with the dwindling of the clan, the stronger the spirit of the relation grew in him. He saw the customs of his ancestors glorified in the mists of the past. What was noble in them appealed to all that was best in his nature and spurred the most generous impulses. The operative force of such influences were first fostered by the teaching of a revered parent, then nourished and tended—with thorough belief and devoted care—by she who shared his authority in life and continued alone to bear the family sceptre. As Alister grew under such nurturing, this primary impulse became a large portion of his religion: he was the shepherd of the much ravaged and dwindled Macruadh-fold; it was his church, in which the love of the neighbor was intensified in the love of the relation and dependent. To aid and guard these, his flock, was Alister's divine service.

But it was only toward the poor of a decayed clan that he had the opportunity of exercising this cherished relation. Almost all who were not poor had emigrated before the lands were sold; indeed, it was only the poor who set store by their unity with the old head. Many of the clan who had moved elsewhere would have smiled, and not without scorn, at the idea of Alister's clinging to any supposed reality in the position he could claim—especially since he was now only a poor farmer. Alister, indeed, lived in a dream; he did not know how far the sea of hearts had ebbed, leaving him alone on the mount of his vision. But he dreamed a dream that was worth dreaming; comfort and help flowed from it to those about him. And all dreams are not false; some dreams are truer than the plainest facts. Let the dreamer only act upon the truth of his dream, and one day he will realize all that was worth realizing in it—and a great deal more and better than it contained. Alister had no far-reaching visions of anything to come out of his. He had, like the true man he was, only the desire to live up to his idea of what the people perceived in him. The one thing troubling him was that his uncle, whom he loved so dearly, had sold the land.

Doubtless there was pride mingled with his devotion, and pride is an evil thing. Still it was a human, not a devilish pride. Pride cannot be defended, nor excused in any shape; it must be destroyed at all costs. Yet a pride that loves cannot be so bad as a pride that hates. But if a good man does not cast out his pride, in the end it will degenerate into a worse pride and sink him lower even than a bad man's pride.

One other point in the character of the Macruadh was in this region at this time, a great peculiarity: he hated whiskey and all the drinking customs associated with it. His father, as a clergyman doing his best for the welfare of his flock, found himself greatly hindered by its deadening influences. And his mother had from his very childhood instilled a loathing of the national weakness into the minds of her sons. In her childhood she had seen its evils in her own father. He was by no means a drunkard, but he was less of a father because he did as others did. Never an evening passed on which he did not drink his stated portion of whiskey-toddy, growing more and more subject to attacks of bad temper and unkindness.

Isobel Macruadh was one of those rare women who preserve in years the influence gained in youth; and the thing that lay at the root of the fact was her justice. For though her highland temper would occasionally burst out in hot flame, everyone knew that if she were in the wrong, she would see it and say so before anyone would tell her of it. This justice, as ready to stand *against* herself as it was to stand *for* another, fixed the influence which her goodness and her teaching of righteousness gained.

Her eldest child, a girl, died in infancy. Alister and Ian were her whole earthly family, and they worshiped her.

5 / An Unsought Encounter_____

Alister strode through the night, revolving no difficult questions through his mind. He had not been to a university like his brother, but he had had a good educational beginning from his father, who was something of a learned man—and better, a man who knew what things were worthwhile, and what were not. His son Alister had made himself able to think about what he did not know by doing the things he did know. But now, as he walked, fighting with the wind, he was thinking mostly of Lachlan, his foster brother, whose devotion had done much to nourish in him the sense that he was head of the clan. He did not have far to go to reach his home—a couple of miles.

He had left the village a quarter of the way behind him when through the darkness he spied an even darker shape by the roadside ahead of him. Going up to it he found an old woman, half sitting, half standing, with a load of peats in a creel upon her back, apparently unable to proceed for the moment. Alister knew at once by her shape and posture who she was.

"Ah, Mistress Conal," he said. "I am sorry to see you resting on such a night so near your own door. You must have filled your creel too full and tired yourself out too much."

"I am not much too tired, Macruadh," returned the old woman, who was proud and cross-tempered and had a reputation for witchcraft, which did her neither much good nor much harm.

"Well, whether you are tired or not, I believe I am the stronger of the two."

"Small doubt of that, Alister!" said Mistress Conal with a sigh.

"Then I will take your creel and you will soon be home. Come along. It's going to be a wild night."

So saying he took the rope from the neck of the old woman and threw the creel with a strong swing over his shoulder, dislodging a few of the topmost of the peats which the poor old thing had been a long way to fetch. She heard them fall and one of them struck her foot.

"Sir, sir!" she exclaimed, half in anger. "What would you be throwing away good peats into the dark for?"

These words, as all that passed between them, were spoken neither in Scotch nor English, but in the more ancient Gaelic—which, if written, would be no more understandable to most readers than Phoenician. If

34

the English translation is deficient compared with Gaelic in vowel sounds, it nevertheless serves to say most things capable of being said.

"I am sorry, Mistress Conal; but we'll not be losing them," returned the laird gently as he began to feel about the road for the fallen chunks.

"How many were there, do you think?" he asked, rising after a vain search.

"How should I be knowing! But I am sure there would be nigh six of them!" answered the woman in a tone of deep annoyance—nor was it much wonder; they were precious to the cold, feeble, aged soul that had gone so far to fetch so few.

Alister again stooped his long back and searched and searched, feeling on all sides around him. He picked up three. Not another could he find.

"I'm thinking that must be all of them, but I find only three," he said. "Come, let us go home. You must not make your cough worse for one or two peats, perhaps none."

"Three, Macruadh, three!" insisted the old woman, in a wavering voice broken by coughing. For having once guessed six she was not inclined to lower her idea of her goods.

"Well, well, we'll count them when we get home!" said Alister, reaching out to help her up.

She yielded, grumbling; still bowed though relieved from her burden, she tottered by his side along the dark, muddy road.

"Did you see my niece tonight at the shop?" she asked; for she was proud of being so nearly related to those who kept the only shop in the hamlet.

"That I did," answered the chief, and a little talk followed about Lachlan in Canada.

No one could have perceived from the way the old woman accepted his service and the tone she spoke to him that she loved her chief. But everybody only smiled at Mistress Conal's rough speech. That night, before she went to bed, she prayed for the Macruadh as she never prayed for one of her immediate family. And if there was a good deal of superstition mingled with her prayer, the main ingredient was genuine—the love prompting it. If God heard only perfect prayers, how could he be the prayer-hearing God?

Her dwelling stood but a stone's throw from the road, and presently they turned up to it by a short steep ascent. It was a poor hut, mostly built of turf. But turf makes warm walls, impervious to the wind, and it was a place of her own! Macruadh set down the creel, and taking out peat after peat, piled them up against the wall where already a good many waited their turn to be laid on the fire. The old woman always said she must carry a few when she could, and get ahead with her store before winter came, or she would be devoured by the cold. Death always prowled about old people, she said, watching for the fire to go out. Many of the Celts are by nature poets, and Mistress Conal often spoke in a manner seldom heard from the lips of a lowland woman. The common forms of Gaelic are more poetic than those of most languages and could have originated only with a poetic people.

As the chief piled the peats, he counted them. She sat watching him from a stone that made part of a rude rampart to the hearth.

"I told you so, Macruadh!" she said the moment she saw his hand return empty from the bottom of the creel. "I was positive there should be three more!"

"I am very sorry!" said the chief, who thought it wiser not to contradict her.

He would have searched his sporran for a coin to make up for the supposed loss of her peats; but he knew well enough there was not a coin in it. He bade Mistress Conal good night, shaking hands with her, and went, closing the door carefully behind him against a great gust of wind struggling to enter. It threatened to sweep off the hearth altogether the fire she was now blowing at with her wrinkled, leather-like lips.

Macruadh ran down the last few steep steps of the path and jumped into the road. Through the darkness came the sound of one springing aside with a great start, followed by the click of a gun lock.

"Who goes there?" cried a voice.

"The Macruadh," answered the chief.

The words apparently conveyed nothing.

"Do you belong to these parts?" said the voice.

A former Macruadh might have answered, "No, these parts belong to me." But Alister curtly replied, "I do."

"Here then, my good fellow, take my game bag and carry it as far as the New House for me—if you know where I mean. I will give you a shilling."

Had he seen how pale and tired the youth with the gun was, Alister would have offered to carry his bag for him. To offer and to be asked, however, most people find much different; and here the offer of payment added to the difficulty. But the word *shilling* had raised the vision of the old woman in her lonely cottage, brooding over the loss, real or imaginary, of her three far-borne peats. What a happy night, through all the wind and rain, would a silver shilling under the chaff pillow give her! The thought froze the chief's pride and warmed his heart. How could he deny her such a pleasure? It would even bring him a little amusement! The chief of Clanruadh carrying his game bag for a Sasunnach fellow to earn a shilling! The idea had a touch of humorous consolation in it, even if mingled with a certain faint sense of shame to so degrade the chieftainship.

"I will carry your bag," he said, "but I must have the shilling first, if you please."

"Oh!" said Valentine Palmer. "You do not trust me! How then am I to trust you?"

"Sir!" said Alister—and, again finding himself on the point of being foolish, laughed.

"I will pay you when the job is done," said Valentine.

"That is quite fair, but it does not suit my purpose," returned Alister.

They were walking along the road side by side, but each could scarcely see anything of the other. The sportsman was searching his pockets to find a shilling. He succeeded, and, groping, put it in Alister's hand.

"All right! It's only a shilling. There it is! But it is not yours yet: here is the bag!"

Alister took the bag, turned, and ran back.

"Hey!" cried Valentine.

But Alister had disappeared, and as soon as he turned up the soft path to the cottage, his steps became inaudible through the wind.

He opened the door, went in, laid the shilling in the old woman's hand, and without a word hurried out again and down to the road. The stranger was some distance ahead, tramping wearily on through the darkness, grumbling at his folly in bribing a fellow with a shilling to carry off his game bag. Alister overtook him.

"Oh, here you are after all!" exclaimed Valentine. "I thought you had made off with both work and wages! What did you do that for?"

"I wanted to give the shilling to an old woman close by."

"Your mother?"

"No."

"Your grandmother?"

"No."

"Some relation, then!" insisted the stranger.

"Doubtless," answered the laird.

They walked on in silence. The youth could hardly keep up with Alister, who thought him illbred and did not much care for his company.

"Why do you walk so fast?" said Valentine.

"Because I want to get home," replied Alister.

"But I paid you to keep me company!"

"You paid me to carry your bag. I will leave it at the New House."

His coolness roused the weary youth.

"You rascal!" he said. "You keep alongside me, or I'll pepper you."

As he spoke he shifted his gun. Again they walked for some distance in silence. Alister began to discover that his companion was weary, and the goodness in his heart spoke.

"Let me carry your gun for you," he said.

"Indeed!" returned Valentine with an angry laugh. "I know a trick worth two of that!"

"You fancy your gun protects your bag?"

"I do."

The same instant the gun was drawn, with swift quiet force, through the loop of his arm from behind. Feeling himself defenseless, young Palmer sprang at the highlander, but Alister eluded him and in a moment was out of his reach, lost in the darkness. He heard the lock of one barrel snap: it was not loaded. The second barrel went off and he gave a great jump, imagining himself struck. The next instant the gun was below his arm again.

"It will be lighter now," said the Macruadh; "but if you like, I will take it."

"By Jove, I wish there was enough light to see what sort of a rascal you are!"

"You are not very polite."

"Mind your own politeness. I was never so roughly treated in my life—by a fellow, too, that had taken my money! If I knew where to find a magistrate in this beastly place—"

"You would tell him that I emptied your gun because you threatened me with it."

"You were going off with my bag!"

"Because I undertook to carry your bag, was I bound to endure your company?"

"Alister!" said a quiet voice out of the darkness.

The highlander started, and then in a tone strangely different, almost trembling yet with a kind of triumph in it, answered, "Ian."

The one word said, he stood still in the darkness. The next moment he flung down the game bag and the two men were in each other's arms.

"Where have you come from, Ian?" said the chief in a voice broken with gladness.

All Valentine understood of the question, for it was spoken in Gaelic, was its emotion, and he scorned any man who showed the least sign of breaking down.

"Straight from Moscow," answered the newcomer. "How is our mother?"

"Well, Ian, thank God!"

"Then, thank God, all is well!"

"What brought you home in such haste?"

"I had a bad dream about Mother and was a little anxious. There were other reasons, too, which I will tell you about later."

"What were you doing in Moscow? Are you on furlough?"

"To tell the truth, I am sort of a deserter. I would have given up my commission, but had not the chance. In Moscow I was teaching in a school to elude the police. But I will tell you all about it."

The brothers had momentarily forgotten the stranger and stood talking until the patience of Valentine was as much exhausted as his strength.

"Are you going to stand there all night?" he said at last. "This is no doubt very interesting to you, but it is rather a bore to one who can neither see you nor understand a word you say."

"Is the gentleman a friend of yours, Alister?" asked Ian.

"Not exactly—but he is a Sasunnach," he continued in English, "and we ought not to be speaking Gaelic."

"I beg his pardon," said Ian. "Will you introduce me?"

"It is impossible; we have never seen one another, and I cannot see him now. But he insists on my company."

"That is a great compliment. How far?"

"To the New House."

"I paid him a shilling to carry my bag," said Valentine. "He took the shilling and was going to walk off with my bag."

"Well?"

"Well indeed! Not at all well! How was I to know—"

"But he didn't—did he?" said Ian, whose voice seemed now to tingle with amusement over the situation. "Alister," he said, turning toward his brother, "you were wrong, you know."

"I know it," he said. "The moment I heard your voice, I knew it. How is it, Ian, that when you are by me, I know what is right so much quicker? I meant to do right, but—"

"But your pride got in the way. I hate to see the devil make a fool of a man like you. Don't you know that in your own country you owe a stranger hospitality?"

"My own country!" echoed Alister with a groan.

"Yes, your own country—and perhaps more yours than it was your grandfather's! You know who said, 'The meek shall inherit the earth'! If it can't be ours God's way, I for one would not care to call it mine any other way. But we must not keep the gentleman standing while we talk!"

"Thank you!" said Valentine. "The fact is, I'm dead beat."

"Have you anything I could carry for you?" asked Ian.

"No, thank you. Yes, here, if you don't mind taking my gun? You speak like a gentleman!"

"I will take it with pleasure."

He took the gun and they started.

"If you choose, Alister," said his brother, again in Gaelic, "to break through conventionalities, you must not expect people to allow you to creep inside them again the moment you please."

But the young fellow's fatigue had touched Alister.

"Are you a big man?" he said, taking Valentine gently by the arm.

"Not as big as you, I'll lay you a sovereign," answered Valentine, wondering why he should ask.

"Then look here!" said Alister. "You get astride my shoulders, and I'll carry you home. I believe you're hungry, and that takes it out of you. Here, Ian, you take the bag; you can manage that and the gun, too."

Valentine murmured some objection; but the brothers took it as a matter of course, and he felt so terribly exhausted—for he had been out since morning and had lost his way—that in the end he yielded.

Alister doubled himself up on his heels, Valentine got his weary legs over his stalwart shoulders, the chief rose with him as if he had been no heavier than Mistress Conal's creel, and bore him along.

The chief and Ian kept up a stream of conversation, every now and then forgetting their manners and gliding off into Gaelic, but as often recollecting themselves, apologizing, and starting again on the path of English. Long before they reached the end of their journey, Valentine came to understand that he had not fallen in with rustics but, whatever their peculiarities, with gentlemen of a noteworthy sort.

The brothers, in the joy of their reunion, talked much of things at home and abroad, but when they saw the lights of the New House, a silence fell upon them. At the door, Alister set his burden carefully down.

"There!" he said with a laugh. "I hope I have earned my shilling!"

"Ten times over," said Valentine. "But I know now better than to offer to pay you. I thank you with all my heart."

The door opened, Ian gave the gun and the bag to the butler, and the brothers bade Valentine a good night.

Valentine had a strange tale to tell. Sercombe refused to accept his conclusions: if he had offered the men half a crown apiece, he said, they would have pocketed the money and fled into the darkness.

6 / Mother Macruadh

The sun shone bright, and the chief was out early in his fields. His oats were nearly ready for the scythe; he was judging where it would be best to begin to cut them.

His fields lay chiefly along the banks of the stream, occupying the whole breadth of the valley on the east side of the ridge where the cottage stood. On the west side of the ridge, nearly parallel to and not many yards from it, a small brook ran to join the stream. This brook was the boundary between the chief's land and Mr. Peregrine Palmer's. Their respective limits were not everywhere so well defined.

The air was clear, clean and full of life. The wind was asleep. A consciousness of work approaching completion filled earth and air—a mood of calm expectation. There was no song of birds—only an occasional crow from the yard or the cry of a blackcock from the hill. The two streams were left to do all the singing, and they did their best, though their water was low. The day was of the evening of the year; even in the full sunshine the twilight and the coming night were present, but there was a sense of readiness on all sides. The fruits of the earth must be housed; that alone remained to be done.

When Macruadh had made up his mind, he turned toward the house—a lowly cottage, more extensive than many farmhouses but appearing no better. It was well built, with an outside wall of rough stone and lime, and another wall of turf within, lined in parts with wood, making it as warm a nest as any house of the size could be. The door, picturesque with abundant repair, opened by a latch into the kitchen.

For many years the floor of the kitchen had been earthen, with the fire on a hearth in the middle of it, as in most cottages. The smoke rose into the roof—keeping it very dry and warm, also very sooty—and then into the air through a hole in the middle. But some ten years before, Alister and Ian, mere lads, had constructed a chimney outside, opened the wall, and built a new hearth in this hole between cottage and chimney, thus giving the smoke its own private way to liberty. They paved the floor with such stones as they could find, smooth and flat enough on one side, and by sinking them according to their thickness, they managed to get a tolerably even surface. Many other improvements followed; although it was still a poor place, it would have been considered a good enough house for an unambitious knight or poor baronet.

41

In the kitchen a plain fir dresser stood under one of the tiny windows, giving enough light for a clean-souled cook. There were only four panes in it, but it opened and closed and so was superior to many windows. On the opposite side of the house was a larger window which, in the winter when the cold was severe, they sometimes filled with a barricade of turf.

A fire was burning on the hearth—small, for the midday meal was not yet on its way. Everything was tidy; the hearth was swept up, the dishes washed. A barefooted girl was placing the last of them on the rack behind the dresser. She was a red-haired, blue-eyed Celt with a pretty face and a refinement of motion and speech.

The chief entered and took down an old-fashioned gun from the wall. He wanted a bird or two, for Ian's homecoming was a great event.

"I saw a big stag last night down by the burn, sir," said the girl, "feeding as if he had been the red cow."

"I don't want him today, Nancy," returned her master. "Did he have big horns?"

"Great horns, sir. But it was too dark to count them."

"When was it?"

"I thought it was morning, sir, and when I got up it was the middle of the night. The moon was so shiny that I went to the door and looked out. Just at the narrow leap I saw him plain."

"If you should see him again, Nancy, scare him. I don't want the Sasunnachs at the New House to see him."

"Hadn't you better take him for yourself, Macruadh? He would make fine hams for the winter!"

"Mind your business, Nancy," said the chief with a smile that took all the harshness from the words. "Don't you tell anyone you saw him. For what you know he may be the big stag."

"Surely no one would kill *him*, sir!" said the girl, aghast.

"I hope not. But get the stoving pot ready, Nancy; I'm going to find a bird or two. In case I should not succeed, have a couple of chickens ready too."

"The mistress has already asked for them."

"That is well. But don't kill them unless I am not back in time."

"I understand, sir."

Macruadh knew the stag as well as the horse he rode, and he knew that his habit had been for some time to come down at night and feed on the small border of rich grass on the south side of the burn, between it and the abrupt heathery rise of the hill. For there the burn ran so near the hill and the ground was so covered with huge masses of gray rock that there was hardly room for cultivation, so the bank was left in grass.

The stalking of the stag was the passion of the highlander in that part of the country. He cared little for shooting the grouse, black or red, and almost despised those whose ambition was a full bag of such game. But he dreamed day and night of killing deer. The chief, however, was in this matter more of a man without being less of a highlander. He loved the deer so much, saw them so much a part of the glory of the mountain and sky, sunshine and storm, that he liked to see them living, not dead. He only shot one now and then when the family had particular need of it. He felt himself the father of the deer as well as of his clan, and mourned greatly that he could do so little now to protect them because of the limited range of his property. Even the creatures that preyed upon others he killed only from a sense of duty and took no pleasure in their death. The heartlessness of the common sportsman was loathesome to him. When there was not much to do on the farm, he would sometimes be out all night, watching the ways and doings of the many creatures that roam while men sleep. One of the reasons he disliked the new possessors of the old land was that he feared a raid upon the wild animals.

Back in the cottage, as he left, his mother sat in the parlor in an old-fashioned easy chair beside the chimney. The room was about fifteen feet by twelve and the ceiling was low. On the white walls hung a few frames containing two or three water colors, several miniature portraits, and one or two silhouettes. Opposite the door hung a target of hide, round and bossed with brass, which Alister had found covering a meal barrel—a service which probably enabled it to elude the search for arms after the battle of Culloden. Under it rested, horizontally upon two nails, the sword of the chief—a long and broad *Andrew Ferrara*, with a plated basket-hilt. Beside it hung a dagger—longer than usual and fine in form, with a carved hilt in the shape of an eagle's head and neck. The sheath, its leather old and flaky with age, was heavily mounted in silver. Below these was a card table of marquetry with spindly legs, holding a workbox of ivory, inlaid with silver and ebony. In the corner stood an Erard harp, golden and gracious, not a string of it broken. In the middle of the room was a small square table, covered with a green cloth.

In middle age Mrs. Macruadh was still beautiful, with the rare beauty that shone from the root of her being. Her hair was of the darkest brown, almost black; her eyes were very dark and her skin very fair, though the soft bloom was gone from her cheek and her hair showed lines of keen silver. Her features were fine, clear, and regular. A more refined and courteous presence could not have been found. The dignity of her carriage in no way detracted from its grace. The falsehood of assuming the look of another's station was impossible to Isobel Macruadh. She wore no cap; her hair was gathered in a large knot near the top of her head. Her gown was of a dark print; she displayed no ornament except a ring with a single ruby. She was working a bit of net into lace.

She could speak Gaelic as well as any in the glen—perhaps better. But to her sons she always spoke English. To them English was their mother-tongue, in the sense that only English came to them from her lips. There were plenty to teach them Gaelic, she said; she must see to their English.

The one window of the parlor, though not large, was of tolerable size, but little light entered because it was so shaded by a rose tree in a pot on the sill. On the opposite wall was a couch, and on the couch lay Ian with a book in his hand—a book in a strange language. His mother and he would sometimes be a whole morning together and exchange no more than a word or two, though many a look and smile. It seemed enough to be in each other's company. There was quite a peculiar bond between the two.

Like so many of the young men of that country, Ian had been intended for the army. But there was in him something of the spirit of the eagle; he passionately loved freedom and had almost a gypsy's delight in wandering. When he left college he became a tutor in a Russian family of distinction, and after that accepted a military commission and served the Czar for three or four years.

But wherever he went he seemed, as he said once to his mother, aware of an almost physical line stretching between him and her, which seemed to vibrate when he grew anxious about her. The bond between him and his brother was equally strong, but different. Between Alister and him it was a cable; between his mother and him a harpstring. In the one case it was a muscle, in the other a nerve. The one retained, the other drew him. Given to roaming as he was, again and again he returned, from pure love-longing, to what he always felt as the *protection* of his mother—protection from his own glooms which nothing but her love seemed able to alleviate.

He was tall—well over six feet, but not of his brother's fine proportion. He was thin, with long slender fingers and feet like his mother's. His small, strong bones were covered with little more than hard muscle, but every motion of limb or body was graceful. His forehead was rather low, freckled, and crowned with hair of a foxy red; his eyes were gray-green; his nose like an eagle. On his short upper lip was a small light moustache, but the rest of his face was clean-shaven. His countenance wore a great calmness, but a calmness that might have seemed rooted in sadness.

While the mother might differ openly with her elder born—whom she admired as well as loved from the bottom of her heart—she was never *known* to say a word of opposition to the younger. It was even whispered that she was afraid of him. It was not so, but her reverence for Ian was such that, even when she felt bound not to agree with him, she seldom had the confidence that—differing from *him*—she was in the right. Sometimes in the middle of the night she would slip quietly into the room where he lay and sit by his bed for hours. The son might be awake all the time, and the mother suspect him awake, yet no word passed between them. Her feeling for her younger son was like that of Hannah for her eldest—intense love mixed with strange reverence.

At one moment she would regard him as gifted beyond his fellows for some great work; at another, she would be filled with a horrible fear that he was in rebellion against the God of his life. Doubtless mothers are far too ready to think *their* sons above the ordinary breed: self, unpossessed of God, will worship itself in its offspring. Yet the sons whom *holy* mothers have regarded as born to great things and who have passed away without a sign of such greatness while in the world, may have gone on toward their great things. Whether this mother thought too much of her son or not, there were questions moving in his mind which she could not have understood—even when he was young and would creep to her bed in the morning to forget in her arms the terrible dreams of the night, or when at evening he would draw his little stool to her knee, unable or unwilling to enjoy his book anywhere but by her side.

What gave him his unconscious power over his mother was, first, what he said, and next, what he did not say; for he seemed to dwell in a rich silence. Yet there remained something between them across which they could not fully meet; a complete union was impossible because of their differing views on spiritual things. Such union is presumed by most people to be impossible without consent of opinion. This mistake on the mother's part rendered her unable to feel entirely at home with him. If she had believed that they understood each other—that is, were of like *opinion*—she would not have been half so unhappy when he went away. Ian, on his part, understood his mother, but knew she did not understand him.

When Ian was gone, she naturally then turned more to Alister, and his love was a strengthening tonic to her sick motherhood. He was never jealous of either. He loved their love for each other. He, too, would mourn deeply over his brother's departure, but it became at the same moment his business to comfort his mother. This drew her with fresh love to her elder born and gave her a renewal of the quiet satisfaction in him which she always felt. Their mutual affection was indeed as true and strong as a mother could desire it.

"Did you not feel the cold very much at St. Petersburg last winter, Ian?"

With a prelusive smile that shone on the mother's heart, Ian lowered his book.

"Yes, Mother, at times," he answered. "But everybody wears fur; the peasant his sheep skin, the noble his silver fox. Nose and toes are in constant danger."

"You will not go back to Russia, will you, Ian? Surely there is work for you at home."

"What can I do, Mother? You have no money to buy me a commission and I am not much good at farm work. Alister says I am not worth a horseman's wages!"

"You could find teaching; or you could go into the church. We might manage that; you would only have to attend the divinity classes."

"Mother, you would put me into one of the priests' offices! As for teaching, there are already too many hungry students for that. I could not take bread out of their mouths. In truth, Mother, I could not endure it. I can live on as little as anyone, but I must have some liberty. I must surely have inherited the spirit of some old sea rover, it is so difficult for me to rest. I am a thistle seed for wandering! I must know how my fellow beings live. I should like to be one man after another—each for an hour or two!"

"Your father used to say there was Norse blood in the family."

"There it is, Mother! I can't help it."

"I don't like the idea of you holding the Czar's commission, Ian— somehow I don't like it. He is a tyrant."

"I am going to give it up, Mother."

"I am glad of that. How did you ever get it?"

"I did a man a good turn, which he was most generous in acknowledging. As he belonged to the court, I was given the offer of a lieutenant's commission. The Scotch are well thought of there."

A cloud settled on the face of the young man. The lady looked at him for a moment with keen mother-eyes. She looked down again to her work and then another question broke from her lips.

"What sort of church did you have to go to in St. Petersburg, Ian?" she said.

Ian was silent a moment, thinking how to be true without hurting her any more than could be helped.

"There are a thousand places of worship there, Mother," he returned with a curious smile.

"Any Presbyterian place?" she asked.

"I believe so," he replied.

"Ian, you haven't given up praying?"

"If ever I prayed, Mother, I certainly have not given it up."

"Ever prayed, Ian! When you were merely a child you prayed like an aging Christian."

"Ah, Mother, that was a sad pity. I asked for things I had no need of. I was a hypocrite. I ought to have prayed like a little child."

The mother was silent. She had taught him to pray—making him pray aloud in her hearing. *And this is the result! The premature blossom has withered!* she said to herself.

"Then you don't go to church!" she said at length.

"Not often, Mother dear," he answered. "When I do go, I like to go to the church of the country I happen to be in. Going to church and praying to God are not the same thing."

"Paul tells us not to forsake the church, Ian."

"*He* commands us to love, Mother—a much higher calling. *He* never uttered a word about going to church."

"Then you say your prayers? Oh, do not tell me you never bow down before your Maker!"

"Shall I tell you where I did once pray to God, Mother?" he said, after a little pause, anxious to soothe her suffering. "At least I did think I prayed!" he added.

"It was not this morning, then, before you left your room?"

"No, Mother," answered Ian. "I did not pray this morning, and I never say prayers."

The mother gave a gasp, but said nothing. Ian went on again.

"I should like to tell you, Mother, about that time."

"I should like to hear about it," she answered with a strange mingling of emotions. On the one hand, she felt parted from her son by a gulf into which she must cast herself to find him, and on the other, that he stood on a height of sacred experience which she could never hope to climb. *Oh, for his father to talk to him*, she said to herself. Ian held a power on her soul which she almost feared.

It was the first time they had come so close in their talk. The moment his mother spoke out, Ian had responded. He was anxious to be open with her so far as he could and forced his natural reticence. Always thoughtful of her, Ian found it hard to talk where there was so much thinking to be done. But wherever he could keep his mother company, he would not leave her.

Just as he opened his mouth, however, to begin his narration, the door opened, flung wide by Nancy, and two young ladies entered.

7 / A Morning Call_____

Had Valentine known who the brothers were or where they lived, he would before now have called to thank them again for their kindness to him. But he imagined they had some distance to go after depositing him. The present visitors, however, had nothing to do with him.

The two elder girls, curious about the pretty cottage, had come wandering down the spur, or hill-toe, as far as the cottage. Beside the door stood a milk pail and a churn, set out to be sweetened by the sun and wind. It was very rural, they thought, and very homely. Thus without hesitation, Christina, followed by Mercy, walked in at the open door, found a barefooted girl in the kitchen, and spoke pleasantly to her. She, in simple hospitality forgetting herself, made answer in Gaelic. Never doubting that the ladies had come to call upon her mistress, she led the way, and the girls, without thinking, followed her into the parlor.

Entering the parlor they did not know what to expect. They had heard of the cowhouse, the stable, even the pigsty, being under the same roof in these parts! For all they knew, the girl might be leading them into the barn! When the opening door disclosed Lady Macruadh, every inch a chieftain's widow, their conventional breeding failed them a little. Though they were incapable of recognizing a refinement beyond their own, they were not incapable of feeling its influence. But when a young man sprang from a couch and the stately lady rose and advanced to receive them, it was too late for retreat. They stood abashed, feeling like intruders.

The behavior of the lady and the gentleman, however, speedily set them at ease. Ian placed chairs for them and invited them to be seated, and the lady began to talk as if their entrance were the least unexpected thing in the world. Leaving them to explain their visit or not as they saw fit, she spoke of the weather, the harvest, the shooting. The birds, though quite healthy, were not numerous, for they had too many enemies to multiply! She asked if they had seen the view from such and such a point. In short, she carried herself as one to whom cordiality to strangers was a duty. But she was not impressed with them. Her order of civilization was higher than theirs, and the simplicity and old-fashioned finish of her consciousness recoiled a little at the young ladies' manner and expression.

Without being able to recognize the superiority of a woman who lived in a cottage, the young ladies felt and disliked it. The matron sensed the commonness of the girls, without knowing exactly what it was. The girls, on the other hand, were very interested in the young man. He looked like a gentleman! Ian, in turn, was interested in the young women. Attributing their airs to shyness, he quickly made them comfortable. His commanding demeanor in the midst of his great courtesy roused their admiration, and they had not been in his company very long before they were satisfied that, however it was to be accounted for, the young man was very much a gentleman. It was an unexpected discovery of northern produce, and "the estate" immediately gained interest in their eyes. Christina did the greater part of the talking, though both did their best to be agreeable.

Ian saw quite as well as his mother what ordinary girls they were, but accustomed to the newer modes in manner and speech, he was not bothered by movements and phrases that annoyed her. The mother noted the mutual fascination and was uneasy, though she did not show it.

When they rose Ian escorted them to the door, leaving his mother anxious, for she was afraid he might accompany them home. Till he returned she did not resume her seat.

The girls walked along the ridge in silence until the ruin was between them and the cottage. Then they burst into laughter. They were ladies enough not to laugh till out of sight, but not ladies enough to see there was nothing to laugh at.

"A harp, too!" said Christina. "Mercy, I believe we are on top of Mount Ararat, and have this very moment left the real Noah's ark, patched into a cottage! Who *can* they be?"

"Gentlefolk evidently," said Mercy. "Perhaps old-fashioned people from Inverness."

"The young man must have been to college! In the north, you know," continued Christina, thinking with pride that her brother was at Oxford. "Even ploughmen send their sons to St. Andrews and Aberdeen to make gentlemen of them!"

"And in this case they have succeeded!"

"I didn't mean *his* father was a ploughman! That would be impossible. Besides, I heard him call that very respectable person *mother*. She is not a ploughman's wife, but surely a lady of the middle class."

Christina did not consider that her own family belonged to the middle class. Perhaps the tone of implied contempt with which her father spoke of the lower classes, and the quiet negation with which her mother would allude to shopkeepers, may have had something to do with her attitude. But the young people of the family imagined themselves to belong to the upper class and on anyone living in a humble house or poor cottage, they looked down with indifference or patronage. They little dreamed how—had she known all about them—the respectable person in the cottage would have looked down with pity upon *them*!

"I will tell you my theory, Mercy," Christina went on. "The lady is the widow of an Indian army officer—perhaps a colonel. Some of their widows are left very poor, but they think highly of themselves. The young man has a military air which he may have got from his father, or he may be an officer himself. Young officers are always poor. That's what makes them so nice to flirt with. I wonder if he really *is* an officer! We've actually called upon the people, and come away too, without knowing their names."

At the cottage, Ian, returning from bidding the ladies good-bye, said, "I suppose they're from the New House!" He had been rewarded with a bewitching smile from the elder and a shy glance from the younger as they left.

"Where else could they be from?" returned his mother. "Come to make our country poorer yet!"

"They're not English."

"Vulgar people from Glasgow, then."

"I think you are too hard on them, Mother. They are not exactly vulgar. I thought there was even a sort of gentleness about them you do not often meet in Scotch girls."

"In the lowlands, I grant, Ian. But the daughter of the poorest tackman of the Macruadhs has a manner and a modesty I have seen in no Sasunnach girl yet. Those girls are bold!"

"Self-possessed, perhaps," said Ian, then paused. "But girls are different from what they used to be, I fancy, Mother," he added thoughtfully.

"The world changes very fast," said the mother sadly. She was thinking, like Rebecca: if her sons took a fancy to these who were not daughters of the land, what good would her life do her?

"Ah, Mother dear," said Ian, "I have never"—as he spoke the cloud deepened on his forehead—"seen more than one woman whose ways and manners reminded me of you!"

"And who was she?" the mother asked, pleased.

But she almost repented of the question when she saw how low the cloud descended on his face.

"A princess, Mother. She is dead," he answered, turning to walk so gently from the room that it was impossible for his mother to detain him.

8 / Alister and Sercombe

The next morning soon after sunrise, the laird began to cut his barley. Ian would gladly have helped, but Alister had a notion that such labor was not fit for him.

Entering the kitchen at dinnertime, Alister had a smile on his face. "I had a comical interview this morning," he said. "I was standing by the side of the burn near the footbridge when I heard somebody shouting. I looked up and there was a big English fellow in gray on top of the ridge with his gun on his shoulder, hollering at me. 'Hey, you there!' he said. 'Come, carry my bag. You don't seem to have anything to do! I'll give you five shillings.' "

"You see what you expose yourself to by your unconventionalities, Alister," said his brother with mock gravity.

"It was not the fellow we carried home the other night, Ian. This man was twice his size. It would have taken all I had to carry *him* home."

"The others must have pointed you out to him!"

"It was much too dark for him to know me again."

"You forget the hall lamp!" said Ian.

"Ah, yes, you're right. I had forgotten. Anyway, the fellow went on by saying, 'You'll want prepayment, no doubt,' putting his hand in his pocket. Those Sasunnach fellows think any highlandman keen as a hawk after their dirty money!"

"They have good reason in some parts," said his mother. "The old breed is fast disappearing. With the difficulty of living even by the hardest work, and the occasional chance of earning a shilling easily, many have turned both idle and greedy."

"That's you and your shilling, Alister!" said Ian.

"I confess," returned Alister, "if I had known what impression of the gentlemen of the country I might give, I would have hesitated. But I'm not yet ashamed of what I did."

"Ashamed, Alister!" cried Ian. "What does it matter what a fellow like that thinks?"

"And Mistress Conal has her shilling," said the mother.

"If the thing was right," pursued Ian, "no harm can come of it; if it was not right, no end of harm may come. But you haven't told us how the thing ended."

"I said to the fellow," resumed Alister, "that I had my shearing to do and I hadn't the time to go with him. 'Is this your season for sheep-shearing?' he asked.

" 'We call cutting the grain shearing,' I answered, 'because in these parts we use the reaping hook.'

" 'That is a great waste of labor,' he returned. I did not tell him that some of our land would smash his machines like toys.

" 'How?' I asked.

" 'It costs so much more,' he said.

" 'But it feeds so many more,' I replied.

" 'Oh, yes, of course, if you don't want the farmer to make a living!'

" 'I manage to make a living,' I said.

" 'Then you are the farmer?'

" 'So it would appear.'

" 'I beg your pardon; I thought—'

" 'You thought I was an idle fellow, glad of an easy job to keep the life in me!'

" 'They tell me you were deuced glad of a job the other night.'

" 'So I was. I wanted a shilling for a poor woman, and I hadn't one to give her without going home a mile and a half for it!'

"By this time he had come down and I had gone a few steps to meet him; I did not want to seem unfriendly. 'The old lady ought to be grateful,' he said.

" 'So ought we all,' I answered, 'I to your friend for the shilling, and he to me for taking his bag. He did me one good turn for my poor woman, and I did him another for his poor legs!' Just then a hare scampered by and up went his gun to his shoulder. 'None of that!' I cried and knocked up the barrel.

" 'What do you mean?' he roared, looking curious. 'Get out of the way or I'll shoot *you*!'

" 'Then you will have murder as well as poaching to contend with,' I said.

" 'Poaching?' he shouted with a scornful laugh.

" 'That rabbit is mine,' I said; 'I will not have it killed.'

" 'You speak rather boldly,' he said, 'especially on Mr. Palmer's land!'

" 'The land is mine, and I am my own gamekeeper!' I rejoined.

" 'You look like it,' he returned.

" 'You put your gun on half-cock, and go after your birds—but not in this direction,' I said, and turned and left him."

"Do you think you handled it the right way?" asked Ian.

"I did almost lose my temper. I almost expected him to fire after I left him, for there was the rabbit lurching slowly away in full view. I'm glad he didn't; I always feel bad after a row."

"Is the conscience getting fastidious, do you think, Alister?" said Ian.

"How is anybody to know that when he's got to obey it?"

"True—so long as we suspect no mistake in what it tells us!"

"So long as it agrees with the Bible, Ian," said the mother.

"The Bible is a big book, Mother, and the things in it are of many sorts," returned Ian. "I am not sure even the Lord would approve of *everything* in it."

"Ian! I am shocked to hear you speak like that!"

Ian rose from the table, knelt by her side, and laid his head on her shoulder. She was silent, pained by his words, and put her arm round him as if to shield him from the evil one. His homage to the Master, apart from the acceptance of certain doctrines, was in her eyes not merely defective but dangerous.

Alister rose and went: there was to him something especially sacred in the communion of his mother and brother. Even though he agreed with Ian, he shrank from any difference with his mother. For her sake he received Sunday after Sunday in silence what was to him a bushel of dust with an occasional bit of moldy bread. But the mother did not imagine any great agreement of opinion between her and Alister any more than between her and Ian. She had not the faintest notion how much genuine faith both of them had, or how it surpassed her own in vitality.

To his brother, Ian seemed hardly touched with earthly stain. But despite his large and dominant humanity, Alister was still in the troublesome condition of one trying to do right against a powerful fermentation of pride. He held noblest principles; but the sediment of generations was too easily stirred up to cloud them. He loved his neighbor, but his neighbor was mostly of his own family or his own clan. He *might* have been unjust for the sake of his own—a small fault in the eyes of the world, but a great fault indeed in a nature like his, capable of being so much beyond it. For while the faults of a good man cannot be as evil as the faults of a bad man, they are more blameworthy, and greater faults than the same would be in a bad man.

Ian was one of those blessed few who doubt many things by virtue of a larger faith—causing consternation among those of smaller faith who wrongly see such doubts as signs of unbelief. But while his roots were seeking a deeper soil, his faith could not show so fast a growth above ground. He doubted most about the things he loved best, while he devoted the energies of a mind whose keenness almost masked its power, to discover possible ways of believing them. To the wise his doubts would have been his best credentials; they were worth ten times the faith of most. It was truth, and higher truth, he was always seeking. The sadness which colored his deepest individuality could be removed only by the conscious presence of the Eternal.

9 / The Plough Bulls

For some time there was no further meeting between any of the chief's family and that of the new laird. Indeed, there was little to draw them together except their common isolation. Valentine would have been pleased to show gratitude to his helpers on that stormy night, but after his sisters' account of their call, he felt not only ashamed, which was right, but ashamed to show his shame, which was a new shame. The girls on their part made so much of what they counted the ridiculous elements of their "adventure" that before long they saw nothing but the ridiculous in it. In the same spirit of facetious wit Mr. Sercombe recounted his adventure with Alister, which annoyed his host, who had but little acquaintance with the boundaries of his land. From the additional servants they had hired, the people of the New House gathered correct information concerning the people at the cottage, but the honor in which the latter were held only added to the ridicule associated with them.

On the other side also there was little inclination toward further interaction. Mrs. Macruadh, from Nancy's account and the behavior of the girls, gathered the reason for their visit; and, as their mother did not follow it up, took no notice of it. In Mercy's mind, however, lurked a little thorn which stung her every time she joined in a laugh at the people of the cottage, feeling that she was not being quite just to them.

The shooting, such as it was, went on, along with the sleeping and the eating, the walking and the talking. Long letters were written from the New House to female friends—letters with the flourishes if not the substance of wit, and funny tales concerning the natives, whom, because of their poor houses and unintelligible language, they represented as semi-savages. The young men went back to Oxford, and the time seemed drawing nigh for the family to return to civilization.

About this time, however, a certain financial speculation of Mr. Peregrine Palmer's failed completely; overnight several thousand pounds were lost, producing in him the feeling a lady of moderate means experiences when she loses her purse. He must find some way to save, and thus gain at least a portion back! For though he spent freely, he placed a great value on money—as well he might, seeing that it gave him the distinction he prized above everything else. He did not know what a poor thing it is to be distinguished among men, and therefore did

55

not like losing his thousands. He must do something, and the first thing that occurred to him was to leave his wife and daughters where they were for the winter. None of them were in the least delicate, and his wife professed herself fond of the country life. It would also give the girls a good opportunity for practice, drawing, and study, and he would find them a suitable governess. And think how much money he would save by not being in London for the social season!

He talked the matter over with Mrs. Palmer. She did not object to the plan. He would spend Christmas with them, he said, and bring Christian, and perhaps Mr. Sercombe, with him.

The girls, however, did not like the idea. It was so cold in the country in winter, and the snow would be so deep! They would be starved to death! But of course if the governor had made up his mind to be cruel, what could they do?

The thing was settled. It was only for one winter. It would be a new experience for them, and they would enjoy their next *season* all the more! The governor had promised to send them new furs and a great box full of novels. He did not tell them that he meant to sell their horses to do it, and to raise additional cash besides. The horses, after all, were his. He was an indulgent father and did not deprive them, but he was not going to ask their permission. But at the same time he did not have the courage to tell them of his plans.

When the time came for him to leave, he took his wife with him as far as Inverness for a day or two that she might purchase a good stock of everything needed for the winter.

When the parents were gone from the house, the girls felt *larky*. They had no wish to do anything they would not do if their parents were at home, but there was a sense of relief in doing whatever they liked. The older two soon resolved on a walk to the village, to see what might be seen—in particular, the young woman at the shop they had heard their brother and Mr. Sercombe speak of.

It was a bright, pleasant, frosty morning, perfectly still, with an air like wine. The harvest had vanished from the fields. The sun shone on millions of tiny dew-suns, threaded on forsaken spider webs. The purple heather was not yet gone, and no snow had yet fallen in the valley. The burn was large, for there had been a good deal of rain, but it was not much darker than its usual brown of smoke-crystal. They tripped gaily along. They had little spiritual, but much innocent natural life, which no great disappointments or keen twinges of conscience had yet damped. They were but human kittens—young, playful, not yet fully awake— and not of the finest breed.

As they crossed the root of the spur and looked down on the autumn fields to the east of it, they caught sight of something they did not understand. Looking more intently they saw what seemed to be a contest between man and beast, but they could still not grasp what was going on. Gradually it grew plain that two of the cattle of the country, wild and shaggy, were rebelling against being subdued. They were in fact two young bulls, of the small black highland breed, accustomed to galloping over the rough hills, jumping like goats, which Alister had set himself the task of breaking to the plough. That was no easy job, or one to be accomplished single-handedly by any but a man of some strength as well as persistence and patience. He had lost a horse a few months earlier which he could hardly afford to replace. If he could make these bulls work, they would not only save him the price of the horse, they would cost less to keep and require less attention.

He had bridled them by the nose, not with rings through their flesh, but with nose bands of iron, bluntly spiked inside so that they could not pull hard without pain. He had made some progress, though he could by no means trust them yet; every now and then a fit of mingled wildness and stubbornness would seize them, and the contest would appear about to begin again from the very beginning. The nose band of one of them had come off and Alister now had him by a horn in each hand. A fierce struggle was going on between them, while the other was pulling away from his companion as if determined to take to the hills. It was a good thing for them that the plough was deep into the ground and thus a help to their master, for had they got away they would probably have killed or at least lamed themselves. Presently he had the nose band on, and by force and persuasion together got the better of them. The shaggy little furries gave in, and Alister quickly gathered up his reins and went back to the plough-stilts, where each hand held at once a handle and a rein. With energetic obedience the little animals began to pull—so vigorously that it took nearly all the chief's strength to hold both his plough and his team.

It was something of a sight to the girls after such a scarcity of events. They were not altogether unused to animals. They had horses they called their own, and would often go to the stables to give their orders, or see that they were carried out. They waited now for some time hoping the fight would begin again. By common consent they left the road, passed the ruin, ran down the steep side of the ridge, and began to work their way through the stubble of the harvested field toward the ploughman. A sharp straw every now and then pierced through their delicate stockings, and the damp soil gathered in great lumps on their shoes. But they plodded on, laughing merrily as they went.

The Macruadh was deep in thought, meditating on the power of the frost to break up the clods of the field, when he saw the girls coming up close to him. He pulled in his cattle, took off his cap with one hand while holding both reins with the other, and said, "Excuse me, ladies. My animals are young and not quite broken. Stand back, please."

They were a little surprised by the reception and concluded from it that the man must be the laird himself. They had heard he cultivated his own land, but had not imagined that to mean he actually labored in the fields himself.

In spite of the blindness produced by their conventional education and training, they could not help but perceive something in the man worthy of their attention. Before them stood a dark, handsome, weather-browned man, with the look of an eagle, yet not so pronounced as his brother's. His hair was long, almost black, in thick, soft curls over a small, well-set head. His glance had the flash that comes with victorious effort; every muscle stood ready. He wore the dark beard that nature had given him; disordered by the struggle with his bulls, it imparted a certain wild look that contrasted with his speech. Christina noted that he did not show the least embarrassment by their presence. A certain Sutherland clan was said to be all gentlemen, and a certain Argyll clan all poets. But the Macruadhs were said to be both. As to Mercy, the first glance of the chief's hazel eyes, looking straight into hers with genial respect, went deeper than any look had yet penetrated.

Ladies in Alister's fields were not an everyday sight. Never before had his work been enlivened by such a presence, and he felt joy at it inside, though his behavior was calm. Christina thought how pleasant and interesting it would be in the days of their winter's banishment to make of him a gentleman who would worship her. He was handsome! Why shouldn't she proceed at once to conquer him? The temptation to patronize another is usually an instinct common to persons of low degree. Therefore, the object of patronage is often superior to the would-be patron, to whom it affords an outlet for the vague activity of self-importance. Miss Palmer worshiped herself, and therefore would fain be worshiped by the country fellow.

She put on a smile—no difficult thing, for she was a good-natured girl. It looked to Alister quite natural. It was nevertheless, like Hamlet's false friends, "sent for" by the false friend of her *self*.

"Do you like ploughing?" she asked.

Had she known the manners of the country, she would have added "laird," or "Macruadh."

"Yes, I do," Alister answered. "But I should plough all the same if I did not. It has to be done."

"But why should *you* do it?"

"Because I must," laughed the laird.

What could she say? It hardly seemed prudent to offer condolences to one who worked at what he obviously enjoyed doing. She would try another tack.

"You had some trouble with your oxen. We saw it from the road and were quite frightened. I hope you are not hurt."

"There was no danger of that," answered Alister with a smile.

"What wild creatures they are! Isn't it rather hard work for them? They are so small."

"They are as strong as horses," answered the laird. "It's hard work to break them. Indeed, I have hardly done it yet! They would very much like to run their horns into me."

"Then it *must* be dangerous! It shows they were not meant to work."

"They were meant to work if I can make them work."

"Then you approve of slavery," said Mercy, speaking up for the first time.

She hardly knew what made her oppose him. As yet she had no opinions of her own, though she did catch an occasional thought sometimes, when it happened to come within her reach. Alister smiled a curious smile, but said nothing.

"You believe, then," she continued, "that we have a right to make lower animals work?"

"I think it is our duty," answered Alister. "In any event, if we do not, we must either kill them off by degrees, or give them this country and leave ourselves. But even that would not be such a good thing for my little bulls here. It is not so many years ago that the last wolf was killed—here, close by! And if we did not subdue the animals, the dogs would turn to wolves again, and then where would my bulls be? The domestic animals would then have the wild beasts for their masters instead of men. No, to have the world a habitable place, man must rule."

"Men are nothing but tyrants to them!" exploded Christina.

"Most are, I admit."

Before he could prevent her, she walked up to the bull nearest her and began to pat him. He poked a sharp wicked horn sideways at her, catching her cloak on it and grazing her arm. She jumped back, her face pale. Alister gave him a terrible tug. The beast shook his head and began to paw the earth.

"It won't do to go near him," he warned. "But you needn't be afraid. He can't touch you. That iron band round his nose has spikes in it."

"Poor fellow!" said Christina. "It is no wonder he is angry. It must hurt him dreadfully!"

"It does hurt him when he pulls against it, but not when he is quiet."

"I call it cruel."

"I do not. He knows what is wanted of him—just as well as any naughty child."

"How can he when he has no reason? The poor thing does not know any better."

"Oh, he knows well enough. And even if he did not, would you allow him to do as he pleased just because he didn't know any better? He wanted to put his horn into you a moment ago."

"But still, it must be hard to want to do something and not be able to do it," said Mercy.

"I used to feel as if I could tear my old nurse to pieces when she wouldn't let me do as I wanted," said Christina.

"I suppose you do whatever you please now, ladies?"

"No, indeed. We wanted to go to London, and here we must stay for the whole winter!"

"And you think it hard?"

"Yes, we do."

"And so you side with my cattle from sympathy?"

"Well—yes."

"And you think I have no right to keep them captive and make them work?"

"None at all," said Christina.

"Then it is time I let them go!"

Alister made for the animals' heads.

"No, no! Please don't!" cried both girls, the one turning white, the other red.

"Certainly not if you do not wish it," answered Alister. "If I did, however, you would be quite safe. For they would not come near me. They would be off up that hill as hard as they could tear, jumping everything that came in their way."

"Isn't it very dull here in the winter?" asked Christina, panting a little, but trying to look as if she had known he was only joking.

"I do not find it dull."

"But you are a man and can do as you please!"

"I never could do as I pleased, and so I please as I do," answered Alister.

"I don't understand you."

"When you cannot do as you like, the best thing is to like whatever comes your way. The secret of happiness is not in doing what one likes, but in liking what one has to do. One's own way is never to be had in this world. There's a better one, though, which *is* to be had."

"I have heard a parson talk like that," said Mercy, "but never a layman."

"My father was a parson as good as any layman," said Alister. "He was strong enough to have laid me on my back in a moment—here as I stand." As he spoke he drew himself up to his full height.

Suddenly he broke into Gaelic, addressing the more troublesome of the bulls. No better pleased to stand still than to go on ploughing, he had fallen to digging at his neighbor, who retorted with the horn, and presently there was a great mixing of bull and harness and cloddy earth. Turning quickly toward them, Alister dropped a rein. In a moment the plough was out of the furrow, and the bulls were straining every muscle trying to send each other into the wilds of the unseen creation. Alister sprang to their heads, and taking them by their noses forced them back into the line of the furrow. Thinking they had broken loose, Christina fled; but Mercy grabbed up the reins and hauled on them with all her might.

"Thank you, thank you!" said the laird, laughing with pleasure. "You are a friend, indeed!"

"Mercy! Mercy! Get away at once!" cried Christina.

But Mercy did not heed her. The laird took the reins, administered a blow each to the animals, and made them stand still.

There are tenderhearted people who would never have force used nor pain suffered, who talk as if kindness could do everything. Yet were it not for suffering, millions of human beings would never develop an atom of affection. It is folly to conclude that a thing ought not to be done because it hurts. There are powers to be born, creations to be perfected, sinners to be redeemed, all through the ministry of pain, that could be born, perfected, and redeemed in no other way. But it was more than her tender heart which now got the best of Christina. She was annoyed at finding the laird not easily to be brought to her feet, and Mercy already advanced in his good graces. She was not jealous of Mercy, for she was beautiful and Mercy plain. But Mercy had by her pluck secured an advantage, and the handsome ploughman looked at her admiringly!

"Oh, you wicked man!" she cried, partly because she was not pleased with him, "you are hurting the poor brutes."

"No more than is necessary," he answered.

"You are cruel!"

"Good morning, ladies."

He just managed to take off his hat to them again, for the four-legged explosions at the end of his plough were pulling madly. He slackened his reins, and away it went like a sharp knife through Dutch cheese.

"You've made him quite cross!" said Mercy.

"What a brute of a man!" said Christina.

10 / The Fir Grove

As the ladies went up the ridge, regarded in the neighborhood as the chief's pleasure ground where nobody went except to call upon the chief, having mounted it lower down than where they descended, they had to pass the cottage. The grove of birch, mountain ash, and fir which surrounded it was planted quite irregularly, and a narrow footpath went winding through the wood to the door. A rough bench stood against one of the firs turned to the west, and seated upon it they saw Ian. He rose, tipped his cap, and sat down again. Christina, who regarded it as a praiseworthy kindness to address anyone beneath her, not only returned his salutation but stopped and said, "Good morning! We have been learning how they plough in Scotland, but I fear we annoyed the ploughman."

"Fergus does sometimes look surly," said Ian, rising again. "He has bad rheumatism, poor fellow! And then he can't speak a word of English, and is ashamed of it!"

"The man we saw spoke English very well. Is Fergus your brother's name?"

"No. My brother's name is Alister—that is Gaelic for Alexander."

"He was ploughing with two wild oxen, and could hardly manage them."

"Then it must have been Alister—only he could manage them perfectly. Alister could break a pair of buffaloes."

"He seemed rather vexed. He did not like to be told he was hard on the animals. I only said the poor things did not know better."

"Ah, I see! He understands animals so well, he doesn't like to be meddled with in his management of them. I imagine he told you that if they didn't know better he had to teach them better. Yes, I confess, he is a little touchy about animals."

Somehow Christina felt herself rebuked and did not like it. He had almost told her that if she had quarreled with his ploughman brother, the fault must be hers!

"But indeed, Captain Macruadh," she said—for she knew the people called him captain, "I know something about animals. We have horses of our own and know all about them. Don't we, Mercy?"

"Yes," said Mercy; "they take apples and sugar from our hands."

"And you would have the chief's bulls tamed with apples and

sugar!'' retorted Ian, laughing. ''But the horses were tamed before you ever saw them. If you had taken them wild, or even when they were foals, and taught them everything, then you would know a little about them. An acquaintance is not a friendship. My brother loves animals and understands them almost like human beings. He understands them better than he does some human beings, for the most cunning of the animals are yet simple. He knows what they are thinking when I cannot read a word of their faces. I remember one terrible night, winters ago—there had been a blinding drift on and off during the day, and my father and mother were getting anxious about him—he came staggering in, and fell on the floor, and a great lump in his plaid blanket on his back began to wallow about, and out of it crept his big collie! They had been to the hills to look after a few sheep and the poor dog was exhausted, and Alister had carried him home at the risk of his own life.''

''A valuable animal, I don't doubt,'' said Christina.

''He had been, but was no more what the world calls valuable. He was an old dog almost past work—but the wisest creature! Poor fellow, he never really recovered from that day on the hills!''

But Christina was not going to give in. Her one idea of the glory of life was the subjugation of men. As if moved by a sudden impulse, she walked up close to him.

''Do not be angry with me,'' she said, almost coaxingly, but with a visible mingling of both boldness and shyness. ''I did not mean to be rude. I am sorry.''

''You mistake me,'' he said. ''I only wanted you to know that you misjudged my brother.''

''Then if you have forgiven me, you will let me sit down for a few minutes. I am *so* tired with walking in the sticky earth!''

''Do, please, sit down,'' responded Ian heartily, and led the way to the bench.

But she sank down gracefully at the foot of the next fir while Mercy sat down on the bench.

Neither beauty nor intellect attracted Ian. Imagination would entice him, but even that would stop the moment he detected the least lack of principle. The simplest manifestation of a live conscience would draw him more than anything. I do not mean the conscience that proposes questions, but the conscience that loves right and turns from wrong.

He was simple, but not free and easy—too sensitive to the relations of life to be familiar quickly with any girl. If she was not one with whom to hold genuine conversation, it was impossible for him to blow dandelions with her, and talk must confine itself to the commonplace.

In the conversation that followed, he soon found the younger capable of being interested, and since he had seen so many parts of the world he had plenty to tell her. Christina smiled sweetly, taking in everything with a bit too much politeness, looking as if the only thing that interested her was that there they were talking about it. At length he thought he might try to raise some response by telling them an adventure he had read about in a book of travels about Persia. As he spoke, Mercy's eyes grew larger and larger, never leaving his face. Christina merely laughed periodically, but showed no interest in the matter.

When he was done and asked if they would like another, it was the older of the two who replied, "No, please! No more for me!" said Christina, laughing as she rose. "That was a horrible tale."

Mercy, however, was silent. Something in the story had set her to thinking, an occupation she indulged in only on rare occasions. She knew she ought to be good, and she knew she was not good. How to be good she did not know, for she had never set herself to be good. But at least the story had turned her mind in that direction. She sometimes wished she were good; but there are thousands of people who would be good if they could without taking the trouble. The kind of goodness they desire, however, would not be worth a life to hold it.

Just then the lady of the house appeared, asking with kind dignity if they would like some refreshment: to a highlander hospitality is a law where it is not a love. Christina declined the offer.

"Thank you. We were only a little tired and are quite rested now," she said. "How beautifully sheltered your house is!"

"On the side of the sea, yes," answered Mrs. Macruadh; "but not much on the east where we want it most. The trees are growing, however."

"Well!" remarked Christina when the sisters were out of sight of the cottage; "he's a nice young man too, is he not? Very well bred! But I never heard anything so disgusting as that silly story of his!"

"But you like to *read* horrid stories, Chrissy. You said so only yesterday. If Colonel Webberly had told you the story, you would have called it charming."

"I would not! You know I would not!" she exclaimed. "Why, I do believe you have fallen in love with the horrid man! Of the two, I declare, I like the ploughman better, even though he is a stupid sort of fellow. But this man! How intently he fixed his eyes on us when he was talking. I almost thought he was a parson."

"He was anxious to make himself understood. I know he made me think what I was about."

"Oh, nonsense! We didn't come into this wilderness to be preached to by a lay John the Baptist. He is an ill-bred fellow!''

She would not have said so much against him had not Mercy taken his side.

Mercy rarely contradicted her sister, but even this brief encounter with a real man had roused the justice in her.

"I don't agree with you, Chrissy," she said. "He seems to me very much of a gentleman."

11 / Among the Hills

When Mr. and Mrs. Palmer reached Inverness, they found they could spend a few days there, one way or another, to good purpose, for they had friends to visit as well as shopping to do. Mr. Palmer's affairs calling him to the south were not immediately pressing, and thus their sojourn extended itself to a full eight days, during which the girls were under no rule but their own. Their parents regarded them as perfectly trustworthy, and the girls themselves were aware of no reason why they should not be.

The window of Christina's bedroom overlooked a part of the road between the New House and the old castle. From there she could see all the ridge as far as the grove that concealed the cottage. If they now saw more of the young men who were their neighbors, I cannot say she had no hand in it. She was at first depressed by a sense of failure. She would have given neither of the men another thought had there been someone else with whom to flirt, and that huckster business had just harm enough in it to make it interesting. Therefore, she sought to relieve her depression by waiting for another opportunity to ply her skills.

One morning two days later, Christina called Mercy, rather imperiously, to get ready at once for their usual walk. She obeyed and they set out. Christina declared that she was perishing with cold, and they walked fast. By and by they saw on the road ahead of them the two brothers walking slowly; one was reading, the other listening. When they came nearer they saw in Alister's hand a manuscript volume; Ian carried an old-fashioned fowling rifle. The hard frost, perhaps, caused Alister's leisure so early in the day.

Hearing the girls' steps behind them, the men turned. The laird was the first to speak. The plough and the fierce bulls were not there to bewilder their judgment, and the young women immediately discovered their perception in the matter of breeding to be more fallible than they had imagined. No well-bred woman could for a moment doubt the man before them was a gentleman. Ian was at once more like and more unlike other people. His manner was equally courteous, but notably stiffer: he was as much at ease, but more reserved.

They walked on together.

"You are a little earlier than usual this morning, ladies," remarked the chief.

"How do you know that, Mr. Macruadh?" rejoined Christina.

"I often see you go by—and till now, always at the same hour."

"And yet we have never met in the morning before."

"The busy and the"—he hesitated a moment—"unbusy seldom meet," said the chief.

"Why don't you say *the idle*?" suggested Christina.

"Because that would be rude."

"Why would it be rude? Most people, I suppose, are more idle than busy."

"*Idle* is a word of blame and I had no right to use it."

"I took you for the kind of man who always spoke his mind."

"I hope I do when it is required and I have something to speak."

"You prefer judging with closed doors!"

The chief was silent: he did not understand her. Did she want him to say he did *not* think them idle—or, if they were, that they were right to be so?

"I think it unfortunate," resumed Christina, with a tone of injury in her voice, "that we should be friendly and open with people, and all the time they are thinking of us in a way that would be rude to say to our faces. It is enough to make one vow never to speak to anybody again!"

Alister looked at her. What could she mean?

"You can't think it hard," he said, "that people should not tell you what they think of you the moment they first see you."

"They might at least tell us what they mean by calling us idle!"

"I said *not busy*."

"Is *every*body to blame that is idle?" persisted Christina.

"Perhaps my brother will answer you that question," said Alister, hoping that he indeed might be able to.

"If my brother and I tell you honestly what we thought of you when we first saw you," said Ian, "will you tell us honestly what you thought of us?"

The girls cast an involuntary glance at each other, and when their eyes met could not keep them from a certain look which gave them away. A twitching also at the corners of Mercy's mouth showed they had been saying more than they would like to be questioned about.

"Ah, you betray yourselves, ladies!" Ian said. "It is all very well to challenge us, but you are not prepared to hold up your end."

Christina would have said something to defend herself, but she could think of no quick reply.

"Then perhaps," Ian went on, "the chance may come for us to speak out plainly what we think of each other when we are about to part, with no probability of meeting again in this world."

"But we shall be coming every summer, though I hope not to stay through the winter."

"Changes come when they are least expected."

"And we could never know," said Alister, "that we shall never meet again."

They had now come to the bottom of the valley and had left the road and were going up the side of the burn, often in single file, so the conversation ceased for a time. Alister was leading and Ian bringing up the rear, for the valley was thickly strewn with lumps of gray rock of all shapes and sizes. They seemed to have rolled down the hill on the other side of the burn, but there was no sign of their origin: the hill was covered with grass below and heather above. The winding of the way among the stones was such that again and again no one of them could see another—for there was no path. The girls felt the strangeness of it, and began to experience a little of the power of solitary places without knowing it.

After walking thus for some distance, their leader stopped.

"Here we have to cross the stream," he said, "and go a long way up the other side."

"You want to be rid of us," said Christina.

"By no means," replied Alister. "We are delighted to have you with us. But we must not let you get tired before turning to go back."

"If you really don't mind, we should like to go a good deal farther. I want to see round the turn there, where another hill comes from behind and closes up the view. We haven't anybody to go with us and have seen nothing of the country. The men won't take us shooting, and Mama is always afraid we will get lost or fall over a cliff or get into a bog or get eaten by wild beasts."

"If this frost lasts, we will have time to show you something of the country. I see you can walk."

"We can walk well enough, and should like to get to the top of a mountain!"

"Well let's make the crossing then," said Alister, and turning to the burn, jumped and rejumped it, as if to let them see how to do it.

The bed of the stream was at that particular spot quite narrow as it went through two rocks, so that, though there was little of it, the water went through with a roar and enough force to knock a man off his feet. It was too wide for the ladies, and they stood eyeing it with dismay, fearing this meant an end to their walk.

"Do not be frightened," said Alister. "It is not too wide."

"You have an advantage over us by the way you are dressed," said Christina.

"I will get you over quite safe," returned the chief.

Christina looked as if she could not trust herself to him.

"I will try," said Mercy.

"Jump high," answered Alister, as he sprang again to the other side and held out his hand across the chasm.

"I can't jump either high or far," said Mercy.

"Don't be in a hurry. I will take you—no, not by the hand; it might slip—but by the wrist. Don't worry about how far you can jump. All you have to do is jump as high as you can."

Mercy could not help feeling frightened—the water rushed so fast and loud below.

"Are you sure you can get me over?" she asked.

"Yes."

"Then I will jump."

She sprang, and with a strong pull on her arm Alister landed her easily on the other side.

"It's your turn now," he said, addressing Christina.

She was rather white, but tried to laugh.

"I—I—I don't think I can," she said.

"It is really nothing," persuaded the chief.

"I am sorry to be such a coward, but I fear I was born one."

"Some feelings no one can help," said Ian, "but you don't need to give in to them. One of the bravest men I ever knew was so afraid of dogs he would always jump aside if the meanest little cur in the street came barking at him. And yet once, when the people were running in all directions, he went straight for a mad dog and held him fast. Come, Alister! You take her by one arm and I will take her by the other."

The chief sprang to her side and the moment she felt the grasp of the two men she had all the courage she needed. The three jumped together and all were presently walking merrily along the other bank, over the same kind of ground in single file—Ian bringing up the rear.

All at once the ladies jumped at the sound of a gun going off close behind them.

"I beg your pardon," said Ian, "but I could not let the rascal go."

"What have you killed?" his brother asked.

"A red-haired fellow," answered Ian, who had left the path and was going up the hill.

The girls looked but saw nothing, and following him a few yards, came to him behind a stone.

"Goodness gracious!" exclaimed Christina with horror, "it's a fox—you shot a fox!"

The men laughed.

"And why not?" asked Alister. "Is the fox a sacred animal in the south?"

"It's worse than poaching to shoot one!" she cried.

"Hardly!" returned Alister. "No doubt you may get a good deal of fun out of him, but you can't make game of him. Why—you look as if you had lost a friend! I admire his intellect, but we can't afford to feed it on chicken and lambs."

"But to *shoot* him!"

"We do not respect him here. He is a rascal."

"What *would* Christian or Mr. Sercombe say to shooting, actually shooting a fox!"

"You treat him as if he were red gold," said the chief. "But we build no temples either to foxes or mammon here. We leave the men of the south to worship them."

"They don't worship them!" said Mercy.

"Do they not respect the rich man because he is rich, and look down on the poor man because he is poor?" said Ian. "Though the rich be a wretch, they think him grand; though the poor man be like Jesus Christ, they pity him."

"And shouldn't the poor be pitied?" said Christina.

"Not unless they need pity."

"Is it not pitiable to be poor?"

"By no means! It is pitiable to be selfish—and that, I venture to suspect, the rich are oftener than the poor. But as to the fox there—instead of shooting him, what would you have had us do with him?"

"Hunt him, to be sure."

"Would he like that better?"

"What he would like is not the question. The sport is the thing."

"That will show you why he is not sacred here: we do not hunt him. It would be impossible to stage a hunt in this country. You could not ride the ground. Besides, there are so many holes, the hounds would scarcely have a chance. No, the only dog to send after the fellow is a lead one."

"There's another!" exclaimed the chief. "There, sneaking away!—and your gun not loaded, Ian."

"I am so glad!" said Christina. "He at least will escape you!"

"But some poor lamb in the spring won't escape him," returned Alister.

"Lambs are meant to be eaten!" said Christina.

"Yes, but a lamb might think it a hard thing to feed such a creature."

"If the fox is no good in the world," said Mercy, "why was he made?"

"He can't be no good," answered the chief. "But what if some things exist just that we may get rid of them?"

"*Could* they be made just to be got rid of?"

"I said that *we* might get rid of them: there is all the difference in that. The very first thing men had to do in the world was to fight beasts."

"I think I see what you mean," said Mercy. "If there had been no wild beasts to fight with, men would never have grown able to do much."

"That's it," said Alister.

"And who knows," suggested Ian, "what good it may do the fox himself to make the best of a greedy nature?"

"But what is the use of talking about such uninteresting things?" said Christina.

The remark silenced the brothers. What, indeed, was the use of talking where there was no interest?

But Mercy felt there was something interesting the men cared to talk about if she could only get at it. They were not like any other men she had ever met!

Christina's whole interest in men was the admiration she looked for and usually received from them.

Silence lasted until they reached the shoulder of the hill that closed the view up the valley. As they rounded it the sun went down behind a cloud and a chill wind, as if from a land where there was no life, met them. They were on the shore of a small lake, out of which ran the burn. The hills behind the lake were very desolate looking, with little heather. Their bloomless heads were mostly white with frost and snow. Their shapes had little beauty; they looked worn and hopeless, ugly and sad— and so cold! The water below was slate gray, in response to the gray sky above: there seemed no life in either. The hearts of the girls sank within them and all at once they felt tired. In the air was just one sign of life: high above the lake wheeled a large fishhawk.

"Don't you think we had better be going, Mercy?" said Christina, drawing her cloak around her with a little shiver. "It has gotten quite cold."

"Look!" said Alister pointing before her sister could answer; "there is the osprey that lives here with his wife! He is just going to catch a fish."

He had hardly spoken when the bird, with a headlong descent, shot into the water, making it foam up all about. He reappeared with a fish in his claws and flew off to find his mate.

"Do you know that very bird?" asked Mercy.

"I know him well. He and his wife have built a nest on that conical rock you see there in the middle of the water and have been there many years."

"Why have you never shot him? He would look well stuffed!" said Christina.

She little knew the effect of her words. The chief *hated* senseless killing, and to hear a lady talk of shooting a high-soaring creature of the air as coolly as of putting on her gloves was nauseous to him. Ian praised him afterward for his unusual self-restraint. But it was a moment or two before he had himself under control.

"Don't you think he looks much better going about God's business?" he said.

"Perhaps, but he is not yours. You have not got him."

"Why should I have him? He seems, indeed, all the more mine the higher he goes. A dead stuffed thing—how could that ever be mine at all? Alive, he seems to soar in the very heaven of my soul!"

"You showed the fox no such pity," remarked Mercy.

"I never killed a fox to *have* him!" answered Alister. "I killed the fox for a higher good, to protect even more life. The osprey does no harm. He eats only fish, and they are very plentiful; he never kills birds or rabbits, or any creature on the land. I do not see how anyone could wish to kill the bird, except from mere love of destruction!"

Mercy did not reply, and it was Christina who spoke in response to this rebuke of her sister. "It has gotten quite cold, Mercy," she said. "Let us turn back."

"I am ready," answered Mercy.

The brothers looked at each other. They had come out to spend the day together, but they could not leave the ladies to go home alone. Having brought them across the burn, they were bound to see them over it again. An imperceptible sign passed between them, and Alister turned to the girls.

"Come then," he said; "we will go back!"

"But you were not going home yet," said Mercy.

"Would you have us leave you in this wild place?"

"We will find our way well enough. The stream will guide us."

"Yes, but it will not jump over for you."

"I forgot the burn!" said Christina.

"Which way were you going?" asked Mercy, looking all around for a road or path through the wilderness which surrounded them.

"This way," answered Ian. "Good-bye."

"Then you are not coming?"

"No. My brother will take care of you."

He turned and went straight up the hill. They stood and watched him go. At what seemed the top, he turned and waved his cap, then vanished.

Christina felt disappointed. She did not much care for either of the peculiar young men, but any company was better than none; a man was better than a woman, and two men were better than one! If these two were not up to admiring her as she deserved, what more rewarding labor than teaching them to do so?

The thing that mainly disappointed her in them was that they had so little small talk. It was so stupid to be always speaking sense! Always polite! Always courteous! Upon occasions of merrymaking the two young men would frolic like unbroken colts. But nevertheless, they had been brought up in a solemn school and had learned to take life as a serious and lovely thing. At the same time, although Ian had from his childhood learned humor from the workshops of the village, he was in himself always rather sad, being perplexed about many things.

Christina was annoyed, besides, that Mercy seemed interested in them. All day she had been on their side against her! She had never been like that before. She must take care she did not make a fool of herself! It might end in unhappiness to the young goose! But of course neither her father nor mother would allow Mercy to draw close to the locals. Nevertheless, she must throw herself into the breach! *Gentlemen* she must admit they were—but of such an old-fashioned type as to be gentlemen by courtesy—not gentlemen in the world's eyes. She was of the world; they of the north of Scotland!

She was not so anxious about her sister, however, as upset that she herself had not gathered a single expression of homage or admiration. Christina's world was a very small one, and in its temple stood her own image. Alister belonged to the land, Ian to the universe. They were gentlemen of the high court. Wherever they might go throughout God's worlds, they would be at home. How could there be much attraction between either of them and Christina?

Alister was more talkative on the way back than he had been all day. Christina thought the change caused by having them, or rather her, to himself alone; but in reality it sprang from the prospect of soon rejoining his brother without them. Mercy found his conversation well worth hearing, and an old Scotch ballad which he repeated appeared to her as beautiful as it was wild and strange. But Christina despised the Scotch language: it was vulgar, she said!

In Mercy's unawakened soul echoed now and then a faint thrill of response to some of the things Alister said, and oftener to some of the verses he repeated. Alister was drawn by the honest gaze of her yet undeveloped and homely countenance; from its childlike look the woman would glance out occasionally and then vanish again just as suddenly, leaving the child to give disappointing answers. She was on the edge of coming awake; all was darkness about her, but something was pulling at her! She had never known before that a lady might be lovely in a ballad as well as in a beautiful gown!

Finding himself listened to, though the listener was little more than a child, the heart of the chief swelled, and when they arrived at the burn and he easily handed them across, he was not quite so glad to turn from them as he had expected.

"Are you going?" said Christina with genuine surprise, for she had not understood his intention.

"Your way will be easy now," he answered. "I am sorry to leave you, but I have to join Ian, and the twilight will be flickering down before I reach the place."

"And there will be no moon," said Mercy. "How will you get home through the darkness?"

"We do not mean to come home tonight."

"Oh, then you are going to join friends?"

"No, we shall be only with each other—not a soul besides."

"There surely can't be a hotel or inn up there?"

Alister laughed as he answered, "There are more ways than one of spending a night on the hills. If you look from a window—in that direction," he said, pointing, "just before you go to bed, you will see at least that we shall not perish with cold."

He sprang again over the burn and with a wave of his cap went, like Ian, straight up the hill.

The girls stood for some time watching him climb as if he had been going up a flight of stairs, until he stood clear against the sky, when, with another wave, he too disappeared.

Mercy did not forget to look from her window in the direction Alister had indicated. There was no room to mistake what he meant, for though the night was a dark one, somewhere on the hill glowed and flamed, reddening the air, a huge crescent of fire, slowly climbing, like a column of attack, up into the sky.

"What does it mean?" she said to herself. "Why do they make such a bonfire—with nobody but themselves to enjoy it? What strange men—out by themselves in the dark night on a cold hill! What can they be doing it for? I *should* like to hear them talk. I wonder what they are saying about *us*!"

The brothers did speak of them, and readily agreed in some notion of their character, but they soon turned to other things—most of which Mercy could not have followed. What would she, for instance, have made of Alister's challenge to his brother to explain the metaphysical necessity for the sine, tangent, and secant of an angle belonging to its supplement as well?

12 / The Wolves

Though the involuntary call of the girls from the New House had interrupted Ian as he was on the point of telling his mother of an important event in his spiritual history, she remained desirous of hearing it. Ian, on the other hand, almost wished he had never brought it up, so sure was he that it would not be satisfactory to her. But his mother could not let the thing rest. More than by interest, she was urged by an anxiety rooted in her ungodlike theories of God. She did not believe that God was unceasingly doing and would do his best for every man; therefore, she was unable to claim the assurance that he was doing his best for Ian. But her longing to hear what her son had proposed telling her was chiefly inspired by the hope of getting nearer to him, of closer sympathy becoming possible between them through her learning more clearly what his views were. Therefore, the night after that spent by her sons on the hill, after Alister had retired, she said to him,

"You never told me, Ian, the story you began about something that made you pray."

"Are you sure you will not take cold, Mother?" he said.

"I am warmly clad, my son; and my heart is longing to hear all about it."

"I am afraid you will not find my story so interesting as you expect, Mother."

"What concerns you is more interesting to me than anything else in the whole world, Ian."

"Not more than God, Mother?" said Ian.

The mother was silent. She was as honest as her sons. The question showed her, however dimly and in shadow, something of the truth concerning herself—even though she could not fully grasp it—namely, that she cared more about salvation than about God. If she could but keep her boy out of hell, she would be content to live on without growing close to the Lord. God was to her an awe, not yet a ceaseless growing delight!

There are centuries of paganism yet in many lovely Christian souls—paganism so deep, therefore so little recognized, that their earnest endeavor is to plant that paganism ineradicably in the hearts of those dearest to them.

As she did not answer, Ian was afraid she was hurt and thought it best to begin his story at once.

"It was one night in the middle of winter—last winter, near Moscow," he began, "and the frost was very bitter—the worst night for cold I have ever known. I had gone with a companion into the depth of a great pine wood. With only our guns we went far into the forest."

"What did you want in such a lonely place at that time of the night?" asked the mother.

She sat with firm-closed lips, and wide, night-filled eyes looking at her son, the fear of love in her beautiful face—fit window for a heart so full of refuge to look out of.

"Wolves, Mother," he answered.

She shuddered. She was a great reader in the long winter nights, and had read terrible stories of wolves—the last of which in Scotland had been killed not far from where they sat.

"What did you want with the wolves, Ian?" she faltered.

"To kill them, Mother. I never liked killing animals any more than Alister. But the wolves are fair game. They are the devils of that country, and I fancy devils do go into them sometimes as they did once into the poor swine. They are the terror of all who live near the forests.

"There was no moon, only starlight, but whenever we came to any open space, there was light enough from the snow to see all about. But the trees were thick and dark. Far away, somewhere in the mystery of the black wood, we could now and then hear a faint howling. It came from the red throats of the wolves."

"You are frightening me, Ian!" said his mother, as if they had been two children telling each other tales.

"Indeed, Mother, they are very horrible when they hunt in droves, ravenous with hunger. To kill one of them, if it be but one, is to do something for humanity. Just when I was oppressed with the feeling that I was doing nothing for anyone, and not knowing anything else I could do at the time, I resolved to go and kill a wolf or two. They had killed a poor woman only two nights before.

"As soon as we could after hearing the howling, we got up into two trees. It took us some time to find two that were fit for our purpose, and we did not get them as near each other as we would have liked. We were rather anxious until we did find them, for if we encountered a pack of the demons while still on foot, we would only last a moment or two alive. Killing one, ten more would be upon us, and a hundred more on the backs of those. But we hoped they would smell us up in the trees, and search for us, when we would be able to give account of a few of them at least. We had double-barreled guns, and plenty of powder and ammunition."

"But how could you endure the cold—at night—and without food?"

"No, Mother. We did not try that! We had plenty to eat in our pockets. My companion had a bottle of vodka—a sort of raw spirit, horrible stuff!—and I had my bottle full of tea. The Russians drink enormous quantities of tea—though not so strong as you make it."

"Go on, then, Ian; go on."

"We sat a long time and there was no sign of the wolves. It was very cold, but our furs kept in our warmth. Before long I fell asleep— which was not dangerous so long as I kept warm, and I thought the cold would wake me before it began to numb me. I began to dream; but my dream did not change the place; the forest, the tree I was in, all my surroundings were the same. I even dreamed that I came awake and saw everything about me just as it was. I seemed to open my eyes to look about me on the dazzling snow from my perch; I was in a small tree on the border of a little clearing.

"Suddenly, from out of the wood to my left came something running fast, but with soundless feet over the snow. In my dream I doubted whether it was a live thing or only a shadow. It came nearer and I saw it was a child, a little girl running for her life. She came straight to the tree I sat in and when she got close to it, but without stopping for a moment, looked up, and I saw a sweet little face, white with terror. But it somehow seemed terrified, not for herself but for me. I called out after her to stop, and I would pull her up into the tree beside me where the wolves could not reach her. But she only shook her head and ran on over the clearing into the forest. Among the trees I watched the fleeting shape appear and disappear and appear again, until I saw it no more. Then first I heard another kind of howl from the wolves—that of pursuit. It strengthened and grew, nearer and nearer, till at last, through the stillness of the night and the motionless forest and the dead snow, came to my ear a kind of soft rushing sound. I don't know how to describe it. The rustle of dry leaves is too sharp; it was like a very heavy rain on a window—a small dull padding: it was the feet of the wolves. They came nearer and grew louder and louder, but the noise was still muffled and soft. Their howling, however, was now loud and horrid. At length, dark as a torrent of pitch, out of the forest flowed a multitude of obscure things, and streamed away, black over the snow, in the direction the child had taken. They passed close to the foot of my tree, but did not even look up, flitting by like a shadow whose substance was unseen. Where the child had vanished, they also disappeared. Plainly they were after her!

"It was only a dream, Mother! Don't be so frightened," interrupted Ian, for here his mother gave a little cry.

"Then first," he went on, "I seemed to recover my self-possession. I saw that though I would certainly be devoured by the wolves and the child could not possibly escape, I still had no choice but to go down and follow, do what I could, and die with her. I jumped down, and began running as I had never run before even in a dream, along the track of the wolves. As I ran I heard their howling, but it seemed so far off that I could not hope to be in time to kill one of them before they were upon her. Still, by their howling, it did not appear they had yet reached her, and I ran on. Their noise grew louder and louder, but I seemed to run miles and miles, wondering what spell was upon me that I could not catch up with them. All at once the clamor grew hideous and I saw them. They were gathered round a tree in a clearing, just like that I had left, and were leaping madly against it, but ever falling back in frustration.

"I looked up, and in the top of the tree sat the little girl, her white face looking down upon them with a smile. All the terror had vanished from it. It was still white as the snow, but, like the snow, was radiating a white light through the dark foliage of the fir. I was enchanted at the sight. But she was not in safety yet, and I rushed into the heap of wolves, striking and stabbing with my hunting knife. I got to the tree and was by her in a moment.

"But as I took the child in my arms I awoke in my own tree, and up against the trunk of it broke a howling, surging wave of black wolves. They leaped at the tree like a wave seems to leap up on the shore when it strikes a huge rock. My gun was to my shoulder in a moment and blazed among them. Howls of death arose. Their companions fell upon the wounded and ate them up. The tearing and yelling at the foot of the tree was like the tumult of devils full of hate and malice and greed. Then for the first time I wondered whether such creatures might indeed be the open haunts of demons. I fired and fired, and still they kept rushing against the trunk of the tree, heaping themselves against it, those behind struggling up on the backs of those next to it, in a storm of rage and hunger and jealousy. Many of those who had just helped to eat some of their fellows were themselves eaten in turn, and not a scrap of them left. But it was a large pack and would have taken a long time to kill enough to satisfy those that remained. I killed and killed until my ammunition was gone and then there was nothing to do but wait for the light. When morning began to dawn, they answered its light with silence, and turning away swept like a shadow back into the wood. Strange to tell, I heard afterward that a child had been killed by them in the earlier part of that same night. But even now sometimes, as I lie awake at night, I grow almost doubtful whether the whole *thing* was not a hideous dream.

"But even if it was, the reality of what I went through between the time my powder came to an end and the dawn of the morning remains a real spiritual fact. And that is really the point of my telling you the story, Mother.

"In the midst of the howling I grew so sleepy that the horrible noise itself seemed to lull me asleep at the same time that it kept me awake, and I fell into a kind of reverie with which my dream came back and mingled. I seemed to be sitting in the tree with the shining little girl, and she had become a picture of my own soul. All the wrong I had in me, and all the wrong deeds I had done, with all the weaknesses and evil tendencies of my nature, had all taken shape in the forms of the howling wolves below, and they were besieging me, to get at me to devour me. Suddenly my soul was gone. Above were the still, bright stars, shining unmoved. Beneath was the white betraying snow and the howling wolves. Away through the forest was my poor soul, ever fleeing in the likeness of a white-faced child!

"All at once came a great stillness, as of a desert place where no life of man or beast breathed. I was alone, frightfully alone—alone as I had never been before. The creatures at the foot of the tree were still howling, but their cry sounded far away and small; they were in some story I had been reading, but nowhere in my life. I was left and lost— in the waste of my own being, without comfort. But left by whom, and lost by whom?

"I looked up to the sky. It was infinite. As I watched, the limitless space came nearer and clasped me. I was at once everything and nothing. I cannot tell you how frightful it was! In agony I cried to God in utter despair. I cannot say whether I believe he answered me. But I know that a great quiet fell upon me—a quiet of utter defeat and helplessness which melted away into a sense of God. It felt as if the great space all about me was God, not emptiness. Neither wolf nor sin could touch me. My very being was at peace. And in my mind—whether an echo from the Bible, I do not know—were the words, 'I, even I, am he that comforteth thee. I am God, thy Savior!' Whereas before I had seemed all alone, suddenly I was with God, the only *with*ness man can really share! I lifted my eyes; morning was in the east, and the wolves were slinking away over the snow."

Mrs. Macruadh did not know how to receive her son's strange experience. She knew she ought to say something, but she sorely questioned the legitimacy of his supposed "revelation," for he had spoken only two words belonging to the religion in which she had reared him: *sin* and *God!* There was nothing in it about the atonement. She was incapable of seeing that it was a dream, or rather a vision, of the atonement itself. She did not yet understand that salvation lies in being one with Christ, even as the branch is one with the vine—that any salvation short of knowing God is no salvation at all. The moment a man feels that he belongs to God utterly, the atonement is there and the Son of God is reaping his harvest.

The good mother was, however, not one of those conceited, stiff-necked souls who have been the curse of the church in all ages; she was but one of those in whom reverence for its passing form dulls the perception of unchangeable truth. Fortunately she was not of the kind who shut up God's precious light in the horn lantern of human theory, whose shadows cast on the path to the kingdom seem to dim eyes like insurmountable obstructions. For the sake of what they count revealed, they refuse all further revelation, and what satisfies them is merest famine to the next generation of believers. Instead of God's truth, they offer man's theory, and accuse of rebelling against God those who cannot live on the husks they call food. But ah, home-hungry soul! God is not the elder brother of the parable, but the father with the best robe and the ring—a God high above all your longing, even as the heavens are high above the earth.

13 / Who Is God?

When Ian ceased, a silence deep as the darkness fell upon them. To Ian, the silence seemed the very voice of God, clear in the darkness. Raised on the doctrines of his parents, he had in recent years taken it upon himself to read the New Testament from a deeper perspective and with more open eyes. The faith he now possessed was indeed a greater and more personal one than he had known in his youth, though his mother did not have eyes to see the true state of his heart. To her the silence and the darkness about them signified a great gulf between her and her boy.

"Are you sure it was the voice of God, Ian?" she said.

"No, Mother," answered Ian, "but I hope it was."

"Hopes, my dear boy, are not to be trusted."

"That is true, Mother, and yet we are saved by hope."

"We are saved by *faith*."

"Indeed, and I know faith."

"You rejoice my heart. But faith in what?"

"Faith in God, Mother."

"That will not save you."

"No, but God will."

"The devils believe in God and tremble."

"I believe in the Father of Jesus Christ, and do not tremble."

"You ought to tremble before an unreconciled God!"

"Like the devils, Mother?"

"Like a sinful child of Adam. Whatever your fancies, Ian, God will not hear you unless you pray to him in the name of his Son."

"Mother, would you take my God from me?"

"What a frightful thing to lay to my charge!"

"Mother, I would gladly perish forever to save God from being the kind of God you would have me believe him. I love God. But I have learned to love him not through your teaching me about him, but by *knowing* him—through the world he made and through the character of Jesus. And I will not think of him other than good. Rather than believe he does not hear every creature that cries to him, whether he knows Jesus Christ or not, I would believe there was no God at all."

"That is not the doctrine of the gospel."

"It is, Mother; Jesus himself says, 'Every one that hath heard and learned of the Father cometh to me.' "

"Why, then, do you not come to him, Ian?"

"I do come to him. I come to him every day. I believe in nobody but him. Only God makes the universe worth being, or life worth living. But my believing does not look like what believing has always meant to you."

"Ian, I cannot understand you. If you believe like that about him—"

"I don't believe *about* him, Mother! I believe *in* him."

"We will not dispute about words! The question is, do you place your faith for salvation in the sufferings of Christ for you?"

"I do not, Mother. My faith is in Jesus himself, not in his sufferings."

"Then the anger of God is not turned away from you."

"Mother, I say again—I love God, and will not believe such things of him as you say."

"Then you do not accept the Bible as your guide."

"I do, Mother, for it tells me of Jesus Christ. There is no such teaching as you say in the Bible."

"How little you know your New Testament!"

"It is one of the few books I *do* know! For the last several years, since I have been trying to understand who God is rather than what people say about him, I have read it constantly. Now I could not live without it. No, I do not mean that. I *could* do without my Testament. Jesus would *be* all the same!"

"Oh, Ian! and yet you will not give Christ the glory of satisfying divine justice by his suffering for your sins!"

· "Mother, to say that the justice of God is satisfied with suffering is a piece of the darkness of hell. God is willing to suffer, and ready to inflict suffering to save from sin, but no suffering is satisfaction to him or his justice."

"What do you mean by his justice, then?"

"That he gives you and me and everybody fair play."

The ordinary sound of the phrase offended the moral ear of the mother.

"How can you speak so lightly of him? You will be speaking against him next!"

"No, Mother. He speaks against God who says he does things that are not good. It does not make a thing good to call it good. I speak *for* him when I say he cannot but give fair play. He knows man is sure to sin; he will not condemn us because we sin; he lets us do that for ourselves. He will condemn us only if we do not turn away from sin, for he has made us able to turn from it."

"He will forgive sin only for Christ's sake."

"He forgives us for his own name's sake, his own love's sake. There is no such word as *for Christ's sake* in the New Testament—except where Paul prays us for Christ's sake to be reconciled to God. It is in the English New Testament, but not in the Greek."

"Then you do not believe that the justice of God demands the satisfaction of the sinner's endless punishment?"

"I do not. Nothing can satisfy the justice of God but absolute fair play. The justice of God is the love of what is right, and the doing of what is right. Eternal misery in the name of justice could satisfy none but a demon whose bad laws had been broken."

"But it is the Holy One who suffers for our sins."

"Oh, Mother! Can justice do wrong to satisfy itself? Did Jesus *deserve* punishment? If not, then to punish him was to wrong him."

"But he was willing; he consented."

"He yielded to injustice—but the injustice was man's, not God's. If justice insisted on punishment, it would at least insist on the guilty being punished, not the innocent. Mind, I say *being punished*, not *suffering*: that is another thing altogether. It satisfied *love* to suffer for another, but it does not satisfy *justice* that the innocent should be punished for the guilty. The whole idea of the atonement in that light is the merest figment of the paltry human intellect to reconcile difficulties of its own invention. The sacrifices of the innocent in the Old Testament were the most shadowy type of the true meaning of Christ's death. He is indeed the Lamb that takes away the sins of the world. But not through an old-covenant sacrifice of the innocent for the guilty. No, the true atonement of Christ is on an altogether higher and deeper plane. And that is the mystery of the gospel. To interpret the mission of Jesus through the eyes of the Old Testament is to ignore his very words. He came bringing freedom from the old, bringing light, bringing good news, bringing the fulfillment of the types! He said, 'Behold, I make all things *new!*' Don't you see, Mother? Jesus is not an Old Testament sacrifice; he is God! He *loves* us! Once, when Alister had done something wrong, Father said, 'He must be punished—unless someone will be punished for him.' I offered to take his place, partly because it seemed expected of me, partly that I was moved by vanity, and partly because I saw what was likely to come next."

"And what did come next?"

"He scarcely touched me, Mother," answered Ian. "The thing taught me something very different from what he had meant to teach by it. That he failed to carry out his idea of justice helped me afterward to see that God could not have done it either, for that was not justice. And if my father could not punish me in my innocence, how much more could God not punish his own son in his far purer innocence."

"Your father believed that he did."

"He accepted it, saturated with the tradition of the elders before he could think for himself. He does not believe it now."

"But why, then, should Christ have suffered?"

"It is the one fact that explains everything else," said Ian. "But I see no reason to talk about that now. So long as your theory satisfies you, Mother, why should I show you mine? When it no longer satisfies you, when it troubles you as it has troubled me, and as I pray God it may trouble you, then I will share my very soul with you."

"I do not see what other meaning you can put upon the statement that he was a sacrifice for our sins."

"Had we not sinned he would never have died; and he died to deliver us from our sins. He against whom was the sin became the sacrifice for it; the Father suffered in the Son, for they are one. But if I could see no other explanation than yours, I would not, could not accept it—for God's sake I would not."

"How can you say you believe in Christ when you do not believe in the atonement!"

"It is not so, Mother. I do not believe what you mean by the atonement. What God means by it, I do believe. But we are never told to believe in the atonement; we are told to believe in Jesus Christ—and, Mother, I do believe in him."

"What do you call believing in him, then?"

"Obeying him, Mother—to say it as briefly as I can. I try to obey him in the smallest things he says—only nothing he says is small—and so does Alister. I strive to be what he would have me. A man may trust in Christ's atonement to his absolute assurance, but if he does not do the things he tells him—he does not yet believe in him. He may be a good man, but if he does not obey—well, you know what Jesus said would become of those who called him, Lord, Lord, but did not do what he said."

Ian was silent. The darkness seemed to deepen around them, and the silence grew keen. His mother began to tremble, for his words had awakened an old anxiety within her.

It was between God and his mother now, thought Ian. Many other would-be counselors would try to persuade the doubter that he does believe. But how much better a thing to convince him that his faith is a poor thing, and that what he must do is rise and go and do the thing that Jesus tells him to do, and so find belief indeed! Men must understand that neither thought nor talk, neither sorrow for sin nor love of holiness is required of them, but obedience! To *be* and to *obey* are one.

A cold hand grasping her heart, Ian's mother rose and went from the room. What she had only feared in her son, she knew now! It broke her heart and she lay down as one sick. Such was the hold the authority of traditional human dogma had on her soul. Instead of glorifying God that she had given birth to such a God-loving, free-thinking man, she wept bitterly because he was on the broad road to eternal condemnation.

But even as she lay weeping, something quiet stole over her. Suddenly there rose up in her a moonlight of peace.

"Can it be God?" she said to herself.

She could tell no more than Ian whether it was God or not. But from that moment on she began to lift up her heart in such prayer as she had never prayed before. And slowly, imperceptibly the feeling awoke in her that if she was not believing in God as she should, he would help her to believe as she ought to believe. Therewith she began to feel as if the gulf between herself and her son were not so wide as she had thought. Doubtless he was in rebellion against God, seeing he would question God's ways, but surely something might yet be done for him! She little suspected the glory of sky and earth and sea eternal that would one day burst upon her, that she would one day see God not only good but infinitely good—infinitely better than she had dared to think him!

As for Ian, he said to himself, "I must go away. I am only paining her. She will come to see things better without me. I will go, and come again."

His heart broke forth in prayer.

"O God, let my mother see that you are indeed truehearted; that you do not give us life by bits and pieces but abundantly; that you do not make men in order to assert your dominion over them, but that they may partake of your life. O God, have pity on me when I cannot understand, and teach me as you would a little earthly son you would carry in your arms. When pride rises in me and I feel as if I ought to walk about without your hand, then think of me and I shall know that I cannot live or think without your self-willing life. Help me to know that I am because you are, that I have no wisdom or insight of my own, that all life exists because you have breathed your being into it. Without your eternity in us, we are so small that we think ourselves great, and are thus miserably contemptible. You alone are true! Make me and my brother strong to be the very men you would have us, as your brothers, Christ, the children of your Father. You are our perfect brother—perfect in love, in courage, in tenderness. Amen, Lord! I am yours!"

14 / The Clan Christmas

By slow degrees, with infinite subdivisions and apparent reversals, autumn had passed into winter indeed. Cloud above, mire below, mist and rain all between, made up many days. The frost at length had brought with it brightness and persuasion and rousing. In the fields it was swelling and breaking the clods; and for the heart of man, it did something to break up that clod too. A sense of friendly pleasure filled all the human creatures. The children ran about like wild things; the air seemed to intoxicate them. Mrs. Palmer went out walking with the girls, and talked of their father and Christian and Mr. Sercombe, who were all coming together. For some time they saw nothing of their neighbors.

They had made some attempts at acquaintance with the people of the glen, but though the manners and addresses of these northern peasants were blameless, they were still not courteous enough for the girls' ideas of good breeding and offended both their pride and their sense of propriety. If Mistress Conal was an exception to the rest of the clan, even she would be more civil to a stranger than to her chief whom she loved—until the stranger gave her offense. And if then she passed to imprecation, she would not curse like an ordinary woman or a hag, but like a poetess, gaining rather than losing dignity. To forgive was a virtue unknown to Mistress Conal, indeed, a special fault of the Celtic character. But this was in no way the same as a desire for revenge. The latter is by no means a specially Celtic characteristic.

Christina and Mercy called upon her one morning and were not ungraciously received. But thinking her ignorant of English, they remarked upon the dirtiness of her floor, they themselves having imported much of the moisture that had turned its surface into a muddy paste. She said nothing, but to the general grudge she bore the possessors of the property which had once belonged to her clan, she now added a personal one. Had the chief offended her, she would have found twenty ways to prove to herself that he meant nothing. But the offense of the strangers lay cherished and smoldering and she had no desire to get rid of it.

The people at the New House did not get on very well with any of the clan. In the first place, they were regarded not merely as interlopers but almost as thieves of the property—though, in truth, they had bought it in good faith. In the second place, rumor had it that they did not behave with sufficient respect to the chief's family, in the point of whose honor the clan was the more exacting because of their common poverty. Hence the inhabitants of the glen, though they were of course polite, showed little friendliness.

But the main obstacle to their reception was in the *selves* of these new people from the south: the human was very little developed in them. They understood nothing of their own beings, had not a notion how poor people feel, did not understand any human feeling, seldom came so near anything as to think about it, and scarcely ever put a question to themselves about anything that mattered. They knew nothing of labor, nothing of danger, nothing of hunger, nothing of cold, nothing of sickness, nothing of loneliness. The realities of life were far from them.

The days passed and Christmas drew near. The gentlemen arrived. There was family delight and a bustling reception. How amazing that such gladness breaks forth in the meeting of persons who, within an hour or so of the joyous welcome, self getting the better of the divine, will begin to feel bored, and will each lay the blame of the disappointment on the other!

Coats were pulled off, mufflers were unwound, every room was bright with a great fire, and dinner was welcomed. After dinner came the unpacking of great boxes, and in the midst of the resultant pleasure the proposal came to be made—none but Christina knew how—that the inhabitants of the cottage should be invited to dinner on Christmas Eve. The idea carried at once, and the next afternoon a formal invitation was sent.

At the cottage it caused no little discussion. The lady of the New House had not called with her girls, it was true; but then neither had the lady of the castle—for that was the clan people's name for the whole ridge on which the cottage stood—called on the newcomers. And if the invitation meant they were ready to throw aside formalities and behave heartily, it would be wrong not to meet them halfway. They resolved therefore to make a counter-proposal. Answer was returned, sealed with no mere crest but with a coat of arms, to the effect that it had been the custom since time forgotten for the chief to welcome his people and friends on Christmas Eve, and the custom could not be broken; but if the ladies and gentlemen of the New House would favor them with their company on the occasion, to dine and dance, the chief and his family would gratefully accept any later offer of hospitality Mr. and Mrs. Peregrine Palmer might do them the honor to send.

This reply occasioned a great deal of talk at the New House, most of it in a humorous vein which the friends of the chief would not have enjoyed hearing. The men burst frequently into laughter at the assumption of the title of *chief* by a man with no more land than he could just manage to live on. The village, they said—and they were right in so saying—was not his at all but belonged to a certain Canadian who was about to turn the whole territory around it into a deer forest. They could hardly be expected to see that the mere loss of the clan property could not cause the genuine patriarchal relation of the chieftainship to cease, any more than could the loss of the silver-hilted Andrew Ferrara sword, descended from father to son for so many generations.

Imagine, they said, that *they* should put off their Christmas party for that of a ploughman in shabby kilt and hobnailed shoes. But in spite of their amused indignation, the thought came to them that they were in a wild part of the country where it would be absurd to expect the *savoir vivre* of the south, and it would be amusing to see the customs of the land. Therefore, a friendly answer was sent: they would not go to dinner, they said, as it was their custom also to dine at home on Christmas Eve; but they would eat early and spend the evening with them.

In the cottage there was no room big enough to receive a large company. The father of the present chief had been well aware of the necessities of entertainment and largely for that purpose had constructed a new barn, in which companionship, feasting, and dancing had been considered even more than the storing and threshing of grain. In that noble race, social relations play an active part in the affairs of men and women. Though some fancy it is only the *well-to-do* who can be hospitable, in actual fact the ideal flower of hospitality is almost unknown to the rich; it can hardly be grown except in the gardens of the poor.

Means in Glenruadh had been shrinking for many years, but the heart of the chief never shrank. His dwelling dwindled from a castle to a house, from a house to a cottage; but the hospitality did not dwindle. As the money vanished, the show diminished; the place of entertainment from a hall became a kitchen, from a kitchen changed to a barn; but the heart of the chief was the same. The entertainment was but little altered, the hospitality not in the least. When things grow hard, most people become frugal in their extensions toward others; the Macruadh began by denying himself. The land was not his except as steward of the grace of God.

Little did the people of England suspect the extremes of poverty which had come to some of the families of the highlands. But poor and crowded though some of the households were, they were the chief's people—they, as well as any guests who came to Glenruadh. Be it in stone hall or thatched cottage, the chief must entertain the stranger as well as befriend his own. This was the fulfilling of his office. And despite the fact that seldom had there been a chief Christian enough or strong enough to fill the full relation of father of his people, that was no reason for him to shrink from such an ideal. Now that the chieftainship had come to a man with a large notion of what it required of him, he was all the more ready to aim at the mark of such a high calling. It was ambition enough for him to be the head of his family, with the highest of earthly relations to realize toward its members.

The fools of greed in the world would have tried to persuade him that a man in his position should not waste himself in the low contest of making and sharing a humble living; he ought to make money and become somebody. "Let the people look after themselves!" such would say. "If they cannot pay their rents, send them about their business. Turn the land into a deer forest or a sheep farm and clear them out. They have no rights. A man is not his brother's keeper!" And indeed, many landowners in the highlands had said and done those very things.

But brought up as he was, Alister yet retained the exalted idea of the chief as a servant to his people. With joy he recognized that the shepherd of a few poor, lean, wool-torn human sheep enjoys a higher dignity than the man who stands for no one but himself. If Alister Macruadh was not in the highest grade of Christianity, he was on his way to it, for he was doing the work that was given him to do, which is the first condition of all advancement. He had much to learn yet, but he was one who, from every point his feet touched, was on the start to go further.

Christmas Eve day rose clear and bright. Snow was on the hills and frost in the valley. There had been a time when at this season great highland games were played between neighboring districts and clans. But there were none here now because there were so few men left. Mistress Macruadh was busy all day with her helpers, preparing a dinner of mutton and beef and fowls and red-deer ham. And the men soon gave the barn something of the aspect of the old patriarchal hall, for which it was not a bad substitute. A long table was covered with the finest linen and when the guests took their places, they needed no arranging—all knew their standing and seated themselves accordingly. Two or three small farmers modestly took the upper places once occupied by immediate relatives of the chief, for of the old gentry of the clan there were none. But all were happy, for their chief was still with them. They reverenced him nonetheless that they were at home with him. They knew his worth, and the roughest among them would mind what the Macruadh said. They knew he feared nothing; he was strong as the red stag after which the clan was named; he was the best shot, the best sailor, and the best ploughman in the clan; and, with genuine respect for every man, he would at the least insolence knock a disrespectful fellow to the ground.

Not many of them, however, understood how much he believed that he had to give an account of his people. He was far from considering such responsibility the clergyman's only. Again and again he had expostulated with some, to save them from the slow gaping hell of drink, and he hoped he did so with success.

In the afternoon the extemporized tables were cleared away, candles were fixed in rough sconces along the walls, with precautions taken against fire, and the floor was rubbed clean—for the barn was floored throughout with pine, in some places polished with use. The walls were already covered with the plaids of the men and women, each kept in place by a stone or two on the top of the wall where the rafters rested. In one end was a great heap of yellow oat straw which had been partly leveled and packed down and made a most delightful divan. What with the straw, the plaids, the dresses, the shining of silver ornaments, and the flash here and there of a jewel on the finger or around the neck, there was a great deal of color in the place. Some of the guests were poorly but all were decently dressed, and the shabbiest behaved as ladies and gentlemen.

The party from the New House walked through the still, starry night, with the motionless mountains looking down on them and a silence which they never suspected as a presence. The little girls were merry. Foolish compliments were not lacking, offered chiefly on the part of Mr. Sercombe and accepted on that of Christina. The ladies, under their furs and hoods, were in their best, with all the jewels they could wear at once, for they had heard that highlanders had a passion for color and that poor people were always best pleased when you visited them in your finery. They did, indeed, make a fine show as they emerged from the darkness of their wraps into the light of the numerous candles.

The approach of the widowed chieftainness to receive them, on the arm of Alister, with Ian on her other side, did not fail in dignity. Mistress Macruadh was dressed in a rich, matronly black silk; the chief was in the full dress of his clan—the old-fashioned coat of the French court, with its silver buttons and ruffles of fine lace, the kilt of Macruadh tartan in which green predominated, the silver-mounted sporran of the skin and adorned with the head of an otter caught with the bare hands of one of his people, and a silver mounted dirk of unusual length, famed for the beauty of both hilt and blade. Ian was similarly, though less showily, clad. When the stately lady advanced between her sons, at least one of the visitors felt a doubt whether their condescension would be fully appreciated.

As soon as their reception was over, the piper—to the discomfort of Mr. Sercombe's English ears—began his invitation to the dance, and in a moment the floor was in a tumult of reels. The girls, unacquainted with the country dances, preferred looking on, and after watching reel and straphspey for some time, altogether declined attempting either. But by and by it was the turn of the clanspeople to look on while the lady of the house and her sons danced a quadrille or two with their visitors, after which the chief and his brother paired with the two elder girls; the ladies were astonished to find them the best they had ever waltzed with, although they did not dance quite in the London way. Ian's dancing, Christina said, was French. Mercy said all she knew was that the chief took the work and left her only the motion: she felt as in a dream of flying. Before the evening was over, the young men had so far gained on Christina that Mr. Sercombe looked a little commonplace.

15 / Ian's Story

The dancing began about six o'clock and at ten, when it was time for supper, the dancing had to cease for a while that the tables might be prepared. The ladies put on their furs and furry boots and gloves and went out into the night with the rest of the company.

The chief and Christina started together, but instead of keeping at her side, Alister went and came, now talking to this couple, now to that, adding to everyone's general pleasure with every word he spoke. Ian and Mercy walked together, and as often as the chief left her side, Christina joined them. Mrs. Palmer stayed with their hostess; her husband took the younger children by the hand; Mr. Sercombe and Christian sauntered along in the crowd, talking now to one, now to another of the village girls.

Ian had said nothing to Mercy, but when the crowd began to break into twos and threes, they found themselves side by side. The company took its way along the ridge, and the road eastward. The night was clear and the two walked for some time in silence. It was a sudden change from the low barn, the dull candles, and the excitement of the dance, to the awful space, the clear pure far-off lights, and the great stillness. Both felt it, though differently; both of them sought after peace. Mercy was only beginning to seek it, not knowing what she needed. Ian sought it in silence with God; she in relation with others of her kind. She was a human chicken that had begun to be aware of herself, but had not yet attacked the shell that enclosed her. Because it was transparent and she could see life about her, she did not know that she was in a shell, or that if she did not exercise the might of her own life, she was sealing herself up to death. Many who think themselves free have never yet even seen the shell that imprisons them—know nothing of the liberty the Lord of life wants to give them. Men and women fight many a phantom when they ought to be chipping at their shells. They think they are getting on in the world, when the "world" is but their shell, killing the infant Christ who houses with them.

Ian looked up to the sky and breathed a deep sigh. Mercy looked up in his face and saw his strangely beautiful smile.

"What are you thinking of, Captain Macruadh?" she said.

"Did you ever feel," he said, "that you could not get enough room?"

"No," answered Mercy, "never."

Ian fell to thinking about how he could wake in her a feeling of what he meant. He had long felt that one of the first elements in human education is the sense of space—of which the heavens are probably the first awakener. He believed that without the heavens we could not have learned the largeness in things below them, the mystery of the high-ascending gothic roof, for instance. Without the greater we cannot interpret the less. And he thought that to have the sense of largeness developed might be to come a little nearer to the truth of things.

"Did you ever see anything very big?" he asked.

"I suppose London is as big as most things," she answered after a moment.

"Did you ever see London?" he asked.

"We generally live there half the year."

"I did not ask if you had ever *been* to London," said Ian, "but if you had ever *seen* London."

"I know the west end pretty well."

"Did it ever strike you as very large?"

"Perhaps not, but the west end is only a part of London."

"Did you ever see London from the top of St. Paul's?"

"No."

"Did you ever see it from the top of Hampstead Heath?"

"I have been there several times, but I don't remember seeing London from it. We don't go to London for the sights."

"Then you have not seen London."

Mercy was annoyed. Ian did not see her irritation, or perhaps he would not have gone on—which would have been a pity, for a little annoyance would do her no harm. At the same time the mood was not favorable to receiving any impression from the region of the invisible. A pause followed.

"Would you like me to tell you a story?" he said at length.

"Anything," answered Mercy, trying to smile.

He began at once, and told her a wonderful tale—told first in Ian's hearing by Rob of the Angels at a winter-night gathering of the women as they carded and spun their wool, and reeled their yarn together. It was one well-known in the country, but Rob had filled it, after his fancy, with imaginative turns and spiritual hints, incomprehensible to the tall child of seventeen walking by Ian's side. Every one of the maidens of the poor village would have understood it better than she. But it took her fancy nonetheless, partly, perhaps, by its uniqueness in comparison to any story she had ever heard before. Her childhood had been starved on the husks of new fairy tales, all invention and no imagination, unnourishing food to offer to God's children.

This story Ian told her under that sky full of stars, as Rob of the Angels had dressed it for the clan matrons and maidens, altered a little again for the ears of the lowland girl:

There was once a woman whose husband was well-to-do, but he died and she sank into poverty. She did her best, but she had a large family and work was hard to find. But she trusted in God, and said whatever he pleased must be right, whether he sent it with his own hand or not.

Now, whether it was that she could not find her children enough to eat, or that she could not keep them warm enough, I do not know. But whatever the cause, they began to die. One after the other became sick and lay down, and did not rise again, and for a long time her life was nothing but waiting upon death. She would have wanted to die herself, but that there was always another to die first and she had to see them all safe home before she dared wish to go herself. At length when the last of them was gone, and she then had no more to provide for, the heart of work went out of her: what was the good of working for herself alone? But she knew it was the will of God she should work and eat until he chose to take her back to himself, so she worked on for her living and comforted herself that every day brought death a day nearer. Then she fell ill herself and could work no more and thought God was going to let her die.

But just as she was going to her bed for the last time, she thought to herself that she was bound to give her neighbor the chance of doing a good deed; any creature dying at *her* door without letting her know he was in want would do her a great wrong. She saw it was the will of God that she should beg. So she put on her clothes again and went out to beg. And beg she did—enough to keep her alive, and no more.

As she went her way begging, one night she came to a farmhouse where a rich miserly farmer lived. She knew about him, and had not meant to stop there, but she was weary and the sun went down as she reached his gate and she felt as if she could go no further. So she went up to the door and knocked and asked if she could have a night's lodging. The woman who opened the door to her went and asked the farmer. Now the old man did not like hospitality, and in particular did not like it toward those that stood most in need of it. At the same time, however, he was very fond of hearing all the country rumors, and he thought to himself that he would invite her in and buy her news with a scrap of something to eat. So he told his servant to bring her in.

He received her kindly enough, for he wanted her to talk, and he let her have a share of the supper, such as it was. But not until he had asked every question about everybody he could think of, and drawn her own history from her as well, would he allow her to have the rest her tired body was so in need of.

Now it was a poor house, like most in the country, and nearly without interior walls, and the man had done little to better his surroundings despite his wealth. He had his warm box-bed and slept on feathers where no wind could reach him, and the poor woman had her bed of short rumpled straw on the earthen floor at the foot of the wall in the coldest corner. Yet the heart of the man had been somewhat moved by her story, for, without dwelling on her sufferings, she had been honest in telling it. He had indeed, before he went to sleep, thanked God that he was so much better off than she. For if he did not think it the duty of the rich man to share with his neighbors, he at least thought it his duty to thank God for being richer than they.

Now it may seem strange that such a man should be privileged to see a vision, especially when the woman saw nothing of it. But she did not require to see any vision, for she had truth in the inward parts, which is better than all visions. His vision was this: In the middle of the night the man came wide awake, and looking out of his bed saw the door open and a light come in, burning like a star. It was a faint rosy color, unlike any light he had ever seen before. Another and another came in, and more still, until he counted six of them. They moved near the floor, but he could not see clearly what sort of little creatures they were that were carrying them. They went up to the woman's bed, walked around it slowly in a hovering kind of way, stopped, moved up and down, and then went on again. And when they had done this three times they went slowly out of the door again, stopping for a moment several times as they went.

The man fell asleep again, and when he woke late the next morning, he was surprised to see his guest still on her hard couch—as quiet as any rich woman on her feather bed. He woke her, told her he wondered how she could sleep so far into the morning, and narrated the curious vision he had had. "Does that not explain it to you," she said, "how I have slept so long? Those were my dead children you saw. They died young and God lets them come and comfort their poor mother. I often see them in my dreams. If, when I am gone, you will look at my bed, you will find every straw laid straight and smooth. That is what they were doing last night." Then she gave him thanks for the good fare and fine rest, and continued on her way, leaving the farmer better pleased with himself than he had been for a long time, partly because there had been granted him a vision from heaven.

At last the woman died also and was carried by angels into Abraham's bosom. She was now with her own people at last, with God and all the good. The old farmer did not know of her death till a long time later, but it was upon the night she died, as near as he could make out, that he dreamed another strange dream. He never told it to anyone but the priest from whom he sought comfort when he lay dying some time later, and the priest told it to no one until everybody belonging to the old man was gone.

The old man was lying awake in his own bed, as he thought, in the dark night, when the poor woman came in at the door. She had in her hand a wax candle, but it was not lit. He said to her, "You extravagant woman! Where did you get that candle?" She answered, "It was put into my hand when I died, with the word that I was to wander till I found a fire at which to light it." "There!" he said, "there's the fire. Blow and get a light; poor thing! It shall never be said I refused a body a light!"

She went to the hearth and began to blow at the smoldering peat; but for all she kept trying she could not light her candle. The old man thought it was because she was dead, not because he was dead in sin, and losing his patience, he cried, "You foolish woman! Haven't you wit enough to light a candle? It's small wonder you came to beggary!"

Still she went on trying, but the more she tried, the blacker grew the peat she was blowing at. It would indeed blaze up at her breath, but the moment she brought the candle near it to catch the flame, it grew black, and each time blacker than before. "Give me the candle!" cried the farmer, springing out of bed; "I will light it for you!" But as he stretched out his hand to take it, the woman disappeared and he saw that the fire was dead and cold.

"This is a fine thing!" he said. "How am I to get a light?" For they were miles from the next house. And with that he turned to go back to his bed. When he came near it he saw somebody lying in it. "What! Has the old hag got into my very bed?" he cried, and went to drive her out of the bed and out of the house. But when he came close, he saw that it was he himself lying there, and at least he knew that he was out of the body, if not downright dead. The next moment he found himself on the moor, following the woman, some distance ahead of him, with her unlighted candle still in her hand. He walked as fast as he could to get up with her, but could not. He called after her but she did not seem to hear.

When he first set out he knew every step of the ground, but by and by he ceased to know it. The moor stretched endlessly before him, and the woman walked on and on. Without a thought of turning back he followed. At length he saw a gate, seemingly in the side of a hill. The woman knocked and by the time it opened he was near enough to hear what passed. It was a grave, and he knew at once that the stately but very happy-looking man that opened it was St. Peter. When he saw the woman he stooped and kissed her. The same moment a light shone from her, and the old man thought her candle was lighted at last. But presently he saw it was her head that gave out the shining. And he heard her say, "I pray you, St. Peter, remember the rich tenant of Balmacoy. He gave me shelter one whole night, and would have let me light my candle but I could not." St. Peter answered, "His fire was not fire enough to light your candle, and the bed he gave you was of short straw." "True, St. Peter," said the woman, "but he gave me some supper, and it is hard for a rich man to be generous. You may say that the supper was not very good, but at least it was more than a cup of cold water." "Yes," answered the saint, "but he did not give it to you because you loved God, or because you were in need of it, but because he wanted to hear your news." Then the woman was sad, for she could not think of anything more to say for the poor old rich man. And St. Peter saw that she was sad and said, "But if he dies tonight, he shall have a place inside the gate, because you prayed for him. He shall lie there." And he pointed to just such a bed of short crumpled straw as she had lain upon in his house.

But she said, "St. Peter, you ought to be ashamed of yourself. Is that the kind of welcome to give a poor man? Where would he have lain if I had not prayed for him?" "In the dog kennel outside there," answered St. Peter. "Oh, then please let me go back and warn him what comes of loving money!" she pleaded. "That is not necessary," he replied. "The man is hearing every word you and I are this moment saying to each other." "I am so glad," rejoined the woman; "it will make him repent." "He will not be a straw better for it," answered the saint. "He thinks now that he will behave differently, and perhaps when he wakes up he will think so still. But in a day or two he will mock it all as a foolish dream. To gather money will seem again to him a good thing to do, and to lay up treasure in heaven will appear as nonsense. A bird in the hand will be to him worth ten in the heavenly bush. And the end of that will be he will not get the straw inside the gate, and there will be many worse places than the dog kennel which will be too good for him!"

And with that the man awoke. "What an odd dream!" he said to himself. "I had better mind what I am about!" So he was better that day, eating and drinking more freely, and giving more to his people. But the rest of the week he was worse than ever, trying to save what he had that day spent, and so he went on growing worse. When he found himself dying, the terror of his dream came upon him, and he told it all to the priest. But the priest could not comfort him.

By the time the story was over, to which Mercy had listened without a word, they were alone in the great starry night on the side of a hill, with the snow high above them and the heavens and the snow and the stars above the heavens, and God above and below everything. Only Ian felt his presence. Mercy had not missed him yet.

She did not see much in the tale. How could she? It was very odd, she thought, but not very interesting. She had expected a tale of a clan feud or a love story. Yet the seriousness of her companion in its narration had made an impression on her.

As Mercy recounted the story Ian had told her to her sister later, it certainly seemed silly enough. She had retained but the withered stalk and leaves; but the strange flower was gone. Christina judged it hardly a story for a gentleman to tell a lady.

They returned almost in silence to find the table laid, a plentiful supper spread, and the company seated. After supper came singing of songs, saying of ballads, and telling of tales. Of several of the old songs Christina begged the tunes, but was disappointed to find that she could not take them down, and neither could the singers set them down. In the tales she found no interest. The hostess sang with her harp and made eloquent music, for her high clear tones had not yet lost their sweetness, and she had some art to accompany her deep emotions. Loud murmurs of delight in the soft strange tongue of the songs themselves followed the profound silence with which they were heard. But Christina wondered what there was to applaud. She could not sing herself without accompaniment, and she left with a regretful feeling that she had not distinguished herself. Naturally, as they went home, the guests from the New House had much fun in their talk over the queer fashions and poverty-stricken company, the harp and the bagpipes, the wild minor-songs, and the unintelligible stories and jokes. But the ladies agreed that the chief was a splendid fellow.

16 / Rob of the Angels

Among the peasantry assembled at the feast were two that had neither danced nor seated themselves at the long table where all were welcome. Mercy wondered about their separation. Her first thought was that they must be somehow in a lower position than the rest, or had perhaps offended against some strange highland law so that the rest were not allowed to keep company with them. Or perhaps they were beggars who did not belong to the clan.

But she soon saw that she must be wrong in both conjectures, for if there was any avoidance, it was on the part of the two; everyone else, it seemed, was almost anxious to wait on them. They seemed, indeed, rather persons of distinction than outcasts, for they were attended with homage. Now one, now another, where all were guests and all were servants, would rise from the table to offer them something, and they partook with the same dignity and self-restraint that was to be noted in all.

The elder was a man about fifty-five, tall and lean, with a wiry frame, dark grizzled hair, and a shaven face. His dress, in the style of the country, was very poor, but decent. His plaid, a present from his clan, was large and thick and bright compared with the rest of his apparel. His eyes were remarkably clear and keen, and the way he used them could hardly fail to attract attention. Every now and then they would suddenly fix themselves with a gaze of earnest inquiry, which would either grow to perception or presently melt away and let his glance go roving, ready to receive but looking for nothing. His face was brown and healthy, with marked and handsome features. Its expression seemed at first a little severe, but soon—to discerning eyes—disclosed patience and tenderness. At the same time there was in it a something indescribably unlike the other faces present—indeed, his whole person and carriage were similarly peculiar. Had Mercy spent on him a little more attention, the peculiarity would have explained itself. She would have seen that, although everybody spoke to him, he never spoke in reply—only made signs, sometimes with his lips, oftener with hand or head. The man was deaf and dumb. But such was the keenness of his observation that he understood everything said to him by one he knew, and much from the lips of a stranger.

His companion was a youth, not far from thirty, who yet looked like a lad. His clothing was much like his father's—poor enough, but with the air of being better than what he wore every day. He was very pale and curiously freckled, with great gray eyes like his father's but with an altogether different expression. They looked dreamy, and seemed almost careless of what passed before them, though now and then a quick sharp turn of the head showed him highly attentive indeed.

The relation between the two was strangely interesting. Day and night they were inseparable. Because the father was deaf, the son gave all his attention to the sounds of his world; his soul sat in his ears, ever awake, ever listening; while such was his confidence in his father's sight that he scarcely troubled himself to look where he set his feet. His expression was also peculiar, partly from this cause, mainly from a deeper. It was a faraway look, which a quick glance would have taken to indicate that he was "not all there." In a lowland village he would have been regarded as little better than a gifted idiot. But in the mountains he was looked upon as a seer, one in communion with higher powers. Whether his people were of this opinion from being all fools together and therefore unable to know a fool, one may judge or misjudge for himself. What the people of Glenruadh thought of him came out in the name they gave him: Rob of the Angels. He was nearly a foot shorter than his father, and very thin. Some said he always looked cold; but that came from the wonderful peace on his face, like the quiet of a lake over which lies a thin mist. Never was stronger or fuller devotion manifested by son to father than by Rob of the Angels to Hector of the Stags. His filial love and faith were perfect. While they were together, he was in his own calm paradise; when they were apart, which was seldom for more than a few minutes, his spirit seemed always waiting. I believe his notions of God his Father and Hector his father were strangely mingled—the more, perhaps, that the two fathers were equally silent. It would have been a valuable revelation to some theologians to see in those two what love might mean.

So gentle was Rob of the Angels that all the women, down to the youngest maid-child, gave him a compassionate mother-like love. He had lost his mother when he was an infant and the father had brought him up with his own hands, and from the moment of his mother's departure had scarcely let him out of his sight. But the whole woman-remnant of the clan was as a mother to the boy. And from the first they had so talked to him of his mother, no doubt from the feeling that from his father he could learn nothing of her, that now his mother seemed to him everywhere: he could not see God; why should not his mother be there too, though he could not see her? No wonder the man-boy was peaceful!

Many would be inclined to call the two poachers and vagabonds—vagabonds because they lived in houses not quite made with hands, for they had several dwellings that were mostly caves—which yet they contrived to make warm and comfortable; and poachers because they lived by the creatures which God scatters on the hills for his humans. The land here had never been preserved with any care, partly from the troubles besetting its owners, but more from their regard for the poor of the clan who needed game to survive. Little notice was ever taken of what was killed or who killed it. At the same time, any wish of the chief with regard to the deer—and Rob's father, for one, knew every antlered head—was rigidly respected. Some parts had over the years become the property of others, but the boundaries between were not very definite, and sale could hardly change habits, especially of highlanders such as the angel watcher and his father. Hector and Rob led their life with untroubled conscience and easy mind.

In a world where the justification of existence lies in money on the one side and work for money on the other, there could be no justification for the existence of these men. But values in the highlands were different, and this father and son lived and enjoyed life, in manner and degree unintelligible to the one for whom money is his consolation. Neither of them could read or write; neither of them had a penny laid by for wet weather; neither of them would leave any memory beyond their generation; neither of the two would leave on record a single fact concerning one of the animals whose ways and habits they knew better than any other man in the highlands. They were nothing and were worth nothing to anybody, according to the judgment of most strangers. But God knew what a life of unspeakable pleasure he had given them—a life which would hardly be distracted when they changed to the life beyond: neither would find himself much out-of-doors when he died. To Rob of the Angels, how could Abraham's bosom feel strange? He was accustomed to lie night after night, star-melting and soft-breathing, or snow-ghastly and howling, with his head on the bosom of Hector of the Stags—an Abraham who could ill do without his Isaac, as his Isaac without him!

The father trusted his son's hearing as implicitly as his own sight. When he saw a certain look come on his face, he would drop instantly and crouch as still as if he had ears and knew what noise was, watching Rob's face for news of some sound wandering through the vast of the night.

Hector seemed at times, however, either not to be quite deaf, or to have some gift that went toward compensating for his deafness. To all motion about him he was sensitive as no other man. From afar the solid earth would convey to him the vibration of a stag's footstep. Rob sometimes thought his cheek could feel the wind of a sound to which his ear was unresponsive. He was occasionally aware of the proximity of an animal and knew what animal it was, though Rob could neither see nor hear it. His corporeal and spiritual being seemed to be a very seismograph to the ceaseless vibration of the great globe. Often he would make his sign to Rob to lay his ear on the ground and listen, when as yet no indication had reached the latter.

He had the keenest eyes in all Glenruadh, and was a dead shot. Even the chief was not his equal. Yet he never stalked a deer, never killed anything for mere sport. They both had the deep-rooted feeling of their chief in regard to the animals. What they wanted for food, they would kill; but they needed little and they had positively not a greed of any kind between them. If they needed meal or potatoes, they would carry grouse or rabbits down the glen, or arrange with some farmer's wife, perhaps Mrs. Macruadh herself, for a side of deer. But they never killed from pleasure of killing. Of creatures destructive to game, they killed enough to do far more than make up for all the game they took; and for the skins of ermine and stoat and fox and otter, they could always get their money's worth in trade for other necessities. Money itself they never sought or had. If the little birds earn the fruit and seed they devour by the snails and slugs they destroy, then Hector of the Stags and Rob of the Angels also thoroughly earned their food.

When a trustworthy messenger was wanted and Rob was within reach, he was sure to be employed. But not even then were his father and he quite parted. Hector would shoulder his gun and follow in the track of his fleet-footed son till he met him returning after his message had been delivered.

For what was life to Hector but to be with Rob? Was his Mary's son to go about the world unattended? He had a yet stronger feeling than any of the clan that his son was not of the common race of mortals. To Hector also, after their own fashion, would Rob of the Angels tell the tales that gave rise to the name his clanspeople gave him—wonderful tales of the high mountain nights, the actors in them for the most part angels. Whether Rob believed he had relations with such beings, heard them speak, and saw them do the things he reported, I cannot tell. Perhaps, like any other poet of good things, he but saw and believed the things his tales meant. To the eyes of those who knew him, Rob seemed just the sort of person with whom the angels might well be pleased to hold converse. Was he not simplicity itself, truth, generosity, helpfulness? Did he not, as a child, all but lose his life in the rescue of an idiot from the swollen burn? Did he not, as a boy, fight a great golden eagle on its nest, thinking to deliver the lamb it had carried away?

His voice had in it a strangely peculiar tone, making it seem not of this world. Especially after he had been talking for some time, it would appear to come from far away, not from the man's lips. It was wonderful with what solemnity of speech and purity of form he would tell his tales. Having been so much in solitude with his mute father, his speech might well be unlike that of other men; but where did the impression of cultivation come from?

When the Christmas party broke up, most of the guests took the road toward the village, the chief and his brother accompanying them part of the way. These included Rob and his father—Hector looking straight before him, Rob gazing up into the heavens as if holding counsel with the stars.

"Are you seeing any angels, Rob?" asked a gentle girl of about ten.

"Well, I'm not sure," answered Rob of the Angels.

"Surely you can tell whether you see anything."

"Oh yes, I see! But it's not easy to tell what will be an angel and what will not. There's so much all blue up there, it might be full of angels and none of us see one of them."

"Do tell us what you see, dear Rob," said the girl.

"Well, and I will tell you. I think I see many heads close together, talking."

"And can you hear what they will be saying?"

"Some of it."

"Tell me, do tell me—just a little."

"Well then, they are saying one to the other—not very plain, but I can hear—they are saying, 'I wonder when people will be good! It would be so easy if only they would mean it, and begin when they are little!' That's what they are saying as they look down on us walking alone."

"That is good advice, Rob," said one of the women.

Rob turned to her.

"And," he resumed, "they are saying now—at least that is what it sounds like to me—'I wish women were as good as they were when they were little girls.' "

"Now I know they are not saying that!" remarked the woman. "How should the angels trouble themselves about us! Confess, dear Rob, you are making it up, because the child asked it of you."

Rob made no answer, but some saw him smile a curious smile. Rob would never defend anything he had said, or dispute anything another said. After a moment or two he spoke again.

"Shall I tell you what I heard them saying to each other last night?" he asked.

"Yes, do, do!"

"It was on the mountain Dorrachbeg; and there were two of them. They were sitting together in the moon—in the correi over the village. I was lying in a bush near them, for I could not sleep and the night was not cold."

"What were they like, Rob dear?" interrupted the girl.

"That does not matter much," answered Rob, "but they were white, and their eyes not so white, but brighter; for so many sad things go in at their eyes when they come down to the earth that it makes them dark."

"How could they be brighter and darker both at once?" asked the girl.

"I will tell you," answered Rob. "The dark things that go in at their eyes burn in the fire of faith; and the fire of that burning makes their eyes bright. It is the fire of their faith burning up the sad things they see."

"Oh yes! I understand now," said the girl. "And what were their clothes like, Rob?"

"When you see the angels, you don't think much about their clothes."

"And what were they saying?"

"I spoke first—the moment I saw them, for I was not sure they knew I was there. I said, 'I am here, gentlemen.' 'Yes, we know that,' they answered. 'Are you far from home, gentlemen?' I asked. 'It is all one for that!' they answered. 'Well,' said I, 'it is true, gentlemen, for you seem as much at home here on the side of Dorrachbeg as if it was a hill in paradise.' 'And how do you know it is not?' said they. 'Because I see people do upon it as they would not do in paradise,' I answered. 'Ah,' said one of them, 'the hill may be in paradise, and the people not! But you cannot understand these things.' 'I think I do,' I said; 'but surely if you did let them know they were on a hill in paradise, they would not do as they do.' 'It would be no use telling them,' he said, 'but oh, how they spoil the house!' 'Are the red deer and the hares and the birds in paradise?' I asked. 'Certainly,' he answered. 'Do they know it?' I said. 'No, it is not necessary for them; but they will know it one day.'

" 'You do not mind your little brother asking you questions?' I said. 'Ask a hundred if you will, little brother,' he replied. 'Then tell me why you came down here tonight?' 'My friend and I came out for a walk, and we thought we would look to see when the village down there will have to be reaped.' 'What do you mean?' I said. 'You cannot see what we see,' they answered; 'but a human place is like a flower, or a field of grain, and grows ripe, or won't grow ripe, and then some of us up there have to sharpen our sickles.' 'What?' I said, for a great fear came upon me. 'Are they so wicked down there?' 'No, not very wicked, but slow and dull.'

"Then I could say nothing more for a while, and they did not speak either, but sat looking in front of them. 'Can you go and come as you please?' I asked at length. 'Yes, just as we are sent,' they answered. 'Would you not like better to go and come of yourselves, as my father and I do?' I said. 'No,' answered both of them, and something in their voice frightened me. 'It is better to go where we are sent. If we had to go and come at our own will, we should be miserable, for we do not love our own will.' 'Not love your own will?' 'No, not at all!' 'Why?' 'Because there is one—oh, ever so much better. When you and your father are quite good, you will not be left to go and come at your own will any more than we are.' And I cried out and said, 'Oh, dear angel, you frighten me!' And he said, 'That is because you are only a man, and not a—' Now I am not sure of the word he said next; but I think it was *Christian*; and I do not quite know what the word meant."

"Oh, Rob dear! everybody knows that!" exclaimed the girl.

But Rob said no more.

While he was talking, Alister had come up behind him, with Annie of the shop.

"Rob, my friend, I know what you mean, and I want to hear the rest of it: what did the angels say next?"

"They said," answered Rob, " 'Was it your will that set you on this beautiful hill, with all these things to love, with such air to breathe, such a father as you've got, and such grand deer about you?' 'No,' I answered. 'Then,' said the angel, 'there must be a better will than yours, for you would never have even thought of such things.' 'How could I when I wasn't made?' said I. 'There it is,' he returned, and said no more. I looked up and the moon was shining and there were no angels on the stone. But a little way off was my father, come out to see what had become of me."

"Now, did you really see and hear all that, Rob?" said Alister.

Rob smiled a beautiful smile—with something in it common people would call idiotic—stopped and turned, took the chief's hand, and carried it to his lips. But not a word more would he speak, and soon they came where the path of the two turned away over the hill.

"Will you not come and sleep at our house?" said one of the company.

But the two declined the offer.

"The hillside would miss us; we are expected home," said Rob— and away they climbed to their hut, a hollow in a limestone rock, with a front wall of turf, there to sleep side by side till the morning came, or as Rob said, "till the wind of the sun woke them."

Rob of the Angels made songs, and would sing one sometimes, but they were in Gaelic, and the more poetic a thing, the more inadequate— if not stupid—is its translation.

He had all the old legends of the country in his head, and many stories of ghosts and of the second sight. These stories he would tell exactly as he had heard them, showing he believed every word of them, but with such of the legends as were plainly no more than poetic inventions, he would take what liberties he pleased. They lost nothing by it, for he not only gave them touches of fresh interest, but sent glimmering through them hints of something higher, of which ordinary natures perceived nothing, while others were dimly aware of a loftier intent: according to his listeners was their hearing. In Rob's stories, as in all the finer work of genius, a man would find as much as, and no more than, he was capable of. Ian's opinion of Rob was even higher than Alister's.

"What do you think, Ian, of the stories Rob of the Angels tells?" asked Alister as they walked home.

"That the Lord has chosen the weak things of the world to confound the mighty," answered Ian.

"Rob confounds nobody!"

"He confounds me," returned Ian.

"Does he believe what he tells?"

"He believes all of it that is to be believed."

"You are as bad as he!" rejoined Alister. "There is no telling sometimes what you mean!"

"Tell me this, Alister: can a thing be believed that is not true?"

"Yes, certainly."

"I disagree. Can you eat that which is not bread?"

"I have seen a poor fellow gnawing a stick for hunger," answered Alister.

"Yes, gnawing! but gnawing is not eating. That's just it! Many a man will gnaw at a lie all his life and perish of want. He may gnaw at it, he may even swallow it, but I deny that he can believe it. There is nothing in it which can be believed; at most it can be supposed to be true. Belief is another thing. Truth alone can correspond with belief, just as air is for the lungs, just as color is for the sight. A lie cannot be believed any more than acid can be breathed. It goes into the lungs, true, and a lie goes into the mind, but both kill; the one is not breathed, the other is not believed. The thing that is not true cannot find its way to the home of faith. If it could, it would be at once rejected. To a pure soul, which alone can believe, nothing is so loathsome as a pretense of truth. A lie is a pretended truth. If there were no truth there could be no lies. As the devil upon God, the very being of a lie depends on that whose opposite and enemy it is. Tell me, Alister, do you believe in the parables of our Lord?"

"Of course, with all my heart."

"Was there any real person in our Lord's mind when he told that one about the unjust judge?"

"I suppose not; but there were doubtless many such as he."

"Many who would listen to a poor woman because she plagued them?"

"Well, it does not matter. What the story teaches is true, and that was what he wanted believed."

"Just so. The truth in the parables is what they mean, not what they say. And it is so, I think, with Rob of the Angels' stories. He believes all that can be believed of them. At the same time, to a mind so simple, the Spirit of God must have freer entrance than to ours—perhaps even teaches the man by what we call the man's own words. His words may go before his ideas—his higher ideas at least—and his ideas follow after his words. The fulfillment of the saying of our Lord, 'Many first shall be last, and the last first,' will cause astonishment nowhere so much as in the highest knowledge of all. A man who has been leader of the age's opinion may be immeasurably behind another whom he would have shut up in a madhouse. Depend upon it, things go on in the soul of that Rob of the Angels which the angels, whether they come to talk with him or not, would gladly look into. The angels may one day be the pupils of such as he."

A silence followed.

"Do you think the young ladies of the New House could understand Rob of the Angels, Ian?" asked Alister at length.

"Not a bit. I tried the younger, and she is the best. They could if they would but wake up."

"You might say that of anybody."

"Yes, but there is this among other differences—that some people do not wake up because they need a new brain first, such as they will get when they die, perhaps; while others do not wake up because their whole education has been a rocking of them to sleep. And there is this difference between the girls: one is full of herself, and the other is not. The one has a closed, the other an open mind."

"And yet," said Alister, "if they heard you say so, the open mind would imagine itself closed, and the closed never doubt but that it was open."

17 / At the New House

The ladies of the New House were surprised the next day when, as they sat with their guests, the door of the drawing room opened and they saw the young highlanders enter with their mother in ordinary evening clothes. The plough-driving chief himself looked to Christina very much like her patterns of Grosvenor-square. It was a long time since he had worn his dress coat, and it was certainly a little small for his more fully developed frame, but he carried himself as straight as a rush, and was not embarrassed with either his hands or his feet. His hands were brown and large, but they were well shaped and as clean as his heart. Out of his hazel eyes, looking in the candlelight, nearly as dark as Mercy's, went an occasional glance which an emergency might at once develop into a look of command.

Ian would have attracted attention anywhere, if only from his look of quiet *unselfness* and the invariable grace of the movement that broke his marked repose. But his entertainers would doubtless have honored him more had they understood that his manner was just the same and he was as much at home in the grandest court of Europe.

The elder ladies got on together pretty well. The widow of the chief tried to explain to her hostess the condition of the country and its people; the latter, though knowing little and caring less about relations beyond those of the family and social circle, was yet interested enough to be able to seem more interested than she was. And her sweet smile and manners were very pleasing to one who seldom had the opportunity of meeting a woman so much on her own level.

The gentlemen, too, were tolerably comfortable together. Both Alister and Ian had plenty of talk and many stories to tell. The latter pleased the ladies with descriptions of northern ways and dresses and manners, and pleased them perhaps more with what pleased the men also—tales of wolf and bear shooting. But when the talk turned upon the home shooting called "sport," both Alister and Ian sat in unsmiling silence.

There was in Ian a certain playfulness, a restrained merriment, which made Mercy doubt her ears after his seriousness of the night before. Life seemed to flash from him on all sides, occasionally in a keen stroke of wit, more often in a humorous presentation of things. His brother alone could see how he would check the witticism on his very lips lest it should hurt. Because of his tenderness toward all life, he was able to give fascinating narratives of what he had seen, such descriptions of persons he had met. He told a story with such quiet participation, seen in the gleam of his gray eyes, that his hearers enjoyed the telling more than the tale. Even the chief listened with eagerness to every word that fell from his brother.

The ladies took note that, while the manners of the laird and his mother were in a measure old-fashioned, Ian's were quite modern; he seemed perfectly at home with social custom. But a certain stateliness in him dominated the ease, and courtesy would not permit friendliness to fall into premature familiarity. He was at ease with his fellows because he respected them, and courteous because he loved them.

The ladies withdrew, and with their departure came the time that tests whether a man be, in truth, a gentleman. In the presence of women, the polish that is not revelation but concealment preserves itself, only to vanish with them. How some women would stand aghast to hear but a specimen of the talk of their heroes at such a time!

It had been remarked throughout dinner that the highlanders took no wine; but it was supposed they were reserving their power. When they now passed decanter and bottle jug without filling their glasses, their abstinence gave offense to the very soul of Mr. Peregrine Palmer. He was not only fond of a glass of good wine, but had the ambition of a fairly well-developed cellar. He would be known as a connoisseur in wines, and kept up a good stock of distinguished vintages, from which he had brought some to Glenruadh as would best bear the carriage. Having not aspiration, there was room in him for any number of petty ambitions, and it annoyed him not to reap the harvest of recognition. *But of course*, he then said to himself, *no highlander understands anything but whiskey!*

"You don't mean you're a teetotaler, Macruadh!"

"No," answered the chief, "I do not call myself one. But I never drink anything strong."

"Not on Christmas Day? Of course you make an exception at times; and if at anytime, why not on the merriest day of the year? You are under no pledge."

"If that were a reason," returned Alister, laughing, "it would rather be one for taking the pledge immediately than for indulging."

"Well, you surprise me! And highlanders too! I thought better of all highlanders; they have the reputation of being good men at the bottle. You make me sorry to have brought my wine where it meets with no consideration. Mr. Ian, you are a man of the world: you will not refuse me?"

"I must, Mr. Palmer. The fact is, my brother and I have seen so much evil arising from the drinking habits of our country, which always get worse in a time of depression, that we dare not give in to them. My father, who was clergyman of the parish before he became head of the clan, was of the same mind before us, and brought us up not to drink. Throughout a whole Siberian winter I kept the rule."

"And got frostbitten for your pains?"

"And found myself nothing the worse."

"It's mighty good of you, no doubt!" said the host, with a curl of his shaven lip.

"You can hardly call that good which does not involve any self-denial," remarked Alister.

"Well," said Mr. Peregrine Palmer, "what *is* the world coming to? All the pith is leaking out of our young men. In another generation we shall have neither soldiers nor sailors nor statesmen!"

"On what do you base such a sad conclusion?" required Ian.

"On the growth of such values as you yourself proclaim in the young men. Believe me, it is necessary for developing manhood that young men should drink a little and gamble a little and sow a few wild oats—as necessary as that a nation should found itself by the law of the strongest. How else can we look for the moderation to follow with responsibilities? The vices that are more than excusable in the young are very properly denied to the married man; the law for him is not the same as for the young man. I do not plead for license, you see; but it will never do for young men to turn ascetics! Let the clergy do as they please; they are hardly to be counted men; at least their calling is not a manly one! Depend upon it, young men who do not follow the dictates of nature—while they are young, I mean—will never make any mark in the world! They dry up like a nut, brain and all, and have neither spirit, nor wit, nor force of any kind. Nature knows best! When I was a young man—"

"Please spare us your confessions, Mr. Palmer," said Ian. "In our case your ideas do not enter willing ears, and I should be sorry if anything we might feel compelled to say should have the appearance of being aimed at you personally."

"Do you suppose I should heed anything you said?" cried the host, betraying the bad blood in his breeding. "Is it manners to prevent a man from speaking his mind at his own table? I say a saint is not a man! A fellow that will neither look at a woman nor drink his glass is not cut out for a man's work in the world!"

Like a sledgehammer came the fist of the laird on the table, and the crystal rang as it shook where it stood.

"My God!" he exclaimed, and rose in indignation.

Ian laid his hand on his arm and he sat down again.

"There may be some misunderstanding, Alister," said Ian, "between us and our host! Pray, Mr. Palmer, let us understand each other: do you believe God made woman to be the slave of man? Can you believe he ever made a woman that she might be dishonored—that a man might caress and despise her?"

"I know nothing about God's intention; all I say is we must obey the laws of our nature."

"Is conscience, then, not a law of our nature? Is it not even on the level of our instincts? Must not the lower laws be subject to the higher? It is a law—forever broken, yet eternal—that a man is his brother's keeper: still more must he be his sister's keeper. In that law is involved all civilization, all national as well as individual growth."

Mr. Peregrine Palmer smiled a contemptuous smile. The other young men exchanged glances that seemed to say, "The governor knows what is best."

"Such may be the popular feeling in this out-of-the-way spot," said Mr. Peregrine Palmer, "and no doubt it is very praiseworthy, but the world is not of your opinion, gentlemen."

"The world has got to come to our opinion," said the laird—at which the young men of the house broke into laughter.

"May we join the ladies?" said Ian, rising.

"By all means," answered the host, with a laugh meant to be good-humored. "They are the fittest company for you."

As the brothers went up the stairs, they heard their host again holding forth, but they would not have been much edified had they been able to hear all of the words he spoke in their absence.

The three from the cottage were halfway home before the gentlemen of the New House rose from their wine. Then first the mother sought an explanation of the early departure they had suggested.

"Something went wrong, sons. What was it?" she asked.

"I don't like the men, Mother; nor does Ian," said Alister gloomily.

"Take care you are not unjust!" she replied.

"You would not have liked Mr. Palmer's doctrine any better than we did, Mother."

"What was it!"

"We would rather not tell you."

"It was not fit for a woman to hear."

"Then do not tell me. I trust you to defend women."

"In God's name we will!" said Alister.

"There is no occasion for an oath, Alister!" said his mother.

"Alister meant it very solemnly," said Ian.

"Yes, but it was not necessary—least of all to me. The name of our

Lord God should lie as a precious jewel in the cabinet of our hearts, to be taken out only at great times and with loving awe.''

"I shall be careful, Mother," answered Alister. "But when things make me sorry or glad or angry, I always think of God first."

"I understand you. But I fear taking the name of God in vain."

"It shall not be in vain, Mother," said the chief.

"Will this mean a breach with our new neighbors?" asked the mother.

"It will depend on them. The thing began because we would not drink wine."

"You did not make any remark?"

"Not until our host's remarks called for our reasons. By the way, I should like to know how the man made his money."

18 / The Brothers

Events after this seemed sorely against any deepening cordiality between the old and the new houses of Glenruadh. But there was a sacred enemy within the stronghold of Mr. Peregrine Palmer, and whether that enemy was his conscience or something else, it kept him from altogether breaking with the young highlanders despite the downright rudeness with which he felt they had expressed their differences with him. He felt, without knowing it, ashamed of the things he had said.

Christian and Sercombe could not but admire the straightforwardness of the brothers. Their conventionality could hardly prevent them from feeling the dignity with which the highlanders stood up for their convictions. And though they could not, after what happened, court their society, they could at least treat them with consideration.

What had taken place could not definitely influence the ideas, feelings, or opinions of the young ladies. Their father would sooner have had his hand cut off than allow any word of his argument with Alister and Ian to reach the ears of his daughters. Some men would rather be burned alive than let those they love know the evil principles they hold.

Mr. Palmer did, however, communicate something of the conversation to his wife, and although she had neither the spirit, the insight, nor the active purity to tell him he was in the wrong, she did not think any the worse of the young highlanders. She even thought it a pity the world should have been so made that they could not be in the right.

But a bird of the air will carry a matter, and some vaguest impression of what had occurred gradually came to alight on the minds of the elder girls, even though nothing was ever said to them—possibly from hints supposed unintelligible passing between Mr. Sercombe and Christian. Now even Mercy had not escaped some notion of the event, and she felt the glow of a conscious attraction toward men who somehow—she knew not how—seemed like old-fashioned knights in their relations to women.

The attachment between the brothers was unusual both in kind and degree. Alister regarded Ian as his better self, through whom he could rise above himself. Ian looked up to his brother as the head of the family, uniting in himself all ancestral claims and representing an ordered and harmonious commonwealth. He saw in Alister virtues and powers he did not recognize in himself. His love blossomed into the deeper de-

116

votion because only he himself had been sent to college. Therefore, he was bound to share with his elder brother what he had learned. Thus Alister got more through Ian than he would have at the best college in the world. For Ian was a born teacher and found intense delight, not in imparting knowledge—for that is a comparatively poor thing—but in leading a mind up to see what it was before incapable of seeing. And, as part of the same gift, he always knew when he had not succeeded. In Alister he found a wonderful teachableness—which crossed occasionally with a great pride, against which he fought sturdily.

No age, however bad, should find it hard to believe in such simplicity and purity as that of these young men; but worse, in our own, we find it difficult to believe in such love between men. Yet a man incapable of loving another man with hearty devotion cannot be capable of loving a woman as a woman ought to be loved.

Alister had a great love of music, which had had little development other than the study of the violin with the assistance of a certain poor performer in the village, and what criticism his brother could afford him. But the late chief, his father, was one of the few clergymen who played the violin, and at the first wail of the instrument in the hands of his son, his widow was seized with such a passion of weeping in the memory of her husband that Alister took care she should never hear it again. He always thereafter carried it to some place too remote for the farthest-traveling tones to reach her. But this was not easy, for sound will travel very far among the hills. At times he would take it to the room behind Annie's shop, at times to the hut occupied by Hector of the Stags: there at least he would not torment his host, and Rob of the Angels would endure anything for his chief. The place he most preferred was too distant to be visited often; but there, soon after Christmas, the brothers now agreed to have a day together, a long talk, and a conference with the violin. On a clear, frosty morning in January they set out, with provisions for a night and two days.

The place was on an upland pasture ground, a good distance inland but still in their possession: no farm was complete without a range in some high valley for the sheep and cattle in summer. On the north of this valley stood a bare hilltop whose crest was a limestone rock which rose about twenty feet out of the heather. Every summer they had spent weeks of their boyhood with the shepherds in the society of this hill, and one day discovered in its crest a shallow cave to which they thereafter often took their food and the book they were reading together. And there they made Gaelic songs in which Alister excelled, while Ian did better in English.

When Ian was at home during university vacations, they were fonder than ever of going to the hill. There Ian would pour out to Alister of the fullness of his gathered knowledge, and there they made their first acquaintance with Shakespeare. Ian had bought some dozen of his plays, and how they reveled in them in the long summer evenings! Every spring, Ian brought with him new books, and these they read in their cave.

Almost from the very first they conceived the idea of developing the hollow into a house. They found serviceable tools about the place at home, and the rock was not quite of the hardest. For the last seventeen years, not a summer had passed without a good deal being done, Alister working alone when Ian was away. The little limestone house grew, sharing in the progress of its occupants, and the cave now assumed notable dimensions. It was called by the people *uamh an ceann*, the cave of the chief, and regarded as his country house. All around it was covered with snow throughout the winter and spring, and supplied little to the need of man beyond the blessed air, and a glorious vision of the sea and land, mountain and valley, falling water, gleaming lake, and shadowy cliff.

Crossing the wide space where recently they had burned the heather so that the sheep might have its young shoots in the spring, the brothers stood and gazed around with delight.

"There is nothing like this anywhere!" said Ian.

"Do you mean nothing so beautiful?" asked Alister.

"No, I mean just what I say. There is nothing like it. I don't care whether one scene be more or less beautiful than another. What I do care for is its individual speech to my soul. I feel toward visions of nature as toward writers. If a book or particular sight produces in my mind a mood that no other produces, then I feel it individual, original, real, therefore precious. If a scene or a song or a poem plays upon my heart as no other scene or song or poem could, why should it matter whether it be beautiful? A bare hill may be more to me than an exquisite garden, but I love them both. Wherever there is something that has power over my heart and soul, I do not ask whether its power be great or small; it is enough that it is a unique power, one by itself."

They were now climbing the last slope of the hill on whose top stood their cave-house, even dearer now than in their boyhood. Alister occasionally went there for a few hours' solitude, and Ian would write there for days at a time; but in general when they visited the place, they went together. Alister unlocked the door and they entered.

The first little room was hardly larger than required for opening the door. But immediately inside another door opened into a room of about eight feet by twelve, with two small windows. Its hearth was a projection from the floor of the live stone; and there, all ready for lighting, was a large pile of peats. The chimney, which had been the most difficult part of their undertaking, went up through the rock. Now and then it smoked inside the room, but peat smoke is sweet.

The first thing after lighting the fire was to fill their kettle, for which they had to take off the snow lid of a small spring nearby. Then they made a good meal of tea, mutton-ham, oatcake, and butter. The only seats in the room were a bench in each of two of the walls, and a chair on each side of the hearth, all of the live rock.

From this opened two more rooms—one a bedroom with a bed in the rock wall, big enough for two. Dry heather stood thick between the mattress and the stone. The third room, of which they intended making a parlor, was not yet more than half excavated; and there, when they had rested a while, they began to bore and chip at the stone. Their progress was slow, for the grain in the rock was tight: never, even when the snow above was melting, had the least moisture seeped through. For a time they worked and talked: both talked better when using their hands. Then Alister stopped and played while Ian went on. Ian stopped next and read aloud from a manuscript he had brought while his brother again worked. No one else would think so well of Ian's verses as did Alister. Ian desired sympathy of feeling, not admiration; from Alister he had both.

Few men would care to hear the talk of those two, for they had no interest in anything that did not belong to the reality of things. To them what most men count real was the merest illusion. They sought what would not merely last, but must go on growing. For them there was no question of choice; they *must* choose what was true, they *must* choose life.

Few men are capable of understanding such love as theirs, of understanding the love of David and Jonathan or of Tennyson and Hallam. These two men, born brothers in body, were also brothers in spirit.

They ceased quarrying and returned to the outer room. Ian took himself to drawing figures on one of the walls, intending to carve them later in dipped relief. Alister proceeded to take their bedding from in front of the fire, where it had been warming, and prepare for the night.

While they were thus busied, Ian began telling Alister of his flight from Russia. Long before he ended Alister came close to him, full of emotion. Ian was perfectly composed, his voice quiet and low.

Having accepted a commission of the Czar, Ian was placed in a post of trust in the palace, where in one apartment lived an imperial princess. Her admitted sympathy with the oppressed masses of her country had given rise to a doubt as to her politics; thus, her movements restricted, she lived as a virtual prisoner in the palace. Her father had fallen into disgrace, her mother was nearly dead of grief, all around her were spies, and love was nowhere. Gladly would she have yielded every rag of her rank to breathe the air of freedom and be a peasant girl on her father's land. But in her present position there was no one in whom she could trust, and her life was miserable.

At certain times of the day Ian was posted to stand guard at one end of a long corridor in one of the wings of the palace which led toward the apartment of the princess. Few passed along this corridor, for the attendants used a back stair and passages. As he stood alone one morning he heard a cry, from whence he never knew, and he immediately darted down the hallway, thinking assistance might be needed. About halfway down it, he saw a lady emerge from the other end and come slowly along. He stood aside, respectfully waiting until she should pass. Her eyes were on the floor, but as she came near she raised them. The sadness of them went to his heart and his very soul rushed into his own eyes. The princess, I imagine, had never before met such an expression, and misunderstood it. Lonely, rejected, helpless, it seemed full of something she had been longing for all her life—a soul to be her refuge from the wind of the cruel world. She stood and gazed at him.

Ian at once perceived who she must be and stood waiting. But she appeared fascinated, her eyes remaining on his, for they seemed to her to be promising help. Her fascination fascinated him, and for some moments they stood thus, regarding each other. Ian felt he must break the spell, even though it was her part to speak and his to obey. "How may I serve your imperial highness?" he asked. She was silent for a moment. "Your name?" He gave it. "Your nation?" He stated it. "When are you here?" He told her his hours. "I will see you again," she said and turned and went back.

From that moment she loved him, and thought he loved her. But though he would willingly have died for her, he did not love her as she thought. Alister was amazed to hear him say so, for his own free heart could hardly have helped itself in such a position. But Ian, with a tenderness for womankind altogether infinite and a compassionate tendency to help and comfort, was not ready to fall in love.

Knowing the ways of the house, the princess contrived to see him often. He talked to her of the best he knew. He did what he could to lighten her loneliness by finding her books and music; best of all, he persuaded her to read a New Testament he gave her. In their few minutes together, he tried to show her the Master of men as he showed himself to his friends. But their time together was always short and their anxiety for each other so great, seeing that discovery would be ruin to both, that they could not go far with anything.

At length came an occasion when at parting they embraced. How it was, Ian could not tell. He blamed himself much, but Alister thought it might not have been his fault. The same moment he was aware that he did not love her and yet that he could not turn back. He was ready to do anything, everything in honor; yet he felt false inasmuch as he had given her ground for believing that he felt toward her as he could not help seeing she felt toward him. Had it been in his power to order his own heart, he might have willed himself to love her. But the princess doubted nothing, and the change that passed upon her as a result of being in love with Ian was wonderful. The power of human love is next to the power of God's love. Like a flower long repressed by cold, she blossomed so suddenly in the sunshine of her happiness that Ian dreaded the suspicion which the evident change might arouse. She began to put on the robes of beauty; the softest tinge of rose began to color her cheek, and within two months she looked years younger than her age. Yet Ian could never be absolutely open with her, haunted by the dread of making her grieve who had already grieved so much and was now so joyfully happy.

One evening they met as usual in the twilight. In five minutes they would hear the steps of the man coming to replace Ian at his post. Few words passed, but they parted with more of lingering tenderness than usual, and the princess put a little packet in his hand. Later that night his only friend in the service came hurriedly into his room, telling him he must flee immediately: something had been discovered and his freedom, if not his very life, was in danger. He must leave at once by a certain coach which would start in an hour. There was just time to disguise him. He must make for a certain port on the Baltic, and there wait in concealment until a chance of getting away turned up.

Ian refused. He feared nothing, had done nothing to be ashamed of! Anxious about the princess, he persisted in his refusal despite his friend's pleading, and the coach went without him. In the early morning hours that followed, every passenger in that coach was murdered. He afterward saw the signs of their fate in the snow.

In the middle of the night a company of men in masks entered his room, muffled his head, and hurried him into a carriage, which drove away rapidly.

When it stopped, he thought he had arrived at some prison to which they were taking him. But instead he soon found himself in another carriage with two of the police. At a certain town his attendants left him, with instructions to make haste out of the country.

But instead of obeying he disguised himself and made his way to Moscow, where he had friends. From there he wrote to his friend at St. Petersburg. Not many letters had passed before he learned that the princess was dead. She had been placed in closer confinement, her health gave way, and by a rapid decline she had at last gained her freedom.

All the night through, hardly closing their eyes until morning, the brothers, with many intervals of thoughtful silence, lay talking.

"I am glad to think," said Alister, after one of these silences, "you do not suffer so much as if you had been downright in love with her."

"I suffer far more," answered Ian with a sigh. "It breaks my heart to think she had not so much from me as she thought she had."

They were once more silent. Alister was full of grief for his brother. Ian at length spoke again.

"Alister," he said, "whether I loved her then or not, I do not know. But beyond a doubt I love her now. It needed only to be out of sight of her, and to have that time only in the memory to know that I loved her. Alister, I do love her!"

"Oh, Ian!" groaned Alister; "how terrible for you!"

"Alister, my dear fellow," returned Ian, "can you understand no better than that? Can't you see I am happy now, though it is a painful happiness? My trouble was that I did not love her—not that she loved me. Now we shall love each other forever!"

"How do you know that, Ian?"

"By knowing that I love her. If I had not come to know that, I could not have said to myself that I would love her forever."

"But you can't marry her, Ian! The Lord said there would be no marrying there!"

"Did he say there would be no love there, Alister? Most people seem to think he did. There are very few who can be said to really believe in any hereafter worth believing in. The life beyond is no factor in the life of such people. I think they fancy the life beyond will be of an utterly different kind than life here. But I look to that life to give me *more* life, *more* strength, *more* love. God is not shut up in heaven, neither is there one law of life there and another here. I desire more life here, and shall have it, for what is needed for this world is to be had in this world. In proportion as I become one with God, I shall have it. This world never did seem my home; I have never felt quite comfortable in it. I have yet to find the perfect home. And does not the Bible itself tell us that we are pilgrims and strangers in the world? This is but a place we come to be made ready for another. Yet it seems that those who *do* regard it as their home are not half so well pleased with it as I. They are always grumbling at it. They complain that their plans are thwarted, and when they succeed they do not give them the satisfaction they expected. Yet they mock him who says he seeks a better country! But I am keeping you awake, Alister! I will talk no more. You must go to sleep."

"It is better than any sleep to hear you talk, Ian," returned Alister. "How far you are ahead of me! I do love this world! When I come to die it will tear my heart to think that this cave which you and I have dug out together must pass into other hands. I love every foot of the earth that remains to us—every foot that has been taken from us. When I stand on the top of this rock and breathe the air of this mountain, I bless God we still have a spot to call our own. It is quite a different thing from the love of mere land. I could not feel the same toward any property, however beautiful, that I had bought. This, our own old land, I feel as if I love in something of the same way as I love our mother. Often in the hot summer days, lying on my face in the grass, I have kissed the earth as if it were a live creature that could return my caresses. The long grass is a passion to me, and next to the grass I love the heather, not the growing grain. I am a fair farmer, I think, but I would rather see the land grow what it pleased than to pass into the hand of another. Place is to me sacred. The love we bear to our friends is something akin to the love we bear to the place in which we were born and brought up."

"That is all very true, Alister. I understand your feeling perfectly. I have it myself. But we must be weaned from that kind of thing; we must not love the outside as if it were the inside! Everything comes that we may know the sender, of whom it is a symbol, a far-off likeness of something in him. And to him it must lead us—the self-existent, true, original love, the making love. But I have felt all you say. I used to lie in bed and imagine the earth alive and carrying me on her back till I fell asleep. Once, the fancy burned itself into a dream."

"Tell me. Can you recall it?"

"I shall try. For I find when a dream does us good, we don't forget it. And I think I shall always remember this one. I thought I was borne on the back of something great and strong—I could not tell what; it might have been an elephant or a great eagle or a lion. It went sweeping swiftly along, the wind of its flight roaring past me in a tempest. I began to grow frightened. Where could this creature of such awful speed be taking me? I prayed to God to take care of me. The head of the creature turned to me and I saw the face of a woman, grand and beautiful. Never with my open eyes have I seen such a face! And I knew it was the face of this earth, and that I had never seen it before because she carries us upon her back. When I woke, I knew that all the strangest things in life and history must one day come together in a beautiful face of loving purpose, one of the faces of the living God. The very mother of the Lord did not for a long time understand him, and only through sorrow came to see true glory. Alister, if we were right with God, we could see the earth vanish and never heave a sigh. God—of whom it was all but a shimmering revelation—would still be ours!''

Early in the morning they fell asleep, and it was daylight, late in the winter, when Alister rose. He roused the fire, asleep all through the night, and prepared their breakfast of porridge and butter, tea, oatcake, and mutton-ham. When it was nearly ready, he woke Ian, and when they had eaten, they read together a portion of the Bible, that they might not forget, and start the life of the day without trust in the life-causing God.

"All that is not rooted in him," Ian would say, "all hope or joy that does not turn its face upward, is an idolatry. Our prayers must rise that our thoughts may follow them."

The portion they read contained the saying of the Lord that we must forsake all and follow him if we would be his disciples.

"It is sometimes almost terrifying," said Ian, "to stop and think of the scope of the demands made upon us as Christians, at the perfection required, at the totality of self-abandonment expected of us. Yet outside of such absoluteness can be no salvation. In God we live every mundane as well as every exalted moment of our lives. To trust in him when no great need is pressing, when things all seem to be going right, may be even harder than when things seem to be going wrong. At no time is there any danger, except in *ourselves* forgetting that it is God who breathes life into everything, that we are nothing—without wisdom or insight—in and of ourselves. Oh Alister, take care you do not love the land more than the will of God. Take care you do not love even your people more than the will of God."

They spent the rest of the day on the hilltop, and as there was no sign of storm, remained till the dark night, when the moon came to light their way home.

"Perhaps when we are dead," said Alister as they walked along, "we may be allowed to come here again sometimes. Only then we shall not be able to dig out any more of the stone, and there is a pain in looking at what cannot go on."

"It may be a special pleasure," returned Ian, "in those new conditions to look into such a changeless cabinet of the past. When we are one with our life so that no prayer can be denied, there will be no end to the lovely possibilities."

"If I have the people I love, I think I could part with all other things, even the land," said Alister.

"Be sure we shall not have to part with them. We shall yet walk, I think, with our father as we did when we were young. The wind of the twilight will again breathe about us like a thought of the living God haunting our goings and watching to help us. 'Be independent!' cries the world. But the Lord says, 'Seek ye first the kingdom of God and his righteousness, and all these things shall be added unto you.' Our dependence is our eternity. We cannot live on bread alone; we need every word of God. We cannot live on air alone; we need an atmosphere of living souls. Should we be freer, Alister, if we were independent of each other? When I am out in the world, my heart is always with mother and you. We must be constantly giving ourselves away, we must dwell in houses of infinite dependence, or sit alone in the waste of a godless universe."

It was a rough walk in the moonlight over the hills, but full of rare delight. And while they walked the mother was waiting for them, with the joy of God in her heart, the joy of beholding how the men she loved loved each other.

19 / The Nail

The next morning on the way to the village, the brothers overtook Christina and Mercy, and they walked along together.

The young men felt more inclined to be friendly with the girls because the men of their own family were so unworthy of them. A man who does not respect a woman because she is a woman cannot have a thorough respect even for his own mother: he is incapable of it and cannot know his own incapacity. Alas for girls in a family where the atmosphere of low thinking and degrading judgments enfolds them! One of the marvels of the world is, that, with such fathers and brothers, there are so few wicked women.

Christina's condescension had by this time dwindled, almost vanishing, and her talk was therefore more natural. The company, conversation, and whole atmosphere of the young men tended to wake in the girls what was best and sweetest. Reality appeals at once to the real, opens the way for a soul to emerge from the fog of the commonplace into the color and air of life. The better things of humanity often need the sun of friendship to wile them out. A well-bred and tolerably clever girl will appear to a man to possess a hundred faculties of which she herself knows nothing; and his belief will help to rouse them in her. A young man will see an angel where those who love her best might only see a nice girl; but he sees not merely what she might be, but what one day she must be.

Christina had been at first rather taken with the ploughman, but she had now turned her batteries mainly on the soldier. During the dinner she had noted how entirely Ian was what she chose to call a man of the world; and it made him in her eyes worthy of conquest. Besides, as elder sister, must she not protect the inexperienced Mercy from him?

All of a sudden as they walked Christina stopped short with a little cry, and grabbed at Ian's arm.

"I beg your pardon," she said, "but I cannot bear it a moment longer. Something in my boot is hurting my foot more and more with each step."

She limped to the side of the road, sat down, accepted the service of Ian to unlace her boot, and gave a sigh of relief when he pulled it off. He inverted and shook it, then searched and found that one of the nails from the sole was projecting through into the inside.

But how to get rid of it? His hand could but just reach it with his fingertips. In vain he tried to knock it down against a small stone put inside. Alister could suggest nothing. But Mistress Conal's cottage was near. There they might find something to help. But Christina could not be left behind, and how was she to walk in a silk stocking over a road frozen hard as glass? The chief would have carried her, but she would not let him. Ian therefore took off his cap, and tied it onto her foot with his handkerchief.

There was much merriment over the extemporized shoe, mingled with apologetic gratitude from Christina, who, laughing at the state of her foot, was yet not displeased with the outcome of the whole affair.

When the chief opened the door of the cottage, there was no one to be seen inside. The fire was burning hot and flameless, a three-footed pot stood in it, but there was no other sign of presence. As Alister stooped down, searching for some implement to fix the boot, in shot a black cat, jumped over his back and disappeared. The same instant they heard a groan, and then first discovered the old woman in bed, seemingly very ill. Ian went up to her.

"What is the matter with you, Mistress Conal?" he asked, addressing her in English because of the ladies.

But in reply she poured out a torrent of Gaelic which seemed to the girls only grumbling but was something considerably stronger. The chief went up and spoke to her, but she was short and sullen with him. He left her to resume his search.

"Let alone!" she cried. "When that nail leaves her brogue, it will be for your heart."

He sought to soothe her.

"She will bring misery on you!" she insisted.

"You have a hammer somewhere, I know," said Alister as if he had not heard her words.

"She shall find no help in *my* house," answered the old woman in English.

"Very well, Mistress Conal!" returned the chief. "The lady cannot walk home, so I shall have to carry her!"

"God forbid!" she cried. "Go and fetch a wheelbarrow."

"Mistress Conal, there is nothing left but to carry her home in my arms."

"Give me the cursed brogue, then. I will pull the nail out."

But the chief would not yield the boot. He went out and searched the hillside until he found a smooth stone of the right size. Using it and a pair of tongs he beat down the nail. Christina put on the boot and they left the cottage. The chief stayed behind for a moment, but the old woman would not even acknowledge his presence.

"What a rude old thing she is! That is how she always treats us," said Christina.

"Have you done anything to offend her?" asked Alister.

"Not that we know of. We can't help being lowlanders."

"She no doubt bears you a grudge," said Ian, "for having what once belonged to us. I am sorry she is so unfriendly. It is not a common fault with our people."

"Poor old thing! What does it matter?" said Christina.

A woman's hate was to her no more than the barking of a dog.

They had not gone far before the nail again asserted itself; it had been but partially subjugated. A discussion was held which resulted in Mercy and the chief going to fetch another pair of boots while Ian remained with Christina.

They seated themselves on a stone by the roadside. The sun clouded over, a keen wind blew, and Christina shivered. There was nothing to do but go back to the cottage. The key was in the door. Ian turned it and they went in. Certainly this time no one was there. The old woman so recently groaning on her bed had vanished. Ian made up the fire and did what he could for his companion's comfort. She was not pleased with the tone of his attentions, but the way she accepted them made her appear more pleased than Ian cared for, and he became colder and more polite. Annoyed by his indifference, she took it nevertheless with a sweetness which belonged to her nature as God had made it, not as she had spoiled it. And even such a butterfly as she felt the influence of a man like Ian and could not help being more natural in his presence. His truth elicited what there was of hers. The longer she was in his company the more she was pleased with him and the more annoyed she became with her failure in pleasing him.

It is generally more or less awkward when a young man and girl, between whom there is not spiritual unity, find themselves alone together. Ian was one of the last to feel such awkwardness, but he thought his companion felt it. He therefore did his best to make her forget herself and him, telling her story after story which she found so interesting that for the moment her self was quieted and she was placed in the humbler and healthier position of receiving the influence of another. For one moment, as he was narrating a hair's-breadth escape he had had from a company of Tartar soldiers by the friendliness of a young girl, the daughter of a Siberian convict, she found herself under the charm of a certain potency of which he was himself altogether unconscious, but which had carried away hearts more indifferent than hers.

In the meantime, Alister and Mercy were walking toward the New

House and, walking, were more comfortable than those who sat waiting. Mercy did not have much to say, but she was capable of asking a question worth answering, and of understanding not a little.

"Would you mind telling me something about your brother?" she said, thinking of her walk with Ian on Christmas Eve.

"What would you like to know about him?" asked Alister.

"Anything you please to tell me," she answered.

Now there was nothing that pleased Alister more than to talk about Ian; and he talked so that Mercy could not help feeling what a brother he himself must be, while on his part Alister was delighted with the girl who took such an interest in Ian. Therefore, for Ian's sake he began to love Mercy, he had never yet been what is called *in love*—he had had little opportunity, indeed, of falling in love. His breeding had been that of a gentleman, and despite the sweetness and gentleness of the maidens of his clan, there were differences which thus far had proved sufficient to prevent the first approaches of love; though, once entertained, they might have added to the depth of it. It was by no means impossible for Alister to fall in love, even with an uneducated girl. But the fatherly relation in which he stood toward his clan had tended rather to prevent such an alliance.

Alister told Mercy how Ian and he used to spend their boyhood. He recounted some of their adventures in hunting and herding and fishing, even in going to and from school, a distance of five miles, in all kinds of weather. Then he began relating the poetry of the people, their legends, their ballads and their songs. At last he came to the poetry of the country itself—the delights of following the plough, the whispers and gleams of nature, her endless appeal through every sense. The mere smell of the earth in a spring morning, he said, always made him praise God.

"Everything we have," he went on, "must be shared with God. Ian says the greatest word in the universe is *one*, the next greatest, *all*. They are but the two ends of a word to us unknowable—God's name for himself."

Mercy had read very little. Most of the poetry she had read was only platitude sweetened with sound; she had never read, certainly never understood, a real poem. But who can tell what a nature may prove to be after feeding on good food for a while? The queen bee is only a better fed working bee. Who can tell what a soul may become when it has been ploughed with the plough of suffering, when the rains of sorrow, the frosts of pain, and the winds of poverty have moistened and swelled and dried its fallow clods?

Mercy did not have such a sweet temper as her sister, but she was less selfish. She was readier to take offense, perhaps, because she was less self-satisfied. Before long they might change places. A little dew from the eternal fountain was falling on them. Christina was beginning to be aware that a certain man, neither rich nor distinguished nor ambitious, had yet a real charm for her. Not that for a moment she would think seriously of such a man! That would be idiotic! But it would be very nice to have a little innocent flirtation with him, or perhaps a "platonic friendship!" as she might say. But what could she have to do with Plato? When she said *I*, she was aware only of a neat bundle of foolish desires, not the God at her heart!

Mercy, on the other hand, was being strongly drawn to the big, strong, childlike heart of the chief. There is always, despite the great gulf between them, an appeal from the childish to the childlike. The childish is but the shadow of the childlike, and shadows are little like the things from which they fall. But to what except the heavenly shall the earthly appeal in its sore need, its widowhood, its orphanage? With what shall the childish take refuge but the childlike? To what shall ignorance cry but wisdom? Mercy felt no restraint with the chief as with Ian. His great, deep, yet refined and musical laugh set her at ease. Ian's smile, with its shimmering eternity, was to Mercy no more than the moon on a rain pool. The moral health of the chief made an atmosphere of conscious safety around her. By the side of no other man had she ever felt so. With him she was at home, therefore happy, and under his genial influence she was already growing.

When they returned and Christina was re-shod and they were leaving the cottage, Ian, happening to look behind him, spied the black cat perched on the edge of the chimney in the smoke.

"Look at her," he said, "pretending innocence when she has been watching us all the time."

"It makes me wonder whether Mistress Conal did not set her to keep her eye on us so that she might be fully acquainted with our doings," said Alister.

Ian laughed a subdued laugh, but said nothing further.

The young men of the New House had not fared well in their hunting in the north. They had neither experience nor competent local guides: none of the chief's men would hunt with them. The men of Clanruadh looked on those from the south as intruders; even those who did not share their chief's disapproval of useless killing nevertheless respected it. Neither Christian nor Sercombe had yet shot a single stag, and the time was drawing near when they would have to return—the one to Glasgow, the other to London. To have no proof of prowess to display was humbling to Sercombe. If he had no stag's head to show, he would have to hide his own! He resolved, therefore, on the next moonlit night to stalk by himself a certain great, wide-horned stag about whose habits he had received information.

At Oxford, where Valentine had made his acquaintance, Sercombe belonged to a fast set, but had distinguished himself notwithstanding as an athlete. He was a great favorite with a few—not the best of the set— and admired by many for his confidence and his stature. His self-assertion, however, made him much disliked by others at the university, a self-assertion based chiefly on his ability to spend money, for he was the favorite son of a rich banker in London. He knew nothing of the first business of life—self-restraint—and had never denied himself anything. He viewed his likings as his rights, but he had not yet in the eyes of the world disgraced himself: it takes a good many disgraceful things to bring a rich man to outward disgrace.

His sole attendant when shooting was a clever vagabond lad belonging to nowhere in particular, and living by any crook except the shepherd's. From him he heard of the great stag, and the spots he frequented in the valleys, often scraping away the snow with his feet to get at the grass. He did not inform him that the animal was a special favorite with the chief of Clanruadh, or that the clan looked upon him as their live symbol, the very stag represented on the vest of the chief's coat of arms. It was the same animal Nancy had reported to her master as eating grass on the burnside in the moonlight. Christian and Sercombe had stalked him day after day, but without success. And now, with one poor remaining hope, the latter had determined to stalk him at night. To take his life from him, his glorious rush over the mountainside, his plunge into the valley; to see that ideal of strength and grace and joyous flight lying nerveless at his feet; to be able to call the huge set of antlers his own, was for the present the single ambition of Hilary Sercombe. He was of the brood of darkness whose delight lies in undoing what God has done.

There was, however, a reason for the failure of the young hunters besides their lack of skill and what they called their bad luck. Hector of the Stags was awake; his keen, everywhere-roving eyes were upon them, as were the keen, all-hearkening ears of Rob of the Angels. They had discovered that the two men had set their hearts on the big stag, *an cabrach mòr* by right of excellence, and every time they went out after him, Hector too was out with his spyglass, the gift of an old seafaring friend, searching the billowy hills. While the men from the south would be toiling along to get the wind of him unseen, for the old stag's eyes were as keen as his velvety nose, the father and son would be lying, perhaps close at hand, perhaps far away on some hillside of another valley, watching now the hunters, now the stag. For love of Macruadh, and for love of the stag, they had made themselves his guardians.

Again and again, when one of them thought he was going to have a splendid shot and had just raised the rifle to his shoulder and had the great pumping heart in his sights, suddenly a distant shot would foil the near one—a shot for life, not death—and the stag, knowing instantly by wondrous combination of sense and judgment where the danger lay, would without once looking round measure straight a hundred yards over hills and rocks before the trigger could be pulled. Another time it would be no shot, but the barking of a dog, the cry of a bird, or some other signal that startled him, for the creatures understand one another's cries. To Christian and Sercombe all the life in the glen seemed in conspiracy to frustrate their heart's desire. Therefore the latter grew all the more determined to kill the great deer, for he had begun to hate him.

The sounds warning the stag were by no means always what they seemed, those of other wild animals; they were often imitations by Rob of the Angels. I fear the animal grew somewhat bolder and less careful from the assurance thus given that he was watched over, and cultivated a little nonchalance. Never, however, did he neglect warning from any quarter, but from feeding peacefully would instantaneously flee, his great horns thrown back over his shoulders, and his four legs just touching the ground with elastic hoof, or tucking themselves almost out of sight as he skipped over rock and gully, stone and bush—whatever lay between him and larger room. Great joy it was to his two guardians to see him, and great game to watch his frustrated enemies. For the sake of *an cabrach mòr*, Hector and Rob would go hungry for hours. But they never imagined how intently the well-fed Sasunnach, incapable, as they thought, of hardship or sustained fatigue, would rise from his warm bed to stalk the lordly animal between snow and moon.

One night Hector of the Stags found he could not sleep—not because of the cold, for the night was a mild one considering the season. The snow, indeed, lay deep around their dwelling, but they owed not a little of their warmth to the snow. It drifted up all about it and kept off the terrible winds sweeping along the side of the hill like sharp swift scythes of death. They were in the largest and most comfortable of their huts— a deepish hollow in the limestone rock, lined with turf and wattles filled in with heather, the tops outward; its front a thick wall of turf, with a strong door of pine. It was indeed so snug as to be far from airy. Here they kept what little store they had—some dried fish and venison; a barrel of oatmeal, seldom full; a few skins of wild creatures, and powder, ball, and shot.

After many fruitless attempts to catch the still fleeting vapor of sleep, Hector, raising himself at last on his elbow, found that Rob was not by his side.

He, too, had been unable to sleep and at last discovered that he was uneasy about something—what, he could not tell. He rose and went out. The moon was shining very clear, its reflection on the snow making the night brighter than many a day. The moon, the snow, the mountains, all dreaming awake, seemed to Rob the same as usual. But presently he fancied the hillside opposite had come nearer than usual: there must be a reason for that. He searched every yard of it with keenest gaze, but saw nothing.

They were high above Glenruadh. Late though it was, Rob thought he saw some light from the New House, which he could not see itself, reflected from some shadowed evergreen in the shrubbery. He stood wondering if someone might be ill, and whether he ought to run down and see whether a messenger was needed, when his father joined him. He had brought his telescope and immediately began to sweep the moonlight on the opposite hill. In a moment he touched Rob on the shoulder, and handed him the glass, pointing with it. Rob looked and saw a dark speck on the snow moving along the hillside. It was the big stag. Now and then he would stop to sniff and search for a mouthful of grass, but was evidently making for one of his feeding places—most likely that by the burn on the chief's land. But the light! Could it imply danger? He had heard the young men were about to leave. Were they going to attempt one last assault on the glory of the glen? He pointed out to his father the dim light in the shadow of the house. Hector turned his telescope in that direction, immediately gave the glass to Rob, went into the hut, and came out again with his gun.

They had not gone far when they lost sight of the stag, but they held on toward the old castle. At every point where a peep could be had in the direction of the house, they stopped to look. If enemies were abroad, they must, if possible, get and keep sight of them. They did not stop for more than a glance, however, but made for the valley as fast as they could walk: the noise of running feet would, on such a still night, be heard too far. The whole way, without uttering a sound, father and son kept interchanging ideas on the matter.

From thorough acquaintance with the habits of the animal, they were pretty certain he was on his way to the haunt near the chief's. If he got there, he would be safe; it was the chief's ground, and no one would dare touch him. But he was not yet upon it and was in danger. And if he should move in any southerly or westerly direction, he would almost at once be out of sanctuary. If they found him feeding, therefore, and any danger threatening, they must scare him eastward or northward. If no peril seemed at hand, they would watch him awhile, that he might feed in safety. Swift and all but soundless in their quiet boots, they paced along, careful not to startle the deer while the hunter was far off, and unknowingly drive him within range of his shot.

They reached the root of the spur and approached the castle; immediately beyond that they would be in sight of the feeding ground. But they were yet behind it when Rob of the Angels bounded forward in terror at the sound of a gun. His father, however, who was in front, was off before him. Neither hearing anything, nor seeing Rob, he knew that a shot had been fired, and caution now being useless, was in a moment at full speed. The smoke of the shot hung white in the moonlight over the end of the ridge. No great brown bulk shadowed the green pasture, no thicket of horns went stalking about over the sod. No lord of creation, but an enemy of life, stood regarding his work, a tumbled heap of death, yet saying to himself, *It is good*. The noble creature lay deformed on the grass, shot through the heart, he had leaped high in the air, fallen with his head under him, and broken his neck.

Rage filled the heart of Hector of the Stags. He could not curse, but gave a roar like a wild beast and raised his gun. But Rob of the Angels caught it before it reached his shoulder. He yielded, and with another roar like a lion bounded barehanded upon the enemy. He took the descent in three leaps and the stream in one. It was not merely that the enemy had killed *an cabrach mòr*, the great stag of their love; he had killed him on the chief's only land! Under the very eyes of him whose business it was to watch over him! It was an unpardonable offense—an insult as well as a wrong to his chief! In fierce majesty of righteous wrath, he threw himself on the poacher. Sercombe met him with a blow straight from the shoulder and he dropped.

Rob of the Angels, close behind the poacher, dropped the gun, and the devil all but got into him as his knife flashed pale in the moonlight. He darted on the enemy. It would have gone ill with the bigger man, for Rob was lithe as a snake, swift not only to parry and dodge but to strike. He could probably not have reached the body of his antagonist without inflicting on Sercombe's arm at least one terrible gash from his razor-sharp *skean-dhu* had not the stern voice of the chief come from the top of the ridge. Rob threw his knife, gleaming in the splendor of the moon, away from him, and himself down by the father. Then Hector came to himself and rose. Rob rose also; and his father, trembling with excitement, stood grasping his arm, for he saw the stalwart form of his chief on the ridge above them. Alister had been waked by the gun, and at the roar of his friend Hector, sprang from his bed. But when he saw his beloved stag dead on his pasture, he came down the ridge like an avalanche.

Sercombe stood on his defense, wondering what devil was to pay, only beginning to think he might have erred. He had taken no trouble to understand the boundaries between Mr. Peregrine Palmer's land and that of the chief, and had imagined himself safe on the south side of the big burn.

Alister gazed speechless for a moment on the slaughtered stag, and then heaved a great sigh.

"Mr. Sercombe," he said, "I would rather you had shot my best horse! Are you aware, sir, that you are a poacher?"

"I had supposed that name inapplicable to a gentleman," answered Sercombe, with entire coolness.

"You would call yourself a gentleman after what you have done?"

"By all means, then, take me before a magistrate," returned Sercombe, nettled at the chief's insinuation.

"You are before a magistrate."

"All I have to answer is that I should not have shot the animal had I not believed myself within my rights."

"On that very point, and on this very ground, I instructed you myself!" said the chief.

"I misunderstood you."

"You should say, rather, that you had not the courtesy to heed what I told you—you had not faith enough to take the word of a gentleman! And for your cruel brutality my poor stag has given his life." He stood for some moments in obvious conflict with himself, then quietly resumed.

"Of course, Mr. Sercombe, I have no intention of pushing the matter," he said.

"I should hope not!" returned Sercombe scornfully. "I will pay whatever you choose to set on the brute."

It would be hard to say which was more offensive to the chief—to have his stag called a brute or be offered blood money for him.

"Stag Ruadh priced like a bullock!" he said with a slow smile, full of sadness. "The pride of every child in the glen! Not a gentleman in the country would have shot Clanruadh's deer."

Sercombe was by this time feeling uncomfortable, and it made him angry. He muttered something about superstition.

"He was taken when a calf," the chief went on, "and given to a great aunt of mine. When he grew up, he took to the hills again and was known by his silver collar till he managed to rid himself of it. He shall be buried where he lies, and his monument shall tell how the stranger Sasunnach served the stag of Clanruadh!"

"Why the deuce didn't you keep the precious monster in a paddock, and let people know him for a tame animal?" sneered Sercombe.

"My poor Ruadh!" sneered the chief. "He was no tame animal! He as well as I would have preferred the death you have given him to such a fate. He lived while he lived. I thank you for his immediate transit. Shot right through the heart. Had you maimed him I should have been angrier."

Sercombe felt flattered, and, attributing the chief's gentleness to a desire to please him, began to condescend.

"Well, come now, Macruadh!" he began, but the chief turned from him.

Hector stood with his arm on Rob's shoulder, the tears rolling down his cheeks. He would not have wept but that the sobs of his son shook him.

"Rob of the Angels," Alister said in their mother tongue, "you must make an apology to the Sasunnach gentleman for drawing the knife on him. That was wrong, if he had killed all the deer on Clanruadh."

"It was not for that, Macruadh," answered Rob of the Angels. "It was because he struck my father, and laid a better man than himself on the grass."

The chief turned on the Englishman.

"Did the old man strike you, Mr. Sercombe?"

"No, by Jove! I took care that he shouldn't. If he had I would have broken every bone in his body!"

"Why did you strike him, then?"

"Because he rushed at me."

"It was his duty to capture a poacher! But you did not know he was deaf and dumb," he added, as if in excuse.

"The deafness makes no difference!" protested Rob of the Angels. "Hector of the Stags does not fight with his hands like a woman!"

"Well, what's done is done!" laughed Sercombe. "It wasn't a bad shot, anyhow!"

"You have little to pride yourself upon, Mr. Sercombe!" said the chief. "You are a good shot, but you need not have been so frightened at an old man as to knock him down."

"Come, come, Macruadh! Enough's enough! It's time to drop this!" returned Sercombe. "I can't stand much more of it! Take ten pounds for the head! Come!"

The chief made one great stride toward him, but turned away, and said, "Come along, Rob! Tell your father you must not go up the hill again tonight."

"Yes, sir," answered Rob. "There's nothing now to go up the hill for! Poor old Ruadh! God rest his soul!"

"Amen!" responded the chief. "But say rather, 'God give him room to run!' "

"Amen! It is better. But," added Rob, "we must watch by the body. The foxes and hooded crows are gathering already—I hear them on the hills; and I saw the sea eagle as white as silver yesterday! We cannot leave him till he is under God's plaid!"

"Then one of you come and fetch food and fire," said the chief. "I will be with you early."

Father and son communicated in silence; and Rob went with the chief.

"These peasants worship the stag just like the old Egyptians did the bull!" said Sercombe to himself as he walked home, full of contempt.

21 / The Stag's Head_____

Alister went straight to his brother's room, his heart bursting with indignation. It was some time before Ian could get the story from him in plain talk. "Oh, Ian! you don't know how it tortures me to think of that interloper, the low brute, killing the big stag, the Macruadh stag—on my land, too! I feel as if I could tear him in pieces!"

"Hadn't you better tell your Master what happened?" asked Ian.

"But for *Him* I would have killed him on the spot. But what am I to do if I must not let off my rage even to you?"

"Let if off to him, Alister. He will give you fairer play than your small brother; he understands you better than I. Come, begin now, and tell me all quietly."

"Word for word then, with all the imprecations!" said Alister, already a little cooler, and soon Ian was in possession of the story.

"Now what do you think I should do?" said the chief, ending his narration, which had been in a measure calm but at various points had revealed the boiling of the floods beneath.

"You must send him the head, Alister," answered Ian.

"Send—what—who—I don't understand you, Ian!" returned the chief, bewildered.

"Oh, well, never mind!" said Ian. "You will think of it presently."

And with the words he turned his face to the wall as if he would go to sleep.

It had been understood between the brothers from far back in the golden haze of childhood that the moment one of them turned his back, not a word more was to be said until he who dropped the subject chose to resume it. To break this unspoken compact would have been to break one of the strands in the ancient bond of their deepest brotherhood. Therefore Alister went at once to his room, leaving Ian praying hard for him with his face to the wall. He went as one knowing well the storm he was about to encounter, but never before had he had such a storm to meet.

He closed the door and sat down on the side of his bed like one stunned. He did not doubt, yet he could hardly in truth believe that Ian had told him to send the antlers of his *cabrach mòr*, the late live type of his ancient crest, the pride of Clanruadh, to that vile Sasunnach who had sent to his death the joyous soul of the fierce, bare mountains.

137

Great were the rushings to and fro in the spirit of Alister, wild and terrible. He never closed his eyes, but fought with himself all night until the morning broke. Could this impossible thing indeed be his duty? And if not his duty, was he called to do it from mere courage of goodness? Would not his action be frightfully misunderstood by such a man? What could he take it for but a mean currying of favor with him? Was it Ian, or was it the Lord that was too hard on him? The more of himself he yielded, the more God demanded! Every time it was something harder than the last! And why did Ian turn his face to the wall? Would he not listen to reason?

But all the time there lay at his door an action to be taken. And what he did not like was *always* the thing he had to do! He *hated* the thought of doing this! It was abominable! Send the grand head to the man who had killed it! Never! It must go to the grave with the fleet limbs, and over it a monument should rise, at sight of which every friendly highlandman would say, *Feuch an cabrach mòr de Clanruadh*! What a mockery of fate it would be for him to allow it to be exposed forever to the vulgar gaze of likeminded southerners, the trophy of a fool, whose boast was to kill! Such a noble beast! To mutilate his remains for the pride of the wretch who killed him! It was too horrible!

He thought and thought until he lay powerless to think anymore. But the cessation of thought gave opportunity for setting his true soul thinking from another quarter. Suddenly he remembered a conversation he had had with Ian a day or two before about Jesus' words, "Whosoever shall smite thee on thy right cheek, turn to him the other also." He had been dissatisfied with Ian's comment, but Ian had answered him, "You must explain it to yourself. There are many things that can be understood only in the doing of them. When you have an opportunity of doing this very thing, do it and see what will follow."

Now it struck him that here was the opportunity of which Ian had spoken.

"This may be just the sort of thing Jesus meant!" he said aloud. "Even if I be in the right, I have a right to yield my right—and to *Him* I will yield it. That was why Ian turned his face to the wall: he wanted me to discover that here was my opportunity to obey! How else but in the name of Jesus Christ could he have dared tell me to forgive Ruadh's death by sending his head to his murderer? But it has to be done! I've got to do it! Here is my chance of turning the other cheek. To do so cannot hurt the stag; it only hurts my pride, and I owe my pride nothing!"

No sooner had he yielded his pride and begun to feel the joy of deliverance from self rushing into his heart than a pity began to awake inside him for Sercombe. Might it be possible to love the man—not for anything he was but for what he might and must someday be in God?

Yet even with the thought again and again swelled again the tide of wrath and unwillingness, making him feel as if he could not carry out his resolve. But all the time he knew the thing was as good as done—it had already been determined and nothing could now turn it aside.

To yield where one may is the prerogative of liberty! he said to himself. *God only can give; whoever would be his child must yield! Abroad in the fields of air, as Paul and the love of God make me hope he is, what will the wind-battling Ruadh care for his old head! Would he not say, "Let the man have it; my hour was come or the Great One would not have let him kill me!"*

Thus argued the chief with himself while yet the darkness lasted, and as soon as the morning began to break, he rose, took with him a shovel, a pick, and a great knife, and went to where Hector and Rob were watching the slain.

It was bitterly cold. The burn crept silently under a continuous bridge of ice. The grass blades were crisp with frost. The ground was so hard it met iron like iron.

He sent the men to get their breakfast from Nancy: no one but himself would do what now must be done for Ruadh! With skillful hand he separated and laid aside the head as in a sacrifice to the living God. Then the hard earth rang with mighty blows of the pickaxe. The labor was severe, and long before the grave was deep enough, Hector and Rob had returned. But the chief would not give them any share in the work. When he laid hold of the body, they did not offer to help him; they understood the heart of their chief. Not without a last pang that he could not lay the head beside it, he began to shovel in the frozen clods, and then at length allowed them to take a part. When the grave was full they rolled great stones upon it that it might not be desecrated. Then the chief went back to his room, and proceeded to prepare the head, that, as the sacrifice, so should be the gift.

"I suppose he would like glass eyes!" he muttered to himself, "but I will not have the mockery. I will fill the sockets and sew up the eyelids, and the face shall be as of one that sleeps."

Having done all, and written certain directions for temporary treatment, which he tied to an ear, he laid the head aside till the evening.

All the day long not a word concerning it passed between the brothers. But when evening came, Alister, with a blue cotton handkerchief in his hand, hiding the head as far as the roots of the huge horns, asked Ian to go for a walk. They went straight to the New House. Alister left the head at the door, with his compliments to Mr. Sercombe.

As soon as they were out of sight of the house, Ian put his arm through his brother's, but did not speak.

"I know now about turning the other cheek!" said Alister. "Poor Ruadh!"

"Leave him to the God who made the great head and nimble feet of him," said Ian. "A God who did not care for what he had made, how should we believe in? But he who cares for the dying sparrow may be trusted with the dead stag."

"Truly, yes," returned Alister.

Before the week was out there stood above the dead stag a growing heap of stones, to this day called *Carn an cabrach mòr*. It took ten men with levers to roll one of the boulders at its base. (Men still cast stones upon it as they pass.)

The next morning came a note to the cottage, in which Sercombe thanked the Macruadh for changing his mind. He said that, although he was indeed glad to have secured such a splendid head, he would certainly have stalked another deer had he known the chief set such store by the one in question.

The note was handed to Alister as he sat at his second breakfast with his mother and Ian: even in winter he was out of the house at six o'clock, to set his men to their work and take his own share in it. He read to the end of the first page, but the moment he turned the leaf, he sprang from his seat with an exclamation that startled his mother.

"The hound!" he cried. "Look at this, Ian! See what comes of taking your advice!"

"I said nothing regarding what would come of following it."

"Look," insisted Alister. "It's a check for ten pounds!"

Ian looked, then burst into loud laughter.

"I told you so! See what comes of it?"

"I daresay the poor fellow was sorely puzzled what to do, and asked everybody in the house for advice."

"You take this check to represent the combined wisdom of the New House?"

"You must have puzzled them all!" persisted Ian. "How could people with no principle beyond that of keeping to a bargain understand you otherwise? First, you perform an action such persons think degrading: you carry a fellow's bag for a shilling and then himself for nothing! Next, in the very fury of indignation with a man for killing the finest stag in the country on your meadow, you take him the head with your own hands! It all comes of that unlucky divine notion of yours to do good that good may come of it. That shilling of Mistress Conal's is at the root of it all!"

Ian laughed again, but the chief was too angry to enter into the humor of the thing.

"Upon my word, Ian. What *are* you laughing at? It all comes of giving him the head!"

"You wish you had not given it him?"

"No!" growled Alister, as from a pent-up volcano.

Now the mother could herself hardly keep from laughing at her eldest son's indignation; he was on his feet, pacing about through the room.

"Think of it," insisted Ian, "a man like him could not think otherwise. What you meant, after all, was not cordiality; it was only generosity; to which his response was giving you ten pounds! All is right between you."

"Now really, Ian, you must not go on teasing your brother so!" said the mother. Alister laughed and ceased his fuming.

"But I must answer the brute!" he said. "What am I to say to him?"

"That you are much obliged," replied Ian, "and will have the check framed and hung in the hall."

"Come, come! No more of that."

"Well then, let me answer the letter."

"That is more than I could hope for!"

Ian sat down at his mother's table and wrote this:

Dear Sir:

My brother desires me to return the check which you unhappily thought it right to send him. Humanity is subject to mistake, but I am sorry for the individual who could so misunderstand his courtesy. I have the honor to remain, sir,

Your obedient servant,
Ian Macruadh

As Ian had guessed, the matter had been openly discussed at the New House and the money was sent with the approval of all except the two young ladies. They had seen the young men in circumstances more favorable to the understanding of their characters. The tone of Ian's rejection of it considerably damaged in their minds the prestige of Sercombe's good looks.

"Why didn't the chief write the letter himself?" asked Christian.

"Oh," replied Sercombe, "his little brother has been to school and could write better!"

Christina and Mercy exchanged glances.

"I will tell you," Mercy said, "why Mr. Ian answered the note: the chief has done with you!"

"Or," suggested Christina, "the chief was in such a rage that he would write nothing but a challenge."

"I wish to goodness he had! It would have given me the chance of giving the clodhopper a lesson."

"For sending you the finest stag's head and horns in the country?" remarked Mercy.

"I shot the stag! Perhaps you don't believe I shot him?"

"I am sure no one else did! The chief would have died sooner!"

"I am sick of your chief!" said Christian. "Some chief, without a penny to his name. A chief, yet glad of the job of carrying a carpetbag. You'll be calling him *My Lord* next!"

"He could write *Baronet* after his name if he pleased," returned Mercy.

"A likely story! Why doesn't he, then?"

"Because," answered Christina, "both his father and himself were ashamed of how the first baronet got his title. It had to do with a sale of a part of the property, and they considered the land the clan's as well as the chief's. They regarded it as an act of treachery to put the clan in the power of a stranger, and the chief looks upon the title as a brand of shame."

"I don't question the treachery," said Christian. "A highlander is treacherous!"

Christina had asked a friend in Glasgow to find out for her anything known among the lawyers concerning the Macruadhs; what she had just recounted was a part of the information she had received.

From that moment on silence covered the whole transaction. Sercombe neither returned the head, sent an apology, nor recognized the gift further than what he had done. That he had shot the stag was enough.

But these things went on shaping the idea of the brothers in the minds of the sisters, and they were beginning to feel a strange confidence in them, such as they had never had in men before. A curious little halo began to shimmer about the heads of the young men in the picture gallery of the girls' fancy. Not the less, however, did they still regard them as fanatics, unfit for this world, incapable of self-protection—in a word, impractical. Because a man would live according to the laws of his being as well as of his body, obeying simple, imperative, essential human necessity, his fellows call him *impractical*! Of all the idiotic delusions of the children of this world, the idea of being practical is one of the most ludicrous.

22 / Annie of the Shop

At the dance in the chief's barn, Sercombe had paired with Annie of the shop oftener than with any other of the girls. That she should please him at all was something in his favor, for she was a simple, modest girl. Yet she had a keen perception both of what respect was due her and what respect she ought to show, and was therefore in the truest sense well-bred. She was one of God's ladies, whom no change of circumstances would cause to alter their manners a hair's-breadth.

Sercombe, though a man of "education," was nevertheless only conventionally a gentleman. To some minds neither innocent nor simple, there is yet something attractive in innocence and simplicity. Perhaps it gives them a pleasing sense of their own superiority. Such a one was Sercombe; he thought himself an exceptionally fine fellow. No one knows what a poor creature he is but the man who makes it his business to be true. The only mistake worse than thinking well of himself is for a man to think God takes no interest in him.

One evening, sorely for lack of anything to do, Sercombe wandered out into the starlit night and along the road to the village. There he went into the general shop, where Annie sat behind the counter. Now the first attention he almost always paid to a woman, when he cared and dared, was a compliment—the fungus of an empty head or a false heart. Annie, accustomed to respectful familiarity from the chief and his brother, showed no repugnance to his friendly approach.

"Upon my word, Miss Annie," said Sercombe, venturing at length a little, "you were the best dancer on the floor that night."

"Oh, Mr. Sercombe! How can you say so, with such dancers as the young ladies of your party?"

"They dance well," he returned, "but not so well as you."

"It all depends on whether you are used to the dance or not."

"No, by Jove! If you had a lesson or two, you would dance out of their sight in the twinkling of an eye. If I had you for a partner every night for a month, you would dance better than any woman I have ever seen."

The grosser the flattery, the surer with a country girl, he thought. But there was something in his tone, besides the freedom of sounding her praises in her own ears, which was displeasing to Annie's ladyhood, and she said nothing.

143

"Come out for a walk," he said. "It is a lovely starlit night. Have you been out today?"

"No, I have not," answered Annie, wondering how to get rid of him.

"You wrong your beauty by keeping it to the house."

"My beauty," said Annie, blushing, "may look after itself. I have nothing to do with it—neither, excuse me, sir, have you."

"Why, who has a right to be offended with the truth? A man can't help but see that your face is as sweet as your voice, and your figure a match for the two."

"I will call my mother," said Annie, and left the shop.

Sercombe did not believe she would, and waited. He took her departure for a mere coquetry. But when a rather grim, handsome old woman appeared, asking him—it took most of the English she knew—"What would you be wanting, sir?" as he had just come into the shop, he found himself in an awkward predicament. He answered, with more than his usual politeness that, having had the pleasure of dancing with her daughter at the chief's ball, he had taken the liberty of looking in to ask how she was. Perplexed, the old woman in her turn called Annie, who came at once, but kept close to her mother. Sercombe began to tell them about a trip he had made to Canada, for he had heard they had friends there. But the mother did not understand him, and Annie more and more disliked him. He soon saw that the best thing he could do was leave, and took himself off, not a little piqued at the repulse from a peasant girl in the most miserable shop he had ever seen.

Two days later he went again—this time to buy tobacco. Annie was short with him, but he went again and again. He would not rest until he had gained some footing of favor with her! Meanwhile, Annie grew heartily offended with the man. She also feared what might be said if he kept coming to the shop—where Mistress Conal had seen him already more than once. For her own sake, for the sake of Lachlan, and for the sake of the chief, she resolved to make the young father of the ancient clan acquainted with her trouble. It was on the day after his rejection of the ten-pound check that she found her opportunity.

"Was he rude to you, Annie?" asked the chief.

"No, sir—too polite, I think. He must have seen I did not want his company. But I shall feel better now, knowing you know."

"I will see to it," said the chief.

"I hope it will not put you to any trouble, sir."

"What am I here for, Annie! Are you not my clanswoman? Is not Lachlan my foster brother? He will trouble you no more, I think."

As Alister walked home from the shop, he met Sercombe on the road, and after a greeting not very cordial on either side, said: "I should be obliged to you, Mr. Sercombe, if you would send for whatever you want instead of going to the shop yourself. Annie Macruadh is not the sort of girl you may have sometimes found in such a position, and you would not wish to make her uncomfortable."

Sercombe was ashamed, perhaps; for the refuge of the fool when dissatisfied with himself is offense with his neighbor, and Sercombe was angry.

"Are you her father—or her lover?" he said.

"She has a right to my protection—and claims it," rejoined Alister quietly.

"Protection! Oh! What the deuce would you protect her from?"

"From you, Mr. Sercombe."

"Protect her, then."

"I will. Force yourself on that young woman and you will have to do with me."

They parted. Alister went home. Sercombe went straight to the shop.

He had been doing what he could to look good in Christina's eyes, but whether from something antagonistic between them, or from unwillingness on her part to yield her position of liberty, she had not given him the encouragement he thought he deserved. He thought himself in love with her, and had told her so. But the truest love such a man can feel is a poor thing. He admired, and desired, and thought he loved her beauty, and that he called being in love with her! He did not think much about her money, but had she been brought to poverty, he would certainly have hesitated about marrying her.

In the family they were nearly regarded as engaged, although nothing was ever *said* and she did not treat him as such, but merely went on bewitching him, pleased that at least he was a man of the world.

While one is yet only *in love*, the real person lies covered with the rose leaves of a thousand sleepy-eyed dreams, and through them come to the dreamer but the barest hints of the real person. A thousand fancies fly out, approach, and cross, but never meet. The man and the woman are pleased, not with each other, but each with the fancied other. The merest common likings are taken for signs of a wonderful sympathy, of a radical unity. But though at a hundred points their souls seem to touch, their contact points are the merest brushings, as of insect antennae. The real man, the real woman, is all the time asleep under the rose leaves. Happy is the rare fate of the true—to wake and come forth and meet in the majesty of the truth, in the image of God, in their very being, in the power of that love which alone is being! They love, not this and that about each other, but each the very other. Where such love is, let the

146

differences of taste, the unfitness of temperament, be what they may, the two must by and by be thoroughly one.

Sercombe saw no reason why a gentleman should not amuse himself with any young woman he pleased. What was the chief to him? Anyhow, he was not *his* chief! If he was a big man in the eyes of his little clan, he was nothing much in the eyes of Mr. Sercombe!

Annie came again to her chief with the complaint that Mr. Sercombe persisted in his attentions. Alister went to see her home. They had not gone far when Sercombe overtook them. The chief told Annie to go on ahead.

"I must have a word or two with you, Mr. Sercombe," he called out.

He turned and came up to the chief with his hands in his pockets.

"I warned you to leave that girl alone!"

"And I warn you now," returned Sercombe, "to leave me alone."

"I am bound to take care of her."

"And I of myself."

"Not at her expense."

"At yours, then!" answered Sercombe, provoking an encounter, to which he was all the more inclined that he saw Ian coming slowly up the ridge.

"Are you saying you have chosen to forget the warning I gave you?" said the chief, restraining his anger.

"I make a point of forgetting what I do not think worth remembering."

"I forget nothing."

"I congratulate you."

"And I mean to help your memory, Mr. Sercombe."

"Mr. Macruadh!" returned Sercombe, "if you expect me not to open my lips to any hussy in the glen without your leave——"

His statement was cut short by a box on the ear from the open hand of the chief. He would not use his fist without warning, but such a word applied to any honest woman of his clan demanded instant recognition.

Sercombe fell back a step, white with rage, then darted forward, and struck straight at the front of his adversary. Alister avoided the blow, but soon found himself a mere child alongside the Englishman. He had not touched Sercombe again, and was himself bleeding rather badly, when Ian came running up.

"Come on, you——" Sercombe began to curse when he saw Ian. "I can fight the precious pair of you!"

"Stop!" cried Ian, laying hold of his brother from behind, grabbing his arms, wheeling him round and taking his place. "Give up, Alister," he went on. "You can't do it, and I won't see you punished when he deserves it. Get back and sit down."

"You can't do it, Ian!" returned Alister. "Let me at him again."

"You are blind with your own blood!" said Ian in a tone that gave Sercombe expectation of too easy a victory. "Sit down there, I tell you."

"If he speaks once again to Annie, I swear I will make him repent it!" said Alister.

Sercombe laughed insultingly.

"Mr. Sercombe," said Ian, "had we better not put off our bout till tomorrow? You have fought already!"

"You coward, come on!"

"Would you not like to catch your breath for a moment?"

"I have all I am likely to need."

"It is only fair," persisted Ian, "to warn you that you will not find my knowledge on the level of my brother's."

"Shut up!" said Sercombe savagely.

For a few moments Ian stood merely to defend himself, and did not attempt to put in a blow. Alister thought he was giving Sercombe time to recover; Sercombe thought him all the more a coward, and became angrier and angrier.

"Mr. Sercombe," said Ian at length, "you cannot serve me as you did my brother."

"I see that well enough."

"Will you give your word to leave Annie of the shop alone?"

Sercombe laughed with a scornful fit of swearing, then rushed at Ian with a fierce blow. Ian swerved and his opponent's fist flew by powerless.

The fight lasted but a moment longer. As his adversary drew back from the failed blow, Alister saw Ian's eyes flash and his left arm shoot out, as it seemed, to twice its length. Sercombe neither reeled nor staggered but fell flat on the ground and lay motionless. They were by his side in a moment.

"I struck too hard!" said Ian.

"Who can think about that in a fight?" returned Alister.

"I could have helped it well enough; a better man would have. But anger shot through me—and the man went down. I hope it wasn't the devil that struck the blow!"

"Nonsense, Ian!" said Alister as they raised him to carry him to the cottage. "It was pure indignation, and nothing to blame yourself for."

"I wish I could be sure of that!"

They had not gone far before he began to come to.

"What are you doing?" he said feebly but angrily. "Set me down."

They did so. He staggered to the roadside and leaned against the bank.

"What's been the row?" he asked. "Oh, I remember! Well, you've had the best of it, I see."

He held out his hand in a vague sort of way, and the gesture went to the hearts of the brothers. Each took the hand.

"I was all right about the girl, though," said Sercombe. "I didn't mean her any harm."

"I don't think you did," answered Alister; "and I am sure you could have done her none. But the girl did not like it."

"There is not a girl of the clan, or in the neighborhood, for whom my brother would not have done the same—or I either," said Ian.

"You're a brace of woodcocks!" cried Sercombe. "It's a good thing you're not out in the world. You would be in hot water from morning to night. I can't imagine how the deuce you get on at all!"

"Get on! To where?" asked Ian with a curious smile.

"Come now! You're not such fools as you want me to think. A man must make a place for himself somehow in the world."

He rose, and they walked in the direction of the cottage.

"There is something better than getting on in the world," said Ian.

"What?"

"To get out of it."

"What! Cut your throats?"

"I mean that to get out of the world altogether is better than merely to get on in it."

"I don't understand you. I begin to think the man who thrashed me is a downright idiot!" growled Sercombe.

"What you call success," said Ian, "we count not worth a thought. Look at our clan. It is but a type of the world itself. Everything is passing away. We believe in the kingdom of heaven."

"Come, come! Fellows like you must know that's all bosh! Nobody nowadays—nobody with any brains—believes such rot."

"We believe in Jesus Christ," said Ian, "and are determined to do what he wants us to do and to take our orders from nobody else."

"I don't understand you."

"I know you don't. You could not until you set about to change your whole way of life."

"What an idea! An impossible idea!"

"As to its being an impossible idea, we hold it and live by it. I know it must seem perfectly absurd to you. But we do not live in your world, and you do not see the light of ours."

"Well, there may be a world beyond the stars. I know nothing about it. I only know there is one on this side of it, a very decent sort of world, too. And I mean to make the best of it!"

"And have not even begun yet."

"Indeed I have! I deny myself nothing. I live as I was made to live."

"If you were not made to obey your conscience, you are differently made from us."

"That's all moonshine! Things are as they appear, nothing more."

The brothers exchanged a look and a smile.

Sercombe said no more. He was silent with disgust at the nonsense of it all.

They reached the door of the cottage. Alister invited him to walk in. But he drew back and would have excused himself and left them right then.

"You had better lie down awhile," said Alister.

"You shall come to my room," said Ian. "We shall meet nobody."

Sercombe yielded, for he felt odd. He threw himself on Ian's bed, and in a few minutes was fast asleep.

When he woke, he had a cup of tea and went away little the worse. The chief could not show himself for several days.

After this Annie had no further molestation. But, indeed, the young man's time at the New House was almost up—which was quite as well, for Annie of the shop, after turning a corner of the road, had climbed the hillside and seen all that transpired between Sercombe and the chief. The young ladies, hearing contradictory statements, called upon Annie of the shop to learn the truth, and the discussion with her that followed was not without influence on them. Through Annie they saw further into the character of the brothers, who, if they advocated things too fine for the world the girls had known up till that time, *did* things also of which it would by no means have approved.

But to Alister and Ian, that world and its judgments lacked all value; indeed, they would rather get out of the world than on in it.

23 / Nature

All the men at the New House left together and the ladies were once again abandoned to the society of Nature, who said little to any of them. For though she recognized her grandchildren and did what she could for them, it was not time that they should make some move toward a more personal acquaintance with her. If you would hear her wonderful tales, or see her marvelous treasures, you must not trifle with her, for her dignity is great. You must not talk as if you could rummage her drawers and cabinets as you pleased. You must believe in her; you must reverence her. Otherwise, though she is everywhere about the house, you may not meet her from the beginning of one year to the end of another.

Conversation with the girls concerning any aspect of nature threatened to bore them. Indeed, many good men and women are bored with common talk about *scenery*; but these ladies appeared unaware of the least expression on the face of their grandmother. Undoubtedly they received some good simply from the power of Granny's operation. But the trumpet of her winds, the stately march of her clouds, and the torrent-rush of her waters were to them poor facts, and had not the vaguest embodiment of truths eternal. What they called *society*, its ways and judgments, in pomps and shows, false, unjust, ugly, was nearly all they cared for. To talk of nature was sentimental. To talk of God was both sentimental and ill-bred. Wordsworth was an old woman; St. Paul an evangelical churchman. They saw no feature of any truth, but, like all unthinkers, wrapped the words of it in their own foolishness, and then sneered at them. They were too much ladies, however, to do it disagreeably. They only smiled at the foolish person who believed things they were too sensible to believe. It must be said in their behalf, however, that they had not yet actually refused anything worth believing. They had not yet looked upon any truth and refused it.

A thaw came. A relationship by degrees established itself between Mrs. Macruadh and the well-meaning, handsome, smiling Mrs. Palmer, and thus the girls naturally went rather frequently to the cottage. The girls had every liberty; their mother seldom interfered. True to her own dim horn lantern, she had confidence in the discretion of her daughters, and looked for no more than discretion. Hence an amount of interaction was possible between them and the young men which would quickly have grown into a genuine intimacy had they inhabited even a neighboring sphere of common life.

Almost unknown to her, however, a change for the better had begun in Mercy. She had not yet laid hold of, had not yet perceived any truth; but she had some sense of the blank where truth ought to be. It was not a sense that truth was lacking; it was only a sense that something was not in her which was in those men. A nature such as hers, one that had not yet turned away from the truth, could not long be near such a warm atmosphere of live truth without the hour approaching when it must chip its shell, open its eyes, and acknowledge the world around it.

One lovely starlit night of keen frost, the two mothers were sitting by a red peat fire in the little drawing room of the cottage and Ian was talking to the girls over some sketches he had made, when the chief came in, bringing with him an air of sharp exhilaration, and proposed a walk.

"Come and have a taste of starlight!" he said.

The girls rose at once and were ready in a minute.

The chief was walking between the two ladies and Ian was a few steps in front, his head bent as in thought. Suddenly Mercy saw him spread out his arms toward the starry vault. The feeling, almost the sense of another presence, awoke in her, and just as quickly vanished.

In a few more minutes she ventured to ask, "Macruadh, Mr. Ian and you often say things about *nature* that I cannot understand. I wish you would tell me what you mean by it."

"By what?" asked Alister.

"By *nature*," answered Mercy. "I heard Mr. Ian say, for instance, the other night, that he did not like *nature* to take liberties with him; you said she might take what liberties with you she pleased; and then you went on talking so that I could not understand a word either of you said."

While she spoke Ian had turned and rejoined them and they were now walking in a line, Mercy between the two men and Christina on Ian's right. The brothers looked at each other; it would be hard to make her understand just that example! Silence fell for a moment, then Ian said, "We mean by *nature* every visitation of the outside world through our senses."

"More plainly please, Mr. Ian. You cannot imagine how stupid I am."

"I mean by *nature*, then, all that you see and hear and smell and taste and feel of the things round about you."

"If that is all you mean, why should you make it seem so difficult?"

"But that is not all. The things themselves hold value for the sake of what they say to us. As our sense of smell brings us news of fields far off, so those fields, or even the smell that comes from them, tell us of things, meaning, thoughts, intentions beyond them, and embodied in them."

"And that is why you speak of nature as a person?" asked Mercy.

"Whatever influences us must be personal. But God is the only real person, being in himself and without help from anybody. And so we talk even of the world, which is his living garment, as if that were a person; we call it *she* as if it were a woman, because so many of God's loveliest influences come to us through her. She always seems to me a beautiful old grandmother."

"But there now! When you talk of her influences, I do not know what you mean. She seems to do and be something to you which certainly she does not and is not to me."

"I think I can let you see into it, Miss Mercy," said Ian. "Imagine for a moment how it would be if, instead of having the sky over us as it is, we only had a roof we could see, with clouds hanging down, as in a theater, only a yard or two from our heads!"

Mercy was silent for a moment, then said, "It would be horribly wearisome."

"It would indeed be wearisome. But how do you think it would affect your nature, your being?"

Mercy held her peace, which is the ignorant man's wisdom.

"We should have known nothing of astronomy," said Christina.

"True; and the worst of it would have been that the soul would have had no notion of heavenly things."

"There you leave me again," said Mercy.

"I mean," said Ian, "that it would have had no sense of outstretching, endless space, no feeling of heights above and depths below. When the soul wakes up, it needs all space for room!"

"Then my soul is not waked up yet!" rejoined Christina with a laugh.

Ian did not reply, and Christina felt that he accepted the proposition, as absurd as it seemed to herself.

"But there is more than that," he resumed. "What notion could we have had of majesty if the heavens seemed scarcely higher than the earth? What feeling of the grandeur of God, of the vastness of his being, of the limitlessness of his goodness? For space is the body to our idea of God. Over and around us we have the one perfect geometrical shape— a dome, or a sphere. I do not say it is put there for the purpose of representing God. I say it is there of necessity, because of its nature in relation to God's nature and character. It is of God's thinking, and that half sphere above our heads is the beginning of all revelation of him to men. We must begin with that. It is the simplest as well as most external likeness of him, while its relation to him goes so deep that it represents things in his very nature that nothing else could."

"You bewilder me," said Mercy.

"Think how it would be if this blue sky was only a solid. Men in ancient times believed that; it is hardly a wonder their gods were so small. But no matter how high it was, if it was limited at all it could not declare the glory of God. But it is a sphere only to the eyes; it is a foreshortening of infinitude that it may enter our sight; there is no imagining its limit. This infinite sphere, then, is the only figure, image, or symbol fit to begin acquainting us with God; it is an idea incomprehensible, and we can only believe it. In like manner, God cannot be found out by searching, cannot be grasped by any mind, yet is ever before us, the one we can best know, the one we must know, the one we cannot help but know. For his end in giving us being is that his humblest creature should at length know him utterly."

"I think I begin to see," said Mercy.

"If it were not for the outside world," resumed Ian, "we should have no inside world to understand things by. Least of all could we understand God without these millions of sights and sounds and scents and motions, weaving their endless harmonies. They come out of his heart to let us know a little of what is in it."

Alister had been listening intently.

"I have never heard you put a thing better, Ian!" he said.

"You gentlemen," said Mercy, "seem to have a place to think in that I don't know how to get into."

She was looking up at Alister, not quite so much afraid of him; Ian was to her hardly of this world. In her eyes Alister saw something that seemed to reflect the starlight, but it might have been a luminous haze about the waking stars of her soul.

"My brother has always been opening doors for me to think in," said Alister. "But here no door needs to be opened. All you have to do is step straight into the temple of nature and let her speak to you."

"Why should we trouble about religion more than is required of us?" interposed Christina.

"Why indeed?" returned Ian. "But then how much is required?"

"You require far more than my father, and he is good enough for me."

"The Master says we are to love God with all our hearts and souls and strength and mind."

"How then can you worship in the temple of nature?" said Mercy.

"Just as he did. It is nature's temple, remember, for the worship of *God*, not of herself!"

"But how am I to get into it? That's what I want to know."

"You *are* in it! True, the innermost places of the temple are open only to such as already worship in a greater temple; but it has courts into which any honest soul may enter. Yet some of nature's lessons you must learn before you can understand them."

"Do you call it learning a lesson if you do not understand it?"

"Yes—to a certain extent. Did you not learn things at school you did not understand, how to do sums, for instance."

"Yes."

"And so one may learn a lesson from nature, too, without at first understanding it. There are many lessons which must be learned first at one level in order to be better learned at another, better understood."

"But how am I to begin? Do tell me. Nothing you say helps me in the least."

"I have all the time been leading you toward the door at which you want to go in. It is not likely, however, that it will open to you all at once. It may not open to you at all, except through sorrow. That is often the case."

"You are a most encouraging master!" said Christina with a light laugh.

"Will you let me ask you a question?" continued Ian.

"You frighten me," said Mercy.

"I am sorry. We will talk of something else."

"I am not afraid of what you may ask me. I am frightened at what you may tell me. I fear to go on if I must meet Sorrow on the way!"

"You make me think of some terrible secret society!" said Christina.

"Tell me then, Miss Mercy, is there anything you love very much? I don't say a person, but any *thing?*"

"I love some animals."

"An animal is not a thing. Tell me, did a flower ever make you cry?"

"No," answered Mercy, with a puzzled laugh; "how could it?"

"Did any flower ever make you a moment later in going to bed, or a moment earlier in getting out of it?"

"No, certainly."

"In that direction, then, I am foiled!"

"You would not really have me cry over a flower, Mr. Ian? Did a flower ever make you yourself cry? Of course not! Only silly women cry for nothing."

"I would rather not bring myself in at present," answered Ian, smiling; "but there is plenty of time," he went on, half to himself.

"But there is so much to learn!" returned Mercy in a hopeless tone.

"That is the joy of existence!" Ian replied. "We are not bound to *know*; we are only bound to *learn*. But to return to our discussion on flowers; a man may really love a flower."

"But how can one love a thing that has not life?" said Mercy.

"The flowers *do* live. They come from the same heart as man himself, and are sent to be his companions and ministers. There is something divinely magical, because profoundly human in them. Our feeling for many of them doubtless comes from certain associations from childhood; but how did they get hold of us even in childhood? Why do they enter our souls at all? It is because they are joyous, inarticulate children, come with vague messages from the Father of all. If I confess that what they say to me sometimes makes me weep, how can I call my feeling for them anything but love? And the flowers are only one example. All nature, from the mountains to the sea to the fog that hangs so low on the hills, the heather in August, the hot, the cold, the rain—everything speaks, like the flower, messages from God, the Father of the universe. The eternal may have a thousand forms of which we know nothing yet!"

Mercy felt Ian must mean something she should understand, but he had not yet told her anything to help her! But he had not reached his end yet; he was leading her on—gently and naturally.

"I did not mean," he resumed, "that you must necessarily begin with the flowers. I was only asking to find out at what point you were nearer to nature. Tell me—were you ever alone?"

"Alone!" repeated Mercy, thinking. "Surely everybody has been alone many times."

"Can you tell me when you were last alone?"

She thought but could not tell.

"What I want to ask you," said Ian, "is, did you ever feel alone? Did loneliness ever press itself so upon you that you felt that if you called nobody would hear? You are not alone while you know that you can have someone with you the instant you choose."

"I don't know if I was ever *that* alone."

"Then what I would have you do," continued Ian, "is to make yourself alone in one of nature's withdrawing rooms, and seat yourself in one of Granny's own chairs. I am coming to the point at last! On a day when the weather is fine, go out by yourself. Tell no one where you are going or that you are going anywhere. Climb a hill. No book, remember. Nothing to fill your thinking place with the thoughts of others.

"When you are quite alone, when you do not even know the nearest point to anybody, sit down and be lonely. Look out on what you see, with the lonely sun in the middle of it all. Fold your hands in your lap and be still. Do not try to think anything. Do not try to call up any feeling or sensation; just be still. By and by, it may be, you will begin to know something of nature, and then possibly of the God whose clothing it is. I do not know you well enough to be sure about it; but if you tell me afterward how you fared, I shall then know you a little better, and could perhaps be able to tell you whether nature had or will soon speak to you."

They were approaching the cottage and little more was said. They found Mrs. Palmer prepared to go, and Mercy was not sorry for she had had enough for a while. Later, as she lay in bed thinking, her own life seemed dull and poor. But as much as she found she liked Alister and Ian, there remained a certain dissatisfaction in being with them. With all their kindness, respect, attention, and even attendance upon them, these men of the hills did not show them the homage which those of their own circle paid them!

24 / Flash Flood

The visits between the men and the ladies were returned in both directions, but somehow there was never the same freedom in the house as in the cottage. Something in the air of the place, the presence of so many commonplace *things*, clogged the wheels of thought. And even with all her knowledge of the world and all her sweetness, Mrs. Palmer did not understand the essentials of hospitality half so well as the widow of the late minister-chief. Even Christina felt something lacking in their reception, and regretted that the house was not grand enough to show the lifestyle they were accustomed to.

Mrs. Palmer seldom understood the talk, and though she sat looking pleased, she was always haunted with a dim feeling that her husband would not be happy with so much interaction between his rich daughters and those penniless country fellows. Yet she more than liked the young men. The relationship between them and their mother delighted her: they were one! They understood each other! Never had she had one such look from either of her own sons as she saw pass every now and then from these to their mother! What it would be like to feel herself loved in that way!

And besides, Mercy had so little chance of marrying well—she was so plain! Would it be an inconceivable idea to her husband for her to marry into an old and once-powerful family like that of the Macruadh? Could he not restore its property as the dowry of his second daughter, stipulating that the chief should acknowledge the baronetcy and use his title? Mercy would then be a woman of consequence, and it would reflect well upon them as her parents as well.

The days went by and Christina had scarcely come any nearer to any understanding with those whose society consoled her, but at least their talk had ceased to sound repulsive. More was needed to wake her than having friends who were awake. It is amazing how long the sleeping may go about with the waking, and never discover any difference between them. But Granny Nature was about to interfere.

The spring drew gently on. But there seemed more of the destructive in the spring itself than of the genial—cold winds, great showers, days of steady rain, assaults of hail and sleet. Still it was spring, and at length, one fine day with a bright sun, snow on the hills, and clouds in the east, but no sign of any sudden change, the girls went out for a walk, taking the younger girls with them.

A little way up the valley, out of sight of the cottage, a small burn came down its own dell to join that which flowed through the chief's farm. Its channel was wide, but except in time of rain had little water in it. About a half mile up its course it divided, or rather the channel did, for in one of its branches there was seldom any water. At the fork was a low rocky mount with an ancient ruin of no great size—three or four fragments of thick walls, within which grew a slender birch tree. To this ruin went the little party, wandering up the stream. The valley was sheltered, no wind but the south could reach it, and the sun, though it could not make it very warm as it looked only aslant on its slopes, yet lighted both sides of it. Great white clouds passed slowly across the sky, with now and then a nearer black one threatening rain, but a wind overhead was carrying them quickly over.

Ian had seen the ladies pass, but made no effort to overtake them, though he was headed in the same direction: at the moment he preferred the company of his book. Suddenly his attention was roused by a peculiar whistle which he knew for that of Hector of the Stags; it was one of the few sounds he could make. Three times it was repeated, and before the third was over Ian had spotted Hector high on a hill on the opposite side of the burn, waving his arms and making eager signs to him. He tried to understand; Hector was pointing with energy, but it was impossible to determine the exact direction. All Ian could gather was that his presence was needed farther on. He resumed his walk at a rapid pace, whereupon Hector pointed still higher. There on the eastern horizon, toward the north, almost down on the very hills, Ian saw a collection of clouds in the strangest commotion such as he had never seen—a mass of dark vapors in appalling unrest. It seemed to be a miniature storm, twisting and contorting with unceasing change—now gray, now black, now mingled with brown through the white. At this season he hardly thought it a thunderstorm and stood watching, absorbed in the unusual phenomenon. But again, louder and more hurried, came the whistling, and again he saw Hector gesticulating more wildly than before. Then he knew someone must be in need of help and set off running as hard as he could. Perhaps the ladies had gotten into some difficulty!

When he arrived at the opening of the valley, Hector's signs made it quite plain it was up there he must go. As soon as he entered it he saw that the cloudy turmoil was among the hills at its head. With that he began to suspect the danger the hunter feared, a flash flood down this little stream bed which stood directly under the fierce isolated storm higher up the mountain. Almost the same instant he heard the merry voices of the children. Running yet faster he came in sight of them on the other side of the stream—not a moment too soon. The valley was full of a dull roaring sound. He called to them as he ran, and the children saw him and came running down the bank, followed by Mercy. She was not concerned, for she thought it only the grumbling of distant thunder. But Ian saw, far up the valley, what looked like a low brown wall across it, and knew what it was—the water from the mountain had been unleashed and was raging toward them.

"Mercy!" he cried, "run up the side of the hill immediately. You will be drowned—swept away if you don't."

She looked incredulous and glanced up the hillside, but still came on as if to cross the burn to join him.

"Do as I tell you!" he cried in a tone few could have ignored.

Mercy did not wait for him to reach her, but took the children, each by hand, and went a little way up the hill that immediately bordered the stream.

"Farther! farther!" cried Ian as he ran toward them. "Where is Christina?"

"At the ruin," Mercy answered.

"Good heavens!" exclaimed Ian and darted off, crying, "Up the hill with you! Up the hill farther!"

Christina was standing by the birch tree in the ruin, looking down the hill. She had heard Ian calling and saw him running, but did not suspect the danger she was in.

"Come, come immediately! for heaven's sake, come!" he cried. "Look up the burn!" he added, seeing her hesitate, bewildered.

She turned, looked, and came running to him, down the channel, white with terror. It was almost too late. The charging water, whose front rank was turf and bushes and rocks, was nearly upon her. It was now at the point of dividing against the rocky mound where the ruin stood, to sweep along both its sides and turn it into an island. Ian bounded to her in the middle of the channel, caught her by the arm and hurried her back to the mound as fast as they could run—they could never have scrambled high enough up the bank to get out of the path of the onrushing flow, and the mound was the highest ground immediately accessible. As they reached it, the water broke with a roar against its rocky base, rose, swelled—and in a moment the island was covered with a brown, seething swirling flood.

"Where are Mercy and the children?" gasped Christina as the water caught her.

"Safe!" answered Ian. "We must get to the ruin!"

The water was halfway up his leg and rising fast. Their danger was but beginning. It was doubtful whether the old walls, mostly made without mortar, would even stand the rush. If a tree coming down the stream should strike them, they would certainly crumble. The water was up to Christina's waist, and very cold. But she recovered at least part of her breath and showed courage. Ian stood between her and the wall and held her tight while he held onto the wall with his other hand. The chief danger to Christina, however, was from the cold. With the water so high on her body and flowing so fast, she could not resist it long. Therefore, Ian took her round the knees and lifted her almost out of the water.

"Put your arms up," he said, "and take hold of the wall."

"I can't help being frightened," she panted.

"We are in God's arms," returned Ian. "He is holding us."

"Are you sure we shall not be drowned?" she asked.

"No, but I am sure the water cannot take us out of God's arms."

This was not much comfort to Christina. She knew nothing about God—did not believe in him any more than most people. The only arms she knew anything about were arms like Ian's—and *they* comforted her, for she could feel them.

How many people actually believe in any support they do not immediately feel? In arms they do not see? But Ian's help was God's help; and though to believe in Ian was not to believe in God, it was a step on the road toward believing in God. He that does not believe in the good man he has seen, how shall he believe in the God he has not seen?

She began to feel a little better. The horrible choking at her heart was almost gone.

"Your poor arms!" she said.

"You are not very heavy," he answered; "and though I am not so strong as Alister, with the help of the wall I can hold you for a long time."

Suddenly in danger, self came less to the front with her than usual. For the first time in her life she was face-to-face with reality. Until this very moment her life had been an affair of unrealities. Solid reality itself is not enough to teach some of nature's reality; they must hurt themselves against its solidness before they realize its solidity, its reality. Looking at a soft river floating away in the moonlight is hardly reality to a dreaming soul. But this river was real! Christina was shivering in its grasp on her body, its omnipresence to her skin; its cold made her gasp and choke; the push and tug of it threatened to sweep her away like a log.

When we are most aware of *fact-ness*, we are most aware of our need of God, and most able to trust him. The recognition of inexorable reality in any shape, or kind, or ways tends to rouse the soul to the yet more real, to its relations with higher and deeper existence. It is not the hysterical alone for whom the great dash of cold water is good. All who dream life instead of living it require some similar shock. Every disappointment, every sorrow, every tragedy of life can work the same way—can drive one a trifle nearer to the truth of being. Hence this sharp contact with nature tended to make Christina less selfish. It made her forget herself so far as to care for her helper as well as herself.

"Oh, if you should be drowned for my sake!" she faltered with white lips.

"I could not wish for a better death," said Ian.

"How can you talk so coolly about it!" she cried.

"What better way of going out of the world is there than by the door of help?"

"Most men would not be quite so willing to leave it for another."

"I don't call such as you speak of men. They are only children. I do care to live, but I don't mind where."

"I can't quite follow you," steamed Christina. "Perhaps it is the cold. I can't feel my hands, I am so cold."

"The water is already falling. It will go as rapidly as it came."

"How do you know that?"

"It has sunk nearly a foot. I have been watching it carefully. It must have been a waterspout, and however much it may bring, it pours it all out at once."

"Oh," said Christina, relieved. "I thought it would go on ever so long."

"We shall get out of it alive! God's will be done."

"Why do you say that? Don't you really mean we are going to be saved?"

"Would you want to live if he wanted you to die?"

"But you forget, Mr. Ian, I am not ready to die, like you."

"Be sure God will not take you away if it be better for you to live here a little longer. But you will have to go sometime, and if you managed to live after God wanted you to go, you would find yourself much less ready when the time came that you must. No one can be living a true life to whom dying is a terror."

Christina was silent. He spoke the truth! Was her life worth anything?

And with the fleeting thought her real self, her spiritual center, had begun to waken. True, that part of her was as yet no more like the divine than the drowsy, arm-stretching, yawning child is like the merry elf about to spring from his couch, full of life, play, and love. She had no faith in God yet; it was more that she felt she was not worth anything.

Only one human being witnessed their danger, and he could give no help. Hector of the Stags had crossed the main valley above where the torrent entered it, and coming over the hill saw the flood-surrounded pair. But the raging torrent blocked the way to both the village and to the chief's house. He could only stand and gaze with his heart in his eyes.

Beyond the stream lay Mercy on the hillside, with her face in the heather. Frozen with dread, she dared not look up. If she had but moved ten yards she would have seen her sister in Ian's arms. The children sat beside her, white as death, with great lumps in their throats and silent tears rolling down their cheeks. It was the first time the possibility of death had come near them.

A sound of rapid steps came through the heather. They looked up: there was the chief striding toward them.

The flood had come upon him at work in his fields, overwhelming his growing crops. He had but time to unyoke his bulls and run for his life. The bulls, not quite equal to the occasion, were caught and swept away. They were found a week later on the hills, none the worse, and nearly as wild as when he had first taken them in hand. The cottage was in no danger, and Nancy got a horse and the last of the cows from the farmyard to the crest of the ridge, against which the burn rushed roaring, just as the water began to invade the cowhouse and stable. The moment he reached the ridge, the chief set out to look for his brother whom he knew to be somewhere up the valley. Having climbed to get a better view, he saw Mercy and the younger girls.

The girls uttered a cry of welcome.

"Mercy," said Alister softly, kneeling down and laying his hand on her, "what has happened?"

She tried to speak but could not.

"Where is Christina?" he went on.

She succeeded in bringing out one word: "Ruin."

"Is anybody with her?"

"Ian."

"Oh," he returned cheerily, as if then all would be right. But seeing Mercy's face, he realized she was still terrified. "But God is with them, Mercy. And where he is, all is well!"

"I wish I could believe that," she said, "but, you know, people *are* drowned sometimes."

"Yes, surely. But if God be with them, what does it matter?"

"It is cruel to talk like that when my sister may be drowning!"

"Mercy," said the chief, his voice trembling a little, "you do not love your sister more than I love my brother, and if he be drowned I shall weep. But I shall not be miserable as if a devil were at root of it all and not one who loves them better than we ever shall. But come, I think we shall find them alive yet! Ian knows what to do in an emergency, and he is very strong."

She rose immediately, and taking the hand he offered, went like a child up the side of the hill with him.

"I see Chrissy! I see Chrissy!" cried one of the children.

"Yes! there she is! I see her too!" cried the other.

Alister hurried up with Mercy. There was Christina. She seemed to be standing on the water. Mercy burst into tears.

"But where's Ian?" she said when she had recovered herself a little. "I don't see him!"

"He is there, all right!" answered Alister. "Don't you see his hands holding her out of the water? The stream is just up to his chest."

And with that he gave a great shout: "Ian! Ian! hold on, old boy! I'm coming!"

Along the hillside went Alister bounding like a deer, then turning sharp sideways, shot headlong, dashed into the torrent—and was swept away like a cork. Mercy gave a scream and ran down the hill.

He was not carried far. In a moment or two he had recovered himself and crept out gasping and laughing, just below Mercy. Ian did not move. He was so numb from the mountain water that to change his position an inch would be to fall.

Trying once again, this time starting higher up, Alister once more rushed into the torrent, and after a fierce struggle, reached the mound, where he scrambled up, put his arms round Ian's legs with a shout, and lifted the two at once.

"Come, come Alister! don't be silly!" said Ian. "Set me down."

"Give me the girl, then."

"Take her."

Christina turned on him a sorrowful gaze as Alister took her.

"I will have been the death of you," she said.

"You have done me the greatest favor," Ian replied.

"What?" she asked.

"Accepted help."

She burst out crying. She had not shed a tear since the ordeal began.

"Get on top of the wall, Ian, out of the wet," said Alister.

"I don't know what the water may have done to my foundations, Alister! I would rather not break my leg. It is so frozen it would never mend again!"

As they talked the torrent continued to fall, rapidly now, so that in a few minutes Hector of the Stags came wading from the other side. A few minutes more and Alister carried Christina to Mercy.

"Now," he said, setting her down, "you must walk."

Ian could not cross without Hector's help. He seemed to have no legs. Nothing could be done for them but get them home; so they all set out for the cottage.

"How will your crops fare, Alister?" asked Ian.

"Some will be spoiled," replied the chief, "part won't be much the worse."

The torrent had rushed halfway up the ridge, then swept along the side of it and round the end to the level on the other side. The water lay soaking into the fields. The valley was desolate. What green things had not been uprooted or carried away with the soil were laid flat. Mud was everywhere, with lumps of turf, heather, brushwood, and small trees scattered all over. But it was early in the year and there was still hope all would mend before summer.

Their return to the cottage brought about great haste and hurrying to and fro in the little house—the blowing of fires, the steaming pails and blankets, the hot milk and tea. Mrs. Macruadh rolled up her sleeves and worked like a good housemaid. Nancy shot throughout the place like a fawn. Alister got Ian to bed and rubbed him with rough towels. Christina fell asleep and slept many hours. When she woke she said she was quite well; but it was weeks before she was like herself. I doubt if ever she was quite as strong again. For some days Ian confessed to an aching in his legs and arms. It was the cold of the water, he said, but Alister was certain it was from holding Christina so long.

"Water could not hurt a highlander!" said Alister.

25 / Change

Christina walked home without difficulty, but the next day did not leave her bed, and it was two weeks before she again left the house. When Ian and she met, her manner was not quite the same as before. She seemed a little timid; her eyes fell, but her face was rosy, and the slight embarrassment disappeared as soon as they began to talk. No affectation or formality, however, took its place: with Ian at least her falseness was gone. The danger she had been in and the sharing of it by Ian had awaked the simpler, the real nature of the girl, till then buried in impressions and their responses. She had lived as a mirror; now something of an operative existence was at length beginning to appear in her. She was growing into a woman. And the first stage in that growth is to become as a little child.

The child, however, did not for some time show her face to any but Ian. In his presence Christina no longer had any self-assertion or guile. Without seeking his notice, she would yet show an almost childish willingness to please him. It was no sudden change. Ever since their adventure she had been haunted, both awake and asleep, by his presence, and it had helped her to some discoveries regarding herself. And the more she grew real, the nearer to becoming a *person*, the more she came under the influence of his truth and his reality. It is only through live relation to others that any individuality crystallizes.

"You saved my life, Ian!" she said one evening for the tenth time.

"It pleased God you should live," answered Ian. "Of course I thank him for that, just as I would give him thanks if we had been drowned."

"How could we have thanked God for being drowned? Must you thank God for everything—thank him if you are drowned or burned or anything?"

"Now you understand me! That is it precisely!"

"Then I can never be good, for I could never bring myself to that!"

"You cannot bring yourself to it; no one could. But we must come to it. I believe we shall all be brought to it."

"Never me! I should not wish it!"

"You do not wish it; but you may be brought to wish it; and without it the potential of your being cannot be reached. No one, of course, could ever give thanks for what he did not know or feel as good. But what *is* good must come to be felt good. Can you suppose that Jesus at any time could not thank his Father for sending him into the world?"

"You speak as if we and he were of the same kind."

"We are so entirely of the same kind that there is no bliss for him or for you or for me but in being the loving obedient child of the one Father."

"You frighten me! If I cannot get to heaven any other way than that, I shall never get there."

"You will get there, and you will get there that way and no other. If you could get there any other way, it would be to be miserable."

"Something tells me you speak the truth; but it is terrible! I do not like it."

"Naturally."

She was on the point of crying, not because she was drawing toward peace, but because of an urging painful sense of separation from Ian. A meeting with him was now to Christina the great event of day or week.

One morning she woke from a sound and dreamless sleep, got up, looked out, and then opened the window. It was a lovely spring morning. The birds were singing loud in the shrubbery. A soft wind was blowing. A presence came to her and whispered something both lovely and sad. The sun was but a little way up and was shining over the hills and snow-covered peaks. Suddenly as she gazed at a little clump of trees against the hillside, nature seemed to come alive with a presence she had never seen before. It was an instinct with a meaning, an intent, a soul; the mountains stood against the sky as if reaching upward, knowing something, waiting for something. Over all was a glory. The change was far more wondrous than merely the change from winter to summer; what could it mean? She was ready to cry aloud, not with joy, not from her feeling of the beauty, but with some sensation she had never known before and which she couldn't even name. She had a new and marvelous interest in the world, a new sense of life in herself, of life in everything, a life-contract with the universe, a conscious flash of the divine in her soul, a throb of the pure joy of being. She was nearer to God than she had ever been before. But she did not know this; she understood nothing of what was going on in her. She only felt it, and thought it was love. And it was love. Whether love was in her or not, she was in love—and it might get inside her.

One might not have expected such a feeling from Christina—and she wondered at it herself. But until a woman is awake, who can tell her nature? The very faculty of loving had been repressed in the soul of Christina, but now at length she was in love.

At breakfast, though she was silent, she looked so well that her mother complimented her on her loveliness. Had she been more of a mother, she would no doubt have seen the cause of the new sparkle in her daughter's eye.

While the chief went on in his humble way, enjoying life in his lowly position and—without knowing it—growing more fond of the poorly educated but simple and open Mercy, a trouble was gathering for him of which he had no warning. We have to be delivered from the evils we are unaware of as well as from those we hate; and the chief had to be set free from his unconscious attachment to mammon. He did not worship mammon by seeking riches. He had no desire to be a millionaire but only to serve his people. But he was so consciously aware of the deteriorating condition of the country and the hundred and fifty souls who still looked to him as their head, that whenever he thought about how to shepherd them should economic matters come to a crisis, his sole comfort in the matter was the money from the last sale of property. It had been accumulating interest in an account ever since and would be his in a very few years. He always thought of this money first, not of God, imagining it an inexhaustible force, a power with which for his clan he could work wonders. It is a common human mistake to think of money as a force and not a mere tool. He never thought of it otherwise than as belonging to the clan. But all the time the very shadow of this money was disappearing from the face of the earth!

Scarcely had it been deposited where the old laird judged it safe— as safe as if he had put it in the Bank of England—when schemes and speculations by the entrusted company brought everything it held into jeopardy. Things had been going from bad to worse ever since. Nothing of this was yet known, for the directors had from the first carefully hidden the truth and went on living in false show with the very money their innocent neighbors had placed in their hands. Annihilation had long closed in upon the fund which the chief regarded as the anchor of his clan: he trusted in mammon, and mammon had played him one of its cruel tricks. The most degrading wrong to ourselves, and the worst eventual wrong to others, is to trust in any thing or person other than the living God. Even those who help us we must regard as the loving hands of the great heart of the universe, else we do God wrong and will come to do them wrong also.

In addition, there was mischief brewing in yet another quarter which was likely to cause further hurt to the ancient clan Ruadh.

Mr. Peregrine Palmer was not now as rich as when he bought his highland property. He was, in addition, involved in several affairs of seriously doubtful outcome. It was natural, therefore, that he should begin to think of his property west of Inverness as no mere ornament of life but as something substantial to fall back upon. He feared nothing, however, more than a temporary embarrassment. Had not he and his family been in the front for three generations? Therefore, he must now see to making the best of his Scotch acres, to make of it a deer forest! He and his other neighbor besides the Macruadh—a Canadian—might together bring about something very worth doing. So all crofters and villagers likely to trespass must be gotten rid of—first and foremost the shepherds, for they had endless opportunities of helping themselves to a deer. Where there were sheep there must be shepherds: they would make a clearance of both!

The neighbor, a certain Mr. Brander, had made his money by sharp dealing in connection with a great Russian railway. Mr. Peregrine Palmer knew him in London, and had been enlightened by him on many things—among others, the shepherd's passion for deer stalking. Being in the company of the deer, he said, the whole day and the whole year through, they were thoroughly acquainted with their habits and were altogether too much both for the deer and for their owners. In short, there was no protecting the deer without uprooting and expelling the peasantry!

The village of the Clanruadh was on Mr. Brander's land and was dependent in part on the produce of small pieces of ground, the cultivators of which were mostly men with other employment as well. Some made shoes of the hides, others cloth and clothes of the wool of the country. Most were shepherds, for there was now very little farming in those hilly and rocky regions. Almost all the land formerly cultivated had been given up to grass and sheep, and much of it was steadily returning to that state of nature from which it had once been reclaimed, producing heather, ling, blueberries, and cranberries. The hamlet was too far from the sea for much fishing, but some of its inhabitants would join relatives on the coast and go fishing with them when there was nothing else to be done. Many of those who looked to the sea for help had just come through a very hard time, in which they would have died but for the seaweed and shellfish the shore afforded them. Yet such was their spirit of independence that when a commission was appointed by the government to look into the plight of these desperate people, hardly a single one was found willing to acknowledge any need. This class of men and women was now doomed to expulsion from the houses and land they had held for generations at the will of two common-minded, greedy men.

Having himself learned the lesson that so long as a man is dependent on anything earthly he is not a free man, Ian was very desirous to have his brother free also. Alister was a good man: why, then, are those who are trying to be good more continuously troubled with lessons of conscience than the indifferent? Simply, as a man advances, more and more is required of him. A wrong thing in a good man becomes more and more wrong as he draws nearer to freedom from it. His friends may say how seldom he offends, but every time he does offend, he is the more to blame—as he himself knows better than any other. The chief was one in whom was no guile, but he was far from perfect: any man is far from perfect whose sense of well-being can be altered by change of circumstance. A man unable to do without this thing or that is not yet in sight of his godly perfection, therefore not yet out of sight of suffering. For it is to the perfection of Christlikeness God calls us, and will bring about in us, no matter how many so-called believers would rather settle for something far less, thinking all God wants from us is that we "be ourselves." Clouds were gathering to burst in fierce hail on the head of the chief, to the end that he might be set free from yet another of the cords that bound him to the earth. He was like a soaring eagle from whose foot hung, trailing on the earth, the line by which his tyrant could at will pull him back to his inglorious perch.

A few acres of good valley land, with a small upland pasturage, and a space of barren hill-country, had developed in the chief a greater love of the land as a possession than would have come of his having suddenly been left an inheritance twenty times its size. He loved his small plot of land, and hung onto what remained him as the last remnant of a vanishing good. Yet the love of possessing a property must, if it goes unchecked, in time annihilate in a man the inheritance of the meek. Thus the Lord had further surgery to perform deep within the soul of young Alister Macruadh.

One day the brothers were lying on the westward slope of the ridge in front of the cottage. A few sheep, small, active, black-faced, were feeding around them: it was no use their running away, for the chief's collie was lying beside him. The laird every now and then buried his face in the short sweet mountain grass—like that of the downs in England, not like the rich sown grass on the cultivated bank of the burn.

"I believe I love the grass, Ian," he said.

"I doubt if grass can be loved so much as a flower."

"Why not?"

"Because the one is a mass, the other an individual."

"I understand."

"I have a fear, Alister, that you are in danger of avarice," said Ian after a pause.

"Avarice, Ian! Me—covetous, hoarding, greedy? What can you mean?"

"Alister, you are as free from the love of money as any man I ever knew. But that is not enough. Did you ever think of the origin of the word *avarice*?"

"No."

"I think it comes from the same root as the verb *have*. It is the desire to call *things* ours—the desire of company which is not of our kind. We call the holding in the hand, or house, or pocket, or purse, or the power, *having*. But things so held cannot really be *had*. *Having* is but an illusion with regard to things. It is only what we can be *with* that we really possess. A love can never be lost; it is a true possession. But who can take his diamond ring, or his piece of land, into the life beyond? These are not possessions. Thus, only love, and only God can be ours perfectly. Nothing called property can be ours at all."

"I know all that—with my head, at least," said Alister; "but I am not sure how you apply it to me."

"Do you not see that the love of our mother earth is meant to be but a beginning; and that such love as yours for the land belongs to that love of things which must perish? I say there is a better way of loving the ground on which we were born than to love it so that the loss of it would cause us torture."

Alister listened as to a prophecy of evil.

"Rather than that cottage and those fields should pass into the hands of others," he said almost fiercely, "I would see them sunk in a roaring tide!"

Ian rose and slowly walked away into the pine trees which sloped down the ridge. Alister lay clutching the ground with his hands.

In a few minutes Alister came to him.

"You cannot mean, Ian," he said, "that I am to think no more of the fields of my fathers than of any other ground on the face of the earth!"

"Think of them as the ground God gave to our fathers, which God may see fit to take from us again," answered Ian.

"Don't be upset with me!" cried Alister. "I want to think and do what is right. But you cannot know how I feel or you would spare me. I love the very stones and clods of the land! The place is to me as Jerusalem to the Jews."

"They loved their land as *theirs*," said Ian, "and have lost it! I am only afraid that your love for the soil will get all the way into your soul. We are here but pilgrims and strangers. God did not make the world to be dwelt in but to be journeyed through. We must not love it as he did not mean we should. If we do, he may have great trouble and we must hurt before we are set free from that misplaced love. Alister, would you willingly turn your back on the house and walk out of it to follow him forever?''

"I don't know about *willingly*," replied Alister, "but if I were sure it was he calling me, I am sure I would walk out and follow him."

"What if your love of house and lands prevented you from being sure that it was he calling you?"

"That would be terrible! But he would not leave me so. He would not turn his back on me in my ignorance."

"No. If he had to take you from everything in order to give you what he had for you, he would take everything from you."

Alister turned and went into the house.

He did not know how much of the worldly mingled with the true in him. He loved his people and was unselfishly intent on helping them to the utmost, but how much self there was in his idea of being their chief was not a question he had considered. In like manner, his love of nature nourished the parasite *possession*. He had but those bare hillsides, and those few rich acres, yet when he stood on top of the mountain over-looking it all, his heart felt a certain satisfaction that it was his brook, his sheep, his glen full of his people. Even with the pure smell of the earth mingled the sense of its possession.

But all is man's only because it is God's. The true possession of anything is to see and feel in it what God made it for, and the uplifting of the soul by that knowledge is the joy of true having. The Lord had no land of his own: his pupils must not care for things he did not care for. He had no place to lay his head—had not even a grave of his own. Once he sent a fish to fetch him money, but only to pay a tax. He even had to borrow the few loaves and little fishes from a boy with which to feed his five thousand.

The half hour which Alister spent in the silence of his room served him well: a ray of light entered his soul in its gloom. He returned to Ian, who had been walking up and down the ridge.

"You are right, Ian," he said. "I do love the world! And oh, how I fear he is going to take the land from me!"

"We must never fear the will of God, Alister. We are not right with him until we can pray heartily, 'Thy will be done!'—heartily, not in sad submission. When we wish what he does not wish, we are not only against him, but against our real selves. Only the will of God is desirable. Nothing else will satisfy us, no matter how it seems that other things can."

It was getting toward summer and the days were growing longer.

"Let us spend a night on the mountain," said Ian; and they fixed a day in the following week.

26 / Mercy Calls on Granny

Although the subject did not come up again, Mercy had not forgotten what Ian had said about listening for the word of nature, and she had resolved to get away the first time she could to see whether Granny, as Ian had called her, would have anything to do with her. It was a fine spring morning when Mercy left the house to seek an interview somewhere among the hills. She took a path she knew well, and then struck into a sheep track she had never tried. Up and up she climbed, spending not so much as a thought on the sudden changes of weather to which that season, especially among the hills, was subject.

Not until she was beyond sight of any house did she begin to feel alone. It was an altogether new sensation. But the slight sense of anxiety and fear was soon overpowered by something like an exhilaration of a child escaping from school. This grew and grew until she felt like a wild thing that had been caught and had broken loose. For almost the first time in her life she began to feel she was free! She might lie in the heather, walk in the stream, do as she pleased. No one would interfere with her. She felt stronger and fresher than ever before, and the farther she went the greater grew the pleasure. The little burn she was walking up, now on one side, now on the other, kept on welcoming her unaccustomed feet to the realms of solitude and liberty. The wind woke now and then and blew on her for a moment, as if tasting her to see what this young maiden was that had floated up into the wild thin air of the hills. The incessant meeting of the brook made it a companion to her, although it could not go her way and was always leaving her. But it kept her from the utter loneliness she sought; for loneliness is imperfect while sound is nearby, especially a sing-song, and the brook was one of nature's self-playing song instruments. But she came at length to a point where the ground was too rough to let her follow its path anymore, so turning from it she began to climb a steep ridge. The growing and deepening silence as she went farther and farther from the brook promised the very place for her purpose on the top of the heathery ridge.

But when she reached it and looked behind her, lo, the valley she had left lay at her very feet! She had not escaped from the world at all—for there it was behind her! It was like being enchanted! She thought she was leaving it far behind, but the nature she sought to escape that she might find *nature* would not let her go! She turned around and made for the next ridge. The danger of losing her way back never suggested itself to her. She had not yet learned that things never look the same when you go back.

When she gained the summit of the second ridge, she looked abroad on a country she knew nothing of. It was like the face of a complete stranger. Not far beyond rose still another ridge: she must see how the world looked from that! On and on she went, crossing ridge after ridge, but no place invited her to stay and be still.

Before long she found that she was tired and sat down on a great stone in the midst of the heather. Though the sun was warm, the air was keen, and, hot with climbing, she turned her face to it and drank in its refreshing with delight. She looked around; not a trace of humanity was visible—nothing but brown and gray and green hills with the clear sky over her head, and in the north a black cloud creeping up from the horizon. Another sense than that of rest awoke in her, and now for the first time in her life the sense of absolute aloneness began to possess her. The silence gathered around her, almost as if it were solid. She was nearer than ever to knowing the presence of the God who is always nearer to us than everything else. Through the very persistence of the silence something seemed to say to her at last, "Here I am!" She sent her gaze out to the horizon. The huge waves of the solid earth stood up against the sky, and on her right lay a blue segment of the ever-restless sea, but so far away that its commotion seemed a yet deeper rest than that of the immovable hills.

She sat and sat, but nothing came to her. Why did she feel so uncomfortable? Was she so silly as to mind being alone? There was nothing in these mountains that would hurt her. Yet something like fear was growing within her! Why should she be afraid? Ian Macruadh must be wrong! How could there be any such bond as he said between nature and the human heart when the first thing she felt when alone with her was fear? The world was staring at her! She did not like it! She would get up and shake off the silly feeling. She rose, but could not stop her thinking.

The terrible, persistent silence—would nothing break it? And yet at the same time there was something inside herself—almost in league with the silence—that kept telling her things were not all right with her; that she ought not to be afraid, yet had good reason for being afraid; that she knew of no essential safety. There must be some refuge, some hiding place, and she ought to know of it! There must be a human condition of not being afraid, of knowing nothing to be afraid of! She wondered whether, if she was good and went to church twice every Sunday and read her Bible every morning, she would grow not to be afraid of—she did not know what. How wonderful it would be to have no fear!

It was all nonsense! The mountain was not really staring at her! She was silly! She would get up and go home: it must be time.

But things were not as they should be. Something was required of her. Did God want her to do something? She had never thought whether he required anything of her. She must be a better girl! Then she would have God with her and not be afraid.

All the time it was God near her who was making her unhappy and ordering her thoughts so. For as the Son of Man came not to bring peace on earth but a sword, so the first visit of God to the human soul is generally in a cloud of fear and doubt, rising from the soul itself at his approach. The sun is the dispeller of clouds, yet often he must look through a fog if he would visit the earth at all. The child, not being a son, does not know his Father. He may know he is called a father; but what the word means he does not know. How, then, should he understand when the Father comes to deliver him from his paltry self and give him life indeed!

She tried to pray. "O God!" she said, "forgive me and make me good. I want to be good!" Then she rose.

She went some little way without thinking where she was going, and then found she did not even know from what direction she had come. A sharp new fear, quite different from the former, now shot through her heart: she was lost! She had told no one she was going anywhere. No one would have a notion where to look for her. She had been beginning to feel hungry, but fear drove hunger away. All she knew was that she must not stay there. *Here* was nowhere; walking she might at least come to somewhere. So she set out on her weary walk from nowhere to some-where, giving nature little thanks. She did not suspect that her "grand-mother" had been doing anything for her by the space around her, or that now, by her very lostness, she was doing yet more. On and on she walked, climbing the one hillside and descending the other, going she knew not where, hardly hoping she drew one step nearer home.

All at once her strength went from her. She sat down and cried. But with her tears came the thought of how the chief and his brother talked of God. She remembered she had heard in church that men ought to cry to God in their troubles. Broken verses of a psalm came to her. She tried to trust him, but could not: he was as far from her as the blue heavens! If only she had God for her friend! What if he was her friend, and she had not known it because she never spoke to him, never asked anything of him, never confided in him? She would pray to God! She would ask him to take her home!

A wintery blast came from the north. The black cloud had risen and was now spreading out across the sky. Again the wind came with an angry burst and snarl. Snow began to fall in hard, sharp little pellets. She jumped up and forgot to pray.

Some sound in the wind or some hidden motion of memory all at once let loose upon her another fear, which immediately became an agony of terror. A rumor had reached the New House the night before that a leopard had broken from a traveling circus and escaped to the hills. It was but a rumor; some did not believe it, and the owners contradicted it. Nevertheless, a party had set out with guns and dogs. It was true! There was the terrible creature crouching behind that stone! He was in every clump of heather she passed, twitching his tail, ready to spring on her! He must be hungry by this time, and there was nothing for him to eat but her! Before long, however, she was too cold to be afraid, too cold to think, and presently half-frozen, scarcely able to go a step farther. She saw a great rock, sank down in the shelter of it, and in a minute was asleep.

She slept for some time and woke a little refreshed. The wonder is that she woke at all. It was dark and her first consciousness was a ghastly fear. The wind had stopped and the storm was over. Little snow had fallen. The stars were all out overhead and the great night was round her, enclosing, watching her. She tried to rise but could hardly move her arms and legs. Had she fallen asleep again, she would not have lived through the night, for with the night came even greater cold. But it is idle to talk of what would have been. Mercy wondered afterward that she did not lose her senses.

It was awful. Surely no one ever needed God's help more! Perhaps God had let her walk into this trouble so that she might learn she could not do without him. She *would* try to be good! How terrible was the world, with such wide spaces and nobody in them!

All the time, though she did not know it, she was sobbing and weeping.

The black silence was all at once torn asunder by the shot of a gun. She startled up with a strange mingling of hope and terror, gave a loud cry, and sank senseless on the ground. The leopard would be upon her!

27 / Rescue

The brothers had that same morning paid their visit to their cavern-home on the mountain and spent the day there as they usually did, intending to go home the same night. As the old moon was very late in rising, they had decided to take the earlier and rougher part of the way in the twilight. Just as they were setting out, however, what they rightly judged a passing storm came on, and they delayed their departure. By the time the storm was over, it was dark and there was no use hurrying. When at length they were getting ready to start out again, they thought they heard something like sounds of distress, but the darkness made search difficult. The chief thought of firing his gun, and Mercy's cry immediately guided them to where she lay. Alister's heart nearly stood still at the thought of what she must have gone through. They carried her in, laid her on the bed, and did what they could to restore her, till she began to come to herself. Then they left her, that she might not see them before she was ready, and sat down by the fire in the outer room, leaving the door open between the two.

"I see what must have happened," said Alister. "You remember, Ian, what you said to her about her giving nature an opportunity of exerting her influence? No doubt Mercy has been following your advice, and lost her way among the hills."

"That was so long ago!" returned Ian thoughtfully.

"Yes—when the weather was not fit for it. It is not fit for it now either, but she has made the attempt."

"You must be right. I thought there was some reality in her! But she must not hear us talking about her."

When Mercy came to herself at first she thought that she lay where she had fallen, but presently perceived that she was covered and had something hot at her feet. Was she in her own bed, was it all but a terrible dream? As she put out her arm, her hand went against cold stone. The dreadful thought rushed into her that she was buried and was lying in her grave. Her first feeling was gladness that she had prayed before she died. She wondered that she was not more frightened, for it was a dreary prospect before her: long and countless years must pass before she heard the sound of voices and again saw the light of the sun. She was half-awake and half-dreaming. The faintness of her swoon was yet upon her, the repose following her great weariness, and the lightness

176

of her brain from lack of food, all combined to make her indifferent—almost happy.

At length she began to hear sounds, and they were human voices. She had companions in the grave! She was not doomed to wait for the judgment alone! She must be in some family vault, among strangers. She hoped they were nice people. It was very desirable to be buried with nice people!

Then she saw a reddish light. It was a fire—far off! Was she in the bad place? Were those shapes two demons, waiting till she had gotten over her dying?

One of them rose and came toward her, growing bigger and blacker as he came, until he stood by the bedside. He laid his hand on her wrist and felt her pulse. It was Ian! She could not see his face, for there was no light on it, but she knew his shape, his movements! She was saved!

He saw her wide eyes, two great spiritual nights, gazing up at him.

"Ah, you are better, Miss Mercy!" he said cheerily. "Now you shall have some tea."

Something inside her was weeping for joy, but her outer self was quite still. She tried again to speak, and uttered a few inarticulate sounds. Then came Alister on tiptoe and they both stood by the bedside, looking down on her.

"I shall be all right presently," she managed to say at length. "I am so glad I'm not dead. I thought I was dead!"

"You would soon have been if we had not found you!" replied Alister.

"Was it you that fired the gun?"

"Yes."

"I was so frightened!"

"The fear saved your life, thank God, for you cried out."

"Fright was your door out of fear!" said Ian.

"I thought it was the leopard!"

"I did bring my gun because of the leopard," said Alister.

"It was true about him, then?"

"He is out."

"And now it is quite dark."

"It doesn't matter. We'll take a lantern. I've got my gun, and Ian has his dirk."

"Where are you going, then?" asked Mercy, still confused.

"Home, of course."

"Oh yes, of course. I will get up in a minute."

"There is plenty of time," said Ian. "You must eat something first. I'm sorry to say we have nothing but oatcakes."

178

"I think you promised me some tea," said Mercy. "I don't feel hungry."

"You shall have tea. When did you last eat?"

"Not since breakfast."

"It's no wonder you are weary! You must try to eat some oatcake."

"I wish I hadn't taken that last slice of deer-ham," said Alister ruefully.

"I will eat if I can," said Mercy.

They brought her a cup of tea and some pieces of oatcake. Then, having lighted her a candle, they left her and closed the door.

She sipped her tea, managed to eat a little of the dry but wholesome food, and soon found herself able to get up. It was the strangest bedroom, she thought. Everything was cut right out from the rock. She kneeled by the bedside and tried to thank God. Then she opened the door. The chief rose at the sound of it.

"What a curious house this is," said Mercy, suddenly feeling very inclined toward tears.

"It is a sort of doll's house my brother and I have been working on for nearly fifteen years. We had planned, when the summer came, to ask you to spend a day with us up here."

"When we first went to work on it," said Ian, "we used to tell each other tales in which the cave always played a key share. Alister's were generally about a lost princess taking refuge in it."

"And now it has come true!" said Alister.

"What an escape I have had!"

"You have been taken care of all the time," said Ian. "Even if you had died in the cold, it would not be because God had forgotten you. You would still not have been lost."

"I wanted to know whether nature would speak to me. But it was of no use! She never came near me."

"I'm sure she did without you knowing her," answered Ian. "But we shall have a talk about that on our way home, when you are quite rested. We must prepare for home now."

Mercy's heart sank. She felt so weak and sleepy. How could she possibly go back over all that rough mountain? But she dared not ask to be left till the morning—with the leopard about!

She soon found that the brothers had never thought of her walking. They wrapped her up in Ian's plaid blanket. Then they took the chief's, which was very strong, and folded it lengthwise; each drew an end of it over his shoulders, letting it hang in a loop between them. In this loop they made her seat herself. After a few shiftings and accomodation, they found they could manage her quite nicely. So they locked the door and left the fire glowing on the solitary hearth.

To Mercy it was the strangest and most wonderful journey—an experience never to be forgotten. The tea had warmed her, and the air revived her. It was not so very cold now, for only now and then blew a little puff of wind. The stars were brilliant overhead, and the wide void of the air between her and the earth below seemed full of wonder and mystery. Now and then she fancied some distant sound to be the cry of the leopard, but even that added to the eerie witchery of the night, making it like a spooky story read in the deserted nursery, with the distant noise of her brothers and sisters outside at play. The motion became very pleasant to her. Sometimes her feet would brush the tops of the heather; but when they came to rocky ground they always shortened the loop of the plaid. In Mercy's inner ear echoed words she had heard at church: "He shall give his angels charge over thee, and in their hands they shall bear thee up, lest at any time thou dash thy foot against a stone." Were not these two men God's own angels?

They scarcely spoke, except when they stopped to catch their breath, but went on and on with a steady, rhythmic, silent trudge. Up and down the rough hill, and upon the less rough hill road, they had plenty to occupy them just heeding their steps. Now and then they would let her walk a little way, but not far. She was neither so strong nor so heavy as a fat deer, they said.

They were yet high among the hills when the pale, withered, wasted shred of the old moon rose above the mountainous horizon. She now accompanied them the rest of their journey, and the witch-like creature brought out the whole character of the night. Rocked in her wonderful swing, Mercy was not always quite sure that she was not dreaming the strangest, pleasantest dream. Were they not fit for a dream, this star-and-moon-filled night—this wind that now and then blew so eerie and wild, yet did not wake her—this gulf around, above, and beneath her, through which she was borne as if she had indeed died, and angels were carrying her through wastes of air to some unknown region afar? Except when she brushed the heather, she forgot that the earth was near her. The arms around her were the arms of men and not angels, but how far above this lower world dwelt the souls that moved within those strong limbs! What a small creature she was beside them! Her awe of the one kept growing; the other she could trust with heart as well as brain; she could never be afraid of him! To the chief she turned to shadow her from Ian.

The men had been watching the sky, and now indeed, just as they reached the valley floor, it began to rain heavily.

So fast did it rain that the men feared for Mercy, turned off the road, and went down a steep descent to make straight across their own fields for the cottage. Just as they reached the bottom of the descent, although they had come all the rough way till then without slipping or stumbling, the chief fell. He rose in consternation; but finding that Mercy had simply dropped on her feet, relieved himself by continued abuse of his clumsiness. Mercy laughed merrily, resumed her place in the blanket, and closed her eyes. She never saw where they were going, for she did not open them again until they stopped a little as they turned into the little clump of firs in front of the door.

"Where are we?" she asked, but for answer they carried her straight into the house.

"We have brought you to our mother instead of yours," said Alister. "To have you get wet from the rain would have been the last straw on the back of such a day. We will let them know at once that you are safe."

Lady Macruadh, as the highlanders generally called her, made haste to receive the poor girl with all the sympathy of her Celtic nature. Mercy's mother had come to her very upset at her daughter's absence and the only comfort she could give her was the suggestion that possibly she had fallen in with her sons. She gave her a warm bath, put her to bed, and then made her eat something to prepare her for a healthful sleep. And she did sleep, but dreamed of darkness and snow and leopards.

The men were out searching in all directions; while Ian went to the New House with the news, Alister lit a beacon on the top of the old castle to signal them to return. By the time Ian had persuaded Mrs. Palmer to leave Mercy in his mother's care for the night, the beacon was blazing beautifully.

By morning Mercy had a bad cold and could not be moved. But the cottage had more than one guest room, and Mrs. Macruadh was delighted to have her to nurse.

When Mercy was able to go down to the drawing room, she found the evenings pass faster than ever before. Although her mother and Christina came often to see her during the day, she had much time and quiet for thinking. And think she must, for she found herself in a region of human life drastically different from any she had ever experienced. Everything said or done seemed to acknowledge something understood. Life went on with a continuous *lean* toward something rarely mentioned, plainly uppermost. The mother and her two sons appeared to know things which her own people did not even suspect.

Under their influence a new idea of life and the world and relationships began to grow in Mercy's mind. There was a dignity, almost a grandeur, about the simple life of the cottage. No one seemed to care for self, but each was always thinking and caring for the others and for the clan. She came to see that such manners are things of the soul, not of *breeding*, as she would have called it. What she had till then heard admired were not even to be compared with the simple, almost peasant-like dignity and courtesy of the chief. And in observing Ian she saw that the moment he began to speak to another, he seemed to pass out of himself and sit in the ears of the other to watch his own words. If his words had to be unpleasant words, they should not hurt except in the nature of what they bore; the truth should receive no injury by mingling with his own personality. He heard with his own soul and was careful over the other soul of his kind. His words and manner were delicate and almost so gracious as to be offensive to a dull or selfish nature.

Through her growing to love Alister, Mercy became able to understand Ian, and finally realized that she disliked him at first only because of her own incapacity and unworthiness. Before she left the cottage springtime had come to her soul; it had begun to put forth the buds of eternal life. In Mercy's case those buds were to grow into spiritual eyes—to open and see, through all the fogs and tumults of this phantom world, the light and reality of the true, the spiritual world everywhere around her. Every throb of true love, however mingled with the foolish and the false, is a bourgeoning of the buds of the life eternal, no matter how far they are yet from leaves, or how much farther from flowers.

Ian seemed high above her, so high that she shrank from him; there seemed a whole heaven between them. She did not realize that this supposed gulf was not one of actual space of personality, but one of motive, of life's attitude, and might be crossed and annihilated at any instant. Nevertheless, it was sweet to Mercy to see in the eyes of Alister, and in his whole bearing, that he was a learner like herself. Though he and Ian were scholars in the same school, toward the chief Mercy felt a kinship while toward Ian she still felt distance.

A hunger after something beyond her awoke in Mercy. She needed something toward which she must grow. She needed a change which she could not understand until it came—the greatest change in the universe.

She began to feel a mystery in the world—a mystery because of a meaning. She came to see jubilance in every sunrise, a sober sadness in every sunset; heard a whispering of strange secrets in the wind of the twilight; perceived a consciousness of unknown bliss in the song of the lark. She was aware of something beyond it all, filling her with wonder, compelling her to ask, "What can it all mean?" Not once did she suspect that nature had indeed begun to deal with her; although from childhood she was accustomed to hear the name of love taken in vain, not once did she suspect that love had anything to do with these inexplicable experiences.

Such experiences can never be explained by saying she was in love! Both are divine mysteries. For who in heaven and earth has fathomed the marvel between man and woman? There is more in this love to uplift us, more to condemn the lie in us, than in any other inborn drift of our being except the heavenly God-bound tide. From it flow all the other redeeming relations of life. It is the hold God has of us with his right hand, while death is the hold he has of us with his left. Love and death are the two marvels, yea, the two terrors—but the one goal of our history.

It was love, in part, that now awoke in Mercy a hunger and thirst after heavenly things. This is a direction of its power little heeded by its historians, for the simple reason that its earthly side occupies almost all their care. Because lovers try to live only in its earthly realm, their very love grows pale and they grow weary—not of love, but of their lack of the fullness of love. The lack of the heavenly in it has caused it to perish: their love had no salt. From those who have not, even what they have is taken away—removed not by a cruel so-called god, but by their own earth-bound selfness. Love without religion is the plucked rose, doomed to wither. Religion without love—there is no such thing. God is the bush that bears all the roses; religion is the natural condition of man in relation to the eternal facts, the truths of his own being. To live is to love; there is no life but love. The poorest love with God is better, because truer, therefore more lasting and more genuine and more possible of infinite development, than the most passionate devotion between man and woman without him.

Thus it was natural that Mercy and the chief should draw together. Mercy regarded Alister as a big brother in the same class with herself, able to help her. In the mere simplicity of his large nature, the chief talked with Mercy as openly as a boy, laying a heart bare to her such that, if the world had many like it, the kingdom of heaven would be more than at hand. Quickly they grew intimate. He talked as to an old friend from whom he had nothing to gain or to fear. There was never a compliment on the part of the man, and never a coyness on the part of the woman. Mercy had never, like her sister, cultivated the woman's part in that low game. She was still an unspoiled girl, with a heart alive though not yet quite awake, that was brought under such good influences. And what better influence for her, or any woman, than an unselfish man? What influence so good for any man than an unselfish woman?

She listened to Ian, and to hear him speak one word about Jesus Christ was to be from that moment truer. To him the Lord was not a theological personage, but a man present in the world, who had to be understood and obeyed by the will and heart and soul, by the imagination and conscience, of every man and woman. If what Ian said was true, this life was a serious affair, and to be lived in downright earnest. She pondered what she heard. But she always went to Alister to have Ian explained; to hear him talk, even as he tried to explain his brother, revealed Alister to her.

When Mercy left the cottage, she felt as if she were leaving home to pay a visit. The rich house was dull and uninteresting. She found that she immediately had to put into practice one of the lessons she had learned—that the service of God is the service of those among whom he has sent us. She tried to be cheerful. But life was harder than before—so much more was now required of her.

The chief was falling thoroughly in love with Mercy, but it was some time before he knew it. With a heart full of tenderness toward everything human, he knew little of love in the particular, and was gradually sliding into it without being aware of it. How little we are our own! Existence is decreed us; love and suffering are appointed us. We may resist, but we cannot help loving, and we cannot help dying. Apart from his choice, the chief was falling in love. The woman was sent him; his heart opened and took her in. Relation with her family was not desirable, but there she was! Ian saw, but said nothing. His mother saw it, too.

"Nothing good will come of it," she said, with a strong feeling of unfitness about the match.

"Everything will come of it, Mother, that God would have come of it," answered Ian. "She is an honest, good girl, and whatever comes of it must be good."

The mother was silent. She believed in God, but not so thoroughly as to repudiate the exercise of a subsidiary providence of her own. The more people trust in God the less they will trust their own judgments or interfere with the ordering of events.

"There is no good that can come of fretting," Ian would say. "True action is the doing of duty, whether heartache, defeat, or success comes of it."

"You are a fatalist, Ian!" said his mother one day.

"Am I? The will of God is my fate. He shall do with me what he pleases."

She took him in her arms and kissed him. She hoped God would not be too hard on him for his peculiar views!

At length came the paternal summons for the Palmers to go to London. For a month the families had been meeting nearly every day. The chief had begun to look deep into the eyes of the girl, as if searching there for some secret joy; and the girl, though she drooped her long lashes, did not turn her head away. Now separation, like death, gave her courage; when they parted, Mercy not only sustained Alister's look, but gave him such a look in return that he felt no need, no impulse to say anything. Their souls were satisfied, for they knew they belonged to each other.

29 / A Terrible Discovery

So completely were the chief and his family out of the world that they had no notion of the worldly relations and business activities of Mr. Peregrine Palmer. But Mrs. Macruadh had an old friend in London, the wife of a certain vice-chancellor, and, thinking it high time to make inquiry as to their neighbor's position and connections, she wrote asking if she knew anything of the family. She was anxious to know that the girl was respectable and worthy of her son. The idea of such an inquiry would have filled Mercy's parents with scornful merriment, ludicrous indeed. People in *their* position, who had family connections with an admiral and a general and some of the oldest names in the country could hardly imagine a yeoman, a man who held the plough with his own hands, inquiring into *their* social standing! Was not Mr. Peregrine Palmer prepared to buy him up the moment he had to sell? Was he not rich enough to purchase an earl's daughter for his son, and an earl himself for his beautiful Christina? Preposterous!

The answer of the vice-chancellor's wife nevertheless burst like a bombshell in the cottage. The Palmers were known, if not in the best, yet in very good society. A distiller in Scotland originally, Mr. Peregrine Palmer had taken to brewing in England. He was the "Palmer" of the firm of Pulp and Palmer, which owned half the public houses in London, and was therefore high in the regard of the English nobility, if not actually within their circle.

Horror fell upon the soul of the mother. The brewer was to her as the publican of the ancient Jew: nothing was half so abominable! Worse yet was a brewer owning public houses, gathering riches a half pence at a time, the coins wet with beer and smelling of gin. And a distiller was even worse. She read the letter, then dropped it from her hands and threw them up in silent appeal to heaven.

To think of the Macruadh marrying the daughter of such a man! In society few questions were asked. Everywhere money was counted a blessed thing, however made. Nonetheless the despicable fact remained that certain moneys were made, not in furthering the well-being of men and women, but in furthering their sin and degradation. Let the world wink its eye blindly, let it hide the roots of the money-plant in layer upon layer of social ascent; the flower for which an earl would give his daughter grew nevertheless in the diseased and dying bodies and souls

185

186

of God's men and women and children.

She started up and paced hurriedly about the room. Her son the son-in-law of a distiller, the husband of his daughter! The very idea was an abhorrence. Was the man not one of the devil's fishers of men, fishing the sea of the world for the souls of men and women? His money was the fungus growth of the devil's wine cellars. How would her son hold up his head if he cast in his lot with a brewer's?

She could not rest. She must find one of her sons. Not a moment longer could she remain alone with the terrible disclosure. If Alister were in love with the girl, he must get out of it at once! Never again would she enter the Palmer's house, never again set foot on their land!

She walked to the end of the ridge and saw Ian with his book on the other side of the stream. She called to him and handed him the letter as she approached. He took it, read it through, and gave it back to her.

"Ian!" she exclaimed, "have you nothing to say to that?"

"I must think about it, Mother. Why should it trouble you so? It is annoying and painful, but we have come under no obligation to them."

"No. But Alister!"

"You cannot doubt that Alister will do what is right!"

"He will do what he thinks right!"

"Is that not enough, Mother?"

"No," she answered angrily. "He must do the thing that is right!"

"Whether he knows it or not? Would you have him do the thing he thought wrong?"

She was silent.

"Mother dear, the only way to get at what is right is to do what seems right. Even if we make mistakes as we go, there is no other way."

"You would do evil that good may come! Oh, Ian!"

"No, Mother. Evil that is not seen to be evil by one willing and trying to do right is not counted evil to him. It is evil only to the person who either knows it to be evil, or does not care whether it is or not."

"That is a dangerous doctrine."

"I will go farther, Mother, and say that for Alister to do what you thought right, if he did not think it right himself—even if you were right and he were wrong—would be for him to do wrong."

"A man may be to blame that he is not able to see the truth," said the mother.

"That is very true, but hardly such a man as Alister. He would sooner die than do something he believed wrong. But why should you take it for granted that Alister will think differently from you?"

"We don't always think alike."

"In matters of right and wrong I never knew him or me to think differently from you, Mother."

"He is very fond of the girl."

"And justly so. I never saw one like her more anxious to learn."

"Nothing would make me trust her."

"Why?"

"She comes of an abominable breed."

"So then is it your part to make her suffer for the sins of her fathers?"

"I make her suffer?"

"Certainly, Mother—by changing your mind toward her and suspecting her, the moment you discover cause to be dissatisfied with her father."

"The sins of the fathers are visited on the children! Will you dispute that?"

"I will grant you even more—that the sins of the fathers are often reproduced in the children. But it is nowhere said, 'Thou shalt visit the sins of the fathers on the children.' God puts no vengeance into our hands. I fear you are in danger of being unjust to the girl. Mother—but then you do not know her so well as we do. The thing is very annoying— let us go and find Alister at once!"

"He will take it like a man of sense, I trust."

"He will! It will trouble him terribly, but he will do as he should. Give him time and I don't believe there is a man in the world to whom the right comes out clearer than to Alister."

The mother only answered with a sigh.

"Many a man," remarked Ian, "has been saved through what men call an unfortunate love affair."

"Many a man has been lost by having his own way in one!" rejoined the mother.

"As to *lost* I would not make up my mind about that for a few centuries or so!" returned Ian. "A man may be allowed his own way for the discipline to result from it."

"I trust, Ian, you will not encourage him in any folly!"

"I shall have nothing to do but encourage him in his resolve to do what he thinks is the truth, Mother!"

They went out but could not find Alister, who had gone to the smithy. It was teatime before he came home. As soon as he entered, his mother handed him the letter.

He read it without a word, laid it on the table beside his plate, and began to drink his tea, his eyes gleaming with a strange light. Ian kept silence also. Mrs. Macruadh cast a quick glance—now at the one, now at the other. She was in great anxiety and could hardly restrain herself.

She knew her boys full of inbred dignity and conscience, but was nevertheless doubtful how they would act. Had she searched herself she might have discovered a latent dread that they might be nearer the right than she.

The reward of parents who have tried to be good may be to learn, with a joyous humility, from their children. Mrs. Macruadh was capable of learning more, and was now going to have a lesson.

When Alister pushed back his chair and rose, she could refrain no longer. She could not let him go on in silence. She must understand something of what was going on in his mind.

"What do you think of *that*, Alister?" she said.

He turned to her with a faint smile.

"I am glad to know it, Mother."

"I was afraid it would hurt you."

"Seeing the thing is so, I am glad to be made aware of it. You cannot expect me to be pleased with the information?"

"No, indeed. I am very sorry for you. After being so pleased with the young woman—"

Alister looked straight in his mother's face.

"You do not imagine, Mother," he said, "that it will make any difference about Mercy?"

"Not make any difference?" echoed Mrs. Macruadh. "What can you possibly mean, Alister?"

The anger that glowed in her dark eyes made her look yet handsomer, proving itself not a mean, though it might be a misplaced anger.

"Is she different, Mother, from what she was before the letter?"

"You did not then know what she was."

"I knew then just as well as I do now. This tells me nothing about *her*. I have no reason to think she is not what I thought her."

"You thought her the daughter of a gentleman!"

"Hardly. I need no information such as this to tell me Mr. Palmer is not a gentleman. I thought Mercy a lady, and such I think her still."

"Then you mean to go on with it?"

"Mother dear," said Alister, taking her by the hand, "give me a little time. Not that I am in any doubt—but the news has been a blow. I do not want to answer out of the soreness of my pride."

"I am quite willing you should do nothing in a hurry."

"I will take time, and here is Ian to help me."

"If only your father were here! He would sooner see a son of his marry the daughter of a cobbler than a brewer."

"So would I, Mother," said Alister.

"You will be back by suppertime, I suppose," said the mother as her sons walked toward the door.

"Certainly. We are only going to the village."

The brothers went.

"I knew everything you were thinking," said Ian.

"Of course you did!" answered Alister.

"I am very sorry."

"So am I."

A pause followed. Then Alister burst into a laugh that was not merry.

"It makes me think of something father said once," he said. "Once at the market he was putting a bunch of unusually dirty bank notes in his pocket. My look must have conveyed that I doubted their value because of the dirt. 'They're better than they look, lad,' he said."

"What *are* you thinking, Alister, not that Mr. Palmer's money is as good as money that had been honorably made!"

"Of course not," said Alister; "just the opposite. Mr. Palmer's money is *worse* than it looks."

"You frightened me for a moment."

"How could I, Ian?"

"You're right. I know you well enough. But I see trouble ahead."

"We shall be called a pack of fools for standing by our principles in this."

"I would rather see you hanged than pocketing a shilling of that man's money."

"It is not the man's money, only his daughter I care about. I wouldn't dare pocket a shilling of his money."

"There will be difficulty, Alister. How much have you said to Mercy?"

"I have *said* nothing definite."

"But she understands."

"I think—I hope so. But don't you think Christina is much improved, Ian?"

"She is more pleasant."

"She is quite attracted to you."

"She is pleased with me for saving her life. She does not like me— and I have just arrived at the point of not disliking her."

"There is a great change on her."

"I doubt if there is much *in* her, though."

"I daresay she is only amusing herself with us in this outlandish place. Mercy, I am sure, is quite different."

"I think you are right. I quite trust her. So what will you do?"

"I will go to Mr. Palmer and say to him: 'Give me your daughter, sir. I am but a poor man, but we shall have enough to live upon. I believe she will be happy.' "

"I will tell you what he will answer. He will say: 'I have the greatest regard for you, Macruadh. You are a gentleman, and that you are poor is not of the slightest consequence to me. Mercy's dowry shall be worthy of the lady of a chief!' What then, Alister?"

"Fathers that love money would be glad to get rid of their daughters without a dowry."

"Perhaps when they are misers, or when money is scarce. But when a poor man of position wanted to marry his daughter, a man like Mr. Palmer would no doubt regard her dowry as a good investment. You will not escape that way, Alister. What would you answer him?"

"I would say, 'My dear sir, I do not want your money. Simply give me your daughter, and my soul will bless you.' "

"Suppose he should reply, 'Do you think I am going to send my daughter from my house like a beggar? No, no, my boy! She must carry something with her. If beggars married beggars, the world would be full of beggars!' What would you say then?"

"I would tell him I had conscientious scruples about taking his money."

"He would tell you you were a fool and not to be trusted with a wife. 'Who ever heard such rubbish!' he would say. 'Scruples, indeed! You must get over them!' What would you say then?"

"If it came to that, I would have no choice but to tell him I had strong objections to the way his fortune was made and could not consent to share it."

"He would protest and consider himself greatly insulted, and swear that if his money was not good enough for you, then neither was his daughter."

"Then I would appeal to Mercy."

"She is too young. It would be sad to set one of her years at variance with her family. I almost think I would rather you ran away with her. It is a terrible thing to go into a house and destroy the peace of those relationships within it."

"I know! I know! That is my trouble. I am not afraid of Mercy's consent, and I believe she would hold out for me till she came of age. I am certain nothing would make her marry the man she did not love. But to turn the house into a hell about her—I can't do that! The whole thing involves delicate and very difficult questions. Do you think I must have every avenue thought out before taking the first step?"

"Indeed I do not. The first step is enough. When that step has been taken, it is time to worry about the next. But above all, you must not lose your temper with the man, however despicable his money. It may be that he will not think you half good enough for Mercy, without mention ever being made of the money."

"That would be a grand way out of the difficulty!"

"In any case, the more you can honestly avoid reference to his money, the better. We are not called upon to rebuke."

Arriving at the village, they found Annie of the shop in a sad way. She had just had a letter from Lachlan saying that he had not been well for some time and that there was little prospect of his being able to fetch her himself. He asked her to come to him, and had sent money to pay her passage and her mother's.

"When do you go?" asked the chief.

"My mother fears the voyage and is very unwilling to turn her back on her own country. But what if Lachlan should die without me with him?"

She could say no more.

"He shall not die for want of you," said the chief. "I will talk to your mother."

He went into the room in the back of the shop, while Ian remained with Annie.

"Of course you must go, Annie," he said.

"I know I must. But I don't know how to persuade my mother. And I cannot leave her, even for Lachlan. No one would nurse him more tenderly than she, but she has a horror of the salt water, and she dreads being buried in it."

"My brother will persuade her."

"I hope so, sir."

In a few moments Alister came from the back room.

"I don't think your mother will see it as quite so difficult now," he said.

The next time the brothers went to the shop, they found Annie and her mother preparing to go.

Ian had nearly finished the book he was writing about Russia and could not begin another all at once. Neither could he stay at home doing nothing. He thought that as things were going from bad to worse in the highlands, he might go to Canada also to visit those of his clan and see what ought to be done for the others who must soon follow. He would presently have a little money in his possession and believed he could not spend it better. Therefore he made up his mind to accompany Annie and her mother. He did not want to leave Alister at such a critical point in his life. But he said to himself that a man might be helped too much, and it might turn out that he and Mercy were in as much need of a refuge in the new world as the clan.

I cannot say *no* worldly pride mingled in the chief's contempt for the distiller's money; his righteous soul was not yet clear of its inherited judgments. He had in him still the prejudice of the landholder, for ages instinctive, against both manufacture and trade, not seeing that nothing the Father of men has decreed can in its nature be contemptible, but must be capable of being nobly done. In all that must be done, the doer ranks in God's sight, and ought to rank among his fellowmen, according to how he does it. The higher the calling, the more contemptible the man who pursues his own ends in it. And the humblest calling, followed on the principles of God, is a true and divine calling, be it handicraft, shopkeeping, shoemaking, or bookbinding. Oh, for the day when God and not the king shall be regarded as the fountain of honor!

But the Macruadh regarded the calling of brewer or distiller as from the devil. From childhood his mother had taught him that the worst of all justifications toward some wrong was the lie, *If I do not do this, another will; there will be just as much harm done, and another instead of me will have the benefit; therefore it cannot defile me, so I will do it.* Imagine our Lord in the brewing trade instead of the carpentering! Much as the Macruadh loved Mercy, he could *not* take such money with her, no matter how clearly she was to him a woman undefiled and straight from God.

After much consideration, it was determined in the family conclave that Ian should accompany the two women to Canada, note how things were going, and decide what had best be done should further exodus be found necessary. As better news of Lachlan followed soon after the previous letter, they planned, for several reasons, to start in the month of September, and a few other of the poorest of the clan resolved to go with them.

30 / Love

Christina went back to London considerably changed. Her beauty was greater, for there was a new element in it—a certain atmosphere of distances and shadows giving her countenance a mystery. She was now subject to changes which made her more attractive to many. Fits of wild gaiety alternated with glooms. She had more admirers than ever, for she had developed points capable of interesting men of higher development than before. But gladly would she have thrown away all the flattery she had once so coveted for one approving smile from the sad-looking, gracious man, whom she knew happier wandering alone over the hills than if she were walking by his side. For an hour she would persuade herself that he cared for her a little; the next she would comfort herself with the small likelihood of his meeting another lady in Glenruadh. But he had, after all, been a traveler and had seen so much of the great world!

She had tried on him her little arts of subjugation, but the moment she began to love him she not only saw their uselessness, but hated them. Her repulsion of her admirers and her occasional oddity caused her mother some anxiety; but as the London season came to a close, and the time approached when they would again make Scotland their temporary abode, she grew gayer and was at times absolutely bewitching. The mother wished to go northward slowly, paying visits along the way. But her plan met with no approval from the girls. Christina longed for the presence and voice of Ian in the cottage parlor, Mercy for a hillside with the chief. And they talked so of the delights of their highland home that the mother began to feel the mountains, the sea, and the islands drawing her to a land of peace where things went well and the world knew how to live. Little did she know that the stormiest months of her life were about to pass among those peaceful, silent mountains!

After a long and eager journey, the girls once more found themselves in their rooms at the New House. Mercy went to her window and stood gazing from it upon the mountain-world, faint-lighted by the northern twilight. She could see the dark bulk of the hills, sharpened to a clear edge against the horizon. By the shape of a small top that rose against the greenish sky between the parting lines of two higher hills, she could see the roof of what Alister and Ian called *the tomb*; she thought how, just below there, away as it seemed in the high-lifted solitudes of heaven, she had lain in the clutches of death, all the time watched and defended by the angel of a higher life who had been with her ever since she first came to Glenruadh, waking her out of such a stupidity of nonexistence as she now could scarcely see possible. True, her waking had been one with her love to that man who was her window to God. But why should that make her doubt? God made man and woman to love each other. Why should not the waking to love and the waking to truth come together? Both were of God. If the chief were never to speak to her again, she would never go back from what she had learned of him. If she ever became careless of truth and life and God, it would only show that she had never truly loved the chief!

As she stood gazing on the hilltop, high landmark of her history, she felt as if the earth were holding her up toward heaven, an offering to the higher life. A deep contentment pervaded her heart. She turned with her weight of peace, lay down, and went to sleep in the presence of her life.

Christina also looked from her window, but her thoughts were not like Mercy's; her heart was mainly filled, not with love of Ian, but with the desire that Ian should love her. She had changed, but not so thoroughly as Mercy. Her soul kept leaning toward Ian; she longed for his arms to shut out the alien nature lying so self-satisfied all about her. To her the presence of God took shape as an emptiness—an absence. She was hungry, not merely after bliss, but after distinction in bliss; not after growth, but after superiority. She had yet to learn the most foundational of all lessons—that she was nobody. Still, by her need of another, God was laying hold of her. As by the law is the knowledge of sin, so by love is selfishness rampantly roused—to be at last, like death, swallowed up in victory—the victory of the ideal self that dwells in God.

All night she dreamed sad dreams of Ian in the embrace of a lovely woman. She woke weeping and said to herself that it could not be. He *could* not be taken from her. Soul, brain, and heart claimed him as hers! How could another possess what her whole consciousness told her was hers and hers alone! Love asserts an innate and irreversible right of profoundest property in the person loved. It is an instinct—but how wrongly and falsely interpreted!

But the girl in her dejection and doubt was worth far more than in her contentment and confidence. She was even now the richer by the knowledge of sorrow; she was on the way to know that she needed help, on the way toward truly knowing herself, and thus on the way toward becoming capable of loving. Life could never be the same as it had been to her, and the farther from it the better.

In the morning Mercy was fresh and rosy, with a luminous mist of loveliness over plain unfinished features. Already they had begun to change in the direction of beauty. Christina's eyes burned; in Mercy's shone something of the light by which a soul may walk and not stumble. In the eyes of both was expectation, one confident, the other anxious.

As soon as they found themselves alone together, eyes sought eyes and met in understanding. They had not made confidantes of each other—each guessed well, and was well guessed at. They did not speculate; they understood.

Without a word they rose, put on their hats, left the house, and took the road toward the valley. About halfway to the root of the ridge, they came in sight of the ruined castle. Mercy stopped with a little cry.

"Look, Chrissy!" she said, pointing.

On the corner of the castle nearest them, up on the turret, sat the two men in what seemed a dangerous position, but what was to the mountaineers a comfortable vantagepoint. The girls both thought, *They are watching for us!*

The men waved their caps. Christina responded with her handkerchief. The men disappeared from their perch and were with the ladies before they reached the ridge. There was no embarrassment on either side, though a few cheeks were rosier than usual. To the chief Mercy was far beyond his memory of her. Not her face only, but her very movement bore witness to a deeper pleasure, a greater freedom in life than before.

"Why were you in such a dangerous place?" asked Christina.

"We were looking out for you," answered Alister. "From there we could see you the moment you came out."

"Why didn't you come and meet us, then?"

"Because we wanted to watch you coming."

"Spies! I hope we were behaving ourselves properly, Mercy."

"We thought you had quarreled; neither of you said a word to the other."

Mercy looked up; Christina looked down.

"Could you hear us all that way?" asked Mercy.

"How could we when there was not a word to hear!"

"How did you know we were silent?"

"We might have known by the way you walked," replied Alister. "But if you had spoken we should have heard, for sound travels far among the mountains."

"It's shameful!" said Christina. "What if we had objected to your hearing us?"

"We never thought of that," said Alister. "I am very sorry."

"Oh, you men always take everything so seriously!" cried Christina, "as if we could have anything to say we should not wish *you* to hear!"

She put a little emphasis on the *you*, but not much. Alister heard it as if Mercy had said it, and smiled a pleased smile.

"But was it not a dangerous place to be in?"

"It is a little crumbly," confessed Ian. "That reminds me, Alister, we must have a bout at repairing the old walls before long! Ever since Alister was ten years old," he went on in explanation to Christina, "he and I have been patching and repairing the old hulk—the stranded ship of our poor fortunes. I showed you, did I not, the ship in our coat of arms—the galley at least, in which, they say, we arrived at the island just near here?"

"Yes, I remember. But you don't mean you do mason's work as well as everything else?" exclaimed Christina.

"Come; we will show you," said the chief.

"What do you do it for?"

The brothers exchanged glances.

"Would you consider it sufficient reason," returned Ian, "that we desired to preserve its testimony to the former status of our family?"

A pang of pleasure shot through Christina's heart. Passion will always twist in its favor whatever can possibly be so twisted. In the eyes of a man of the world like her father, an old name was nothing beside new money! Still, an old castle was always an old castle! And that he cared about it for her sake made it to her at least worth something. Before she could make an answer, Ian went on, "But in truth," he said, "we have always had a vague hope of its restoration. The dream of our boyhood was to rebuild the castle. Every year it has grown more hopeless and keeps receding. But we have come to see how little it matters, and thus we content ourselves with keeping up, for old love's sake, what is left of the ruin."

"How do you get up on the walls?" asked Mercy.

"Ah, that is a secret!" said Ian.

"Do tell us," pleaded Christina.

"If you want very much to know—" answered Ian, a little doubtfully.

"I do, I do."

"Then I suppose we must tell you! There is a stair," Ian went on, "no one but our two selves knows anything about. Such stairs are common in old houses—far commoner than people in towns have a notion of. But there would not have been much of it left by this time if we hadn't taken care of it. We were little fellows when we began, and it needed much effort, for we were not able to remove the remnants of the broken steps and replace them with new ones."

"Do show us," begged Christina.

"We will keep it for some warm twilight," said Alister. "Mornings are not for ruins. Yon mountainside is calling to us. Will you come, Mercy?"

"Oh yes!" cried Christina. "That will be much better! Come, Mercy! You are up to a climb, I am sure!"

"I ought to be, after such a long rest."

"You may have forgotten how to climb!" said Alister.

"I dreamed too much of the hills for that! And always the noise of London was changed into the rush of waters."

They had dropped a little behind the other pair.

"Did you always climb your dream-hills alone?" asked Alister.

She answered him with just a lift of her big dark eyes.

They walked slowly down the road till they came to Mrs. Conal's path, passed her door unassailed, and went up the hill.

31 / Ian and Christina

It was a glorious morning, and as they climbed, the air made their spirits rise with their steps. Great masses of cloud hung beyond the edge of the world. The sun was strong and poured down floods of light, but his heat was deliciously tempered by the mountain atmosphere. There was no wind—only an occasional movement as if the air itself were breathing—just enough to let them feel they moved in no vacuum, but in the heart of a gentle ocean.

They came to the hut chiefly inhabited by Hector of the Stags and Rob of the Angels. It commanded a wonderful view. In every direction rose a cone-shaped hill. The world lay in colored waves before them, wild, rugged, and grand, with sheltering spots of beauty between and the shine of lowly waters. They tapped at the door of the hut, but there was no response. They lifted the latch—it had no lock—and found neither of the men inside.

Alister and Mercy wandered a little higher, to the shadow of a great stone. Christina went inside the hut and looked from its door upon the world. Ian leaned against the side of it and up to the sky. Suddenly a few great drops fell—it was hard to say from where. The scattered clouds had been drawing a little nearer the sun, but had hardly looked threatening. But suddenly a swift rain, like a rain of the early summer, began to fall, and grew to a heavy shower. They were glorious drops that made that shower, for the sun still shone and every drop was a falling gem, shining, sparkling like a diamond as it fell. It was a bounteous rain, falling in straight lines from heaven to earth. It needed only sound to complete its charm, and that the bells of the heather gave, set ringing by the drops. The heaven was filled with blue windows, and the rain seemed to come from them rather than from the clouds. Into the rain rose the heads of the mountains, each clothed in thin mist. They seemed rising on tiptoe heavenward, eager to drink of the highborn comfort; for the rain comes down not upon the mown grass only, but upon the solitary and desert places also where grass will never be—"the playgrounds of the young angels," Rob called them.

"Do come in," said Christina; "you will get all wet!"

He turned toward her. She stepped back and he entered. Like one a little weary, he sat down on Hector's old chair.

"Is anything the matter?" asked Christina with concern.

She saw that he was not quite like himself, that there was an unusual expression on his face. He gave a faint apologetic smile.

"As I stood there," he answered, "a strange feeling came over me—a foreboding, I suppose you would call it."

He paused, and Christina grew a little pale.

"Won't you tell me what it was?"

"It was an odd kind of feeling that the next time I stood there, it would not be in the body. I think I shall not come back."

"Come back!" echoed Christina, fear beginning to tug at the edges of her heart. "Where are you going?"

"I start for Canada next week."

She turned deadly white and put out her hands, feeling blindly after support. Ian jumped to his feet.

"We have tired you out!" he said in alarm, taking her by both hands to place her in the chair.

She did not hear him. The world had grown dark about her. The moment she felt supported she began to come to herself. There was no pretense, however, in her faintness. And there was nothing but misery and affection that made her lay her head on Ian's shoulder and burst into a fit of weeping. Unused to real emotion, when it came she did not know how to deal with it, and it overpowered her.

"Oh! oh!" she cried between her sobs. "I am ashamed of myself. I can't help it! What will you think of me!"

Ian had not even guessed the state of things. The cold shower seemed to flood his soul; the bright drops descending with such swiftness of beauty turned at once into points of icy steel that pierced his heart. But he must not worry about himself! He must speak to her. He must say something through the shroud that enfolded them.

"You are safe with me," he faltered, "—as safe as with your mother."

"I know it," she answered, still sobbing, but looking up with an expression of genuine integrity such as he had never seen on her face before. "But I *am* sorry!" she went on. "It is very weak, and very, very un—un—womanly of me. But it came upon me all at once! Why didn't you prepare me for it? You might have known what it would do to me to hear it so suddenly."

Ian grew all the more aghast! What was to be done? What was left for a man to do when a woman laid her soul before him? Was he to lie to save her from bitterest humiliation? Once he had found it impossible to refuse a woman even where he could not give, and had let her take his soul! But that was once, and forever. It could not be done again!

"I am very sorry!" he murmured, and the words and their tone sent a shiver through Christina's heart.

But now that she had betrayed her secret, the pent-up tide of her emotion rushed to the door. She was reckless. Passion, like a lovely wild beast, had mastered her, and she did not try to tame it.

"If you speak to me like that," she cried, "my heart will break! Must you go away?"

"Dear Miss Palmer—" faltered Ian.

"Oh!" she cried, with a world of bitterness in the protest.

"—do let us be calm," continued Ian. "We shall not come to anything if we lose ourselves this way!"

The *we* and *us* gave her little hope.

"How can I be calm?" she cried. "I am not coldhearted like you! You are going away and I shall never see you again to all eternity!"

She burst out weeping afresh.

"Do love me a little before you go," she sobbed. "You gave me my life once, but does that make it right to take it from me again!"

"God knows," said Ian, "if my life could serve you, I should count it a small thing to yield! But this is useless talk. A man must not pretend anything. We must not be untrue."

She thought he did not believe in her.

"I know! I know! You may well distrust me!" she returned. "I have often betrayed you horribly. But I am being true now. I dare not tell you a lie! To you I *must* speak the truth, for I love you with my whole soul."

Ian stood dumb. His look of consternation and misery brought her a little to herself.

"What have I done!" she cried, and stepping back a step, stood looking at him shaking. "I am disgraced! I told a man I love him, and he leaves me to the shame of it! How can you do this to me, Ian?"

"I must be true!" said Ian in a voice altogether unlike his own.

"You will not love me! You despise me!"

Ian took her hand. It trembled as if she would pull it away and her eyes flashed in an angry fire. She looked more nearly beautiful than he had ever seen her. His heart was about to break. He drew her to the chair, and taking a stool, sat down beside her.

"Let me speak to you, Christina Palmer," he said with a voice that gathered strength as it went, "as in the presence of him who made us. To pretend I love you would be easier than to bear the pain of giving you such pain. If I was selfish enough I could take delight in accepting your love. But my love is not mine to give."

It was some relief to her proud heart to imagine he would have loved her had he been free. But she did not speak.

"If I thought," pursued Ian, "that by some behavior of mine I had been to blame for this—" He stopped, not wanting to seem to lay blame on her. "I think," he resumed, "I could help you if you would listen to me. Ah, Christina, if you but knew my Father in heaven and could tell him everything, you would not break your heart that a man did not love you just as you loved him."

Had not her misery been so great, and had she not been so humbled before herself, Christina would have been indignant with the man who refused her love and dared speak to her of religion. But she was now too broken for resentment.

The diamond rain was falling, the sun was shining in his strength, but to Christina the world was as black and blank as the gloomy hut in which they sat. When first her love blossomed, she saw the world open; she looked into its heart; she saw it alive. Now the vision was over, the desert was dull and dry, the bush burned no more. There was no God nor man anymore. Time had closed and swept the world into the limbo of vanity. For a time she sat without a thought, as in a mental sleep. She opened her eyes, but the emptiness and loneliness overpowered her. Hardly aware of what she was doing, she slid to her knees at Ian's feet, crying, "Save me, Ian, save me! I shall go mad. Help me!"

"All a man may be to his sister, I am ready to be to you. I will write to you from Canada; you can answer me or not as you please. My heart cries out to me to take you in my arms and comfort you. But I must not. It would not comfort you."

"You do not despise me, then? Oh, thank you!"

"Despise you! No more than my dead sister! I would cherish you as I would her were she in similar sorrow. I would die to save you from this grief—except that I hope good will come of it."

"Forget all about me," said Christina, summoning pride to her aid.

"I will not forget you. It is impossible. And I wouldn't even if I could."

"You forgive me then, and will not think badly of me?"

"Forgive you? What have you done? Is it an offense that you trust me?"

"I have lost your good opinion! How could I degrade myself so?"

"On the contrary, you are fast gaining my good opinion. You have begun to be a true woman!"

"What if it should be only for—"

"Whatever it may have been for, now that you have tasted truth, you will not turn back."

"But now that I know you do not care for me, I fear I shall soon sink back into my old self."

"I do care for you, Christina, and you will not sink back into your old self. God means you to be a strong, good woman. Believe me, you and I may come nearer to each other in the ages ahead of us by being both true than would be possible in any other way whatever."

"I am miserable at the thought of what you must think of me. Everyone would say I had done a shameless thing in confessing my love!"

"I am not in the habit of thinking as everybody thinks. You are safe with me."

"You will not tell anybody?"

"You must trust me. Your confession, instead of putting you in my power, makes me your servant."

By this time Christina was calm. There was a great load on her heart, but somehow she was aware of the possibility of carrying it. She looked gratefully into Ian's eyes, already beginning to feel for him a reverence which made it easier to let go of the desire to put her arms round him. And with that feeling arose the first movement of divine relationship, though it appeared first as resistance. But complaint against God is far nearer to God than indifference about him.

"Ian Macruadh," said Christina solemnly, "how can you believe there is a God? If there were, would he allow such a dreadful thing? How am I to blame? I could not help it."

"He will let you see the why of it in his time. But you can be sure there is nothing in it but his truth and goodness toward his child. The thing is between him and you."

"It will be hard to convince me it is either good or loving to make anyone suffer like this!" protested Christina, "and all the disgrace of it too!"

"I see no disgrace," returned Ian. "But I will not try to convince you of anything about God. I cannot. You must know him. I only tell you I believe in him with all my heart. You must ask him to explain himself to you, and not take it for granted that he has done you a wrong because he has done what you do not like. Whether you seek him or not, he will do you justice. But he cannot explain himself unless you seek him."

"I think I understand. Believe me, I am willing to understand."

A few long seconds of silence followed. Christina came a little nearer.

"Will you kiss me once," she said, "as you would a little child?"

"In the name of God," answered Ian, and stooped to kiss her gently and tenderly.

"Thank you," she said, "and now the rain is over, let us join Mercy and the chief. I hope they are not soaked."

"Alister will have taken care of that. There is plenty of shelter around here."

They left the cottage, drew the door closed, and went up the hill through the heather, sparkling with a thousand raindrops, the sun shining hotter than ever through the rain-mist.

They found the other pair sheltered by the great stone which was not only a shadow from the heat but sloped sufficiently to be a cover from the rain. They did not know it had ceased; perhaps they did not know it had rained.

On a fine morning of the following week, the emigrants began the first stage of their long journey, the women in two carts, the men walking—Ian with them, a stout stick in his hand. They were to sail from Greenock near Glasgow.

Ian and Christina met several times before he left, but never alone. No conference of any kind, not even of eyes, had been sought by Christina, and Ian had resolved to say nothing until he reached Canada. From there he would write things which pen and ink would say better and carry nearer home than could speech. And by that time, too, the first bitterness of her pain would have dulled and left her mind more capable of receiving them. He was greatly pleased with the general calm of her behavior. No one else could have seen any difference, but he read in her carriage that of a child who had been humbled but was not angry. Her mother noted that her cheek was pale and that she seemed thoughtful. To Ian it was plain she had made up her mind to be reasonable.

32 / The Chief's Quandary_____

Ian's mother, now that the light of her eyes was gone, felt forsaken. Alister was too much occupied with Mercy to feel his departure as on former occasions, yet he missed him every hour of the day. Mercy and he met, but not for some time in open company, as Christina refused to go near the cottage. Things were moving toward a change.

Alister's occupation with Mercy did not keep him from increasing his attention to his mother, but she was not quite the same to him now. At times she was even more tender; at other times she seemed to hold him away from her. The fear came to him that she might speak to one of the Palmers so as to raise a barrier between the families, and this fear made him resolve to come at once to an understanding with Mercy. That his mother did not like the alliance had to be braved, for a man must leave father and mother to cleave to his wife—a principle commonly inverted by male presumption.

Talking over possibilities among themselves, Mr. Peregrine Palmer had agreed with his wife that, Mercy being so far from a beauty, it might not be such a bad match, at least not one to be ashamed of, if she did marry the impoverished chief of a highland clan, with a baronetcy in his pocket. Having bought the land so cheap, he could afford to let a part of it, perhaps even the whole, go back with his daughter, thus restoring to its former position an ancient and honorable family. The husband of his younger daughter would then be head of one of the very few highland families in possession of their ancestral acres—a distinction he would owe to Peregrine Palmer! The thought was pleasant to the kindly, common, little man. Mrs. Palmer, therefore, when the chief called upon her, received him with more than her previous cordiality.

His mother would have been glad to see him return from his call somewhat dejected, but he entered so radiant and handsome that her heart sank within her. Was she actually on the point of being allied through the child of her bosom to a distiller and brewer—a man who had grown rich on the ruin of thousands of his fellow countrymen? She was prepared for any poverty, she said, but how was she to endure disgrace? Alas for the clan whose history was about to cease!

Thus bitterly spoke the mother. She brooded and scorned and raged inwardly, and the chief's heart was troubled by it. He must make haste to have the whole thing settled!

204

He had arranged to meet Mercy the same evening, and long before the time went to watch for her coming. He climbed the hill and lay down in the heather where he could see the door of the New House. He lay there until the sun was down and the stars began to appear. At length he saw the door open and Mercy walk slowly to the gate. He rose and went down the hill. She saw him, watched him as he came, and the moment he reached the road, went to meet him. They walked slowly down the road without a word spoken, until they felt themselves alone.

"You look so lovely!" said the chief.

"In the twilight, I suppose," said Mercy.

"Perhaps; you are a creature of the twilight with your great black eyes."

"I don't like you to speak to me so. You never did before. You know I am not lovely. I am very plain!"

She was evidently not pleased.

"What have I done to upset you, Mercy?" he asked. "Why should you mind my saying what is true?"

She bit her lip and could hardly speak to answer him. Often in London she had been sickened by the false rubbish talked to her sister and had boasted to herself that the chief had never paid her a compliment. Now he had done it!

She took her hand from his arm.

"I think I will go home," she said.

Alister stopped and turned to her. The last gleam of the west was reflected from her eyes and all the sadness of the fading light seemed to gather in them.

"My child," he said, all that was fatherly in the chief rising at the sight, "who has been making you unhappy?"

"You," she answered, looking him in the face.

"How? I do not understand."

"You have just paid me a compliment—a thing you never did before—a thing I never heard before from anyone but a fool. How could you say I was beautiful? It breaks my heart to think *you* could say what you don't believe."

"Mercy!" said the chief, "if I said you were beautiful, and to my eyes you were not, it would yet be true; for to my heart, which sees deeper than my eyes, you are more beautiful than any other ever was or ever will be. I know you are not beautiful in the world's meaning, but you are very lovely, and it was *lovely* I said you were!"

"Lovely because you love me! Is that what you meant?"

"Yes, that and more. Your eyes are beautiful, and your hair is beautiful, and your expression is lovely. But I am not flattering you—I am not even paying you compliments, for those things are not yours. God made them and has given them to me."

She put her hand in his arm again, and there was no more talk in that direction.

"But, Mercy," said the chief when they had walked some distance without speaking, "do you think you could live here always and never see London again?"

"I would not care if London ceased to exist," she answered.

"Could you be content to be a farmer's wife?"

"If he was a very good farmer," she answered.

"Am I a good enough farmer, then?"

"Good enough if I were ten times better. Do you really mean it, Macruadh?"

"With all my heart. Only there is one thing I am very anxious about."

"What is that?"

"How your father will take my condition."

"I think he will allow that it is good enough for me—and more than I deserve."

"That is not what I mean. It is—that I have a certain condition to make."

"Else you won't marry me? That seems strange. Of course, I will do anything you would wish me to do. *A condition!*" she repeated ponderingly.

"Yes," rejoined Alister, "a condition. I hope with all my heart it will not offend him. I don't think it will offend you."

"Let me hear your condition," said Mercy, looking at him curiously, her honest eyes shining in the faint light.

"I want him to let me take you just as you are, without having to take a shilling of his money to spoil the gift. I want you in and for yourself."

"I dare not think you one who would rather not be obliged to his wife for anything!" said Mercy. "That cannot be it!"

She spoke with just a shade of displeasure. He did not answer. He was in great dread of hurting her and his plain reason could not fail to hurt her.

"Well," she resumed, "there are fathers, I daresay, who would be grateful for a condition like that."

"Of course your father will not like the idea of your marrying so poor a man!"

"If he should insist on your having something with me, you will not refuse, will you? Why should you mind it?"

Alister was silent. The thing had already begun to grow dreadful. How could he tell her his reasons? Was it necessary to tell her? If he had to explain, it must be to her father, not to her. How could he reveal the horrible fact that her father was despised by her lover? She might believe it her part to refuse such a love. He trembled lest Mercy should urge him to explain. But thinking she had already been too bold, she held her peace.

They tried to talk about other things, but without success, and when they parted it was with a sense on both sides that something had come between them. Mercy could hardly sleep through the night for trying to discover what his aversion to her dowry might mean. It was impossible his great soul should grudge his wife's superiority in the one poor trifle of money! Was not his whole family superior to money? What else could it be that the chief despised the origin of her father's riches?

But she had no suspicion of anything more than landed pride looking down upon manufacture and trade. She suspected no moral root of even a share in the chief's difficulty. Naturally, she was offended. But was the chief, whatever his pride, capable of being ungenerous? Questions like these kept coming and going throughout the night. The morning came, the sun rose, and she could not find rest. She had come to see how ideally delightful it was just to await God's will of love, yet, in this first trouble, she actually *forgot* to think of God, never asked him to look after the thing for her, never said "Thy will be done."

Alister missed Ian sorely. He prayed to God but was too troubled to feel him near. Imagined trouble may seem easy to meet; actual trouble is quite another thing. His mother, perhaps, was to have her desire; perhaps Mercy would not marry a man who disapproved of her family. The thing had already come between them. It could not be talked about; he could not set free his heart to her!

When Mercy woke, the old love was awake also: let Alister's reasons be what they might, she had no reason to resent it! The life he led was so much grander than a life spent in making money that he must feel himself superior. And was he not, indeed, in a far nobler position in being allowed to influence the hearts and characters of men than money could give him? From her night of doubt and bitterness, Mercy came out more loving and humble. *What would I be like now*, she said to herself, *if Alister had not taught me*? He had been better to her than her father or brothers. She would trust him! She would believe him right! If he had hurt her pride, it was well her pride should be hurt!

Alister knew he would continue in pain and anxiety until he had spoken to her father. But he felt that the time for such a meeting was not yet, not until Mercy had had more time to understand principles

which, born and brought up as she had been, she might not yet be able
to see into. Then it would be time to explain to her, and then to her
father. Till her father came north, therefore, he would avoid the subject!

All morning he was busy in the cornyard—preparing new stances
for ricks with his hands, while with his heart he tried to content himself
beforehand with whatever fate the Lord might intend for him. As yet he
was more of a Christian philosopher than a philosophical Christian. He
was working in the region of his own imagination rather than in the
revealed will of God. If this should not prove to be the will of God
concerning him, then he was spending his strength for nothing. There
is something in the very presence and actuality of a thing to make one
able to bear it; but a man may weaken himself for bearing what God
intends him to bear, by trying to bear what God does not intend him to
bear. The chief was being anxious about the morrow like an unbeliever—
not without some moral advantage, I daresay, but with spiritual loss.
We have no right to school ourselves concerning an imaginary duty.
When we do not know, then what he lays upon us is *not to know* and to
be content not to know. The philosopher lives in the thought of things,
the Christian lives in the things themselves. The philosopher occupies
himself with God's decree, the Christian with God's will; the philosopher with what God may intend, the Christian with what God wants *him
to do*.

The chief looked up, and there were the young ladies! It was the
first time Christina had come near the cottage since Ian's departure.

"Can you tell me, Macruadh," the elder sister said, "what makes
Mrs. Conal always so spiteful? When we said good morning to her a
few minutes ago, she overwhelmed us with a torrent of abuse."

"How did you know it was abuse?"

"It is hardly necessary to understand Gaelic to know she was not
exactly blessing us. It is not necessary to know cat-language to distinguish between purring and spitting. What harm have we done her? Her
voice was fierce and her eyes were like two live peats flaming at us. Do
speak to her."

"It would be of no use."

"What's the good of being chief, then? I don't ask you to make the
old woman civil, but I think you might keep her from insulting your
friends. I am beginning to think your chiefdom a sham."

"I doubt indeed if it reaches to the tongues of the clan! But let us
go and tell my mother. She may be able to do something with her."

Christina went into the cottage; the chief drew Mercy back.

"What do you think the first duty of married people, Mercy—to
each other, I mean?" he said.

"To always be what they look," answered Mercy.

"Yes, but I mean actively. What is their first duty to do toward each other?"

"I can't answer that without thinking."

"Isn't it to help the other to do the will of God?"

"I would say *yes* if I were sure I really meant it."

"You will mean it one day."

"Are you sure God will teach me?"

"I think he wants to do that more than anything else."

"More than to save us?"

"What is saving but taking us out of the dark into the light? There is no salvation but to know God and grow like him."

33 / A Generous Dowry

At length Mr. Peregrine Palmer arrived, and the next day the chief called upon him. The father received the Macruadh, if a little pompously, yet with kindness; and the moment they were seated Alister laid his request before him.

"Mr. Palmer," he said, "I come to ask the hand of your daughter Mercy. I have not much beyond myself to offer her, but I can tell you precisely what there is."

Mr. Peregrine Palmer sat for a moment looking important. Not prepared for the proposal of the chief, Mercy's father had nothing to urge against it. Her suitor's name was almost a historical one, and the new laird was not unwilling that a man of the Macruadh's pedigree should supply an ancient name to his daughter's children.

"Well, Macruadh," he said at length, hesitating with hum and with haw, "the thing is—well, to speak the truth, you take me a good deal by surprise. I do not know how the thing may appear to Mrs. Palmer; and then the girl herself, you will admit, ought in a free country to have a word in the matter! We give our girls absolute liberty. Their own hearts must guide them—that is, where there is no serious exception to be taken. Honestly, it is not the kind of match we should have chosen. It is not as if things were as once they were with you, when the land was all your own, and—and—you—pardon me—did not have to work with your own hands."

Had he been there on any other errand, the chief would have stated his opinion that it was degrading to a man to draw income from anything he would count it degrading to put his own hand to. But there was so much he might be compelled to say to the displeasure of Mr. Palmer while asking of him the greatest gift he had to bestow that he would say nothing unpalatable which he was not compelled to say.

"My ancestors," he answered, willing to give the objection a pleasant turn, "would certainly have preferred helping themselves to the produce of lowland fields rather than here. My great-great-grandfather, scorning to ask any man for his daughter, carried her off without a word!"

"I am glad the peculiarity has not shown itself hereditary," said Mr. Palmer, laughing.

"But if I have little to offer, I expect nothing with her," said the

210

chief abruptly. "I want only herself."

"A very lovely way of speaking! But needless to say, no daughter of mine shall leave me without a certainty of suitable maintenance. You know the old proverb, Macruadh, 'When poverty comes in at the door—' "

"There is hardly a question of poverty in the sense the proverb intends," answered the chief, smiling.

"Of course! of course! At the same time you cannot keep the wolf too far from the door. I would not, for my part, care to say I had given my daughter to a poor farmer in the north. Two men, I believe, you employ, Macruadh?"

The chief answered with a nod.

"I have other daughters to settle—not to mention my sons," pursued the great little man. "But—but I will find a time to talk the matter over with Mrs. Palmer and see what I can do for you. Meanwhile, you may reckon me a friend. All I have seen makes me judge well of you. Where we do not think alike I can yet say for you that your faults lean to virtue's side, and are such as my daughter at least will be no loser by. Good morning, Macraudh."

Mr. Peregrine Palmer rose, and the chief, perplexed, rose also.

"You scarcely understand me, Mr. Palmer," he said. "On the possibility of being honored with your daughter's hand, you must allow me to say distinctly beforehand that I must decline receiving anything with her. When will you allow me to call upon you again?"

"I will write. Good morning."

The interview certainly did not do much to relieve the chief's anxiety. He went home with the feeling that he had been patronized, almost insulted, by a paltry fellow whose only importance rested on his money. But everything would all be in vain in the end anyway, for he could not lie! Indeed, truth, if not less of a virtue, was less of a heroism in the chief than in most men, for he *could not* lie. Had he been tempted to try, he would have reddened, stammered, and broken down with shame.

For a week he heard nothing. Then came a letter. It implied, almost said, that some difficulty had been felt about his reception by *every* member of the family—which the chief must himself see as only natural. But while money was of no consequence to Mr. Palmer, it was of the greatest consequence that his daughter should seem to make a good match. Therefore, he had concluded that the best course of action to make all aspects of the alliance right was that, in giving him his daughter, to restore the chief's family to its former dignity by turning over to him the Clanruadh property he had purchased. While he thus did his duty by his daughter, he hoped the Macruadh would accept the arrangement as a mark of esteem for himself. Two conditions only he would make—the first, that as long as he lived the shooting rights should be Mr. Palmer's to use or rent out to others, and should extend over the whole estate; the second, that the chief should assume the baronetcy which belonged to him.

It was clearly a generous proposition, notwithstanding that the greater part of the money-value of the gift lay in the shooting. As Alister left his mother for the night, he gave her the letter.

She took it, read it slowly, laughed angrily, smiled scornfully, wept bitterly, crushed it in her hand, and walked up to her room with her head high. All the time she was preparing for bed she was talking in her spirit with her dead husband. For the first time in her life she distrusted her son. She did not know what he would do! The temptation would surely be too strong for him! Two good things were set over against one evil thing on the other side—the woman he loved and the land of his ancestors on the one side, and only the money that bought the land on the other—would he be able to hold out? He must take all three together or have none of them! Henceforward and forever there would be a gulf between them. The poor religion he had would never serve to keep him straight! There was but one excuse for the poor boy—and that a miserable one: the blindness of love. Yet there was more excuse than that: to be lord of the old lands, with the old clan growing and gathering again about its chief—it was a temptation fit to ruin an archangel! Oh, what he would be able to do for his people then! But God forbid such bliss should be bought at such a cost?

But before the night was done her thoughts began to flow around the other way. She began to make the best of it in her mind, for the sake of her son, and for the sake of the bond between them. Then she began to excuse it for the sake of the clan. Everything that could favor the acceptance of the offer came up clearly to her. The land was the same as it had always been! It had never been in the distillery! *It* was clean, whatever had been transacted concerning it. A good cow was a good cow no matter how many times it had been stolen. For Mr. Palmer to give and Alister to take the land back would be some amends to the nation. The deed would restore to the redeeming and uplifting influence of her son many who were quickly perishing from poverty and whiskey. Hundreds who had gone abroad could return to replenish the old glens with the true national wealth. The glorious time she had herself seen would return! The dream of her boys would come true! They would rebuild the old castle and make it a landmark in the history of the highlands!

But while she thought thus, suddenly in her mind's eye rose the face of her husband, and his voice was in her ear; he seemed to stand above her in the pulpit, reading from the prophet Isaiah—the four *woes*: "Woe to the crown of pride, to the drunkards of Ephraim! Woe to Ariel, to Ariel, the city where David dwelt! Woe to the rebellious children, saith the Lord, that take counsel, but not of me! Woe to them that go down to Egypt for help; and stay on horses, and trust in chariots, because they are many; and in horsemen, because they are very strong; but they look not unto the holy one of Israel, neither seek the Lord!"

She covered her face with her hands and wept—ashamed before God, ashamed before her husband. It was a shame unutterable that the thing should have even looked tempting! She cried for forgiveness, rose, and went to Alister's room.

Seldom since he was a man had she gone to her elder son in his chamber. She cherished for him, as chief, something of the reverence of the clan. The same familiarity had never existed between them as between her and Ian. Now she was going to wake him and hold a solemn talk with him.

She found him awake, and troubled, though not with an eternal trouble such as hers.

"I thought I should find you asleep, Alister," she said.

"It was not very likely, Mother," he answered gently.

"You, too, have been tried with terrible thoughts?"

"I have been tried, but hardly with terrible thoughts. I know that Mercy loves me."

"Ah, my dear son! Love itself is the terrible thing! It has drawn many a man from the way of peace."

"Did it draw you and my father from the way of peace?" asked Alister.

"Not for a moment!" she answered. "It made our steps firmer in the way."

"Then why should you fear it will draw me from it? I hope I have never made you think I was not following my father and you."

"Who knows what either of us might have done with such a temptation as yours!"

"I don't think I am tempted to anything just now."

"There it is, you see! The temptation is so subtle that you do not suspect its character!"

"I am confident my father would have done just as I mean to do."

"What do you mean to do?"

"Is it my own mother who asks me? Does she distrust her husband and her son together?"

It began to dawn on the mother that she had fallen into her own temptation through the distrust of her son. Because she distrusted him, she sought excuse for him and the excuse had turned to all but justification. But she must be sure about Alister! She must not trust her impressions! The enemy might even now be bent on deceiving her afresh! For a moment she kept silence, then said: "It would be a grand thing to have the whole countryside your own again—wouldn't it, Alister?"

"It would, Mother!" he answered.

"And to have all your people under your own care?"

"A grand thing indeed, Mother."

"How then can you say it is no temptation to you?"

"Because it is none."

"How is that?"

"I would not have my clan under a factor of Satan's, Mother."

"I do not understand you."

"What else should I be if I accepted the oversight of them on terms of allegiance to him! That was how he tempted Jesus. I will not be the devil's steward, to call any land or any people mine."

His mother kissed him on the forehead, walked erect from the room, and went to her own to humble herself afresh.

In the morning Alister took his dinner of bread and cheese in his pocket and set out for the tomb on the hilltop. There he remained until the evening, and wrote his answer.

He begged Mr. Peregrine Palmer to dismiss the idea of enriching him, thanked him for his great liberality, but declared himself entirely content, and determined not to change his position: he could not and would not avail himself of his generosity.

Mr. Palmer, unable to suspect the reasons at work in the chief's mind, pleased with the genuineness of his acknowledgment, and regarding him as a silly fellow who would quixotically outdo him in magnanimity, answered in a more familiar, almost jocular strain. He must not be unreasonable, he said; pride was no doubt a good thing, but it might be carried too far. Men must act upon realities, not fancies. He must learn to eschew heroics: what was life without money? The property was a mere trifle to him. He hoped the Macruadh would live long to enjoy it, and make his father-in-law the great-grandfather of chiefs, perpetuating his memory to ages unborn. There was more to the same effect, not without eloquence and a certain good-heartedness, which the laird both recognized and felt.

It was again his painful turn. He now had to make his refusal as positive as words could make it. He said he was sorry to appear headstrong, perhaps uncivil and ungrateful, but he could not and would not accept anything beyond the priceless gift of Mercy's hand.

Not even then did Peregrine Palmer guess that his offered gift was despised; it was to him an idea all but impossible of conception. He merely read opposition, and was determined to have his own way. Next time he, too, wrote positively, though not unkindly—the Macruadh must take the land with his daughter, or leave both.

The chief replied that he could not yield his claim to Mercy, for he loved her and believed she loved him. He therefore begged Mr. Peregrine Palmer, of his generosity, to leave the decision to his daughter.

The next was a letter from Mercy, begging Alister not to hurt her father by seeming to doubt the kindness of his intentions. She assured him her father was not the man to interfere with his management of the estate; the shooting was all he cared about, and if that was the difficulty, she imagined even that might be overcome. She ended praying he would, for her sake, cease making much of so little a thing.

The chief answered her in the tenderest way, assuring her that if the property had been hers, he would only have blessed her for it; that he was not making much ado about nothing; that pride or unwillingness to be indebted had nothing to do with his determination; that the thing was with him in very truth a matter of conscience. He implored her therefore from the bottom of his heart to do her best to persuade her father, to save him who loved her more than his own soul from a misery only God could make him able to bear.

Mercy was bewildered. She neither understood nor suspected. She wrote again, saying her father was now thoroughly angry; that she found herself without argument, for the thing was as incomprehensible to her as to her father. She could not see where the conscience of the thing lay. She was afraid that if he persisted she would have no choice but to think he did not care for her. She had tried in vain to reconcile his behavior with what he had taught her. If he destroyed her faith in him, all her faith might go, and she be left without God as well as without him!

Alister saw now that necessity had culminated, that it was no longer possible to hold anything back. Whatever other suffering he might cause her, he must not leave Mercy thinking him capable of sacrificing her to some foolish idea. She must know the truth of the matter and why it was to him of the deepest conscience.

The man without a tender conscience cannot imagine the state to which another may come, who carries it about with him, stinging and accusing him all day long with demands to obey it.

So out of a heart aching with very fullness, Alister wrote the truth to Mercy. And Mercy, though it filled her with grief and shame, had so much love for the truth, and for the man who had waked that love, that she loved him through all the pain of his words; loved him yet more for daring the risk of losing her; loved him yet the more for cleaving to her while loathing the mere thought of sharing her wealth; loved him most of all that he loved the truth.

She carried the letter to her father's room, laid it before him without a word, and went out again.

The storm gathered swiftly, and burst at once. Not two minutes seemed to have passed when she heard his door open and a voice of wrathful displeasure call out her name. She returned—in fear, but in strength.

Then first she knew her father! Seldom did wrath and injustice show themselves in him. Now he treated her as a willing party to an unspeakable insult from a highland boor to her own father. To hand him such a letter was the same as to have written it herself! She identified herself with the writer when she became the bearer of the mangy hound's insolence! He raged at Mercy as in truth he had never raged before. If she ever spoke to the fellow again, he would turn her out of the house.

She would have left the room. He locked the door, set a chair in front of his writing table, and ordered her to sit there and write what he told her. But no power on earth or under it would have prevailed to make Mercy write as her own the words that were not hers.

"You must excuse me, Papa!" she said in a tone he had never heard from her before.

This raising of the rampart of human dignity, crowned with refusal, between him and his own child, galled him afresh.

"Then I will make you!" he said with an oath through clenched teeth.

Mercy stood silent and motionless.

"Go to your room. By heaven, you shall stay there till you do as I tell you!"

He was between her and the door.

"You need not think to gain your point by obstinacy," he added. "I swear that not another word shall pass between you and that blockhead of a chief, not if I have to turn watchdog myself!"

He made way for her, but did not open the door. She left the room, too angry to cry, and went to her own. Her fear of her father had vanished. With Alister on her side she could stand against the world! She went to the window. She could not see the cottage from it, but she could see the ruin and the hill of the crescent fire, on which she had passed through the shadow of death. Gazing on the hill she remembered what Alister would have her do, and with her Father in heaven she knelt down and sought shelter from her father on earth.

34 / Mistress Conal

Mr. Peregrine Palmer's generosity had, in part, rested on the idea of securing the estate against a reversal of fortune, sufficiently possible though not expected. In the hands of Macruadh the land would be out of reach of his creditors should his fortunes in the south go from bad to worse! At the same time, with the improvements he hoped to make, the shooting would be excellent and would make him a large return. He felt all the more wronged by the ridiculous scruples of the chief because he did not quite believe them. It never occurred to him that, even if the chief accepted the gift of the land, upon discovery that it had been maneuvered out of reach of the donor's creditors, he would have at once insisted on placing it at their disposal.

His wrath proceeded to vent itself in hastening his schemes for improvement of the property, for he was well aware how much worse than distasteful they would be to the Macruadh. He and his Canadian neighbor had agreed to turn the whole of their property into a deer forest, and his first requirement was the removal of every peasant within his tenancy who was capable of violating its sanctity. He chuckled with wrath to think how entirely he had the chief in his power for justifiable annoyance. Mr. Palmer believed himself about to do nothing but good to *the country* by removing its miserable inhabitants; the sentimental indulgence of their so-called chief had kept them contented with their poverty, and interference would now enrage him. How he hated the whole wretched pack of ridiculous highlanders!

Mr. Palmer's "good" to the country consisted in making the land yield more money into the pockets of Mr. Brander and himself by feeding wild animals instead of men. To tell such landowners that they are going against the very creative energy of the land can be of no use. They do not believe in God anyway, no matter how much they may imagine they do. Belief that is not lived by is no belief at all, for belief involves what we *do* more than it does *ideas*.

Two days later he sent Mistress Conal the message that she must be out of her hut, goods and gear, within two weeks. He was not sure that the thing was legally correct, but he would risk it. She might go to the law, if she would, but he would make a beginning with her. The chief might take her quarrel upon himself if he chose. Nothing would please Mr. Palmer more than to involve him in a lawsuit, clear him out, and send him adrift! His money might be contemptible, but the chief would find it dangerous at least!

With rage and scorn that made her feel every inch a witch, Mistress Conal, accompanied by her black cat which might or might not be an innocent animal—though the neighbors did not think him so—hurried to the Macruadh and informed him that "the lowland thief" had given her notice to quit the house of her fathers within a fortnight.

"I fear there is not much we can do; the house is on his land!" said the chief sorrowfully.

"His land!" echoed the old woman. "Is the nest of the old eagle his land? Can he make his heather white or his ptarmigan black? Will he dry up the lochs and stop the rivers? Will he remove the mountains from their places or make the generations of men to cease from the earth? Defend me, chief! I come to you for the help that was never sought in vain from the Macruadh!"

"What help I have is yours without the asking," returned the chief. "I cannot promise to do more than is in my power. Only one thing I can promise you— that you shall not lack food or shelter."

"My chief will abandon me to the wolf!" she cried.

"Never! But I can only protect you, not your house. He may have no right to turn you out at such short notice, but he can turn you out; it would only be a matter of weeks. To go to law against him could only be to leave me without roof to shelter you when your own was gone!"

"The dead would have shown him into the dark before he turned me into the cold!" she muttered, and turned and left him.

The chief was greatly troubled. He had heard nothing of such an invention on the part of his neighbor. Was it for revenge? He had heard nothing yet of his answer to Mercy. All he could do was represent to Mr. Palmer the trouble the poor woman was in and let him know that the proceeding threatened would make him very unpopular in the surrounding area. This he thought it best to do by letter.

It could not enrage Mr. Palmer more, but it enraged him afresh. He vowed that the moment the time was up, out the old witch should go; and with the help of Mr. Brander he provided men who did not belong to the immediate neighborhood to enforce his purpose.

The chief kept hoping to hear from the New House, but neither his letter to Mercy nor to her father received any answer. How he wished for Ian to confide his troubles to! His mother could not help him. He saw nothing for it but to wait for events.

Day after day passed and he heard nothing. He would have tried to find out the state of things at the New House, but until war was declared that would not be right. Mr. Palmer might, for all he knew, be seeking how to move with dignity in the matter, for certainly the chief had placed him in a position even more unpleasant than his own. He must continue to wait!

Exactly two weeks after the notice had been given, about three o'clock in the afternoon, a ragged little urchin of the village came flying to the chief's, almost too breathless to make his news intelligible—that there were men at Mistress Conal's who would not leave her house, and she and her old black cat were swearing at them.

The chief ran. Could the new laird actually be unhousing the aged, helpless woman? It was the action of a devil, not a man! As he neared the place, her poor possessions were already on the roadside: her one chair and stool, her bedding, her three-footed pot, her big chest, all that she could call hers in the world! As he came in sight of the cottage, she was being brought out of it, struggling, screaming, and cursing in the grasp of two men! Fierce in its glow was the torrent of Gaelic that rushed from the crater of her lips, molten in the volcanic depths of her indignant soul.

"Set her down!" cried the chief. "I will take care of her."

When she heard the voice of her champion, the old woman let loose a cat-like screech of triumph, and her gliding Gaelic, smoothness itself in articulation, flowed yet more fiery in word and more fierce in tone. But the men who were thus ejecting her—hangers-on of the sheriff-court in the county town, employed to give a color of law to the doubtful proceeding—did not know the chief.

"Oh, we'll set her down," answered one of them insolently, "and glad enough, too! But we'll have her on the public road with her sticks first!"

Infuriated by the man's disregard of her chief, Mistress Conal struck her nails into his face and with a curse he flung her from him. She turned instantly to the other with the same painful argument, and found herself staggering on her own weak limbs toward a severe fall, when the chief caught and saved her. She struggled hard to break from him and rush again into the hut, declaring she would not leave it if they burned her alive in it, but he held her fast.

There was a pause, for one or two who had accompanied the men employed knew the chief, and their reluctance to go on with the ruthless deed in his presence influenced the rest. Report of the eviction had spread, and the neighbors came running from the village. A crowd seemed to be gathering. Again and again Mistress Conal tried to escape from Alister and rush into the cottage.

"You too, my chief!" she cried. "You turned against the poor of your people!"

"No, Mistress Conal," he answered. "I am too much your friend to let you kill yourself."

"We have orders, Macruadh, to set fire to the hovel," said one of the men, touching his hat respectfully.

"They'll roast my black one!" shrieked the old woman.

"Small fear for him," said a man's voice from the little crowd, "if half be true—!"

Apparently the speaker dared no more.

"Fire won't singe a hair of him, Mistress Conal," said another voice. "You know it; he's used to it!"

"Come along, and let's get it over!" cried the leader of the eviction party. "It won't take many minutes once it's well a-going, and there's fire enough on the hearth to set Ben Cruachan in a blaze!"

"Is everything out?" demanded the chief.

"All but her cat. We've done our best, sir, and searched everywhere, but he's not to be found. There's nothing else left."

"It's a lie!" screamed Mistress Conal. "Is there not a great pile of peats, carried on my own back from the moss! Ach, you robbers! Would you burn the good peats?"

"What good will the peats be to you, woman," said one of them not unkindly, "when you have no hearth?"

"I will burn them on the road," she said. "They will keep me a few hours from the dark. When I die I will go straight up to God and implore his curse upon you, on your bed and board, your hands and tools, your body and soul. May your every prayer be lost in the wide murk, and never come at his ears! May—"

"Hush, hush," interposed the chief with great gentleness. "You do not know what you are saying. But you do know who tells us to forgive our enemies."

"It is well for *him* to forgive!" she screamed, "sitting on his grand throne, and leaving me to be turned out of my blessed house on the cold road."

"Nannie!" said the chief, calling her by her name, "because a man is unjust to you, is that a reason for you to be unjust to him who died for you? You know as well as he that you will not be left out on the cold road. He knows and so do you that while I have a house over my head, there is a warm corner in it for you. And as for his sitting on his throne, you know that all these years he has been trying to take you up beside him, and can't get you to set your foot on the first step of it. Be ashamed of yourself, Nannie!"

She was silent.

"Bring out her peats," he said, turning to the bystanders. "We have small need, with winter on the way, to waste any of God's gifts.''

They obeyed. But as they carried them out and down to the road, the number of Mistress Conal's friends kept growing; a laying together of heads began, and a gathering of human fire under the glooming eyebrows, threatening. Suddenly Mistress Conal broke out in a wild yet awful speech, wherein truth indeed was the fuel, but earthly wrath supplied the prophetic fire. Her friends suspended their talk, and her foes their work, to listen.

English is by no means equally poetic with the Gaelic, regarded as a language, and hardly serves to represent her utterance. Much that seems natural in the one language seems forced and unreal amidst the less imaginative forms of the other. English provides little better than an imitation of her prophetic outpouring. It was like a sermon, in that she began with a text:

"Woe unto them," she said—and her voice sounded like the wind among the great stones of a hillside—"that join house to house, that lay field to field, till there be no place, that they may be placed alone in the midst of the earth!"

This woe she followed with woe upon woe, and curse upon curse, now from the Bible, now from some old poem of the country, now from the bitterness in her own heart. Then she broke out in purely native eloquence:

"Who art thou, O man, born of a woman, to say to thy brother, 'Depart from this earth: here is no footing for thee?' Who art thou to speak thus to your fellow, as if he entered the world by another door than thyself! Because thou art rich, is he not also a man—a man made in the same image of the same God? For that saying, God will brand thee with the brand of Cain. Yea, the hour will come when those ye will not give room to breathe will rise up and cry, 'If we may neither eat nor lie down by their leave, lo, we are strong. Let us take what they will not give! If we die, we die!' Then shall there be blood to the knees of the fighting men, and the earth shall be left desolate because of you, foul feeders on the flesh and blood, on the bodies and souls of men. In the pit of hell you will find room enough, but no drop of water; and it will comfort you little that ye lived merrily! Which of us has coveted your silver or your gold? Which of us has stretched out our hand to take of your wheat or your barley? All we ask is room to live! But because ye would see the dust of the earth on the head of the poor, ye have crushed and straitened us till we are ready to cry out, 'God, for thy mercy's sake, let us die, lest we be guilty of our own blood!' ''

A solitary man had come down the hill behind, and stood alone listening to her speech. He was the mover of the wickedness. In the old time, the rights of the people in the land were fully recognized. When the chiefs of Clanruadh sold it, they could not indeed sell the rights that were not theirs, but they forgot to secure them for the helpless, and they were now in the grasp of the selfish and greedy devourers of the poor. He did not understand a word the woman said, but he was pleased to look on her rage and see the man who had insulted him suffer with her. When he began to notice the glances of lurid fire which every now and then turned upon him during Mistress Conal's speech, he scorned the indication. Under what he counted the chief's contempt, he had already grown worse; and the thought that perhaps the great world might one day look upon him with like contempt wrought in him bitterly. He was crueler now than before the chief's letter to his daughter.

When Mistress Conal saw him, she addressed herself to him directly. What he would have felt had he understood, I cannot tell. Never in his life did he know how the weak can despise the strong, how the poor can scorn the rich.

"Worm!" she said, "uncontent with holding the land, eating the earth that another may not share! The hour is at hand when the earth will swallow thee, and thy fellow worms will eat thee as thou hast eaten men. The holy and beautiful house of my fathers—" she spoke of her poor little cottage, but in the words lay a spiritual fact— "mock not its poverty! Is it not to me sacred as the cottage at Nazareth to the poor man who lived there with his peasants? Old and despised I am, but once I was younger than any of you, and ye will be old and decrepit as I, if the curse of God does not cut you off too soon. You man-trapping, land-stealing, house-burning Sasunnach, do your worst! I care not."

She ceased, and the spell was broken.

"Come, come!" said one of the men impatiently. "Tom, get a peat and set it on the top of the wall, under the roof. You too, George!—and be quick. Peats all round! There are plenty on the hearth. How's the wind blowing? You, Henry, make a few holes in the wall here, outside, and we'll set live peats in there. It's time there was an end to this!"

"You're right; but there's a better way to end it!" returned one of the clan, and gave him a shove that sent him to the ground.

"Men, do your duty!" cried Mr. Palmer. "Never mind the old woman! Of course she thinks it hard; but hard things have got to be done! It's the way of the world, and all for the best."

"Mr. Palmer," said another of the clan, "the old woman has the right of you. She and her family have lived there, in that cottage, for nearly a hundred years."

"She has no right. If she thinks she has, let her go to the law for it! In the meantime, I choose to turn her off my land. *What's mine's mine*, as I mean every jack of you to know—chief and beggar!"

The Macruadh walked up to him.

"Pardon me, sir," he said. "I doubt much if you have a legal right to disturb the poor woman. She has never paid rent for her hut, and it has always been looked upon as her own property."

"Then the chief that sold it swindled both me and her!" stammered Mr. Palmer, white with rage. "But as for you who call yourself a chief, you are the most insolent, ill-bred fellow I ever had to do with, and I have not another word to say to you!"

A silence like that before a thunderstorm succeeded. Not a man of the clan could believe what he had just heard! There is nothing the Celtic nature resents like rudeness. Suddenly half a dozen of the Macruadhs rushed at once upon the Sasunnach insulter of their chief, intent on his punishment.

"One of you touch him," cried Alister, "and I will knock him down."

Each eager assailant stood still in his tracks.

"Finish your work, men!" shouted Palmer.

To do him justice, he was no coward.

"Clansmen," said the chief, "let him have his way. I do not see how to resist the wrong without bringing more evil upon our own heads than we can meet. We must leave it to him who says 'Vengeance is mine.'"

The Macruadhs murmured their obedience, and stood silently and sullenly looking on. The men went into the hut and carried out the last of the fuel. They then scooped holes in the turf walls, inside to leeward, outside to windward, and taking live peats from the hearth put them in the holes. A few minutes later Nannie's "poor and beautiful" house was a great fire.

When they began to apply the fire, the chief would at once have taken the old woman away, but he dreaded an outbreak and lingered. When the fire began to run up the roof, Mistress Conal broke from him and darted to the door. Everyone rushed to seize her, Mr. Palmer with the rest.

"Blackie! Blackie! Blackie!" she shrieked like a madwoman.

While the men did their best to get her away, down shot the cat from the blazing roof, a fizz of fire in his black fur, his tail as thick as his neck, an infernal howling screech of hatred in his horrible throat, and, wild with rage and fear, flung himself straight upon Mr. Palmer. A roar of delighted laughter burst forth. He bawled out—and his bawl was mingled with a scream—to take the brute off him. His own men hurried to his rescue; but the frantic animal had dug his claws and teeth into his face and clung to him so that they had to choke him off. The chief caught up Mistress Conal and carried her off. There was no danger of anyone hurting Mr. Palmer now!

He bore her on one arm like a child; indeed, she was not much heavier. But she kept her face turned and her eyes fixed on her burning home and, leaning over the shoulder of the chief, poured out, as he carried her farther and farther from the scene of the outrage, a flood of maledictory prophecy against the doers of the deed. The chief never said a word, never looked behind him, while she, almost tumbling down his back as she cursed with outstretched arms, deafened him with her raging. He walked steadily down the path to the road, where he stepped into the midst of her pile of goods. The sight of them diverted a little the current of her wrath.

"Where are you going, Macruadh?" she cried as he walked on. "Don't you see my property? Don't you know the greedy Sasunnach will carry everything away!"

"I can't carry them and you too, Mistress Conal!" said the chief.

"Set me down, then. Who ever asked you to carry me? And where would you be carrying me? My place is with my things!"

"Your place is with me, Mistress Conal! I belong to you and you belong to me, and I am taking you home to my mother."

At the word, silence fell, not on the lips, but on the soul of the raving prophetess: the chief she loved, his mother she feared.

"Set me down, Macruadh!" she pleaded in a gentle tone. "Don't carry me to her empty-handed. Set me down immediately. I will load my back with my goods and bear them to my lady, and throw them at her feet."

"As soon as we get to the cottage," said the chief, as he strode on with his reluctant burden, "I will send up two men with wheelbarrows to bring them home."

"*Home*, did you say?" cried the old woman, and burst into the tearless wailing of a child. "There is a home for me no more! My house was all that was left of my people, and it is your own that makes a house a home! In the long winter nights, when I sat by the fire and heard the wind howl, and the snow pat, pat like the small hands of my little brothers on the window, my heart grew glad within me, and the dead came back to my soul! When I took the book, I heard the spirit of my father reading through my own lips! And oh, my mother! My mother!"

She ceased as if in despair.

"Surely, Nannie, you will be at home with your chief," said Alister. "My house is your house now, and your dead will come to it."

"It is their chief's house!" she returned. "They loved their chief. Shall we not make a fine clan when we're all gathered to our fathers,

we Macruadhs! No man nor woman can say I did anything to disgrace
it!"

"Lest we should disgrace it," said the chief, "we must bear with
patience what is sent upon it."

He carried her into the drawing room and told her story, then stood,
to the delighted amusement of his mother, with his little old sister in his
arms, waiting for her orders, like a big boy carrying the baby, who now
and then moaned a little but did not speak.

His mother called Nancy and told her to bring the tea tray and get
ready for Mistress Conal the room next to Nancy's own, that she might
be near to wait on her.

But the terrible excitement had so thinned the mainspring of Mistress
Conal's time-watch that it soon broke. She did not live many weeks.
From the first she sank into great dejection and her mind wandered. She
said her father never came to see her now, that he was displeased with
her for leaving the house, and that she knew now she ought to have
stayed and been burned in it. The chief reminded her that she had had
no choice, but had been carried bodily away.

"Yes, yes," she answered, "but they do not know that! I must make
haste and tell them. Who can bear for her own people to think ill of
her? I'm coming, I'm coming. I'll tell you all about it. I'm an honest
woman yet!"

Another thing troubled her sorely, for which she would hear no
consolation: Blackie had vanished! Whether he was killed at the time
of his attack on Mr. Palmer, or was afterward shot, or whether he fled
the strath and went to the wild cats among the hills, or back to the place
which some said he had come from, no one could tell.

Nancy was more than uneasy at having the witch so near, but by no
means neglected her duty to her. One night she woke and for some time
lay listening, when suddenly quavered through the dark the most horrible
cat-cry she had ever heard. In abject terror she covered her head and lay
shuddering. The cry came again and kept coming at regular intervals,
drawing nearer and nearer, with an expression of intense and increasing
pain. The creature seemed to come close to the house, then with difficulty to scramble up on the roof, where it went on yowling and screech-
ing and throwing itself about, Nancy said, until at last it gave a great
choking, gobbling scream, and fell to the ground, after which all was
quiet. Persuading herself it was only a cat, she tried to sleep and finally
succeeded. When she woke in the morning the first thing she did was
to go out, fully expecting to find the cat lying at the foot of the wall.
No cat was there. She went then as usual to attend to the old woman.
She was dead and cold.

The clan followed Mistress Conal's body to the grave, and the black
cat was never seen.

35 / Confrontation

It was plainly of no use for the chief to try to mollify Mr. Palmer. So long as he was what he was, it would be impossible for him to understand the conscience which lay behind the chief's actions. When a man's own conscience is content, how shall he listen to another man's? It was now a lonely time for Alister. Ian was not within reach even by letter. He had heard nothing from Mercy since writing his explanation. And his mother did not sympathize with his dearest earthly desire. Alister's light was thus left to burn in very darkness that it might burn the better. As strength is made perfect through weakness, so does the light within grow by darkness: the people who walked in darkness saw a great light. He was brought closer than ever to first principles and had to think all the harder about what the right thing was to do. There was, of course, no thought of giving Mercy up, but the chief did not want to interfere with her love for her father. Somehow or other he must manage to speak with her!

First of all, however, he must learn how she was being treated. It was not in fiction only or the ancient clan histories that cruel things were done! There were several of the clan employed about the New House of whom Alister might have sought information. But he scorned to learn anything through those of a man's own household. Therefore he fired a gun, and ran up a flag on the old castle, which brought Rob of the Angels at full speed, and comforted the heart of Mercy sitting disconsolate at her window: it was her chief's doing, and might have to do with her!

The chief told Rob the state of matters between him and the New House. "From this moment, Rob," he concluded, "every hour your father does not actually need you, be somewhere on the hills where you can see the New House. I want to learn first whether she goes out at all. With the dark you must draw nearer the house. But do not question the servants or anyone employed about the house. I will not have anyone used unconsciously as a traitor."

Rob understood and departed; but before he had news for his master, an event occurred which superseded his service.

The neighbors, Mr. Peregrine Palmer and Mr. Brander, had begun to enclose their joint estates, bordering in a few places—mostly with the chief's small remaining land between—for a deer forest, and had

226

hired men to act as curators. They were from the neighborhood but none of them belonged to Strathruadh, and not one knew the boundaries of the district they had to patrol. And indeed, the boundaries were nowhere very precisely determined. Why should they be where all was heather and rock? Until the space grew valuable with game, who should care whether this or that lump of limestone rooted in the solid earth were the actual property of one or the other?

There was just one person who knew all about the boundaries: Hector of the Stags. He could not in all places draw their lines with absolute assurance, but he had better grounds for his conclusions than anyone else could have. For who was so likely to understand the boundary lines as he who knew the surface within them as well as the clay floor of his own hut? If he did not everywhere know where the march-line between properties fell, at least he knew perfectly well where it ought to fall.

It happened just at this time that Mistress Macruadh told Hector she would like a deer, intending to cure part of it for winter use. Therefore the next day—the first day of Rob's secret service—he stalked one across the hill farm, got a shot at it near the cave house, brought it down, and was busy preparing it when two men came creeping up behind him, threw themselves upon him, and—luckily for themselves—managed to tie him up before he had a chance of defending himself. Finding he was deaf and dumb, one of them knew who he must be and would have let him go. But the other, eager to ingratiate himself with the new laird, prevailed with his companion, and they set out for the New House with Hector between them, his hands tied. Annoyed and angry at being treated like a common thief, Hector was comforted when he realized where they were taking him, for Rob would be certain to see him. Wherever he was, he was watching the New House! He went composedly along with them therefore, fuming and snorting, but not caring to escape.

When Rob caught sight of the three, he looked through his telescope, and, discovering that his father's hands were bound behind his back, was overwhelmed with fiercest indignation in his soul. His father—the best of men—bound like a criminal! What could the devils mean! He shut up the telescope and ran down toward the house, sharpening his knife on his hand as he went.

The moment they were near enough, signs, unintelligible to the keepers, began to pass between father and son: Rob's meant that he must let him pass unnoticed. So, with but the usual salutation of a stranger, Rob passed them. But the same moment he turned, and with one swift sweep of his knife, severed the bonds of his father. The old man stepped back, and father and son stood facing the enemy.

"Now," said Rob, "if you are honest men, tell me how you dared bind Hector of the Stags."

"Because he is not an honest man," replied one of them.

Rob answered him with a blow. The man made at him, but Hector stepped between.

"Say that again of my father," cried Rob, "who has no speech to defend himself, and I will drive my knife into you!"

"We are only doing our duty!" said the other. "We came upon him there cutting up the deer he had just killed on the new laird's land."

"Who are you to say which is the stranger's and which is the Macruadh's? Neither my father nor I have ever seen your faces in the country! Will you pretend to know the boundaries better than my father, who was born and bred in the heather, and knows every stone on the face of the hills?"

"We can't help where he was born or what he knows! He was on our land!"

"He is the Macruadh's keeper, and was on his own land. You will get yourselves into trouble!"

"We'll take our chance!"

"Take your man then!"

"If he tries to escape, I swear by the bones of my grandfather," said the more angry of the two, the inheritor of a clan-feud with the Macruadhs, "I will shoot him."

Rob of the Angels burst into a scornful laugh.

"You will! Will you?"

"I will not kill him; I don't want to be hanged for him. But I will empty my shot-barrel into his legs. So take your chance; you have been warned!"

They had Hector's gun and Rob had no weapon but his knife. And he was hardly inclined to use it now that he had cooled a little. He turned to his father. The old man understood perfectly what had passed between them and signed to Rob that he would go on to the New House, and Rob might run and let the chief know what had happened. The same thing was in Rob's mind, for he saw how it would favor the desires of the chief, bringing them all naturally about the place. But he must first go with his father on the chance of learning something.

"We will go with you," he said.

"We don't want *you*!"

"But I mean to go! My father is not able to speak for himself."

"You know nothing!"

"I know what he knows. The lie does not grow in these hills."

"You crow high, my cock!"

"No higher than I strike," answered Rob. In the eyes of the men Rob was small and weak; but there was something in him that looked dangerous nevertheless, and though far from cowards, they thought it best to leave him alone.

Mercy at her window saw them coming and instinctively connected their appearance with her father's new measure of protection. When the men turned toward the kitchen, she ran down to learn what she could. Rob greeted her with a smile as he entered.

"I am going to fetch the Macruadh," he whispered, and turning went out again.

He told the chief that at the word her face lighted up as with the rise of the moon.

One of the maids went and told her master that they had brought a poacher into the kitchen.

Mr. Palmer's eyes lightened under his black brows when he saw the captive whom he knew by sight and by report. His men told him the story their own way, never hinting a doubt as to whose was the land on which the deer had been killed.

"Where is the nearest magistrate?" he inquired with grand severity.

"The nearest is the Macruadh, sir," said a highlander who had come from work in the garden to see what was going on.

"I cannot apply to him; the fellow is one of his own men!"

"The Macruadh does what is just!" rejoined the man.

His master gave no further reply. He would not show his wrath against the chief; it would be undignified.

"Take him to the toolhouse and lock him up till I decide what to do with him. Bring me the key."

The butler led the way, and Hector followed between his captors. They might have been showing him to his bedroom, he was so calm. Rob had gone to fetch the chief; his imprisonment could not last—and he was in the right!

As Mr. Palmer left the kitchen, his eye fell on Mercy.

"Go to your room," he said angrily, and turned from her.

She obeyed in silence, consoling herself that from her window she could see the arrival of the chief. Nor had she watched long when she saw him coming along the road with Rob. At the gate she lost sight of them. But presently she heard voices in the hall and crept down the stairs far enough to hear.

"I could commit you for a breach of the peace, Mr. Palmer," she heard the chief say. "You ought to have brought the man to me. As a magistrate, I order his release. But I give my word he shall be forth-coming when legally required."

"Your word is no bail. The man was taken poaching. I have him, and I will keep him."

"Let me see him, then, that I may learn from himself where he shot the deer."

"He shall go before Mr. Brander."

"Then I beg you to take him at once. I will go with him. But listen a moment, Mr. Palmer. When this same man, my keeper, took your guest poaching on my ground, I let Mr. Sercombe go. I could have committed him as you would commit Hector. I ask you in return to let Hector go. Being deaf and dumb, and the hills the joy of his life, confinement will be terrible to him."

"I will do nothing of the kind. You could never have committed a gentleman for a mistake. This is quite a different thing!"

"It is a different thing, indeed, for Hector cannot have made a mistake. He could not have followed a deer onto your ground without knowing it."

"I make no question of that!"

"He says he was not on your property."

"Says!"

"He is not a man to lie."

Mr. Palmer smiled.

"Once more I pray you, let us see him together."

"You shall not see him."

"Then take him at once before Mr. Brander."

"Mr. Brander is not at home."

"Take him before *some* magistrate—I care not who. There is Mr. Chisholm!"

"I will take him when and where it suits me."

"Then as a magistrate, I will set him at liberty. I am sorry to make myself unpleasant to you. Of all things I would have avoided it. But I cannot let the man suffer unjustly. Where have you put him?"

"Where you will not find him."

"He is one of my people. I must have him."

"Your people! A set of idle, poaching good-for-nothings! By heaven, the strath shall be rid of the pack of them before another year is out!"

"While I have land in it with room for them to stand upon, the strath shall not be rid of them! But this is useless! Where have you put Hector of the Stags?"

Mr. Palmer laughed.

"In safe keeping. There is no occasion to be uneasy about him. He shall have plenty to eat and drink, be well punished, and show the rest of the rascals the way out of the country."

"Then I must find him. You compel me!"

So saying, the chief, with intent to begin his search at the top of the house in the hope of seeing Mercy, darted up the stairs. She heard him coming, went a few steps higher, and waited. On the landing he saw her, white, with flashing eyes. Their hands clasped—for a moment only, but the moment was of eternity, not of time.

"You will find Hector in the toolhouse," she said aloud.

"You shameless hussy!" cried her father, following the chief in a fury.

Mercy ran up the stairs. The chief turned and faced Mr. Palmer.

"You have no business in my house!"

"I have the right of a magistrate."

"You have no right! Leave my house at once!"

"Allow me to pass."

"You ought to be ashamed of yourself, making a girl turn traitor to her own father!"

"You ought to be proud of a daughter with the conscience and courage to stand up for the truth."

The chief passed Mr. Palmer, and running down the stairs, joined Rob of the Angels where he stood at the door in a group composed of the keepers and most of the servants.

"Do you know the toolhouse?" he said to Rob.

"Yes, Macruadh,"

"Lead the way, then. Your father is there."

"Don't let them open the door!" cried Mr. Palmer. "They may talk through it if they please."

"It will be difficult to say much to a deaf man through inch-thick boards," remarked one.

Mr. Palmer hurried after them and his men followed.

Alister found the door locked and solid, without a handle. He looked at his companion and was about to throw his weight against the lock.

"It is too strong," said Rob. "Hector of the Stags must open it."

"But how? You cannot even let him know what you want."

Rob gave a smile, and going up to the door, laid himself against it, as close as he could stand, with his face upon it, and so stood silent.

Mr. Palmer came up with his attendants and all stood for a few moments in silence, wondering what he was doing. He must be holding communication with his father—but how?

Sounds began inside—first a tumbling of tools about, then an attack on the lock.

"Come! Come! This won't do!" said Mr. Palmer, approaching the door.

"Prevent it then," said the chief. "Do what you will, you cannot make him hear you, and while the door is between you, he cannot see you! If you do not open it, he will!"

"Run!" said Mr. Palmer to the butler; "you will find the key on my table. I don't want the lock ruined!"

But there was no stopping the thing! Before the butler came back the lock fell, the door opened, and out came Hector, wiping his brow with his sleeve, and looking as if he enjoyed the fun.

The keepers darted forward.

"Stand back!" said the chief, stepping between them. "I don't want to hurt you, but if you attempt to lay hands on him, I will."

One of the men dodged round and laid hold of Hector from behind; the other made a move toward him in front. Hector stood motionless for an instant, watching his chief, but when he saw him knock down the man in front of him, he had his own assailant by the throat in an instant, gave him a shake, and threw him beside his companion.

"You shall suffer for this, Macruadh!" cried Mr. Palmer, coming up close to him and speaking in a low, determined tone.

"It is no use telling you how sorry I am to have to make myself disagreeable to you," returned the chief; "but I give you fair warning that I will accept no refusal of the hand of your daughter from any but herself. As you have chosen to break with me, I accept your declaration of war, and tell you plainly that I will do all I can to win your daughter without asking your leave about anything I may think it good to do. You will find there are stronger forces in the world than money. Henceforward, I hold myself clear of any personal obligation to you except as Mercy's father."

From very rage Mr. Palmer was incapable of answering him. Alister turned and followed Rob, who was turning a corner of the house. It was not the way to the gate, but Rob had seen Mercy peeping round that same corner—anxious about her father; she feared nothing for Alister.

He came at once on Mercy and Rob talking together. Rob withdrew and joined his father a little way off. They retired a few more paces, and stood awaiting their chief's orders.

"How *am* I to see you again, Mercy?" said the chief hurriedly. "Can't you think of some way? Think quickly!"

Now Mercy, as she sat alone at her window, had often imagined the chief standing below on the walk, or just beyond in the belt of shrubbery; and now once more in her mind's eye she suddenly saw him there. She answered hurriedly,

"Come under my window tonight."

"I don't know which it is."

"You see it from the castle. I will put a candle in it."

"What hour?"

"Any time after midnight. I will sit there till you come."

"Thank you," said the chief, and departed with his attendants.

Mercy hastened into the house by a back door, but had to cross the hall to reach the stairs. As she ran up, her father came in at the front door, saw her and called her. She went down again to meet the tempest of his rage, which now broke upon her in gathered fury. He called her a treacherous, unnatural child, with every name he thought bad enough to characterize her conduct. She stood pale, but looked him in the face. Her mother came, trembling, as near as she dared, withered by her terror to almost twice her age. Mr. Palmer in his fury took a step toward Mercy as if he would strike her. Mercy did not move a muscle, but stood ready for the blow. Then love overcame her fear, and the wife and mother threw herself between, her arms round her husband, as if rather to protect him from the deed than her daughter from its hurt.

"Go to your room, Mercy," she said.

Mercy turned and went. She could hardly understand herself. She used to be afraid of her father, but suddenly she found herself calm. But the thing that quieted her in reality was her sorrow that he should conduct himself so wildly. She sat down at her window to gaze and brood.

When her father cooled down he was annoyed with himself, not that he had been unjust, but that he had behaved with so little dignity. With brows black as evil, he sat degraded in his own eyes, and blamed the degradation on his daughter. Every time he thought of her, fresh rage arose in his heart. He had been proud of his family autocracy. So seldom had it been necessary to enforce his authority that he never doubted his wishes would always be obeyed. Born tyrannical, the characterless submission of his wife had nourished the tyranny in him. Now all at once, his daughter—the ugly one—dared to defy him for a clown in a worn-out rag of a chieftainship—the musty fiction of a clan of half a dozen shepherds, crofters, weavers, and shoemakers, not the shadow of a gentleman among them! For the sake of such a fellow, with a highland twang that disgusted his fastidious ear, his own daughter made a mockery of his authority. In his own house she had risen against him and betrayed him to the insults of his enemy! His conscious importance, partly from doubt in itself, boiled and fumed, bubbled and steamed in the caldron of his angry brain. Not one, but many suns would go down upon such a wrath!

"I wish I might never set eyes on the girl again!" he said to his wife. "A small enough loss the sight of her would be, the ugly thing! She makes me feel as if I should go out of my mind! So calm, so meek, so self-sufficient! Oh, quite a saint! And so strong-minded! Quite equal to throwing her father over for a fellow she never saw till a year ago!''

"She shall have her dinner sent up to her, as usual," answered his wife with a sigh. "But really, Peregrine, my love, you must compose yourself! Love has driven many women to extremes!"

"Love! Why should she love such a fellow! I see nothing in him to love! *Why* should she love him? Tell me that! Give me one good reason for her folly, and I will forgive her—anything but let her have the rascal! That I *will not*! Take for your son-in-law an ape that loathes your money, calls it filthy lucre—and means it! Not if I can help it! Don't let me see her! I shall come to hate her, and that I would rather not. A man must love and cherish his own flesh! I must go away!"

"You can't suppose that I shall be able to prevent her from seeing him!"

"Lock her up in the coal cellar—bury her, if you like. I shall never ask what you have done with her. Never to see her again is all I care about!"

"Ah, if she were really dead, you would want to see her again— sooner or later."

"Then I wish she were dead that I might want to see her again. It won't be sooner. Ten times rather than know her married to that beast, I would see her dead and buried."

The mother held her peace. He did not mean it, she said to herself. It was only his anger. But he did mean it; at that moment he would with joy have heard the earth fall on her coffin.

In spite of her faculty for shutting out the painful, her persistent self-assurance that it would blow over, and her confidence that things would by and by resume their course, Mrs. Palmer was for the next several days very unhappy. The former quiet once restored, she would take Mercy in hand, reason with her, and soon persuade her to her own way of thinking. It was her husband's severity that had brought it all to this!

But Mrs. Palmer did not understand that influence works only between those who inhabit the same spiritual sphere. Her daughter had been lifted into a region above all the arguments of her mother, and the life-poverty she had so long endured could never attract her to its death again.

36 / Midnight

Mercy sat alone but not lonely at her window. A joy in her heart made her independent of the need for human interaction. Life with the expectation of seeing Alister was livable without company.

The evening drew on. They sent her food, but she forgot to eat it and sat looking out, till the lines of the horizon seemed to grow in her mind to an etching. She watched the slow dusk swell and gather—with delicate, soft-blending gradations in the birth of the night. Through palest eastern rose, through silvery gold and golden green and brown, the daylight passed into the shadow of the light. And the stars, like hope in despair, began to show themselves where they always were. As the night came on, deeper and deeper sank the silence. Household sounds grew quiet, and no step came near her door. Her father had given orders and was obeyed. Christina had stolen down the hall to listen at her door, but hearing no sound from within had concluded it better for Mercy, as well as safer for herself, to return.

Still Mercy sat. She could now barely trace the meeting of earth and sky, each the evidence of the other. Sound itself seemed asleep. Absolute silence the soul cannot grasp; therefore, deepest silence seems ever, in Wordsworth's lovely phrase, wandering into sound, for silence is but the thin shadow of harmony. There may be yet another reason, beyond its great depth or height or strength, why we should be deaf to the spheral music; perhaps the absolute perfection of its harmony can be to our ears only the shape of silence.

Content and patient, Mercy sat watching.

It was just past midnight, but she had not yet lighted a candle, when something struck the window as with a blow soft as a moth's wing. Her heart gave a great leap. She listened breathless. Nothing followed for several moments.

It came again! She dared not speak. She softly opened the window. The darkness had thinned on the horizon and the half-moon was lifting a corner above the edge of the world. Something in the shrubbery answered her shine, and without the rustle of a branch, quiet as a ghost, the chief stepped into the open space. Mercy leaned toward him and said, "Hush, speak low."

"There is no need to say much," he answered. "I came only to tell you that I am always with you."

235

"How quietly you came! I did not hear a sound."

"I have been in the shrubbery two hours."

"And I didn't suspect it once! You might have given me some hint. A very small one would have been enough."

"It was not your time, but it is twelve now. I came early for the luxury of expectation and the delight of knowing you are better looked after than you thought."

"My chief!" she said softly. "I shall always find you nearer and better than I was able to think. You are even better than I can imagine man to be."

"I am good toward you, Mercy! I love you!"

A long silence followed.

"Have you been to a ball?" said Mercy.

"No. I doubt if there will be any more dancing in Strathruadh!"

"Then why are you in court dress?"

"When should the Celt, who loves radiance and color, put on his gayest clothes? For the ball, for the crowd—or for the one most cared about above all?"

"Thank you. Is it a compliment? But after your love, everything fine seems only natural."

"In love there are no compliments. Truth only walks the sacred path between the two doors. I will love you as my father loved my mother, and loves her still."

"I do like to see you shining. It was kind of you to dress for me."

"Whoever loves the truth must love shining things! God is the father of lights, even of the lights hid in the dark earth—sapphires and rubies, and all the families of splendor."

"I shall always see you like that."

"There is one thing I want to say to you, Mercy—don't think me indifferent, however long I may be in proposing a definite plan for our future. We must wait upon God!"

"I shall think nothing you would not have me think. Not long ago I was so dead till you waked me. If I were what girls call *in love*, I should probably be impatient with you, but I love you much more than that and do not need to be always with you. You made me able to think. I was but a child, and you made a woman of me."

"God and I and Ian did," said Alister.

"Yes, but the others through you."

"Then will you always trust me?"

"I will. When one really knows another, then all is safe."

"Then I want to know how your father treats you."

"Must we talk about him? He *is* my father. And he has had no one to teach him, Alister. He has always been rich and accustomed to having his own way. I think one's punishment of making money in a wrong way is to be prosperous in it.''

"I am sure you are right. But will you be able to bear poverty, Mercy?''

"Yes," she answered, but so carelessly that she seemed to speak without having thought.

"You do not know what poverty means!" rejoined Alister. "We may have to endure much for our people."

"It still means *you*, does it not? If you and poverty come together, then I will welcome them both!"

All at once there was a little noise—like a sob. Mercy started and when she looked again, Alister had vanished—as noiselessly as he had come. For a moment she sat afraid to move. A wind came blowing upon her from the window: someone had opened her door behind her! With great dread that her father had discovered her, she slowly turned her head.

It was Christina! She came to her through the shadow of the moonlight, put her arms round her, and pressed to her face a wet cheek. For a moment or two neither spoke.

"I heard a little, Mercy," sobbed Christina. "Forgive me. I meant no harm. I only wanted to know if you were awake. I was coming to see you."

"Thank you, Chrissy! That was good of you."

"You are a dear, and so is your chief. Forgive me for listening."

"I don't mind your hearing a bit. I am glad you know the chief loves me."

"But you must be careful! Papa might pretend to take him for a robber and shoot him."

"Oh no, Chrissy! He wouldn't do that."

"I would not be too sure. I never had an idea what Papa was like before this. Oh, what men are like!"

With this statement, to Mercy's astonishment, she burst into tears. Mercy tried to comfort her but she did not know how. She had seen for some time that her sister was troubled. Now perhaps she would tell her about it.

She was weeping like a child on her shoulder. Mercy coaxed her into her bed where she lay down beside her. Before the morning, with many breaks of sobbing and weeping, Christina had told Mercy her story.

"He is going to write to me," she sobbed as soon as she could speak again.

"Perhaps he will love you yet, Chrissy."

"No, no! He will never love me that way! Don't even hint at such

a thing. I am all done with tricks and pretendings. I mean to be worthy
of his friendship. His friendship is better than any other man's love. I
will be worthy of it!"

The poor girl burst yet again into tears—not so bitter as before, and
ended them all at once with a kiss to Mercy.

"For his sake," she said, "I will take care of Alister and you."

"Thank you, thank you, Chrissy! Only you must not do anything to
offend Papa. It is hard enough on him as it is! I cannot give up the chief
to please him, for he has been a father to my better self. But we must
do nothing to trouble him that we can help."

Alister did not feel like going home. Not anxious to leave the dream-
like circumstances surrounding his visit to Mercy's house, he turned
toward the castle, climbed the broken steps, and sat on the corner of
the wall watching the moonlight reflecting from Mercy's window under
which he had stood such a few moments ago. He sat for an hour, then
came down and went straying down the road, into the valley, along the
burnside, up the steep slope beyond it, and away to the hill farm and
the tomb.

The moon was with him all the way. He wandered along, paying no
attention to time, to the moon, to the stars, or to the sunrise, thinking
about many things. And by the time he reached the tomb, he was weary
with excitement and lack of sleep. Taking the key from where it was
hidden, he unlocked the door and entered.

He started back, thinking he saw a gray-haired old man seated on
one of the stone chairs and leaning sadly over the fireless hearth: his
uncle! But the same moment he saw that it was nothing but a ray from
the moon, entering by the small, deep window and shining feebly on
the chair. He struck a light, lit a fire, and went for water. Returning
from the well, he found the house dark as before; the fire had gone out
and there again seemed to be the old man leaning over the extinguished
peats! The idea lasted but a moment, and once more the level light of
the moon revealed itself. He tried to laugh at his imagination, but did
not quite succeed. Several times on the way up the hill he had thought
of his old uncle: this must have given the shape to the moonlight! He lit
the fire again and put on the kettle. Going then for a book to read till
the water boiled, he remembered a letter which, in the excitement of
the afternoon, he had put in his pocket unread and forgotten. It was
from the family lawyer in Glasgow, informing him that the bank in
which his uncle had deposited the proceeds of his sale of the land was
in a state of absolute and irrecoverable collapse. There was not the
slightest hope of retrieving any portion of the money.

Alister did not jump up and pace the room in rage; neither did he sit as one stunned and forlorn. He felt bitter disappointment in the loss of the hope of making up to his people for his uncle's wrong. But it was clear that if God had cared for his having the money, he would have cared that he should have it. Here was an opportunity for absolute faith and contentment in the will that looks after all our affairs, the small as well as the great.

What is money, after all? said the chief to himself. *It was discontent with poverty that began the ruin of the highlands! If the heads of the people had but lived pure, active, sober lives, satisfied to be poor, poverty would never have overwhelmed them. The highlands would have made Scotland great with the greatness of men dignified by high-hearted commitment and strong with the strength of men who could do without!*

With these thoughts it dawned upon Alister that when he longed to help his people, his thoughts had always turned first, not to God, but to the money his uncle had left him. He had trusted in a fancy; in God alone can trust rest. All along he thought he had loved God as the first and last, the beginning and end, and yet he had been trusting, not in God, but in uncertain riches, in mammon. It was a painful and humiliating discovery.

"It was well," he said, "that my false deity should be taken from me! Perhaps without it to lean on, God may be able to send some other good gift to my people. I must be more to them than ever, to make up to them for their loss with more than money."

He fell on his knees and thanked God for the wind that had blown cold through his spirit and slain at least one evil thing. When he rose all that was left of his trouble was a lump in his throat, for he had to admit that things looked bad for the clan. But even that lump melted away as he walked home through the morning air on the hills. For he could not delay; he must let his mother know their trouble, and, as one who had already received help from on high, help her to bear it.

For a moment dejection at their plight threatened to overcome him afresh. He could not enjoy the glory of the morning, for he was troubled!

But would a single note in the song of the sons of the morning fail because God did or would not do a thing? Could God deserve less than perfect thanks from any one of his creatures? A man could not truly know God if he thanked him only for what appeared to be good.

He was upset with himself, and lifted up his heart. As he reached the brow of his last descent, the sun rose, and with it his soul arose and shone, for its light was come, and the glory of the Lord was risen upon it. "Let God take from us what he will," he said; "himself he can only give!

Joyful he went down the hill. God was, and all was well!

37 / The Power of Darkness

He found his mother at breakfast, wondering what had become of him.

"Are you up to a bit of bad news, Mother?" he asked with a smile.

The mother's thoughts flew instantly to Ian.

"Oh, it's nothing about Ian," said the chief, answering her look.

Her expression changed; she hoped now it was some new obstacle between him and Mercy.

"No, Mother, it is not that either!" said Alister, again answering her look. "It is only that uncle's money is gone—all gone."

She sat silent for a moment, gave a little sigh, and said, "Well, it will all be over soon! In the meantime, things are no worse than they were. His will be done."

"I had hoped to do some good with the mammon, at least before we were turned out naked!"

"We shall have plenty," answered the mother. "God himself, and a few besides. If you can do good with the mammon, you can do good without it."

"Yes, that is happily true."

As they spoke Nancy entered.

"Please, Laird," she said. "Donald the shoemaker is wanting to see you."

"Tell him to come in," answered the chief.

Donald entered and stood up by the door with his hat under his arm—a little man with puckered face. The chief shook hands with him and asked how he could serve him.

"It will not be to your pleasure to know, Macruadh," said Donald, humbly declining to sit, "that I have received notice to leave my house and garden."

The house was a turf cottage, and the garden might grow two bushels and a half of potatoes.

"Are you far behind with your rent?"

"Not a quarter, Macruadh."

"Then what does it mean?"

"It means, sir, that Strathruadh is to be given to the red deer, and the son of man have nowhere to lay his head. I am the first at your door with my sorrow, but before the day is over you will have—"

Here he named four or five who had received like notice to quit.

"It is a sad business," said the chief sorrowfully.

"Is it lawful, sir?"

"It is not easy to say what is law, Donald; certainly it is not gospel! As a matter of course, you will not be without shelter, so long as I may call stone or turf mine, but things are looking bad! Things as well as souls are in God's hands, however."

"I have learned from the new men on the hills," resumed Donald, "that the new lairds have conspired to exterminate us. They have discovered, apparently, that the earth was not made for man, but for rich men and beasts." Here the little man paused and his insignificant face grew grandly expressive. "But the day of the Lord will come," he went on, "as a thief in the night. Vengeance is his. But what would you have us do, Laird?"

"I will go with you to the village."

"You should stay here, if you please, sir. Better men will be at your door presently to ask you the same question, for they will do nothing without the Macruadh. We are no more on your land, to our great sorrow, Chief, but we are of your blood, you are our lord, and your will is ours. You have been a father to us, Macruadh!"

"I only wish I could be!" answered the chief.

"They will want to know whether these strangers have the right to turn us out, and if they do not, whether we have the right to resist. If you would have us fight, and will head us, we will fall to a man, for fall we must if they—"

"No, no, Donald! It is not a question of the truth. That, of course, we should be bound to die for. But it is only our rights that are concerned, and they are not worth dying for. That would be mere pride and denial of God who is fighting for us. At least it seems so to me at the moment."

"Some of us would rather fight and have it done with, sir."

The chief could not help smiling with pleasure at the little man's readiness. He knew it was no empty boast. What there was of him was good stuff.

"You have a wife and children, Donald," he said. "What would become of them if you fell?"

"My sister was turned out in the cold spring," answered Donald, "and died in Glencalvu! It would be better to die together!"

"But, Donald, none of you will die of cold, and I can't let you fight, because the wives and children would then all be on my hands, and I would have more than my meal could feed. No, we must not fight. We may have a right to fight, I do not know. But I *am* sure we have the right to abstain from fighting. Don't let us confuse right and duty, Donald.''

"Will the law not help us, Macruadh?"

"The law is a slow coach! Our enemies are rich, and the lawyers have little love of righteousness! Most of them would see the dust on our heads to have the picking of our bones. No stick or stone would be left us before anything came of a legal recourse.''

"But, sir," said Donald, "is it the part of brave men to give up their rights?"

"No man can take our rights from us," answered the chief, "but any rich man may keep us from getting the good of them. Again I say, we are not bound to insist on our rights. If we decline to do so, that may give God the opportunity to look after us all the better.''

"God does not always give men their rights, sir. I don't believe he cares about our small matters.''

"Nothing that God does not care about can be worth our caring about. But, Donald, how dare you say what you do? God *does* care for our rights. He cares about *all* parts of our lives. We need not claim our rights, for a day is coming when he will judge the oppressors of their brethren.''

"We shall all be dead and buried long before then!''

"As he pleases, Donald. He is my chief. I will have what he wills, not what I should like. I will wait a thousand years for my rights if he chooses. I will trust him. I will have no other way than his. He alone can set everything straight.''

"You must be right, sir, only I cannot help wishing for the old times when a man could strike a blow for himself.''

With all who came Alister held similar talk. Though they were not all so warlike as the cobbler, they keenly felt the wrong done them, and most preferred to oppose force with force.

"The case is before a higher tribunal," said the laird. "The wise thing is to submit to wrong.''

Although many of the villagers spoke in wrath, not one of them truly wanted to see death come to the glen. Heartily did Rob of the Angels insist on peace, but his words had less force because he was puny in person, and although capable of great endurance, unnoted for deeds of strength. Evil birds carried the words of their righteous anger to the ears of the new laird, and he concluded that the chief had instructed them to resist.

On all sides the horizon was dark about the remnant of Clanruadh. Poorly as they lived in Strathruadh, they knew no place else where they could live at all. It was a great comfort to the chief that in the matter of his clan, his mother agreed completely with him; to their last penny they must help their people. The land was not theirs to *have*, but to use. Things are ours that we may use them for all—sometimes that we may sacrifice them. God had but one precious thing, and that he gave.

The chief, although he saw that the proceedings of Mr. Palmer and Mr. Brander must have been determined upon while his relation to Mercy was yet undeclared, could not help imagining how differently it might have gone with his people had he been married to Mercy and in good understanding with her father. Had he crippled his reach toward men by the narrowness of his conscience toward God? But as long as he did what seemed to be right, he could regret no consequences. God would take care of others as well as him.

One thing was clear—it would only do more harm to beg from Mr. Palmer any pity for his people. It would but give more zest to his rejoicing in iniquity! Nevertheless, something must be done, and quickly, for winter was at hand.

The Macruadh had to consider not only the immediate housing of the ejected, but how they were to maintain themselves. He began to long for some news from Ian which might justify an exodus from their own country to a home in the wilderness. But what would the land of his fathers be then without its people? Even he could not stay then. It would be no more worthy the name of Macruadh, no longer fit to be called a possession! For he knew that the true love of the land is one with the love of its people. The poor are blessed because by their poverty they are open to divine influences; they are the buckets set out to catch the rain of heaven; they are the salt of the earth. The poor are with a nation for its best blessing or for its condemnation and ruin. The chief saw the valleys desolate of the men readiest and ablest to fight the battles of his country. Because of greedy, low-minded men, from sheiling, cottage, or clachan would spring no kilted warriors with battle response as in days of old! The pride of the highlands was no more! The red deer and the big sheep had taken the place of men over countless miles of mountain and moor and strath. His heart bled for the sufferings and wrongs toward those ancestors who had died to keep the country free.

But vengeance had begun to gather, though neither his generation nor our own has seen it. Offenses must come, but woe unto them by whom they come!

38 / The New Village

The Macruadh turned his eye upon the small strip of ground on the west side of the castle ridge, between it and the tiny tributary of the strath burn which was here the boundary between the lands of the two lairds. The slope of the ridge on the chief's side was not so steep and was nearly level before it sank into the alluvial soil of the valley. With a little smoothing and raising it would serve as a tolerable building foundation, while in front was a narrow but rich piece of ground going down to the bank of the little brook.

Therefore, before many days were over, men were at work there, in full sight of the upper windows of the New House. It was not at first clear what they were about, but soon began to rise, plain enough, the walls of cottages—some of stone, some of turf. Mr. Palmer saw a new village already in the process of construction to take the place of that about to be destroyed! The despicable enemy had moved his camp to pitch it under his very walls, hardly more than a stone's throw from his very property! It filled him with the rage of defeat. The poor man who scorned him was going to be too much for him. He thought he would be rid of all those hateful, ridiculous highlanders, and here instead was their filthy little hamlet of hovels growing like a fungus just under his nose, expressly to spite him! Thinking he was destroying it, the thing had come even closer! When the wind was from the northwest, the smoke of their miserable cabins would be blown right in at his dining room window!

It would be useless to argue with the chief now. He had chosen that very spot to mock him. The fellow had stolen a march upon him! He himself had done nothing beyond what was absolutely necessary for the improvement of his property. And here their chief had brought them almost into his garden!

He let his whole household see how annoying the thing was to him. He never doubted it was done purely to irritate him. What right had the man to interfere between a landlord and his tenants? Christina dared to hint that, evicted by their landlord, they ceased to be his tenants. Even were he not their chief, he could hardly be said to be interfering in giving help to the destitute. He burst at her in a way that terrified her. The man seemed entirely changed. In truth, he was not a bit changed; things had only occurred which were capable of bringing out the true facts of his

244

nature. Her mother, who had not dared to speak at the time, tried to reason with her afterward.

"Why shouldn't Papa be told the truth?" objected Christina.

Her mother was about to reply, "Because he will not hear it," but she saw she owed more to her husband than to his child, and did not.

Mercy said to herself, *It is not to annoy my father he does it, but to do what he can for his people. He does not even know how unpleasant it is to my father to have them so near.* She longed to see Alister. Something might perhaps be done to lessen the offense. But her father would never consent to use her influence. Perhaps her mother might!

She therefore suggested that Alister would do nothing for the sake of annoying her father, and could have no idea how disagreeable this thing was to him. If her mother could contrive her seeing him, she would talk to him about it.

Mrs. Palmer was of Mercy's opinion regarding Alister's intent, and promised to think the matter over.

The next night her husband was going to spend at Mr. Brander's. The project might be carried out in safety! They would go together, in the hope of persuading the chief to change the site of his new village.

When it was dark they walked to the cottage, and knocking at the door, asked Nancy if the chief were at home. The girl invited them to enter, though not with her usual cordiality. Mrs. Palmer declined to come in, however, simply requesting her to let the chief know they were there.

Alister was at the door in a moment.

"I am *so* sorry for all that has happened!" said Mrs. Palmer. "You know I have nothing to do with it. There is not a man I should like for a son-in-law better than yourself, Macruadh; but I am helpless."

"I quite understand," replied the chief, "and thank you heartily for your kindness. Is there anything I can do for you?"

Mercy told him her father thought he was building the new village to spite him, seeing the smoke from its chimneys could hardly help blowing in at door and windows as often as the wind was from the sea.

"I am sorry, but hardly surprised your father should think so, Mercy. I do not want to trouble him. And certainly it is no convenience or comfort to my mother and me to have the village immediately below us."

"I thought you might—" Mercy stopped, then resumed, "but I suppose you chose that spot for some reason that cannot be helped."

"Indeed it is. I must think of my people. If I put them on the other side of the ridge, they would be exposed to the east wind, and you know yourself how bitterly it blows down the strath from the mountains. Besides, there we should have to use up too much good land, every foot of which will be needed to feed them. Where I have chosen they will be on the rock, and the ground, not being so damp, will be healthier. I have no other place so sheltered as here. Would it be reasonable, Mercy, to sacrifice the good of so many poor people to spare one rich man a single annoyance which will not even hurt him? Would it be right?"

"No, Alister, no!" cried Mercy. "You must not change anything. I am only sorry my father cannot see that you have no ill will toward him in what you do."

"I cannot think it would make much difference. He will never give you to me, Mercy. But be true, and God will."

"Would you mind letting the flag fly, Alister? I should like to have something of you to look at."

"I will. And when I want particularly to see you, I will haul it down. Then, if you hang a handkerchief from your window, I will come to you."

39 / The Peat Moss

For the first winter the Clanruadh had not much to fear. They had their small provision of potatoes and meal, and some poor trifle of money. But Lady Macruadh was anxious that the new cottages be completely dry before being occupied, and gave a general order that fires were to be burned in them for some time before the villagers took up residence in them. To do so would require their present stock of dry peats; therefore, many more would have to be provided for the winter.* Every available member of the clan would be required to get the fresh stock cut, hauled down to the village, and under the cover before the weather broke.

The peat moss from which they cut their fuel was at some distance from the castle, on the outskirts of the hill farm. It was the nearest moor to the glen which had a thick covering of peat. And the old chief, when he parted with so much of the land, took care to keep it, knowing full well that his remaining people could not live without it through a single winter. But his brother, the minister, who succeeded him, as well as the present chieftain, his nephew, had freely allowed all the tenants on the land sold to supply themselves from it. Therefore, the mistaken notion had arisen that the moss was not part of the chief's property at all. Never before had the question of ownership of the barren moor come up in anyone's mind.

Report was carried to Mr. Peregrine Palmer that the tenants Mr. Brander and he were about to evict were providing themselves with a stock of fuel greatly in excess of what they usually laid in for the win-

---

*In the highlands of Scotland, where the terrain is mountainous and the weather very wet, decaying organic matter—shrubbery, heather, grass, etc.—simply rots on top of a subsoil layer of rock, and is unable, because of the moisture and the lack of drainage, and because of the conditions of the soil, to return fully to the soil. It becomes instead "peat" or "peat moss," which, after centuries of accumulated build-up, becomes very deep, in some cases up to ten feet. This black *peat*, which, after perhaps many more thousands of years, would ultimately become coal, has long been used in the highlands as fuel. It is removed from under the surface with long knives, cut into manageable shapes approximately the size of bricks, looking simply like brick-shaped clods of dirt, dried, and then burned. It burns very hot and slowly, indeed, much like coal, but also very clean, giving off a unique and, some think, pleasant odor. To this day peat is cut in the highlands with little thought of monetary value or ownership. There remains sufficient supply for thousands of winters to come.

ter—that, in fact, they were cutting large quantities of peat, besides the turf for their new cottages. He determined, after a brief consultation with the men, who knew nothing but said anything, to put an immediate stop to the supposed presumption and violation.

A few of the peats cut in summer had not yet been removed, not having dried so well as the rest, and one day two widows, the owners of these small stacks of drying peats, went to fetch them home to the new village. As it happened, there were none of their fellow villagers working in the moss at the time.

They filled their creels, helped each other to get them on their backs, and were setting out on the weary tramp home when two of Mr. Palmer's men who had been watching them, walked up, cut their ropes, and took their loads, emptied the peats into a pool of water, and threw the creels in after them. The poor women poured out their wrath on the men, telling them they would go straight to the chief, but were answered only with mockery of their chief and themselves. They turned in despair, bemoaning the loss of the peats they had worked so hard for and their creels, and raging at the wrong they had received. One of them had faith in her chief; she would go to him at once: he always had a word and a smile and a handshake for her. The other, commonly called Craftie, was unwilling to face him: her character did not stand high in the glen, and she feared the Macruadh.

"He does not like me," said Craftie.

"When a woman is in trouble," said the other, "the Macruadh asks no questions. You come with me! He will be glad of the chance to do something for you."

In her confidence she persuaded her companion, and together they went to the chief.

Having gathered courage to appear, Craftie needed none to speak: where that was the call, she was never slow to respond.

"Craftie," said the chief, "is what you are telling me true?"

"Ask *her*," answered Craftie, who knew that her own words were not all-convincing.

"She speaks the truth, Macruadh," said the other. "I will take my oath to it."

"Your word is enough," replied the chief, "as Craftie knew when she brought you with her."

"Please, Laird, it was myself brought Craftie. She was not willing to come."

"Craftie!" said the chief, "I wish I could make a friend of you. But you know I can't."

"I do know it, Macruadh, and many is the time I am sorry for it.

But my door never had any latch, and the word is out before I can think to keep it back!''

"And so you send another and another to back the first! Ah, Craftie! If purgatory doesn't do something for you, then—!''

"Indeed, and I hope I shall fall into it on my way farther, Chief!'' said Craftie, who happened (like many in the highlands) to be Catholic.

"But now," resumed the chief, "when will you be going for the rest of your peats?''

"They're sure to be on the watch for us, and there's no saying what they mightn't do another time!'' was the direct and hesitating answer.

"I will go with you.''

"When you please then, Chief.''

So the next day the poor women went again and the chief went with them, their guard and servant. If anyone was on watch they did not appear. The Macruadh fished their creels out of the water and put them on the ground to dry, then helped them to fill those they had borrowed. On the way back he carried now the one, now the other creel, so that one of the women was always free. The new laird met them on the road, and recognized with a scornful pleasure the chief bending under his burden. This was the fellow who would be his son-in-law!

About this time Sercombe and Valentine came again to the New House. Although lately he had had no encouragement from Christina, Sercombe was not prepared to give her up, and was, in fact, prepared to press the siege. He found the lady's reception of him so cool that he could not but suspect some new adverse influence. He saw, too, that Mercy was in disgrace, and as Ian was gone, concluded there must have been something between them. Therefore, his final conclusion in the matter was that the chief had been "trying it on'' with Christina. The brute was always getting in his way! But some chance of getting rid of him was certain to turn up!

On the first suitable day Alister had arranged an expedition from the village to the moss, with all the carts they could gather, to bring home as many peats as horses and men and women could carry together. The company was seen setting out, and news of it carried at once to Mr. Palmer; for he had set men to watch all the doings of the clan. Within half an hour he, too, set out with the messenger, accompanied by Sercombe, in grim delight at the prospect of a row. Valentine went also, willing enough to see what would happen, though with no particular ill will toward the chief. They were all furnished as for a day's shooting, and expected to be joined by some of the keepers on their way.

The chief, in view of possible assault, had taken care that not one of his men should have a gun. Even Hector of the Stags was requested to leave his at home.

They went in little groups, some about the creeping carts, in which sat the older women and younger children, some a good way ahead, some scattered behind, but the main body with the chief who talked to them as they went. They looked like a very poor company indeed, but God saw past their poverty. All their clothes, including the chief's, were shabby, with a crumpled, dirty look, through their many faded colors. They had about them all a forgotten air,—looking thin and wan like a ghostly funeral to the second sight—as if they had walked so long they had forgotten how to sleep, and the grave would not have them. Except in their chief there was nothing left of the grand and proud glance and gait and show, once so notable in every gathering of the Clanruadh, when the men were all soldiers born and the women were mothers, daughters, and wives of soldiers. Their former stately grace had vanished from the women; they were weather-worn and bowed with labor too heavy for their strength, too long for their endurance. They were weak with lack of food, from lack of hope, and the dreariness of the outlook, the ever-gray spiritual horizon. They were numbed with the cold that had ceased to be felt, the deadening sense of life as a weight to be borne, not a strength to rejoice in. But they were not beaten into the ground yet; there was one that loved them—their chief and their friend!

The carts were small, with puny horses, long-tailed and droop-necked, in harnesses of more rope than leather. They had a look of old men, an aspect venerable, as of life and labor prolonged after due time, as of creatures kept from the grave and their last sleep to work a little longer. Scrambling up the steep places, they were like that rare seabird which, unable to fly for shortness of wing, makes of its beak a third leg to help it up the cliff: these horses seemed to make fifth legs of their necks and noses. The chief's horses alone, always at the service of the clan, looked well fed, well kept, and strong, and the clan was proud of them.

They reached the moss. It lay in a fold of the hills, deserted and dreary, full of hollows and holes from which the peat had been taken, now filled with water, black and terrible—a land lonely by day, at night full of danger. Everywhere stood piles of peats set up to dry, with many openings through and through, windy drains to gather and remove their moisture. Here and there was a tuft of dry grass, a bush of heather, or a few slender-stalked, hoary heads of *cannach*, or cotton grass. It was a land of devoted desolation, doing nothing for itself, this bountiful store of life and warmth for the winter-sieged houses of the strath.

They went heartily to work. They cut turf for their walls and peats from under it for their fires. They loaded the carts from the driest piles and made new piles of the fresh wet peats they dug. It was approaching noon, and some of the old women were getting the food out of Lady Macruadh's well-filled baskets, when over the nearest ridge beyond rose seven men, carrying guns. Rob of the Angels was the first to spot them. He pointed them out to his father, and presently the two disappeared together. The rest went on with their work, but the chief could see that they were now and then casting upward and sidelong glances at them, reading hostility in their approach. Suddenly, as if by common consent, they all ceased working, stood erect, and looked out like men on their guard. But the chief made a sign, and they resumed their labor as if they saw nothing.

Mr. Peregrine Palmer had laid it upon himself to act with calmness and dignity. But no self-restraint, indeed, no civilized habits and manners, can kill the savage in a man. The savage is there all the time till the man pass through the birth from above.

Mr. Palmer was in the worst of positions for protection against his own nature. Possessed of a large property, he owed his position to evil and not to good. Not only had he done nothing to raise those through whom he made his money, but in the process of making his money, he plunged them deeper and deeper into poverty and vice. His success was the ruin of many. Yet he was full of his own imagined importance—or had been until he felt that contempt of one man for his wealth and position. Well might such a man hate such another—and all the more that his daughter loved him! All the chief's ways were founded on such opposite principles to his own that by very nature they filled him with anger. And now here was his enemy insolently daring, as Mr. Palmer fully believed, to trespass in person on his land and steal its wealth in front of its owner's very eyes!

In addition, here Mr. Peregrine Palmer was in a place whose very remoteness and wildness tended to rouse all the old savage in him—its very look suggested to the city man that law was different here, and that he might commit an unlawful deed for his own righteous ends. Persons more *respectable* than Mr. Palmer are capable of doing the most wicked and lawless things when their selfish sense of their own right is uppermost.

"Are you not aware that you are trespassing on my land, Macruadh?" cried the new laird across several holes full of black water which obstructed his closer approach.

"On the contrary, Mr. Palmer," replied the chief, "I am perfectly aware that I am not."

"You have no right to cut peats there without my permission!"

"I beg your pardon. You have no right to stand where you speak the words without my permission. You are on my land. But you are quite welcome."

"There is not a word of truth in what you say," rejoined Mr. Palmer. "I desire you to order your people away at once."

"That I cannot do. It would be to ask them to die of cold."

"Let them die! What are they to me—or to anybody! Order them off, or it will be the worse for them—and for you, too!"

"Excuse me; I cannot."

"I give you one more warning. Go yourself, and they will follow you."

"I will not."

"Go, or I will make you." As he spoke he half raised his gun.

"You dare not!" said the chief, drawing himself up indignantly.

Together Mr. Palmer and Mr. Sercombe raised their guns to their shoulders, and one of them fired. To give Mr. Palmer the benefit of the doubt, he was not quite at home with his gun. The same instant the two men found themselves floundering, gun and all, in the black bog water on whose edge they had been standing a moment before. There now stood Rob of the Angels, gazing down upon them with the look of an avenging angel, with his father, grim as a gratified Fate, beside him.

Such a roar of rage rose from the clansmen with the shot, and so many came bounding with sticks and shovels over the rough ground, that the two keepers judged it prudent to do nothing against them. Only Valentine came running in terror to help his father.

"Don't be frightened," said Rob; "we only wanted to wet their powder."

"But they'll be drowned!"

"Not a chance of that," answered Rob. "We'll have them out in a moment. But please tell your men that if they dare to lift a gun, we'll serve them the same. It wets the powder horn and cools the man!"

A moment later and the two men lay coughing and gasping on the crumbly bank. With his first breath Sercombe began to swear.

"Drop that, sir, if you please," said Rob, "or in you go again."

He replied with a volley of oaths, but the same instant the black water was again choking him. Had Hector of the Stags had his way, he would have kept the murderer of *an cabrach mòr* there till he had to be dived for. Rob was determined this time that he should not come out until he gave his word that he would not swear.

"Come! Come!" gasped Sercombe at length, after many attempts to get out—which the other bystanders easily foiled—"you don't mean to drown me, do you?"

"We mean to drown your bad language. Promise to use no more," returned Rob.

"The promise you get from me will rest in hell!" he gasped.

"Men must have patience with a suffering brother!" remarked Rob, and saying a few words in Gaelic which drew a hearty laugh from the men about him, seated himself on a heap of turf to watch the unyielding flounder in the peat hole. He had almost begun to fear the man would drown before giving in when his ears welcomed the despairing words— "Take me out, and I will promise anything!"

He was so cold he could hardly move till one of the keepers gave him some whiskey, but in a few minutes he was crawling homeward after his host, who was doing his best to walk over rocks and through bogs with the help of Valentine's arm, muttering something about "proper legal fashion."

In the meantime, the chief lay shot in the right arm and chest, but not dangerously wounded by the scattering lead from the shotgun.

He had lost a good deal of blood and was faint—a new sensation to him. The women had done what they could, but that was only binding his arm, laying him in a dry place, and giving him water. He would not let them call the men till the enemy was gone.

When they knew what had happened, they were in dreadful grief— especially Rob of the Angels. The chief would have had him try to get the shot out of his arm with his knife; but Rob, instead, started off at full speed, running as no other man in the country could run, to fetch the doctor.

At the chief's desire they made a hurried lunch, and then resumed the loading of the carts, preparing one of them to take him back down. When it was half full, they covered the peats with a layer of dry, springy turf, then made on that a bed of heather. More to please them than because he could not walk, Alister then consented to be laid on this luxurious invalid-carriage and borne home over the rough roads like a disabled warrior.

They arrived some time before the doctor.

Mercy soon learned that some sort of encounter had taken place between her father's shooting party and some of the clan; also that the chief was hurt, but in what manner she was not told. She had heard enough to fill her with anxiety. Her window looked out over the ridge by the castle, and she seated herself there with her opera glass to watch. When the hill party came from behind the ruin, she could not see his tall figure among his people but soon discovered him lying on one of the carts looking very white. Her heart nearly stopped, and she began contriving in her mind how she might see him.

In a few minutes Christina came to tell her she had just heard from one of the servants that the Macruadh was shot. Having seen him alive, Mercy was able to bear the frightful news with tolerable calmness. Christina said she would do her best to discover how badly he was hurt; no one in the house seemed to be able to tell her. To avoid implicating her sister, Mercy said nothing about her own plans.

As soon as it was dark she prepared to steal from the house, afraid of nothing but being prevented. When her dinner was brought to her and she knew everyone would be safely in the dining room, she drew her scarf over her head, left her food untasted, stole halfway down the stairs, and from there watched for an opportunity between the comings and goings of the servants. Presently she got away unseen, crept softly past the windows, and when out of the shrubbery, darted off at her full speed. Her breath was all but gone when she knocked, panting, at the door of the cottage.

It opened and there stood the mother of her chief. But the moment Mrs. Macruadh saw her, leaving her no time to say a word, her anger got the better of her and she began pushing her from the door and trying to pull it shut behind her, stern as righteous Fate. But Mercy was not going to give in so easily; she was doing nothing wrong.

"How is the Macruadh, please?" she managed to say.

"Alive, but terribly hurt," answered his mother, still trying to oust her visitor.

"Please," said Mercy, standing her ground, "how is he hurt?"

She turned upon her almost fiercely.

"This is what *you* have done for him!" she said with anger in her tone. "Your father fired at him, on my son's own land, and shot him in the chest."

"Is he in danger?" gasped Mercy, leaning against the wall, trembling.

"I fear he is in great danger. If only the doctor would come."

"You wouldn't mind my sitting in the kitchen till he comes?" whispered Mercy, her voice all but gone.

"I could not allow it. I will not condone your coming here without the knowledge of your parents. It is not at all a proper thing for a young lady to do!"

"Then I will wait outside," said Mercy, her temper beginning to waken in spite of her anxiety. "There is one, I think, Mrs. Macruadh, who will not find fault with me for it."

"At least he will not tell you so for some time."

The door opened behind her.

"She does not mean me, Mother," said Alister; "she means Jesus Christ. He would say to you, *Let her alone.* He does not care for society. Its ways are not his ways, nor its laws his laws. Come in, Mercy, I am sorry my mother's worry about me should have made her inhospitable to you."

"I cannot come in, Alister, if she will not let me," answered Mercy.

"Please, walk in! I can sit in the kitchen until you are gone!" said Mrs. Macruadh.

"There is no need!" insisted Mercy. "Just tell me how you are, Alister, and I will go, and come again tomorrow."

Alister told her what had happened, making little of the affair, and saying he was sure it was an accident.

"Oh, thank you!" she said with a sigh of relief. "I meant to sit by the castle wall till the doctor came; but now I shall get back before they discover I am gone."

Without a word more she turned and ran from the house, and reached her room unmissed and unseen.

The next was a dreary hour for the mother and son—the most painful they had ever passed together. The mother was all the time buttressing her pride with her grief, and the son was cut to the heart that he should have to take part against his mother. When the doctor at length came and she saw him take out his instruments, her pride melted away.

"Forgive me, Alister!" she whispered, and his happy kiss comforted her repentant soul.

When the small operations were over and Alister was in bed, she would have gone to let Mercy know all she could tell her. But it would work mischief in the house. So she sat down by Alister's bedside and watched him all night.

He slept well. His body was in such a healthful condition that the loss of blood and the presence of the few pieces of shot found in him did him little harm. He yielded to his mother's pleading to spend the morning in bed, but was up long before the evening in the hope of Mercy's coming again. When she came, the mother took her in her arms and begged her forgiveness. And having once taken her in her arms, she could no longer treat her relationship with her son with coldness. If the girl was ready, as her conduct showed, to leave everything for Alister, she could certainly not be one of the enemy!

Thus was the mother repaid for her righteous education of her son: through him her pride received almost a mortal blow, her justice grew more discriminating, and her righteousness more generous.

In a few days the chief was out and looking quite himself.

The time was drawing near when the warning of eviction would no doubt begin to be put in force. Hearing through Rob of the Angels that attempts were being made to stir the people up and get them into trouble, the chief instituted measures of his own. Discussing the matter with the best of the villagers, both women and men, it was decided that they all had better leave together before the limit of the earliest notice had expired. They agreed that the people should be told to get themselves in readiness to move at a moment's notice. In the meantime, he pushed on their labor at the new village.

In the afternoon preceding the day on which certain of the clan were to be cast out of their homes, the chief went to the village, from house to house, telling his people to have everything in order for fleeing that very night, so that in the morning there should not be so much as an old shoe left. He told them to be careful that no rumor of their purpose got out. They would thus have a good laugh at the enemy who was reported to have applied for military assistance as a precautionary measure. His horses should be ready and as soon as it was dark, they would begin to cart and carry, and be snug in their new houses before the morning.

All agreed, and a tumult of preparation began. Lady Macruadh came to help and counsel and took the children in charge while the mothers bustled. It was amazing how much had to be done to remove such a small amount of property. The chief's three carts were loaded first; then the men and women loaded each other's. The chief took on his back the biggest load of all, except for Hector's. To and fro went the carts, and to and fro went the men and women, I do not know how many journeys, upheld by companionship, merriment, hope, and the clan-mother's plentiful provision of tea, coffee, milk, bread and butter, cold mutton and ham—luxurious fare to all. As the sun was rising they closed every door and walked for the last time, laden with the last of their goods, out of the place of their oppression, leaving behind them not a scrap worth stealing—all removed in such order and silence that no one at the New House had a suspicion of what was going on. Mercy, as she sat at her window, did think she heard strange sounds coming faintly through the night from the shadowy valley below—even thought she caught glimpses of a shapeless gnome-like train moving along the road. But she only wondered if the highlands had suddenly gifted her with the second sight, and these were the brain-phantasms of coming events. She listened and gazed, but could not be sure she heard or saw anything.

When she looked out in the morning, however, she understood, for the castle ridge was almost hidden in the smoke that poured from every chimney of the new village. Her heart swelled with joy to think of her chief with all his people under his eyes and within reach of his voice. From her window of solitude, they seemed almost like the camp of an army come to set her free.

Hector and Rob, with one or two more of the clan, hid themselves to watch those who came to evict the first of the villagers. There were no military. Two sheriff's officers, a good many constables, and a few vagabonds made up the party. Rob's keen eye enabled him to distinguish the very moment when they first began to be aware of something unusual about the place. He saw them halt and look at each other as if something was a little uncanny. There were seldom many signs of life in the poor hamlet, but there would always be some sounds of handicraft, some shuttle or hammer going, some cries of children, some noises of animals, some smoke, a person or two.

They feared an ambush, a sudden attack. Warily they stepped into the place, looking sharply about them in the street. Slowly they opened door after door, afraid of what might be lurking behind to pounce on them. Only after searching every house and finding not the smallest sign of living creature did they recognize their foolish errand for what it was. And all the time there was the new village, smoking hard, under the very windows, as he chose himself to say, of its chief adversary!

41 / Laying Down of Arms

The winter came down upon them early and the chief and his mother had a sore time of it. They had known of the poverty of their people before, but now they understood more clearly just how poor they were. Unable to endure the sight of it, he spent more and more of his own money to combat it, and soon realized it would be impossible for them to hold out much longer. For some time his hope had rested in the money from Glasgow he would soon receive from his uncle's investment. Now that hope was gone, yet the need was greater than ever. He was not troubled, for his faith was simple and strong. But his faith made him all the more eager to work toward the deliverance of his people. He was now waiting for Ian's opinion concerning the prospects of the settlers in Canada.

In the meantime, the clan was more comfortable and passed the winter more happily than for many years. First of all, they had access to the chief at any moment. He had prepared a room in his own house where there was always a fire and a light for any who would read the books he was able to lend them, or play at quiet games. To them its humble arrangements were sumptuous. And best of all, he would, in the long dark *fore-nights,* as the lowland Scotch call them, read aloud, sometimes in Gaelic, other times in English, poems and stories that gave them great delight. *If only this state of things could be kept up—with Ian back and Mercy married to the chief!* thought the mother.

Mr. Palmer would gladly have left his family again and spent the winter somewhere else. But as things were he could not leave them, and as certain other things were, he did not care to take them to London. Besides, for them all to leave now would be to confess defeat, and who could tell what might happen in his absence? He was resolved to see the thing out. And above all, he must keep that worthless girl, Mercy, under his own eye!

Both Mercy and the chief thought it better not to meet much, but they did occasionally arrange to see one another for a few minutes—usually by the help of Christina. Only twice was Mercy's handkerchief hung from the window. The signal brought him both times through the wild wintry storm, joyous as a bird through the summer air. Once or twice they met just outside the gate.

At length came the much-desired letter from Ian, full of news to help the chief in his decision.

Two things had been clear to Alister: even if the ground he had could grow enough to keep his people alive, it certainly could not keep them all employed; and if they went elsewhere, especially to any of the surrounding towns, it could produce a descent in the moral scale. He was their shepherd and must lose none of them! It was now clear to him that the best thing was that the poor remnant of the clan should leave their native country and move where many of their own people, among them Lachlan and Annie, would welcome them, probably to ease and comfort. There he would buy land, settle with them, and build a village. Some would work the soil under their chief; others would pursue their trades for the good of the community and themselves.

Now again, the chief's love of the land came face-to-face with his love of men. For the first time, the two seemed opposed to one another. For there was but one way to get the money necessary to carry out his plan: the last of the Macruadh property must go! Yet it did not rouse a grudging thought in the chief, for it was for the sake of the men and women and children whose lives would be required of him. The land itself must yield them wings to leave it and fly beyond the sea.

He wrote to Ian, and determined that, if he agreed with the plan, he would negotiate the sale of the land at once in order to carry the clan to Canada.

Reflecting on the plan, he saw no reason why he should not give Mr. Peregrine Palmer the first chance of purchase. He thought also, with his usual hopefulness, that time might come when the clan, laying its savings in Canada together, might be able to return and purchase back its ancient homesteads. Such things had been, and might be again!

Two months passed, and then came Ian's answer. Because of the loss of their uncle's money and the good prospect of comfort in return for hard work in Canada, Ian entirely approved of the proposal. From that moment the thing was no longer merely discussed, but plans as to how to carry it out were made. The chief assembled the clan in the barn, read his brother's letter, and in a simple speech told them exactly what the situation was. He told them of the loss of the money he had long hoped for, reminding them that there was neither employment nor subsistence enough on the land for all of them. He stated his resolve to sell the last of the land in order to provide the means for their migrating as a body to Canada, where many of their old friends were eager to welcome them. There they would buy land, he said, of which every man should have a portion to cultivate and live on. He believed they would fare well in exchange for hard work. There was even a possibility, he hoped, that if they lived and labored well, one day they might buy back the home they had left. And if not they, perhaps their sons and daughters might return from their captivity and restore the house of their fathers. If anyone would not go, he would do for him what was fair.

Donald the shoemaker rose, unpuckered his face, and said, "Where my chief goes, I will go; where my chief lives, I will live; where my chief is buried, God grant that I may be buried also."

He sat down, and wept.

One voice rose from all present: "We'll go, Macruadh! Our chief is our home!"

The chief's heart swelled with mingled gladness and grief, but he answered quietly, "Then you must at once begin preparations; we ought not to be in a hurry when the time comes."

An immediate stir, movement, bustle, followed. There was much talking and many sunny faces, over which kept sweeping the clouds of sorrow.

The next morning the chief went to the New House and asked to see Mr. Palmer. He was shown into what the new laird called his study. Mr. Palmer's first thought was that he had come to call him to account for firing at him. He neither spoke nor advanced a step to meet him. The chief stood still some yards from him.

"You are surprised to see me, Mr. Palmer," he said as pleasantly as he could.

"I am."

"I have come to ask if you would like to buy my land?"

"Already!" said Mr. Palmer, and cast on his enemy a glare of victory. The chief did not reply.

"Well!" said Mr. Palmer.

"I await your answer," returned the chief.

"Did it never strike you that insolence might be carried too far?"

"I came for your sake more than my own," rejoined the chief without a shadow of anger, "I have no particular desire that you should have the land, but I thought it only right that you should have the first offer. If you decline, I can sell it elsewhere."

What a dull ox the fellow must take me for! said Mr. Palmer to himself as he stood looking the chief over from head to foot. *It's all a dodge to get into the house. As if he would ever sell me his land! Buy his land! It's some trick, I'll wager my soul! The infernal scoundrel! Takes an ounce of shot in the chest and never says, "What the devil did you mean by that?" I don't believe the savage ever felt it!*

"If you cannot make up your mind at once," said Alister, "I will give you till tomorrow to think it over."

"When you have learned to behave like a gentleman," answered the new laird, "let me know, and I will refer you to my factor."

He turned and rang the bell. Alister bowed and did not wait for the servant to show him out.

In the afternoon Alister set out for London.

42 / Another Expulsion

Mr. Peregrine Palmer brooded more and more upon what he counted the contempt of the chief. It became such an obsession with him that it had already sent out several shoots, and had, among others, developed the notion that he was despised by his own family as well. He grew moody, and his moodiness and distrust developed suspicion. He told himself he cared not a straw what such a fanatical fool as the chief thought of him; but he reflected that if one could so despise his money because of its source, there might be others, even many, who did so. His smoldering, unmotivated anger, and the fierce resentment of the chief's judgment revealed how closely the offense clung to his consciousness.

Flattering himself that Mercy's calmness indicated she had gotten over her foolish liking for the "boor," he had listened to the prayers of her mother and had at last submitted to her company at the dinner table. But he continued to treat her shamefully.

That evening he could hardly eat for the wrathful memories of the Macruadh's interview. Perhaps his most painful reflection was that he had not been quick enough to seize the opportunity to annihilate his enemy. Thunder lowered portentous in his black brows, and not until he had drunk several glasses of wine did a word come from his lips. His presence was purgatory without the purification.

"What do you think that fellow was here about this morning?" he said at length.

"What fellow?" asked his wife unnecessarily, for she knew very well what visitor had been shown into the study.

"The highland fellow," he answered, "who claims to do what he pleases on my property!"

Mercy's face grew hot.

"Came actually to offer me the purchase of his land! The merest trick to get into the house—confound him! As much as told me if I did not buy the land, I should not have the chance again! The brute! To dare show his face in my house after trifling with my daughter's affections on the pretense that he could not marry a girl whose father was in trade!"

Mercy felt she would be false to the man she loved if she did not speak. She had no thought of defending him, but simply of bearing witness to the truth.

"I beg your pardon, Papa," she said, "but the Macruadh never trifled with me. He loves me, and has not given me up. If he told you he was going to part with his land, he is going to part with it, and came to you first because he must return good for evil. I saw him from my window ride off as if he were going to meet the afternoon coach."

She would not have been allowed to say so much had not her father been speechless with rage. This was more than he or any man could bear! He rose from the table, his eyes blazing.

"Return *me* good for evil!" he thundered. "A beast who has done me more wrong than ever I did in all my life! A scoundrel bumpkin who loses not a single opportunity of insulting me! You are an insolent, depraved girl—ready to sacrifice yourself, body and soul, to a man who despises you and your family with the pride of a savage! You hussy, I can hardly keep my hands off you!"

He came toward her with a threatful stride. She rose, pushed back her chair, and stood facing him.

"Strike me if you will, Papa," she said in a choking voice, "but Mama knows I am not what you call me! I would be false and cowardly if I did not speak the truth for the man whom I owe—" She was going to say "*more than to any other human being,*" but she checked herself.

"If the beggar is your god," said her father, and struck her on the cheek with his open hand, "you can go to him!"

He took her by the arm and pushed her before him out of the room and across the hall. Then, opening the door, he shoved her from him into the garden and flung the door closed behind her. The rain was pouring down in torrents, the night was very dark, and when the door shut, she felt as if she had lost her eyesight.

Without a moment's hesitation—while her mother wept and pleaded, while Christina stood burning with anger, while two little ones sat white with open mouths, and while the servants hurried about scared but trying to look as if nothing had happened—Mercy fled into the dark. She stumbled into the shrubbery several times, but at last reached the gate, and while they imagined her standing in front of the house waiting to be let in, she was running from it down the road to her refuge. The pouring rain was sweet to her whole indignant person, especially to the cheek which burned from her father's blow. The way was deep in mud, and she slipped and fell more than once.

Mrs. Macruadh was sitting in the little parlor with no one but Nancy in the house when the door opened and in came the wild-looking girl, bedraggled and spent. Great masses of long black hair hung dripping with rain about her shoulders. Her dress was torn and wet, dirty with clay from the road. One cheek was white, and the other had a red patch on it.

"My poor child!" cried the mother. "What has happened? Alister is away."

"I know," panted Mercy. "I saw him go, but I thought you would take me in—though I know you do not like me much."

"Not like you, my child!" echoed the mother tenderly. "I love you! Are you not my Alister's choice? There are things I could have wished otherwise, but—"

"I could wish them otherwise too!" interposed Mercy. "I do not wish another father, but I wish he hadn't struck me and put me out into the dark and rain, and—"

"Struck you and put you out! My child! What did he do it for?"

"Perhaps I deserved it. It is difficult to know how to behave to a father. A father is supposed to be one whom you not only love, but of whom you can be proud as well! I love mine, but I can't be proud of him, and don't quite know how to behave to him. Perhaps I ought to have kept silent, but when he said things that were not true about Alister, I felt it false to hold my tongue."

She ceased and sank to the floor, kneeling at Mrs. Macruadh's knee. All the compassion of the woman, all the protective pride of the chieftainess, woke in the mother. She raised the girl in her arms and vowed that not one of Mercy's house should set eyes on her again without her son's consent. He would see how his mother cared for what was his. How wide her arms, how big her heart, to take the one he loved! They would, of course, repent and want her back, but they would not have her. She would be in peace until Alister came. Thank God, they had turned her out, and that made her free of them! They would not have her again; Alister would have her—and from the hand of his mother!

She got her to bed and sent for Rob of the Angels. With injunctions to silence, she told him to fetch his father, and be ready as soon as possible to drive a cart to the chief's cave, there to make everything comfortable for herself and Miss Mercy Palmer.

Mercy slept well, and as the day was breaking, Mrs. Macruadh woke her and helped her to dress. Then they walked together through the lovely spring morning to the turn of the valley road, where a cart was waiting for them, half filled with oat-straw. They got in and were borne up at a walking pace to the spot Mercy knew so well. Never by swiftest coach had she enjoyed a journey so much as that slow crawl up the mountains in the rough springless cart of her ploughman lover! She felt so protected, so happy, so hopeful! Alister's mother was indeed a hiding place from the wind and the storm. Having consented to be her mother, she could mother her no way but completely. An outcast for the sake of her Alister, she should have the warmest corner of her heart next to him and Ian!

Into the tomb they went, finding everything strangely comfortable—the stone floor covered with warm and wooly skins of black-faced sheep, a great fire glowing, plenty of provisions, and the deaf, keen-eyed father with the swift keen-eared son for attendants.

"You will not mind sharing your bed with me—will you, my child?" said Mrs. Macruadh. "Our accommodation is scanty. But we shall be safe from intrusion. Only those two faithful men know where we are."

"Mother will be terribly frightened," said Mercy.

"I thought of that and left a note with Nancy to give to her, telling her you were safe and well, but giving her no hint of where. I said that her dove had flown to my bosom for shelter, and there should have it."

Mercy answered her with a tearful embrace.

43 / The Chief's Princess_____

Ten peaceful days they spent in the cave house. It was cold outside, but the clear air of the hilltop was delicious, and inside it was warm and dry. There were plenty of books, and Mercy never was bored. The mother talked freely of her sons and of their father, of the history of the clan, of her own girlhood, and the hopes and intentions of her sons.

"Will you go with him, Mercy?" she asked.

"I would rather be with him than remain at home; there is no life there," Mercy stated.

"There is life wherever there is will to live—that is, to do the thing that is given one to do," Mrs. Macruadh responded.

In writing to London, she told Alister nothing of what had happened: she did not want him to hurry home without completing his business. There he was able to settle everything, parted with his property to an old friend of the family, and received what would suffice for his further intents. He also chartered a ship to take them over the sea, arranging for it to go northward and take the clan on board at a certain bay on the coast.

When at length he reached home, Nancy informed him that his mother was at the hill house. He was naturally perplexed: she went there so seldom! And she had never gone there for the night. He set out immediately.

It was twilight when he reached the top of the hill. That day Mercy had been amusing Mrs. Macruadh with charades of a sort, and when the mother heard her son's approaching step, a thought came to her.

"Here, quick!" she said, "put on my cap and shawl, and sit in this chair. I will go into the bedroom. Then do as you like."

When the chief entered, he saw the form of his mother, as he thought, bending over the peat fire, which had sunk rather low. In his imagination he saw again the form of his uncle as on that night in the low moon light. She did not move, did not even look up. He stood still for a moment; a strange feeling possessed him of something not being as it ought to be. But he recovered himself with an effort, and kneeling beside her, put his arms around her—not a little frightened at her continued silence.

"What is the matter, Mother dear?" he said. "Why have you come to this lonely place?"

When Mercy first felt his arms, she could not have spoken if she would—her heart seemed to grow too large for her body. But in a moment or two she controlled herself and was able to say—sufficiently in his mother's tone and manner to keep up the charade, "They put me out of the house, Alister."

"Put you out of the house?" he returned, like one hearing and talking in a dream. Something in the voice sounded wrong, yet he knew the voice like his own. Whose could it be but his mother's? Was the night playing tricks on his ears as well as his eyes? "Who dared interfere with you, Mother? Am I losing my senses? I do not seem to understand my own words."

"Mr. Palmer."

"Mr. Palmer! Was it to him I sold the land in London? What could he have to do with you, Mother? Oh, I see! He came and worried you so about Mercy that you were glad to take refuge from him up here."

"No, that was not it. But as we are going soon, there would have been no good fighting it out. We *are* going soon, aren't we?"

"Indeed we are, please God!" replied the chief, who had again relapsed into utter bewilderment.

"That is well—especially for you. Would you believe it—the worthless girl vows she will never leave her mother's house!"

"Ah, Mother, *you* never heard her say so. I know Mercy better than that. She will leave it when I say *come*. But that won't be long now. I must wait, and come fetch her when she is of age."

"She is not worthy of you."

"She is worthy of me if I were twenty times worthier than I am. Mother, Mother, what has made you so changeable?"

"To whom are you talking, Alister? Yourself, or a ghost?"

Alister started up, and saw his mother coming from the bedroom with a candle in her hand. He stood stupefied. He looked again at the seated figure, still bending over the fire.

With a wild burst of almost hysteric laughter, Mercy sprang to her feet and threw herself in his arms. This new bewilderment became an unspeakable delight. Was he awake or dreaming? His princess had arrived! The dream of his boyhood come true! She was here in his cave to be his own!

By the time Alister left them to go home, the night was far advanced. But even then he did not go home but wandered about all night, like an angel sent to hover and watch until the morning. When he astonished them by entering as they sat at breakfast and told them how he had passed the night, it thrilled Mercy's heart to know that while she slept and dreamt of him, he was awake and thinking about her.

After breakfast he went to see the clergyman of the parish who lived some miles away; in a few days they were married. Before that, however, he went once more to the New House to tell Mr. Palmer what was about to be done. He refused to see him, and would not even allow his wife or Christina to go to him.

The wedding was held at noon within the ruined walls of the old castle. The withered remnant of the clan, with pipes playing, guns firing, and shouts of celebration, marched to the cave house to fetch the bride and bring her down the hill to her waiting bridegroom. After the ceremony a feast was ready for all in the barn, and much dancing followed.

Evening came, with a half-moon hanging faint in the limpid blue, and the stars looking large through the mist of nature's ungathered tears. The wind breathed easily like a sleeping child, sweet and soft and full of dreams of summer; the mountains and hills stood around them like a flock of day-wearied sheep, haunted by the angels of Rob's visions. The lovers stole away to walk through the heavenly sapphire of the still night, up the hills and over the rushing streams of the spring, to the cave of their rest—no ill omen, but a lovely symbol to such as could see in the tomb the porch of paradise. Where should true lovers make their bed but on the threshold of eternity?

44 / The Farewell

A month passed, and the flag of their ship of exile was seen flying in the bay. The same hour the chief's horses were hitched, the carts loaded, and their last things gathered. Few farewells had to be made, for the whole clan, except two that had deserted, turned out at the very minute appointed. The chief arranged them in marching column. Foremost went the pipes; the chief and his wife and mother came next; Hector of the Stags, carrying the double-barreled rifle the chief had given him, and Rob of the Angels followed. Then came the women and children; next the carts, with a few who could not walk on top of the baggage; the men brought up the rear. Four or five favorite dogs were the skirmishers of the column.

The road to the bay led them past the gate of the New House. The chief called a halt, and went with his wife to seek a last interview. Mr. Peregrine Palmer kept to his room, but Mrs. Palmer bade her daughter a loving farewell. The children wept. Christina bade her sister good-bye with a hopeless, almost envious look: Mercy, who did not love him, would see Ian! She, who would give her soul for him, was never to look on him again in this world!

Kissing Mercy once more, she choked down a sob and whispered, "Give my love—no, my heart—to Ian, and tell him I *am* trying."

They all walked together to the gate and there took leave of the ladies of the New House. The pipes struck up; the column moved on.

When they came to the corner which would hide from them their last view of their native strath, the march changed to a lament; and with the opening wail, all stopped and turned for a farewell look. Men and women, the chief alone excepted, burst into weeping, and the sound of their lamentation went wandering through the hills with an adieu to every loved spot. And this was what the pipes said:

We shall never see you more,
  Never more, never more!
Till the sea be dry, and the world be bare,
And the dews have ceased to fall,
And the rivers have ceased to run,
We shall never see you more,
  Never more, never more!

269

270

As they stood and gazed, the pipes went on lamenting and the women, weeping.

At length Alister stopped the piper. "My friends," he cried (in Gaelic of course), "look at me. My eyes are dry! Where Jesus, the Son of God, is—there is my home! He is here, and he is over the sea, and my home is everywhere. I have lost my land and my country, but I take with me my people and make no moan over my exile! Hearts are more than hills. Farewell, Strathruadh of my childhood! Place of my dreams, I shall visit you again in my sleep! And again I shall see you in happier times, please God, with my friends around me!"

He took off his cap. All the men too uncovered their heads for a moment, then turned to follow their chief. The pipes struck up Macrimmon's lament, *Till an crodh a Dhonnachaidh*. Not one looked behind him again till they reached the shore. There, out in the bay, the biggest ship any of the clan had ever seen was waiting to receive them.

When Mr. Peregrine Palmer saw that the land might in truth be for sale, he would gladly have bought it, but found to his chagrin that he was too late. It was just like the fellow, he said, to mock him with the chance of buying it! He took care to come himself, rather than sending a man he might have believed with the offer!

45 / Epilogue

The clan thrived in the clearings of the Canadian pine forests. The hill men stared in disbelief at the growth of their harvests. Their many children were strong and healthy, and called Scotland their home.

In an outlying and barren part of the chief's land, they came upon rock oil. It was so plentiful that as soon as transport of it became possible, the chief and his people began to see their poverty as a thing of the past.

News came to them that Mr. Peregrine Palmer was in difficulties and desirous of parting with his highland estate. The chief was now able to buy it, and gave his agent in London directions to secure it for him, with any other land in the area that might come on the market. But he would not at once return to occupy it, for his mother dreaded the sea, and he would rather have his boys grow where they were, and face as men the temptations beyond. He was not anxious, moreover, to take them away from such teaching as that of their uncle Ian! Both father and uncle would have them *alive* before encountering what the world calls *life*.

But the Macruadh continued to dream of the time when those of the clan then left in the world, accompanied, he hoped, by some of those who had left Scotland before, would go back to repopulate the old waste places, and from a wilderness of white sheep and red deer, make the mountain land a nursery of honest, unambitious, brave men and strong-hearted women, loving God and their neighbor. There no man would think of himself at his brother's cost, no man grow rich by his neighbor's ruin, no man lay field to field to treasure up for himself wrath against the day of wrath. There no man would say, "What's mine's mine!" but where all would say to God, *"What's mine is yours."*

271

THE
Gentlewoman's
Choice

George MacDonald

THE
Gentlewoman's Choice

Michael R. Phillips, Editor

BETHANY HOUSE PUBLISHERS
MINNEAPOLIS, MINNESOTA 55438
A Division of Bethany Fellowship, Inc.

Published by Bethany House Publishers
A Division of Bethany Fellowship, Inc.
6820 Auto Club Road, Minneapolis, Minnesota 55438

Printed in the United States of America

Library of Congress Cataloging-in-Publication Data
Macdonald, George, 1824-1905.
    The gentlewoman's choice.

    Originally published: Weighed and wanting. London : Sampson Low, 1882.
    I. Phillips, Michael R., 1946-   . II. Title.
PR4967.W48   1987   823'.8   87-6556
ISBN 0-87123-941-8 (pbk.)

Contents

Introduction _____

It fell to one of George MacDonald's lesser known novels, *Weighed and Wanting*, published in 1882, to manifest more fully than any of his other works one of the strongest driving forces in MacDonald's spiritual vision: the theme of godly service to the poor. Certainly MacDonald stresses the necessity for Christian charity and sacrifice in a number of his other books, notably *The Vicar's Daughter, Robert Falconer*, and *Sir Gibbie*, and infuses nearly everything he wrote with the imperative of actively *living* one's faith. However, in *Weighed and Wanting* (here republished as *The Gentlewoman's Choice* in the Bethany House series of MacDonald reprints), this is the dominant theme throughout the story.

Hester Raymount, a sort of feminine counterpart to Robert Falconer and one of MacDonald's few leading ladies who carries a book all on her own, wants to grow beyond the threshold of her own salvation. As she takes her first steps in this direction, she struggles with the question of how to live out that faith toward those around her. Her eventual capacity to choose the life God has marked out for her comes only with much soul-searching along the way. The quest of Falconer's heart had primarily to do with the truth of the gospel, but Hester's choices are concerned with what obedience to the gospel means regarding her fellowman.

Hester's family is a so-called religious one, yet without deep convictions. Hester has grown up in an environment where the words of life were present but had not penetrated into action. It is this empty shell of pseudo spirituality, exemplified by Hester's father, and the negative fruit revealed in the character of one of her brothers, which has been "weighed" and found "wanting" in the end—the unconverted heart that gives only lip service to a faith in God, but which puts self-interests first when the test comes.

Hester, however, rising above her parental training, chooses a different road—reminiscent of Falconer and the adult Sir Gibbie in their ministrations to the forsaken masses of the city—and ultimately discovers her fulfillment in the path of selflessness, the path of laying down one's life in service to God and his people. In so doing, she exemplifies one of the most profound lessons MacDonald emphasizes in nearly all of his books—letting God use you where you are, with the talents you possess, to help and minister to those around you. Also, in so doing,

9

Hester helps raise her family to an increased consciousness of God.

The gift that God wanted Hester to use in his kingdom was a simple one—her voice raised in song, along with her piano playing. Singing was not considered, in the late 19th century, a great "witnessing" tool in comparison with the mighty proclamations of the well-known evangelists and preachers of the day. Yet Hester's music was the tool God had given *her*, and was the tool he wanted *her* to use for him. He had given her the gift, and she faithfully put it to use. That was all God required of her—nothing more. God was able to work by his Spirit in the lives around Hester as she obediently used these gifts for his glory. In our own lives, God's tools are the things he has placed in our hand.

In addition to MacDonald's constant theme of living one's faith in active ministry, a number of sub-themes capture our attention in *The Gentlewoman's Choice* as well. One is particularly struck with MacDonald's forerunning social convictions on marriage and his significant position on the role of women in positions of ministry—ideas far in advance of his time. In a Victorian era in which women were often relegated to a subservient role, Hester stands firm and tall as a woman of God who comes to know where she is going and confidently occupies that role without fear. Similarly, MacDonald reveals that his views of marriage ran counter to the accepted Victorian norms. "You have very different ideas," says one of Hester's acquaintances, "from such as were taught in my girlhood concerning the duties of wives. A woman, I used to be told, was to fashion herself for her husband; fit her life to his life, her thoughts to his thoughts, her tastes to his tastes."

"Absurd indeed," answers MacDonald to the notion of Hester marrying the man in question according to such a pattern. He concludes the discussion: "Instead of walking on together in simple equality, in mutual honor and devotion, each helping the other to be better still, the ludicrous notion would instead have the woman—large and noble though she might be—come cowering after her husband—spiritual pigmy though he might be—as if he were the god of her life."

But even more memorable, again like the paths of ministry marked out for Robert Falconer and Mary St. John, Hester's story speaks to those he does not lead into marriage in their ministries, confirming that often God lays out a single road for his children.

In one sense, this book capsulizes MacDonald's urgent message to the Christian body. He urges us to worry less about doctrine, theology, and the forms and trappings of religion. Instead he advises us to *do* the work God has put before us. In that sense, *The Gentlewoman's Choice* is one of the least theological of MacDonald's works. It illustrates that faith without works is no faith at all—it will be weighed, and in the end found to be lacking substance or value. MacDonald summarizes this theme at the book's close with the words, "Let every man or woman work out the thing that is in him. Whoever uses the means that he has, great or small, and does the work that is given him to do, stands by the side of Jesus and is a fellow worker with him."

This, then, is Hester's pilgrimage into a faith of her own; as she confronts the options before her, as she contemplates the future course of her life, and as she makes the choice and puts that faith into action.

Michael Phillips
1707 E Street
Eureka, CA 95501

1 / A Bad-Weather Holiday_____

It was a gray, windy noon in early autumn—certainly not the sort of day one would choose for a holiday. The Raymounts had come to Burcliff on the east coast of England to enjoy the blue sky, the blue sea, and the bright sun overhead. So far, however, they had scarcely seen any of the three. It was hardly surprising, then, that their moods were somewhat disagreeable.

The sky and the sea were almost the same dull color. Where they met, troops of waves broke into white crests as they rushed toward the shore. On land the trees and the smoke were greatly troubled—the trees because they would rather stand still, the smoke because it would rather ascend. But the wind kept tossing the former and beating down the latter. None of the hundreds of fishing boats belonging to the coast were to be seen, nor a single sail visible—not even the smoke of a solitary steamer ploughing through the rain and fog south to London or north to Aberdeen.

To the thousands who had come to Burcliff to enjoy a holiday, the weather was depressing. But no matter how much time the labor-weary were allotted, to them the holiday had looked short from the beginning. Because of the gloomy dreariness, the time of relaxation was growing shorter and shorter, while the days seemed longer and longer. The vacationers found themselves wrapped in a blanket of fog, out of which intermittent rains of the wettest kind poured down upon them. To those who hated work, this joyous holiday, which by every right and reason belonged to them, seemed snatched away by that vague enemy against whom the grumbling of the world is continually directed. For were they not born to be happy, and how could a human being possibly fulfill that destiny in such miserable circumstances?

Some can be happy in such circumstances by securing the corner of a couch near a good fire. With the help of an intriguing novel, they are able to forget the world around them—the noise of the waves on the sands, or the storm resounding through the chimney, or the rain on the windows serving to deepen still further the calm of their surroundings. But there are others, an exceptional class of mortals indeed, who can be content even in worse circumstances—without a novel, without a cheerful fire, without pleasing smells from the kitchen—content with a calm of spirit that comes from within. Such persons, patient and pleasant to those around them, are well worth knowing. Mrs. Raymount, half the head and more than half the heart of the family staying in a certain lodging house in the forefront of Burcliff, was one of these.

The Raymount family was not large, yet it contained perhaps as many varieties of character and temperament as some larger ones. These varieties gave rise to several ways of dealing with such misfortunes as rainy weather. For misfortune it must seem to poor creatures who are slaves of the elements, especially when the weather ought to be sunny. When it is not, something must be out of order, giving ground for complaint. The father met it with tolerably good humor; but he was busy writing a paper for one of the monthly reviews and would have stayed inside regardless of the weather. Therefore, he could take no credit for his genial mood, and his disposition must for the moment pass as not tested. But, if you had taken from the mother her piece of work—she was busy embroidering a pinafore—and given her nothing to do, she would yet have been as peaceful as she now looked, for she knew who made her.

A tall lad stood at one of the windows in smoldering rebellion against the order of events. He was such a creature of moods that individual judgments of his character might well have proved irreconcilable. He had not yet begun to use his will—constantly mistaking, as do many, impulse for will—to blend the conflicting elements of his nature into one. As a man he was, therefore, much like the mass of flour and raisins, etc., before it becomes a plum pudding. He would have to pass through something comparable to boiling before he would become worthy of the name *man*. But to himself he seemed virtuous enough, and never bothered to discern his bad moods. He substituted forgetfulness for failure to pay his debts, a return of good humor for repentance, and at best a joke for apology. Time would tell in which direction he chose to go.

Mark, a pale, handsome boy of ten, and Josephine, a rosy girl of seven, sat on the opposite side of the fire amusing themselves with a puzzle. The gusts of wind and the great splashes of rain on the glass only made them feel cosier and more content.

"Beastly weather!" Cornelius blurted, turning toward the room rather than the persons in it.

"I'm sorry you don't like it, Corney," his elder sister sympathized, as she sat beside her mother trimming what promised to be a pretty bonnet. A concentrated effort to draw her needle through an accumulation of silken folds seemed to take something off the bloom of her smile.

"Oh, it's all very well for girls!" snapped Cornelius. "You don't do anything worthwhile. And besides, you've got so many things you like to do, and so much time to do them in, that it's all the same to you whether you go out or stay home. But when a fellow has only a miserable three weeks and then it's back to a job he hates, it is rather hard to have it turn out like this. Day after day, as sure as the sun rises—if it does rise—the weather is as abominable as rain and wind can make it!"

"My dear boy!" chided his mother without looking up.

"Oh yes, Mother! I know! You're so good you would have had Job himself take it coolly. But I'm not like you. Only you needn't think me so very—what do you call it? It's only a breach in the laws of nature I'm grumbling at. I don't mean anything to offend you."

"Perhaps you mean more than you think," answered his mother with a deep sigh.

"Oh, I know," returned the youth in a tone that roused his sister's anger, "and you think I should be more thankful. I've heard you say so many times before, like the three children in the fiery furnace you so often remind me about."

"They would have been glad enough for some of the weather you call beastly," said Hester, again pulling through a stiff needle, this time without any smile, for sometimes her brother was more than she could bear.

"Oh, I daresay! But then, they knew when they got out they wouldn't have to go back to a wretched bank with nothing but figures before their eyes from morning till night."

The mother's face grew sad.

"I am afraid, Cornelius, my dear son, that you will need the furnace yourself to teach you that the will of God, even in unpleasant weather, is a thing for rejoicing in. But I dread the fire for your sake, my boy!"

"I should have thought this weather, and the bank waiting after it, furnace enough, Mother!" he answered, trying to laugh off her words.

"It does not seem to be," she stated with some displeasure. "But then," she added with a sigh, "you do not have the same companion the three holy children had."

"Who is that?" rejoined Cornelius, for he had partly forgotten the story he knew well enough in childhood.

"We will not talk about him now," answered his mother. "He has been knocking at your chamber door for some time: when he comes to the furnace door, perhaps you will open that to him."

Cornelius returned no answer; he felt awkward at his mother's seriousness, and told himself she was unkind. Why couldn't she make some allowance for a fellow? He meant no harm . . .

Since working at the bank, he had become still less patient with his mother's infrequent admonitions, for, much as he disliked the job, he considered himself quite a man of the world because of it. But a completely wordly man he was not—not yet at least—even though he was totally incapable of perceiving the kind of thing his mother cared about. This came not from moral lack alone, but from dullness and lack of imagination as well. He was like the child so sure he can run alone that he snatches his hand from his mother's and sets off through dirt and puddles, acting the part of the great person he considers himself.

With all her peace of soul, Mrs. Raymount was very anxious about her son, but she said no more to him now. She knew that a sudden drenching shower is not the best way of making a child friendly with cold water.

"Well, for my part," declared Cornelius at length, partly to justify himself and partly to divert the conversation, "I don't desire to be better than my neighbor. I think it downright selfish."

"Do you want to be as good as your neighbor, Corney?" asked his mother. "More importantly, are you content with being as good as you are now, or do you want to be better?"

"To tell you the truth, Mother, I don't trouble my head about such things. Philosophers are agreed that self-consciousness is the bane of the present age. Therefore, I mean to avoid it. If you had let me go into the army, I might have had some time to think about such matters, but that horrible bank takes everything out of me—except a burning desire to forget it at any cost till the time comes when I must endure it again. If I didn't have some amusement in between, I would kill myself, or take to opium or drinking. I wonder how the governor would like to be in *my* place!"

Hester rose and left the room, indignant with him for speaking so of his father.

"If your father were in your place, Cornelius," said his mother with dignity, "he would carry out his duties without grumbling, however irksome they might be."

"How do you know that, Mother? He never had such a job."

"I know it because I know him," she answered confidently.

Cornelius acknowledged this with a grunt.

"If you think it hard," his mother resumed, "that you have to follow a way of life you did not choose, you must remember that we could get you to express no preference for anything. Furthermore, your father had to strain everything to send you to college. I am sorry to say it, but you did not make it any easier by your mode of living while there."

"I didn't run up a single bill!" he cried indignantly.

"Your father knows that; but he also knows that your cousin Robert did not spend two-thirds of what you did, and made more of his time, also."

"He was in *rather* a different group," sneered the youth.

"And you know too," his mother continued, "that your father's main reason for placing you in your uncle's bank was to give you a knowledge of the business that will help you to properly manage the money he will leave behind him. When you have gained that knowledge, there will be time to look for something else to do . . . you are young yet."

His father's money was a continual annoyance to Cornelius, for it was no secret how he meant to dispose of it after he died. He intended to leave it under trustees, with his son as one of them until he married. At that time his estate was to be divided equally among his children, without any particular provision made for Cornelius as his father's "heir."

Cornelius did not agree with this arrangement, for he could not see any advantage, then, in being the eldest son of the family.

"Now, Mother," he complained, "do you think it fair that I should have to look after the whole family as if they were my own?"

This was by no means his real cause of complaint, but he chose to use it as his grievance for the present.

"You will not be the only trustee," said his mother. "It need not weigh on you."

"Well, of course, I could do better with it than anyone else in the family."

"If you have your father's love of fair play, Cornelius, you will. What you can do to prepare yourself is to become thoroughly trained in business."

"A bank's hardly the place to get the business knowledge necessary for that sort of thing!"

"Your father has his reasons. How well prepared you are will depend on you. And when you marry, your responsibility will cease."

"What if I should marry before my father's death?"

"Indeed, I hope you will, Cornelius. The arrangement your father has made is merely a provision against the unlikely. When you are married, I don't doubt he will make an entirely new will to meet the new circumstances."

I believe, Cornelius thought to himself, *that if I were to marry a woman with money—and why shouldn't I—my father would divide my share among the rest and not leave me a farthing!*

Full of the injury of the idea, he rose and left the room. His mother wept as he vanished. She dared not allow herself to ask why she wept, dared not admit to herself that her firstborn was not lovely in her eyes, dared not ask where he could have gotten such a selfish nature.

Although since coming to Burcliff, Cornelius attributed his sour spirits to the weather, and had expended them on the cooking, the couches, the beds, and twenty different things that displeased him, he had nevertheless brought his disposition with him. And his mother had sad doubts, not only about his conduct, but about his attitude and his conscience, which lay lazily undisturbed under both of them.

He had always been temperamental and wayward, but had only recently begun to behave so unpleasantly. Yet among his companions, he bore the character of the best-natured fellow in the world. To them he never showed any of the peevishness of his mental discomfort. He kept that for home, for those who loved him a thousand times better and would have cheerfully parted with their own happiness for his. Cornelius was but one of a large group of youths who possessed no will of their own yet enjoyed the reputation of a strong one. He would become obstinate over any foolish notion his pettiness decided to latch on to. And the common mind always takes obstinacy for strength of will, even when it springs from an utter inability to exercise the will as it was meant to be used.

Mr. Raymount knew little of the real nature of his son. The youth was afraid of his father—even though he spoke of him with so little respect. To his face he dared not show his true nature. He knew that his mother would not betray him—at least he would have considered it betrayal—to his father. And to be sure, no one who had ever heard Mr. Raymount give vent to his judgments would have wondered why either of them hesitated to mention the thing to him.

Whether in his own youth he would have done better in a position similar to his son's, as his worshiping wife believed, may be doubtful.

2 / An Eventful Walk

Gerald Raymount was a man with an unusual combination of qualities. His character contained such contradictions that one would think there was almost a savage strain in him. On the other hand, he possessed a sharp mind, which seemed to indicate a heritage of culture. At the university he had read widely outside his specific requirements and thus had developed a broad knowledge of literature.

He had inherited a few thousand pounds from his father, a country attorney. However, he had found that as his family had increased, his income was not sufficient for their accustomed style of living. There were no extravagant tastes among them, but they did not have the ability to save money and were rather too free with it in small things. The result was that Mr. Raymount was compelled to rouse himself out of his self-indulgence, and discover whether he could write articles that might add to his shrinking income.

Though Mr. Raymount was driven to this extreme by necessity, it did serve to make a man of him. But the question is not whether a man works because he has to, but whether the work he does is good, honest work for which the world is better off. In this matter there are many first that shall be last. The work of a baker for instance, must stand higher in the judgment of the universe than that of a brewer, no matter how good his ale might be. Because the one trade brings in more money than the other, many in the world count it more honorable. But there is another judgment at hand.

In the exercise of his calling, Mr. Raymount was compelled to think more carefully than before, and so not only his mind but his moral and spiritual nature took a fresh start. More and more he wrote of the feelings and experiences of his own heart and history, and so, by degrees, gained power to rouse the will, not merely the emotions, or even the aspirations of men—the only true kind of power. The poetry of his college days now came to the service of his prose, and the deeper poetic nature, which is the prophetic in every man, awoke in him. His wife grew proud of him and of his work. Even though she looked upon her husband as a great man, she was still the practical wisdom of the house. He was not a great man—only a growing man; yet she was nothing the worse for thinking so highly of him, because he *was* a growing man. Had he

19

not been a growing man, her admiration would have caused her growth to deteriorate as well.

The daughter of a London barrister, of a good family, she had known something of life before she married. From mere dissatisfaction she had early begun to withdraw from the show and self-assertion of social life. Instead, she sought within herself that quiet chamber unknown to most. For a time she had paid no attention to a certain soft knocking of one who would enter and share it with her. But now for a long time he who knocked had been her companion in the chamber whose walls are infinite. Why is it that men and women will welcome any romance or tale of love, devotion, and sacrifice from one to another of themselves, but turn from the least hint at the existence of a perfect love at the root of it all? Is it not because their natures are yet so far from the ideal, the natural, the true, that the words of the prophet rouse in them no vision, no slight perception of spiritual truth?

Helen Raymount was now a little woman of fifty, clothed in a sweet dignity with plentiful gray hair and great, clear, dark eyes. She had the two daughters and two sons already introduced, of whom Hester was the eldest.

Although a wise mother and a far-seeing father, they had made the mistake common to many parents of putting off teaching their children obedience until it was more or less too late. If this is not begun at the first possible moment, it will be harder every hour it is postponed. The spiritual loss and injury caused to the child by their waiting till they decide he's ready to reason with is immense. Yet there is nothing in which parents are more stupid and cowardly, and even stubborn, than this. A home where children are humored and scolded and coaxed and punished instead of being taught obedience is like a moral slaughterhouse instead of the training ground it was meant to be. So-called "Christian homes" can be the worst of all in this regard.

The dawn of reason as a child grows will no doubt help to develop obedience; but obedience is even more necessary to the development of reason. Where there has been no prior obedience there can be no rightly directed reason. For a parent to require of a child only what that child can understand is simply to help him to make himself his own god— that is a devil. That some children mature well enough and seem so little the worse for their bad training is no justification for lack of disciplines. So many others display attitudes and behavior that clearly reveal the consequences of their parents' foolishness.

Cornelius was one of these. He had not been taught obedience, and both he and his parents were now reaping the fruit of their neglect. He was a youth of good abilities, even a few good qualities. Yet he was full of self. He was not incapable of generosity, and was even tempted occasionally toward kindness. But he did not care whom he hurt as long as he did not see the suffering. He was incapable of controlling himself, yet was full of weak indignation whenever control was placed upon him. Supremely conceited, his view of the essentials of life were a good carriage, good manners, self-confidence, and plenty of money to spend freely. In his foolish brain he had fashioned a god into the likeness of what he considered a *gentleman*—and it was this image he was trying to become. To any wisdom in his father and mother he was so far blind that he even looked down upon it. Their opinion was hardly to be compared with that of one Reginal Vavasor, who, though so poor as to be one of his fellow clerks, was heir apparent to an earldom.

Angrily leaving his mother, Cornelius took refuge in his room. Although he had occupied it only two weeks, the top of its chest was covered with cheap novels—the only literature he cared for. He read largely of these, if indeed his mode of swallowing could be called reading. But though he had read them all, he was too lazy to face the wind and rain between him and the nearest bookshop. None of his father's books interested him, whether science, philosophy, history, or poetry. A drearier soul in a drearier setting could hardly be imagined than the soul of this youth in that day's weather at Burcliff.

It may seem that one could hardly be blamed for such a reaction to his circumstances. The truth is when a man cares for nothing that is worth caring for, the fault must indeed lie within himself—in the character the man has made, and is making, out of the nature God has given him. If Cornelius had begun at any time to do something he knew he ought to do, he would not now have been the poor slave of circumstances he was—at the mercy of the weather. When men can *act,* can *obey,* can face a duty, not only will that duty become less unpleasant to them, but life itself will *immediately* begin to gather interest. For only in duty, action, and obedience does a person begin to come into real contact with life; and only in them can he see what life is, and grow fit for it.

Cornelius threw himself on the bed—for he dared not smoke with his father so near—and dozed away the morning till lunch. He then returned to his room and fell asleep again till tea time. This was his only resource against the unpleasantness of the day. When tea was over, he rose and sauntered once more to the window.

"Hullo!" he cried. "I say, Hester, the sun's shining! The rain's over—at least for a quarter of an hour! Come, let's go out for a walk. We'll go hear the band at the castle gardens. I don't think there's anything going on at the theater."

"I would rather walk," said Hester as she went to put on her hat and cloak, and soon they were in the street.

It was one of those misty clearings in which sometimes the day seems to gather up its careless skirts that have been sweeping the half-drowned world as it prepares for the waiting night. There was a great lump of orange color half melted in the watery clouds of the west, but dreariness still hung everywhere else. As they walked along, Hester's eyes were drawn upward into the sky. Suddenly she cried out in pain when her foot turned awkwardly on a stone.

"That's what you get, Hester," Cornelius scolded, pulling her up like a horse that stumbled, "from your stargazing. You are always coming to grief by looking higher than your head!"

"Oh, please stop a minute, Corney," returned Hester, for he continued to walk on as if nothing had happened. "My ankle hurts!"

"I didn't know it was that bad," he answered stopping. "There, take my arm."

After resting a few minutes she said, "Now I can go on again. How stupid of me to be so careless!"

They walked on, but within minutes Hester stopped again.

"Corney," she grimaced, "my ankle feels so weak I am afraid I will twist it again."

"Just my luck," complained her brother. "I thought we were going to have some fun!"

They stood silent—she looking nowhere in particular, and he staring about in all directions.

"What's this?" he cried, fixing his gaze on a large building opposite them. " 'The Pilgrim's Progress,' it says on the board. It must be a lecture. Let's go in and see! We may at least sit there till your ankle is better. 'Admission—sixpence.' Come along. We may get a good laugh, who knows?"

"I don't mind," Hester said as they crossed the road.

It was a large, dingy, dirty, water-stained and somewhat dilapidated hall to which the stone stair, ascending immediately from the door, led them. Some twenty-five or thirty people were present in the gloomy place. An old man, like a broken-down clergyman, wearing a dirty white neckcloth, kept walking up and down the platform, flaunting a pretense of lecture on Bunyan's allegory. Whether he was a little drunk or greatly in his dotage, it was impossible to determine without getting closer. A sample of his mode of lecturing will reveal that a few lingering rags of scholastic achievement yet clung to the poor fellow.

"And then came the terrible battle between Christian—or was it Faithful?—I used to know, but trouble has played old hookey with my memory. It's all here, you know"—and he tapped his bald head—"but there's Christian and Apollyon. When I was young, and that wasn't yesterday, I used to think, but that was before I could read, that Apollyon was one and the same with Bonaparty—Nap-poleon, you know. And I wasn't just so far wrong neither, as I shall readily prove to those of my distinguished audience who have been to college like myself, and learned to read Greek like their mother tongue. For what is the very name Apollyon but a prophecy concerning the great conqueror of Europe! Nothing can be plainer. N stands for nothing . . . a mere veil to cover the prophecy till the time of revealing. I challenge any Greek scholar who may be here present to set me right—that is, to show me wrong. Would any one in the company oblige me? I take that now for an incontrovertible"—he stammered over the word—"proof of the truth of the Bible. But I am wandering from my subject, which error, I pray you, ladies and gentlemen, to excuse me."

He rambled on in this way, uttering even worse nonsense, and mingling with it soiled and dusty commonplaces of religion, every now and then dwelling for a moment or two upon his own mental and physical decline from the admirable being he once was.

Cornelius was in fits of near laughter. The only thing that kept his merriment within bounds was the dread that the poor old soul, who smelled abominably of strong drink, might address him personally and so draw upon him the attention of the audience.

Hester's mood was quite different. To the astonishment of Cornelius, when at last they rose to go, there were tears in her eyes. The misery of the wretched man, no doubt once a clergyman, had overcome her heart. It was a reaction one such as Cornelius could never have understood. Hester's nature of sympathy and compassion went out to the man. Worst of all, to the heart of Hester, was the fact that so few people were present, many of them children at half-price, most of whom were far from satisfied with the amusement offered them. When the hall and the advertising were paid for, what would this poor, old remnant of humanity, with his yellowing neck-cloth, have left for his supper? Did he have anyone to look after him? The poor man! Hester's eyes were full of tears to think she could do nothing for him. She remembered the fat woman with curls hanging down her cheeks who had taken their money at the door. Apparently she was his wife. The misery of the whole situation was unbearable to Hester!

When they emerged breathing again the clean, rain-washed air instead of the musty smells of the hall, Hester's eyes involuntarily rose to the vault above her, the top of whose arch is the will of the Father, whose endless space alone is large enough to picture the heart of God. How was that old man to get up into the high regions and grow clean and wise? He must belong there as well as she! And were there not thousands equally and more miserable in the world—people who knew no tenderness, to whom none ministered, people who were pitifully alone? Was there nothing she could do to help, to comfort, to lift up one such person of her own human family, to rescue a heart from the misery of hopelessness, to make one feel there was a heart of love and refuge at the center of things?

The ambition to minister to her fellow beings had long lain dormant in Hester's heart. The sight of the poor man in the hall had suddenly awakened something within her and she would never be the same again. She found the feeling growing inside that the whole human family was depending upon her, and that she could not rise in life—even with all the advantages her favored station seemed to offer—without desiring to raise them along with her. For the necessities of our deepest nature do not allow us contentment in mere personal satisfaction. We were not made to live alone. I well remember feeling as a child that I did not want God to love me if he did not love everybody. I had been taught that God chooses some but not others. My very being recoiled from the hint of such a false idea. Even were I one of the few, the chosen, the elect, I could not accept love from such a God. The kind of love I needed was essential to my nature—the same love that *all* men needed, the love that belonged to them as the children of the Father, a love he could not give me unless he gave it to all men.

Hester's sympathy and love for people were only a crystallization of long-growing roots in her being, which would continue to extend downward into God's soil until they bore fruit on the tree of her life. And though at the age of twenty-three she had little fruit to show yet, the tree would be nonetheless abundant in the end. She was one of the strong ones that grow slowly.

"There you are, staring up into the sky again!" Cornelius ranted. "You'll be spraining your other ankle next!"

"I had forgotten all about my ankle, Corney," returned Hester quietly; "but I will be careful."

"Well, I think between us we got the worth of our shilling! Did you ever see such a ridiculous old bloke?"

Hester did not reply, but sighed inwardly. What would be the use in trying to let her brother know how she felt inside so long as he recognized no dignity in life, never set himself *to be*!

Cornelius burst out laughing. "To think of that old codger trying to interpret the muffs going through the river, and the angels waiting for them on the bank like laundresses with their clean shirts!"

"The whole thing was pitiful," said Hester. "That old man made me very sad."

"How you could see anything pathetic, or 'pitiful,' as you call it, in that disreputable old humbug, I can't even imagine," replied her brother. "A more ludicrous specimen of broken-down humanity would be hard to find! A drunken old thief, I'll bet you anything!"

"And you don't count that pitiful, Cornelius? A man so low, so hopeless, yet you feel no pity for him?"

"Oh, don't trouble your head about him. He'll have his hot supper when he gets home, and his hot tumbler of whisky—swearing, too, if it's late."

"That seems to me the most pitiful of all. Is it not pitiful to see a human being, made in the image of God, sunk so low?"

"It's his own doing," returned Cornelius coldly.

"And is not that the worst of it all? If he were not to blame, it would be sad enough. But to be as he is and to be to blame for it seems to me a misery unbearable."

Cornelius again burst into laughter, and Hester held her peace. That her own brother's method of dealing with the suffering in the world should be to avoid as much as possible adding to his own was to her heart humiliating.

3 / The Aquarium _____

After the family separated for the night, Hester went to her room and began thinking again.

She was one of those women who, from the first dawn of consciousness, have all their lives tried, with varying degrees of success, to do the right thing. In this she followed in the footsteps of her mother, who also walked steadily along the true path of humanity. But Hester was young and did not consider herself as caring as she wanted to be, and was frequently irritated by her failure; for it is impossible to satisfy the hard master *self*. While he flatters some, he requires of others more than they can give.

God seems to take pleasure in working by degrees. The progress of the truth is as the permeation of leaven, or the growth of a seed: a multitude of successive small sacrifices may work more good in the world than many a large one. What would even our Lord's death on the cross have been except as the crown of a life in which he died daily, giving himself, soul, body, and spirit, to his men and women? It is the *being* that is precious. Being is the mother to all little *doings* as well as the grown-up *deeds* and the mighty heroic *sacrifice*. Hester had not had time, neither had she prayed enough to *be* quite yet, though she was growing well toward it. She was a good way up the hill, and the Lord was coming down to meet her, but they had not quite met yet so as to go up the rest of the way together.

What had gradually been rising in Hester was the feeling that she must not waste her life! She must *do* something! Her deep awareness of the misery around her told her she should do something to help those in need. But what?

That evening the thought of the miserable, ruinous old man kept haunting Hester, making her very sad. From there her thoughts wandered abroad over the universe of misery. For was not the whole world full of men and women who groaned, not merely under poverty and cruelty, weakness and sickness, but under dullness and stupidity? And now, on this night for the first time, the idea came to Hester that she might, in some way, make use of the one gift she was aware she possessed. Her passion for music had resulted in her learning both organ and piano. She was also gifted with a fine contralto voice which, she hoped, could comfort and uplift humanity.

26

But sheer pity for her kind was not the only impulse moving Hester in this direction of ministry. Hers was an honest and active mind. She could not have gone to church regularly as she did without gaining some glimpses of the mightiest truth of our being, that we belong to God in actual face of spiritual property and profoundest relationship. She had much to learn in this direction. This night she remembered a sermon she had heard on the text, "Glorify God in your body, and in your spirit, which are God's." It was a dull enough sermon, yet not so dull that it hindered her from gleaning its truth. When she had gone out of the dark church into the sunshine on that day and heard the birds singing, something new had dawned on her.

She realized that the voice lying like an unborn angel in her own throat belonged not to herself but to God, and must be used in some way for his will in the world he had made. She had no real notion yet of the glory of God. She did have a lingering idea—a hideously frightful one—that God thought so much of himself that he required homage from his creations. So she first thought of devoting her voice to some church choir. With her incomplete notion of God and of her relation to him, how could she yet have escaped the poor pagan fancy—good for a pagan, but beggarly for a Christian—that church and its goings-on are synonymous with serving God? She had not begun to ask how these were to do God any good, or how they were to do anything for God.

She had not begun to see that God is the one great servant of all, and that the only way to serve him is to be a fellow servant with him— to be, say, a nurse in his nursery, tending this or that lonely person, this or that sickly child of his. It is as absurd to call song and prayer serving God as it would be to say the thief on the cross did something for Christ in consenting to go with him to paradise.

But now some dim perception of this truth began to awaken in her a feeling that perhaps God had given her this voice, this delight and power in music and song for some reason. What if she, like the birds who are the poets of the animal world, were intended to be a doorkeeper in the house of God, opening windows in heaven that the air of the high places might reach the low, swampy ground? Might not truth go forth from her throat to those who could hear and respond to the cry? How she did not yet see, but the truth had begun to dawn that serving God in any true sense meant serving him where he needs service—among his children lying in the heart of sin and pain and sorrow.

The cry of the human heart in all ages and in every moment is, "Where is God and how shall I find him?" I know multitudes are incapable of knowing that this is their heart's cry. But if you are one of these, I would ask if you have ever yet made one discovery in your heart.

To him who has been making discoveries in it for fifty years, the depths of his heart are yet a mystery. The roots of your heart go down beyond your knowledge—whole eternities beyond it—into the heart of God. I repeat, whether you know it or not, your heart in its depths is ever crying out for God. Where the man does not know it, it is because the unfaithful self, a would-be monarch, has usurped the consciousness—the carnal man, almost the demon-man, is uppermost, not the Christ-man. If ever the true cry of the heart reaches that self, it calls it childish, and tries to trample it out. It does not know that a child crying to God is mightier than a warrior armed with steel.

If there was nothing but fine weather in our soul, the carnal self would be too much for the divine self, and would always control it. But bad weather, misfortune, adversity, or whatever name men may call it, sides with the Christ-self deep inside, and helps to make its voice heard.

To the people at Burcliff there came at last a lovely morning, with sky and air like the face of a thoroughly repentant child who has been so cleansed from sin that he is no longer even ashamed. The water danced in the joy of a new birth, the wind whispered in gentle breezes, and the sun beamed merrily down on the happy commotion the Creator's presence caused.

As Mrs. Raymount looked out she could not help but think of her boy, wishing that the light who created the sun was shining in his heart too. She was perhaps the only one able to love him fully, for the mother's heart more than any other God has made is similar to his in the power of loving.

Alas, that it is not so in wisdom, for it often thwarts the work of God, forcing him to deal more severely with the child because the mother attempts to shield him from God's law, thinking to save him from sorrow. From his very infancy, she gets between him and the right consequences of his conduct, as if with her one feeble, loving hand she would stop the fly-wheel of the universe. It is the law that the man who does wrong shall suffer; it is the only hope for him and the neighbor he wrongs. When he forsakes his evil, his suffering will drop away. When the mother attempts to keep him from the consequences of his selfishness, she only impedes the redemptive work of salvation that God plans to carry out in her child.

As soon as breakfast was over the whole family set out for a walk. Mr. Raymount seldom left the house till after lunch, but even he, who cared comparatively little for the open air, had grown eager for it. Streets, hills and the sandy beaches were swarming with human beings—all drawn out by the sun.

Mrs. Raymount saw her son, now cheerful because of the change of weather, and looked upon him as good. She was one of the best of women herself: her lamp was sure to have oil in it. Yet ever since he first lay in her arms, I doubt if she had ever done anything to help the youth conquer himself. Now it was too late, even if she had known what to do. Her other children had so far turned out well. Why should not this one also? The moment his surly disposition was temporarily over, she looked upon him as reformed. And when he spoke worldliness, she persuaded herself he was joking. But, unfortunately, she had no adequate notion—not even the shadow of an idea—of the selfishness of the man-child she had given to the world. And where self is king, there is no room for God, however righteous an individual's parents. This matter of the black sheep in the white flock is one of the most mysterious facts of spiritual generation.

His father had just as little notion that Cornelius was a black sheep. It was only to the rest of the family that Cornelius showed his true self. He was afraid of his father; and that father, being proud of his children, would have found it hard to believe anything bad of them: like his faults, they were his own! The discovery of any serious fault in one of them would be a sore wound to his vanity.

It never entered Mr. Raymount's mind that any member of his family might think differently than he did about anything. But both his wife and Hester were able to think, and did think for themselves. They walked in considerably different paths from those he had trod. He supposed that both they and Cornelius read what he wrote and agreed with all of it. And while his wife and daughter did read most of it, his son read little. What he did read, he held in silent contempt. The bond between the father and son was by no means as strong as the father thought. Indeed, because of Mr. Raymount's intentions regarding the division of his property, his son looked upon him as his enemy.

"Let's go see the aquarium," Cornelius suggested.

"What do you think of that, Saffy?" the father asked the bright child walking hand in hand with him. It was Josephine, with eyes so blue he would have called her Sapphira but for the association. Between the two he contented himself with the pet name *Saffy*.

"Oh, yes, let's go see the fish, Papa!"

Since they were nearby, it did not take long before they entered and began the descent into the fascinating place. About halfway down, Cornelius gave a cry of recognition and darted down to the next landing. With a degree of respect he seldom showed, he approached a gentleman leaning over the balustrade and shook hands with him. He was several years older than Cornelius, a couple of inches taller, and quite good-looking—one who would hardly fail to attract notice, even in a crowd.

Cornelius looked on Mr. Vavasor with almost a jealous admiration, when the rest reached the landing.

Cornelius had been in the bank eighteen months but had never mentioned the fellow clerk. This troubled son was one of those youths who cover their emptiness by pretending importance through concealment and pretended mystery. And even now had his father not requested it of him, he would not have presented his bank friend to him or any of the family.

Mr. Vavasor's manners and approach insured him a friendly reception by all, from Mr. Raymount to little Saffy, who had the rare charm of being shy without being rude. His manners if not genial were yet friendly, and his bearing if not graceful was easy—a kind of company posture, hedged with indifference, except when he desired to commend himself. He shook hands with little Saffy as respectfully as with her mother, but with guarded respect to either. He was definitely handsome, with a Grecian nose, giving him an aristocratic look. This was emphasized also by the simplicity of his dress. He turned with them and redescended the stairs.

"Why didn't you tell me you were coming, Mr. Vavasor? I could have met you," Cornelius said, slightly stretching the degree of familiarity common between them.

"I didn't know myself until the last minute," answered Vavasor. "It was a sudden decision of my aunt's. I had not the remotest idea you were here."

"Have you been looking at the fish?" asked Hester, at whose side their new acquaintance was walking, now that they had reached the subterranean level.

"Yes, but they are not very well kept. The glass is dirty and the water too. They seemed to look unhappy. I can hardly bear it. It would be a good deed to poison them all."

"Wouldn't it be better to give them fresh water?" suggested little Saffy. "That would make them happy."

To this wisdom there was no response.

"We were just talking," Hester said, "before we had the pleasure of meeting you, about people and fish—comparing them in a way."

"Look at that dogfish!" Vavasor exclaimed, pointing to the largest in the tank. "What a brute! I wouldn't want to be compared to him. Don't you just hate him, Miss Raymount?"

"I am not willing to hate any living thing," answered Hester.

"Why shouldn't you hate him? You would be doing the wretch no wrong."

"How can you tell that unless you knew all about his nature and life?"

"You seem to imply motive and choice, even for an ugly fish, where I see no ground for either. The ugly things are ugly just because they are ugly. We must take things as we find them. We ourselves are just what we are and cannot help it. We are made so."

"Then you think we are all just like the dogfish—except that destiny has made none of us quite so ugly?" asked Hester. "You do not believe in free will, or that something higher has made us to become something more than that fish?"

"I see no ground for believing in it. We are but random forces. Everyone does just what is in him."

"I say *no*. Everyone is capable of acting better than he does," she asserted.

"And why does he not then?"

"Ah, why? That is indeed the question."

"Then you actually believe we can make ourselves different from what we are made?" Vavasor asked incredulously.

"Yes. We are made with the power to change. We are meant to take a share in our own making. We are made so and so, it is true, but not made to be that way forever. We are made with a power inside us that can lay hold of the original power that made us. We are not made to remain as we are. We are bound to grow."

She spoke rapidly, her eyes bright with earnest conviction.

"You are too much of a philosopher for me, Miss Raymount," Vavasor smiled. "But just answer me one question. What if a man is too weak to change?"

"He *must* change," insisted Hester. "No one is too weak to change. We were born to grow. Growth is part of our true nature."

Beginning to feel the conversation was becoming much too serious, Vavasor asked, "But don't you think this is rather—ah—serious for an aquarium?"

Hester did not reply. Nothing was too serious for her in any place. She was indeed a peculiar girl.

"Let us see the octopus," suggested Vavasor, trying to inject a lighter mood.

Mr. Raymount followed as they went and gradually drew even with his son's friend. He had heard the last turn of their conversation and now proceeded to pick up the edge of it, relating the ugliness of the fish around them to his rather oblique observations concerning art.

What a peculiar family! Vavasor thought as they were leaving the place some time later. *There's a bee in every one of their bonnets! An*

*odd, irreverent way the old fellow has about him—pretending to believe
everything he says.*

As for the existence of God, Vavasor was not one of the age who
came out with a firm denial. Like his fellows at the bank, he never took
the trouble to deny him. They all went their own way and asked no
questions. When a man has not the slightest intention that the answer
shall influence his conduct, why should he bother to ask if there is a
God? Vavasor cared more about the top of his cane than the God whose
being he did not take the trouble to deny. He believed a little less than
the maiden aunt with whom he lived; she believed less than her mother,
and her mother had believed less than hers. For generations the so-called
faith of the family had been dying down, simply because all that time
it had sent out no fresh root of obedience. It had really been no faith at
all, only assent. Miss Vavasor went to church because it was the right
thing to do: God was one of the heads of society, and his drawing rooms
had to be attended. That she should come out of it all as well as other
people when this life was over, she saw no reason to doubt. She was
devoted to her nephew, as she counted devotion, but would make sure
that he reciprocated her devotedness.

4 / Amy Amber

Ever since her experience at the lecture on "The Pilgrim's Progress," the tide of human affection had risen all the more rapidly in Hester. It had been like a mirror in which she saw the misery of her kind, including her brother Cornelius. Being several years older than he and having had a good deal to do with him as a baby and child, she had always loved him dearly. But now the plain revelation of his heartlessness had given her devotion to him a rude shock. Every day she grew more anxious about him, and tried to act toward him as a sister ought.

The Raymounts could not afford one of the most expensive lodgings in Burcliff, but were content with a floor in an old house in an unfashionable part of town, looking across the red roofs of the port and out over the flocks of Neptune's white sheep on the blue-gray German ocean. It was kept by two old maids whose hearts had been flattened under the pressure of poverty—no, I am wrong. Our Lord never mentions poverty as one of the obstructions to his kingdom. It was *anxiety* over their poverty that caused the sisters Witherspin to wear away their lives in scraping together provision for an old age they were destined never to see.

They were a small, meager pair with hardly a smile between them. One waited, the other cooked, and Hester's heart was full of compassion for them. It looked as if God had forgotten them—toiling for so little all day long, but the fact was they had forgotten God. They should have sought the kingdom of heaven, and trusted him for their future while they did their work with might. Instead, they exhausted their spiritual resources by sending out armies of ravens, with hardly a dove among them, to find and secure a future still submerged in the waves of a friendly deluge. Nor was Hester's own faith in God so vital yet as to reproduce itself in the minds of those she knew. She could only be compassionate and kind.

The day after the visit to the aquarium dawned bright and cheerful. Hester was still in the dining room trimming her mother's bonnet with a new ribbon and glanced up as woeful Miss Witherspin entered to remove the ruins of breakfast. The spinster wore a sadder expression than usual. It was a glorious day and she was like a live shadow in the sunshine.

"Is anything the matter, Miss Witherspin?" Hester asked.

"Indeed, miss. There never come nothing to sister and me but what's the matter. But it's the Lord's will and we can't help it," she sighed.

"Is there some new trouble," Hester questioned further, "if you will excuse my asking?"

"Well, I don't know, miss, if trouble can ever be called new. But now our sister-in-law's passed on after her husband an' left her girl, brought up in her own way an' every other luxury, on our hands to take charge of. The responsibility will be the death of me."

"Is there no provision for her?"

"Oh yes, there's provision! Her mother kept a shop for fancy goods at Keswick—after John's death, that is—an' scraped together a good bit o' money, they do say. But that's under trustees—not a penny to be touched till the girl comes of age!"

"But the trustees must make you a proper allowance for bringing her up. And anyhow, you can refuse the charge if you choose, can't you?"

"No, miss, that we can't. It was John's wish, when he lay dyin', that if anything was to happen to Sarah, the child should come to us. It's the trouble of the young thing, the responsibility—havin' to keep your eyes on her every blessed moment for fear she'll do the thing she ought not to—that's weighing on me. Oh yes, they'll pay so much a quarter for her! It's not that . . . But to be always at the heels of a young sly miss after mischief—it's more'n I'm up to."

"When did you see her last?" asked Hester.

"Not since she was three years old!" answered Miss Witherspin.

"Then perhaps she may be wiser by this time," Hester suggested. "How old is she now?"

"Sixteen. It's awful to think of!"

"But how do you know she will be troublesome? You haven't seen her for thirteen years!"

"I'm sure of it. I know the breed, miss! She's took after her mother, you may take your mortal oath! The sly way she got round our John—an' all to take him away from his own family. You wouldn't believe it, miss!"

"Girls are not always like their mothers," Hester assured her. "I'm not half as good as my mother. When is she coming?"

"She'll be here this blessed day, miss!"

"Your house is filled with lodgers. Perhaps you will find her a help instead of a trouble. It won't be as if she had nothing to do."

"She'll be no good to mortal creature," sighed Miss Witherspin as she put the tablecloth on top of the breakfast things.

The girl did arrive that day. She sprang into the house like a loud sunbeam—loud for a sunbeam, not for a young woman of sixteen. She was small and bright and cheerful, with large, sparkling black eyes. Her face was rather small, her hair a dead brown, almost black. Her figure was, if not essentially graceful yet, thoroughly symmetrical, and her head, hands, and feet were all small and well-shaped. She had as little shyness as forwardness, being at once fearless and modest, gentle and merry, noiseless and swift—a pleasure to eyes, nerves, and mind. Her sudden appearance in rosebud print, to wait upon the Raymounts the next morning at breakfast, startled them all with a sweet surprise. Every time she left the room she was the topic of conversation, and Hester's information about her was a welcome addition to their astonishment. A more striking contrast than that between her and her two aunts could hardly have been found in the whole town. She was like a star between two gray clouds of twilight. But she had not so much caused her own cheerfulness as her poor aunts had caused their misery. She so lived because she was so made. She was a joy to others as well as to herself, but as yet she had no merit in her own peace or its rippling gladness. So strong was the life in her that, although she cried often over the loss of her mother at night, she was fresh as a daisy in the morning, opening like that to the sun of life, ready not merely to give smile for smile but to give smile for frown. In a word, she had one of those lovely natures that need only to recognize the eternal to fly straight to it. But, on the other hand, such natures are usually very hard to awaken to a recognition of that unseen eternal. They assent to every good thing, but for a long time seem unaware of the need of a perfect Father. To have their minds opened to the truth, they must suffer like other mortals less amiable. Suffering alone can develop in such any spiritual insight, or cause them to care that the living God is concerned about them.

She was soon a favorite with every one of the family. Mrs. Raymount often talked to her. And on her side, Amy Amber was so much drawn to Hester that she never lost an opportunity to wait on her, and never once missed going to her room to see if she wanted anything, last of all before she went to bed. The only one of the family that professed not to think much of her was Cornelius. Even Vavasor, who soon became a frequent caller, if he chanced to say some admiring word about the pretty creature after she had just flitted from the room, would only draw from his friend a grunt and a half sneer. Yet now and then he might have been caught looking at her, and would sometimes, in spite of himself, smile on her sudden appearance.

5 / Cornelius and Vavasor

If you had chanced to meet Cornelius in any other company than that of his own family, whom he treated with contempt, you would probably have taken him for an agreeable young man. The slouch and hands-in-pocket mood—those signals that self was at home to nobody but himself—vanished whenever he left his family. By going to the same tailor as Vavasor, he always managed to be well dressed in the latest European fashion—paying twice as much as his father for his irreproachable coats and linen shirts. But this side of his existence he kept hidden from his family. He never spoke to them about anything he did away from home. And he gloried in the vulgar mystery that he did this or that of which neither the governor, the mother, nor Hester knew anything. As a result, he felt large and powerful and wise, and if he was only the more of a fool, what did it matter so long as he did not know it?

From the first day that Cornelius began working in the bank, Mr. Vavasor, himself not the profoundest of men, had been taken with the youth's easy manners and his obvious worship of himself. Therefore he had allowed the one who aspired to his favor to enter by degrees into his charmed circle. He began to make Cornelius an occasional companion for the evening, and would sometimes take him home with him. There Cornelius at once laid himself out to please Miss Vavasor. Flattery went a long way with her, because she had grown to suspect herself no longer young or beautiful. Cornelius soon learned what he must admire and what he must look down on if he would be in Miss Vavasor's favor. As much energy as he expended on ingratiating himself to the man and his aunt, none of his own family had even heard of Mr. Vavasor before the encounter at the aquarium.

From Miss Vavasor's, Cornelius had been invited to several other houses, resulting in his increasing contempt for his own family, seeing them as unfit for the grand company to which his merits, unappreciated at home, had introduced him. He began to take private lessons in dancing and singing, and though he developed a certain facility of imitation and was thus able in time to do well enough when he wanted to please, he took no delight in music for its own sake. Whenever he heard his sister practicing he would call it *an infernal row*.

Cornelius was inwardly astonished, even a little annoyed, at the

36

seemingly favorable impression made by his family, Hester in particular, upon one in whose judgment he had placed unquestioned confidence. And he did not conceal from Vavasor that his opinion of them was different, for he felt that his friend's admiration of them gave him the advantage to be seen as a free-thinker, as one who disdained what his friend admired.

"My mother's the best of the lot," he conceded. "She's the best woman in the world, I do believe; but she's nobody except at home—don't you know? Why, just look at her and your aunt together! No comparison!"

What Vavasor thought had better be left unsaid. He went on to give him a lecture, well meant and shallow, on what was good in a woman. In his view, not only Cornelius's mother, but Hester herself, possessed qualities which approached this strange virtue.

"She's a very good girl—of her sort—Hester is," Cornelius continued, modifying his opposition somewhat. "I don't need you to tell me that. But she's too serious. Half an hour in one of her moods is enough to destroy one's peace of mind forever. And there's no telling when the spell may come over her."

Vavasor laughed. But he thought to himself what a great woman might be made of her! To him she seemed fit—with a little developing assistance—to grace the best society in the world. It was not polish she needed, but experience and insight, Vavasor mused. He would have her learn to look on the world and its affairs as they who viewed them under the artificial light of fashion. Thus Vavasor almost immediately conceived the ambition of having a personal hand in the worldly education of this young woman, grooming her to shine as she deserved in the fashionable circles of the city—the only circles worth anyone's while. Through his aunt he could gain Hester's entrance where he pleased. Compared with her family, he seemed to himself a man of power and influence.

Hester took to Vavasor from the first, in an external, meet-and-part sort of fashion. His bearing was so dignified, yet his manner so pleasing, that he brought out the best side of her nature. He roused no inclination to oppose, which poor, foolish Corney always roused in her. He could talk well about music and pictures and novels and plays. She not only let him talk freely, but was inclined to put a favorable interpretation on things that she did not agree with, trying to see humor where another might find cynicism. For Vavasor, being in his own eyes the model of an honorable and well-behaved gentleman, had of course only the world's way of regarding and judging things. Instead of giving a poor woman in the street money for a pair of shoes, he would give her a half-worn pair of gloves while he was on his way to buy a new pair for himself.

It would have enlightened Hester a little to watch him for half an hour where he stood behind the counter of the bank. There he was more discourteous than any of the bank clerks. But he never forgot to take up his manners with his umbrella as he left the bank. He also resumed his airy, cheerful way of talking, which was more natural to him than his rudeness, and sparkled pleasantly against the more somber texture of Hester's manner. She suspected he was not profound, but that was no reason for not being pleasant to him and allowing him to be pleasant to her. So by the time Vavasor had spent three evenings with the Raymounts, Hester and he were on an external intimacy, if there be such a relation.

On the last of these evenings, he heard Hester sing for the first time. He had not even known she cared for music; for Hester, who did not regard her faculty as an accomplishment but as a gift, treated it as a treasure to be hidden for the day of the Lord rather than a flag to be flown in a public procession. She was jealously shy over it, thinking it would be profanity to perform before any but loving eyes. To sing to any but the right persons would have for her been immodest.

Vavasor was astonished, yet delighted, at what he heard. He was in the presence of a power! But all he knew of power was society related. It was not a spirit of might he recognized, for the opening of minds and the strengthening of hearts, but only an influence of pleasing for self-aggrandizement. The best thing in him was his love of music. He did not really believe in music—he did not really believe in anything except himself. He professed to adore it, and imagined he did, because his greatest pleasure lay in hearing his own verses well sung by a pretty girl who would nod and then try to steal a glance at the poet from under her eyelids as she sang.

On his way home he mused over the delight of having his best songs sung by such a singer as Hester.

"But why did you never tell me your sister was such a singer?" he asked of Cornelius, who was walking halfway with him.

"Do you think so? She ought to feel very flattered! Why I didn't tell you?—Oh, I don't know. I never heard her sing like that before. I suppose it was because you were there. A brother's nobody, you know."

This flattered Vavasor, as how should it not? So he continued to go as often as he dared—that is, almost every night—to the Raymounts' lodging. He knew a good song, sometimes, when he heard it, and had himself a very tolerable voice and knew quite a bit about music. Therefore, it came about very naturally that he found himself, to his satisfaction, relating to her as a pupil relates to a teacher. Hester dedicated herself to improving the quality of his singing—his style, his expression, and his tone. The relationship between them developed and, had it then lasted, might have soon led to genuine intimacy. At least it might have led to some truer understanding on the part of each of the kind of person the other was. But the day of separation arrived first; and it was only on his way back to London that Vavasor began to discover what a hold Cornelius's sister had taken of his thoughts—indeed, of his heart, the existence of which organ he had never before had any very convincing proof.

6 / Hester and Amy

Hester did not miss Vavasor quite so much as he hoped she might, or as much, perhaps, as he believed she did. She had been interested in him mainly because she found him both receptive and capable of development in the area of music—ready to understand, that is, and willing to be taught. To have such a man listen with respect to every word she said could not fail to be pleasant, even flattering to her. It is unfortunate how often a man such as Cornelius and his rude behavior at home will lead a sister such as Hester to place a higher value upon the civility of other men than they deserve. But the nearer persons come to each other in a family setting, the greater is the room and more frequent are the opportunities for courtesy. It is within the family that more gentleness should be shown, not less.

Sad to say, such was not the case in the Raymount household. The father could not bear rudeness any more than wrong in his children. Yet such a statement is inaccurate, for rudeness is a great and profound wrong, a wrong to the noblest part of the human being. And a mere show of indifference is sometimes almost as bad as the rudest of words. The more guilty a man is of such faults, the less he is conscious of it.

But, despite his pleasant contrast with her brother, Vavasor did not move the deepest in Hester. How should he? With that deepest he had developed no relation. There were worlds of thought and feeling already in motion in Hester's universe, while the vaporous mass in him had hardly yet begun to stir. He was living on the surface of his being, all the more exposed to earthquake and volcanic eruption because he had never yet suspected the existence of the profound depths from which they rose. Hester, on the other hand, was already beginning to discover some of the abysses of the nature gradually unfolding in her. When Vavasor was gone she turned with greater diligence to her musical studies.

Amy Amber continued to be devoted to her, and when Hester was practicing would come around for as long as she could. Hester's singing seemed to enchant and fascinate the girl. But a change had already begun to show itself in Amy. The shadow of an unseen cloud was occasionally visible in her expression. As the days went by, the signs of her discomfort grew deeper. She moved about her work with less energy, and her smile did not come as readily. Both Hester and her mother noticed the change. In the morning, when Amy was always the first one up, she was generally cheerful; but as the day passed, the cloud came. Happily, however, her diligence did not let up. Sound in health, and active by nature, she took a positive delight in work. In another household she would have been invaluable. But as it was, she was growing daily less and less happy.

One night she appeared in Hester's room, as usual, before going to bed. Her small face had lost, for the time, most of its beauty, and was dark as a thundercloud. She tried to smile, but only a wounded smile would come.

"My poor Amy! What is the matter?" cried Hester.

The girl burst into tears.

"Oh, miss, I *would* like to know what you would do in my place!"

"I'm afraid if I were in your place, I would do nothing as well as you do, Amy," said Hester. "But tell me what is the matter. What has made you so miserable?"

"It's not one thing nor two, nor even twenty things!" answered Amy, ceasing her crying and now looking sullen with the feeling of heaped-up wrong. "What *would* my mother say to see me treated so! *She* used to trust me. I don't understand how those two prying, suspicious old maids can be *my* father's sisters!"

She spoke slowly and sadly, without raising her eyes.

"Don't they treat you well?"

"It's not that they watch every bite I put in my mouth," returned Amy. "I don't complain about that, for they're poor—at least they're always saying so. But not to be trusted one moment out of their sight—to be always suspected, and followed and watched, and me working my hardest—that's what drives me wild, Miss Raymount. I'm afraid they'll make me hate them before long—and them my own flesh and blood, too. It was easier to take at first. I said to myself, 'They'll get to know me better!' But when I found they only got worse, I got tired of it altogether, and grew more and more cross, till now I can't stand it. If there isn't a change somehow soon, I shall run away—I shall, indeed, Miss Raymount. Oh, how I wish I could have kept the good temper I used to have—you're going away so soon, miss! Let me do your hair tonight."

"But you are tired, my poor child!" Hester protested.

"Not too tired for that . . . It will relax me and bring back my good temper. Maybe some of yours will flow into me through your hair."

"No, no, Amy. I have none to spare. But do what you like with my hair."

As Amy lovingly brushed Hester's long waves, Hester tried to help her understand that she must not think of a happy disposition merely as something that could be put into her and taken out of her. She tried to make her see that everyone has a large supply of good temper at hand, but that it was not theirs until it was made personally theirs by choosing and willing to be good-tempered—by holding it fast with the hand of determination when the hand of wrong would snatch it away.

"Because I have a book on my shelves," she explained, "does not make it mine. When I have read and understood it, then it is a little mine; when I love it and do what it tells me, then it is altogether mine. It is like that with good temper: if you have it sometimes and not at others, then it is not yours. It lies in you like that book on my table— a thing priceless if it were your own, but as it is, a thing you can't even keep against your poor, weak old aunts."

As she said all this, Hester felt like a hypocrite, remembering her own weakness and sins. But Amy listened quietly, brushing steadily all the time. Yet scarcely a shadow of Hester's meaning crossed her mind. If she was in a good temper, she was in a good temper; if she was in a bad temper, she was in a bad temper. She had no knowledge of the possibility of having a hand in making her own temper—not a notion that she was in any way accountable for the temper she might find herself in.

Hester kissed her, and though she had not understood, Amy went to bed a little comforted. When the Raymounts departed two or three days later, they left her at the top of the cliff-stair, weeping quietly.

Hester had no sooner reached home, hardly taking time to unpack her box, before she went to see her music teacher to make arrangements for taking up her study with her once again.

Miss Dasomma was one of God's angels, one of those live fountains that carry his gifts to their thirsting fellows. Of Italian descent, English birth, and German training, she had known well some of the greatest composers of her day. But the enthusiasm for her art was mainly the result of her own genius. It was natural, then, that she should exercise a great influence on every pupil who was worthy of her. Without her Hester could never have become what she was. Miss Dasomma was ready to begin at once, and Hester gradually increased her hours of practice, indulging her musical inclinations to the full.

They had not been home more than a week when, one Sunday afternoon, Mr. Vavasor called. This was not quite agreeable to Mrs. Raymount, who liked to spend their Sundays quietly. But he was shown to the study.

Mr. Raymount was pleased with him afresh, for he spoke modestly and seemed by his manner to acknowledge the superior position of the elder man. They talked about the prominent questions of the day, and Mr. Raymount was even more pleased when he found the young aristocrat ready to receive enlightenment from his own lips. But the fact was that Vavasor cared very little about the matter. He simply had a light, easy way of touching on things, as if all his concessions, conclusions, concurrences were the merest matter of course. By this he made himself seem a master of a situation over which he merely skimmed on insect wing. Mr. Raymount took him not merely for a man of thought, but even of some originality—capable at least of forming an opinion of his own.

In relation to the wider circle of the country, Mr. Vavasor was so entirely a nobody that the acquaintance of a writer even so partially known as Mr. Raymount was something to him. There is a tinselly halo about the writer of books, and this attracted the young man. Since his return he had begun inquiries concerning Mr. Raymount, and finding both him and his family in good repute, he had told his aunt as much about them as he judged prudent. Miss Vavasor, however, being naturally skeptical of the opinions of young men, made inquiries for herself. From these she learned that there was a rather distinguished-looking girl in the family. Having, however, her own ideas for the nephew whose interests she had, for the sake of the impending title, made her own, she put off any visit, hoping his interest in the family would taper off. But, though she declined to call, he went all the more often to see them.

On this, his first visit, he stayed the evening and was installed as a friend of the family all over again. Although it was Sunday, and Hester's ideas were a little strict as to religious proprieties, she received him cordially while her mother received him with a somewhat detached kindness. Falling into the old ways, he took his part in the hymns, anthems, and what other forms of sacred music followed the family tea. And so the evening passed without annoyance—partly because Cornelius was spending it with a friend.

The tone, expression, and power of Hester's voice astonished Vavasor once again. After she had played a sacred song on the piano, he was so moved he even felt more kindly disposed toward religion—by which he meant "going to church, and all that sort of thing"—than ever in his life before. He did not call the next Sunday, but came on Saturday; and the only one present who was not pleased with him was Miss Dasomma, who happened also to spend the evening there.

Devout as well as enthusiastic, human as well as artistic, Hester's teacher was not an angel of music only, but had, for many years, been a power in the family for good. She did not find her atmosphere gladdened by Mr. Vavasor's presence. With tact enough to take his cue from the family, he treated her with studious politeness; but Miss Dasomma did not like Mr. Vavasor. She had to think before she could tell why, for there is a spiritual instinct which often supersedes the understanding, and has to search and analyze itself for its own explanation. She sought that explanation by watching his countenance as she sat off to the side while Hester was playing. She tried to read it—trying to read, that is, what the owner of the face never meant to write. For what a man is lies as certainly upon his countenance as in his heart, though none of his friends may be able to read it.

Miss Dasomma concluded that Vavasor was a man of good instincts, but without moral development, pleased with himself, and desirous of pleasing others—at present Hester Raymount.

7 / A Beginning in Hester_____

The Raymounts did not live in a highly fashionable part of London, but in a very serviceable house in Addison Square in the dingy, smoky, convenient, healthy district of Bloomsbury. One of the advantages of this position to a family with soul in it, that strange essence which will go out after its kind, was that on two sides it was closely pressed by poor neighbors. Artisans, small tradespeople, outdoor servants, poor actors and actresses lived in the narrow streets thickly branching away in certain directions. Hence, most happily for her, Hester had grown up with none of that uncomfortable feeling so many have when brought into contact with the poor. It was in a measure because since childhood she had been used to the sight of such that her sympathies were so soon and so thoroughly aroused on the side of suffering humanity.

Those who would do good to the poor must attempt it in the way in which they could best do good to people of their own standing. They must make their acquaintance first. They must know something of the kind of the person they would help, to learn if help be possible from their hands. Only man can help man; money without man can do little or nothing. As our Lord redeemed the world by being a man, the true Son of the true Father, so the only way for a man to help men is to be a true man to his neighbor. But to seek acquaintance with the poor with ulterior design is a perilous thing, likely to result in disappointment. We must be aware of and follow the leadings of the Lord, and get familiar with the so-called lower classes by the natural working of the social laws that bring men together. What is the divine intent in the many needs of humanity, and the consequent dependence of the rich on the poor, even greater than that of the poor on the rich, but to bring men together that in far-off ways at first they may be compelled to know each other? The man who treats his fellow as a mere means for the supply of his own desires, and not as a human being with whom his heart is to have interaction, is an obstructing clot in the human circulation.

Does anyone ask for rules of procedure in getting close to those about him? There are none to be had. Such must be discovered by each for himself. The only way to learn the rules of anything practical is to begin to do the thing. We have enough knowledge in us—call it insight, instinct, inspiration, or natural law—to begin anything required of us. The only way to deal with the profoundest mystery that is yet not too profound to draw us is to begin to do some duty revealed by the light from its golden fringe. If it reveals nothing to be *done*, there is nothing there for us to do.

Let the simplest relation toward a fellow human being, even if it is only embodied in the act of buying from the market, passing on the street, or meeting during some transaction, be recognized as a true heart-meeting of that human soul. Let our eyes perceive deeper than the surface. Let us see into the hearts of the men and women and children around us. Whatever the simple or seemingly insignificant degree of such interaction, let its outcome be in truth and friendliness. Allow nature her course, and next time let the relation go further.

To follow such a path is the way to find both the persons to help and the real modes of helping them. In fact, to be true to a man or woman in any way is to help him. He who goes out of common paths to look for opportunity leaves his own door and misses that of his neighbor. It is by following the paths we are in that we shall first reach somewhere. He who does this will find that his acquaintance widens and grows quickly. His heart will be full of concern for humanity, and his hands will eagerly help. Such care will be death to one's own cares, such help balm to one's own wounds.

In a word, to be a true *minister*, a true *servant*, a true man or a true woman in the fullest sense, one must cultivate, in a simple human manner, the acquaintance of his neighbors. He must be a neighbor where a neighbor is needed. So shall he fulfill the part left behind of the work of the Master, which He desires to finish through mankind.

Of course I do not imagine that Hester understood all this. She had no theory of action toward the poor, and did not confine her hope of helping people in general to the poor. There are as many in every other class needing help as among the poverty-stricken, and the need, although it wears different clothes, is essentially the same in all. To make the light go on in the heart of a rich man, if a more difficult task, is just as good a deed as to make it go on in the heart of a poor man. But with her strong desire to carry help where it was needed, and with her genuine feeling of the fundamental relationship between all human beings, Hester was in the right position to begin.

She went one morning into a small shop in Steven's Road to buy a few sheets of music paper. The woman who kept the shop had been an acquaintance almost from the day they had moved to the neighborhood. In the course of their talk, Mrs. Baldwin mentioned that she was anxious about a woman in the house who was not well and whom she thought Mrs. Raymount would be interested in.

"Mama is always ready to help when she can," offered Hester. "Tell me about her."

"Well, you see, miss," replied Mrs. Baldwin, "we're not in the way of having to do with such people, for my husband's rather particular about whom he rents the top rooms to. But, rent them we must, for times is hard an' children is many, an' it's all we can do to pay our own way; only thank God we've done it up to this present. An' this man looked so decent, as well as the woman, but pitiful-like, that I didn't have the heart to send them away on such a drizzly, cold night as it was. They had four children with them, the smallest o' them ridin' pickaback on the biggest—an' it always goes straight to yer heart, to see one human being lookin' after another like that. But my husband, as was natural, he bein' a householder, was reluctant about the children. For children, you know, miss, 'cept they be yer own, ain't nice things about a house. An' them poor things wouldn't be a credit nowheres, for they were ragged enough—only they were pretty clean, as children go, an' there was nothing, as I said to him, in the top-rooms, as they could do much harm to. The man said theirs weren't like other children, for they had been brought up to do things as they were told, an' to remember that things belongin' to other people was to be handled as such. An', he said, they were always too busy earnin' their bread to be up to tricks, an' in fact were always too tired to have much spare powder to let off. So the long an' the short of it was we took 'em in, an' they've turned out as quiet an' well-behaved a family as you could desire; an' if they ain't got just the most respectable way o' earnin' their livin', that may be as much their misfortune as their fault, as my husband said."

"What is their employment, then?" asked Hester.

"Somethin' or other in the circus way, as far as I can make out from what they tell me. Anyway, they didn't seem to have no engagement when they come to the door, but they paid the first week down afore they entered. You see, miss, the poor woman she give me a kind of look up into the face that reminded me of my Susie, as I lost, you know, miss, a year ago—it was that as made me feel to hate the thought of sendin' her away, an' she was plainly in no condition to go wanderin' about, but I hardly knew how far her condition was. An' the very next day the doctor had to be sent for, an' there was a baby! The doctor come from the hospital, as nice a gentleman as you'd wish to see, miss, an' waited on her as if she'd been the first duchess in the land. 'I'm sure,' said my good husband to me, 'it's a lesson to all of us to see how he do look after her as'll never pay him a penny for the care he's taking of her!' But my husband he's that soft-hearted, miss, where anything in the baby-line's a goin' on! Now the poor mother's not at all strong, an' ain't gettin' back her strength, though we do what we can with her an' send her up what we can spare. You see, they pay for their house-room, an' then ain't got much over," added the woman in excuse of her goodness. "They're not out o' money yet quite, I'm glad to say, though he don't seem to have got nothing to do yet, so far as I can make out. That sort o' trade, ye see, miss, the demand's not steady in it. It's not like skilled labor, as my husband says—though to see what them young ones has to go through, it's labor enough. Would you mind goin' up an' havin' a look at her, miss?"

Hester told Mrs. Baldwin to lead the way, and followed her up the stairs.

The top rooms were two poor enough garret ones. In the largest, the ceiling sloped to the floor till there was only height enough for the small chest of drawers of painted pine to stand against the wall. A similar washstand and a low bed completed the furniture. The bed was immediately behind the door, and there lay the woman, with a bolster heightened by a thin petticoat and threadbare cloak under her head. Hester saw a pale, patient, worn face, with large eyes, thoughtful and troubled.

"Here's a kind lady come to see you," said her landlady.

It annoyed Hester to be called kind, but she spoke perhaps the more kindly to the poor woman because of Mrs. Baldwin's words.

"It must be dreary for you to lie here all alone," she said softly, taking the thin hand into hers. "May I sit a few minutes beside you? I was once in bed for a whole month and found it very tedious. I was at school then. I don't mind being ill so much when I have my mother nearby."

The woman gazed up at her with eyes that looked like the dry wells of tears.

"It's very good of you, miss," she murmured weakly. "It's a long stair to climb up."

She lay and gazed and said nothing more. Her child lay asleep on her arm, a poor little washed-out rag of humanity, but dear to the woman from the way she now and then tried to look at it, which was not easy for her.

Hester sat down and tried to talk, but found it hard to keep on. After a few moments a dead silence prevailed.

What can be the good of a common creature like me going to visit people? she asked herself. *I have nothing to say. I would help them if I could, but what can I do?*

For a few moments she sat silently, growing more and more uncomfortable, and thinking how to begin. The baby woke and began to whimper. The mother, who rarely let him off her arm, because then she was not able to get him again until help came, drew him up to her, and began to nurse him. Suddenly the heart of the young, strong woman was pierced to the quick at the sight of how ill-fitted was the mother for what she had to do. *If only I could help her!* she thought desperately.

She had yet to learn that the love of God is so deep he can be satisfied with nothing less than getting as near as it is possible for the Father to draw nigh to his children—and that is into absolute contact of heart with heart, love with love, being with being. And as that must be wrought out from the deepest inside, divine law working itself up through our nature into our consciousness and will, and claiming us as divine, who can tell by what slow certainties of approach God is drawing nigh to the most suffering of his creatures? Only, if we so comfort ourselves with such thoughts as to do nothing, we, when God and they meet, shall find ourselves out in the cold—a cold infinitely worse than any trouble this world has to show.

The baby made no complaint against the slow fountain of his life, but made the best he could of it, while his mother every now and then peered down on him as lovingly as ever a happy mother looked on her firstborn. The same God is at the heart of all mothers, and all sins against children are against the one Father of children, against the Life itself.

A few moments more passed, and then Hester began to sing—low and soft. Having no song planned for the occasion, she took a common hymn, sung in all churches and chapels. She put into it as much of sweetness and soothing strength as she could make the sounds hold. She sang with trembling voice, and with more shyness than she had ever experienced before. It was neither a well-instructed nor critically disposed audience she had, but the reason was that never before had she been so anxious for some measure of success. Not daring to look up, she sat with the music flowing over her lips like the slow water from the mouth of some statue of stone in a fountain. And she had her reward; for when the hymn was done and at length she ventured to raise her eyes, she saw both mother and babe fast asleep. Her heart ascended on a wave of thanks to the giver of song. She rose softly, crept from the house, and hastened home to tell her mother what she had heard and seen. The same afternoon a basket of nice things arrived at the shop for the poor lodger in the top room.

The Raymounts did not relax their care until the woman was fairly on her feet again. And not until then did a day pass when Hester did not see her and sing to her and her baby. Several times she dressed the child, singing to him all the time. It was generally in the morning she went, because then she was almost sure to find them alone. Of the father she had seen next to nothing. All she had ever had time to see was that he was a man of middle height, with a strong face and frame, dressed like a workman. His three elder boys always left with him in the morning. The eldest was about twelve, the youngest about seven. They were rather sickly looking, but had intelligent faces and inoffensive expressions.

Mrs. Baldwin continued to bear the family good witness. She said they never seemed to have much to eat, but said they paid their lodgings regularly, and she had nothing to complain of. The place had indeed been untidy at first, but as soon as the mother was about again, it began to improve, and now, really, for people in their position, it was wonderfully well kept.

8 / The Frankses

Hester had not been near the woman and her child for two or three days. Dusk was approaching, but tomorrow was Sunday and she felt as if she could not go to church without again seeing the little family committed, in a measure, to her humble charge. She decided, in spite of the hour, to visit them. Finding Mrs. Baldwin busy in the shop, she nodded as she passed her and went up the stair. But she hesitated when she opened the door, and saw the father and the three boys standing together near the fire, like gentlemen on a hearth rug expecting visitors. Also, a man she did not know sat in a chair next to the bed where her friend lay. It was immediately clear to Hester that she had walked in, upon a performance of some kind.

Before she had a chance either to speak or to turn and go, the woman's husband said, "Come in, miss, please."

"Oh, I—I don't want to interrupt," faltered Hester.

"Just do us the honor to take a seat, miss" he urged. "We shall be happy to show you as much as you may please to look upon. This is Mr. Christopher, the kind doctor who's helped Mother an' me an' all us in our trouble—which I'm sure no lady in the land could have been better attended to than she has been. We thought we'd do our best for him, an' try an' see whether amongst the boys an' me we couldn't give him a pleasant evenin', as it were, just to show we was grateful. So we asked him to tea, an' he come, like the gentleman he be, an' so we was showin' him a bit o' our craft, just a trick or two, miss—me and the boys here. Stan' forward, Robert, an' the rest of you an' make your bows to the distinguished company."

Before, the man had always hastened to disappear when Hester came, so she was astonished by this outpouring of information. But the moment he was through his wife said, "Now you be careful, John Franks! Any more falls like that last one, cushion on the floor or no, an' I'll faint dead away, I tell you. Evenin' to you, miss," she added, turning her face toward Hester with a smile.

Franks, flourishing a stage-bow, immediately offered Hester a chair. She hesitated a moment, for she felt shy around Mr. Christopher. But as she had more fear of not behaving as she ought to the people she was visiting, she sat down, and became for the first time in her life a spectator of the feats of an acrobatic family.

The display may have seemed unremarkable to one in the habit of seeing such things. But to Hester it was positively astonishing at what each was capable of. As to the mother's anxiety over hard falls and broken bones, there hardly seemed any bones in the boys to break. Gelatine, at best, seemed to be what was inside their muscles, so wonderful were their feats and their pranks so strange. Amidst the marvels of their performance, in which their agile bodies responded to their wills, the occasional appearance of a strangely mingled touch of pathos chiefly interested Hester.

After some twenty or thirty minutes, the master of ceremonies suddenly drew himself up, wiped his forehead, then gave a deep sigh, as much as to say, *I have done my best, and if I have not pleased you, the more is my loss, for I have tried hard.* The performance was over.

The doctor rose, and in a manly voice proceeded to point out to Franks one or two precautions which his knowledge of anatomy enabled him to suggest, especially regarding the training of the youngest. At the same time, he expressed his great pleasure with what his host had been so kind to show him.

"It mayn't be the best o' livin's for a family man," Franks replied, almost apologetically. "But at least I managed to keep life in the kids. It wasn't much more, you see; but life's life, though it be not tip-top style. An' if they're none o' them doin' just so well as they might, there's none o' them in trouble with the magistrate yet. An' that's a comfort as long as it lasts. An' when folk tell me I'm doin' no good, an' my trade's o' no use to nobody, I says to them, 'Beggin' your pardon, sir, or ma'am, but do you call it nothin' to fill four hungry bellies at home afore I was fifteen, after my mother and father died?' After that, they ain't in general said nothin'. An' one gentleman, watching me once perform on the street, he gave me half a crown."

"That was the best possible answer you could have given, Franks," affirmed Mr. Christopher. "But I think perhaps you hardly understood what such objectors meant to say. They might have gone on to explain, only they hadn't the heart after what you told them, that most trades did something on both sides. The trade not only fed the little ones at home, but did good to the persons for whom the work was done. The man, for instance, who cobbled shoes gave a pair of dry feet to some old man at the same time that he filled his own child's hungry little stomach."

Franks was silent for a moment, thinking.

"I understand you, sir," he said. "But I think I knows trades as makes a lot of money, and them they makes it from is the worse for it, not the better. It's better to stand on a fellow's own head like a clown as I do than to sell whiskey."

"You are quite right: there's not a doubt of it," responded Mr. Christopher. "But mind you," he went on, "I don't for a moment agree with those who tell you your trade is of no use. I was only explaining to you what they meant; for it's always best to know what people mean, even when they are wrong."

"Surely, sir, and I thank you kindly. Everybody's not so fair."

Here he broke into a quiet laugh, so pleased was he to have the doctor take his part.

"I think," Mr. Christopher went on, "that to amuse people innocently is often the only good you can do them. When done lovingly and honestly, it is a Christian service."

This rather shocked Hester—acrobatics a Christian service! With the grand ideas of service beginning to dawn within her, there still mingled some foolish notions. She still felt as if going to church and, while there, trying to fix her thoughts on the prayers and the sermons and the hymns was *serving* God.

"Suppose," he went on, "somebody walking along Oxford Street was brooding over an injury that had been done to him by another, and thinking of how he might get his revenge. He passes many persons and things and takes no notice of anything. But then he comes upon a small crowd watching a man perform some tricks—we won't say as good as yours, Mr. Franks—he stops and stares and forgets for a moment or two that there is one brother-man he hates and would kill if he could."

Here Hester found words to respond. "But he would only go away as soon as he had had enough of it, and hate him all the same."

"I know very well," answered Christopher, turning now to her, "that it would not make a good man of him. Yet it must count for something to have the evil mood in a man stopped even for a moment, just as it is something to a life to stop a fever. It gives the godlike spark in the man, feeble, perhaps nearly exhausted, a fresh opportunity of revival. For the moment at least, the man is open to influences from a source other than his hate. If the devil may catch a man unawares when he is in a bad or unthinking mood, why should not the good Power take his opportunity when the evil spirit is asleep through the harping David or the feats of a Franks?"

Hester said nothing further, but still caught only a glimpse of the doctor's meaning. We are surrounded with things difficult to understand, and the way most people take it is to look away lest they should find out they have to understand them. Hester suspected scepticism in his remarks: most doctors, she believed, leaned in that direction. But she herself had begun to have a true notion of serving man. Therefore, there was no fear of her not coming to see, sooner or later, what serving God meant. She did serve him, so she could not fail to discover the word that belonged to the act: only by serving can one discover what serving him means. Some people are constantly rubbing at their skylights, but if they do not keep their other windows clean also, there will not be much light in the house. God, like his body, the light, is all about us, and prefers to shine in upon us sideways, for we could not endure the power of his vertical glory. No mortal man can see God and live, and he who does not love his brother whom he has seen will not love his God whom he has not seen. He will come to us in the morning through the eyes of a child when we have been gazing all night at the stars in vain.

Hester rose. She was a little frightened of this very peculiar man and his talk. She had made several attempts in the dull light to see him as they watched the contortions of the acrobats.

He was a rather thick-set man about thirty, in a rough coat of brownish gray with many pockets, a striped shirt, and a black necktie. His head was big, with rather thick, long and straggly hair. He had a large forehead and large gray eyes. The remaining features were well formed but rather fat, like the rest of his not elegant person, with a pale complexion. His voice was somewhat gruff but not unmusical, a thread of sadness in it. Hester declined his offer to see her home.

The next time she went to see the Frankses, which was not for four or five days, she found they were gone. They had told Mrs. Baldwin that they were sorry to leave, but they had to look for a cheaper place. Hester was very disappointed. In later years the memory of them was always precious to her because it had been with Mrs. Franks that she had first experienced the hope of her calling by many times giving sleep and rest to her and her babe. And if it is a fine thing to delight a concert room full of well-dined, well-dressed people, surely it is not a little thing to hand God's gift of sleep to a poor woman weary with the lot of women, and having so little pleasure in life.

Mrs. Franks would undoubtedly have differed from Hester in this judgment of her worldly condition, on the ground that she had a good husband and good children. Some people are always thinking others better off than themselves. Others feel as if the lot of many about them must be absolutely unbearable because they themselves could never bear it, they think. But things are unbearable only until we have them to bear; the possibility of carrying them comes with them. For we are not the roots of our own being.

9 / Vavasor and Hester

Vavasor continued to visit Hester. His frequent presence was disturbing to both her mother and Miss Dasomma. They noted also, with some anxiety, that he began to attend their church, a dull enough place, without any possible attraction of its own for a man like Vavasor. After two or three Sundays, he began to join them as they came out and walk part way home with them. Next, he went all the way and was invited to stay to lunch.

It may seem strange that Mrs. Raymount would allow things to progress like this if she was truly anxious about the result. But in the first place, she had complete confidence in Hester; in the second place, she was not adverse to a possible union. It is amazing what weakness may coexist with what strength, what worldliness stand side by side with what spirituality—for a time, that is, till one overcomes the other. Mrs. Raymount was pleased with the idea of a possible marriage of such distinction for her daughter, which would give her just the position she counted her fit for. These mutually destructive considerations were, with whatever logical inconsistency, both certainly operative in her.

Also, they knew nothing against the young man. He made himself agreeable to everyone in the house. In Addison Square he showed not the faintest shadow of the manner which made him almost hated at the bank. Not only was he on his good behavior, but his heart and his self-respect, as he would have called his self-admiration, were equally concerned in his looking his best—which always means looking better than one's best. He seemed to be improving in Hester's company. Hester had whatever elevating influence on him he was yet capable of receiving, and this fact said more for him than anything else. She seemed to be gaining a power over him that could not be for good. Both glad and proud to see her daughter this powerful, Mrs. Raymount felt she could not interfere.

Miss Dasomma was more aware, however. She knew better than Mrs. Raymount the kind of soil in which this human plant had been reared and saw danger ahead. She feared the young man was merely amusing himself, or at best enjoying Hester's company as some wary winged thing enjoys the flame, courting a few singes but being careful not to turn a delightful fantasy into a consuming reality. Miss Dasomma could not believe him as careless of himself as of Hester. She was afraid he was flirting with her student, which held danger for Hester since she was unaware of any such idea. I am sure he never questioned his intentions, or where they were leading, because of the difference between his social position and that of the lady. Possibly he regarded himself as honoring the low neighborhood of Addison Square by the frequency of his shining presence; but, at the same time, I think he was feeling the good influences of Hester more than he knew, or would have liked to admit.

Hester was, of course, greatly interested in him. She had been but little in society, had not studied men in the least, and could not help being pleased with the power she plainly had over him. Even Corney, not very observant or penetrating, remarked on the gentleness of Vavasor's behavior in their house. He followed every suggestion Hester gave concerning his singing, and showed himself even anxious to win her praise by the pains he took to improve. He ceased to bring forward his heathenish notions about human helplessness and fate; instead, he listened to her statements about the individual mission of every human being with an almost humble and attentive manner. Whether any desire of betterment was now awake in him through the power of her spiritual presence, I cannot tell. At first Hester thought only of doing him good. And it was not until she imagined some success in that vein that the true danger to her began.

After that, with every fresh encouragement the danger grew—for in equal proportion grew the danger of *self* coming in and getting the upper hand.

I do not suppose that Vavasor once consciously planned to actually deceive her, or make her think him better than he thought himself. With a woman of Hester's instincts, there might have been less danger if he had. But if he had any, he had but the most rudimentary notion of truth in the inward parts, and could deceive another all the better because he did not know he was deceiving. He had just as little understanding of the nature of the person he was dealing with, or the reality to her of the things she spoke about—belief was, to him, the mere difference between opinions. She spoke the language of a world whose existence he was incapable of recognizing, for he had never obeyed one of its demands. His natural inborn proclivities to the light had, through his so seldom doing the deeds of the light, become so weak that he hardly knew such a thing as reform was required of, possible to, or desirable in him.

He was certainly falling more and more into what more people call *love*. As to what he meant he did not himself know. When intoxicated with the idea of her, that is when thinking what a sensation she would make in his grand little circle, he felt it impossible to live without her.

Some way must be found! Had he anything worthy the name of property coming with the title, he would have proposed to her at once, he told himself. But it would be raging madness, even with the most beautiful wife in the world, to encounter an earldom without a penny. And her family could not have great money. No one with anything would slave as the governor did from morning till night. To marry her would be to live on his salary, in a small house in St. John's wood, or Park Village, ride home in the omnibus every night like one in a tin of sardines, wear half-crown gloves, cotton socks, and cheap hats. The prospect was too hideous even to be ludicrous! No, there must be some way other than that. Thus would Vavasor's emotions work themselves back and forth.

It was some time before he risked an attempt to please her with a song of his own. There was just enough unconscious truth in him to make him a little afraid of Hester. Commonplace though his thoughts were, he would still not risk encountering her scorn. He knew she was capable of it, for Hester had not yet gathered the sweet gentleness that comes of long breathing the air of the high countries. It is generally many years before a strong character learns to think of itself as it ought to think. While there is left in us the possibility of scorn, we know not quite the spirit we are of—still less if we imagine we may keep this or that little shadow of a fault.

But Vavasor had come to understand Hester's taste enough to know her likes and dislikes in a song. And so, by degrees, he had resolved to venture something that would please her. He flattered himself that he knew her *style*. He was very fond of the word, and imagined that all writers and speakers and musicians, to be of any worth, must fashion their style after this or that great master. How the master got his style, it never occurred to him to ask. He never thought about having something worth saying or writing or singing. To make a good speech was the grand thing. Whether it was right or wrong was unthinkable with him. Even whether a given speaker believed what he said was of no consequence—except that, if he did not, his speech would be the more admirable, as the greater *tour de force*, and himself the more admirable as the cleverer fellow.

Knowing that Hester was fond of a good ballad, he decided to try his hand at one, thinking it could not be so difficult. But he found that, like everything else, a ballad was easy enough if you could do it, and more than difficult if you could not. After several attempts he wisely yielded the ambition; his gift did not lie in that direction! He had, however, been so long in the habit of writing drawing-room verses that he had better ground for hoping he might produce something similar that might please her. It would be a great stroke toward placing him in a right position with her.

By degrees, therefore, he began to show her things, and if she saw very little in their meaning, she hoped there was more than she was able to appreciate. For her interest in Vavasor was growing, though slowly, as was natural with a girl of her character. She had no suspicion of how empty he was, even after she began reading some of his verses. It was impossible to imagine a person so indifferent to truth, or without interest in his own character and growth. Being of one piece herself, she had no conception of a nature all in pieces—with no unity except that of pleasing self. Though her nature did now and then receive a jar and a shock from him, she generally attributed it to his lack of development— a condition which she hoped her influence might change.

Women are constantly being misled by the hope of being the saviors of men! Such is natural to goodness and innocence, but, still, the error is disastrous. Is it good that a life of supreme suffering should result only in an increase of guilt? It is said that patience reaps its reward, but I fear too many patiences fail and the number of resultant saints is small. Once marriage to a worthless man is committed, and irretrievable, fresh obedience is born and divine goodwill result from what suffering may then arise.

But it may well be that a woman does more to redeem a man by declining his attentions than by encouraging them to the point of matrimony. I dare not say that a woman cannot play a role in the redemption of a man. But I think one who obeys God will scarcely imagine herself free to lay herself and her happiness in the arms of a man who denies him. Good Christians not Christian enough to understand this may have to be taught by the change of what they took for love into what they know to be disgust. Women who merely hope to keep their men within the bounds of respectability will almost certainly fail. God cares nothing about keeping a man respectable apart from making him a true man. Indeed, he has given his very self, his own Son, for that purpose. It takes God to make a true man. A woman is not enough for it. Marrying a good woman cannot be God's way of saving bad men.

10 / The Concert Room_____

Because of his economic condition, Vavasor eventually realized he could not continue to visit Hester so often, and thus he began to lessen the number of his appearances at Addison Square.

But in so doing he became more aware of her influence on him, and had come to feel differently about certain things. He had not really begun to change in a fundamental way, but was only a little infected with her goodness. He took the change, however, as one of great moral significance and was wonderfully pleased with himself. His natural kindness, for instance, toward the poor was quickened, causing him to give out a penny more often to those who begged. On one occasion he prided himself that he had walked home in order to give his last shilling to a poor woman, whereas in truth he walked home because he found he had given her his last. Yet there was a little more movement of the sap of his nature, as even his behavior in the bank would have testified.

Hester was annoyed to find herself disappointed when he did not appear, and applied herself all the more diligently to her growing vocation. She began to widen her sphere a little by going about with a friend belonging to a sisterhood. But in her own neighborhood—not wishing her special work to be crossed by any prejudices—she always went alone, and seldom entered a house of the poor without singing. To the children she would frequently tell a fairy tale, singing the little rhymes she made come into it. Of course, she had to encounter rudeness from time to time, but was determined to get used to it and learn to let it pass.

The house in which the Raymounts lived, which was their own, was somewhat remarkable. Besides the ordinary accommodation of a good-sized London house with three drawing rooms on the first floor, it had unusual provisions for receiving guests. At the top of the first landing, rather more than halfway up the stair, there was a door through the original wall of the house to a long gallery, which led to a large and lofty room, apparently intended for concerts and dancing. Since they had owned the house, this room had been used only as a playroom for the children. Mr. Raymount always intended to furnish it, but had not yet done so.

The house, obtained at a low price, was larger than they required, but Mr. Raymount had a great love for room. Beneath this concert room

59

was another equally as large but so low it was difficult to find any use for it and it continued even more neglected than the other. Below this again were cellars of alarming extent and obscurity, reached by a long vaulted passage. They would have held coal and wood and wine, everything natural to a cellar, enough for one generation at least. The history of the house was unknown. There was a nailed-up door in the second of the rooms I have mentioned, which was said to lead into the next house. But as the widow who lived there took every opportunity of making herself disagreeable, they had not ventured to investigate. There was no garden, for this addition to the original house took up all the room. The great room was now plaguing Hester's mind: if only her father would allow her to use it to give a concert to her lowly friends and acquaintances!

Hester's father was also concerned about the poor in the cities, and believed he was enlightening the world on the important social condition of the day. He little suspected that his daughter was doing more for the poor, almost without knowing it, than he with all his conscious wisdom. She could not, however, have made her request at a more favorable moment, for he was just then feeling especially benevolent toward them and had written an article expressing himself powerfully on behalf of the poor. Though he was far from being unprejudiced, he had a horror of prejudice, and hunted it as uncompromisingly in himself as in another. He was not like most people who, surmising a fault in themselves, rouse every individual bristle of their nature to defend and retain the very thing that degrades them. He, therefore, speedily overcame his initial reluctance and agreed to his daughter's strange proposal. He was willing to make that much of an attempt toward the establishment of relations with the class he befriended in print. It was an approach which, if not altogether free of condescension, was still kindly meant.

Hester was greatly delighted with his ready compliance with her request, and for two weeks was busy preparing the house for the concert. A couple of charwomen were turned loose to thoroughly clean the great room. But before long, Mr. Raymount realized that no amount of cleaning could remove the dirty look of the place, so he committed the dingy room to painters and paperhangers. Under their hands it was wonderful to see how it gradually took on a gracious look.

The day for the concert was finally set for a week off, and Hester began to invite her poorer friends and neighbors to spend that evening at her father's house, when her mother would give them tea and she would sing to them. The married women were to bring their husbands if they would come, and each young woman might bring a friend. Most of the men turned up their noses at the invitation, but were nevertheless inclined to go out of curiosity. Some responded doubtfully: they *might* be able to go, they were not sure.

In requesting the presence of some of the small tradespeople, Hester asked it as a favor, begging their assistance in entertaining their poorer neighbors. And so put, the invitation was heartily accepted.

The hall and gallery were brilliantly lighted, and the room itself looked charming—at least in the eyes of those who had been so long watching the process of its resurrection. Tea was ready before the company began to arrive, and was served by men and women of the tradespeople. The meal went off well, with a good buzz of conversation. The only unpleasant thing was that several of the guests, mindful of their cubs at home, slipped large pieces of cake into their pockets to take to them. But this must not be judged without a just regard to their ways of thinking. It was, in reality, not a tenth part so bad as many of the ways in which well-bred persons appropriate slices of other people's cake without once suspecting they are in the same category.

After the dinner, the huge urns and the remnants of food were removed, and the windows opened for a minute to freshen the air. As the guests conversed quietly, a curtain rose at the end of the room, revealing a small stage decorated with green branches and artificial flowers. A piano had been placed in the center where Hester sat, now seen for the first time, having reserved her strength for her special duty.

When the assembly caught sight of her turning over the leaves of her music, a great silence fell. The moment she began to play, however, all began to talk again. But with the first tone of her voice, they quieted again, for she had chosen a ballad with a sudden and powerful opening, and, further, nervous and a little irritated at the same time with their talking while she played, had begun in a voice that would have compelled attention from a herd of cattle.

But the ballad was a little too long for them, so by the time it was half sung they had resumed talking again and exchanging opinions concerning the song. All agreed that Miss Raymount had a splendid voice. But several, who were there by second-hand invitation, said they could find a woman to beat her easily! I believe most of this group regarded their presence as a favor to her, providing her an audience that she might show off her talents. Among the poor, you see, as in more so-called respectable circles, the most refined and the coarsest-grained natures are to be met side by side.

Hester had not told Vavasor about the gathering—in part from doubt of his sympathy, in part from dislike of talking instead of doing. When she lifted her eyes at the close of her ballad, a little disappointed in having failed to interest her audience, she was extremely pleased to see him standing near the door. She assumed that he had heard of her purpose and had come to help her. Even at that distance she could see that he was looking very uncomfortable; annoyed, she did not doubt, by the behavior of her guests. A rush of new strength and courage made her bold. She rose, advanced to the front of the little stage, and called out in a clear, ringing voice, "Mr. Vavasor, will you come and help me?"

Now Vavasor was in reality a little disgusted at what he beheld. He had called without any idea of what was going on, and, seeing the lights along the gallery as he was heading for the drawing room, he had changed his direction, not knowing about the room to which it led. Bewildered by the unexpectedness of the sight, he did not at first discern the kind of company he had entered. Presently his eyes revealed the fact that he was in the midst of a great number of the unwashed. He had often talked with Hester about the poor, for they were now even a rather fashionable subject in some of the minor circles of the world's elect. But in the poor themselves he could hardly be said to have the most rudimentary interest; and that a lady should so degrade herself by singing to them and exposing both her voice and her person to their abominable remarks was to him simply incomprehensible. The admission of such people to a respectable house, and the entertainment of them as at a music hall, could have its origin only in some wild semipolitical scheme of the old fellow, who had more eccentricities in his head than brain could well hold! It was a proceeding as disgraceful as extraordinary!

And then, of all things, with the ballad at an end, the voice he had grown so to delight in came to him across the hall, clear and brave and quiet, asking him, the future earl of Gartley, to come and help the singer! Was she in trouble? Had her father forced her into the awkward situation in which she found herself? These reflections flashing through his brain caused a moment's delay in Vavasor's response. Then with perfect command, and with no shadow of expression on his face beyond that of a perfect equanimity, he proceeded toward the stage.

With smiling face but shrinking soul he walked forward, hiding his inner disgust, and sprang on the stage, making her a rather low bow.

"Come and sing a duet with me," she said, indicating one on the piano before her that they had sung together several times.

He smiled but said nothing, and almost immediately the duet began. They sang well, and the assembly, for whatever reason, acted a little more like an audience than before.

Hester next requested Vavasor to sing a certain ballad she knew was a great favorite with him. Inwardly protesting, he obeyed, and rendered it as expressively as could be expected under the circumstances. Even so, they were all talking again before he had finished.

After a brief pause, Hester invited a gentleman prepared for the occasion to sing them something patriotic. He responded with Campbell's magnificent song, "Ye Mariners of England!", which was received with hearty cheers. He was followed by another who, well acquainted with the predilections of his audience, gave them another to their liking, which was not only heard in silence but followed by tremendous cheering. Thus the occasion was gradually sinking to the intellectual level of the company—with an unforeseen consequence.

Now that the tail of the music-kite had descended near enough to the earth to be a temptation to some of the walkers afoot, they must try to catch it! The moment the last song was ended, one of the uninvited friends was on his feet. Without a word of permission he called out in a loud voice, "Ladies an' gen'lemen, Mr. William Blaney will now favor the company with a song."

Immediately a pale pock-marked man, with high retreating forehead and long, thin hair, rose and at once proceeded to make his way through the crowd: he would sing from the stage, of course! Hester and Vavasor looked at each other, one whisper passing between them, after which they waited the result in silence.

Scrambling with knee and hand upon the stage, the poor, feeble fellow stood erect and faced the audience with glowing anticipated triumph. Plunging into his song, if song it could be called, he executed it in a cracked and strained falsetto. The result, enhanced by the nature of the song, which was pathetic and dubiously moral, must have been excruciation to every good ear in the place. Long before it was over Hester had made up her mind, the moment the end came, to let loose the most thunderous music of which she was capable.

But vanity is suspicious as well as vain, and Mr. Blaney, stopping abruptly in the middle of his song's final note, changed from the sung to the spoken word without a pause before she could strike the first chord, and screeched aloud, "I will now favor the company with a song of my own composure!"

But before he had gotten his mouth into its singing place in his left cheek, Hester had risen: when she knew what had to be done, she never hesitated.

"I am sorry to have to interfere," she said, not visibly trembling, "but my friends are in my house and I am accountable for their entertainment. Mr. Blaney must excuse me if I insist on keeping the management of the evening in my own hands."

The vanity of the would-be singer was sorely hurt. He was too selfish and arrogant to see himself in a true light, and spoke up the moment Hester had ended.

"The friends as knows me and knows what I can do will back me up. I have no right to be treated as if I didn't know what I was about. I can warrant the song homemade and of the best quality. So here goes."

Vavasor made a stride toward him, but a second later Mr. Raymount spoke from somewhere near the door.

"Come off the stage!" he shouted, making his way through the company as fast as he could.

Vavasor drew back and stood like a sentinel on guard. Hester resumed her seat at the piano. Blaney, fancying that he would be allowed to finish if he began before Mr. Raymount reached him, got his mouth into position and began to howl. But his host jumped on the stage from behind, reached him at his third note, took him by the back of the neck, and proceeded to walk him through the company and out of the room like a naughty boy. Propelling him thus out of the house, Mr. Raymount reentered the concert room and was greeted by a great clapping of hands as if he had performed a deed of valor. But in spite of the man's impudence, seeing his puny form in her father's mighty clutch had gone right to Hester's heart.

The moment silence was restored, up rose a burly honest-looking bricklayer.

"I beg your pardon, miss, but will you allow me to make one remark?"

"Certainly, Mr. Jones," answered Hester.

"It seems to me, miss," said Jones, "as it's only fair on my part as brought Blaney here, to make my apologies and to say for him that I know he never would have done what he done if he hadn't had a drop as we come along to this 'ere tea party. That was the cause, miss, an' I hope as it'll be taken into account as poor enough reason of his conduct. It takes very little, I'm sorry to say, miss, to upset his behavior—not more'n a pint. But there's not a morsel of harm in him, poor fellow. I know him well, bein' my wife's brother—leastways half brother. When he's got a drop in his nob, it's always for singing, he is—an' that's the worst of him. Thank you kindly, miss."

"Thank *you*, Mr. Jones," returned Hester. "We'll think no more of it."

Loud applause followed, and Jones sat down, well satisfied.

The order of the evening was resumed, but once the harmony of the assembly was disturbed, all hope of quiet was gone. They now had something to talk about!

Hester sang again, but no song seemed quite right. Vavasor also sang several times—as often as Hester asked him. But inwardly he was repulsed by the whole affair—as was natural, for could any fish have found itself more out of the water than he? Everything annoyed him—most of all that the lady of his thoughts should have addressed herself to such an assembly. How could a woman of refinement seek appreciation for her songs from such a detestable assemblage!

One main test of our dealings in the world is whether the men and women we associate with are better or worse for it. Vavasor had often been where at least he was the worse and no one the better for his presence. For days a cloud hung over the fair image of Hester in his mind.

He called on the first possible opportunity to inquire how she was after her exertions, but avoided any further allusion to the events of the evening. She thanked him for the help he had given her, but was so far from satisfied with her experiment that she too let the subject rest.

Mr. Raymount was so disgusted that he said nothing of the kind should ever again take place in his house. He had not bought it to make a music hall out of it!

If any change was about to appear in Vavasor, a change in the fortunes of the Raymounts prevented it.

What people call *luck* seems to have odd predilections and prejudices regarding families as well as individuals. Some seem invariably successful, whatever they take in hand; others go on, generation after generation, struggling without a ray of success. On the surface there appears no reason for inequality. But there is one thing in which preeminently I do not believe. The world calls it by many names—luck, chance, or fortune—but all are names which reveal they do not know what they are talking about.

The Father of families looks after his families—and his children too.

11 / Sudden Change _____

Light and shade, sunshine and shadow pursue each other over the moral as well as the material world. Every soul has a landscape that changes with the wind that sweeps its sky, with the clouds that return after its rain.

The middle day of March had been dreary all over England—dreariest of all, perhaps, in London. Great blasts had blown under a sky whose miles-thick vault of clouds they never touched, but instead hunted and drove and dashed earth clouds of dust into all unwelcoming places, throats and eyes included. Now and then a few drops would fall on the stones as if the day's fierce misery were about to yield to sadness. But it did not so yield. Up rose again a great blundering gust, and repentance was lost in rage. The sun went down on its wrath, and its night was tempestuous.

But the next morning rose bright and glad, looking as if it would make up for its father's wildness by a gentler treatment of the world. The wind was still high, but the hate seemed to have gone out of it. It swept huge clouds across the sky, never granting a pause of motion. But the sky was blue and the clouds were white, and the dungeon-vault of the world was broken up and being carried away.

Everything in the room stood ready when the Raymounts assembled for breakfast—the fire in the hearth, crocuses in a vase on the table. Mr. Raymount was very silent, almost a little gloomy. Mrs. Raymount's face, in consequence, was a shade less peaceful. There was nothing the matter, only he had not yet learned to radiate. It is hard for some natures to let their light shine. Mr. Raymount had some light, but let it shine mostly in reviews, not much at home.

The children were rosy, fresh from their baths, and ready to eat like breakfast-loving English. Cornelius was half of his breakfast ahead of the rest. He made the best of the hardship of having to be at the bank by nine o'clock each day by claiming immunity from the niceties of the breakfast table. Never did he lose a moment in helping anybody. Even little Saffy had to stretch out a very long arm after the butter without his even looking up—except if it happened to cross his plate, when he would sharply rebuke her breach of manners. Mark would sooner have gone without salt for his egg than ask Corney to pass it.

This morning the pale boy sat staring at the crocuses.

"Why don't you eat your breakfast, Mark, dear?" asked his mother.

"I'm not hungry, Mama," he answered simply.

The mother looked at him a little anxiously. He was not a very vigorous boy physically. But unlike his father's, his light was almost always shining, making the faces about him shine.

After a few minutes of staring at the crocuses, he said almost without realizing it, "I can't imagine how they come."

"They grow!" exclaimed Saffy.

"Didn't you see Hester make the paper flowers for her party?" added their father, willing to set them thinking.

"Yes," replied Saffy, "but it would take such a long time to make all the flowers in the world that way!"

"So it would; but if a great many angels took it in hand, I suppose they could do it."

"That can't be how," Saffy laughed. "You know the flowers come up out of the earth, and there isn't room to cut them out there."

"I think they must be cut and put together before they are made!" said Mark, very slowly and thoughtfully.

The supposition was greeted with a great burst of laughter from Cornelius. In the midst of a refined family he behaved as the blind and stupid generally behave to those who see what they cannot see. Mockery is the share they choose.

"Stop, Cornelius!" his father admonished. "I suspect we have a young philosopher here, where you see only the silly little brother. He has, I believe, got a glimpse of something he does not yet know how to say."

"In that case," Cornelius growled, "he had better hold his tongue till he does know how to say it."

It was not often he dared to speak so to his father, but he was growing less afraid of him, though not through increase of love. *Everything the little idiot says, they think clever,* he complained to himself. *Nobody made anything of me when I was his age!*

The mail was soon brought in. Among the letters was one for Mr. Raymount with a broad black border. He looked at the postmark.

"This must be the announcement of cousin Strafford's death!" he said. "Someone told me she was not expected to live."

"You did not tell me she was ill," reproved his wife.

"I forgot to. It has been so many years since I had the least communication with her, or even heard anything of her. She was a strange old soul!"

"You used to be close to her, didn't you, Papa?" asked Hester.

"Yes, at one time. But we differed so entirely it was impossible for that closeness to last. She would think the most peculiar things about what I thought and meant, and then accuse me of being in favor of things I disliked quite as much as she did. She took no trouble to try to understand what I was really saying. But that is often the way with people. They hardly know what they think themselves and can hardly be expected to know what other people mean."

He picked up the letter, slowly broke the large black seal and began to read. His wife sat looking at him, waiting in expectation.

He had scarcely read half the first page when she saw his countenance change a little, then flush. He folded the letter, laid it down by the side of his plate, and began to eat again, with a fixed expression on his face.

"Well, dear?" urged his wife.

"It is not quite what I thought," he answered with a curious smile, then ate his toast in a brooding silence. Never in the habit of making secrets like his son, he nevertheless had a strong dislike of showing his feelings. Besides, he was too proud to reveal his interest in the special contents of this letter.

The poor, yet hopeless and hardly indulged, ambition of Mr. Raymount's life was to possess a portion of earth—even if only an acre or two. He came of families possessing property, but none of it had come anywhere near him except what belonged to cousin Strafford. He was her nearest relation, but he had never hoped to inherit anything from her. After a final quarrel had put an end to their quarrelling, he had stopped seeing her altogether. For many years there had not been the slightest communication between the cousins. But in the course of those years, all the other relatives of the old lady had died, and, as the letter he now held informed him, he was after all heir to her property—a small estate in a lovely spot among the roots of the Cumberland hills. Quite a few thousand pounds in government securities accompanied the property.

But while Mr. Raymount was not a money lover in any notable sense, his delight in having land of his own was almost beyond expression. This enormous pleasure had nothing to do with the money value of the property; he scarcely thought of that. The gratification was in large part because of a new sense of room and freedom. It made him so excited he could hardly get his toast down.

Mrs. Raymount was by this time tolerably familiar with her husband's moods, but she had never before seen him look just the way he looked now, and was puzzled. The fact was, he had never before had such a pleasant surprise, and sat absorbed in a foretaste of bliss.

Presently he rose and left the room, his wife following him. The moment she entered his study behind him, he turned and took her in his arms.

"Here's news, my dear!" he blurted, unable to contain his joy any longer. "You'll be just as happy as I. Yrndale is ours—at least so my old friend Heron says, and he ought to know. Cousin Strafford left no will. He is certain there is none. She persistently put off making one, with the full intention, he believes, that the property should come to me, her lawful heir and next of kin. He thinks she did not have the heart to leave it to anyone else. Thank God! It is a lovely place. Nothing could have given me more pleasure."

"I am indeed glad, Raymount," said his wife—who called him by his family name on important occasions. "You always had a fancy for playing the squire."

"A great fancy for a little room, rather," replied her husband—"not much, I fear, for the duties of a squire. There is money as well, I am glad to say—enough to keep the place up, anyhow."

"I have no doubt you will turn into a model farmer and landlord," encouraged his wife.

"You must take the business part—at least till Corney is fit to look after it," he returned.

But his wife's main thought was what influence the change would have on Hester's marriage prospects. In her heart she hated the thought that property should have anything to do with marriage—yet this was almost her first thought. Inside us are played more fantastic tricks than any we play in the face of the world.

"Are the children to be told?" she asked.

"I suppose so. It would be a shame not to let them share in our happiness. And yet I hate to think of them talking about it, as children will."

"I am not afraid of the children," objected his wife. "I must simply tell them not to talk about it. I am as confident in Mark as if he were fifty. Saffy might forget, but Mark will keep her in line."

When she returned to the dining room, Cornelius was gone, but the rest were still at the table. She told them that God had given them a beautiful house in the country with hills and woods and a swift flowing river. Saffy clapped her hands, crying, "Oh, Mama!" and could hardly sit on her chair. Mark was perfectly still, but his eyes spoke volumes. The moment her mother ceased, Saffy jumped down and made a rush for the door.

"Saffy, Saffy, where are you going?" cried her mother.

"To tell Sarah," answered the happy child.

"Come back, my child. Your papa and I wish you to say nothing whatever about this to anyone."

"O-oh!" groaned Saffy. Both her look and tone said, *What's the good of it then?*

Mark spoke not a word, but his face shone as if it had been heaven he was going to, breaking into the loveliest smile. When Mark smiled, his whole body and being smiled.

Hester's face flushed a rose red. Her first thought was of the lovely things of the country and the joy of them. Her next thought was of the poor: *Now I shall really be able to do something for them!* But then immediately followed the thought that now she would be able to do less than ever for them. Yrndale was far from London. Maybe her father and mother would let her stay behind, but she hardly dared even hope for that. Perhaps it was God's will to remove her from London because she was doing more harm than good. Now her endeavors would be at an end! So her pleasure was quickly dampened.

"You don't like the thought of leaving London, Hester?" asked her mother with concern, thinking it was because of Vavasor.

"I am very happy for you and Papa, Mother," answered Hester. "I was thinking of my poor people and what they would do without me."

"I have sometimes found," returned her mother, "that the things I dreaded most serve me best in the end. I don't mean because I got used to them, or because they did me good. I mean they furthered what I thought they would ruin."

"Thank you, Mother! For myself I could not imagine anything more pleasant. If only it were near London!"

"I suppose, Father," said Cornelius when his father had told him the news that same evening, "that it will no longer be necessary for me to work at the bank."

"It will be more necessary than ever," countered his father. "There will be far more to look after when I am gone. What do you imagine you could employ yourself with down there? You have never taken to study, or, as you know, I would have sent you to Oxford. When you leave the bank, it will be to learn farming and the management of an estate."

Cornelius made no reply. His father's words annoyed him. He was hardly good at anything except taking offense, and he looked on the estate as nearly as much his as his father's. What right had his father to keep from him what he deserved—a share in the good fortunes of the family? He left the study almost hating his father because of what he counted his injustice. Despite his father's request that he would say nothing of the matter until things were more settled, he made not the slightest effort to obey him, taking the first opportunity to pour out his righteous indignation to Vavasor.

His friend responded very sensibly, congratulating him so warmly on his good fortune that a vague hope rose in him at the same time. For Cornelius had used large words in telling him of the estate; and in the higher position which Mr. Raymount would now occupy as one of the proprietors of England, therefore as a man of influence in his country and its politics, Vavasor saw the gulf beginning to close between him and Hester. She would no doubt come in for a personal share in this large fortune; and if he could but see the possibility of living without his aunt's money, he would, he almost said to himself, marry Hester and risk his aunt's displeasure. At the same time, she would doubtless now look with more favor on his choice. There could be nothing terribly offensive to her pride in his proposing to marry the daughter of a country squire. In the meantime he would, as Cornelius had begged him after the first burst of his rage was over, be careful not to mention the matter.

Mr. Raymount went to look at his property, returning more delighted with house, land, and landscape than he had expected. He seldom spoke of his good fortune, however, except to his wife, or betrayed his pleasure except by the sparkle in his eyes. As soon as the warm weather came, they would migrate. Immediately they began their preparations—the young ones by packing and unpacking several times a day a most unlikely assemblage of things. The house was to be left in charge of old Sarah, who would also wait on Cornelius.

12 / Yrndale

It was a lovely morning when they left London. Because trains did not travel so fast in those days, it was late in the afternoon before they neared the station from which they had to journey by road. The weather had now turned cold and dismal, the sky changing from sunshine to one mass of clouds and steady, falling rain. For some time they had been traveling in the hills, but those they were passing through were neither lofty nor lovely—only dreary through the rain and mist. They were mostly bare, except for a little grass, interrupted by huge brown and yellow gulleys.

Saffy had been sound asleep through this part of the journey, but Mark had been standing at the window of the railway carriage, gazing out on an awful world. What would he do, he wondered, if he were lost there? Would he be able to sit still all night without being frightened, waiting for God to come and rescue him? As they rushed along, it was not through the brain alone of the child the panorama flitted, but through his mind and heart as well. There, like a glacier, it marked its passage, or rather, it left its ghosts behind it, ever shifting forms and shadows, each atmosphered in its own ethereal mood. They were hardly thoughts, but a strange other awareness of life and being.

Hills and woods and valleys and plains and rivers and seas, entering by the gates of sight into the live mirror of the human, are transformed into another nature—to a living wonder, a joy, a pain, a breathless marvel as they pass. Nothing can receive another thing; not even a glass can take into its depth a face without altering it. In the mirror of man, things become thoughts, feelings, life, and send their streams down the cheeks, or their sunshine over the countenance.

Before Mark reached the end of that journey, he had gathered a great amount of fuel in the bottom of his heart, stored there for the future consumption of thinking and for reproduction in forms of power. He was unaware of this phenomena, for he took nothing consciously. Things just kept sinking into him. The sole sign of his reception was an occasional sigh—of which he could not have told either the cause or the meaning.

Arriving at the station, the Raymounts got into their own carriage. The drive was a long and tedious one, for the roads were rough, muddy and often steep. For some time they drove along the side of a hill and could see next to nothing except in one direction. When at length the road ran into a valley and along the course of the swollen river, it was getting so dark and the rain was coming down so fast that they could see nothing at all. Long before they reached their new home, Saffy and Mark were sound asleep, Hester was deep in her own thoughts, and the parents sat holding hands in unbroken silence.

Hester's mind was on the places they had left. Ah, that city—so full of fellow creatures struggling in the toils of numerous foes! Many sorrows had entered in at Hester's ears—tales of oppression and want, giving rise to sympathy in her bosom. From the spray that reached her on its borders, she knew how that human sea tossed and raged afar. Yet now she was gone away from it, unable to plunge into its midst with what little help she was able to give.

It was pitch dark when they arrived at their destination. They turned and went through a gate, then passed through the trees, which made the night yet darker. By and by the faint lights of the house appeared, with blotchy pallors thinning the mist and darkness. Presently the carriage stopped.

Both the children continued sound asleep and were carried off to bed. The father and mother knew the house from times past and revived for each other old memories. But to Hester all was strange. With the long journey, the weariness, the sadness, and the strangeness, she entered the old hall as if walking in a dream. It had a quiet, dull, dignified look, as if it expected nobody; as if it was here itself because it could not help it and would rather not be here; as if it had seen so many generations come and go that it had ceased to care much about new faces. Everything in the house looked somber and solemn, seeming not to have forgotten its old mistress. They had supper in a long, low room, with furniture almost black, against whose window heavy roses every now and then softly patted, caught in the fringes of the rain gusts. The dusky room, the perfect stillness inside, the low mingled sounds of swaying trees and pattering rain outside, the sense of the great darkness—all grew together into one possessing mood, which rose and sank, like the water in a sea-cave, in the mind of Hester. But who by words can fix the mood that comes and goes unbidden? A single happy phrase, the sound of a wind, the odor of the mere earth may send us into some lonely, dusky realm of being. I doubt if even the poet ever conveys just what he means to the mind of his fellow. We can truly meet in spirit only in God.

But the nearest mediator of feeling, the most potent, the most delicate, and perhaps the most similar to the breath moving upon the soft face of the waters of chaos, is music. It rose like a soft, irrepressible tide in the heart of Hester. It mingled and became one with her mood; together they beat at the gates of silence. She rose and looked around her for such an instrument as had always been within her reach—walked about the shadowy room searching. But there was nothing musical among the aged furniture. She returned and sat again at the table, the mood vanishing in weariness.

But the family did not linger there long. The fatigued ladies were glad to be shown to the room prepared for them. The housekeeper, the ancient authority of the place, in every motion and tone expressing herself wronged by their intrusion, conducted them. Every spot they passed was plainly far more hers than theirs; only the law was a tyrant, and she dared not assert her rights!

Tired as she was, Hester was charmed with her room, and the more charmed the more she looked around. It was old fashioned to her heart's content, and seemed full of shadowy histories, as if each succeeding occupant had left behind an ethereal record, a memorial imprint of presence of walls and furniture—to which she would now add hers. In weary haste she undressed, ascending with some difficulty the high four-post bed which stood waiting for her like an altar of sleep.

She awoke to a blaze of sunlight. The night had passed and carried the tears of the day with it. Ah, how much is done in the night when we sleep and know nothing! Things never stop. The sun was shining as if he too had wept and repented. All the earth beneath him was like the face of a child who has ceased to weep and begun to smile, but has not yet wiped away his tears.

Raindrops everywhere! millions of them! every one of them with a sun in it! Hester had sprung from her bed and opened the curtains. How different was the sight from what she saw when she looked out in Addison Square. If heaven be as different from this earth, and as much better than it, we shall indeed be happy children. On each side she saw green, undulating lawn, with trees and meadows beyond; but just in front, the grassy lawn sloped rapidly, grew steep, and fell into the swift river—which, now swollen from the rains, went rolling and sliding, brown and heavy toward the far-off sea. Beyond the river, the bank rose into a wooded hill. She could see walks winding through the wood, here appearing, there vanishing, and a little way up the valley, the rails of a rustic bridge that led them to it.

It was a paradise! In place of the roar of London along Oxford Street, there was the sound of the river; in place of the cries of rough human voices, the soprano of birds and the soft mellow bass of the cattle in the meadows. The sky was a shining blue. Not a cloud was to be seen upon it. Quietly it looked down as if saying to the world over which it stood, *Yes, you are welcome to it all!*

She thanked God for the country, but soon was praying for the town. The neighborly country offered to console her for the loss of the town she received, but then she remembered that God cared more for one miserable, selfish, wife-and-donkey-beating ironmonger in London than for all the hills and dales of Cumberland, and all the starry things of his heavens.

Dressing quickly, she then went to her mother's room. Her father was already outdoors, but her mother was having breakfast in bed.

"What a lovely place it is, Mama! You did not say half enough about it," exclaimed Hester.

"Wasn't it better to let you discover for yourself, my child," answered her mother. "You were so sorry to leave London that I did not want to praise Yrndale for fear of prejudicing you against it."

"Yes, it was hard for me to leave," Hester admitted quietly. "I was never one to turn easily to new things. And I believe you may already know that my calling is among my fellow creatures in London—at least that conviction has been growing in me."

She had never before spoken so plainly to her mother about the things on her heart and mind. She was a little timid to do so even now. What if her mother thought the mere idea of having a calling was presumptuous?

"Two things, I think, go to make up a call," said her mother, to Hester's relief. "You must not imagine that because you have said nothing, I have not known what you were thinking. Mother and daughter are too near not to be able to hear each other without words. There is between you and me a constant undercurrent of communication."

"Oh, Mother!" cried Hester, overjoyed to find her mother felt close to her, "I am so glad. Please tell me the two things you mean."

"I think, to make up a true call," replied Mrs. Raymount, "both desire and possibility are required. The first you know well, but have you considered the second? Even if you have a desire to help people, the other half of being so used needs an open door. And in addition, a desire to do a thing in itself does not always determine fitness to do it."

"I can't believe, Mama, that God would give any gift, especially when accompanied by a desire to use it for some special purpose, without intending it should be used."

"You must admit there are some who never find a use for their special gifts."

"Yes; but could that be because they have not sufficiently cultivated their gifts or have not done their best to put them to use? Or could they have wanted to use them for their own ends instead of God's? I feel as if I must stand up against every difficulty lest God should be disappointed in me. Surely any frustration of the ends to which their very being points must be their own fault. Could it be that they have nothing but unsatisfied longings because they have not yielded to the calling voice? They have gone picking and choosing what *they* would like to do instead of obeying?"

"There must be truth in what you say, Hester, but it cannot explain every case. Sometimes there might be delay in carrying out a calling without that calling being frustrated. You think yours is to help the poor. But is it for you to say when you are ready? Willingness is not everything. May not part of the preparation for work be the mental discipline involved in the imagined postponements? Remember how long Moses was prepared for his work—eighty years. And Jesus. And what about our life beyond the grave? This life is but a beginning. While cultivating your gift and waiting the call, you may be in active preparation for the work in the coming life for which God intended you when he made you."

Hester gave a great sigh. Indefinite postponement is terrible to the young and eager.

"That is a dreary thought, Mother," she said mournfully.

"Is it, my child?" returned the mother. "Painful the will of God may be—that I well know. But *dreary*, no. Have patience. Your heart's deepest desire must be the will of God, for he cannot have made you so that your heart should run against his will. Let him have his own way with you and he will give you your desire. He delights in his children. As soon as they can be indulged without ruin, he will heap upon them their desires; they are his too."

Hester was astonished at her mother's grasp and wisdom. The child may for years have but little idea of the thought and life within the form and face he knows and loves better than any. But at last the predestined moment arrives, the two minds meet, and the child understands the parent.

Hester threw her arms around her mother, kissed her, and went to her own room, understanding that if God has called, he will also open the door.

Scarcely had she reached her room, however, when she heard the voices of the children shouting along the same corridor on their way to breakfast. In their eagerness to rush into the new creation, the garden of Eden around them, they could hardly be prevented from bolting their breakfast like puppies.

I will attempt no description of the beauties that met them at every turn. I doubt if some of the children in heaven are always happier than Saffy and Mark were that day. Hester had thoughts which kept her from being so happy as they, but she was more blessed. Glorious as is the child's delight, the child-heart in the grown woman is capable of tenfold the bliss. Saffy pounced on a flower like a wild beast on its prey; she never stood and gazed at one like Mark. Hester would gaze until tears filled her eyes.

Mark was in many things an exception—a curious mixture of child and youth. He had never been strong and had always been thoughtful. God is the God of little children, and God had always been especially so with little Mark.

Saffy, on the other hand, expressed smiles and tears just as they chose to come. She had not a suspicion yet that the exercise of any operative power on herself was possible to her—and even required of her. Many men and women are in the same condition who have grown cold and hard in it; she was soft and warm, on the way to wakefulness and action. Even now, when a good thought came she would give it a stranger's welcome; but the first appeal to her sense would drive it out-of-doors again.

Before the three had finished their ramble, what with the sweet twilight gladness of Mark, the merry noonday brightness of Saffy, and the loveliness all around, the heart of Hester was quiet and hopeful as if waiting in the blue night for the rising of the moon. She had some things to trouble her, but none of them had touched the quick of her being. She was at last beginning to see that it is God who means everything as we read it, however poor or mingled with mistake our reading may be. And the soothing of his presence in what we call nature was working on Hester, helping her toward that quietness of spirit needed to perceive the will of God.

13 / Down the Hill_____

When Franks, the acrobat, and his family left Mrs. Baldwin's garret to go to another yet poorer lodging, it was with heavy hearts: they crept silently away to go down another step of the world's stair. And yet how often on the steps of this world, when you think you are going down, you are really ascending. I think it was so with the Frankses and the stair they were on.

I think God has a thousand times more to do with the fortunes of the poor than with those of the rich. With the poor there are many more changes, and they are of greater significance as coming closer to the heart of their condition—more variations of weather, more sunshine and shade, more storms and calms, than lives passed on airier slopes.

The Frankses were on the down-going side of the hill Difficulty, and down they must go, unable to help themselves. They had found a cheaper lodging, but Franks was beginning to feel his strength and elasticity not quite what they had been. Certainly strength has ever to be made perfect in weakness, and old age is one of the weaknesses in which it is perfected. But poor Franks had not got so far yet as to see this, and the feeling of the approach of old age helped to relax the springs of his hopefulness. Also, his wife had not recovered from her last confinement. The baby, too, was sickly. And there was little receptivity for acrobatics in the streets; coppers came in slowly. But his wife's words were always cheerful, though their tone was a little mournful. Their tone came of temperament, the words of love and its courage. The daughter of a gamekeeper, she was regarded by the neighbors as throwing herself away when she married Franks. But her husband was an honest and brave man, and she never repented of giving herself to him, even when life was the hardest.

For a few weeks they did quite well in their new lodging. They managed to pay their way, and had food enough—though not quite so good as husband and wife wished each for the other and both for their children. The boys had a good enough time of it. They had not yet exhausted their own wonder in London. The constant changes around made of their lives a continuous novel, a romance, and being happy they could eat anything and thrive on it.

The lives of parents are like an umbrella over those of their children, shutting out all care if not all sorrow, and every change is welcomed as a new delight. This is true in all classes, yet I suspect perhaps that imagination, fancy, perception, insight into character, the sense of adventure, and many other powers and feelings are more likely to be active in the children of the poor, to the greater joy of their existence, than in others.

John Franks, according to his light, was a careful and conscientious parent. His boys were strongly attached to him, never thought of shirking their work, and endured a good deal of hardness and fatigue without grumbling. Their mother had caused them to see that their father took more than his full share and did his best for them. They were very proud of their father and believed him not only the top man in his profession, but the best man that ever lived in the world besides. To believe so of one's parent is a stronger aid to righteousness than all other things combined, until the day-star of the knowledge of the great Father rises in the heart.

The Frankses were now reduced to one room, with the boys sleeping on the floor. This was no hardship now that summer was near, only the parents found it interfered a little with their freedom of speech. Nor did it change anything to send them to bed early, for the earlier they went to bed, the longer they were in going to sleep.

One evening after the boys were in bed, the father and mother sat talking. The mother was busy patching young Moxy's garment. The man's work for the day was over, but not the woman's!

"Well, I dunnow . . ." he said at last, and stopped.

"What don' ye know, John?" asked his wife.

"I was jist thinkin' that Mr. Christopher was such a friend. You remember as how he used to say a man could no more get out o' the sight o' the eyes o' the Almighty than a child could get out o' sight o' the eyes o' his mother as was watchin' him?"

"Yes, John, I do remember, and a great comfort it was to me at the time."

"Well, I dunnow!" said Franks again, and paused. But this time he resumed. "What troubles me is this: that if there was a mother lookin' after yer child an' was to see him doin' no better'n you an' me, an' day by day gettin' further an' further behind, I should say she wasn't much of a mother to let us go on in that way."

"She might have got her reasons for it, John," suggested his wife. "Perhaps she might see a little farther down the road, and might know that the child was in no danger o' harm. When the children want their dinner very bad, I have heard you say to them sometimes, 'Now, kids, have patience. Patience is a fine thing. What if ye do be hungry? You ain't dyin' o' hunger. You'll wear a bit longer yet!' Ain't I heard you say that, John?"

"I ain't goin' to deny it. But you must allow this is drivin' it jist a little too far. Here we come to Lon'on thinkin' to better ourselves—not wantin' no great things, but jist thinkin' as how it were time to lay a shillin' or two to keep us out o' the workhouse—that's all we was after. An' here sin' we come, first one shillin' goes, an' then another, till we ain't got one, as I may almost say, left! Instead o' gettin' more we get less, an' that with harder work, as is wearin' me an' the boys out; an'—"

"I ain't wore out, Father. I'm good for another go," interrupted little Moxy from the bed.

"I ain't neither, gov'nor. I got a lot more work in me!"

"No, nor me!" cried the third. "I likes London. I can stand on my head twice as long as Tommy Blake, an' he's a year older'n me."

"Hold yer tongues, you rascals, an' go to sleep," growled the father, pretending to be angry with them. "What right have you to be awake at this time o' the night—an' in Lon'on too? It's not like the country, you know. In the country you can do much as you like, but not in the town! You've no call to be awake listenin' to what yer father an' mother was sayin' to theirselves."

"We wasn't listenin', Father. We was only hearin' 'cause we wasn't asleep. An' you didn't speak down as if it was secrets."

"Well, you know there's things as fathers and mothers can understand an' talk about as no boys can see to the end. So they better go to sleep and wait till their turn comes to be fathers and mothers theirselves. Go to sleep direc'ly, or I'll break every bone in your bodies!"

"Yes, Father," they answered together, in no way terrified by the awful threat—which was not a little weakened by the fact that they had heard it every day of their lives and not yet known it to be carried out.

But having become aware that his children were awake, the father, without the least hypocrisy, conscious or unconscious, changed his tone: in the presence of his children he preferred looking at the other side of the argument. After a few moments' silence he began again.

"Yes, as you was sayin', Wife, an' I knows as yer always in the right, if the right be anyhows to be got at—there's no sayin' when that same as we was speakin' of—the Almighty is the man I mean—no sayin', I say, when he may come to see as we have, as I may say, had enough o' it, an' turn an' let us have a taste o' luck again."

"So it do seem to me, John," answered the mother.

"Well," said Franks, apparently, now that he had taken up the defense of the ways of the Supreme with men, warming to his subject, "I daresay he do the best he can, an' give us as much luck as is good for us. Leastways that's how the rest of us would do. We can't always do as well as we would like for to do for our little ones, but we always do the best we can. We'll suppose yet a little while, anyhow, as how he's a lookin' after us. It can't be for nothin', as he counts the hairs on our head, as the sayin' is!"

There are many who think to reverence the Most High by assuming that he can and should do anything or everything that pleases him in a mere moment. In their eyes power is a grander thing than love. But his Love is higher than his omnipotence. See what it cost him to redeem the world! He did not find that easy, or to be done in a moment without pain or toil. Yes, God is omnipotent—awfully omnipotent. For he wills, effects, and perfects the thing which, because of the bad in us, he has to carry out in suffering and sorrow. Evil is a hard thing, even for God to overcome. Yet thoroughly and altogether and triumphantly will he overcome it. But not by crushing it underfoot—any god of man's idea could do that!—but by conquest of heart over heart, of life over life, of life over death, of love over all. Nothing shall be too hard for God that fears not pain, but will deliver and make true and blessed at his own severest cost.

For a time, then, the Frankses went on, with food to eat and money to pay their way, but going slowly down hill, and finding it harder and harder to keep their footing. By and by the baby grew worse. They sought help at the hospital, but saw no Mr. Christopher. The baby did not improve. Still they kept on, and every day the husband brought home a little money. Several times they seemed on the point of an engagement, but every time something happened to prevent it, until at length Franks almost ceased to hope, growing more and more silent.

Poor Franks struggled in his own way with life's conflicts having not much of a philosophy to assist him. Yet he had much affection, which is the present God in a man—and so he did not go far in the evil direction. The worst sign of his degenerating temper was the more frequently muttered oath of impatience with his boys—never with his wife. But not one of them was a moment uneasy in consequence—except when the *guv'nor* wasn't jolly, neither were they.

14 / Out of the Frying Pan

The tide of Amy Amber's destiny seemed now to have caught her in its swell, bearing her more swiftly along. No longer able to endure a life bounded by the distrust and ill temper of her two aunts, Amy did at last what she had threatened. One morning when she was very late, they went to her room, received no answer, and could find her nowhere either inside or out of the house. She had some time before written to a friend in London, and following her advice, had taken the cheap overnight train to go to her. The friend had taken her home and helped her find a job. Before many days had passed Amy stood behind a counter in a large shop, hard at work. Though the hours of business were long, the labor was by no means too much for her fine health and spirits, which now quickly blossomed.

At first, her aunts raised an outcry of horror and dismay, then of reprobation, accusing her of many things. In reality, the things they accused her of, they were guilty of themselves; for as to the gratitude and affection we are so ready to claim and so slow to pay, the debt was great on their part, and very small indeed on hers. They wrote to her guardians, of course, to acquaint them with the shocking fact of her flight, but dwelt far more upon her bad behavior toward them, her rapid deterioration, and their convictions as to the depth of the degradation she had preferred to the shelter of their (very moth-eaten) wings.

The younger of the two guardians was a man of business and at once took proper measures to locate Amy. Several months elapsed before he was successful. By that time her employers were so satisfied with her that, after an interview with them, followed by one with the girl herself, he was convinced that she was much better off where she was than with her aunts, whose dispositions were unknown to him. So he left her in peace.

Knowing nothing of London and busy with her new way of life, Amy did not go at once to find Miss Raymount. She often recalled her kindness and always intended to seek her out as soon as she had the time. But the days and weeks wore away, and still she had not gone.

She continued to be a well-behaved girl, went regularly to church on Sundays, had many friends but few close ones, and lived with the girl who had been her friend before her mother's death. Her new life was, no doubt, from its lack of ties to a home and the restraining influences of older people, dangerous: no kite can soar without the pull of the string. But danger is less often ruin than some people think. He who can walk without falling will learn to walk the better that his road is not always smooth.

Such were the respective conditions of Amy Amber and the Frankses when the Raymounts left London. Hester knew nothing of the state of either, nor had they ever belonged to her flock. It was not at all for them that she was troubled in the midst of the peace and rest of her new life. One good thing, however, that came of the change was that she and her father were drawn closer together through the quiet of this country life. When Mr. Raymount's hours of writing were over, he missed the more busy life into which he had been able to turn at will, and needed a companion. His wife not wishing to go with him, he naturally turned to his daughter, and they took many walks together.

During these walks Hester learned much. Though her father was not chiefly occupied with the best things, he did have both a learning and a teaching nature. There are few who can be described as truly alive. Of Mr. Raymount it might be said that he was coming alive, and it was no small consolation to Hester to get nearer to him. Like the rest of his children, she had been a little afraid of him. Fear, though it may dig deeper foundations of love, chokes its passages. Before a month was over, she was astonished to find how much they had become companions as well as friends.

Most fathers know little of their sons and less of their daughters. Because they are familiar with every feature of their children's faces and every movement of their bodies, they take it for granted they know them. But now Mr. Raymount began to make some discoveries of a deeper nature in Hester.

She kept up a steady correspondence with her music teacher, Miss Dasomma, and that also was a great help to her. She had a note now and then from Mr. Vavasor, but that was not a help. A little present of music was generally its pretext. He dared not trust himself to write to her about anything else. Hester was always glad when she saw his writing, and always disappointed with the letter—she could hardly have said why, for she never expected it to go beyond the surface of things.

In her absence Vavasor found himself haunted by her face, her form, her voice, her music, and the uplifting influence she exercised upon him. It is possible for a man to fall in love with a woman he is centuries from being able to understand. But how the form of such a woman must be dwarfed in the camera of such a man's mind. He is but a telescope turned wrong end upon her. To see how he sees her—to get a glimpse of the shrunken creature he has to make her before he can get her through

the proud door into the straightened cellar of his poor, pinched heart—
would be enough in itself to keep any such woman from falling in love
with that type of man.

At length, in one of his brief communications, he mentioned that
his yearly resurrection was at hand—a month of holiday. He must go
northward, he said, to brace him for the autumn city heat. The memories
of Burcliff drew him. He had an invitation to the opposite coast, which
he thought he might accept instead. He did not know exactly where
Yrndale lay, but if he found it within accessible distance, he hoped her
parents would allow him to call some morning for an hour or two.

Hester answered that her father and mother would be glad to see
him, and that if he were inclined to spend a day or two, there was a
beautiful country to show him. If his holiday happened to coincide with
Corney's, perhaps they would come together.

By return mail came a grateful acceptance. About a week after, they
heard from Cornelius that he could not take a holiday before November.
He did not inform them that he had exchanged vacations with another
clerk whose time fell in the undesirable month late in the year.

One lovely evening in June, when her turn came to get away a little
earlier, Amy Amber decided to find Miss Raymount. She learned the
address from a directory and was now well-enough acquainted with
London to know how to reach Addison Square.

In every motion and feeling Amy Amber was a little lady—from her
stylish dress to the daintiest little bonnet, to her gloves neatly covering
her petite hands. She did not have much experience, and therefore was
ignorant of some of the small ways and customs of the higher social
strata. But such knowledge is not essential to ladyhood, though half
ladies think themselves whole ladies because they have it. To become
ladies indeed, they have to learn what those things and the knowledge
of them are really worth. Another way in which Amy was unlike many
who would have counted themselves her superiors was her inability to
be disagreeable. Without knowing it, she held the main secret of all
good manners: she was simple. She never pretended, never wished to
appear anything other than what she was.

Eager to locate her friend, Amy got into an omnibus and found
Addison Square and the Raymount house. It looked dingy and dull—
for many of its shutters were closed—and held an indescribable air of
departure. Nevertheless, she knocked and the door was opened. She
asked if Miss Raymount was at home.

"They are all out of town, miss," replied Sarah, "—except Mr.
Cornelius, of course."

At that moment Mr. Cornelius, on his way to go out, stepped on the landing of the stair and stood for an instant looking down into the hall, wondering who might be at the door. He could not see Amy's face, and had he seen it, I doubt if he would have recognized her, but the moment he heard her voice he knew it, and hurried down, his face glowing with pleasure. But as he drew near, the change in her seemed to him so great that he could hardly believe with his eyes what his ears had told him.

From the first, Corney, like everyone else in the family, was taken with Amy, and Amy was not less than a little taken with him. He was good-looking and, except with his own people, ready enough to make himself agreeable. Amy's face beamed with pleasure at the sight of him, and she almost involuntarily stepped within the door to meet him.

"Amy! Who would have thought of seeing you here? When did you come to town?" he asked, shaking her hand.

"I have been in London a long time," she answered.

Corney thought she indeed looked as if she had.

How deuced pretty she is! he said to himself. *Quite ladylike, by Jove.*

"Come upstairs," he said, "and tell me all about it."

He turned and led the way. Without a second thought, Amy followed him. Sarah stood for a moment staring, wondering who the lady could be. "A cousin from Australia," she concluded: they had cousins there.

Cornelius went into the drawing room, Amy following him, and opened the shutters of a window, congratulating himself on his good luck. Not often did anything so pleasant enter the stupid old place! He made her sit on the sofa in the half dark, sat down beside her, and in a few minutes had all her story. After a conversation of about half an hour, she rose.

"What!" exclaimed Corney, "you're not going already, Amy?"

"Yes, sir," replied Amy. "I think I had better go. I am sorry not to see Miss Raymount. She was very kind to me."

"You mustn't go yet," insisted Corney. "Sit down and rest a little. Come—you used to like music: I will sing to you and you shall tell me whether I have improved since you heard me last."

Amy sat down again as he went to the piano and sang her half a dozen songs. Next he showed her a book of photographs, chiefly portraits of the more famous actresses of the day, and told her about them. He kept her occupied with one thing and another until Sarah grew fidgety and was on the point of stalking up from the kitchen when she heard them coming down. Picking up his hat and stick, Cornelius said he would walk with her. Amy made no objection; she was pleased to have his company. He went with her all the way to the lodging she shared with her friend in a quiet little street in Kensington. Before they parted, her manner and behavior had begun to fill what little there was of Corney's imagination, and he left her with a feeling that he knew where a treasure lay. He walked with an exaggerated strut as he went home through the park, and swung his cane with the air of a man who had made a conquest of which he had reason to be proud.

15 / Waiting a Purpose

The hot, dreamy days came and went in Yrndale. Hester would wake in the morning oppressed with the feeling that there was something she ought to have begun long ago, and must positively get started on this new day. Later in the day she would seek out a shady spot with a book for her companion. Under the shadow of some rock, the tent-roof of some great beech tree, or the solemn gloom of some pine grove, the brooding spirit of the summer would day after day find her when the sun was at the height of his great bridge and fill her with a sense of repose. On and off she would be haunted with a vague sense of guilt at enjoying the leisure, but then faith would rouse itself and say: *But God will take care of you in this thing, too. You do not have to watch lest he should forget, only be ready when he calls you, however softly. You have to keep listening.*

Every evening Hester would regularly sit at her piano, which had by then arrived. There, through all the sweet atmospheric changes of the brain—for the brain has its morning and evening, its summer and winter as well as the day and the year—she would meditate aloud. And, more often than she knew, especially in the twilight when the days had grown shorter, Mark would be somewhere in the dusk listening to her, a lurking cherub, feeding on her music—sometimes ascending on its upward torrent to a solitude where only God would find him.

Occasionally a thought of Vavasor would come, but mainly as one who would be a welcome helper in her work. Then when she had had enough of music, she would softly close her piano as she would have covered a child, and glide into the night to wander about through the gloom without conscious choice. These were the times she would imagine what it would be like to have a man for a friend, one who would strengthen her heart and make her bold to do what was needful and right.

To cherish the ideal of a man with whom to walk through life is as right for a woman as it was for God to make them male and female. It is not the building of castles in the steepest heights of air that is to be blamed, but the building of such as inspector conscience is not invited to enter. And if occasionally Hester did indulge in such fantasies along the lines of the natural architecture of most young maidens, and if through these airy castles went flitting the form of Vavasor, who will wonder?

One evening, toward the end of July, when the summer is at its peak and makes the world feel as if there had never been and never ought to be anything but summer, Hester was sitting under a fir tree on the gathered leaves of numberless years, pine odors filling the air around her, as if they, too, stole out with the things of the night when the sun was gone. The sweet melancholy of the hour moved her spirit. So close was her heart to nature that when alone with it, she seldom longed for her piano. She *had* the music and did not need to hear it.

A slight rustling sound on the dry carpet around her interrupted her thoughts. Looking intently into the gloom she saw the dark form of a man. She was startled, but he spoke instantly; it was Vavasor. She was so surprised that she could not answer for a moment.

"I am sorry I frightened you," he apologized.

"It is nothing," she returned. "But how did you find me?"

"They told me at the house you were somewhere in this direction. Mark had apparently followed you some distance. So I ventured to come and look for you, and something led me right."

"I hardly know myself where I am going sometimes. And it is so dark we ought to be moving back to the house before we can't see at all."

"Do let us risk it a few minutes longer," coaxed Vavasor. "This is my first escape out of the dungeon-land of London for a whole year! This is paradise. I feel as if I'm dreaming."

As they talked, Vavasor had seated himself on the fragrant carpet beside her. She asked him about his journey and about Cornelius. Presently they rose, found their way without difficulty back to the house, and were soon at the piano.

Vavasor remained the next two weeks at Yrndale. In those days Nature had the best chance with him she had ever had. For a man is a man however he may have been injured by society trying to substitute itself for both God and Nature. A man's potentially a man no matter how far he may be from actual manhood. Who knows what may not sometimes be awakened in a man when placed under the right influences.

During that fortnight, sensations came upon Vavasor of which he had never been aware. The most remarkable event of the time, which would have seemed unbelievable to those who knew him best in London, was that one morning he got up in time to see—and *for the purpose of seeing*—the sun rise. It was a great stride forward. And that was not all: he really enjoyed it! He had poetry enough to feel something of the indwelling greatness that belonged to the vision itself. He felt a power of some kind present to his soul in the sight—though he counted it merely as a poetic feeling. It was, in fact, the drawing of the eternal nature in him toward God, of whom he knew so little.

Under the influence of the lovely place, of the lovely weather, and of his admiration for Hester, the latent poetry of Vavasor's nature came quickly alive, with the result that he was growing more and more in love with Hester. It became plain to him that now his aunt could no longer look upon the idea of such an alliance in the same unfavorable light that she would naturally have before. It was very different to see Hester, now, in the midst of such grounds and in such a house, with all the old-fashioned comforts and luxuries of an ancient and prosperous family around her. If he could get his aunt to see her in the midst of these surroundings, then her beauty would have a chance to work its natural effect upon her.

By degrees, therefore, and without any transition noticed by Hester, emboldened mainly by the influences of the soft dusky twilight, he came to speak with more warmth and openness.

"How strangely this loveliness seems to sink into the soul," he commented lyrically one evening. "How love exalts the whole being."

Hester sat quietly. There are women, like Hester, who have had their minds constantly filled with true and earnest things and so have, over the years, fully matured, without having even speculated on what it may be to be in love. Such women, therefore, are somewhat in the dark when love first begins to blossom. Having never invited its presence, finding it within them adds to their perplexity. Yet, though Vavasor's experience was scarcely so valuable as her ignorance, he judged he might venture a little further. But with all his experience in the manufacture of compliments, he was now at a loss; he had no fine theories of love to talk from!

"If one might sit forever like this," he almost whispered, "—forever and ever, needing nothing, desiring nothing! lost in perfect bliss! If only God would make this moment eternal."

He ceased and was silent.

Hester could not help being moved by the hint of the poetic thought that pervaded the utterance. But she was not altogether pleased. Never had she ever felt, even in a transient mood, like praying, "Let it last forever!"

"I do not quite understand you," she said. "I can scarcely imagine the time should ever come when I would wish that it should last forever."

"Have you had so little happiness?" he asked sympathetically.

"I do not mean that," she replied. "Indeed, I think I have had a great deal. But I do not think much of happiness. And no amount of happiness that I have known yet would make me wish to stand still. I want to be always growing—and while one is growing Time cannot stand if he would: you drag him on with you! I want to be always becoming more and more capable of happiness."

"Ah!" returned Vavasor, "as usual you are out of sight beyond me. You must take pity on me and pull me along with you or else you will leave me miles behind and I shall never be able to look at you again."

"But why should it be so?" answered Hester, almost tenderly. "Our fate is in our own hands. It is ours to determine the direction in which we shall go. I don't want to preach to you, dear Mr. Vavasor, but why should not every one be reasonable enough to seek the one best thing, and then there would be no parting? All the love and friendship in the world would not suffice to keep people together if they were inwardly parted by such difference as you imply."

Vavasor's heart was touched in two ways by this simple speech. First, in the best way—he could not help thinking for a moment what a blessed thing it must be to live in perfect peace about whatever might happen to you. Religion would be better than endurable in the company of such people as Hester! Secondly, he was pleased in the way of self-satisfaction; for clearly she was not opposed to terms of closer intimacy with him. And as she made the advance, why should he not accept the offer of the help she had *almost* made?

From that night he placed himself more than ever in the position of a pupil toward her, hoping in the natural effect of the intimacy. To keep up and deepen their relationship, he would go on imagining himself in this and that difficulty. He was no conscious hypocrite in the matter— only his intellect alone was concerned, while he talked as if his whole being was. No answer given to him would have had the smallest effect on the man—Vavasor only thought about what he would say next. Hester kept trying to meet him as simply and directly as she could, never supposing that what she said made no difference to him. So long as she would talk, he cared not a straw whether she understood what he had said. Thus her desire to wake something better in him brought her into relations with him which had an earthly side, as everything heavenly of necessity has. For this life also is God's, and the very hairs of our head are numbered.

16 / Major H. G. Marvel_____

One afternoon when everyone was occupied with his own pursuit—
Vavasor in his room writing a letter to his aunt, Mr. Raymount in his
study, his wife in her own room, and the children out-of-doors—a gentleman was shown into the drawing room as Hester sat alone at her
piano. The servant apologized, saying he thought she was out. Since
the visitor was already in the room, the glance she threw at the card the
servant had given her informed her little as to the man's identity. The
card simply read *Major H. G. Marvel.* She vaguely thought she had
heard it, but in the suddenness of the meeting was unable to recall a
single clue concerning the owner.

Advancing to meet him, she saw before her a man whose decidedly
podgy figure yet bore a military air and was not without a certain grace
of confidence. His bearing was marked by the total absence of any
embarrassment, anxiety, or air of apology. His carriage spoke of self-
assertion, but his person beamed with friendship. Notably above average
height, his head looked a little too small for the base from which it rose,
all the smaller that it was round and smooth and shining bald like ivory,
and the face upon it was brought by the help of the razor into as close
a resemblance with the rest of the ball as possible. His was a pleasant
face to look at, in spite of—or maybe because of—his irregular features.
A retreating and narrow forehead sat above keen gray eyes that sparkled
with intelligence and fun.

"Cousin Hester!" he exclaimed as he approached her, holding out
his hand.

Mechanically she gave him hers. The voice that addressed her was
a little husky, and very cheery; the hand that took hers was small and
soft, yet kind and firm. A merry, friendly smile lit up his eyes and face
as he spoke. Hester could not help liking him at first sight—yet felt a
little shy of him. She thought she had heard her mother speak of a cousin
somewhere abroad: this must be he.

"You don't remember me," he stated, "seeing you were not yet in
this world for a year or two after I left the country. And, to tell the truth,
had I been asked, I should have objected to your coming on any terms."

As his words did not seem to carry much enlightenment, he went
on to explain. "The fact is, my dear young lady, that I left the country
because your mother and I were too much in agreement."

"In agreement?" Hester's bewilderment was growing.

"The thing, you see," explained the major, standing before her with polite, yet confident, bearing, "was this: I loved your mother better than myself, but it was not to be. I had the choice between two things— staying at home and breaking my heart by seeing her marry another man, or going away and getting over it the best I could. So I must, by nature, be your sworn enemy—only it's of no use, for I've fallen in love with you at first sight. So now if you will ask me to sit down, I will swear to let bygones be bygones, and be your true knight and devoted servant as long as I live. How you do remind me of your mother, only by Jove, you're twice as lovely!"

"Do please sit down, Mr. Marley—"

"Marvel," interrupted the major, "and if you could let me have a glass of water with a little sherry just to take the taste off it, I should be greatly obliged to you."

As he spoke he wiped his round head with a red silk handkerchief.

"I will get it at once, and let my mother know you are here," Hester obliged, turning to the door.

"No, no, never mind your mother. I daresay she is busy or lying down. She always went to lie down at this time of the day. I shouldn't wonder if she thought me troublesome in those days. But I bear no malice now, and I hope she doesn't, either. Tell her I say so. It's more than twenty-five years ago, though to me it hardly seems more than so many weeks. Don't disturb your mother, my dear. But if you insist on doing so, tell her old Harry has come to see her—very much improved since she sent him about his business."

Hester told a servant to take the sherry and the water to the drawing room, and, much amused, ran to find her mother.

"There's the most interesting gentleman downstairs, Mama, calling himself 'old Harry.' He's having some sherry and water in the drawing room. I never saw such an odd man!"

Her mother laughed—a pleased little laugh.

"Go and tell him I shall be down directly."

"Is he really a cousin, Mama?"

"To be sure—my second cousin. He was very fond of me once."

"Oh, he has told me all about that already. He says you sent him about his business."

"If that means that I wouldn't marry him, it is true enough. But he doesn't know what I went through for always standing up for him, though I could never bear him near me. He was such an odd, good-natured bear! Such a rough sort of creature, always saying the thing he ought not to and making everybody, ladies especially, uncomfortable.

He never meant any harm, but never saw where fun should stop. I daresay he's much improved by this time."

"He told me to tell you he was. But I like him, Mama, so don't be too hard on him."

"I won't, dear. Did he tell you that since he left he has been married to a black, or at least a very brown, Hindu woman?"

"No. Has he brought her home with him, I wonder?"

"She has been dead now for some ten years. I believe he had a large fortune which by judicious management he has increased considerably. He is really a good-hearted fellow."

The major's wife was the daughter of an English merchant by a Hindu wife, a very young girl when he first made her acquaintance. She had been kept almost in slavery by the relatives of her deceased father, who had left her all his property. Major Marvel had become interested in her when her relatives attempted to lay the death of her father at her door. The major had taken her part and helped win her complete acquittal. But, though nobody believed her in the smallest degree guilty, society looked askance upon her. True, she was rich, but was she not black? And had she not been accused of a crime? So the major said to himself: *Here I am a useless old fellow, living for nobody but myself. It would make one life at least happier if I took the poor thing home with me. She's too old for adoption, but perhaps she would marry me.*

He did not know, even then, what a large fortune she had. That the major rejoiced over what he found when he came to inquire into things, I do not doubt. But I am entirely sure he would have been an honorable husband had he found she had nothing. When she left him the widowed father of a little girl, he mourned sincerely for her. When the child followed her mother, he was for some time a sad man indeed. He had now returned to his country to find almost every one of his old friends dead, or so changed as to make them all but dead to him.

Little as anyone would have imagined it from his conversation or manner, it was with a kind of heart-despair that he sought the cousin he had loved. And scarcely had he seen the daughter of his old love than he was immediately taken with her. He saw at once that she was a grand sort of person and gracious—different from anyone he had ever seen before. At the same time he unconsciously began to feel a proprietary claim on her; to have loved the mother seemed to give him a right in the daughter. But all this was as yet only in the region of the feelings, not at all in that of the thinking.

"Well," said Hester, turning to leave, "I shall go back to him, Mama, and tell him you are coming as soon as you have got your wig and your newest lace-cap on, and your cheeks rouged and pearl-powdered, to look as much like the young lady he left as you can."

Her mother laughed merrily and pretended to give her daughter a swat. It was not often any mood like this rose between them, for not only were they serious in heart, but from temperament and history and modes and directions of thought, their ways were serious as well.

"Look what I have brought you, Cousin," Major Marvel announced the moment Hester reentered the room, holding out to her a small necklace. "You don't mind such a gift from an old fellow like me. Of course I don't mean that I want to marry you straightaway before I know what sort of temper you've got. Here, take them."

Hester drew near and looked at the necklace.

"Take them," the major urged.

"How strangely beautiful it is!—all red, pear-shaped, dull, scratched stones, hanging from a savage-looking gold chain. What are they, Mr. Marvel?"

"You have described it like a book!" he said. "It is a barbarous native necklace, but they are fine rubies—only rough, neither cut nor polished."

"It is beautiful," repeated Hester. "Did you really mean it for me?"

"Of course I did!"

"I will ask Mama if I can keep it."

"Why do that? I hope you don't think I stole it?—But here comes your mother!—Helen, I'm so glad to see you again!"

Hester slipped away with the necklace in her hand, and left her mother to welcome her old admirer before she would trouble her about the offered gift. They met like trusting friends whom the years had done nothing to separate. While they were still talking of times gone by, Mr. Raymount entered, received him cordially, and insisted on his remaining with them as long as he could. They were old friends, although rivals, and there had never been any bitterness between them. The major readily agreed, as Mr. Raymount sent to the station for his luggage, and showed him to a room.

Major Marvel was, in one sense, and that not a slight one, a true man. There was no discrepancy between his mental condition and the clothing in which he presented that condition to others. His words, looks, manners, tones, and everything that goes to express man to man expressed what was inside him. What he felt, he showed. I think he was unaware of the possibility of doing otherwise. At the same time, he had very little insight into the feelings of others, and almost no sense of the possibility that the things he was saying might affect his listeners otherwise than they affected him. If he boasted, he meant to boast. He had no very ready sympathy with other people, especially in any suffering he had never himself experienced, but he was scrupulously fair in what he said or did in regard of them, and nothing would make him angrier than any injustice or show of deception. He would have said that a man's first business was to take care of himself, as so many think but do not have the courage to say—and so many more who do not even think it. But one thing caused him to dislike another quicker than anything; that was when they found the heel of his all but invulnerable vanity and wounded it. Not accustomed to being hurt, he resented hurt all the more sorely when it came.

During dinner he dominated the conversation and evidently expected to be heard. But that was nearly all he wanted. Let him talk, and hear you laugh when he was funny, and he was satisfied. He was fond of telling tales of adventure, some wonderful, some absurd, and just as willing to tell a joke against himself as at the expense of another. Every now and then throughout the dinner he would say, "Oh, that reminds me!" and then tell something that happened when he was at such-and-such a place, when so-and-so "of our regiment" was out tiger-shooting, or pig-sticking, or whatever the sport might be. "And if Mr. Raymount will take a glass of wine with me, I will tell him the story," he would say, for he was constantly drinking wine, after the old fashion, with this or that one of the company.

When he and Vavasor were introduced to each other, he glanced at him, drew his eyebrows together, made his military bow, and included him among the listeners to his tales of exploit and adventure by sea and land.

Vavasor was much annoyed by his presence. So while he retained the blandest expression and was ready to drink as many glasses of wine with the newcomer as he wished, he set him down in his own mind not only as an ill-bred man and a boaster, in which there was some truth, but as a liar and a vulgar-minded man as well, in which there was little or no truth.

Now, although Major Marvel had not much ordinary insight into character because of his inability to feel a deep enough interest in his neighbor, if his suspicion or dislike was roused, he was just as likely as anyone to arrive at a correct judgment concerning a man he did not love.

He had been relating a thrilling adventure with a man-eating tiger. He saw, as they listened, the eyes of little Mark and Saffy almost surpassing the use of eyes and becoming ears as well. He saw Hester also, who was still child enough to prefer a story of adventure to a love tale, sitting entranced as if her hair would stand on end. But at one moment he caught also a certain expression on the face of Vavasor, which that experienced man of the world certainly never intended to be seen, only at the moment he was annoyed to see Hester's attentiveness; she seemed to have eyes for no one but the man who shot tigers as Vavasor would have shot grouse.

The major, who, upon fitting occasion, could be as quarrelsome as any turkey cock, said: "Ha, ha, I see by your eyes, Mr. Passover, you think I'm drawing the long bow—drawing the arrow to the head, eh?"

"No, upon my word!" Vavasor denied earnestly. "Nothing was further from my thoughts. I was only admiring the coolness of the man who would actually creep into the mouth of the—the jungle after a—what-do-you-call-him?—a man-eating tiger."

"Well, you see, what was a fellow to do," returned the major, still suspicious. "The fellow wouldn't come out! and, by Jove, I wasn't the only one that wanted him out! Besides, I didn't creep in; I only looked in to see whether he was really there. That I could tell by his shining eyes."

"But is not a man-eating tiger a horrifying beast? Once he takes to that kind of diet, don't you know—they say he likes nothing else half so well. Good beef and mutton will no longer serve him, so I've been told at the club."

"It is true he does not care for other food after once getting a passion for the more delicate, but it does not increase either his courage or his fierceness. The fact is, it ruins his moral nature. He does not get many Englishmen to eat, and it seems as if the flesh of women and children and poor cowardly natives undermines his natural courage. He is well known as a sneak. I sometimes can't help thinking the ruffian knows he is a rebel against the law of his Maker, and a traitor to his natural master. The man-eating tiger is the devil of his kind. The others leave you alone unless you attack them; then they show fight. These attack you—but run when you go out after them. You can never get any sport out of him. If there's a creature on earth I hate, it's a coward!" concluded the major.

"But why should you hate a coward so?" asked Hester, feeling at the moment, with the vision of the man-eating tiger in her mind, that she must herself come under the category. "How can a poor creature made without courage help being one?"

"Such as you mean, I wouldn't call cowards," returned the major. "Nobody thinks worse of the hare or the fox for running away from the hounds. Even men whose business it is to fight will run from the enemy when they have no chance, and when it would do no good to stand and be cut down. There is a time to run and a time to fight. But the man will run like a man, and the coward like a coward."

Vavasor's only reply was to himself, but he took care not to allow the slightest expression to cross his face which the major might detect.

"What can harmless creatures do but run?" resumed the major, filling his glass with old port. "But when the wretch that has done all the hurt he could will not show fight for it, but turns tail the moment danger appears, I call him a contemptible coward. That's what made me go into the place to find the brute."

"But he might have killed you, though he was a coward," said Hester, "when you did not leave him room to run."

"Of course he might have, my dear! What else would be the fun of it? Without that the thing would be no better than this shooting of pigeons and pheasants that men do in this country under the so-called name of sport. You *had* to kill him, you know."

As much as he was taken with the daughter of the house, he disliked the fine gentleman visitor that seemed to be dangling after her. Who he was, or in what capacity he was there, he did not know; but almost from first sight, he profoundly disliked him. His dislike grew as he saw more of Vavasor's admiration for Hester. He might be a woman-eater himself, like the tiger, and after her money—if she had any. Such suspects must be watched and followed and their haunts marked.

"But," persisted Hester, "I would like to understand this a little better. I am not willing to set myself down as a coward. Tell me, Major Marvel—when you know that a beast may have you down, and begin eating you at any moment, what is it that keeps you up? What have you to fall back upon? Is it principle, or faith, or what is it?"

"Ho, ho!" laughed the major, "a metaphysician in the very bosom of my family! I had not reckoned upon that! I cannot exactly say that it is principle, and I am sure it is not faith. You don't think about it at all. Well, I daresay there comes in something of principle!—that as an Englishman you are sent to that benighted quarter of the world to kill their big vermin for them, poor things! But no, you don't think of it at the time. You've got to kill him—that's all. And then when he comes roaring on, your rifle jumps to your shoulder of its own accord."

"Do you make up your mind beforehand that if the animal should kill you, it is all right?" Hester questioned further.

"By no means," answered the major with a chuckle.

"Unless I had made up my mind that if I was killed it was all right," Hester admitted, "I couldn't meet the tiger."

"But you see, my dear," explained the major, "you do not know what it is like to have confidence in your eye and your rifle. It is a form of power that you soon come to feel as resting in yourself—a power to destroy the thing that opposes you."

Hester fell to thinking and the talk went on without her. She never heard the end of the story, but was roused by the laughter that followed it.

"It was no tiger at all—that was the joke of it," said the major. "Everyone roared with laughter when the brute—a great lumbering, floundering hyena, rushed into the daylight."

"And what became of the man-eater?" asked Mark, looking disappointed.

"Lost in the jungle till it was safe to come out and go on with his delicate meals."

"Just imagine that horrible growl behind you when you didn't suspect it," said Saffy, her eyes big as saucers.

"By George! for a young lady," exclaimed the major, "you have an active imagination! Too much of that, you know, won't make you a good hunter of tigers."

"Then perhaps you own your coolness to lack of imagination?" suggested Hester.

"Perhaps so. Perhaps after all," returned the major with a merry twinkle in his eye, "we hunters are but a set of stupid fellows—too stupid to be frightened."

"I didn't mean that exactly. I think that perhaps you do not know so well as you might where your courage comes from. For my part I would rather be courageous to help the good than to destroy the bad."

"Ah, but we're not all good enough ourselves for that," the major replied with a serious expression, looking at her out of his clear eyes, from which their habitual twinkle of fun had for the moment vanished. "Some of us are only fit to destroy what is even worse than ourselves."

"To be sure we can't *make* anything," said Hester thoughtfully, "but we can help God to make. To destroy evil things is good, but the worst things can only be destroyed by being good, and that is so hard!"

"It *is* hard," agreed the major—"so hard that most people never try it!" he added with a sigh and a gulp of his wine.

Mrs. Raymount rose, and with Hester and the children, withdrew. After they were gone the major rattled on again, his host putting in a word now and then, while Vavasor sat silently with an expression that seemed to say, "I am amused, but I don't eat all that is put on my plate."

17 / A Walk Along the River_____

The major had taken a strong fancy to Hester, and during the whole of his visit kept as near her as he could, much to the annoyance of Vavasor. Doubtless it was, in part, to keep the major from her that he himself sought her, for there was a natural repulsion between the two men. Vavasor thought the major a most objectionable, indeed low fellow, a vulgar braggart, and the major thought Vavasor a supercillious idiot. It is curious how differently a man's character will be read by two people in the same company. If you like a man, you will judge him with more or less fairness; if you dislike a man, you cannot fail to judge him unjustly.

Without ceasing for a moment to be conventionally polite, Vavasor allowed Major Marvel to see unmistakably that his society was not welcome to him. Entirely ignorant each of the other's pursuits, and nearly incapable of agreement on any point, each would gladly have shown the other to be the fool he thought him. Each watched the other— the major annoyed with the other's silent pretention, and Vavasor regarding the major as a narrow-minded and overgrown schoolboy— though, in fact, his horizon was very much wider than his own.

After breakfast the next day, all but Mr. Raymount went out for a little walk together.

It seemed destined to be a morning of small adventures. As they passed the gate of a nearby farm, out rushed a half-grown pig. Heading right for the major, the animal shot between the well-parted legs of the man, throwing him backwards into a humiliating heap. A look of keen gratification rose in Vavasor's face, but he was too well-bred to allow it to remain. He proceeded to offer assistance to the fallen hero. Marvel, however, heavy as he was, did not require help, but got on his feet again with a cheerfulness which showed either a sweetness or a control over his temper, which gave him a great lift in Hester's estimation.

"Confound the brute!" he laughed. "He can't know how many of his wild relatives I have stuck, else he should never have done it. What a mess he has made of me!"

Saffy laughed merrily over the fun he made of his fall, but Mark looked concerned. He ran and pulled some grass and proceeded to brush him off.

"Let us go into the farmhouse," suggested Mrs. Raymount. "Mrs. Stokes will help us."

"No, no," returned the major. "Better let the mud dry. It will come off much easier then. Why shouldn't piggy have his fun as well as anyone, eh, Mark? Come along. You shan't have your walk spoiled by my carelessness."

There seemed to be more creatures than the pig wanting to escape the bounds. A spirit of liberty was abroad. Mark and Saffy went rushing away like wild rabbits every now and then, making a round and returning. It was one of those cooler of warm mornings that rouse all the life in heart, brain, and nerves, making every breath a pleasure and every movement a joy.

They had not gone much farther when a horse that had been turned into the fenced field to graze came sailing over the fence. Unaccustomed to horses, except when equipped and held ready by the hand of the groom, the ladies and children started and jumped back. Vavasor also stepped a little aside, making way for the animal. But as he alighted from his jump, carrying with him the top bar of the fence, he stumbled and almost fell. While the horse was yet a little bewildered, the major hurried up to him, and before the animal could recover his wits, Major Marvel had him by the nose and ear and was leading him to the gap in the fence. He made the horse jump in again and replaced the bar that had been knocked off.

"Thank you! How brave of you, Major Marvel!" said Mrs. Raymount, genuinely impressed.

The major laughed with his usual merriment.

"If it had been the horse of the Rajah of Rumtool," he said humbly, "I should have been brave indeed! Only by this time there would have been nothing left of me to thank. A man would have needed courage to take him by the head! But a quiet, good-tempered carriage-horse like this one none but a cockney would be frightened of him!"

With that, to the delight of the children, he began telling them the most amazing and, indeed, horrible tales about the Rajah's horse as they continued their walk. Whether it was all true or not I cannot tell. All I can say is that the major only told what he heard and believed, or had himself seen.

Vavasor was annoyed with himself for the very natural nervousness he had shown, for it was nothing more, and turned his annoyance on the major, who, by such an insignificant display of coolness had gained a great advantage over him in the eyes of the ladies.

Following the course of the river, the group gradually descended from the higher grounds to the immediate banks, which spread out into a small meadow on each side. Saffy pulled stalks of feathery-headed grasses along the bank while Mark walked quietly by the brink of the stream, stopping every now and then to look into it. Some distance behind the children, and a little way from the bank, the ladies and gentlemen strolled in the meadow. Suddenly startled by Saffy's scream of agony they looked up as she came running toward them shrieking. No Mark was in sight. All rushed toward her, but Mrs. Raymount soon sank on the grass overcome by emotion. As Hester ran back to her, Mrs. Raymount motioned her on.

Vavasor reached Saffy first. Unable to answer any questions, she continued to shriek. Right on the heels of Vavasor the major quickly surveyed the scene and surmised Mark had fallen in. He had to react fast! Keeping close to the bank, he looked for some sign of the spot where the boy could have fallen in.

Just then Hester cried from behind him, "Across! Across!"

He looked across the river and saw halfway over, slowly drifting down the current, something dark, appearing and then disappearing again. The major's experienced eye knew at once it was Mark. Throwing off his coat, he plunged in, swam toward the object he had seen. But he surfaced so little and so seldom that he hardly knew if he was going in the right direction.

In the meantime, Hester, followed by Vavasor, ran along the bank till she came to a spot where she could safely climb down to the river. Rendered absolutely fearless by her terrible fear, Hester flew down without a slip, leaving Vavasor behind, for he was neither very surefooted nor very sure-headed. But by the time she had reached the river, the major was already trying to heave the unconscious form up onto the bank. Not having swum much for many years, the poor man was nearly exhausted.

Hester hurried to him, knelt down and grabbed Mark. Together they managed to get the body onto the shore. By the time Vavasor arrived, the major had pulled himself up on the bank. Hester turned to Vavasor and commanded, "Go tell my mother we have Mark, and that we are just above the old mill. Then tell my father to send for the doctor!"

Vavasor obeyed, feeling a little small. But Hester thought none the worse of him. Her only thought was for Mark and her mother.

In a few minutes they had the boy up on the high bank, and the major, who knew well what to do, for he had been in almost every emergency under the sun, began resuscitating him.

Vavasor assured Mrs. Raymount that Mark was safe and would be all right in a little while. She rose and with Saffy's help managed to walk home. But after that day she was never so well again. Vavasor ran on to the house and before long Mr. Raymount was on the spot—just as the first signs of returning life appeared. After about half an hour the boy opened his eyes, looked at his father, smiled in his own angelic way, and closed them again with a deep sigh. They covered him up with their own wraps and left him to sleep until the doctor came.

That same night, as Hester was sitting beside him, she heard him talking in his sleep: "When may I go and play with the rest by the river? Oh, how sweetly it talks! it runs all the way through me and through me! It was such a nice way, God, of fetching me home! I rode home on a water-horse!"

He thought he was dead, that God sent him home, and that he was now safe, only tired. It sent a pang to Hester's heart. What if, after all, he was going to leave them! For the child had always seemed more fit for heaven than earth, and any day it seemed, he might be sent for.

Mark recovered by degrees, but continued very sleepy and tired. He never fretted or complained, received every attention with a smile, and told his mother not to worry, for he was not going away yet. He had been told that under the water, he said. Before winter he was able to go about the house and was soon reading all his favorite books again, especially *Pilgrim's Progess*, which he had already read through five times.

The major left Yrndale the next morning, but Vavasor stayed a day or two longer, much relieved at Marvel's departure. He could not go until he saw Mark well on the road to recovery.

In reality, the major went because he could no longer endure the sight of "that idiot," as he called Vavasor, assured that in London he had only to inquire to learn enough to discredit the fellow. He told the Raymounts to tell Mark he had gone to fetch tiger skins and a little statue with diamond eyes and would tell him all about them as soon as he was well again.

Before leaving he informed Mr. Raymount that he had no end of business to look after, but now that he knew the way to Yrndale he might be back any day. He also informed Mrs. Raymount about some pearls he had for her—he knew she was fond of pearls—and was going away to fetch them. He made Hester promise to write to him at the Army and Navy Club every day until Mark was well. And so he departed, much blessed by all the family for saving the life of their precious boy.

When he reached London the major hunted up some of his old friends, and through them sent out inquiry after inquiry concerning Vavasor. He learned some things about him—nothing very bad, and nothing especially to his credit. That he was heir to an earldom he liked least of all, for he was only the more likely to marry his beautiful cousin, and he thought her a great deal too good for him.

Vavasor was relieved when he was gone, but as the days passed and he expected the enthusiasm for the major's heroics to have died down, he was annoyed to find that Hester was just as impressed with the objectionable character of the man. That Hester should not be shocked with him was almost more than he could bear. He could not understand that just as to the pure all things are pure, so the common mind sees far more vulgarity in others than the mind developed to genuine refinement. It understands, therefore forgives. Hester was able to look deeper than he, and she saw much that was good and honorable in the man, even though he might have the bridle of his tongue too loose for safe riding in the crowded paths of society.

A day or two before the end of Vavasor's visit, as he was sitting together in the old-fashioned garden with Mrs. Raymount and Hester, the mail arrived—one letter for Vavasor with a great black seal. He read it through, then said quietly: "I am sorry I must leave you tomorrow. Or is there a train tonight? But I daresay it does not matter, only I ought to be present at the funeral of my uncle, Lord Gartley. He died yesterday, from what I can figure out. It is a tiresome thing to succeed to a title with hardly property enough to pay the servants."

"Very tiresome," assented Mrs. Raymount; "but a title is not like an illness. If you can live without, you can live with one."

"True. But there's society, you see. There's so much expected of a man in my position. What do you think, Miss Raymount?" he asked, turning toward Hester.

"I do not see why a mere name could have any power to alter one's way of life. Of course if the change brings new duties, they must be attended to, but if the property is as small as you say, it cannot need much looking after. To be sure, there are the servants, but they cannot be many. Why shouldn't you go on as you are?"

"I must go a good deal by what my aunt thinks best. She has a sort of right, you see. Her one fixed idea, knowing that I was likely to succeed, has always been the rehabilitation of the earldom. She has been like a mother to me, and will more than likely make me her heir too, though she might change her mind at any moment. She is a kindhearted woman, but a little peculiar. I wish you knew my aunt, Mrs. Raymount."

"I should be very pleased to know her."

"She would be delighted with this lovely place of yours. It is a perfect paradise. I feel its loveliness even more that I am so soon to hear its gates close behind me."

"You must bring your aunt some time, Mr. Vavasor. We would make her very welcome," Mrs. Raymount offered cordially.

"Unfortunately, with all her good qualities, my aunt, as I have said, is a little peculiar. For one thing, she shrinks from making new acquaintances."

By this time Vavasor had resolved to make an attempt to gain his aunt's approval of Hester and felt sure she could not fail to be taken with her if only she saw her in proper surroundings; with her the frame was more than half the picture. And now, in the setting of Yrndale, the family would be of so much more importance in her eyes. He also had the advantage of being more important now with his new title: he was, finally, the Earl of Gartley. She must either be of one mind with him now, or lose the cherished purpose of so many years.

That same evening he left them in high spirits, and without any pretense of decent regret for the death of one he had never seen. To say that Hester was not interested in the news would be untrue. She and Vavasor had been thrown together so much of late, and in circumstances so favorable to close friendship, that she could hardly have been a woman at all and not care what might happen to him. Neither was she altogether indifferent to the idea of wearing a distinguished historical name, or of occupying an exalted position in the eyes of the world. But I must say this for her, she thought of it first of all as a buttressing help to the work that, come what might, she hoped to follow among her poor friends in London.

So, again, the days passed quietly. Mark grew a little better. Hester wrote brief but regular bulletins to the major, which were seldom acknowledged. The new earl wrote that he had been to the funeral, and described, with an attempt at humor, the house and lands to which he had fallen heir. The house might, he said, with unlimited money, be made fit to live in, but what was left of the estate was merely a savage mountain.

18 / An Unpleasant Interview_____

Mr. Raymount went to London occasionally but never stayed long. In the autumn he had his books brought to Yrndale, saying in London he could always get what books he wanted, but must have his own about him in the country. When they were all arranged, he began to feel for the first time in his life as if he had a permanent home, and talked of selling the house in Addison Square.

In October, when the sun shone a little sadly and the hints of the coming winter might be felt hovering in the air, Major Marvel again made his appearance at Yrndale. But this time he had a troubled expression on his face that Mrs. Raymount had never seen before. It was the look of one who had an unpleasant duty to discharge—a thing he would rather not do, but felt compelled to do just the same. He had brought the things he promised, which brightened Mark up amazingly. At the dinner table he tried to be merry as before, but failed rather conspicuously. He drank more wine than usual, and laid the blame on the climate.

The next morning after breakfast the major followed Hester out of the dining room. He quietly asked her to walk with him alone, as he wished a private conversation with her. Hester at once consented, in spite of a vague sense of anxiety, but first consulted her mother.

"What can he want to talk to me about, Mama?"

"How can I tell, my dear?" answered her mother with a smile. "Perhaps he will dare the daughter's refusal too."

"Oh, Mama! How can you joke about such a thing! I wouldn't go with him."

"You had better go, dear. You need not be afraid. He really is a gentleman, and you must not forget how much we owe him for saving Mark's life."

"Do you mean, Mama, that I ought to marry him if he asks me?" Hester was sometimes oddly dense for a moment as to the intent of those she knew best.

Her mother laughed heartily.

"What a goose you are, my darling! Don't you know your mother from a villain yet?"

But in truth her mother so rarely jested that there was some excuse for her. Relieved by her mother's laugh, she still was not comfortable about going, but put on her bonnet and went without more words. Until they were some distance from the house, she and the major walked in absolute silence, which seemed a bad sign to Hester. How changed the poor man was, she thought. He marched steadily along, his stick under his arm like a sword, his eyes straight before him.

"Cousin Hester," he ventured at length, "I am about to talk to you very strangely. Can you imagine a man making himself intensely, unpardonably disagreeable, from the very best of motives?"

They were words very different from what she expected.

"I think I could," answered Hester, thinking whatever he had to say, the sooner it was said the better.

"Tell me," he said suddenly then paused awkwardly. "Let me ask you first," he resumed, "whether you are able to trust me a little. I am old enough to be your father—let me say your grandfather. Imagine I am your grandfather. In my soul I believe neither could wish you well more truly than I do myself. Will you trust me? What is your relationship with Mr. Vavasor?"

Hester remained silent.

Before she had time to consider an answer, he resumed.

"I know," he said, "ladies think such things are not to be discussed with gentlemen; but there are exceptions to every rule." He paused, then spoke directly. "Are you engaged to Mr. Vavasor?"

"No," answered Hester promptly.

"What is it, then? Are you going to be?"

"I don't know—how can I say?" replied Hester.

"Thank God you are still free!"

"But why should you be so anxious about it?"

"Has he never said he loved you?" asked the major eagerly.

"No," she stated. She felt instinctively it was best to answer directly. Her answer was hesitant, mingled with doubt, though literally true. "We are friends," she added. "We trust each other a good deal."

"Trust him with nothing, least of all your heart, my dear," advised the major earnestly. "He is not worthy of you."

"Do you say that to flatter me or to disparage him?"

"Entirely to disparage him. I never flatter."

"Major Marvel, you surely did not bring me out to say evil things of one of my best friends?" she asked, now growing angry.

"I certainly did—if the truth be evil—but only for your sake. The man is a nobody."

"That only proves you do not know him: you would not speak so if you did."

"I am sure I would have worse to say if I knew him better. It is you who do not know him. It astonishes me that sensible people like your father and mother let a fellow like that come prowling after you."

"Major Marvel, if you are going to abuse my father and mother as well as Lord Gartley—" cried Hester, but he interrupted her.

"Ah, there it is!" he exclaimed. "Lord Gartley! I have no business to interfere—no more than your gardener or coachman—but to think of an angel like you in the arms of a—"

"Major Marvel!"

"I beg ten thousand pardons, Cousin Hester! But I am so desperately in earnest I can't pick and choose my phrases. Believe me, the man is not worthy of you."

"As his friend I ask you, what do you have against him?"

"That's the pity of it. I can't tell you anything specifically very bad of him, other than that no one has anything good to say—of whom never a warm word is uttered. I do not say he has disgraced himself openly; he has not."

"I assure you, Major Marvel, he is a man of uncommon gifts and—"

"Great attractions, no doubt—to me invisible," blurted the major. Hester turned from him.

"I am going home," she said flatly. "Luncheon is at the usual hour."

"Just one word more," he begged hurrying after her. "I swear I have no purpose in interfering but to save you from a miserable future. Promise me not to marry this man and I will settle on you a thousand pounds a year."

At those words she turned on him with a glance of contempt. But there were tears in her eyes and her heart smote her. Though he had abused her friend he was plainly being honest. Her countenance softened as she looked at him. She stopped and he came up to her. Laying her hand on his arm, she said: "Dear Major Marvel, I will speak to you without anger. Such a promise I cannot give, whether it be an earl or a beggar. How am I to know the will of God for the remainder of my life?"

"Yes, yes, my dear! You are quite right—absolutely right," the major agreed humbly. "I only wanted to make you financially independent so you would not *have* to marry. But will you have liberty otherwise? Will your father settle any of his estate upon you?"

"I don't know. I have never thought about anything of the kind."

"How could they let you go about with him so much and never ask what he meant by it?"

"You would have them shut me up and make my life miserable to keep me safe? If a woman has any sense, Major Marvel, she can take care of herself; if she has not, she must learn the need of it."

"Ah!" said the major sadly, "but I would sooner see my child dead with a husband she loved than living a merry life with one she did not."

Hester began to feel she had not been doing the major justice.

"So would I!" she said heartily. "You mean me well, and I shall not forget how kind you have been. Now, let us go back."

"Just one thing more: if you ever think I can help you, you *will* let me know?"

"That I promise with all my heart," she answered. "I mean if it be a thing I think I should trouble you about."

The major's face fell.

"I see!" he said. "You won't promise anything. Well, stick to that, and *don't* promise."

"You wouldn't have me come to you for a new bonnet, would you?"

"By George! shouldn't I be proud to fetch you the best one in Regent Street!"

"Or saddle the pony for me?"

"Try me. But I trust you to remember there is an old man that loves you, and has more money than he knows what to do with."

"I think," said Hester, "that the day is sure to come when I shall ask your help. In the meantime, if it will be any pleasure to you to know it, I trust you heartily. You are all wrong about Lord Gartley, though. He is not what you think him."

"I sincerely hope you are right, for your sake."

She gave him her hand. He took it in his own and pressed it to his lips. She did not draw it away, and he felt she trusted him.

Now that the hard duty was done, and if not much good at least no harm had resulted, he went home a more peaceful man. His host congratulated him on looking so much better as a result of his walk, and Hester recounted to her mother their strange conversation.

"Just think, Mama," she said; "he offered me a thousand a year not to marry Lord Gartley!"

"Hester!"

"He does not like the earl, and he does like me; so he wants me not to marry him. That is all!"

"I thought I could have believed anything of him, but this goes almost beyond belief!"

"Why should it, Mama? The odd thing is that instead of hating him for it, I like him better than before."

"Are you sure he has no notion of making room for himself?"

"Quite sure. He said he was old enough to be my grandfather. But you know he is not that!"

"Maybe it is time we knew what Lord Gartley intends," said her mother in a more serious vein.

"Oh, Mama, don't talk like that!"

"It does sound disagreeable, but I cannot help being anxious about you. If he does not love you, he has no right to court your company so much."

"I encourage it, Mama. I like him."

"That is what makes me afraid."

"There will be time enough to think about it if he continues to come and visit now that he has the earldom."

"Would you like to be a countess, Hester?"

"I would rather not think about it, Mother. It may never make any difference whether I like it or not."

"I can't help thinking it strange that he is with you so often and never says a word of his intentions."

"It is no more strange than that I am so often with him, or that you let him come so often to the house."

"It was neither your place nor mine to say anything. Your father has always said he would not ask a man his intentions: either he was fit to be in his daughter's company or he was not. Either he must get rid of him or leave his daughter to manage her own affairs. He is quite American in his way of looking at such matters."

"Don't you think he is right, Mother? If I let Lord Gartley come, surely he is not to blame for coming!"

"Only if you became fond of him and it led to nothing."

"Well, I don't even know exactly what *I* think. I am afraid you must think me very cool. But all I can do is try to do right as things come up, and leave my understanding of things to follow in time. But of one thing you may be sure, Mother. I will try to do what is right."

"I am sure of that, my dear—quite sure; and I won't trouble you more about it."

19 / Corney's Holiday

Major Marvel was in no hurry to leave, but he spent most of his time with Mark, and was in nobody's way. Mark was very happy with the major. The nature of the man was so childlike that, although he knew little of the deep things in which Mark was at home, his presence was never an interruption to the child's thoughts. When the boy made a remark in the upward direction, the major would look so grave and hold such a peace that the child never missed the lacking words of response. Who knows what the man may have gained even from silent communication with the child?

One day he was telling the boy how he had been out alone on a desolate hill all night; how he heard the beasts roaring round him, and not one of them came near him. "Did you see *him*?" asked Mark.

"See who, Sonny?" returned the major.

"The one between you and them," answered Mark, his tone subdued. And from his tone the major understood.

"No," he replied; and taking into his the spirit of the child, went on. "I don't think anyone sees him nowadays."

"Isn't it a pity?" said Mark. "I wish God would call me. I know he calls some children, for he said, 'Samuel, Samuel!' "

"What would you say?" asked the major.

"I would say, 'Here I am, God! What is it?' We mustn't keep God waiting, you know!"

The major wondered if God had ever called him and he had not listened? Of course it was all a fancy! And yet as he looked at the child and met his simple, believing eyes, he could not help wondering if there were things in the world of which he was unaware. Could there be things this child understood but he did not? Happily there were no conventional religious phrases in the mouth of the child to repel him; his father and mother had a horror of formal Christianity. They had both seen in their youth too many religious prigs to endure temple white-wash on their children. Except what they heard at church, hardly a specially religious phrase ever entered their ears. Those of the New Testament were avoided from reverence, lest they should grow too common and fail their purpose when the children read them for themselves.

How such a plan could have succeeded with Hester and Mark and not with Cornelius is a hard question. One must consider each person's own bent of choice when they respond to the influences before them. Hester and Mark had responded by making right choices, that is, unselfish ones. Cornelius had responded by making wrong, that is, selfish ones. But had the common forms of a so-called religious education been added to that youth's upbringing, he would have been a far more offensive fellow, and harder to influence for the good. The best true teaching for children is persons, history, and doctrine in the old sense of the New Testament—instruction in righteousness, that is—not human theory about divine facts.

The major was still at Yrndale when, in the gloomy month of November, Cornelius arrived for his holiday. He was more than usually polite to the major: he was, after all, in the army, the goal of Corney's aspiration! But he laughed privately at what he called the major's vulgarity. Because Cornelius prized nothing of the kind, he could see nothing of his essential worth, and took note merely of his blunders, personal ways, and oddities. The major was not truly vulgar, only ill-bred, for there are many ladylike mothers whose children do not turn out to be ladies and gentlemen because they do not teach them as they were taught themselves. But the feelings of the major went far deeper than those of Cornelius, though the latter's surface manners may have shown to better effect in the society of London. The one was capable of genuine sympathy, the other not yet of any. The major would have been sorry to find he had hurt the feelings of a dog; Cornelius would have whistled on learning that he had hurt the feelings of a woman.

In respect of Cornelius the major was more careful than usual not to make himself disagreeable, for his feelings against the conceit of the lad put him on his guard: many behave better to those they do not like than to those they do. By this he flattered, without intending it, the vanity of the youth, who did not, therefore, spare his criticism behind his back. Hester usually answered in his defense, but tried to do so calmly. One day she lost her temper with her beam-eyed brother. "Cornelius, the major may have his faults," she said, "but you are not the man to find them out. He is ten times the gentleman you are."

She did not see the major enter the room as she said this. Afterward he made himself known and asked Cornelius to go with him for a walk. Hoping he had only just come in, but a little anxious, Cornelius agreed. As they walked, he behaved better than usual—until he had persuaded himself that the major had heard nothing. He then relapsed into his former manner—one of condescension and thin offense. But all the time the major was studying him, and saw into him deeper than his mother or Hester—making out a certain furtive anxiety in the youth's eyes when he was silent, an unrest as of trouble he would not show. *The rascal has been doing something wrong*, he mused; *he is afraid of being found out.*

The weeks went on. Cornelius's month ran out, but he seemed rest-less for it to be over, making no response to the lamentations of the children that Christmas was so near and their new home such a grand one for keeping it in, and Corney not to be with them! He did not show them much kindness, but a little went a long way with them, and they loved him.

"Better be well before I come again, Markie," he said as he left. "You're not a pleasant sight moping about the house!" Tears came to the child's eyes. He was not moping; he only looked a little sad, even when he was quite happy.

"Never mind, Markie dear," Hester consoled him later. "He meant no harm. It's only that you are not very strong—not up to a game of romps as you used to be. You will be merry again one day."

"I am merry enough," replied Mark; "only somehow the merry goes all about inside me and doesn't want to come out—like the little bird, you know, that wouldn't go out of its cage though I left the door open for it."

He was indeed happy enough—more than happy when the major was there. They would be together most days all day long. And the amount of stories Mark, with all his contemplativeness, could swallow was amazing.

But the family party was soon to be broken up—not by subtraction but by addition. The presence of the major had done nothing to spoil the homeness of home, but that very homeness was now for a time to be disturbed.

There is something wrong with anyone who, visiting a house of any kind, makes it less of a home. The angel-stranger makes the children of a house all the more aware of their home; they delight in showing it to him, for he takes an interest in all that belongs to its family life, and sees the things as the children see them. But the stranger of this world makes the very home by his presence feel chilly and less comfortable and homey than before.

20 / A Distinguished Guest_____

A letter came from Lord Gartley, begging Mrs. Raymount to excuse the liberty he took, and allow him to ask whether he might presume upon her wish, casually expressed, to welcome his aunt to the hospitality of Yrndale.

> I am well aware of the seeming rudeness of this suggestion. If you have not room for us, or if our presence would spoil your Christmas party, do not hesitate to put us off, I beg. I shall understand you, dear Mrs. Raymount, and say nothing to my rather peculiar but most worthy aunt, waiting a more convenient season.

An invitation was immediately dispatched—with some wry faces on the part of the head of the house who, however, would not oppose what his wife wished.

Despite his knowledge of human nature, Mr. Raymount was not good at reading a man who made himself agreeable and did not tread on the toes of any of his theories. I would not have you think of him as a man of theory only; but while he thought of the practice, he too sparingly practiced the thought. He laid too much upon words altogether, especially words in print, attributing more power to them for the regeneration of the world than was reasonable. Perhaps knowing how few of those who admired his words acted upon them would have made him think how little he struggled *himself* to do the things which, by persuasion and argument, he drove home upon the consciences of others. He had not yet believed that to do right does more for the regeneration of the world than any quality or amount of teaching can.

He did not see deeply into Gartley, who was by no means an intentional hypocrite. But Vavasor was a gentlemanly fellow, and that went a long way with him. He did not oppose him, and that also went a long way. He forgot that the difficulty is not so much in recognizing the truth of a proposition, but in doing what that truth demands.

The day before Christmas Eve the expected visitors arrived—just in time to dress for dinner.

The family was assembled in the large, old drawing room of dingy white and tarnished gold when Miss Vavasor entered. She was tall and handsome and had been handsomer, for she was not of those who, growing within, grow more beautiful without as they grow older. She was dressed in the plainest, handsomest fashion—in black velvet, fitting

113

well her fine figure, and half covered with lace. The only stones she wore were diamonds. Her features were regular, her eyes a clear gray, her expression very still, and her hair more than half gray but very plentiful. She had a look of distinction and to the merest glance showed herself wellborn, well nurtured, well trained, and well kept, hence well preserved. Her manner was as simple as her dress—without a trace of condescension or more stiffness than was becoming with persons she had just met. She spoke with readiness and simplicity, looked with interest but without curiosity at Hester, and had the sweetest smile at hand for use as often as wanted.

Lord Gartley was in fine humor. He had never before appeared to so great an advantage. Vavasor had not put off his company manner with Hester's family; however, Gartley was almost merry, quite graciously familiar. But how shall I describe his face when Major Marvel entered! He had never even suspected his presence. A blank dismay came over him, hardly visible, a strange mingling of annoyance, contempt and fear. But in a moment he had overcome the unworthy sensation and was again seemingly cool.

The major was presented to Miss Vavasor by their hostess as her cousin. Seated next to her at dinner, he did not once allude to pig-sticking or tiger-shooting, to elephants or Hindus, or even to his regiment or India, but talked about the last opera and the last play, with some good criticisms on the acting he had seen. He conducted himself in such manner as would have made Lord Gartley quite grateful to him had he not disliked him so much.

All day the major had been tempted toward very different behavior. Remembering what he had heard of the character of the lady and of the relation between her and her nephew, he knew at once that Lord Gartley was bringing her down with the hope of gaining her consent to his asking Hester to marry him. *The rascal!* he thought. And with this realization arose his temptation to so behave before the aunt as to disgust her with the family and save his lovely cousin from being sacrificed to a heartless noodle.

I'll settle the young ape's hash for him! he thought belligerently. *What jolly fun it will be to send her out of the house in a rage—and a good deed done too!*

But before the day was through he had begun to have his doubts. Would it not be dishonorable? He would turn Mark and Hester away from him in the very process. His heart continued to go against his plans, and by the time he dressed for dinner he had resolved to drop the idea and behave like a gentleman. But now as they sat at the table, with every sip of wine the temptation came stronger and stronger. The spirit of fun kept stirring in him. Not merely for the sake of Hester, but for the joke of the thing, he was tempted, and had to keep fighting the impulse all evening. From this inner struggle came the subdued character of his demeanor. What had threatened to destroy his manners for the evening actually corrected his usual behavior. Miss Vavasor, being good-natured, was soon interested and eventually pleased with him. This reacted upon him and he began to feel pleased with her and more at his ease. And with his ease came the danger some at the table had foreseen: he began to tell one of his stories. But he saw Hester look anxious and that was enough to put him back on his careful honor. Before dinner was over he said to himself that if only the nephew were half as good as the aunt, he would be happy to give the young people his blessing.

By Jove! thought Gartley, *the scoundrel is not such a low fellow after all.* Now and then he would listen across the table to their talk, and everything the major said that pleased his aunt pleased him as well. At one little witticism of hers in answer to one of the major's, he burst into such a hearty laugh that his aunt looked up.

"You are amused, Gartley," she said.

"You are so clever, Aunt," he returned.

"Major Marvel has all the merit of my wit," she answered.

After dinner they sat down to whist and cribbage and within another hour the fear of Lord Gartley as to the bad influence of the major vanished entirely.

Now that he was more at his ease, and saw that his aunt was pleased with both Hester and the major, Lord Gartley began to radiate his fascinations. All his finer nature appeared. He grew playful, even teasing; gave again and again a quick repartee; and sang as his aunt had never heard him sing before. But when Hester sang, the thing was done. The aunt knew at once what a sensation such a singer would make in her circle! She would be a decided gain to the family, even contributing something herself to the title. Then who could tell but this cousin of hers—who seemed to have plenty of money the way he so cheerfully parted with it at the gaming table—might be moved to make a poor countess a rich one. The issue was settled, so far as Gartley was concerned.

Christmas was a merry day to all but the major, who did not like things any better than before. He found refuge and consolation with Mark, who was merry in a mild and reflective way.

Lord Gartley now began to pursue his courtship in earnest, with full intent and purpose. "How could she listen to him?" I can hear some readers say. But to explain the thing is more than I am bound to undertake. How a certain woman will have a certain man is one of the deepest mysteries of the world. All I can say is that when a woman like Hester of high hopes and aims—a woman filled with eternal aspirations—gives herself to such a one, I cannot help thinking she must have seriously mistaken some things both in him and in herself, the consequence perhaps of some self-sufficiency or other fault which requires the correction of suffering.

Hester found her lover now very pleasant. If sometimes he struck a jarring chord, she was always able to find some way of accounting for it or explaining it away. This way she was able to go on hoping, like most self-deceiving women, that she would have greater influence over him as his wife. But where there is not already a far deeper unity than marriage can give, marriage itself can do little to bring two souls together—and may do much to drive them apart.

For Hester the days now passed in pleasure, though the closer contact with Lord Gartley negatively influenced the rate of her growth toward the upper regions. We cannot be heart and soul and self in the company of the untrue without loss. Her prayers were not so fervent, her aspiration not so strong. But the Lord is mindful of his own. He does not forget because we forget. Pain may come, but not because he forgets—nay, just because he does not forget. That is a thing God never does.

There are many women who would have bewitched Gartley more, yet great was his delight in the presence of Hester, and he yielded himself with pleasing grace. Inclined to rebel at times when wearied with her demands on his attention and endeavor, he yet condescended to them with something of the playfulness with which one would humor a child. His turn would come by and by. Then he would instruct her in many things she was now ignorant of. She had never moved in his great world: he must teach her its laws, instruct her how to shine, how to make the most of herself, how to do him honor! He had but the vaguest idea of the *folly* that possessed her about ministry. He thought of her relation to the poor as but a passing phase of a previously objectless life. That she should even imagine continuing her former pursuits after they were married would have seemed utterly incredible to him. And Hester would have been equally staggered to find that he had so totally failed to understand her after the way she had opened her heart to him. So things went on upon a mutual misunderstanding—each falling more and more in love with the other, while in reality they were separating further and further, each caught up in thoughts and motives that were alien to the other.

Miss Vavasor continued to be the most pleasant and unexacting of guests. Though the time passed slowly with such primitive people, she found the company of the major agreeable for her nephew's sake. Mr.

Raymount would not leave what he counted his work for any goddess in creation. Hester had inherited her fixedness of purpose through him, and its direction through her mother. But it was good he did not give Miss Vavasor much of his company. If they had been alone together for a quarter of an hour discussing almost anything imaginable, they would have parted sworn foes. So the major, instead of putting a stop to the unworthy alliance, found himself actually furthering the affair, doing his part with the lady on whom the success of the enemy depended. He was still now and then tempted to break through his self-imposed shell of restraint; yet he remained a man of honor and behaved like one.

After almost two weeks, Miss Vavasor took her leave for a round of visits, and Lord Gartley went back to town, intending to pay a visit to his property, such as it was. He would return to Yrndale in three or four weeks, when the final arrangements for the wedding would be made.

A correspondence naturally began and Hester received his first letter joyfully. But the letter was nothing like the man's presence. There was no *life* in it. With Hester in person, she suggesting and leading, his talk seemed to indicate the presence of what she would have in him. But alone with his own thoughts, without the stimulus of her presence or the sense of her moral atmosphere, the best things he could write were poor enough. They had no bones in them, and no other fire than that which the thought of Hester's loveliness could supply. So his letters were disappointing. Had they been those of a person indifferent to her, she would have thrown them down, called them stupid, and thought no more of them.

But all would be well when they met again. She assumed it was her absence that oppressed him, poor fellow! He was out of spirits and could not write! He had not the faculty for writing that some had! Her father had told her that some men were excellent talkers, but could not write a word. Was it not to his praise rather than blame? Was not the presence of a man's own kind the best inspirer of his speech? She tried to persuade herself that it was his loving human nature that made utterance in a letter impossible to him. But she could not quite succeed in believing it.

She *would* have liked a little genuine, definite response to the things she wrote!

21 / Calamity

One afternoon the post brought a letter from Lord Gartley and two for Mr. and Mrs. Raymount. The one to Mrs. Raymount was written in a strange-looking cramped hand, which she immediately recognized.

"What can Sarah be writing about?" she wondered aloud, a sudden foreboding of evil crossing her mind.

Hester rose to leave the room; she did not like to read Gartley's letters around her mother—not from shyness, but from shame: she did not want anyone to know how poor her Gartley's utterances were on paper. But before she was six steps away, she heard a cry from her mother and turned.

"Good heavens, what can it be?" cried Mrs. Raymount. "Something has happened to him!"

Her face was pale, almost as white as the paper she held.

"Mother, Mother! what is it?" Hester asked, suddenly afraid.

"I knew we were too happy," she moaned. "I knew something would happen to ruin it all."

"Let's go to Papa," said Hester, still frightened but quiet, taking her mother by the hand to lead her. But Mrs. Raymount stood as if fixed to the ground.

In the meantime, Mr. Raymount's letters had been carried to him in the study and one of them had similarly perturbed him. He was pacing up and down the room almost as white as his wife, but his pallor was from rage.

"The scoundrel!" he cried. "I had the suspicion he was a mean dog! Now all the world will know it—and that he is my son! What have I done that I have given life to a vile hound like this?"

He threw himself in a chair and wept with rage and shame. He had for years been writing of family and social duties; now here was his illustration! His own son! How could he ever show himself again? He would leave the country, forget the property! The rascal would never succeed to it! Mark would have it—if he lived! And now Hester was going to marry an earl! Not if the truth would prevent it! Her engagement must be broken at once! Lord Gartley would never marry the sister of a thief!

While he raged on, a knock came to the door and a maid entered.

"Please, sir," she said, "Miss Raymount says will you come to Mis'ess. She's taken bad!''

This brought him to himself. The horrible fate was hers too! He must go to her. But how could she have heard the vile news? She must have heard it! What else could have made her ill? He followed the maid to where his wife stood in his daughter's arms. He asked no questions, but took her himself, carried her to her room, and laid her on the bed. Then he sat down beside her, hardly caring if she died—the sooner they all died the better! Hester followed them in, and eventually the doctor came.

Hester had picked up the letter, and as her father sat there, she handed it to him . . .

Dear mistress, it is time to let you know of the goings on here. I never held with bearing tales, and perhaps it's worse to bring tales against Master Cornelius, as is your own flesh and blood, but what am I to do as was left in charge, and to keep the house respectable? He's not been home this three nights; and you ought to know as there is a young lady, his cousin from New Zealand, as is come to the house three or four times since you went away, and stayed a long time with him, though it is some time now that I ain't seen her. She is a pretty, modest-looking young lady; though I must say I was ill-pleased when Mr. Cornelius would have her stay all night; and I up and told him if she was his cousin, it wasn't as if she was his sister and it wouldn't do, and I would walk out of the house if he insisted on me making up a bed for her. Then he laughed in my face and told me I was an old fool, and he was only making game of me. But that was after he had done his best to persuade me and I wouldn't be persuaded. I told him if neither he nor the young lady had a character to keep, I had one to lose, and I wouldn't. But I don't think he said anything to her about staying all night; for she come down the stair as innocent-like as any dove, and bid me good night smiling, and they walked away together. And I wouldn't have took upon me to be a spy, nor I wouldn't have mentioned the thing, for it's none of my business so long as nobody doesn't abuse the house as is my charge; but he ain't been home for three nights, and there is the feelings of a mother! And it's my part to let her know as her son ain't slept in his own bed for three nights, and that's a fact. I hope dear mis'ess it won't kill you to hear it. O why did his father leave him alone in London, with none but an old woman like me, as he always did look down upon, to look after him! Your humble servant for twenty years,

S.H.

Mrs. Raymount had not read half of this. It was enough to learn he had not been home for three nights. How strange it is that parents with no reasonable ground for believing their children good are yet incredulous when they hear they are going wrong. Helen Raymount concluded her boy had turned into bad ways because he was left in London, although she knew he had never taken to good ways while they were all with him. If he had never gone right, why should she wonder that he had gone wrong?

The doctor was sitting by the bedside, watching the effect of something he had given her. Mr. Raymount rose and led Hester from the room—sternly almost, as if she had been to blame for it all. But Hester understood and did not resent it.

"Is this all your mother knows, Hester?" inquired her father, pointing to the letter in his hand. She told him her mother had read only the first sentence or two.

He was silent as he returned to the bedside, and stood there quietly. The life of his dear wife had been suddenly withered at the root, and she had not even yet heard the worst!

His letter was from his wife's brother, in whose bank Cornelius was a clerk. A considerable deficit had been discovered in his accounts. He had not been to the bank for two days, and no trace of him was to be found. His uncle, concerned about the feelings of his sister, had requested the head of his office to be silent. He would wait for his brother-in-law's reply before taking any steps. He feared the misguided youth had counted on the forbearance of an uncle; but for the sake of his own future, if for no other reason, this could not be passed over.

Passed over! Gerald Raymount would never have considered such a thing. If not for his wife's illness, he would already have been on his way to London to repay the missing money!

But something must be done. He must send someone. Who was there to send? There was Hester! She was a favorite with her uncle! And she would not dread the interview, which to him would be an unendurable humiliation. For he had had many arguments with this same brother-in-law concerning the way he brought up his children. They had all turned out well and here was his miserable son a felon, disgracing both families! Yes, let Hester go! There were things a woman could do better than a man! Hester was no child now but a capable woman. While she was gone he could be making up his mind what to do with the wretched boy!

He led Hester again from her mother's room and gave her the letter to read. He watched her as she read—saw her grow pale, then flush, then turn pale again. What she was thinking he could not tell, but he made his proposal at once.

"Hester," he began earnestly, "I cannot leave your mother. You must go for me to your uncle and do the best you can. If it were not for your mother, I would have the rascal prosecuted; but it would break her heart."

"Yes, Papa," she agreed solemnly, "I shall be ready to catch the evening train. Am I to say anything to Corney?"

"You have nothing to do with him," he answered sternly. "What is the good of keeping a villain from being as much of a villain as he has within him to be? I will sign you a blank check, which your uncle can fill in with the amount Cornelius has stolen."

On her way to her room Hester met the major. He had just heard of her mother's attack, as he had been out for a long walk.

"But what did it, Hester?" he asked. "I can smell in the air that something has gone wrong. What is it?"

They had met in a dark part of the corridor and had now, at a turn, come opposite a window. It was then the major saw Hester's face. He had never seen her look like that!

"Is your mother in danger?" His tone became gentle, for his heart was, in reality, a most tender one.

"She is very ill. The doctor has been with her now for three hours. I am going to London for Papa. He can't leave her."

Going to London—and by the night train! the major mused. *Then there has been bad news! It must be that scoundrel Corney up to some mischief—I wouldn't be surprised to hear anything bad of him.* But before he had a chance to say something to her, she was gone.

She went to her room to get a few things together. Then she drank a cup of tea, went to her father to get the check, and was ready by the time the carriage came to the door with a pair of horses. In only a few minutes more she was on her way through the gathering dusk to the railway station.

While the lodge-gate was being opened, she thought she saw someone get up on the box beside the coachman, and figured it must be a groom going with them. The drive was a rather long and anxious one for Hester. When at last the carriage stopped and the door opened, there was the major in a huge fur coat, holding out his hand to help her down. It was as great a pleasure as a surprise, and she showed both.

"You didn't think I was going to let you travel alone?" he said. "Who knows what wolf might be after my Red Riding Hood!"

Hester told him she was only too glad of his escort. Careful not to seem the least bent on the discovery of the cause of her journey, he seated himself in the farthest corner of the train car, for there was no one else in it, and pretended to go to sleep.

And now Hester began, as a result of the general misery of the family, to contemplate her own situation with a little more honest introspection than before. A mist had slowly been gathering around her, though she had put off looking into it at the undefined forms in the distance. Now these forms slowly began to reveal themselves in shifting yet recognizable reality. The doubts she had tried to ignore when reading Vavasor's letters now at last demanded recognition. Even if this miserable affair with Cornelius were to be successfully hushed up, there was yet one who must know of it: she would have to acquaint Lord Gartley with what had taken place.

With this realization one of the shapes in the mist settled into solidity: if the love between them had been an ideal love, she would not have had a moment's anxiety as to how her fiancé would receive the painful news. But she realized she shrank from telling him, for fear of how he might respond. Yet with the insight into her own anxiety came a decision: if he hesitated, that would be enough. His response would involuntarily reveal whether their love was a true one or not. Nothing could make her marry a man who hesitated whether to draw back from her or not. It was impossible.

22 / In London

Arriving in the city, they went directly to Addison Square. When they had roused Sarah, the major took his leave of Hester, promising to be with her in a few hours, and went to his hotel.

She did not want to rouse speculation at the bank by being recognized as the sister of Cornelius. When the major returned, she asked him to be her messenger to her uncle and tell him that she had come representing her father. The major was to inquire where it would be convenient for them to meet. He undertook the commission at once, and went without asking a question.

Early in the afternoon her uncle came, and behaved to her very kindly. He was chiefly a man of business and, thus, made no particular attempt to show sympathy for the trouble she and her parents were in. Yet sympathy was revealed unconsciously by his manner. He was careful to avoid any remark on the conduct or character of the youth. When she had at last given him her father's check, with the request that he would himself fill it in with the amount Cornelius had stolen, and he with a slight deprecatory smile and shrug had taken it, she ventured to ask what he was going to do with regard to her brother.

"When I take this check," answered her uncle, "it indicates that I treat the matter as a debt paid in full, and I leave him entirely in your father's hands. He must do as he sees fit. I am sorry for you all, and for you, especially, that you should have had to take an active part in the business. I wish your father could have come."

"I am glad he could not come," Hester admitted, "for he is so angry with Cornelius that he would probably have insisted that you prosecute him. You never saw such indignation as my father's at any wrong done by one man to another—not to say by one like Cornelius to one like you, Uncle, who have always been so kind to him. It is a terrible blow to my father!"

She broke down and wept bitter tears—the first she had shed since learning the news. She wept not only for the rest of her family, but for Cornelius as well. How was one who cared so little for righteousness to be brought to contrition? If this issue were passed over and he was not brought to open shame, he would hold his head as high as ever. And then how would even what regenerative power that might lie in the shame ever be brought to bear upon him?

When her uncle left her, she sat motionless a long time, thinking much but hoping little. The darkness gathered deeper and deeper around her. But the human heart has to go through much before it is able to house even a suspicion of the superabounding riches of the creating and saving God. The foolish child thinks there can be nothing where he sees nothing; the human heart feels as if where it cannot devise help, there is none possible to God, as if God, like the heart, must be content to botch the thing up, and make, as we say, the best of it.

But as the heavens are higher than the earth, so are his ways higher than our ways, and his thoughts than our thoughts.

It was a sore and dreary time for Hester, alone in the room where she had spent so many happy hours. She sat in a window seat, looking out upon the leafless trees and the cold, gloomy old statue in the midst of them. Frost was upon every twig. A thin, sad fog filled the comfortless air. There might be warm, happy homes somewhere, but they no longer belonged to her world. The fire was burning cheerfully behind her, but her eyes were fixed on the dreary square. She was hardly thinking— only letting thoughts and feelings come and go. What a thing is life and being, when a soul has become but the room in which ghosts hold their revel; when the man or woman is no longer master of himself, and can no more say to this or that thought, you shall come, and you shall go. That person is a slave to his own existence; he can neither cease to be, nor order his being. He is able only to entangle himself even more in the net he has knotted around him! Such is every soul who is parted from the essential life, who is not one with the Power by which he lives. God is all in all, and he made us out of himself. He who is parted from God is a live discord, an antitruth. Not such was Hester, and although her thoughts now came and went without her, they did not come and go without God, and a truth from the depths of her own true being was on its way to console her.

How would her fiancé receive the news? That was the agitating question. What would he do?

She would liked to have written at once, but she did not know exactly where he was. However, a far stronger reason against writing was that if she wrote, she could not know how he received her sad story; and if he had to make a decision about her, which was what she feared, he would have time for it. She must, then, communicate the dread message with her own lips. She must see how he took it! If he showed the slightest change toward her, the least tendency to regard the relationship now as an entanglement that he regretted, she could not marry him. If he could not be her earthly refuge in this trouble, she would have none of him. The behavior of Cornelius had perhaps made her more capable of doubt;

possibly her righteous anger with him inclined her to imagine grounds of anger with another. Probably this feeling of uncertainty regarding her fiancé had been prepared for by things that had passed between them since their engagement, but upon which she had not allowed herself to dwell. Now she was almost in a mood to quarrel with him. Brought to moral bay, she stood with her head high, her soul roused, and every nerve strung to defense. She had not yet cast herself on the care of her Father in heaven. But he was not far from her.

Yet deeper into the brooding fit she sank. Weary with her journey and the sleepless night, her brain seemed to work itself. Then suddenly came the thought that here she was again in the midst of her poor. But how was she to face them and hold her head up among them now? Who was she, of a family of sinners, to speak a word to them? How lightly the poor bore such ills. Even the honest of them would have this cousin or that uncle in jail for so many months, and think no less of him when he was out again. Nothing could degrade them beyond the reach of their sympathies! They had no thought of priding themselves against another because they themselves had not broken the law.

Suddenly Hester felt nearer her poor than ever before, and it comforted her. The bare soul of humanity comforted her. She was not merely of the same flesh and blood with them—not even of the same soul and spirit only, but of the same failing, sinning, blundering breed. Their shame was hers: the son of her mother, the son of her father was a thief! She was and would be more one with them than ever before. If they made less of crime in another, they also made less of innocence from it in themselves! Was it not even better to do wrong, she asked herself, than to think it a great thing not to do it? What merit was there in being what it would be contemptible not to be? The Lord could get nearer to the publican than the Pharisee, to the woman who was a sinner than the self-righteous, honest woman. The Pharisee was a good man, but he thought it such a fine thing to be good that his pride came between him and God. The other, who thought it a sad thing to be bad, was able to be reached by God in his humility. Let her just get among her nice, honest, wicked, poor ones, out of this atmosphere of pretense and appearance, and she would breathe again!

She dropped on her knees and cried to her Father in heaven to make her heart clean altogether, to deliver her from everything mean and faithless, to make her turn from any shadow of evil as thoroughly as she would have her brother repent of the stealing that made them all so ashamed. Like a woman in the wrong, she drew near the feet of her master; she too was a sinner; her heart needed his cleansing as much as any!

And then came another God-given thought. For suddenly she perceived that her self had made her severe and indignant to the son of her own mother, while she was indulgent toward those whose evil did not touch her. If God were to do like her, how many would be redeemed? Corney, whom she had taken care of as a baby—was he not equally to be loved in his sin as the poor who so occupied her heart? But God knew all the difficulties that beset men, and gave them fair play even when sisters did not: he would redeem Corney yet!

True, it seemed impossible that he should ever wake to see how ugly his conduct had been. But there were powers in God's heart that had not yet been brought to bear upon him. Perhaps this was one of them— letting him disgrace himself. If he could only be made ashamed of himself, there would be hope! In the meantime she must get the beam out of her own eye that she might see to take the mote or beam, whichever it might be, out of Corney's! Again she fell upon her knees and prayed God to enable her. Corney was her brother, and must forever be her brother, even if he were the worst thief under the sun! God would see to their honor or disgrace; what she had to do was to be a sister! She rose determined that she would not go home until she had done all she could to find him.

Presently the fact, which at various times cast a dim presence upon her horizon without thoroughly attracting her attention, became plain to her—that she had in part been drawn toward her fiancé because of his social position. Certainly without loving him, she would never have consented to marry him for that, but had she not come the more readily to love him because of it? If he had not been a prospective earl, would not some things in him have possibly repelled her a little more? Would she, for instance, have tried so hard to like the verses he brought her? Clearly, she must take her place with the sinners!

23 / A Talk with the Major

While she thus meditated, Major Marvel made his appearance. He had been watching outside, saw her uncle go, waited another hour, then came to the door and was shown to the room where she still sat, staring out on the frosty trees of the square.

"Why, my child," he said with almost paternal tenderness, "your hand is as cold as ice! Why do you sit so far from the fire?"

She rose and went to the fire with him. He put her in an easy chair and sat down beside her. Common, pudgy, red-faced, bald-headed as he was, she came to him with a sense of refuge. Unity of opinion on things is not necessary to confident friendship and warm love.

As they talked, the major could see that she was depressed, and began to tell her some of the more personal parts of his own history. Becoming interested, she began to ask questions and drew from him much that he would never have thought of volunteering. Before their talk was over, she had come to regard the man with a greater respect than she would have imagined possible before. In a high sense the major was a true man. He knew nothing of the slang of the Pharisees, knew little of the language of either the saints or the prophets. He had, like most Christians, many worldly ways of looking at things, and yet I think our Lord would have said there was no guile in him.

Hester began to question whether she would not be justified in taking the major into her confidence regarding Cornelius. She had received no injunctions to secrecy from her father. She was certain the man would be prudent and keep quiet whatever ought to be kept quiet. Therefore, she told him the whole story, hiding nothing that she knew. The major listened intently, said nothing, betrayed nothing, till she had ended.

"My dear Hester," he said solemnly, after a few moments' pause, "the mysteries of creation are beyond me!"

Hester thought the remark irrelevant, but waited.

"It's such a mixture," he went on. "There is your mother, then Cornelius, then yourself—such differences within the same family! And then little Mark—I will not say too good to live, but too good for any of the common uses of this world! I declare, sometimes he terrifies me!"

"What about him terrifies you?" asked Hester, a little shocked.

"I suppose it's because I'm not made of the stuff of saints—good saints, I mean."

Hester laughed in spite of the gnawing unrest in her heart.

"I think," she said softly, "that one day you will be as good a saint as love can wish you to be."

"Give me time, give me time," replied the major. "But the main cause of my unpopularity—with religious people, you know—was that I hated pretense and humbug—and I do hate humbug, Cousin Hester, and shall hate it till I die—and so want to steer clear of it."

"I hate it, I hope almost as much as you do, Major Marvel," responded Hester. "But whatever it may be mixed up with, what is true, you know, cannot be false itself."

"Yes, yes! But how is one to know what is true, my dear? There are so many differing claims to the quality! How is one to separate the humbug from the true?"

"I have been told, and I believe it," replied Hester, "that the only way to *know* what is true is to *do* what is true."

"But you must *know* what is true before you can begin to *do* what is true."

"Everybody knows something that is true to do—that is, something he ought to lose no time in setting about. The true thing to any man is that which must be done, not ignored. It is much easier to know what is true to do than what is true to think. But those who do the one will come to know the other—and none else, I believe."

The major sat for a few moments silent and thoughtful. At last he rose.

"Is there anything you want me to do in this sad affair, Cousin Hester?" he offered.

"I want you to help me find my brother."

"Why should you want to find him? You cannot do him any good."

"Who can tell that? If Christ came to seek and save his lost, we ought to seek and save our lost."

"But to mix yourself up in his affairs may bring trouble upon yourself."

"That matters little to me now," replied Hester.

There was still so much the major was incapable of understanding. The idea of a woman like Hester being in any sense defiled by knowing what her Lord knows while she fills up what is left behind of the sufferings of Christ is contemptible. As wrong melts away and vanishes in the heart of Christ, so does the impurity she encounters vanish in the heart of the pure woman: it is there burned up.

"I hardly see what is to be done, regardless," said the major, after a moment's silence. "What do you say to an advertisement in *The Times* to the effect that if C. R. will return to his family, all will be forgiven?"

"That we must not do. There is surely some other way of finding persons."

"What do you think your father would like done?"

"I do not know. But as I am Corney's sister, I will venture as a sister may."

"Well, I will do what I can for you—though I greatly fear your brother will never prove worth the trouble."

"People have repented who have gone farther wrong than Corney," said Hester.

"True!" responded the major; "but I don't believe he has character enough to repent of anything. However, I will do what I can to find out where he is."

Hester thanked him heartily, and he took his leave.

Having no idea what she would do if she did find Cornelius, whether he would go home with her, or how he would be received if he did, she sat down and wrote to her father, giving him all the details and ending by saying she was doing what a sister was able to do and that Major Marvel was doing his best to find him.

The next day she heard from her father that her mother was slowly recovering. On the following day, another letter came saying that her letter had been a great comfort to her mother, but beyond that her father made no remark. Even his silence, however, was something of a relief to Hester.

In the meantime she was not idle. The moment the letter had been sent, she set out to visit her old friends. She went to Mrs. Baldwin's shop and had a little talk with her. Mrs. Baldwin told her that the Frankses had been seen once or twice going about their acrobatics on the street, but she feared they were not getting on. Hester was sorry, but had many more to think of in addition.

There was much rejoicing at her return. There were many changes also—new faces, and not the best news of some who remained. One or two were in prison. Some were getting on better. One man of whom she had been hopeful had disappeared—it was supposed with another man's wife. All the little ones gathered around her again, but with less confidence, both because she had been away, and because they had grown more than they had improved. But soon things were nearly on the old footing with them.

Every day she visited the poor. Certain of the women were as warmly her friends as before. There was only one who had some experience of the Christian life, but there seemed to be no corresponding influence from this one onto those even who lived in the same house. Who can trace the slow working of leaven?

She heard no news of Cornelius—only rumor of a young woman in whose company he had lately been seen, but she, too, had disappeared from sight.

It had rained one afternoon, but the sun was now shining and Hester's heart felt lighter as she took deep breaths of the clean-washed air. She decided to visit the wife of a bookbinder who had been long laid up with rheumatism. They lived in a large, run-down building, occupied by many people much poorer than themselves.

When she knocked at the door, it was opened by the parish doctor.

"We cannot have you come in, Miss Raymount," he said. "We have a bad case of smallpox here. You good ladies must make up your minds to keep away from these parts for a while. Their bodies are in more danger than their souls now."

"I'm not worried about myself, Doctor. I would like to see my friends."

"I'm afraid I cannot allow that. You will only carry the infection."

"I will take every precaution."

"While the parish is my responsibility," cautioned the doctor, "I must object to anything that increases the risk of infection. I know your motives are the best, but I cannot have you going from one house to another. How are we to keep it out of the West End if you ladies carry the seeds of it?"

He turned and closed the door. Hester went back down the stair. Her plan thwarted, she did not know what to do next. Instinctively she sat down on the stairs and began to sing. It was not a wise thing to do, but for the moment she was unable to see its impropriety.

In big cities the children are like flies, gathering swiftly as from out of the woodwork. In a moment the stair below Hester was half filled with them. The tenants above opened their doors and came out. Others began to come in from the street to listen, and presently the stair and entrance were filled with people, all shabby and almost all dirty—men and women, young and old, good and bad, listening to the voice of the singing lady, as she was called in the neighborhood.

By this time the doctor had finished his visit and appeared on the stair above. It was hardly any wonder, when he saw who the singer was, that he should lose his temper. He thought she was deliberately trying to spite his refusal of her request to visit her friends by bringing half the neighborhood into contact with the infected family. Hurriedly he walked through the crowd and down to where Hester sat. When he reached her he seized her arm from behind and began to raise her and push her down the stair. Some of the faces below grew red with anger. A loud murmur arose and several began to force their way up to rescue her. But the moment Hester saw who had seized her, she rose and began to descend the stair of her own accord, closely followed by the doctor. It was not easy, for many gave a disorderly and, indeed, rather threatening look to the assemblage because of what the doctor had done.

As she reached the door, on the opposite side of the passage, she saw the pale face and glittering eyes of Mr. Blaney, who had already had the pint which, according to his brother-in-law, was more than he could tolerate.

"Serves you right, miss!" he cried, when he saw who was the center of the commotion; "serves you right! You turned me out o' your house for singin', an' now you've got no right to come a singin' an' a misbehavin' in ourn!"

The crowd had been gathering from both ends of the passage, for high words draw people even faster than sweet singing, and the place was so full that it was hardly possible to leave. The doctor was almost wishing he had left well enough alone, for he was now a little worried about Hester. Some of the rougher ones began pushing. The vindictive little man kept crying. All at once Hester spied a face she knew, though it was considerably changed since last she had seen it.

"Now we shall have help!" she said to her companion, making common cause with him despite his antagonism. "Mr. Franks!"

The acrobat was not so far off that she needed to call very loud. He heard and started with eager interest. He recognized the voice. With his great muscular arms he parted the crowd right and left like the Red Sea, and reached her in a moment.

"Come now! Don't you hurt her!" shouted Mr. Blaney. "She's an old friend o' mine."

"You shut up!" yelled Franks. Then turning to Hester, pulled off his fur cap, made a slight bow, and said briefly, "Miss Raymount—at your service!"

"I am very glad to see you again, Mr. Franks," said Hester with relief. "Do you think you could get us out of the crowd?"

"Easy, miss. I'll carry you out of it, if you'll let me."

"No, no; that will hardly be necessary," returned Hester with a smile.

"Go on before, and make a way for us," said the doctor.

"There is no occasion for you to trouble yourself about me further, Doctor," said Hester. "I am perfectly safe with this man. I am sorry to have caused you all this trouble."

She took Franks' arm, and in a minute they were out of the crowd, which speedily made room for them, and onto the street.

But as if everybody she knew was going to appear, who should meet them face-to-face as they turned into Steven's Road, with a fringe of the crowd still at their heels, but Lord Gartley! He had written and Mrs. Raymount had let him know that Hester was in London. His lordship went at once to Addison Square, and had just left the house disappointed when he met Hester on Franks' arm.

"Miss Raymount!" he exclaimed.

"My lord!" she returned.

"Who would have expected to see you here?"

"Apparently you did, my lord."

He tried to laugh.

"Come then; I will see you home," he said.

"Thank you. Come, Franks."

As she spoke she looked round, but Franks was gone. Finding she had met one of her own family, as he supposed, he had quietly withdrawn, feeling embarrassed. But he lingered around a corner, to be certain she was going to be taken care of. Seeing them walk away together he was satisfied, and went with a sigh.

24 / Lord Gartley

The two were silent on their way, but for different reasons. Lord Gartley was uneasy at finding Hester in such a situation. For a woman of her refinement, she had the strangest proclivity for low company! Hester was silent, thinking how to begin her story about Cornelius. Uncomfortable and even slightly irritated at the tone in which his lordship had expressed the surprise he could not help feeling at the sight of her, she realized it would be good to come to a clearer understanding at once concerning her life-ideal and projects. But she would make up her mind to nothing until she saw how he was going to carry himself when she said what she had to say.

These thoughts hardly passed logically through her mind; it was filled, rather, with a confused mass of tangled thought and feeling, which tossed about in it like the nets of a fishing fleet rolled together by a storm.

Neither spoke before they reached the house, and Hester began to wonder if he had already heard about Cornelius. It was plain he was troubled, plain he was only waiting for the cover of the house to speak. It should be easy, very easy for him to get rid of her.

They entered, and she led the way up the stair. Not a movement of life was audible in the house. The stillness was almost painful.

"Did no one come with you?" he asked.

"No one but Major Marvel," she answered, opening the door of the drawing room.

As she closed it, she turned and said, "Forgive me, Gartley. I am in trouble; we are all in trouble. When I have told you about it, I shall be more myself again."

Then without introduction or any attempt to influence the impression of the news, she began her story—telling first of her mother's distress at Sarah's letter, then the contents of that letter, and then those of her uncle's. She could not have done it with greater fairness to her friend: his practiced self-control had opportunity for perfect operation. But the result was more to her satisfaction than she could have dared to hope. He held out his hand with a smile and said, "I am very sorry. What can I do?"

She looked up into his eyes. They were looking down kindly and lovingly.

"Then—then—" she faltered, "you don't—I mean there's no—I mean, you don't feel differently toward me?"

"Toward you, my angel!" exclaimed Gartley, and held out his arms.

She threw herself into them and clung to him. It was the first time either of them had shown anything like abandonment. Gartley's heart swelled with delight, for until that moment he had been painfully conscious now and then that he played second fiddle. But he was now no longer the second person in the compact.

They sat down and talked the whole thing over.

Now that Hester was at peace, she began to look at it from his point of view.

"I am sorry," she apologized. "It is very sad you should have to marry into a family so disgraced. What *will* your aunt say?"

"My aunt will treat the affair like the sensible woman she is," replied the earl. "But there is no fear of disgrace; this scandal will never be known. Besides, where is the family that hasn't one or more such loose fishes about in its pond?"

From the heaven of her delight Hester almost fell. Was this the way her almost-husband looked at these things? But, poor fellow! how could he help looking at them so? This was the way he had been taught from earliest childhood to look at them.

"But we won't think more about it just now," he added. "Let us talk of ourselves!"

"If only we could find him!" returned Hester.

"Depend upon it, he is not where you would like to find him. Men don't come to grief without help! We must just wait till he turns up."

Far as this was from her purpose, Hester was not inclined to argue the point: she could not expect him or anyone out of her own family to be much interested in the fate of Cornelius. They began to talk about other things; and if they were not the things Hester would most readily have talked about, neither were they the things Lord Gartley had entered the house intending to talk about. He too had been almost angry; only by nature he was cool and even good-tempered. To find Hester, the moment she came back to London, yielding all over again to her diseased idea of doing good; to come upon her in the street of a low neighborhood, followed by a low crowd, and accompanied by a low fellow—well, it was far from agreeable! He could not fail to find it annoying, especially with their marriage so near! Something must be done about her habits!

But when he had heard her trouble, he knew this was not the time to say what he had meant to say about it.

He had risen to go and was about to take a loving farewell, when Hester, suddenly remembering, drew back with an almost guilty look.

"Oh," she gasped, "I should not have let you come near me!"

"What *can* you mean, Hester?" he exclaimed, and would have laid his hand on her arm, but again she drew back.

"There was smallpox in the house I had just left when you met me," she explained.

He started back and stood speechless—showing no more cowardice than anyone in his circle would have justified.

"Has it never occurred to you what you are doing in going to such places, Hester?" he faltered. "It is against all social claim. I am sorry, but—really—I—I—cannot help being a little surprised at you. I thought you had more—more—sense!"

"I am sorry to have frightened you."

"Frightened!" repeated Gartley, with an attempt at a smile, which closed in an even more anxious look, "—you do indeed frighten me! Don't imagine I am thinking of myself; *you* are the one that is in most danger! And you might carry the infection without getting it yourself!"

"I didn't know it was there when I went to the house—but I would have gone all the same," asserted Hester. "But I should have had a bath as soon as I got home. Seeing you so suddenly made me forget. I *am* sorry I let you come near me."

"One has no right either to get or carry infection," insisted Lord Gartley. "But there is no time to talk about it now. I hope you will use what preventives you can. It is very wrong to trifle with such things!"

"Indeed it is!" Hester agreed; "and I say again I am sorry I forgot. You see how it was—don't you? It was you that made me forget!"

But his lordship was by no means now in a smiling mood. He bade her a rather cold good night, then hesitated, thinking that he must not look too much afraid, and held out his hand. But Hester drew back a third time, saying, "No, no, you must not," and with a solemn bow he turned and went, his mind full of conflicting feelings and perplexing thoughts. What a glorious creature she was! and how dangerous! What a spirit she had! but what a pity it was so ill-directed! It was horrible to think of her going into such places—and all alone too! How ill she had been trained!—in such utter disregard of social obligation and the laws of nature. It was preposterous! He little thought what risks he ran when he fell in love with *her*! If he got off now without an attack, he would be lucky! But—good heavens! if she were to take ill herself! "I wonder when she was last vaccinated!" he muttered. "I was last year; I daresay I'm all right! But if she were to die, I would kill myself!" Philanthropy had gone mad! To sympathize with people like that was only to encourage them! Vice was like hysterics—the more kindness you showed, the worse it grew. They took it all as their right! And the more you gave, the more they demanded—never showing any gratitude as far as he knew!

His lordship was scarcely gone when the major came. But Hester was not to be seen at the moment, for she had already begun her bath, taking what measures seemed advisable for her protection and those about her. But she had no fear, for she did not believe in chance. The same and only faith that would have enabled the major to face the man-eating tiger enabled her to face the smallpox; if she did die by going into such places, it was all right.

The major sat down and waited.

"I am at my wits' end!" he blurted when at length she entered the room. "I can't find the fellow. I've had a detective on it, but he hasn't got a trace of him yet. Don't you think you had better go home? I will do what can be done, you may be sure of that."

"I *am* sure," answered Hester, "but I would rather be here than have Papa leave Mama. And he won't as long as I stay."

"But it must be dreary for you."

"I go about among my people," she said.

"Ah," he returned. "Then I hope you will be careful what houses you go into, for I hear smallpox is in the neighborhood."

"I have just come from such a house," she replied. The major rose in haste. "But," she went on, "I have changed all my clothes and had a bath since."

The major sat down again.

"My dear young lady!" he said, the roses a little ashy on his cheek-bones, "do you know what you are doing?"

"I hope I do—I *think* I do," she answered.

"Hope! Think!" repeated the major.

"Well, *believe*," said Hester.

"Come! come!" he rejoined almost rudely; "you may hope or think or believe what you like, but you have no business to act but on what you *know*."

"I suppose *you* never act where you do not know the outcome!" returned Hester. "You always *know* you will win the battle, kill the tiger, beat the smallpox."

"It's all very well for you to laugh!" the major said, exasperation in his voice, "but what is to become of us if you catch it? Why, my dear cousin, you might lose every scrap of your good looks! Really, this is most imprudent!"

"Is the smallpox worse than a man-eating tiger?" she asked.

"Ten times worse," he answered. "You can fight the tiger, but you can't fight the smallpox. You really ought not to run such fearful risks.

It is your life, not only your beauty you are imperiling."

"I think," stated Hester, "that whoever lives in constant fear of infection might just as well catch it and have done with it. I know I would rather die than live in the fear of death. What we've got to do we must just go and do without thinking about the danger. I believe it is often the best wisdom to be blind and let God be our eyes as well as our shield. God took complete care of Jesus. And yet he allowed the worst man could do to overtake him. That was the consequence of his obedience. I don't want my obedience to be any less in the work God has called me to do."

When the major left, he could not help being filled with admiration for "Cousin Helen's girl."

By Jove! he said to himself, *it's a good thing I didn't marry Helen; she would never have had a girl like that if I had! Things always work out for the best. The world needs a few such in it—even if they be fools—though I suspect they will turn out the wise ones, and we the fools!*

That same evening the major sent her word that one answering the description of Cornelius had been seen in the neighborhood of Addison Square.

25 / Further Down

The Frankses had finally reached the point of being unable to pay for their lodging. They were two weeks' rent behind. Their landlady did not want to be too hard on them, but what could a poor woman do? she said. So, the day finally came when they had to go forth like Abraham without a home. The still weak wife had to carry the sickly baby who, with many ups and downs, had been slowly wasting away. The father went laden with the larger portion of the goods yet remaining to them, leading the boys bearing the small stock of implements belonging to their art.

They had delayed their departure until after dusk, for Franks could not help a vague feeling of blame for the condition of his family, and shrank from being seen by anyone. The world was like a sea before them—a prospect of ceaseless motion through the night, with the hope of an occasional rest on a doorstep or the edge of the curbstone when the policeman's back was turned. They set out with no place to go—to walk on and on with no goal before them.

At length as they wandered they came to an area where there seemed to be only small houses. Presently they found themselves in a little lane with no street, at the back of some stables, and had to return along the rough-paved, neglected way. It was such a quiet and secluded spot that Franks thought they should find its most sheltered corner to sit down and rest, and possibly sleep. But nearly the same moment he heard the measured step of a policeman on the other side of the stables. Instinctively, hurriedly, they looked around for some place of concealment, and saw, at the end of a blank wall, belonging apparently to some kind of warehouse, a narrow path between that and the wall of the next property. Taking no thought to where it led, anxious only to escape the policeman, they turned quickly into it. Scarcely had they done so when little Moxy, whose hand his father had let go, disappeared with a little cry, and then a little whimper came up from somewhere through the darkness.

"Hold your noise, you rascal!" his father sharply whispered. "The bobby will hear you and have us all in the lock-up!"

Not a sound more was heard, and the boy did not reappear. "Good heavens, John!" cried the mother in an agonized whisper; "the child has fallen down a sewer!"

"Hold your noise," Franks commanded again.

" 'Tain't a bad place," cried a little voice in a whisper broken with repressed sobs. " 'Tain't a bad place, I don't think, only I've broken one o' my two legs; it won't move."

"Thank God, the child's alive!" cried the mother.

By this time the steps of the policeman were fading in the distance. Franks turned and climbed down a few steps into the opening through which Moxy had fallen. When he found him he lifted him, but the child gave a low cry of pain. It was impossible to see where or how much he was hurt. The father sat down and took him on his knees.

"You'd better come down an' sit here, Wife," he said in a low dull voice. "The boy's hurt, an' down here you'll be out o' the wind at least."

They all got as far down the stair as its room would permit—the elder boys with their heads hardly below the level of the wind. But by and by one of them crept down past his mother, and began to feel what sort of place they were in.

"Here's a door, Father!" he said.

"Well, 'tain't no door open to the likes o' us. 'Tain't no door open for the likes o' us but the door o' the grave."

The boy's hand came upon a latch; he lifted it and pushed.

"Father," he cried, "it *is* open!"

"Get in then," said his father.

"I daren't. It's so dark!" he answered fearfully.

"Here, you come an' take Moxy," instructed the father with faintly reviving hope, "an' I'll see what sort of place it is. If it's any place at all, it's better than bein' in the air all night at this freezin' time."

So saying he gave the injured boy to his bigger brother and went to learn what kind of place they had stumbled into. Feeling with foot and hand, he went in. The floor was earthen and the place had a musty smell: *it might be a church vault,* he thought. He went farther in, sliding his foot on the soundless floor, and sliding his hand along the cold wall—on around two corners, past a closed door, and back to that by which he had entered, where the family sat waiting his return.

"Wife," he said, "we can't do better than to take the only thing that's offered. The floor's firm an' it's out o' the air. It's some sort of a cellar—perhaps at the bottom of a church. It did look as if it was left open just for us!"

He took her by the hand and led the way into the darkness, the boys following, one of them with a hold of his mother, and his arm round the other, who was carrying Moxy. Franks closed the door behind them. They had gained a refuge. Feeling about, one of the boys came upon a large packing case. Franks laid it down against the inner wall, sat down, and made his wife lie upon it with her head on his knees, and took Moxy again in his arms, wrapped in one of their three thin blankets. The boys stretched themselves on the ground and were soon fast asleep. The baby moaned by fits all night long.

In about an hour Franks, who did not fall asleep for some time, heard the door open softly and stealthily, and seemed aware of a presence beside themselves in the place. He concluded some other poor creature had discovered the same shelter; or, if they had got into a church vault, it might be some wandering ghost. But he was too weary for further speculation, or any uneasiness. However, when the slow light crept through the chinks of the door, he found they were quite alone.

It was a large dry cellar, empty except for the old packing case. They would have to use great caution, and do their best to keep their hold of this last retreat! Misfortune had driven them into the earth; it would be fortune to stay there.

When his wife woke he told her what he had been thinking. He and the boys would creep out before it was light and return after dark. She must not even put a finger out of the cellar door all day. He laid Moxy down beside her, woke the two elder boys, and went out with them.

They were so careful that for many days they continued undiscovered. Franks and the boys went and returned, and gained bread enough to keep them alive, but it may well seem a wonder they did not perish with cold. It is amazing what even the delicate can sometimes go through when survival is at stake.

26 / Differences Come to Light_____

About noon the next day Lord Gartley called. Whether he had got over his fright, thought the danger now less imminent, or was vexed with himself that he had appeared to be afraid, I do not know. Hester was very glad to see him again.

"I think I am a safe companion today," she said. "I have not been out of the house yet. But until the bad time is over among my people, I think we had better be content not to meet."

Lord Gartley mentally gasped. He stood for a moment speechless, gathering his thoughts, which almost refused to be gathered.

"Do I understand you, Hester?" he asked in disbelief. "It would trouble me more than I can tell you to find I do. You don't mean to say you are going out—again!"

"Is it possible you thought I would abandon my friends to the small-pox, as a hireling his sheep to the wolf?"

"There are those whose business it is to look after them."

"I am one of those," returned Hester.

"Well," answered his lordship, "for the sake of argument, we will allow it *has* been your business up till now. But how can you imagine it is your business any longer?"

The fire of Hester's indignation burst into flame and she spoke as Gartley had never heard her speak before.

"You mean, I presume, that because of my engagement to one of your *position*, I should no longer have to do with such people!"

"Of course. You didn't think that—?"

"I am aware, my lord," she said, trying to remain calm, "that I must have new duties to perform, but I never considered that they would have to displace the old. The claims of love surely cannot obliterate those of friendship! The new should make the old better, not sweep it away!"

"But, my dear girl, this is preposterous!" exclaimed his lordship. "Don't you see you will enter on a new life! The duties of a wife are altogether distinct from those of an unmarried woman."

"But if the position of a wife is the higher, then it must enable her to do even better those things which are her duty as a human being— such as helping the poor."

"But to try to do what you are doing now, in the station you are about to occupy, would be absurd. You will be the wife of a lord! You will have your own duties, and will find that both cannot be done."

"You have given me more than I can manage all at once," she replied in a troubled voice. "I must think."

"The more you think, the better satisfied you will be of what I say. I am certain your good sense will convince you I am right."

He paused a moment. Hester did not speak. He resumed: "There are sick in every class. You would have those of your own to visit. Why not leave others to visit those of theirs?"

"Then of course you would have no objection to my visiting a duchess who had smallpox?"

Lord Gartley was on the point of saying that duchesses never got smallpox, but he did not, afraid that Hester might know something to the contrary.

"There could be no occasion for that," he hedged. "She would have everything she could want."

"And the others are in lack of everything! To desert them would be to desert the Lord. He would count it so."

"And in your naive fancy to help the poor, you would be careless of those of your own class to whom you might spread the disease!" His voice took on the hint of a sneer.

"Don't imagine that because I trust in God I have no fear of what the smallpox can do to me and that I would therefore neglect any necessary preventive. That would be to tempt God."

"You will bathe and wash your clothes, but you will not keep away! Those so-called preventives in the face of such a brazen challenge to fate seem to me foolish rather than prudent!"

Hester felt as if a wall rose suddenly across the path between them. It became clear to her that he and she had been going on without any real understanding of each other's views in life. Her expectations tumbled about her like a house of cards. If he wanted to marry her, full of designs and aims in which she did not share, and she was going to marry him, expecting sympathies and helps which he had not the slightest inclination to give her, where was the hope for success?

She sat silent. She wanted to be alone to think. It would be easier to write than to talk further. But she must know more clearly what was in his mind.

"Do you mean, then, that when I am your wife, if ever I am, that I shall have to give up all the friendships to which I have devoted my life?"

Her tone was dominated by the desire to remain calm, to discern his real feeling. Gartley mistook it, and supposed she at last was yielding to his influence. He concluded that now he had only to be firm so there would be no future discussion on the matter.

"I would not for a moment act the tyrant, or say you must never go into such houses again. Your own good sense will guide you. But of one thing I am certain. In the circle to which you will in the future belong, nothing is considered more out of place than to speak of these persons, whatever regard you may have for their spiritual welfare, as your *friends*. You know well enough that such persons *cannot* be your friends."

This was more than Hester could bear. She broke out with a passion for which she was afterward sorry, though by no means ashamed.

"They *are* my friends. There are twenty of them who would do more for me than you would!"

Lord Gartley rose. He was hurt. "Hester, you think so little of me or my concern for your best interests that I suppose it will be a relief to you if I go."

She answered not a word—did not even look up, and his lordship walked gently but unhesitatingly from the room.

It will bring her to her senses! he told himself.

Long after he was gone, Hester sat motionless, thinking. What she had vaguely dreaded—she knew now that she had dreaded it all along— had come! They were not, never had been, never could be at one about anything! He was a mere man of this world, without relation to the world of truth. And yet she loved him—would gladly die for him if by so doing he could be saved from himself and given to God instead. But she could not marry him! That would be to swell his worldly triumphs, help gild the chains of his slavery. It was one thing to die that a fellow creature might have all things good—another to live a living death that he might persist in the pride of life! She could not throw God's life to the service of Satan!

Was it then all over between them? Might he not come again and say he was sorry he had left her? He might indeed. But would that make any difference to her? Had he not beyond a doubt disclosed his real way of thinking and feeling? If he could speak as he had now, after they had talked so much, what spark of hope was there in marriage?

To forget her friends that she might go into *society* as a countess! The very thought was contemptible. She would leave such ambition to women that devoured novels and studied the peerage! One loving look from human eyes was more to her than the admiration of the world. If only the house were her own. Then she might turn it into a hospital! She would make it a hope to which anyone sick or sad, any outcast of the world might flee for shelter! She would be more than ever the sister and helper of her own, cling tighter than ever to the skirts of the Lord's garment, that the virtue going out of him might flow through her to them!

How easy is it, in certain moods, to think thoughts of unselfish devotion. But how hard is the doing of the thought in the face of a thousand unlovely difficulties! Hester knew this, but was determined not to withdraw hand or foot or heart as God helped her. She rose and made herself ready to visit her people. First of all she would go to the bookbinder's and see how his wife was attended to.

The doctor was not there and she was readily admitted. The poor husband, unable to help, sat by the scanty fire, a picture of misery. A neighbor, not yet quite recovered from the disease herself, had taken upon herself the duties of nurse. Hester gave her what instructions she thought she might carry out, told her to send for anything she wanted, then rose to leave.

"Won't you sing to her a bit, miss, before you go?" asked the husband. "It'll do her more good than all the doctor's stuff."

"I don't think she's well enough," said Hester.

"Not to get all the good out of it, I daresay," rejoined the man; "but she'll hear it like in a dream, an' she'll think it's the angels a singin'; an' that'll do her good, for she do like all them creatures!"

Hester gave in and sang, thinking all the time how the ways of the open-eyed God look to us like things in a dream, because we are only in the night of his great day, asleep before the brightness of his great waking thoughts. The woman had been tossing and moaning in discomfort, but as Hester sang she grew still, and when the singing stopped she lay as if asleep.

"Thank you, miss," said the man. "You can do more than the doctor, as I told you! When he comes, he always wakes her up; you make her sleep soundly!"

27 / Deliverance

In the meantime, even worse trouble had come upon the poor Frankses. About a week after they had taken possession of the cellar, little Moxy, who had been weak ever since his fall down the steps, became seriously ill and grew worse and worse. For some days they were not much alarmed, for the child had often been ailing—oftener lately since they had not been faring so well; and even when they were better off they dared not get a doctor to look at him for fear of being turned out and having to go to the workhouse.

By this time they had managed to make the cellar a little more comfortable. They got some straw and with two or three old sacks made a bed for the mother, the baby, and Moxy on the packing case. By the exercise of their art they had gained enough money to keep them in food, but never enough to pay for even the poorest room. The parents loved Moxy more tenderly than either of his brothers, and it was with heavy hearts they saw him getting worse. The sickness was a mild smallpox—so mild that they did not recognize it, yet it was more than his weary body could bear, and he was gradually sinking. When this became clear to the mother, then indeed she felt the hand of God heavy upon her.

Religiously brought up, she had through the ordinary troubles of a married life sought help from the God in whom her mother had believed. But with every fresh attack of misery, every step further down on the stair of life, she thought she had lost her last remnant of hope. Now Moxy was about to be taken from them, and no deeper misery seemed, to their imagination, possible! Nothing seemed left—not even the desire of deliverance. Margaret Franks, in the cellar of her poverty, the grave yawning below it for her Moxy, felt as if there were no heaven at all, only a sky.

But a strange necessity now compelled her to rouse all the latent hope and faith and prayer that were in her.

By an inexplicable insight, the child seemed to know that he was dying. For one morning, after having tossed about all night long, he suddenly cried out in the most pitiful tone, "Mother, don't put me in a hole!"

As far as any of them knew he had never seen a funeral—at least to know what it was—and had never heard anything about death or burial:

145

his father had a horror of the subject.

The words went like a knife to the heart of the mother.

Again came the pitiful cry, "Mother, don't put me in a hole!"

Most mothers would have sought to soothe the child, their own hearts breaking all the while, with the assurance that no one would put him into any hole or anywhere he did not want to go. But this mother could not lie in the face of death, and before she could answer, a third time came the cry, this time in despairing though supressed agony—"Mother, don't let them put me in a hole!"

The mother gave a cry like the child's and her heart melted.

"Oh, God!" she gasped, and could say no more.

But with the prayer—for what is a prayer but a calling on the name of the Lord—came a little calm, and she was able to speak. She bent over and kissed him on the forehead.

"My darling Moxy, Mother loves you," she said, soothingly.

What that had to do with it she did not ask herself. The child looked up in her face with dim eyes.

"Pray to the heavenly father, Moxy," she went on—and there stopped, thinking what she should tell him to ask for. "Tell him," she resumed, "that you don't want to be put in a hole, and tell him that Mother does not want you to be put in a hole, for she loves you with all her heart."

"Don't put me in the hole," begged Moxy, again.

"Jesus Christ was put in the hole," said the voice of the next oldest boy from behind his mother. He had just come in softly. It was Sunday, and he had strolled into a church somewhere and had heard the wonderful story of hope. It was remarkable that he had taken it in as he did, for he went on to add, "but he didn't mind much, and soon got out again."

"Ah, yes, Moxy!" said the poor mother, "Jesus died for our sins, and you must ask him to take you up to heaven."

But Moxy did not know anything about sins, and just as little about heaven. What he wanted was an assurance that he would not be put into the hole. And the mother, now a little calmer, thought she knew what she ought to say.

"It isn't your soul, it's only your body, Moxy, that they put in the hole," she told him truthfully.

"I don't want to be put in the hole," Moxy almost screamed.

The poor mother was at her wits' end; but here the child fell into a troubled sleep, and for some hours a grave-like silence filled the dreary cellar.

On this same particular Sunday Hester had been to church, and had then visited some of her people, carrying them words of comfort and hope. They received them from her, but none of them, had they gone, would have found them at church. How seldom is the man in the pulpit able to make people feel that the things he is talking about are relevant to them! Neither when the heavens are black with clouds and rain, nor when the sun rises glorious in a blue perfection, do many care to sit down and be taught astronomy! But Hester was a live gospel to them—most of all when she sang. Even the name of the Savior uttered in her singing tone and with the expression she gave it, came nearer to them than when she spoke it.

How many things there are in the world in which the wisest of us can hardly perceive the hand of God! Who not knowing could ready the lily in its bulb, the great oak in the pebble-like acorn? God's beginnings do not *look* like his endings, but they *are*; the oak *is* the acorn, though we cannot see it.

This Sunday, in her dejection and sadness about Gartley, over whom—not her loss of him—she mourned deeply, Hester felt more than ever how little she was able to touch her people. There came upon her a heavy hopelessness that sank into the very roots of her life. She was having to learn that even in all dreariness, of the flesh and of the spirit, the refuge is the same—he who is at once the root and crown of life.

The day was an oppressive, foggy, cold, dreary day. The service at church had not seemed interesting. She laid the blame on herself, not on the prayers, the lessons, or the preacher, though in truth some of these could have been better. The heart seemed to have gone out of the world—as if God had gone to sleep and his children had waked before him and found the dismal gray of the world's morning. She tried her New Testament, but Jesus, too, seemed far away. She tried some of her favorite poems, but all were infected with the same disease—with commonplace nothingness. Everything seemed mere words! words! words! Nothing was left her in the valley but the last weapon—prayer. She fell upon her knees and cried to God for life. "My heart is dead within me," she said, and poured out her lack into the hearing of him from whom she had come. But even in her prayers Hester could not get near him. It seemed as if his ear was turned away from her cry, and she sank into a kind of lethargic stupor.

There are times, in order to give us the spiritual help we need, when it is necessary for God to cast us into a sort of mental quiescence, that the noises of winds and waters of the questioning intellect and roused feelings may not interfere with the impression the master would make upon us. But Hester's lethargy lasted long, and was not so removed. She rose from her knees in a kind of despair she had never known.

It had been dark for hours, but she lit no candle, sitting in bodily as well as spiritual darkness. She was in her bedroom, which was on the second floor, at the back of the house, looking out on the top of the gallery that led to the great room. She had no fire. One was burning away unheeded in the drawing room below. She was too miserable to care whether she was cold or warm. When she had got some light in her body, then she would go and get warm!

She did not know what time it was. She had been summoned to the last meal of the day, but had forgotten the summons. It must have been about ten o'clock. The streets were silent, the square deserted—as usual. The evening was raw and cold, one to drive everybody indoors that had doors to go in.

A shriek chilling her with horror pierced the cold and darkness. Yet it seemed as if she had been expecting it—as if the cloud of misery that had all day been gathering deeper and deeper above and around her had at length reached its fullness and burst forth. It was followed by another and yet another. She could not tell where they came from. Certainly not from the street, for all outside was still. And there was a certain something in the sound of them that made her sure they rose from within the house. Was Sarah being murdered? She was halfway down the stairs before the horrible thought crystallized in her mind.

The house seemed unnaturally still. At the top of the kitchen stairs she called aloud to Sarah—as loud, that is, as a certain tremor in her throat would permit. There came no reply. Down she went to face the worst: she was a woman of true courage—that is, a woman whom no amount of apprehension could deter when she knew she ought to seek the danger.

In the kitchen stood Sarah, motionless, frozen with fear. A candle was in her hand, just lighted. Hester's voice seemed to break her trance.

She started, stared, and began trembling. Hester made her drink some water, and then she came to herself.

"It's in the coal cellar, miss!" she gasped. "I was that minute going to fetch a scuttleful! There's something buried in them coals as sure as my name's Sarah!"

"Nonsense! Who could scream like that from under the coals? Come. We'll go and see what it is."

"Laws, miss, don't you go near it now! It's too late to do anything. Either it's the woman's spirit as they say was murdered there, or it's a new one."

"And you would let her be killed without interfering?"

"Oh, miss, all's over by this time!" persisted Sarah with trembling white lips.

"Then you are ready to go to bed with a murderer in the house?"

"He's done his business now, an' 'll go away."

"Give me the candle. I will go alone."

"You'll be murdered, miss—as sure's you're alive!"

Hester took the light from her and went toward the coal cellar. The old woman sank on a chair.

I have already alluded to the subterranean portion of the house, which extended under the great room. A long vault, corresponding to the gallery above, led to these cellars. It was a rather frightful place to go into in search of the source of a shriek. Its darkness was scarcely affected by the candle she carried; it seemed only to blind her own eyes. The black tunnel stretched on and on, like a tunnel in a feverish dream, before the cellars began to open from it. She walked on, I cannot say fearless, but therefore only the more brave. At last she reached the coal cellar, the first that opened from the passage, and looked in. The coal pile was low and the place looked large and black—she could see nothing. She went in and moved about until she had thrown light into every corner, but no one was there. She was about to return when she remembered that there were other cellars—one the wine cellar, which was locked. She would go ask Sarah if she knew where the key to it was. But just as she left the coal cellar, she heard a moan followed by several low sobs. Her heart began to beat violently, but she stopped to listen. The light from her candle fell upon another door, a step or two from where she stood. She went to it, laid her ear against it and listened. The sobs continued a while, ceased, and all became silent again. Then clear and sweet, but strange and wild, as if from some unearthly region, came the voice of a child: "Mother," it rang out, "you *may* put me in the hole."

Immediately the silence fell deep as before.

Hester stood for a moment horrified. Her excited imagination suggested some deed of superstitious cruelty in the garden of the adjoining house. And the sobs and cries lent themselves all the more toward something in that direction. She recovered herself instantly and ran back to the kitchen.

"Do you have the keys of the cellars, Sarah?"

"Yes, miss, I think so."

"Where does the door beyond the coal cellar lead to?"

"Not to nowhere, miss. That's a large cellar as we never use. I ain't been into it since the first day when they put some of the packing cases there."

"Give me the key," said Hester. "Something is going on there we ought to know about."

"Then pray send for the police, miss!" answered Sarah, trembling. "It ain't for you to go into such places!"

"What! Not in our own house?"

"It's the police's business, miss!"

"Then the police are their brothers' keepers, and not you and me, Sarah?"

"It's the wicked as is in it, I fear, miss."

"It's those that weep anyhow, and they're our business. Quick! Show me which is the key."

Sarah sought the key in the bunch, and noting the coolness with which her young mistress took it, gathered a little courage from hers to follow, a bit behind.

When Hester reached the door, she carefully examined it, so she would be able to do what she had to do as quickly as possible. There were bolts and bars upon it, but not one of them was fastened: it was secured only by the bolt of the lock. She set the candle on the floor and inserted the key as quietly as she could. It turned without much difficulty, and the door fell partly open with a groan of the rusted hinge. She grabbed the light and went in.

It was a large, empty place. For a few moments she could see nothing. But presently she saw, somewhere in the dark, a group of faces, looking white through the surrounding blackness, the eyes of them fixed in amazement—if not terror—upon herself. Advancing toward them, she almost immediately recognized one of them—then another; but what with the dimness, the ghostliness, and the strangeness of it all, felt as if surrounded by the veiled shadows of a dream. But whose was that pallid little face whose eyes were not upon her with the rest? It stared straight ahead into the dark, as if it had no more to do with the light! She drew nearer to it. The eyes of the other faces followed her.

When the eyes of the mother saw the face of her Moxy, who had died in the dark, she threw herself into a passion of tears and cries. When Hester turned in pain from the agony of the mother, she saw the man kneeling with uplifted hands of supplication at her feet. A torrent of divine love and compassion filled her heart, breaking from its deepest God-haunted caves. She stooped and kissed the man on his forehead.

Franks burst out crying like a child. All at once in the depths of hell, the wings of a great angel were spread out over him and his! No more starvation and cold for his poor wife and the baby! The boys would have plenty now! If only Moxy—but he was gone where the angels came from. Theirs was a hard life! Surely the God his wife talked about must have sent her to them! Did he think they had borne enough now? Only he had borne it so poorly! So thought Franks, in dislocated fashion, as he remained kneeling.

Hester was now kneeling also, with her arms around the mother who held the body of her child. She did not speak to her, did not attempt a word of comfort, but wept with her. She, too, had loved little Moxy! She, too, had heard his dying words. In the midst of her own loneliness and seeming desertion, God had these people already in the house for her to help! The back door of every tomb opens on a hilltop.

With awestruck faces the boys looked on. They, too, could not see Moxy's face. They had loved Moxy—loved him more than they even knew.

The woman at length raised her head and looked at Hester.

"Oh, miss, it's Moxy!" she said, bursting into a new passion of grief.

"The dear child!" said Hester quietly.

"Oh, miss, who's to look after him now?"

"There will be plenty to look after him. You don't think he who provided a woman like you for his mother before he sent him here would send him there without having somebody ready to look after him?"

"Well, miss, it wouldn't be like him—I don't think!"

"It would *not* be like him," Hester assured her.

Then she asked them a few questions about their history since she last saw them, and how it was they had sunk so low. The answers she received were more satisfactory than her knowledge had allowed her to hope.

"But oh, miss!" exclaimed Mrs. Franks, "you ought not to ha' been here so long. The little angel there died o' the smallpox, as I know too well, an' it's no end o' catching!"

"Never mind me," replied Hester; "I'm not afraid. But," she added, rising, "we must get you out of this place immediately."

"Oh, miss! where would you send us?" asked Mrs. Franks in alarm. "There's nobody as'll take us in! An' it would break both our two hearts to be parted at such a moment, when us two's the father an' mother o' Moxy. An' they'd take Moxy from us, an' put him in the hole he was so a feared of!"

"You don't think I would leave my own flesh and blood in the cellar!" answer Hester. "I will go and make arrangement for you above, and be back presently."

"Oh, thank you, miss!" said the woman as Hester set the candle down beside them. "I do want to look on the face of my blessed boy as long as I can. He will be taken from me altogether soon."

"Mrs. Franks," rejoined Hester, "you mustn't talk like a heathen."

"I didn't know I was saying anything wrong, miss!"

"Don't you know," said Hester, smiling through her tears, "that

Jesus died and rose again that we might be delivered from death? Don't you know that it's *he* and not death that has got your Moxy? He will take care of him for you until you are ready to have him again."

"The Lord love you, miss! An angel o' mercy you been to me an' mine."

"Goodbye then for a few minutes," said Hester. "I am only going to prepare a place for you."

Only as she said the words did she remember who had said them before her. And as she went through the dark tunnel, she sang with a voice that seemed to beat at the gates of heaven, "Thou didst not leave his soul in hell."

Mrs. Franks threw herself again beside her child, but her tears were not so bitter now.

"She'll come again for us," she murmured. "An' Christ'll receive my poor Moxy to himself! If he wasn't, as they say, a Christian, it was only as he hadn't time—so young, an' all the hard work he had to do— with his precious face a grinnin' like an angel between the feet of him, a helpin' his father to make a livin' for us all! If ever there was a child o' God's makin' it, it was that child!"

Thoughts like these kept flowing through the mind of the bereaved mother as she lay with her arm over the body of her child—now more lovely to her than ever. The smallpox had not been severe—only severe enough to take a feeble life from the midst of privation. He lay like a sacrifice that sealed a new covenant between his mother and her Father in heaven. We have yet learned but little of the blessed power of death. We call it an evil, but it is a holy, friendly thing. We are not left shivering all the world's night in a stately portico with no house behind it. Death is the door to the temple-house, whose God is not seated aloft in motionless state, but walks about among his children, receiving his pilgrim sons in his arms, and washing the sore feet of the weary ones. Either God is altogether like Christ, or the Christian religion is a lie.

Not a word passed between husband and wife. Their hearts were too full for speech, but their hands found and held each other's. It was the strangest combination of sorrow and relief! The two boys sat on the ground with their arms about each other. So they waited. . . .

28 / On the Way Up

Hearing only the sounds of a peaceful talk, Sarah had ventured near enough to the door to hear something of what was said. Her mind was set to rest by finding that the cause of her terror was only a poor family that had sought refuge in the cellar. She woke up to the situation and was ready to help. More than sufficiently afraid of robbers and murderers, she was not afraid of infection. "How could an old woman like me get the smallpox! I've had it bad enough once already!" She was rather staggered, however, when she found what Hester's plan for the intruders was.

Since the night of the concert, nothing more had been done to make the great room habitable by the family. It had been well cleaned out and that was all. But what better place, thought Hester, could there be for a smallpox ward!

She told Sarah to light a big fire as quickly as possible, while she settled what could be done about beds. Almost all in the house were old-fashioned wooden ones, hard to take down, heavy to move, and hard to put up again. With only her and Sarah it would take a long time! For safety, too, it would be better to use iron beds which could be easily purified—only it was Sunday night, and late! But she knew the merchant in Steeven's Road. She would go to him and see if he had any beds and if he would help her put them up at once.

The raw night made her rejoice all the more that she had got hold of the poor creatures drowning in the social swamp. It was a consolation against her own sorrows to know that virtue was going out of her for rescue and redemption.

She had to ring the bell many times before the door opened, for it was now past eleven o'clock. The man was not pleased at being taken from his warm bed to go out and work—on such a night, too! He made what objections he thought he could, to no avail. Finally assenting to Hester's arguments, he went to find the beds she wanted. Having got the two beds extracted piecemeal from the disorganized heaps in his back shop, he and Hester proceeded to carry them home—no easy job, for she made three trips back and forth and they were heavy. It was long after midnight before the beds were ready—and a meal of coffee, toast, bread and butter was spread in the great room. Then, at last, Hester went back to the cellar.

"Now, come," she said, taking up the baby, which had just weight enough to lie and let her know how light it was, and led the way.

Franks rose from the edge of the packing case, on which the body of Moxy still lay, with his mother yet kneeling beside it, and put his arm round his wife to raise her. She yielded, and he led her away after their hostess, the boys following hand in hand. But when they reached the cellar door, the mother gave a heartbroken cry, and, turning, ran and threw herself again beside her child.

"I can't! I can't!" she cried. "I can't leave my Moxy lyin' here all alone! He ain't used to it. He never once slept alone since he was born!"

"He is not alone," Hester reminded her. "—But we're not going to leave the darling here. We'll take him too, of course, and find him a good place to lie in."

The mother was satisfied, and the little procession passed through the dark passage and up the stair.

The boys looked pleased at sight of the comforts that waited them, but a little awed with the great lofty room. And over the face of Franks passed a gleam of joy mingled with gratitude. Much had not yet begun to be set to rights between him and the high government above. But the mother's heart was with the little boy lying alone in the cellar. Suddenly with a wild gesture she made for the door.

"Stop! stop, dear Mrs. Franks!" cried Hester. "Here, take the baby. Sarah and I are going immediately to bring him out of the cellar, and lay him where you can see him when you please."

Again she was satisfied. She took the baby and sat down beside her husband.

I have mentioned a room with a low ceiling under the great one. In this Hester had told Sarah to place a table covered with white. They would lay the body there as a sweet remembrance to the mother.

As they went, Hester asked, "But how can the Frankses have got into the place?"

"There is a back door to it," answered Sarah. "The first load of coals came in that way, but master Raymount wouldn't have it used. He didn't like a door to his house he never set eyes on, he said."

"But how could it have been open to let them in?" Hester wondered.

When they reached the cellar, she took the candle and went to look at the door. It was pushed closed, but not locked, and had no fastening upon it except the lock, in which was the key. She turned the key, took it out, and put it in her pocket.

Then they carried up the little body, washed it, dressed it in white, and laid it, as a symbol of a peace more profound, on the table. They lighted six candles, three at the head and three at the feet, that the mother might see the face of her child, and because light not darkness befits death. Then they went to fetch the mother.

She was washing the things they had used for supper. The boys were already in bed. Franks was staring into the fire. The poor fellow had not even looked at one for some time. Hester asked them to go and see where she had laid Moxy, and they went with her. The beauty of death's courtly state comforted them.

"But I can't leave him alone!" moaned the mother "—all night too!—he wouldn't like it! I know he won't wake up no more; only, you know, miss—"

"Yes, I know very well," replied Hester.

"I'm ready," Franks volunteered.

"No, no!" returned Hester. "You are worn out and must go to bed, both of you. I will stay with him tonight and see that no harm comes to him."

After some persuasion the mother consented, and in a little while the house was quiet. Hester threw a fur cloak around herself and sat down in the chair Sarah had placed for her beside the dead boy.

When she had sat there awhile, she began to think about the dead Christ. What would it have been like to sit beside that body all the night long! Oh, to have seen it come to life! To see it move and wake and rise with the infilling God! Every dead thing belonged to Christ, not to something called *death*! This dead body was his! It was dead as he had been dead, and not otherwise. There was no reason for the fear which had begun to steal over her. There was nothing dreadful here, any more than in sitting beside the cradle of a child yet unborn! In the name of Christ she would fear nothing! He had abolished death!

Thus thinking, she lay back in her chair, closed her eyes, and thanking God for having sent her relief through helping his children, fell fast asleep.

She started suddenly awake, seeming to have been roused by the opening of a door. The fringe of a departing dream lay yet upon her eyes: Was the door of the tomb in which she had lain so long burst from its hinges? Was the day of the great resurrection come? Swiftly she came to her senses, and saw plainly and remembered clearly. Yet could she be really awake? For in the wall opposite stood the form of a man!

She neither cried out nor fainted, but sat gazing. She was not even afraid, only dumbstruck with wonder. The man did not look fearful. A smile she seemed to have seen before broke gradually from his lips and spread over his face. The next moment he stepped from the wall and came toward her.

Then sight and memory came together: in that wall was a door, said to lead into the next house. For the first time she saw it open!

The man came nearer and nearer. It was Mr. Christopher! She rose and held out her hand.

"You are surprised to see me!" he greeted her, "—and well you may be. Am I in your house? And what does this all mean? I seem to recognize the sweet face on the table. I must have seen you and it together before! Yes! it is Moxy!"

"You are right, Mr. Christopher," she answered. "Dear little Moxy died of the smallpox in our cellar. He was just gone when I found them there."

"Is it wise of you to expose yourself so much to the infection?" he asked.

"We have our work to do; life or death is the care of him who sets the work. But tell me how you came to be here. It almost looked to my sleepy eyes as if an angel had melted his own door through the wall!"

"No, I came here in the simplest way in the world," he replied; "though I am no less surprised than you to find myself in your presence. I was called to see a patient. When I went to return as I came, I found the door by which I had entered locked. Then I remembered passing a door on the stair and went back to try it. It was bolted on the side to the stair. I withdrew the bolts, opened the door gently, and beheld the wonderful sight of you sitting beside the white body of Moxy. I think I must have unconsciously pushed the door against the wall, for somehow I made a noise with it and you woke."

Christopher stood silent. Hester could not ask him to sit down, but she must understand how he had gotten into the house. Where was his patient? In the next house? This puzzle certainly must be looked into! That door must be secured on their side. Their next midnight visitor might not be so welcome as this, whose heart burned to the same labor as her own!

"I never saw that door open before," she said, "and none of us knew where it led. We took it for granted it was into the next house, but the old lady was so cross—"

Here she checked herself; for if Mr. Christopher had just come from that house, he might be a friend of the old lady's.

"It goes into no lady's house, so far as I understand," said Christopher. "The stair leads to an attic—I should fancy over our heads here—much higher up though."

"Would you show me how you came in?" Hester asked.

"With pleasure," he answered, and taking one of the candles, led the way.

"I would not let the young woman leave her husband to show me out," he went on. "When I found myself a prisoner, I thought I would try this door before interrupting the sleep of a patient with smallpox. You seem to have it all around you here!"

Through the door so long mysterious Hester stepped on a narrow, steep stair. Christopher turned downward and trod softly. At the bottom he passed through a door admitting them to a small cellar, a mere recess. From there they came into that which the Frankses had occupied. Christopher went to the door Hester had locked and said, "There is where I came in. I suppose one of your people must have locked it."

"I locked it myself," replied Hester, and told him briefly the story of the evening.

"I see!" said Christopher. "We must have passed through just after you had taken them away."

"And now the question remains," said Hester, "—who can be in our house without our knowledge? The stair is plainly in our house."

"Beyond a doubt, but how strange it is you should know your own house so imperfectly! I fancy the young couple, having gotten into some difficulty, found entrance the same way the Frankses did; only they went farther and fared better!—to the top of the house, I mean. They've managed to make themselves pretty comfortable too! There is something peculiar about them—I can hardly say what."

"Could I not go up with you tomorrow and see them?" asked Hester.

"That would hardly do. I could be of no further use to them if they were to think I betrayed them. You have a perfect right to know what is going on in your house, but I would rather not be involved in the discovery. One thing is plain, you must either go to them or unlock the cellar door. You will like the young woman. She is a capable person— an excellent nurse. Shall I go out this way?"

"Will you come tomorrow? I am alone and cannot ask anybody to help me because of the smallpox. And I shall need some help for the funeral. You do not think me troublesome?"

"Not in the least. It is all part of my business. I will manage it for you."

"Come then, I will show you the way out. This is No. 18, Addison Square. You need not come in the cellar way next time."

"If I were you," advised Christopher, stopping at the foot of the kitchen stair, "I would leave the key in that cellar door. The poor young woman would be terrified to find they were prisoners."

She turned immediately and went back; he followed, replacing the key.

"Now let us lock up that door I came in by," suggested Christopher. This was soon done, and he left.

What a strange night it had been for Hester! For the time she had forgotten her own troubles! Ah, if she had been of one mind with Lord Gartley, where would those poor creatures be now? Woe for the wife whose husband has no regard to her deepest desires, her highest aspirations!—who loves her so that he would be the god of her idolatry, not the friend and helper of her heart, soul, and mind! Many of Hester's own thoughts were revealed to her that night by the side of the dead child. It became clear to her that she had been led astray, in part by the desire to rescue one to whom God had not sent her, in part by the pleasure of being loved, and in part by worldly ambition. Marriage might be the absorbing duty of some women, but was it necessarily hers? Certainly not with such a man. Might not the duties of some callings be incompatible with marriage? Did not the providence of the world ordain that not a few should go unmarried? Was a husband to take the place of Christ and order her life for her? Was man enough for woman? Did she not need God? It came to that! Was he or God to be her master? It grew clearer and clearer. There was, there could be, no relation of life over which the Lord was not supreme!

When the morning came and she heard Sarah stirring, she sent her to take her place, and went to get a little rest.

29 / The Attic Room

Hester was restless and could not sleep. She rose, went back to the room where Moxy lay, and sent Sarah to get breakfast ready. But an urgent desire came upon her to know the people who had come, like swallows, to tenant in the space overhead. She opened the door through which the doctor had come when she first saw him the night before. Gently she stole up the stair—steep, narrow, and straight—which ran the height of the two rooms between the walls. A long way up she came to another door and, peeping through a chink in it, saw that it opened to the small orchestra high in the end-wall of the great room. Probably, at one time, the stair had been an arrangement for the musicians.

Going higher yet, until she almost reached the roof, the stair brought her to a door. She knocked. No sound of approaching footsteps followed, but after some little delay it was opened by a young woman, with a finger on her lip and a scared look in her eye. She had expected to see the doctor, and was startled to see Hester, instead. There was little light where she stood, but Hester could not help feeling as if she had seen her somewhere before. She came out on the landing and shut the door behind her.

"He is very ill," she explained; "and he hears a strange voice even in his sleep. The voice is dreadful to him."

Her voice was not strange, and the moment she spoke it seemed to light up her face. With a pang she could scarcely account for, Hester recognized Amy Amber.

"Amy!" she exclaimed.

"Oh, Miss Raymount!" cried Amy joyfully, "is it indeed you? Have you come at last? I thought I was never to see you anymore!"

"Amy," said Hester, "I am bewildered. How do you come to be here? I don't understand."

"*He* brought me here."

"*Who* brought you here?"

"Why, miss!" exclaimed Amy, as if hearing the most unexpected of questions, "who else should it be?"

"I have not the slightest idea," returned Hester.

But the same instant a feeling strangely mingled of alarm, discomfort, indignation, and relief crossed her mind.

Through her palor Amy turned whiter still, and then turned a little away, like a person offended.

"There is but one, miss," she stated flatly. "Who should it be but him?"

"Speak his name," said Hester almost sternly. "This is no time for hide-and-seek. Tell me whom you mean."

"Are you angry with me?" faltered Amy. "Oh, Miss Raymount, I don't think I deserve it!"

"Speak out, child! Why should I be angry with you?"

"Do you know what it is?—Oh, I hardly know what I am saying! He is dying! He is dying!"

She sank on the floor and covered her face with her hands. Hester stood a moment and looked at her weeping, her heart filled with sad dismay. Then softly and quickly she opened the door of the room and went in.

Amy jumped to her feet, but too late to prevent her, and followed trembling, afraid to speak, but relieved to find that Hester moved so noiselessly.

It was a large room, but the roof came down to the floor nearly all around. It was lighted only with a skylight. In the farthest corner was a screen. Hester crept gently toward it, and Amy after her, not attempting to stop her. She came to the screen and looked behind it. There lay a young man in a troubled sleep, his face swollen and red and blotched with the smallpox; but through the disfigurement she recognized her brother. Her eyes filled with tears. She turned away and stole out again as softly as she came in. Amy had been looking at her anxiously, and when she saw the tenderness of her look, she gathered courage and followed her. Outside, Hester stopped, and Amy again closed the door.

"You *will* forgive him, won't you, miss?" she begged pitifully.

"What do you want me to forgive him for, Amy?" asked Hester, suppressing her tears.

"I don't know, miss. You seemed angry with him. I don't know what to make of it. Sometimes I feel certain it must have been his illness coming on that made him weak in his head and talk foolishness; and sometimes I wonder whether he has really been doing anything wrong."

"He must have been doing something wrong; otherwise, how should *you* be here, Amy?" said Hester with hasty judgment.

"He never told me, miss, or of course I would have done what I could to prevent it," answered Amy, bewildered. "We were so happy, miss, till then! And we've never had a moment's peace since! That's why we came here—to be where nobody would find us. I wonder how he came to know the place!"

"Then do *you* not know where you are, Amy?"

"No, miss, not in the least. I only know where to buy the things we need. He has not been out once since we came."

"You are in our house, Amy. What will my father say! How long have you—have you been—"

Something in her heart or her throat prevented Hester from finishing the sentence.

"How long have I been married to him, miss? You surely know that as well as I do, miss!"

"My poor Amy! Did he lead you to believe we knew about it?"

Amy gave a little cry.

"Alas!" Hester cried, "I fear he has been more wicked than we know! But, Amy, he has done something else very wrong."

Amy covered her face with her apron, through which Hester could see her soundless sobs.

"I have been doing what I could to find him," continued Hester, "and here he was close to me all the time! But it adds greatly to my misery to find you with him, Amy!"

"Indeed, miss, how was I to suspect he was not telling me the truth? I loved him too much for that! I told him I would not marry him unless he had his father's permission. And he pretended he had got it, and read me such a beautiful letter from his mother! Oh, miss, it breaks my heart to think of it!"

Suddenly a new fear came upon Hester: had he also deceived the poor girl with a pretended marriage? What her father would say to a marriage was hard to think; what he would say to a deception, she knew!

Such thoughts passed swiftly through her mind as she stood half turned from Amy, looking down the steep stair that sank like a precipice before her. She heard nothing, but Amy started and turned to the door. She was following her when Amy said, in a voice almost of terror, "Please, miss, do not let him see you until I have told him you are here."

"Certainly not," answered Hester, and drew back, "—if you think the sight of me would hurt him!"

"Thank you, miss; I am sure it would," whispered Amy. "He is frightened of you."

Frightened of me! Hester thought amazed, when the girl had gone in. *I thought he only disliked me. I wonder if he would have loved me a little if he had not been afraid of me! Perhaps I could have made him love me if I had tried. It is easier to arouse fear than love.*

It may be very well for a nature like Corney's to fear a father; fear does come in for some good where love is in short supply; but I doubt if fear of a sister can do any good.

Then it began to dawn upon Hester that there was in her a certain hardness of character different from unbending devotion to the right, which is necessary—belonging, actually, to her area of weakness—fear for self, which is of death, not of life. But she was one of those who, when they discover a thing in them that is wrong, take refuge in the immediate attempt to set it right—with the conviction that God is on their side to help them.

She went down to the house to get everything she could think of to make the place more comfortable. It would be a long time before the patient could be moved. Poor Amy! She was but the shadow of her former self, but a shadow very pretty and pleasant to look at. Hester's heart ached to think of such a bright, good, honest creature married to a man like her brother. She was sure Amy could have done nothing to be ashamed of. Where there was blame, it must all be Corney's.

It was with strangely mixed feelings of hope and dismay that, having carried everything she could for the time up to Amy, she gave herself to the comfort of her other guests.

Left alone in London, Corney had gone idly roaming around the house when another man would have been reading or doing something with his hands. Eventually he discovered the door in the wainscot of the low room and the room to which it led. Contriving often to meet Amy, he had grown rapidly more and more fond of her—became indeed as much in love with her as was possible to him. Without a notion of denying himself anything he desired and could possibly have, he determined she would be his, but from fear as well as the deceit so natural to his being, he avoided the direct way of winning her. He judged that the straight line would not be the shortest: his father would never consent to his marriage with a girl like Amy. Ultimately he contrived to persuade her to agree to a private marriage—contrived also to prevent her from communicating with her sister.

His desire to please her, and his passion for showing off, soon brought him into straits for money. He could not ask his father for any; he would have insisted on knowing how it was that he suddenly found his salary so insufficient. He went on and on, changing none of his habits, until he was positively without a shilling. Then he borrowed, and went on borrowing small sums from those about him, till he was ashamed to borrow more. The next thing was to *borrow* a trifle of what was passing through his hands in the bank. He was only borrowing, and from his own uncle. After all, his uncle had so much, and he was in such straits! It was the height of injustice! Of course he would replace it long before anyone knew!

Thus, by degrees, the poor weak creature, deluding himself with excuses, slipped into the consciousness of being a thief. There are some, I suspect, who fall into vice from being so satisfied with themselves that they think it impossible for them to ever do wrong.

He went on taking and taking, until, at last, he was obliged to confess to himself that there was no possibility of returning the money before the time came when his *borrowing* was discovered as out-and-out embezzlement. Then, in a kind of cold despair, he grabbed a large sum and left the bank an unconvicted felon. What story he told Amy, who was now his wife, I do not know; but once convinced of the necessity for concealment, she was as careful as he. He brought her to their refuge by the back way. She came and went only through the cellar, and knew no other entrance. When they found that, because Amy left the door unlocked when she went out to shop, others had taken refuge in the cellar, they dared not, for fear of attracting attention to themselves, warn them off the premises.

30 / Ministry in Addison Square ─────────────

The Frankses remained at rest until the funeral was over, and then Hester encouraged the father and sons to go out and follow their calling while she and the mother did what could be done for the ailing baby, who could not linger long behind Moxy. And the very first day, though they went out with heavy hearts and could hardly have played with much spirit, they brought home more money than any day for weeks before.

The same day Lord Gartley called, but was informed by Sarah, who opened the door just a crack, that the smallpox was in the house and that she could admit no one but the doctor. She said that her young mistress was perfectly well, but was in attendance upon the sick and could and would see nobody. So his lordship was compelled to go without seeing her, not without a haunting doubt that she did not *want* to see him.

The major also made his appearance that day. Sarah gave him the same answer, adding by her mistress's directions that in the meantime there was no occasion to make further inquiry about Mr. Cornelius. It was all—as Sarah put it—explained, and her mistress would write to him.

But what was Hester to tell her father and mother? Until she knew with certainty that Amy and Cornelius were married, she shrank from mentioning Amy; and for the present it was impossible to find out anything from Cornelius. She decided to simply write that she had found him, but very ill; that she would take the best care of him she could, and as soon as he was able to be moved, she would bring him home.

The big room was, for the time, given over to the Frankses. The wife kept everything tidy, and they managed things their own way. Hester inquired about their needs now and then, to be sure they had everything necessary, but left them to provide for themselves.

She did her best to help Amy without letting her brother suspect her presence, and gradually she made the room more comfortable for them. Corney had indeed taken a good many things from the house, but had been careful not to take anything Sarah would miss.

He was covered with the terrible infection, and if he survived, which often seemed doubtful, would probably be much changed in appearance, for Amy could not keep his hands from his face. In small trifles is the lack of self-control manifested, and its consequences are sometimes grievous.

Cornelius did, however, at last begin to recover, but it was long before he could be treated as anything but a child—he was so feeble and unreasonable. The first time he saw and knew Hester, he closed his eyes and turned his head away as if he would have no more of such an apparition. She left, but watched to see him, in his own sly way, looking through half-closed lids to know whether she was gone. When he saw Amy where Hester had stood, his face beamed. "Amy," he said, "come here." When she came, he took her hand and laid it on his cheek, little knowing what a disfigured cheek it was.

Thank God! thought Hester. She had never seen him look so loving toward anyone, despite his disfigurement.

She took care not to show herself again until he was more accustomed to the idea of her presence.

The more she saw of Amy the better she liked her. She treated her patient with good sense, and was so carefully obedient to Hester and the doctor that she rose every day in Hester's opinion, at the same time finding an even deeper place in her heart.

His lordship wrote, making apology for anything he had said, from anxiety about one he loved. He would gladly talk the whole matter over with her as soon as she would allow him to. For his part, he had no doubt that her good sense would eventually convince her of the reasonableness of his ideas for her. As soon as she was able, and judged it safe to admit a visitor, his aunt would be happy to call upon her. For the present, as he knew she would not admit him, he would content himself with frequent and most anxious inquiries after her, reserving discussion for a happier, and, he hoped, not very distant time.

Hester smiled curiously at the prospect of a call from Miss Vavasor. Was she actually going to plead her nephew's cause?

As her brother grew better and things became a little easier, the thought of Lord Gartley came more often, with something of the old feeling for the man himself, but mingled with sadness and a strange pity. She would never have been able to do anything for him! If God cannot save a man by all his good gifts, a woman's giving of herself as a slave to his lower nature can only make him all the more unredeemable. But the withholding of herself *may* do something—may at least, as the years go on, wake in him some sense of what a fool he had been. The man who would go to the dogs for lack of the woman he fancies will go to the dogs when he has her too—and may possibly drag her to the dogs with him. Hester at last began to see something of this. She recalled how she had never once gained from him a worthwhile reply to anything she had said; she had, in her foolishness, supplied from her own imagination the defective echoes of his response! And now that her spirit was awakened toward the truer nature of things, it was Cornelius, no longer Vavasor, who occupied the thoughts of her ministering heart.

But his poor mother! Would she even recognize him—so terribly scarred and changed? He was young, and might in time grow more like his old self, but for now he was anything but pleasant to look at. Corney had always been one who took pleasure in his own looks, regarding himself as superior on most grounds, and particularly on that of good looks. But now he had to admit that he was anything but handsome. It was a pain that in itself could do little to cast out the evil spirit that possessed him; but it was something that the evil spirit, while it remained in him, should be deprived of one source of its nourishment. It was a good thing that from any cause, the transgressor should find his ways hard. After his first look at himself, he threw the mirror from him and burst into tears, which he did not even try to conceal.

From that time he was more dejected and less peevish. Still Hester found it difficult to bear with his remaining peevishness and bad temper, knowing what he had made of himself, and that he knew she must know it. But at such hard moments she had the good sense to leave him to the soothing ministrations of his wife. Amy never set herself against him. First of all she would show him that she understood what was troubling him, then would say something sympathetic or coaxing, and always had her way with him. She had the great advantage that he had not once quarrelled with her.

That gave a ground of hope for her influence with him that his sister had long lost. Amy had less trouble from selfishness than most people. Hester, on the other hand, had far more trouble than Amy in conquering her self-assertiveness. In Hester it was, no doubt, associated with a loftier nature, and the harder victory would have its greater reward, but until finally conquered it would continue to hinder her walk in the true way. So Hester learned from the sweetness of Amy, as Amy from the unbending principles of Hester.

She at last made up her mind that she would take Cornelius home without giving her father the opportunity of saying he should not come. She would presume that he must go home after such an illness. The result she would let take care of itself, even though the first meeting between father and son could in no case be a happy one.

With gentle watchfulness she regarded Amy, and was more and more satisfied that she could have had no hand in the wrongdoing. But she could not believe that had Amy known before she married him what kind of person Cornelius was, she would have given herself to him. It hardly occurred to her how nearly the man she had once accepted stood on the same level of manhood. But Amy was the wife of Cornelius, and that made an eternal difference. Her duty was as plain as Hester's—and the same—to do the best for him!

When he was able to be moved, Hester brought them into the house, and placed them in a comfortable room. She then moved the Frankses into the room they had left, giving it over to them, for a time at least. With their own entrance through the cellar, they would be able to live there as they wished. Hester's only stipulation was that they were to let her know if they found themselves in any difficulty. And now, for the first time in her life, Hester wished she had some financial resources of her own so she might act with freedom in the ministry the Lord had given her.

31 / Miss Vavasor

About three weeks after Lord Gartley's call, during which he had left a good many of his calling cards in Addison Square, Hester received the following letter from Miss Vavasor:

My dear Miss Raymount:

I am very anxious to see you, but fear it is hardly safe to call on you yet. I do not want to willingly be the bearer of infection into my own circle, but I must communicate with you somehow, for your own sake as well as Gartley's, who is pining away for lack of the sunlight of your eyes. I will leave the matter entirely in your judgment. If you tell me you consider yourself out of quarantine, I will come to you at once; if you do not, please propose something, for we must meet.

Hester pondered the matter well before returning an answer. She replied that it was impossible to say there was no danger; for her brother, who had been ill, was still in the house, too weak for the journey to Yrndale. She would rather suggest that they meet in some quiet corner of one of the parks. She need hardly add that she would take every precaution against carrying infection.

The proposal proved acceptable to Miss Vavasor. She wrote suggesting a time and place that worked out well for both of them.

Hester appeared on foot. Miss Vavasor, who had remained seated in her carriage, got down as soon as she saw her, and advanced to meet her with a smile: she was perfect in surface hospitality.

"How long is it now," she began, "since you last saw Gartley?"

"Three weeks or a month," replied Hester.

"I am sadly afraid you cannot be much of a lover, not to have seen him for so long and still look so contented," smiled Miss Vavasor, with gently implied reproach.

"When one has one's work to do—" Hester began.

"Ah, yes!" returned Miss Vavasor, not waiting for the rest of the sentence. "I understand you have some peculiar ideas about work. That kind of thing is spreading very much in our circle, too. I know many ladies who visit the poor. No one can tell where such things will end."

"No," Hester replied evenly. "Nothing has ever stopped yet. We know nothing about the ends of things—only the beginnings."

"You and Gartley had a small misunderstanding, he tells me, the last time you met," said Miss Vavasor, returning to her original subject after a short pause.

"I think not," answered Hester; "at least I think I understood him very well."

"My dear Miss Raymount, you must not be offended with me. I am an old woman, and have had to soothe over differences that have divided many couples. I am not boasting when I say I have had considerable experience in that sort of thing."

"I do not doubt it," said Hester. "What I do doubt is that you have had any experience of the sort necessary to set things right between Lord Gartley and me. The fact is, for I will be perfectly open with you, that I saw then—for the first time plainly—that to marry him would be to lose my liberty."

"Not more than every woman does who marries, my dear."

"But he would require me to turn away from obeying a higher calling even than the natural calling of a woman to marriage."

"I am not aware of any higher calling."

"I am. God has given me gifts to use for my fellowman, and use them I must until he, not man, stops me. That is my calling."

"But you know that of necessity a woman must give up many things when she accepts the position of a wife, and possibly the duties of a mother."

"I would heartily acknowledge the natural claims upon a wife or mother."

"But one of the duties of a wife is the claim society has upon her. Gartley thought you understood."

"I thought I had done and said more than was necessary to make Gartley understand my ideas of what was required of me in life, and I thought he would be what help to me he could. Now I find instead that he never believed I meant what I said, but all the time intended to put a stop to the aspiration of my life—ministry to the poor—the moment he had it in his power to do so."

"Ah, my dear young lady, you do not know what love is!" sighed Miss Vavasor, as if *she* knew what love was. "A woman really in love," she went on, "is ready to give up everything, yes, my dear, *everything*, for the man she loves. She who is not equal to that does not know what love is."

"Suppose he should prove unworthy of her?"

"That would be nothing, positively nothing. If she had once learned to love him, she would see no fault in him."

"*Whatever* faults he might have?"

"Whatever faults: love has no second thoughts. A woman who loves gives herself to her husband to be molded by him."

"I fear that is the way men think of us," said Hester sadly. "With all my heart I say a woman ought to be ready to die for the man she loves: she cannot really love him if she would not. But that she should agree with all his thoughts, feelings, and judgments, even those that she would despise in others, is to me something no true woman could do who had not first lost her reason."

I see, Miss Vavasor concluded inwardly; *she is one of the strong-minded who think themselves superior to any man. Gartley will be well rid of her—that is my conviction! I think I have done nearly all he could require of me.*

"I tell you honestly," continued Hester, "I love Lord Gartley so much that I would gladly yield my life to do him any worthy good. Of course I would do that to redeem any human creature from the misery of living without God. Perhaps I would even marry Lord Gartley if only I knew that he would not try to prevent me from being the woman I ought to be and have to be. But I could never marry one who opposed my being what I ought to be, what I desire, determine, and with God's help will be! Certainly a wife must love her husband grandly—passionately. But there is one to be loved immeasurably more grandly, even *passionately*—he whose love creates all other loves."

Heavens! exclaimed Miss Vavasor to herself, *what an extravagant young woman! She won't do for us!*

But what she said to Hester was, "Don't you think, my dear, all that sounds a little—just a little extravagant? You know as well as I do that that kind of thinking is out-of-date—does not belong to today's world. Nothing will ever bring in that way of life again. It is all very well to go to church, but really it seems to me that such extravagant notions about religion must have a great deal to do with the present sad state of affairs."

"What do you take God for?" asked Hester. "What did Jesus Christ mean when he said that whoever loved anyone else more than him was not worthy of him? Or do you confess the ideas of 'religion,' as you call it, true—but then say they are of no consequence? If you do not care about what God wants of you, I can simply say that I care about nothing else; and if ever I should change, I hope he will soon teach me better—no matter what I have to go through to learn. I desire not to care a straw about anything he does not care about."

"It is very clear to me," said Miss Vavasor, "that you do not love my nephew as he deserves to be loved. You have very different ideas from such as were taught in my girlhood concerning the duties of wives. A woman, I used to be told, was to fashion herself for her husband; fit her life to his life, her thoughts to his thoughts, her tastes to his tastes."

The idea would have seemed absurd, to anyone really knowing the two, of a woman like Hester fitting herself into the mold of a man like Lord Gartley. For what would be done with the quantity of her that would be left after his lordship's small mold was filled! Instead of walking on together in simple equality, in mutual honor and devotion, each helping the other to be better still, the ludicrous notion that Miss Vavasor held would have the woman—large and noble though she may be—come cowering after her husband—spiritual pigmy though he might be—as if he were the god of her life.

"You are right," Hester agreed with a nod. "I do not love Lord Gartley sufficiently for that. Thank you, Miss Vavasor. You have helped me come to the thorough conviction that there could never have been any real union between us. Can a woman truly love a man who does not care whether she ever grows as God intended? *He* would have been quite content that I should remain forever the poor creature I am. He would not have sought to raise me above myself. And I could never fully love a man who could be so satisfied with the imperfect . . . I wish you a good morning, Miss Vavasor."

She held out her hand. Miss Vavasor drew herself up and looked with cold annihilation into her eyes. The warm blood rose from Hester's heart to her brain, but she quietly returned her gaze. It seemed minutes where only seconds passed. Hester smiled at last and said, "I am glad you are not going to be my aunt, Miss Vavasor. I am afraid I would cause you nothing but grief."

"Thank goodness, no!" cried Miss Vavasor, with a slightly hysterical laugh. Unused to having such a strong, full, pure look fixed fearlessly upon her without defiance, it had unnerved her. In spite of her educated self-command, she felt cowed before the majesty of Hester. She now had to go back to her nephew and confess that she had utterly failed where she had expected an easy victory. She had to tell him that his lady was the most peculiar, most unreasonable young woman she had ever had to deal with, and that she was not only unsuited to him, but quite unworthy of him.

She turned and walked away, attempting a show of dignity but instead displaying haughtiness—an adornment only the possessor does not recognize as counterfeit. Then Hester turned and walked in the opposite direction, feeling that one part of her life had drawn to a close.

She did not know that she was constantly attended at some distance by a tall, portly gentleman of ruddy complexion and military bearing. He had seen her interview with Miss Vavasor and had beheld with delight the unmistakable signs of serious difference that culminated in their parting.

Since coming to London with Hester he had, as much as possible, kept guard over her, and had known a good deal more of her whereabouts than she was aware of—all with completely unselfish devotion. He was willing to follow at a distance, ready to intervene at any moment when intervention may have proved desirable. She had let him know that she had found her brother, that he was very ill, and that she was helping to nurse him; but she had not yet asked his help. As if in obedience to orders, then, he did not even now call on her. But the next day he found a summons waiting for him at his club.

Thinking it better to prepare him for what she was about to ask of him, Hester mentioned in her note that in a day or two she was going to Yrndale with her brother and his wife.

"Marriage and embezzlement!" exclaimed the major when he read it. "This complicates matters. Poor devil! If he were not such a confounded ape, I should pity him! But the smallpox and a wife may perhaps do something for him!"

When he reached the house Hester received him warmly, and at once asked him to go with them. He agreed immediately, but thought she had better not say he was coming, as under the circumstances he would not receive a proper welcome.

32 / Mr. Christopher

On the last Sunday evening before she was to leave for Yrndale, Hester had gone to see a poor woman in a house she had not been in before. Walking up the dirty, dismal stair, she heard moans coming from behind a slightly open door. Peeking in she saw a poor old woman, yellow and wrinkled, lying on a bed, apparently at the point of death. A man knelt by her bedside, his arm under the pillow to hold her head higher, his other hand clasping hers.

"The darkness! the darkness!" moaned the woman.

"Are you lonely?" asked the man with quiet sympathy.

"All, all alone," sighed the woman.

"I can do nothing for you. I can only love you."

"Yes, yes," said the woman hopelessly.

"You are slipping away from me, but my Master is stronger than I am and can help you yet. He is not far from you, though you can't see him. He loves you too, and only wants you to ask him to help you. He can cure death as easy as any other disease."

No reply came for a moment. Then she cried out from the depths of her being, "Oh, Christ, save me!"

Suddenly Hester was seized with an impulse toward song. The words which came to her mouth were the same words, over and over again, which the poor dying woman had just spoken: "Oh, Christ, save me!"

They seemed to rise from some well deep within her, yet not of her own making. She felt as if she were in the immediate presence of Christ, pleading with him for the consolation and strength his poor dying creature so sorely needed.

The holy possession lasted but a minute or so and left her without further words. She turned away and continued up the stairs. The good doctor's tear-filled eyes followed her as she left the room.

"The angels! the angels! I'm going now!" the woman whispered feebly.

"The angel was praying to Christ for you," said Christopher. "Oh, Father, save our dying sister."

"Oh, Christ, save me!" she murmured again, and they were her last words.

Christopher laid the body gently back on the pillow. A sigh of relief passed from his lips and he went from the room to give notice of the death. He must go on to help the living!

Such may seem nothing but empty religious sentiment to the man of this world. But when the inevitable Death has him by the throat, when he lies like that poor woman, lonely in the shadow, though his room be crowded with friends and possessions, whatever his theories about the afterlife, it may be an awful hour in which no one but Christ will be able to comfort him.

Hester's heart was full when she found the woman she went to see. She spoke of Christ, the friend of men, who came to save everyone by giving him back to God, as one gives back to a mother the stray child who has run from her to escape obeying her. The woman listened intently. Then Hester sang to her for a while, and took her leave.

Hester was walking home when, passing through a court on her way, she heard the voice of a man, which she again recognized as that of Mr. Christopher. Glancing about her she discovered that it came from a room half under ground. She went to the door. A little crowd of dirty children was making noise around it, and she could not hear all of what was going on, but she did hear enough to tell that the doctor was speaking to a small group of the poor, pleading with his fellows not to sink in misery but to live and rejoice, even in their present state. She went in.

The room had a low ceiling and though the crowd was not large, the air was stifling. The doctor stood at the far end. Some of his congregation were decently dressed, but most wore their ordinary clothes. Only a handful seemed to be listening to him. That the speaker was in earnest there could be no doubt. His eyes were glowing, his face was gleaming with a light of its own, and his gestures were eloquent. The whole rough appearance of the man was elevated into dignity. Simplicity and forgetfulness of himself were manifest in both manner and speech, and he kept saying the simplest things to them about God's desire to love them. He told them that they were like orphan children, hungry in the street, raking the gutter for what they could get, while behind them stood a grand, beautiful house where their father lived, waiting for any one of them to turn and run in to him.

"He is certainly sending out messengers to tell them to come in," he went on. "But they mostly laugh at them. 'It's not likely,' they say, 'a man like that would trouble his head about such as us, even if we were his children!' And are some of you thinking inside now, 'We wouldn't do that! We would be only too glad to believe it'? But there's the rub. These children who won't go into the house are just like you: they won't do anything about it. Why, here I am, sent to you with this very message, and you fancy I am only talking without meaning. I am one of those who have been in the house and have found my father to be oh so grand! And I have come out again to tell you that if you go in, you will have the same kindness that I have had. All the servants of the house will rejoice over you with music and dancing—so glad that you have come home. But you will not take the trouble to go.

"There are certain things required of you when you go," he went on. "Perhaps you are too lazy or dirty in your habits to want to do such things. I have known some to refuse to scrape their shoes when they went in, and then complain loudly that they were refused admittance. A fine house it would be if they were allowed to run in and out as they pleased! In a few months the grand beautiful house would be as wretched and dirty as the houses they live in now. Those are the people that keep grumbling about not being rich. They want to loaf about and drink and be a nuisance to everybody, doing anything that takes their fancy. But their father is not one to let such disagreeable children work whatever mischief they like. He is a better father than that. And the day is coming when, if he can't get them to mind him any other way, he will put them where they will be ten times more miserable than ever they were at the worst time of their lives, and make them mind. Out of the same door whence came the messengers to ask them in, he will send dogs and bears and lions and tigers and wild cats out upon them.

"Now, some of you will say, 'But that's not the sort of thing we care about. We know you're just dressing up religion in your little fable about the beautiful house, and we don't need it.' I know this is not the kind of thing some of you care for. I know the kind of thing you *do* care for—low, dirty things. You are like a child that prefers mud and the gutter to all the beautiful toys in a grand shop. But though these things are not the things you want, they are the things you need. And the time will come when you will say, 'Ah, what a fool I was not to look at the precious things and take them when they were offered me!' "

After about twenty minutes he finished, led them in a simple hymn, in which Hester joined in, prayed for two or three minutes, and then sent them away. Being near the door, Hester went out with the first ones, and walked home, filled with the joy of such preaching. She did not yet know that Christopher taught them there every Sunday, and that this sermon, if such it could be called, was but one wave in the flow of a great river.

She was on the point of turning into the square when she heard a quick footstep behind her, and was presently overtaken by Mr. Christopher.

"I was so glad to see you come in!" he said. "It made me able to speak all the better, for I was then sure of someone agreeing with what I said. It is not easy to go on when you doubt whether anyone is listening."

"I do not see," said Hester, "how anyone could help understanding what you were saying."

"Ah!" he returned, "the one incomprehensible thing is ignorance. To understand why another does not understand seems to me beyond the power of our humanity. I have been trying now for a good many months to teach these people, but I am not sure a single thought has passed from my mind to theirs. I sometimes wonder if I am just beating the air. But I must tell you how your singing comforted the poor woman at whose door you stopped this afternoon. I saw it in her face. She thought it was the angels. And it was one angel, for did not God send you? She died just a minute or two later."

They walked some distance before either spoke again.

"I was surprised," said Hester at length, "to find you taking the clergyman's part as well as the doctor's. Your profession has to do with the bodies of men, but you seem to care more for their souls."

"I began to study medicine so I would have a good, ostensible reason for going about among the poor. It was not primarily from the desire to alleviate their sufferings, but in the hope of starting them on the way toward victory over all evil. I saw that the man who brought them physical help had a chance with them that no clergyman ever would."

"How well I understand you!" Hester exclaimed with enthusiasm. "But would you mind telling me how you first began? I started thinking of these things because I saw how miserable so many people were, and longed to do something to make life better for them."

"That was not quite the way with me," replied Christopher. "In the first place, you may suppose I could not have followed my wishes if I did not have money. I did have a good deal—left me by my grandfather. My father died when I was a child, I am glad to say."

"Glad to say!" Hester's voice revealed her shock.

"Yes. If he had lived, he may have followed in my grandfather's footsteps. Not that my grandfather was considered a bad man. On the contrary, he stood high in the world's opinion. When he died and left me his money it was necessary that I look into his business affairs, for it was my mother's wish that I should follow the same. In the course of my investigation I came across things which I considered to be dishonest in the way the business had been run. And where there had been wrong, I felt there must be atonement, restitution. I could not look on the money that had been left me as mine, for part of it at least, I cannot say how much, ought not to be mine at all.

"Then the truth dawned on me and I saw that my business in life must be to send the money out again into the channels of right. I could claim a workman's wages for that. The history of the business went so far back that it would have been impossible to return the sums to the same people from whom they had been taken. Therefore something else, and that a large something, must be done. Little by little it grew clearer to me that the greatest good I could do lay in doing what Christ himself did, giving the energy of my life to delivering men out of their lonely self-centeredness into the liberty of becoming sons of God. So I continued to study medicine and then, by the doctor's art, have gradually learned how God would have me spend the money upon humanity itself, repaying to mankind what had been wrongfully taken from its individuals much earlier.

"That is my story. I now try to work steadily, without haste, and have this very day gotten a new idea that may have some true possibilities in it."

"Will you tell me what it is?" asked Hester.

"I don't like talking about things before they are begun," answered Christopher.

"I know what I would do if I had money!" said Hester.

"You have given me the right to ask what—though perhaps not the right to an answer."

"I would have a house of refuge to which anyone might run for shelter or rest or warmth or food or medicine or whatever he needed. It would have no society or subscription or committee, but would be my own to use as God enabled me. It would be a refuge for the needy, those out of work, to the child with a cut finger. I would not take in drunkards or ruined speculators—at least not before they were very miserable indeed. The suffering of such is the only desirable consequence of their doing, and to save them from it would be to take away their last chance."

"It is a lovely idea," said Christopher heartily. "One of my hopes is to build a small hospital for children in some lovely place, near some sad, ugly one. But I am in no hurry. If it is to be, God will see to it. Small beginnings with slow growings have time to root themselves thoroughly. God's beginnings are always imperceptible, whether in the region of soul or of matter. How the devil would have laughed at the idea of a society or an organization for saving the world. But when he saw *one* man take it in hand, one who was in no haste even to do that, one who would only do the will of God with all his heart and soul, and cared for nothing else, then, indeed, he might tremble for his kingdom!

"It is the individual Christians forming the church by their obedient individuality that have done all the good since men for the love of Christ began to gather together. No organization, not even a religious organization, can ever accomplish anything. It is individual love alone that can combine into a larger flame. There is no true power but that which has individual roots. Neither custom nor habit nor law nor foundation is a root. The real roots are individual conscience that hates evil, individual faith that loves and obeys God, individual heart with its kiss of charity."

"I think I understand you. I am sure I do in part, at least," Hester added quietly.

They had unconsciously walked twice around the square as they talked, and had now a third time reached the house. He went in with her and saw his patient, then went home to an evening with his New Testament, greatly refreshed from his talk with one who shared his convictions.

33 / Preparations_____

Second causes are God's just as much as first. We are always disbelieving in him because things do not go as we intend and desire them to go. We forget that God has larger ends for us than we can see; so his plans do not fit ours. If God were to always answer our prayers as we want them answered, he would not be God our Savior, but the ministering genius of our destruction.

Since her homecoming, Hester had not yet been to see Miss Dasomma because of the smallpox danger. But now she thought she might visit her friend. After telling her of herself and Lord Gartley, Hester told her teacher that her brother Cornelius had been behaving very badly, and had married a young woman without letting them know. Her father and mother were yet unaware of the fact and she dreaded having to tell them of it. He had been very ill with smallpox and she was now planning to take them home. But she did not know what to do with his wife until after she had broken the matter to them since she knew her father would be very angry.

"Could I see the young lady?" asked Miss Dasomma thoughtfully.

"Surely; any time," replied Hester, "now that Corney is so much better."

Miss Dasomma called, and was so charmed with Amy that she suggested to Hester that Amy should stay with her.

Now came the painful necessity of breaking to the young wife that her husband had deceived her, and that, as a result, she must be parted from him for a while.

Had Cornelius not been ill and helpless, he would probably have refused to go home. But he did not venture a word of opposition to Hester's determination. Notwithstanding his idiotic pretense of superiority, he had a kind of thorough confidence in Hester. In his sickness something of the old childish feeling about her as a refuge from evil had returned to him, and he was now nearly ready to do whatever she pleased, trusting her to get him out of the scrape he was in.

"But now tell me, on your word of honor," she said to him that same night when they were alone talking, "are you really and truly married to Amy?"

She was delighted to see him blaze up in anger.

"Hester, you insult us both!" he raged with indignation.

179

"No, Cornelius," returned Hester calmly, "I have a right to distrust you because of all that has happened. But I do not distrust Amy in any way."

At this Cornelius swore a solemn oath that Amy was as much his lawful wife as he knew how to make her.

"Then what is to be done with her when you go home? You cannot expect that she will be welcomed. I have not dared tell them of your marriage—only of your illness."

"I don't know. How should *I* know!" answered Cornelius with a return of his old manner. "I thought you would manage it for me! This cursed illness—"

"Cornelius!" said Hester, "this illness is the greatest kindness God could have shown you."

"Well, we won't argue about that!—Sis, you must get me out of this scrape!"

Hester's heart swelled at the sound of the old loving nursery word. She turned to him and kissed him.

"I will do what I honestly can, Cornelius," she promised.

"All right!" replied Corney. "What do you want me to do?"

"Before anything else, Amy must be told what you have done. She will have to know all about it someday, but it ought to come from you, not me. You will never be fit for honest company until you have told your wife how you have deceived both her and your family."

"Then I'm not going! I'd rather stay here and starve if they won't receive my wife!"

"After what you have done, it is hardly any wonder that our father should be angry with you. It is possible he may refuse even to see you."

Hester thought she must not let him fancy that things would now go back into the old grooves—that his crime would become a thing of no consequence and pass by, ignored and forgotten. Evil cannot be destroyed without repentance.

He was silent as one who had nothing to answer.

"So now," Hester continued, "will you, or must I, tell Amy that she cannot go home with us, and why?"

He thought for a moment.

"I will," he said.

Hester left and sent Amy to him. In a few minutes she returned. She had been weeping, but now looked quite in control of herself.

"Please, miss—"she said—but Hester interrupted her.

"You must not call me *miss*, Amy," she corrected. "You must call me *Hester*. Am I not your sister?"

A gleam of joy shone from the girl's eyes, like the sun through red clouds.

"Then you have forgiven me!" she cried.

"No, Amy. I had nothing to forgive you of. You may have been foolish, but everybody can't always be wise. And now we must have time to set things straighter without doing more mischief, and you mustn't mind staying a little while with Miss Dasomma."

"You won't be too hard on him when he hasn't me to comfort him, will you, Hester?" and as she called her sister by her name, she blushed.

"I will think of my new sister who loves him," replied Hester. "But I love him too, Amy. Oh, Amy! you must be very careful over him. You must help him to become good, for that is the highest duty of everyone toward a neighbor, particularly of a wife toward a husband."

In the meantime things had been very gloomy at Yrndale. Mrs. Raymount was better in health but hardly more cheerful. She could not get over the sadness of what her boy had become. But the thing that most oppressed her was to see the heart of his father so turned from the youth. Cornelius had not been pleasant since he first approached manhood. But she had always looked to the time when growing sense would prevail; and now this was the outcome of her hopes and prayers for him! Her husband went about sullen and listless. He wrote no more. How could one thus disgraced in his family presume to teach the world anything? How could he any longer hold his head up? Cornelius's very being cast doubt on all he had ever said or done!

He had been proud of his children. But now all was falling into ruin around him. For hours he would sit with his hands in his pockets, scarcely daring to think, because the thoughts that came crowding out the moment the smallest chink was opened in their cage were so miserable. He had become short, I do not say rough, in his speech to his wife. He would break into sudden angry complaints against Hester for not coming home. The sight of the children was a pain to him. Though he had been told nothing of the cause of his parents' misery, Mark had sympathy and insight enough to perceive that something was badly amiss. He would sometimes stand and gaze at his father, but the solemn, far-off, starry look of the boy's eyes never seemed to disturb him. He loved his father as few boys love, and yet had a certain dread of him and discomfort in his presence, which he could not have explained, and which would vanish at once when he spoke to him.

He had never quite recovered from the effects of his near drowning. He had grown thinner and his food did not seem to nourish him. His being seemed slowly slipping away from its hold on the world. He was full of dreams and fancies, all of the higher order of things where love is the law. He spent many happy hours alone, seeming to the ordinary eye to be doing nothing, because his doing was with the unseen. When such as Mark die, we may well imagine them wanted for a special work in the world to which they go. Some of us may one day be ashamed of our outcry after our dead when we discover why they were called.

Mark seldom talked about his brother. Before he went away he had begun to shrink from him a little, as with some instinct of an inward separation. He would stand a little way off and look at him as if he were a stranger in whom he was interested, and as if he himself were trying to determine what attitude to assume toward him. When he heard that he was seriously ill, the tears came into his eyes, but he did not speak.

The mother saw it and thought the boy must be looking toward a region to which she herself had been longing. The way her husband took their grief made them no more a family, just a mere household. He brooded alone and said nothing. They did not share sorrow as they had shared joy.

At last came a letter from Hester saying that in two days she hoped to start with Corney to bring him home. The mother read the letter, and with a faded gleam of joy on her countenance, passed it to her husband. He took it, glanced at it, threw it from him, rose, and left the room. For an hour his wife heard him pacing up and down his study; then he took his hat and stick and went out. What he might have resolved to do had Corney been returning in good health, I do not know—possibly kick him out of the house for his impudence in daring to show his face there. But even this wrathful father could hardly turn from his sickly child— even if he was the greatest scoundrel under the sun. But that still could not make him acknowledge him! Swine were the natural companions of the prodigal, and the sooner he was with them the better! Truly the heart of the father had turned from his son. The Messiah came to turn the hearts of the fathers to their children. Strange it should have ever needed doing! But it needs doing still.

Gerald Raymount went walking through the pine woods on his hills, but there was now little satisfaction to be found in his land. He had taken honesty as a matter of course in his family. Were they not *his* children? Yet he had never known anything of what was going on in the mind of his son. He had never asked himself if his boy loved the truth. And now he was astonished to find *his* boy no better than the common sort of human animal!

But often an act of open disgrace is the quickest road toward repentance. Few seem to understand that the true goal is not to keep their children from doing what is wrong, but to train them to be incapable of doing wrong. While one is capable of doing wrong, he is no nearer right than if that wrong were actually done—and not so near the right as if the wrong *were* done and repented of. Some minds are never roused to the true nature of their selfishness until they have done some monstrous wrong. Happy he will be if he then repents and begins to turn from the evil itself! This Cornelius had not yet begun to do, but his illness made it all the more likely that when the notion of repentence did at last present itself to his consciousness, he would be able to look it in the face.

The father came back from his lonely walk in no better frame of mind—just as determined that his son should no more be treated as a son. He could not refuse him shelter in his house for a time, but it would be only a concession, not from any right of sonship!

The heart of the mother, however, was longing after her boy, like a hen whose chick has run from under her wing and come to grief. He had sinned, he had suffered, and was in disgrace. The very things that made his father feel he could not speak to him again worked in the deeper nature of the mother in the opposite direction. Was he unlovely?—she must love him the more! Was he selfish and repellent?—she must get the nearer to him! Everything was reason to her for love and more love. She would clasp him so close that evil could not touch him! Satan himself could not get at him with her whole mother-being folded round him! Now that sickness and shame had cast down his proud spirit, love would have room to enter and minister! The good of all evil is to make a way for love, which is essential good. Therefore evil exists, and will exist, until love destroys and casts it out.

34 / The Return

The day finally came. The invalid was carefully wrapped up for the journey. Miss Dasomma and Amy saw Hester, Corney, and the major off at the station and then returned to the teacher's home. When the three travelers reached the station, the major got on the box of the carriage Hester's mother had sent to meet them. And so Hester bore her lost sheep home—in little triumph and much anxiety. When they arrived no one was waiting for them. The hall was not lighted and the door was locked. The major rang the bell and, when the door was opened, carried the youth in his arms into the dining room, which also appeared dark and friendless. Hester hurried from room to room and returned to the major in a moment.

"I was sure of it," she whispered to him. "There is a glorious fire in his room and everything is ready for him. The house is my father, but the room is my mother."

The major carried him easily up the stair—he had become so thin and light. The moment they were past the door of her room, out came the mother into the corridor, gliding pale and noiselessly after them. Hester looked around and saw her, but her mother laid a finger on her lips, and continued to follow without a word. When they were in Corney's room, she came to the door, looked in, and watched them, but did not enter. Cornelius did not open his eyes. The major laid him down on the sofa near the fire. The moment she saw his face a fresh rush from the inexhaustible fountain of motherlove came upon her. Her whole wounded heart seemed to go out to him in one trembling sigh as she turned to go back to the room where her husband sat gazing hopelessly at the fire. She had only enough strength to reach the side of her bed where she fell in a faint. He jumped up with a sting of self-accusation, thinking that the promise he had exacted from her to utter no word of welcome that night must have killed her.

He lifted her onto the bed and in a little while her eyelids began to tremble. "My baby!" she murmured, and the tears began to flow.

"Thank God!" he said as she came to herself, and he got her into bed.

But he did not feel fit to lie down beside his wife. He would stay awake and watch: she might have another bad turn! Soon she fell asleep from the exhaustion which follows intense emotions. He sat by the fire, awake and disturbed. For sorrow is sleepy, pride and remorse are wakeful.

Hester and the major got Corney to bed, and instantly he was sound asleep. The major arranged himself to pass the night by the fire; Hester went to the adjoining room where she, too, was presently fast asleep. There was no gnawing worm of duty undone or wrong unpardoned in her heart to keep her awake.

The night began differently with the two watchers. The major was troubled in his mind at what seemed the hardheartedness of the mother, for he loved her with a true brotherly affection. He brooded long over the matter, but by degrees forgot her and fell to thinking about his own mother.

As the major sat thinking, the story came back to him which she had told him and his brothers, all now gone but himself, as they sat around her one Sunday evening in their room. The story was about the boy who was tired of being at home, and asked his father for money to go away. His father gave it him, thinking it better he should go than grumble at the best he could give him. The boy had grown naughty and spent his money in buying things that were not worth having, and in eating and drinking with greedy, coarse people until at last he had nothing left to buy food with and had to feed swine to earn something. Then finally he had begun to think about going home.

It all came back to the major's mind just as his mother used to tell it—how the poor prodigal, ragged and dirty and hungry, had set out for home, and how his father had seen him coming a great way off and knew him at once, and ran out to meet him, welcoming him with a kiss. True, the prodigal came home repentant, but the father did not wait to know that—he ran to welcome him without condition.

As the major thus reflected, he kept coming nearer and nearer to the Individual lurking at the keyhole of every story. Only he had to go home; otherwise, how was his father to receive him?

I wonder, he mused, *if when a man dies, that is counted as going home. I hardly think so, for that is something no man can help. I would find myself no better off than this young rascal when he goes home because he can't help it!*

The result of this thinking was that the major, there in the middle of the night, got down on his knees and tried, as he had not done in years, to say the prayers his mother had taught him—speaking from his heart as if one was listening, one who, in the dead of the night, did not sleep, but kept wide awake in case one of his children should cry.

In his wife's room, Gerald Raymount sat on into the dead of the night. After a long while, as his wife continued to sleep soundly, he thought he would go down to his study and find something to turn his thoughts from his misery. None such had come to him as to his friend. He had been much more of a religious man than the major, but it was the *idea* of religion, and the thousand ideas it broods, more than the practice of it daily, that was his delight. He philosophized and philosophized well of the relations between man and his maker, of the necessity to human nature of a belief in a God, of the disastrous consequences of having none, and such like things. But having an interest in God is a very different thing from living in such a close relationship with the father that the thought of him is an immediate and ever-returning joy and strength. He was so busy understanding with his intellect that he missed the better understanding of heart and imagination. He was always so pleased with the thought of a thing that he missed the thing itself—whose *possession*, not its thought, is essential. Thus when the trial came, it found him no true parent, because the resentment he bore the youth for having sinned against *his* family was stronger than the longing for his son's repentance. Love is at the heart of every right way, and essential forgiveness at the heart of every true treatment of the sinner.

He rose, and treading softly, went to his study. The fire was not yet out; he stirred it and made it blaze, lighted his candles, took a book from a shelf, sat down, and tried to read. But it was no use; his troubled thoughts could hold no company with other thoughts. The world of his kind was shut out; he was a man alone because he was unforgiving and unforgiven. His soul slid into the old groove of misery, and so the night slipped away.

The nominal morning, if not the dawn was near, when the door of the old library opened so softly that he heard nothing, and before he was aware of it a child gowned in white stood by his side. He started violently. It was Mark—walking in his sleep. He had seen his mother and father more than usually troubled all day and their trouble had haunted him in his sleep. It had roused him without waking him from his dreams, and the Spirit of love had directed him to the presence of his father. There was in the look on his face something like idiocy, for his soul was not precisely with his body. His eyes, though open, evidently saw nothing; and so he stood for a little time.

There had never been tender relations between Mark and his father like those between the boy and his mother and sister. His father was always kind to him, but between him and his boys he had let grow a kind of hard skin. Even when as tiniest children they came to be kissed before going to bed, he did not like the contact of their faces with his. No woman, and perhaps not many men will understand this, but it was always a relief to Mr. Raymount to have the nightly ceremony over. He thought there was nothing he would not do for their good; and I think his heart must in the main have been right toward them. But the clothes of his affections somehow did not sit easy on him, and there was a good deal in his behavior to Cornelius that had operated unfavorably on the mind of the youth. Even Mark, although, as I have said, he loved him dearly, was yet a little afraid of him—never went to him with a confidence, never snuggled close to him, never sat down by his side to read his book in a heaven of twilight peace, as he would with his mother. He would never have gone to this father's room for refuge from sleeplessness.

Not recognizing his condition, his father was surprised and even annoyed, as well as startled: he was in no mood for such a visit. He felt also strangely afraid of the child, but did not know why. Wretched about one son, he was dismayed at the nocturnal visit of the other. The cause was, of course, his wrong condition of mind. Lack of truth and harmony in ourselves alone can make us miserable; there is a cure for everything when that is cured.

There was an unnatural look, at the same time pitiful and lovely, about the boy as the father sat staring in gathering dread. He had nearly imagined him an angel of some doom.

Suddenly the child stretched out his hands to him and came close to his knee. Remembering how once before, when a tiny child, he had gone into a kind of fit when awakened suddenly, and anxious to avoid anything of the kind again, the father took the child softly in his arms, lifted him to his knees, and held him. An expression of supreme delight came over the boy's face—a look of absolute contentment mingled with hope. He put his thin hands together as if saying his prayers, but lifted his look to that of his father. How could his earthly father know that in his dreams, the boy thought he was sitting in the lap of his heavenly Father? And now his lips began to move, and a murmur came from them, which grew into barely audible words. He was indeed praying to his Father, but a father closer to him even than the one upon whose knees he sat.

"Dear God," the child prayed, "I don't know what to do for Papa and Corney. I am afraid they are both naughty. I would not say so to anybody but you, for you know all about it. When Corney came home tonight, neither went and said 'How do you do,' or 'Good night' to the other. Oh, God, you are our big papa! Please put it all right. Please, dear God, make Papa and Corney good. You know they must love each other. I will not pray a word more, for I know you will do just what I want. Goodbye, God. I'm going to bed now—down there. I'll come again soon."

With that he slipped from his father's knee, who did not dare to detain him, and walked from the room with slow, stately step.

By now the heart of the strong, hard man was swelling with the love that was at last coming awake. He could not weep, but felt dry, torturing sobs welling up from within him that seemed as if they would kill him. He rose to see the boy safely in bed.

In the corridor he breathed more freely. Through an old window, the bright moon, shining in peace with no one to see, cast a shadow in the shape of a cross, partly on the wall and partly on the floor. Severe Protestant as Gerald Raymount was, he found himself on his knees in the passage in front of the shadow—not praying, not doing anything he knew, but under some spiritual influence known only to God.

When the something had reached its height and the passion was over and his soul was clearing of the storm that had swept through it, he rose from his knees and went up to Mark's room, two stories higher. The moonlight was there too, and the father saw the child's white bed glimmering like a tomb. He drew near. The boy seemed in his usual health, and was sleeping peacefully—dreaming pleasantly, for the ghost of a smile glinted about his just-parted lips. Then upon the father—who with all his hardness, yet had a sound imagination—came the wonder of watching a dreamer. What might be going on within that brain? Splendid visions might be gliding through the soul of the sleeper—his child, born of his body—and not one of them was open to him!

But how much nearer to him in reality was the child when awake and about the house? Even then, how much did he know of the thoughts, the loves, the imaginations, the desires, the aspirations that moved in the heart and the brain of the child? The boy was sickly: he might be taken from him before he had made any true acquaintance with him! He was just the sort of child to die young! Certainly he might see him in the other world, but the boy would have so few memories of him, so few associations with him, that it would be hard to tie the new to the old!

He turned away and went back to his room. There, with a sense of loneliness deeper than he had ever felt before, he went down on his knees to beg the company of God whose existence he had so often defended but whom he had so little regarded as practically and immediately existent that he had not yet sought refuge with him. All the house was asleep—the major had long ended his prayers and was slumbering by the fire—when Raymount knelt before the living source of his life, and rose from his knees a humbler man.

35 / A Sad Beginning

Toward morning he went to bed and slept late. Alas, when he woke the old feeling had returned! How *could* he forgive the son that had so disgraced him!

Instead of going once again to the living strength, he began to try to persuade himself on philosophical grounds that the best thing would be to forgive his son, that it was the part of the wise man to abstain from harshness. But he had little success with himself. Anger and pride were too much for him. His breakfast was taken to him in the study, and there Hester found him an hour later, his food still untouched. He submitted to her embrace, but scarcely spoke and asked nothing about Corney. Hester felt sadly chilled and hopeless. But she had begun to learn that one of the principal parts of faith is patience, and that the setting of wrong things right is so far from easy that not even God does it all at once. Time is nothing to him who sees the end from the beginning.

The only way in such stubbornness of the spirit, when we cannot feel that we are wrong, is to open our hearts, alone in silence and prayer, to the influences from above. Mr. Raymount, however, like most of us, was a long way from being able to do this yet. He strove hard to reconcile the memories of the night with the feelings of the morning—strove to realize a state of mind in which a measure of forgiveness to his son blended with a measure of satisfaction to the wounded pride he called paternal dignity. How could he take his son to himself as he was? he asked. But he did not ask how he was to draw him to repentance! He did not think of the tender entreaty with which God pleads for his people to come back to him.

For a father not to forgive is far worse than for a son to need forgiveness; and such a father, as well as the son, will of course go from bad to worse unless he repents. The shifty, ungenerous spirit of compromise awoke in Raymount. He would be very good, very gentle, very kind to everyone else in the house. He would walk softly, but he would postpone his forgiveness. He knew his feelings toward Corney were wearing out the heart of his wife—but he would not yield. There was little Mark, however; he would make more of him, know him better, and make the child know him better.

He went to see how his wife was. He was annoyed to find that she was a trifle better. In the selfishness of his misery, he looked upon her

189

happiness at having her worthless son home as a lack of sympathy with himself. He did not allude to Cornelius, but said he was going for a walk, and went to find Mark—with a vague hope of consolation in the child who had clung to him so confidently in the night. He had forgotten it was not to him that the boy's soul had clung, but to the Father of both of them.

Mark was in the nursery, as the children's room was still called. When Mark heard his father's step, he bounded to meet him; and when his sweet moonlit (rather than sunshiny) face appeared at the door, the gloom on his father's face yielded a little; the gleam of a momentary smile broke over it, and he said kindly: "Come, Mark, I want you to go for a walk with me."

He was not doing the right thing in taking him out, but he was not thinking of that just now. He ought to have known that the boy was still too weak for anything like a walk; neither was the weather fit for his going out. But absorbed in his own trouble, the father did not think of his boy's weakness; and Hester was not there to object. So away they went. Mark was delighted to be his father's companion, never doubting all was right, and forgot his weakness as entirely as his father did.

With his heart in such a state, the father naturally had next to nothing to say to the boy, and they walked on in silence. But that did not affect Mark; he was satisfied to be with his father whether or not he spoke to him. From God he had learned not to dislike silence. Without knowing it, he was growing tired as they walked. When weariness at last became conscious, it came upon him all at once and poor Mark found he could scarcely put one leg in front of the other.

The sun had been shining when they started—a beautiful but not very warm spring sun. But now it had grown cloudy and rain threatened. They were in the middle of a bare, lonely moor, easily reached from the house but of considerable size in all directions, and the wind had begun to blow cold. Sunk in his miserable thoughts, all the more miserable now that he had relapsed into total unforgiveness, the father was oblivious to his child's failing strength, and kept trudging on. All at once he became aware that the boy was not by his side. He looked around, but he was nowhere to be seen. Alarmed, he stopped, turned, and called his name. The wind was blowing the other way and at first he heard no reply. He called again and this time thought he heard a feeble response. He retraced his steps rapidly.

Some four or five hundred yards back, he came to a hollow where Mark sat on a tuft of brown heather, looking as white as the moon in daylight.

His anxiety relieved, the father felt annoyed, and berated the little fellow for stopping.

"I wasn't able to keep up, Papa," replied Mark. "So I thought I would rest a while, and meet you as you came back."

"You ought to have told me. I wouldn't have brought you if I had known you would behave so. Come, get up, we must go home."

"I'm very sorry, Papa, but I don't think I can."

"Nonsense!"

"There's something wrong with my knee."

"Try," urged his father, growing frightened again.

He obeyed and rose, but with a little cry dropped on the ground. He had somehow injured his knee and could not walk a step.

His father stooped to lift him.

"I'll carry you, Markie," he said in a kinder voice.

"Oh, no, you must not Papa! It will tire you!"

His father was already walking homeward with him.

The next moment Mark saw the waving of a dress.

"Oh!" he cried, "there's Hessie! She will carry me!"

"You little goose!" said his father tenderly. "Can she carry you better than I?"

"She is not stronger than you, Papa, because you are a big man. But I think Hessie has more carry in her. She has such strong arms!"

Hester was running, and quite out of breath when she came near.

She had feared how Mark would be when she discovered her father had taken him for a walk. Her first feeling was of anger, for she had inherited not a little of her father's spirit: indirectly the black sheep had roused evils in the flock unknown before. However, when she saw the boy's arms around his father's neck and his cheek laid against his, her anger left her and she was sorry and ashamed, even though from his face she could tell that Mark was suffering greatly.

"Let me take him, Papa," she offered.

But the father had no intention of giving up the child. Before he knew it, however, the boy had stretched out his arms to Hester and was out of his and into hers, and he was left to follow in distressed humiliation.

"He is too heavy for you, Hester," he protested. "Surely it is my fault. I ought to bear the penalty!"

"It is no penalty—is it, Markie?" said Hester merrily.

"No, Hessie," replied Mark. "You don't know how strong Hessie is, Papa!"

But by and by Hester found, with all her goodwill, that her strength was not quite up to it, and was obliged to yield him to her father. It was much to his relief, for a sense of moral weakness had invaded him as he followed his children: he was rejected by his family and had become a nobody in it.

When at length they reached home, Mark was put to bed and the doctor sent for.

36 / Corney and Amy_____

In the meantime, Corney kept to his bed. When his mother could, without her husband knowing it, she went to her son and knelt down by his bedside. With his mother, Corney had never pretended to the same degree as with other people, and his behavior toward her now was more genuine than toward anyone but his wife. He clung to her embrace as he had never clung since his infancy, feeling that, however his father might treat him, he still had a home. Now that his mother so clearly showed her unqualified love toward him, he was more content, or rather less discontented, than he had even been with Hester. Mrs. Raymount was greatly consoled, and he was so happy with her that he began to wish he did not have a secret from her. For the first time in his life he was sorry that he was in possession of one. He even grew anxious for the time, when she would know it, but nonetheless eager that he should have to tell it.

A great part of the time when her husband supposed her asleep, Mrs. Raymount had been lying wide awake, thinking of the Corney she had lost and the Corney that had come home to her instead. She was miserable over the altered looks of her disfigured child. His sad, pockmarked face held a torturing fascination for her. It was almost pure pain, yet she could not turn her eyes from it. She reproached herself that it gave her pain, yet was almost indignant with the face usurping the place of her boy's beauty. Through that mask she must force her way to the reality beneath it. At the same time, pity made her love with a new and deeper tenderness the poor, spoiled visage, pathetic in its ugliness.

Hester could not help, a little like the elder brother in the divine tale, looking upon the sight with concern, especially since she could not confidently look on the prodigal as a repentant one. However, it was not long before she herself was encouraged by a softness in Corney's look and a misty expression in his eyes, which she had never seen before. Doubtless had he been as in former days, he would have turned from such overflow of love as womanish gush; but disgraced, worn out, and even to his own eyes an unpleasant object, he was not so much inclined to repel the love of the only one who knew his story and who did not feel contempt for him.

Slowly, slowly, something was working on him—now in the imagined judgment of others, now in the thought of his wife, now in the devotion of his mother. There was little result for earthly eye to see, but the mother's perceived or imagined a difference in him. If only she could see something clear enough to tell her husband! If only the ice that froze up the spring of his love would but begin to melt! For to whom are we to go for refuge from ourselves if not to those through whom we were born into the world, and who are to blame for more or less of our unfitness for a true life! The mother still carried in her soul the child born of her body, preparing for him the new and better, the all-lovely birth of repentance unto life.

Hester had not yet said a word about her own affairs. No one but the major knew that the engagement to Lord Gartley was broken. She did not want to add still another element of perturbance to the over-charged atmosphere; she would not add disappointment to grief.

In the afternoon the major, who was staying in the village two miles off, made his appearance. No sooner did he learn of Mark's condition than he insisted on taking charge of him. Hester was pleased with the proposal, for she had so much else to see to. So the major took the position of head nurse, with Saffy for his aide and one of the servants for an orderly.

Hester's mind was almost constantly occupied with wondering how to let her father and mother know about Cornelius and Amy's marriage. They ought to know as soon as possible. She would tell her father first; her mother should not know until he did. But she could not see how to begin. Everything seemed at a standstill. So she waited, as she ought; for much harm comes of the impatience that outstrips guidance. People are too ready to think *something* must be done, and forget that the time for action may not have arrived, that there is seldom more than one thing fit to be done, and that doing the wrong thing before that one right thing is revealed is always worse than doing nothing.

Cornelius gradually grew better and at last was able to go downstairs. But the weather continued so unfavorable that he could not go outside. He had not yet seen his father, and his dread of seeing him grew to a terror. He never left his room unless he knew his father was not in the house, and, even then, would sit at some window that commanded a view of the door by which he was most likely to enter. He enticed Saffy to be his scout and bring him word in what direction his father went. The father was just as anxious to avoid him, fully intending, if he met him, to turn his back upon him. But it was a rambling and roomy old house, and there was plenty of space for both. A whole week passed and they had not met—to Hester's disappointment, who cherished some hope in a chance encounter.

She had just one consolation. Ever since Cornelius had been safe under her wing, their mother had been noticeably improving. But even this was a source of irritation to the father's brooding selfishness—who thought to himself, *Here I have been nursing her through the illness in vain, and the moment she gets the rascal back, she begins to improve! She would be perfectly happy with him if she never saw me again!*

Miss Dasomma was quite as pleased with Amy as she had expected to be, and found her very quick to pick up whatever new came her way. She began at once to teach her music. She understood quickly, but the doing of what she understood she found very hard—the more so that her spirit was still ill at ease. Corney had deceived her, and had done something very wrong besides. Now she was separated from him. All was very different from what she had expected in marrying her Corney. Also, from her weariness and anxiety in nursing him, and from other causes as well, her health was not what it had been. Then too, Hester's letters were a little stiff. She felt it without knowing what she felt or why they made her uncomfortable. It was from no pride or lack of love they were such, but from Hester's uncertainty—the discomfort of knowing they were no nearer a solution of their difficulty than when they parted. She still did not know what she was going to do in the matter! This prevented the free flow of communication, because Hester was unwilling to tell Amy just how uncomfortable things actually were at Yrndale. Amy naturally surmised that the family was not willing to receive her, and wrongly assumed that this same unwillingness was in Hester also. But it was not so, for Hester saw that the main hope for her brother lay in his love for Amy and her devotion to him. But Amy could not discern this from Hester's letters.

Amy noted, for love and anxiety made her very sharp, that Miss Dasomma did not read to her every word of Hester's letters. Once she stopped suddenly in the middle of a sentence, and after a pause went on with another. There must have been something she was not to know! Something must not be going right with her husband! Was he worse and they were afraid to tell her? Perhaps they were treating him as her aunts treated her—making his life miserable—and she was not with him to help him bear it!

She brooded over the matter, but not for long. At last she threw herself on her knees and begged her friend to tell her all that her sister's letter had said.

"But, my dear," said Miss Dasomma, "Hester and I have been friends for many years, and we may well have things to say to each other we do not want even one we love as much as you to hear. A lady must not be inquisitive, you know."

"Just tell me it was nothing about my husband and I shall be quite content."

"But think a moment, Amy," returned Miss Dasomma, who began to find herself in the midst of a difficulty; "there might be things between his family and him which they are not quite prepared to tell you until they know you better."

"What kind of things?" asked Amy in growing anxiety. "If it is anything affecting him, his wife has a right to know about it—and no one has a right to conceal it from her!"

"Why do you think that?" Miss Dasomma was anxious to shift the track of the conversation, for she did not see how to answer Amy's appeal. She could not lie, but neither did she feel at liberty to tell her the truth of Corney's involvement with his uncle, and if she continued to evade her question, the poor child might imagine something even more dreadful.

"Why, miss, I have to do what I can for him, and I have a right to know what there is to be done."

"But can you not trust his own family?"

"Yes, surely," replied Amy, "if they were not angry with him. But he's mine, miss! And I've got to look after him. If anybody's not doing right by him, I ought to be there to see him through it!"

Here Miss Dasomma's prudence left her for a moment.

"That's all you know, Amy!" she blurted out—and bit her lip almost the same moment, angry with herself for her hasty remark.

"What is it?" Amy cried. "I *must* know what it is! You *shall* not keep me in the dark! I *must* do my duty to my husband! If you do not tell me, I will go to him."

In terror at what might be the result of her hasty remark, Miss Dasomma faltered, reddened, and betrayed considerable embarrassment. Amy saw, and was all the more convinced and determined. She persisted, and Miss Dasomma knew that she would not give up.

"How can you wonder," she asked with confused vagueness, "when you know he deceived you and never told them he was going to marry you? How can you wonder that one who could behave like that would be only too likely to do other things?"

"Then there *is* something more—something I know nothing about!" exclaimed Amy. "I suspected it from Hester's face. I *must* know what it is! I may be young and silly, but I know what a wife owes to her husband!"

Miss Dasomma was silent. She had awakened a small volcano, which, though without intending harm against vineyards and villages, would go to its ends regardless of them. She must either answer her questions or persuade her not to ask any.

"I beg you," she said, "not to do anything rash. Can you not trust friends who have proved themselves faithful?"

"Yes, for myself," answered Amy; "but it is my *husband*!"—she almost screamed the word—"And I will trust nobody to take care of *him*. They can't know how to treat him or he would love—"

She did not finish the sentence, for the postman's knock came to the door, and she bounded off to see what he had brought. She returned with a look of triumph—a look so wildly exultant that her hostess was momentarily alarmed, thinking that she may have appropriated a letter not addressed to her.

"Now I shall know the truth!" she declared. "This is from *him*!"

And with that she flew to her room. Miss Dasomma should not hear a word of it! How dared she keep from her what she knew about her husband!

It was Corney's first letter to her. It was filled, not with direct complaints, but a general grumble. Here is a part of it.

> I do wish you were here, Amy, my own dearest! I love nobody like you—I love nobody but you. What comforts me for any wrong I have done is that I have you. That would make up to a man for anything short of being hanged. My mother is very kind to me, of course—ever so much better company than Hester! She never looks as if a fellow had to be put up with, or forgiven, or anything of that sort, in her high and mighty way. But you do get tired of a mother always telling you how much she loves you. You can't help thinking there must be something behind it all. Depend upon it, she wants something of you—wants you to be good, I daresay—to repent, don't you know, as they call it! They're all right, I suppose, but it isn't nice nevertheless. And that Hester has never told my father yet.
>
> I haven't even seen my father. He has not come near me once. Saffy would hardly look at my face for a long time. She shrieked when they first made her come to me. So you may see how I am used! But I've got her under my thumb at last, and she's useful. Then there's that prig Mark! I always liked the little wretch, though he is such a precious humbug! He's in bed—put out his knee, or something. He never had any stamina in him! Scrofulous, don't you know! They won't let me go near him—for fear of frightening him! But that's that braggart Major Marvel! He comes to me sometimes and makes me hate him—talks as if I wasn't as good as he—as if I wasn't even a gentleman! Many's the time I long to be back in the garret—horrid place! along with my little Amy."

So went the letter.

When Amy next appeared she was in another mood. Her eyes were

red and her hair was in disorder. She had been lying now on the bed,
now on the floor, pulling at her hair, and stuffing her handkerchief in
her mouth.

"Well, what is the news?" asked Miss Dasomma, as kindly as she
could speak, and as if she saw nothing peculiar in her appearance.

"You must excuse me," replied Amy, with the stiffness of a woman
of the world resenting intrusion. "Do not think me unkind, but there is
positively nothing in the letter that would interest anyone but me."

Miss Dasomma said nothing more. Perhaps she was going to escape
without further questioning! And though she was anxious about what
the letter might have contained to have put the poor girl in such a state,
she would not risk the asking of a single question more.

The solemn fact was that his letter, in conjunction with the word
Miss Dasomma let slip, had at last begun to open Amy's eyes a little to
the real character of her husband. She herself had seen a good deal of
his family, and found it hard to believe they would treat him unkindly.
Something must be at the root of it all, something she did not know
about, the same thing that made him take to the garret and hide there!
The more she thought about it, the more convinced she was that he had
done something hideously wrong.

From the first glimmer of certainty as to the uncertain facts, she saw
with absolute clearness what she must do. *I must know all about it!* she
said to herself, *or how am I to help him?* It seemed to her the most
natural thing that when one has done a wrong, he should confess it—
thus having done with it, disowning and casting away the cursed thing.
But this Cornelius did not seem inclined to do! She was determined to
learn the truth of the thing.

By degrees her mind grew calm in settled resolve. Should she tell
Miss Dasomma what was in her thoughts? Neither she nor Hester had
trusted her with what they knew: need she trust them? She must take
her own way in silence, for they would be certain to oppose it. Could
they be trying to keep her and Corney apart?

All the indignant strength and unalterable determination of the little
woman rose in arms. She would see who could keep them apart now
that she had made up her mind! She had money of her own—and there
was the jewelry Corney had given her! It must be valuable, for Corney
hated fake things. She would walk her way, work her way, or beg her
way if necessary, but nothing would keep her from Corney!

Not a word more concerning their differences passed between her
and Miss Dasomma. They talked cheerfully and kissed as usual when
parting for the night.

The moment she was in her room, Amy began to pack a small

carpetbag. When that was done she made a bundle of her cloak and shawl and then lay down in her clothes. Long before dawn she crept softly down the stairs, and sneaked out.

Thus for the second time she was a fugitive—the first time *from*, now *to*.

When Miss Dasomma had been up for some time, she went up to see why Amy was making no appearance. One glance around the room told her that she was gone. At first she was dreadfully anxious, not suspecting where she had gone, thinking that perhaps the letter which had made her so miserable contained the announcement that their marriage was not a genuine one. If so, then in the dignity of her true heart, she must have at once forever taken her leave of Cornelius. She wrote to Hester, but the post did not leave before evening, and would not arrive until the afternoon of the next day.

When Amy got to the station she found she was in time for the first train of the day. There was no third class on it, but she found she had enough money for a second-class ticket, and without a moment's hesitation, though it left her almost penniless, she took one.

37 / Vengeance Is Mine_____

At Yrndale things went on in the same dull way, anger burrowing like a mole in the heart of the father, a dreary spiritual fog hanging over all the souls, and the mother longing for some glimmer of a heavenly dawn. Hester felt as if she could not endure it much longer. But there was one bright spot in the house yet—Mark's room, where the major sat by the bedside of the boy, reading, telling him stories, or now and then listening to him as he spoke childlike wisdom in childish words. What seemed to add to the misery of everyone else, though it made Mark merry, was that the weather had again put on a wintry temper. Sleet and hail, and even snow fell, alternating with rain and wind, day after day for a week.

One afternoon the wind rose almost to a tempest. The rain came in sheets, beating unmercifully against Mark's windows. His was a cheerful room, though low-pitched and very old, with a great beam across the middle of it. There were colored prints, mostly of Scripture subjects, on the walls; and the beautiful fire burning in the grate shone on them and reflected from the polished floor. The major sat by it in his easy chair. A bedroom had been prepared for him next to the boy's, and Mark had a string close to his hand whose slightest pull rang a little bell that woke the major like a cannon on the field of battle.

This afternoon, with the rain-charged wind rushing in fierce gusts against the windows, and twilight coming on all the sooner because the world was wrapped in blankets of wet clouds, the major was reading, but soon grew sleepy. A moment more and he was far away, following an imaginary tiger, when Mark woke him with the question: "God will make Corney good, won't he, Majie?"

The major sat bolt upright, rubbed his eyes, stretched himself, but quietly enough that Mark might not know he had waked him, and gave a *hem* as if pondering deeply instead of trying hard to gather wits enough to understand the question. When he trusted his voice not to betray him, he answered: "Well, Mark, I hope so." The answer was not really so deep for the amount of thought he put into it.

"But don't you think we ought to do something to help make Corney good? I don't think we ought to leave Corney to Mother all alone: it's too hard for her! Corney never was willing to be good! I can't understand that! Why doesn't he like to be good?"

"Mark, some people like their own way even when it's wicked and selfish, better than God's way when it's nice."

"But God must be able to let them know what foolish creatures they are, Majie! It just won't do for you and me to be so safe from all the storm and wind, wrapped in God's cloak, and poor Corney out in the wind and rain. You may say it's his own fault—it's because he won't let God take up and carry him. That's very true, but then that's just the pity of it! It is all so dreadful! I can't understand it!"

The boy could understand good, but was perplexed with evil.

While they talked in their comfortable nest, there was one out in the wind and rain, all but exhausted, who hastened with what poor remaining strength she had to do His will. Amy, left at the station with an empty purse, had set out to walk through the wet darkness, up hill and down dale to find her husband—the man God had given her to look after.

That same morning, Mr. Raymount had found it necessary, or had chosen to imagine it necessary, to start out early for the county town on something he called business, and was not expected home before the next day. In his absence Cornelius wandered freely about the house, lunching with his mother, Hester and Saffy like one of the family. His mother, wisely or not, did her best to prevent his feeling different from old times. Their conversation at the table was neither very interesting nor very satisfactory. How could it be? A child of Satan might just as well be happy in the house of God, as the unrepentant Cornelius in the house of his mother, even in the absence of his father. Their talk was poor and intermittent. Well might the youth long for his garret and the company of the wife who had nothing for him but smiles and sweetest attentions!

After dinner he sat alone for a while at the table. He had had a little wine during his recovery and was already in danger of adding a fondness for it to his other weaknesses. But the mother, wise and aware of the danger, had kept the administration of the medicine in her own hands. Today, however, she had been called from the room and had not put away the decanter. Thus Cornelius had filled his glass repeatedly without interruption. When his mother reentered the room, she noticed the nearly empty decanter, but thought it better to say nothing.

Cornelius tried to conceal the effects of the wine as he left the room, sauntering into the library and then into the study, where his father's collection of books was kept. He lit a lamp, took down a volume of poetry, threw himself into his father's chair, and began to read. He had never been able to read long without weariness, and from the wine he had drunk and his weakness, he was presently overcome with sleep. His mother came and went, but would not disturb him. I fear that her satisfaction in having him under her roof was beginning to wane from the constant stress of a presence that showed no more signs of growth than a dead man. But her faith was strong and she waited in hope.

The night was now very dark. Above, the major and the boy talked of sweet, heavenly things. Down below, the youth lay snoring, where, had his father been at home, he would not have dared show himself. The mother was in her own room, and Hester in the drawing room— where she never now played her piano, due to the oppression of these times. The house was quiet except for the noise of the wind and the rain, and those Cornelius did not hear.

Suddenly he started awake and sat up in terror. A hand was on his shoulder, gripping him like a metal instrument, not a thing of flesh and blood. The face of his father was staring at him through the lingering vapors of his stuporous sleep.

Mr. Raymount had started out in the morning with a certain foolish pleasure in the prospect of getting wet through and through and being generally ill-used by the atrocious weather, as he called it. Thinking to shorten the way, he took a certain shortcut he knew, but found the road very bad. The mud drew off one of his horse's shoes, but he did not discover it for a long way—not until he came to a piece of newly mended road where the poor animal fell suddenly lame. He dismounted and made for an inn a mile or two farther on, where he stayed and had some refreshment while his horse was being attended to by a local smithy. By the time he was again mounted, the weather was worse than ever and it was so late that he could not have hoped to reach the town in time to do his business. He, therefore, gave up his intended journey, and turning aside to see a friend in the neighborhood, resolved to go home again that same night.

His feelings when he saw his son asleep in his chair were evil indeed. He had been giving place to the devil for so long that the evil one was now able to do with him as he would. Nor would the possessed ever have been able to recognize the presence of the devil had he not, for a minute or two, committed his full will to him. Or does the miserable possessed go further than the devil means him to go? I doubt if he cares that we commit murder. I imagine he is satisfied if all we do is hate well.

"The sneak!" he growled at the sight of his unpleasant son asleep in *his* chair. "He dares not show his face when I'm at home, but the minute he thinks it safe, gets into my room and lies in my chair! Drunk, too, by Jove!" he added, as a fume from the sleeper's breath reached the nostrils of the angry father. "What can that wife of mine be about, letting the rascal go on like this!"

The devil saw his chance, sprang up, and mastered him.

"The snoring idiot!" he growled louder yet, seizing his boy by the shoulder and neck and roughly shaking him awake.

The father had been drinking, not too much by some people's standards, but enough to add to the fierceness of his wrath. He had come into the study straight from the stable, and when the poor creature looked up half awake and saw his father standing over him with a heavy whip in his hand, he was filled with a terror that nearly paralyzed him. He sat and stared with white, trembling lips and red eyes, and a look that confirmed to the father that his son was drunk.

"Get out of there, you dog!" cried his father, and with one sweep of his powerful arm, half dragged, half hurled him from the chair. He fell on the floor, and in weakness mixed with cowardice lay where he fell. The devil—I am sorry to have to refer to him so often, but he played a notable part in the affair, and I would be more sorry not to acknowledge his part in it—rushed at once into the brain and heart and limbs of the father.

When Raymount saw the creature who had turned his previously happy life into a shambles lying at his feet, he became instantly conscious of the whip in his hand, and without a moment's pause of hesitation, raised his arm high over him and brought it down with a fierce lash on the quivering flesh of his son. The boy richly deserved the punishment, but God would not have struck him that way. There was the poison of hate, not the leaven of love, in the blow. He again raised the whip, but as it descended, the piercing shriek that broke from Corney's lips startled even the possessing demon, and the violence of the blow was broken. But the lash of the whip found his face and marked it for a time worse than the smallpox.

What the father would have done next I do not know. While the cry of his son yet sounded in his ears, another cry—almost an echo from another world—rang ghastly through the storm like the cry of a banshee. It seemed to come from far away, but the next instant a spectral face flitted swift as a bird up to the window and laid itself close to the glass of the French window. A moment more and it burst open with a great clang and clash and wide tinkle of shattering glass, and a small figure leaped into the room with a second cry that sounded like a curse in the ears of the father.

She threw herself on the prostrate youth, and covered his body with hers, then turned her head and looked up at the father with indignant defiance in her flashing eye. Cowed with terror and smarting with keenest pain, the youth took his wife in his arms and sobbed like the beaten thing he was. Amy's eye gleamed; protection grew fierce and fanned the burning sense of wrong. The father stood over them like a fury rather than a fate—stood as the shock of Amy's cry and her stormy entrance, like that of an avenging angel, had fixed him.

But presently he began to recover his senses, jumping to the conclusion that this worthless girl had drawn Cornelius into her evil ways and was the cause of ruining him and his family forever! The thought set the geyser of his rage roaring and spouting in the face of heaven. He heaved his whip and a punishing blow fell upon her. But instead of another shriek following the lash, nothing came but a shudder and a silence, and the unquailing eye of the girl fixed itself like a spectre upon her assailant. He struck her again. Again came the shivering shudder and the silence. Cry she would not, even if he killed her! The sense that she had kept the blows from falling upon Corney upheld the brave creature. She once drew in her breath sharply, but never took her eyes from the man's face. Then, suddenly, the light in them began to fade and went quickly out. Her head dropped like a stone upon the breast of her cowardly husband. Now, even mute defiance was gone.

What if he had killed the woman, thought Raymount, as he stood with subsiding passion looking down on the miserable pair.

Amy had walked all the long distance from the station and had lost her way and had to ask directions several times. Again and again she had all but lain down to die on the moorland waste onto which she had wandered. Then the thought of Corney and his need would rouse her again. Wet all the way through, blown about by the wind so that she could hardly breathe, and faint with hunger and cold, she struggled on. When at last she got to the lodge gate, the woman in charge of it took her for a common beggar and could hardly be persuaded to let her pass. But then she heard her husband's cry. She saw the lighted window, ran into the grounds and straight toward it, smashed it open and entered. It was the last expiring effort of the poor remnant of her strength. She had not life enough left to resist the shock of her father-in-law's blows.

While the father was still looking down on his children, the door opened softly and the mother entered. She did not even know that her husband had returned and had come in merely to know how her unlovely but beloved child was faring in his sleep. She stood still. She saw what looked like a murdered heap on the floor, and her husband standing over it. Behind her came Hester, who looked over her shoulder and understood at once.

She nearly pushed her mother aside as she sprang to help. Her father tried to prevent her. "No, Father!" she cried with determination. "It is time to disobey!"

All was clear to her! Amy had come, and died defending her husband from her father! Hester put her strong arms around the dainty little figure and lifted the limp body, its long wet hair and helpless head hanging over the crook of her arm. She gave a great sob. Was this what Amy's lovely, brave womanhood had brought her to! What creatures men were! She glanced down and saw on Amy's neck a frightful swollen welt. She looked to her father. There was the whip in his hand. "Oh, Papa!" she screamed. She could not look him in the face. As she dropped her eyes, she saw the terrified face of Cornelius open its eyes.

"Oh, Corney!" said Hester, in the tone of an accusing angel, and ran from the room with Amy in her arms.

The mother darted to her son.

But the wrath of the father rose afresh at the sight.

"Let the hound lie!" he commanded, stepping between them. "What right has he to walk the earth like a man?"

"You've killed him, Gerald!—your own son!" accused the mother with a cold, still voice.

She saw the dreadful mark on his face, began to stagger, and would have fallen. But the arm that, through her son, had struck her heart caught and supported her. The husband carried his wife once again to her room, and the foolish son was left alone on the floor, smarting in pain, ashamed, and full of fear for his wife, whom his father had so violently whipped.

A moment later he rose. But as he did, he realized that all at once the terror of his father was gone. They had met, face-to-face, and by his actions, his father had put himself in the wrong. Corney was no longer afraid. It consoled him that he had been so treated by his father. Having seen his father in a rage, the childhood feeling of reverence and fear had begun to give way: they were suddenly more on the same level. And his father's unmerciful use of the whip seemed to him a sort of settling of scores, and so in a measure, a breaking down of the wall between them. He felt as if the storm had passed and the sun had begun to appear. He did not yet know what poor condition his wife was in, but he knew she was safe with Hester.

He listened, and finding all quiet, stole, smarting and aching, slowly to his room and there tumbled into bed, longing for Amy to come to him. He was an invalid, after all, and could not go about looking for her! It was her job to find him! In a few minutes he was fast asleep once more, and forgot everything in dreams of the garret with Amy.

When Mrs. Raymount came to herself, she looked up at her husband. He stood expecting such reproaches as never yet in their married life she had given him. But she stretched out her arms to him and drew him to her. Her pity for the misery that could have led him to behave so horribly joined to her sympathy in the distressing repentance she did not doubt must have already begun.

It went deep to the man's heart. His wife's embrace was like balm to the stinging wound of the deep sense of degradation that had seized him—not for striking his son, who, he continued to say, entirely deserved it, but for striking a woman, whoever she might be. But it was only when, through Hester, he came to know who Amy was, that the iron, the beneficial spearhead of remorse, entered his soul. Strange that the mere fact of our knowing *who a person is* should make such a difference in the way we think of and behave to that person! A person is a person just the same, whether one of the few of our acquaintances or not, and his claim on us for all kinds of human compassion just the same. Our knowledge of anyone is a mere accident, and should only make us feel more of what we *should* feel toward everyone.

But recognition of Amy showed his crime all the more hideous. It brought back to Mr. Raymount's mind the vision of the bright girl he used to watch in her cheerful service at Burcliff, and with that vision came the conviction that not she but Corney must be primarily to blame. He had twice struck the woman his son had wronged!

He pronounced himself the most despicable and wretched of men: He had lifted his hand against a woman that had been but in her right in following his son, and had shown herself ready to die in his defense! His wife's tenderness confirmed these feelings, and he lay down in his own room a few moments later a humbler man than he had ever been.

38 / Father and Daughter-in-law_____

Hester carried poor little Amy to her own room, laid her on her own bed, and did for her all she could. With hands tender as a mother's, and weeping eyes, she undressed her, put her in a warm bath, then got her into bed, using every enticement to induce her to take some nourishment. She had poor success, however, for the heart seemed to have gone out of her. She lay like one dead and seemed to care for nothing. She scarcely answered when Hester spoke, though she tried to smile. It was the most pitiful smile Hester had ever seen. Her brain was haunted with the presence of Corney's father, who seemed ever and always standing over her and Corney with his terrible whip. The only thing she could think of was how to get her husband away from the frightful place. Hester did her best to reassure her, telling her Corney was fast asleep and little the worse, and finally, shortly after midnight, was successful in getting the exhausted girl to sleep. Then she herself lay down on the sofa beside her.

In the gray of the morning Mr. Raymount awoke. He was aware of a great silence about him. He looked out the window and saw in the east the first glimmer of a lovely spring day. The stillness awed, almost frightened him. His very soul seemed hushed, as if in his sleep a Voice had said, "Peace! Be still!" Yesterday seemed far away—only the shudder of it was left. Had some angel been by his bedside to soothe him?

Then rose in his mind's eye the face of Amy Amber. What had become of the poor girl? Surely his wife and daughter would be taking care of her. But still he must do something for her, and somehow make atonement for treating her so brutally. Hope dawned feebly on his murky horizon. He would be good to her. There was something to be done for everybody. If she had gone back out into the night, he would spend every penny he had to find her! Cornelius would know where she was. He must see him! And he would tell him he was sorry he had struck him, too. What could have gotten into him that he had whipped his own son!

In the still, dark gray of the morning he went to his son's room.

When he reached the door he saw it was open a little. The next instant he heard a soft voice inside speaking persuadingly. He went closer and listened. It was Amy Amber's voice!—in his house! in his son's room!

And after the lesson he had given them the night before! The devil began to stir again within him.

He looked in quietly. The dainty little figure was half lying on the bed, with an arm thrown around his son. He could not see her face, but he could clearly hear her words through the dusk.

"Corney darling, you must get up. You must come away. I have come to take you away from them. I knew they were not treating you well. That was what made me come. I know you have done something very wrong to make your father so angry with you. It doesn't matter to me. But you cannot have said you were sorry or he would have forgiven you. He can't be a bad man—though he did hurt me dreadfully!"

"He is a good man," muttered Corney from the pillow. "He didn't hurt me much. Beside, Amy—I will confess it to you—I only gave him too good a reason."

"Come, then, come. We will go somewhere. Perhaps when you are sorry, we will come back and tell him so. Then perhaps he will forgive me and we shall all be happy again."

The cunning creature! thought Raymount. This was her trick to entice him from his home!—And just as the poor boy was beginning to repent, too! She knew her trade! She would fall in with his better mood and pretend to be good. All to lure him away!

But as he thought like this, his conscience smote him. How could Cornelius help but prefer going with one who loved him and talked to him like that, whatever she was, to staying with a father who treated him as he had been doing ever since he came home? But he would behave very differently after this. He, too, would repent! But first he must interfere now with the wicked girl's schemes. What else was a father for?

He pushed the door wide open and barged in.

Amy heard him and raised herself from the bed to face him. There was just enough light to see that it was the father, and the horrid idea shot through her mind that he had come to lash his son again. She roused every fevered nerve to do battle with the strong man for his son. Clenching her little hand hard, she stood like a small David between the bed and the approaching Goliath.

"Get out of this room!" he stormed with the sternness of rising wrath.

"I came to take him away," said Amy, but standing her ground trembling, continued. "It is my business to take care of him."

"Your business! When he has his own family? His own mother!"

"If a man is to leave father and mother and cleave to his wife," answered Amy, "the wife can at least protect him from his father!"

Mr. Raymount stood confounded. What could the hussy mean? Was she now going to pretend she was married to him?

Indignation and rage began to rise afresh. Yet almost the same instant came the memory of what he had been guilty of the night before. He must not give way a second time! For an instant he struggled within himself. And with the self-restraint came wholesome doubt: could it be possible? Could Corney have married her? Would it not have been just like him to have done so and never told his family?

In his doubt the shell of wickedness surrounding the true heart of the man at last began to fracture.

"Do—do you mean to tell me," he faltered, "that he has married you—without a word to his own father or mother?"

Then at last Cornelius spoke, rising on his elbow in the bed: "Yes, Father," he said with slow determination, "I have married her. It is all my fault, not a bit hers."

"Why did you not let us know then?" cried the father.

"Because I was a coward," answered Corney, speaking the truth with more courage than he had ever summoned in his life. "I knew you would not like it."

"Little *you* know of what I like or dislike!" blurted out the pride of the man, now struggling for its very life in the midst of the approach of *true* life that was threatening to overtake him.

"Forgive us! Forgive us both!" cried Amy. "Forgive us, and take me too. I was so happy to think I was going to belong to you all! I would never have married him if I had known—without your consent, I mean."

Now, at last, the full horror of what he had done broke upon the mind of Gerald Raymount. He stood for a moment appalled.

"You will let me take him away then?" asked Amy, thinking his hesitation meant he was unwilling to receive her.

Now whether it was from an impulse of honesty toward her, of one final last-gasp of justification of himself, or whether he blurted out the fact without thinking, I cannot tell, but he instantly returned: "Do you know that his money is stolen?"

"If he stole it," she replied, displaying no shock but only deeper love, "then we will return it. He will never steal again."

"He will never get another chance. He can get no job now."

"I will work for both of us! He belongs to me as much as I do to him. I will help him to set everything right."

And this is the woman I was such a savage to last night! groaned Mr. Raymount, inwardly chastising himself.

"Forgive me, Amy!" he begged, his pride caving in at last, and as he said the words he stretched out his arms to her. "I have behaved like a brute. To strike my son's wife! I deserve to be hanged for it. I shall never forgive myself. But you must forgive me!"

The strong man was now the weaker. The father, not the daughter, wept as he clasped her to his chest. After a moment she drew back her head.

"Come, Corney, out of your bed and down on your knees to your own blessed father, and confess your sins to him. Tell him you're sorry for what you did."

Corney obeyed. In some strange, lovely way she had become mistress of his conscience as well as his heart. He got out of bed at once, got down on his knees, and, though he did not speak, was presently weeping like a child. It was a strange group in the gray of the new morning—ah, indeed, a new morning for them!

After a few moments Gerald Raymount closed the door on his son and his son's wife and hastened to his own to tell her everything.

Immediately when the emotional strain was off her, Amy fell into a severe and fevered illness, brought on by her exposure to the cold and rain, and intensified by her hunger and the pain of her father-in-law's whip. Before her strong body was once more able to gather its strength, she was brought almost to death's door. Corney in his turn became nurse, and improved himself from this service of love, coupled with her sweetness and the new sympathy of his father toward them both. Such was her constitution that when she began to recover she recovered rapidly and was soon ready for the share lovingly allotted her in the duties of the house.

39 / The Message

But the precious little Mark did not get better, and it soon became very clear to the major that, although months might elapse before he left them, he would not live long. It was the only cloud that now hung over the family. But the parting drew upon them so softly, with so little increase of suffering, and with such a mild but genuine enjoyment of existence that only he was thoroughly aware that death was at the door. The rest said the summer would certainly restore him; but the major expected him to die with the first of the warm weather. The child himself believed he was going soon.

Most of his dreams, which now seemed to be coming with greater frequency, he told to the major. One day he said, "I was trying to tell Saffy a dream I had while you were resting. And when I told her she said, 'But it's all nonsense, you know, Mark! It's only a dream!'—What do you think, Majie?"

"Was it a dream, Mark?" asked the major.

"Yes, it was a dream, but do you think a dream is nothing at all? I think if it is a good dream, it must be God's. For you know every good thing is from God. He made the thing that dreams and the things that set it dreaming, so he must be the master of dreams—at least when he pleases—and surely always of those who obey him."

Here he began to cough and could talk no more for the present.

A great silent change had been overtaking the major, for the child's and the soldier's souls had gotten nearer to each other than until that time any two other souls in the house had been able to. Mark was not only an altogether new influence on him, but he had helped to stir up and bring alive in him a thousand influences besides. Those were not merely of things hitherto dormant in him, but memories of unconscious memories—words of his mother, a certain Sunday evening with her, her last blessing on his careless head, the verse of a well-known hymn she repeated as she was dying, old scraps of things she had taught him. Dying little Mark gave life to these and many other things. The major had never properly been a child but now lived his childhood over again with Mark in a better fashion.

"I have had such a curious, such a beautiful dream, Major," Mark said, waking up in the middle of one night. The major was sitting up with him: he was never left alone now.

211

"What was it, Markie?" asked the major.

"I should like Corney to hear it," returned Mark.

"I will call him and you can tell us both together."

"Oh, I don't think we should wake Corney up. He would not like that! He must hear it sometime—but it must be at the right time; otherwise he would laugh at it and I could not bear that. You know Corney always laughs without thinking first whether the thing was made for laughing at."

By this time Corney had been to see Mark often. He always spoke kindly to him now, but always as a little goose; and Mark, the least assuming of mortals, always being in earnest, did not want his dream made light of. Hence he was not often ready to speak freely to Corney.

"But I'll tell you what, Majie," he went on"—I'll tell *you* the dream, and then, if I should go away without having told him, you must tell it to Corney. He won't laugh then—at least I don't think he will. Do you promise to tell him, Majie?"

"I will," answered the major, drawing himself up with a mental military salute, ready to obey to the letter whatever Mark would require of him.

Without another word the child began.

"I was somewhere," he said. "—I don't know where. Jesus was there too. 'Ah, little one,' he said when he saw me, 'I have been getting your eyes open as fast as I could all the time! We're in our father's house together now! But, Markie, where's your brother Corney?' And I answered and said, 'Jesus, I'm very sorry, but I don't know. I know very well that I'm my brother's keeper, but I can't tell where he is.' Then Jesus smiled again and said, 'Never mind, then. I didn't ask you because I didn't know myself. But we must have Corney here—only we can't get him until he chooses to believe and obey! You must tell Corney, only not just yet, that I want him. Tell him that he and I have got one father, and I couldn't bear to have him out in the cold, with all the horrid creatures that won't be good! Tell him I love him so that I will be very sharp with him if he doesn't hurry and come home. Our father is *so* good, and it is dreadful to me that Corney won't mind him! He is *so* patient with him, Markie!' 'I know that, Jesus,' I said. And I don't know what came next.—Now, what am I to do, Majie? You see why I couldn't bear to have that dream laughed at. Yet I must tell it to Corney because there is a message in it for him!"

The major did not speak, but looked at the child with his soul in his eyes.

"I do not think," Mark went on, "that he wanted me to tell Corney the minute I woke. I think when the time comes he will let me know it is come. But if I found I was dying, you know, I would try and tell him, whether he laughed or not, rather than go without having done it. But if Corney knew I was going, I don't think he would laugh."

"I don't think he would," returned the major. "Corney is a better boy—a little—I do think, than he used to be."

A feeling had grown upon the household as if there was in the house a strange lovely spot in direct communication with heaven—the room where Mark lay shining in his bed, a Christ-child, if a child might bear the name. Whenever the door opened, loving eyes would seek first the spot where the sweet face, the treasure of the house, lay.

That same afternoon, as the major dozed in his chair, the boy suddenly called out in a clear voice, "Oh, Majie, there was one bit of my dream I did not tell you. I've just remembered it for the first time."

"What was it?" asked the major, who was now in the habit of recovering his wakefulness almost instantly.

"After we spoke, Jesus looked at me for one minute—no, not a minute like on Mama's watch—but perhaps just a few seconds, and then said just one more thing, 'Our father, Markie!' and then I could not see him anymore. But it did not seem to matter the least tiny bit. There was a rock near me, and I sat down upon it, feeling as if I could sit there without moving forever, I was so happy. And it was because Jesus' father was touching me everywhere. My head felt as if he were counting the hairs of it. And he was not only close to me, but far and far and farther away, and all between. Everywhere was the father! I couldn't see or feel or hear him, yet I felt I was one with him. I am talking nonsense, Majie, but I can't do it better. It was God, God everywhere, and there was no nowhere anywhere. All was God, God, God. And I felt I could sit there forever, because I was right in the middle of God's heart. That was what made everything look so right that I was anxious about nothing and nobody."

Here he paused a little.

"And then after a while," the boy resumed, "I seemed to see a black speck somewhere. And I could not understand it. I did not like it, and it made me miserable. *But*, I said to myself, *whatever the black speck may be, God will rub it white when he is ready!* For you know, he couldn't go on forever with a black speck going about in his heart. And when I said this, all at once I knew the black speck was Corney, and I started to cry. But with that the black speck began to grow dim, and it grew dimmer and dimmer till all at once I could see it no more. The same instant Corney stood beside me with a smile on his face, and the tears running down his cheeks. I stretched out my arms to him, and he caught me up in his, and then it was all right. And then I woke, Majie."

The days went on. Every day Mark said, "Now, Majie, I do think today I shall tell Corney my dream and the message I have for him." But each day passed and the dream was not told. The next and the next and the next passed and he seemed to the major not likely ever to have the strength to tell Corney. Still, even his mother, who was almost constantly in the room during the day, did not perceive that his time was drawing nigh. Hester also was much with him now, and sometimes his father, occasionally Corney and Mrs. Corney, as Mark called her with a merry look—very pale on his almost transparent face; but none of them seemed to think his end quite near. When several were in the room, he would lie looking from one to another like a miser contemplating his riches—and well he might! For such riches neither moth nor rust corrupt, and they are the treasures of heaven also.

One evening most of the family were in the room. A vague sense had diffused itself that the end was not far off, and an unspoken instinct had gathered them.

A lamp was burning low, but the firelight was stronger.

Mark spoke. In a moment the major was bending over him.

"Majie," he whispered, "I want Corney. I want to tell him."

The major went to find the brother, and on his way met the father and told him that the end was near. With a sorely self-accusing heart, for the vision of the boy seated in the middle of the cold moor the day of their walk haunted him, he went quickly to the boy's room, the anteroom of heaven.

Mark kept looking for Corney's coming, his eyes turning every other moment to the door. When his father entered, he stretched out his arms to him. The strong man bent over him and could not repress a sob. The boy pushed him gently back far enough to see his face.

"Father," he said, "you must be glad, not sorry. I am going to your Father and my Father. He is waiting for me."

Then seeing Corney come in, he stretched his arms toward him past his father. "Corney! Corney!" he cried, just as he used to call him when he was a little child. Corney bent over him, but the outstretched arms did not close around him; they fell.

But he was not yet ascended. Feebly he signed to the major.

"Majie," he whispered, with a look and expression for which the major tried the rest of his life to find the meaning. "Majie! Corney! You tell!"

Then he went.

The major alone did not weep. He stood with his arms folded, like a sentry relieved and waiting the next order. Even Corney's eyes filled with tears and he murmured, "Poor Markie!" It should have been "Poor

Corney!'' He stooped and kissed the silent face, then drew back and gazed with the rest.

Saffy, who had been seated gazing into the fire, called out in a strange voice, ''Markie, Markie!'' Hester turned to her at the cry and saw her apparently following something with her eyes along the wall from the bed to the window. At the curtained window she gazed for a moment, and then her eyes fell and she sat like one in a dream. A moment more and she sprang to her feet and ran to the bed, crying again, ''Markie! Markie!'' Hester lifted her and held her to kiss the sweet white face. It seemed to content her. She went back to her stool by the fire, and there sat staring at the curtained window with the look of one gazing into regions unknown.

That same night, before the solemn impression should pass, the major took Corney to his room and, recalling every individual expression he could of the little prophet-dreamer, carried out the commission entrusted him, not without the shedding of tears. And Corney did not laugh. He listened with a grave, even sad face; and when the major ceased, his eyes too were full of tears.

''I shall not forget Markie's dream,'' he promised.

Thus everything was working together to help the youth who had begun to mend his ways.

And shall we think the boy found God not equal to his dream of him? He made our dreaming. Shall it surpass in its making his mighty self? Shall God's love be inferior to man's imagination or his own?

40 / A Birthday Gift

When Mark's little cloak was put in the earth, for a while his room felt cold—as if the bit of Paradise had gone out of it. But before long the major requested that it might continue to be called Mark's, but should be considered the major's. He would like to put some of his things in it, and occupy it when he came for visits. Everyone was pleased with the idea.

Mark's books and pictures remained undisturbed. Every day the major read in Mark's Bible. His own sword that the boy had always so admired for its brightness he had placed unsheathed upon the wall. He slept in Mark's bed, and in the solitude of Mark's chamber he learned a thousand things his busy lifetime had prepared him for learning. The master had come to him through the child. In him was fulfilled a phase of the promise that whosoever receives a child in the name of Jesus receives Jesus and his father. Through ministering to the child, he had come to know the child's elder brother and master. It was the presence of the master in the child, that without his knowing it, opened his heart to him, and he had thus entertained more than an angel.

Time passed, and under the holy influences of duty and love and hope their hearts began to cover with flowers their furrows of grief. Hester's birthday was at hand. The major went to London to buy her a present, determined if he could to make the occasion a cheerful and memorable one.

He wrote to his cousin, Helen Raymount, asking if he might bring a friend with him. He did not think, he said, she or her husband knew him, but Hester did. He was a young doctor by the name of Christopher. He had met him among "Hester's friends" and admired him a great deal. He had been ailing for some time and had persuaded him to take a little relaxation. After Hester told them something of the man's history, saying that she had the highest esteem for him and the work he was doing among London's poor, Mr. and Mrs. Raymount expressed their delight in the major's proposal.

Corney gradually began to show a little practical interest in the place—first in the look of it, and then in its yield. Next he took to measuring the land and the major gave him no end of help. Having found a point of common interest, they began to be drawn a little together and to develop a mild liking for each other's company. By degrees, Corney

216

saw that the major knew much more than he, and the major discovered that Corney had more brains than he had given him credit for.

Hester informed her parents of the dissolution of her engagement to Lord Gartley. Her mother was troubled, for the simple reason that she knew how the tongue of the world would wag against her daughter. But the world and its judgments will pass. The tongue is a fire, but there is a stronger fire than the tongue. Mr. Raymount and the major cared little for this aspect of the matter, for they felt that the public is only a sort of innocent, whose behavior may be troublesome or pleasant, but whose opinion is worth considerably less than that of a wise hound. The world is a fine thing to save, but a wretch to worship. Though the father had liked Lord Gartley, neither man cared much for him.

There was nothing left her now, Hester said to herself, but the best thing of all according to Paul—a single maiden life devoted to the work of her Master. She was not willing to again run the risk of losing her power to help the Lord's creatures in order to pursue marriage. The events of the past months had served to solidify the calling she felt upon her life to minister wholeheartedly to the downtrodden and even the well-to-do in their own miserable weakness and vices. She would keep herself free. What a blessed thing it was to be her own mistress and the slave of the Lord, externally free! Like St. Paul, who abstained from marriage that he might better do the work given him by the Lord, her decision was for the sake of the kingdom of heaven.

Her spirits soon returned even more buoyant than before. Her health improved. In a few weeks, in the prime of health and feminine strength, she looked yet a grander woman than before. There was greater freedom in her carriage and she seemed to have grown. The humility that came with the discovery of her mistake over Gartley had only made her more dignified: true dignity comes only of humility. Pride is the ruin of dignity, for it is a worshiping of self. She was able to look on the whole business calmly, with a thankfulness that kept growing as the sting of her blunder lost its burning.

Everybody felt her more lovable than before. Her mother began to feel an enchantment of peace in her presence. Her father sought her company more than ever in his walks, and talked about his own wrong feelings toward Corney and how he had been punished for them by what they wrought in him. He had begun, he told her, to learn many things he had supposed he knew; he had only thought and written and talked about them before! Even Corney perceived a change in his sister. Scarcely a shadow of what he used to feel of "superiority" remained in her. She became more and more Amy's ideal of womanhood, and she showed her husband how few sisters would have tried to protect and deliver him as she had done. So, altogether, they were growing toward becoming a true family as God intended families to be.

Along with Mr. Christopher, Hester invited Miss Dasomma to come and spend a few days to help her celebrate her birthday. When the day came, it was the sweetest of summer days, and Hester looked a perfect summer-born woman. After breakfast all except the mother went out for a walk. Hester was little inclined to talk, and the major was in a thoughtful, brooding mood. Miss Dasomma and Mr. Raymount alone conversed. Mr. Raymount had taken them to a certain spot for the sake of the view, but Hester had fallen a little behind, and Christopher went back to meet her.

"You are thinking of your brother," he said, in a tone full of understanding.

"Yes," she answered.

"I knew by your eyes," he returned. "Why don't you tell me something about him?"

As they walked and talked, he drew her from her sadness with gentle words about children and death, and the look and reality of things. And so they wandered about the moor for a little while before joining the others.

The day went on simply, in a pleasant relaxed fashion. After lunch Hester opened her piano and asked Miss Dasomma to sit and play for them.

Following an early dinner, the major stood, raised his glass, and proposed the health of his cousin Hester, and then made a little speech in her honor. But his praise did not make Hester feel awkward, for praise which is the odor of love is genuine and true and therefore does not sicken its hearers.

"And now, Cousin Hester," concluded the major, "you know that I love you like a child of my own. But it is a good thing you are not, for if you were, then you would not be half so good or so beautiful or so wise or so accomplished as you are! Will you honor me by accepting this little gift, which I hope will serve to make this blessed day yet a trifle more pleasant to look back on when I am gone and when Mark has got his old Majie back. I hope you will fill this gift with many good deeds of the sort which only you know how to perform."

With this mysterious introduction, the major made Hester a low bow and handed her a small piece of white paper, twice folded, and tied with a bit of white ribbon. She took it with a sweetly radiant curiosity.

It was the title deed of the house in Addison Square. She gave a cry of joy, got up, threw her arms around Majie's neck, and kissed him.

"Ah!" said the major, "if I was a young man now, I should not have had that! But I know what she means by it: the collective kiss of all the dirty men and women in her dear slums, glorified into that of an angel of God!''

Hester was not a young lady given to weeping, but she did here break down and cry. Her long-cherished dream had come true! She knew she had no money to go with the house, but that did not trouble her. There was always a way of doing when one was willing to begin small!

And this is, indeed, a divine law. Success never comes to the man or woman who is not willing to begin small, to begin where he is at the moment. Small is strong, for it only can grow strong. Big at the outset is but bloated and weak. There are thousands willing to do great things for everyone who is willing to do a small thing. But there never was any truly great thing that did not begin small.

In her delight, without unfolding it all the way, Hester handed the paper to Mr. Christopher. He took it and, with a questioning look, opened it farther.

The major had known for some time that Mr. Raymount wanted to sell the house, and believed from the way Hester spent her time in London that he could give her no greater joy than to purchase it for her.

"There is more here than you know," said Christopher, handing her back the paper. She opened it and saw several notes, amounting to something around a thousand pounds. But before the evening was over she learned that it was not a thousand pounds the dear major had given her, but the thousand a year he had offered her if she would give up Lord Gartley. Thus a new paradise of Godly labor opened on the horizon in the delighted eyes of Hester.

In the evening, when the sun was setting, they all went for another walk in the long twilight. They climbed westward full in the face of the sunset, which was barred across the trees in gold, blue, rosy pink, and a lovely indescribable green, such as is not able to live except in the twilight. As they reached the top of the ridge, the major and Christopher and Hester found themselves together. A little way beyond stood the dusky group of their companions. And the whole world lay beneath them.

All three were silent for a moment. Then the major spoke.

"Who would live in London who might live here?" he said.

"It is beautiful," replied Hester. "Sometimes I think that I could go on and on staying in this peaceful place. But then I remember my people."

"And then you realize that you do prefer London to the country?" asked the major.

"I do not think it is that I *prefer* it. But if God chooses that I live in London, then that is my home."

"Surely Jesus would have liked better to go on living in his father's house," said Christopher, "than to go where so many did not know either him or his father. But he could not go on enjoying his heaven while so many lived what was a death in the midst of life. He knew he had to go and start them for home! Who could possibly, seeing even a little of what Jesus sees and feeling but a little of what he feels, rest in the enjoyment of beauty while so many are unable even to desire it? We are not true men and women until we are of the same mind with Christ."

Mr. Christopher spoke quietly in contrast to the fervor of his words.

"I would take as many in with me," he said, "as I possibly could, even if it meant my own entrance at the gate of the sunset—the sunrise rather, should be delayed a thousand years. It would be such sorrow to go in alone!"

And so the two did return from those peaceful valleys and hills to London, to the people who drew their hearts, and to whom God had sent them to minister. And though the major was not always by Hester's side, he too, never quite knowing how greatly the Lord was using him, was from then on more in London than at Yrndale.

Hester labored and Christopher labored, toiling joyfully in the eternal harvest of men. And if one was the heart and the other the head, the major was the right hand. But what they did and how they did it would require another book, and no small one, to itself.

It does not matter that I cannot here tell their story. No man ever did the best work who merely copied another. Let every man or woman work out the thing that is in him. Whoever uses the means that he has, great or small, and does the work that is given him to do, stands by the side of Jesus and is a fellow worker with him.

CHRISTIAN HERALD
People Making A Difference

Christian Herald is a family of dedicated, Christ-centered ministries that reaches out to deprived children in need, and to homeless men who are lost in alcoholism and drug addiction. Christian Herald also offers the finest in family and evangelical literature through its book clubs and publishes a popular, dynamic magazine for today's Christians.

Our Ministries

Family Bookshelf and **Christian Bookshelf** provide a wide selection of inspirational reading and Christian literature written by best-selling authors. All books are recommended by an Advisory Board of distinguished writers and editors.

Christian Herald magazine is contemporary, a dynamic publication that addresses the vital concerns of today's Christian. Each monthly issue contains a sharing of true personal stories written by people who have found in Christ the strength to make a difference in the world around them.

Christian Herald Children. The door of God's grace opens wide to give impoverished youngsters a breath of fresh air, away from the evils of the streets. Every summer, hundreds of youngsters are welcomed at the Christian Herald Mont Lawn Camp located in the Poconos at Bushkill, Pennsylvania. Year-round assistance is also provided, including teen programs, tutoring in reading and writing, family counseling, career guidance and college scholarship programs.

The Bowery Mission. Located in New York City, the Bowery Mission offers hope and Gospel strength to the downtrodden and homeless. Here, the men of Skid Row are fed, clothed, ministered to. Many voluntarily enter a 6-month discipleship program of spiritual guidance, nutrition therapy and Bible study.

Our Father's House. Located in rural Pennsylvania, Our Father's House is a discipleship and job training center. Alcoholics and drug addicts are given an opportunity to recover, away from the temptations of city streets.

Christian Herald ministries, founded in 1878, are supported by the voluntary contributions of individuals and by legacies and bequests. Contributions are tax deductible. Checks should be made out to Christian Herald Children, The Bowery Mission, or to Christian Herald Association.

Administrative Office: 40 Overlook Drive, Chappaqua, New York 10514
Telephone: (914) 769-9000

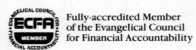 Fully-accredited Member
of the Evangelical Council
for Financial Accountability